# Then Spoke the Thunder

ALSO BY ELWYN CHAMBERLAIN

*Gates of Fire*
*Hound Dog*

# *Then Spoke the Thunder*

BY

ELWYN CHAMBERLAIN

GROVE PRESS
*New York*

The name Grove Press and the colophon printed on the title page and
the outside of this book are trademarks registered in the U.S. Patent and
Trademark Office and in other countries.

Published by Grove Press
841 Broadway
New York, N.Y. 10003

Excerpt from "The Waste Land" in *Collected Poems 1909–1962* by T. S. Eliot,
copyright 1936 by Harcourt Brace Jovanovich, Inc., copyright © 1963, 1964
by T. S. Eliot, reprinted by permission of the publisher.

Library of Congress Cataloging-in-Publication Data

Chamberlain, Elwyn M.
    Then spoke the thunder.
    I. Title.
PS3553.H249T5   1988        813'.54        88-11178
ISBN 0-8021-1060-6

Designed by Irving Perkins Associates

Manufactured in the United States of America

This book is printed on acid-free paper.

First Edition 1989

10   9   8   7   6   5   4   3   2   1

*For Sally*

# Acknowledgements

The author wishes to acknowledge his great debt to his many Indian friends the world over. And to specially thank Joan Creigh, Dechen Fitzhugh, Barbara and Herbert Kouts, Camilla and Earl McGrath, Caterine Milinaire, Rameshwar Das, Heidi Spielhagen, and Michael Zimmer—friends for all seasons; Bo and Sylvia Sax for the trip to Kedarnath; Tony and Jan Heiderer and Sara Chamberlain for their invaluable first-hand accounts of events in Delhi after Mrs. Gandhi's assassination; Sam Chamberlain, for his advice and suggestions, and Fred Jordan of Grove Press, who brought it all together.

Ganga was sunken, and the limp leaves
Waited for rain, while the black clouds
Gathered far distant, over Himavant.
The jungle crouched, humped in silence.
Then spoke the thunder.

    T. S. Eliot, "The Waste Land," 1922

*Part
One*

# I

JUNE 1984. Storm clouds gathered in the sky above Bombay's Victoria Station as David Spencer Bruce, former Captain, Indian Army, Burma, a graying centurion with an athletic stride, and his wife Philippa got down from a taxi. The damp heat was oppressive. In the crumbling railway station, several thousand people were huddled together on bits of cloth and straw mats, cooking their meals, nursing their children, begging, defecating. Valiantly determined to preserve a sense of humor that had never before failed her, Philippa Bruce, at forty-seven looking much younger than she had a right to expect, covered her mouth with a handkerchief and clung to her husband's hand. Her passionate blue eyes, their beauty exaggerated by sudden isolation, darted anxiously from side to side.

A pack of shouting coolies converged on them, demanding to carry their luggage: "What is your good name, your train number, what class will you be traveling in?" The press of sweating bodies was overwhelming. Suddenly the lights went out; a moan, escalating into a collective scream, shattered the fetid gloom and they were shoved unceremoniously against a wall. Philippa's lustrous blond hair, caught in a bun at the back of her neck, came undone and fell over the shoulders of her fashionable Liberty bush jacket. At any moment she felt she could be awfully sick.

"What the devil?" shouted David, fending off the crush of half-naked bodies.

"No problem, sir." One of the coolies grinned. "On your luggage please sit down, we will protect."

Her soigné confidence crumbling, Philippa slid down onto one of the old Louis Vuitton cases while David, refusing to be jostled, stood his ground. The coolies locked arms in front of them.

"It is a strike, sir." They laughed as the crowd surged by, fists clenched, shouting slogans. Lights flickered on and off, revealing swarthy police in khaki shorts beating back hordes of angry people.

Philippa closed her eyes. The moment they'd touched down at Bombay airport, she'd realized she was totally unprepared for the reality of India. Was it a kind of cosmic retribution for the sins committed here by her viceregal great-grandparent? Had the powers that regulated such things returned her to the scene of his crimes?

In decreasing waves the noise finally subsided. Lights came on. David helped her up. "Don't you think we're a bit out of shape for this sort of thing?" She smiled grimly, trying to repair her coif.

"Nonsense," he replied, his face taut with excitement. "Some minor disturbance. Come on, they want us to move out now."

His attitude mystified her. He seemed to be enjoying the whole thing.

"Sir," barked one of the coolies, jerking his head in a military fashion.

They followed in his wake as he fought his way skillfully through the packed station. Inside the train, ten well-dressed people were shouting angrily over the possession of a first-class sleeping compartment meant for two. The coolies stowed their bags and departed. An official arrived, examined everyone's tickets, and glanced sheepishly at them.

"All valid," he mumbled. "Overbooking."

"Quick," whispered David, "into the upper berth with you. Take possession."

Six people squeezed themselves onto the lower berth. A couple with two young children spread out a mat and claimed the floor. Outside, the departure bell clanged and they began to move. Safe on their perch, Philippa found herself still holding David's hand. How many years since that had happened? Pleasant, but unsettling too.

From the speakers of innumerable transistor radios, a stress-filled woman's voice echoed through the train as it picked up speed. It was Mrs. Gandhi, David said, and translated from a reservoir of Hindi remembered over forty years. "Even at this late hour . . . to call off their threatened agitation and accept . . . Punjab is uppermost in our minds . . . deeply concerned." The atmosphere in the compartment became charged. Why were people listening so intently?

Philippa put her bag under her head and tried to visualize Dunwell, their farm in Surrey, southwest of Guilford toward Frensham Common: the beech woods thick with bluebells, the cowslips lining the lazy stream. Now she was driving in the gate, and there were the towers of the great old Elizabethan house looming up beyond the lawns and gardens. If she could remain focused on this blissful vision, perhaps she would be able to forget India and fall asleep. Someone in the lower berth began to snore fretfully. Her friends had all warned her against making this trip. But David had so wanted to come, so wanted to show her what he called "the real India," India as he had known it as a young man, not the India she'd been brought up on, quaint butt of jokes over old photo albums on cold winter nights in her grandfather's azure-domed library. And then she had thought an adventure might possibly revitalize a marriage gone stale. Adventure, indeed!

Beside her, David tried to sleep, but a lurid blue light which could not be turned off kept him awake as the events of the past weeks percolated through his numbed brain. His sixtieth birthday dinner. All the ridiculous explanations he'd had to make to Philippa's friends and relations for dragging her off on a journey everyone thought was mad. A fight with his son, Edward, which left him feeling helpless and miserable. The attitude of his daughter, Belinda, who had humored him as though he'd gone off the deep end. Suddenly it all seemed too much, only reinforced the inexplicable feeling of meaninglessness which had haunted him now for some time, and made him more determined than ever to make this trip to the land where he'd spent the happiest years of his life. He turned restlessly on the hard berth and wondered whether he would be able to locate his old friend and comrade-in-arms, Madho Dev Singh. Philippa's calm breathing was annoying. How did she manage to simply turn off the world when she grew tired of it? Why had he not thought to remove his sleeping pills from his luggage before they boarded the train? The graffiti-covered green walls glowed with a nightmarish phosphorescence. Overhead fans rattled, and the foul-smelling wind blew in hot, fitful gusts through the open windows. Lying there, he recalled the trains of his childhood, the pleasure of riding in them, and wondered what could have happened here in India that such a great people had been reduced to being transported in this hellish manner.

*    *    *

THE next morning Philippa returned trembling from a trip to the bathroom. "Can you believe I had to climb over twenty sleeping people to get to the loo? Darling, it's awful, hasn't been cleaned in months. We really should have flown or hired a car."

"Never occurred to me it would be like this; sorry." He avoided her gaze. "We always used to go by train, all very luxurious, a great adventure." He waved his hand in despair.

The day wore on and many of the passengers debarked. Finding themselves alone at last in the dingy compartment, they took seats by the window and looked disconsolately out at the monotonous landscape as it slipped past. Separated for the first time from all the trappings of her fashionable life, Philippa felt like a piece of rare porcelain thrown into a dustbin by mistake. Tiny balls of soot blew in through cracks at the windows as she watched David's reflection in the glass. After almost thirty years of marriage, he was still an enigma to her. His past, his adventures in India, had always overshadowed their life together. But if she had ever resolved the mystery that seemed to surround him, really understood this attractive man, wouldn't she have left him? Probably. Certainly he had given her enough provocation: his long silences; women attracted to him like moths to a flame. Yet he had never ceased to intrigue or surprise her. And realizing finally that boredom might be a far worse fate than suffering through his infidelities, she had taken her own lovers and hoped for the best. A modern marriage, she believed it was called.

Awakened from a nap late that afternoon after a day of maddening heat, David imagined himself on the train back from London, fresh from the arms of his current mistress, a young French girl whom he kept there in an expensive flat. As he gazed out the train window, he thought he saw the awful commuter housing that had swallowed up the home counties south of London and was startled by the conductor's voice as he pounded on the compartment door. Kotagarh! The train had stopped. Coolies charged in and took command of their luggage. Outside on the platform the heat was like dragon's breath. Dazed, he looked around and tried to get his bearings. Thirty-eight years since he'd stood on this platform: 1946. He'd accompanied Madho Dev, who'd come home to ask his father's permission to marry Devika, daughter of a neighboring raja. He could still hear the jolly music of the state band welcoming the heir apparent, see the red carpet and retinue of servants sent to greet them. Now as he came to his senses, his thick hair damp with perspiration, everything looked

drab and strangely desolate. Hordes of young men in tight pants and
ill-fitting shirts strutted back and forth, staring arrogantly at them,
while poor countryfolk squatted stoically in small groups like
wounded birds. Leaving Philippa to watch the luggage, he strode off
in search of the stationmaster.

"But the Government Rest House is for government officials only."
The stationmaster was protesting loudly as David maneuvered him
toward Philippa a few minutes later. Philippa smiled blandly. "Memsahib would most probably prefer the Tourist Bungalow," he added,
nervously eyeing her. "Just a few kilometers outside of town, the
guesthouse of the former Raja of Kotagarh," he added proudly.

"Then I've stayed there," replied David.

The man's half-veiled crocodile eyes lit up. "Achcha?" He smiled
inquisitively.

"In 1946," David explained. "I was in the army with the Yuvaraj,
Madho Dev. Perhaps you could tell me where I can find him."

"Yes, yes, of course, he is living just nearby." The man grinned
obsequiously and dispatched a flunky for tea. "Please come into my
office. I shall call him. I have a fan; you must be hot and tired. You
have come from Bombay, I presume?"

The stationmaster's domain was piled high with faded papers and
records. In one corner an antiquated wireless ticked out messages taken
down in longhand by a young clerk on a high stool. There were various
religious calendars, a framed picture of Indira Gandhi holding up her
hand with the word UNITY written across it, a gigantic old Remington,
and an equally ancient telephone on which the stationmaster now tried
to reach an operator. Rattling the receiver up and down, he yelled
"Hallo!" into the mouthpiece, but there was no response.

"How are they expecting us to keep the trains running on time
when an important office like this must bribe the repairmen to do
their duty? I am telling you, if I was in charge. . . ." He cursed the
system and seemed about to throw the phone through the window,
when tea arrived.

The muddy-looking concoction served in old stained cups was not
the kind of tea Philippa was accustomed to. She grimaced slightly and
hoped she would not have to drink it.

Suddenly David remembered how difficult it had been to drink tea
in Kotagarh without swallowing some of the flies that formerly
swarmed over everything. Where were they? he wondered.

The stationmaster smiled enigmatically. "I think you must be film
star," he said. "Have I seen you at the cinema?"

David shook his head and chewed thoughtfully on a Britannia

biscuit. "Where have all the flies gone?" he asked. "I seem to remember clouds of them everywhere."

The man's face brightened. "You must be noticing the difference. Very good, isn't it?" He gestured toward an emaciated barefoot youth who sauntered along the platform, delicately dispensing white powder from a large straw basket. "It is the magic powder, DDT." He grinned, trying the phone again. "Flies gone."

David glanced at Philippa. One of the many committees she served on was dedicated to educating the British public on the dangers of various pesticides, agitating to have them outlawed. She looked faint.

"I think it would be best if we went directly to the Tourist Bungalow," said David. "It's getting late. I wouldn't want to disturb the Yuvaraj at this hour. Mind you, it'll be quite a shock for him to see me after all these years."

"He does not expect you?" asked the stationmaster with surprise.

"Afraid not," said David. "We came on the chance that he might be here or that someone would know where he was."

"Ah, well, in that case." The stationmaster dismissed the matter with a disparaging wave of his hand and called in a boy to carry their luggage. "Madho Devji's house is near the irrigation canal, about four kilometers from the Bungalow." He stood up. "You can go there easily in the morning. If there is anything I can do for you, I am at your service. I hope the Tourist Bungalow will be to your satisfaction, but I have heard things have gone down there recently." His eyes rolled in their sockets. "You see, the problem is, sir, nobody wants to work."

With that poignant observation, one to which David found he had no rejoinder, he ushered them to the street, where two dilapidated bicycle rickshaws had been commandeered. There was a sharp exchange over why a taxi could not be found. Alas, the only one which had a luggage rack had apparently broken down that morning. The stationmaster explained that except for the people who came to see the tigers at the game preserve and were picked up by the Forestry Department jeeps, and Russians who came to inspect a new factory they had built, Kotagarh rarely had visitors.

In one rickshaw the coolies loaded their luggage; the other, its high double seat upholstered in sky-blue plastic, adorned with representations of voluptuous film stars, gods and goddesses, and the cryptic motto LOVE IS GOD, stood waiting for them. Two barefoot men with blank expressions on their faces lounged on the handlebars of their bikes.

"Take sahib and memsahib to the Tourist Bungalow and see that you stay awake and don't get hit," the stationmaster commanded.

They climbed into the flimsy contraption and moved off around the town square, where a few battered palms rattled in the wind above weed-choked flower beds and a cement fountain from which no water flowed.

Down narrow streets they glided, the rickshaw wallahs furiously ringing their bicycle bells, past shops and stalls selling pots and pans, vegetables, grains, and cheap saris embossed with gold. With the approach of evening, the townspeople had come out of their houses, and thousands of expressionless eyes followed them with an intensity Philippa found unnerving. Only when they left the bazaar and were speeding along between rows of windowless mud walls and houses did she relax enough to smile at the herds of homeward-bound water buffaloes and cows.

Cow-dust hour, thought David, and was instantly transported to his childhood days in Bengal when the heat of day gave way to twilight and he would be bathed by his nurse, Savitri, and allowed to play games with his older cousins. It was then when the cooking fires were lit that for a few hours India became a place of magic. Later, when he was sent back to public school at Winchester, he remembered sitting at his dormitory window thinking of the smells, the sounds of the night birds, the singing of the cook, and the distant beating of drums in the nearby villages. To his surprise, he now suddenly realized how much he'd really hated England then.

Rounding a corner, they narrowly missed crashing into a parade of men in tattered uniforms carrying Coleman lanterns adorned with tinsel shades. Behind them walked a group of musicians playing battered trumpets and saxophones to the syncopated beat of drums. Next came a group of young men singing and dancing with one another around a flower-decked young man in a white suit astride an old nag of a horse. A claque of boys throwing firecrackers and rockets darted back and forth, clearing the way.

"Shadi." The rickshaw driver grinned, turning to see if David and Philippa were appreciating the spectacle.

"Wedding," explained David. "Not a very big one, judging from the groom's mount. He's on his way to the bride's house. If you're rich, you may come in a carriage pulled by white horses or you may sit on an elephant as my friend Madho Dev did in this very street almost forty years ago." He glanced at Philippa and was startled to see in the strange half-light that her face seemed suddenly drawn and gray.

The procession passed, and they reached the meeting of several roads. Here, half-naked men bathed at a community faucet and fires burned fitfully in the open hearths of shops where sweaty young boys fried bits of food in huge cauldrons of rancid-smelling fat. Then they were out of town, gliding swiftly along under an avenue of huge trees. Yet the road was still clogged with people and animals: old women, ravaged beauties of another day, laboring under huge bundles; families in carts whipping the horses that pulled them. They passed a camel hitched to a wagonload of sugar cane and despite her fatigue, Philippa, who had never seen a camel outside a zoo, poked David and smiled. Now and then a truck came honking its way by them at breakneck speed, belching black diesel smoke, its sides gaily painted with buxom goddesses. At every turn, like apparitions, people's faces materialized out of the crepuscular gloom—determined, stoic faces, inward-looking, expressionless. Long afterward, Philippa would remember this first night on the dark Indian road and wonder what had moved her so. In any other country it would have been sordid. Here it seemed apocalyptic.

The two drivers veered off the road up an overgrown driveway, and a large building loomed up against the evening sky.

"That's it!" shouted David eagerly and stopped—or was it? A neglected garden withered between two wings of a crumbling art deco building. As they got out of the rickshaw, a peacock screamed and scuttled across a veranda cluttered with leaves and refuse. The drivers rang their cycle bells, and presently an old man in khaki shorts and a torn white kurta shuffled out, waving a flashlight.

"He doesn't look too happy to see us," whispered Philippa. "Are you quite sure this is the place?"

"We'd like a room for the night," said David in Hindi.

The old man looked blank, then jerked his head condescendingly. They followed him inside, to one of the rooms. A bare bulb flickered on, revealing a large room with peeling paint, curved mirrors, an enormous half-moon bed, and worn peach-colored carpets.

David winced and closed his eyes. A darkened corner of his brain was suddenly illuminated. Years ago he'd slept in this very room, and not alone. His heart skipped. Philippa must not see that he remembered anything. Terrible mistake, this going back. How could he have pushed it out of his mind so completely? How could he have forgotten the night he made love there on that impossible bed?

The caretaker turned on a ceiling fan. Philippa busied herself opening closets and drawers, inspecting the loo. "There's no toilet," she said wearily. "Just a hole in the floor."

"There certainly used to be one," he replied absentmindedly. There, he'd done it, let the cat out of the bag.

"You've been here before, I take it?"

"Of course," he said, trying to sound casual. "Used to stay here when I visited Madho Dev. This was the royal guesthouse. There were very proper loos then." He peered into the bathroom, discovered the Western toilet had been replaced by a Hindu one. "That's a squatter; guess you'll have to learn how to use it."

"It would be easier if there was some water." She rattled the flush chain.

"Pani?" David asked the caretaker helplessly. "There must be running water for the bathroom."

"Pani nahin," he replied, shaking his head. "I will bring buckets. Will you be requiring anything to eat?"

David studied the man's unwashed clothes and hands. The light flickered and went out. The fan stopped.

"Outage." The old fellow disappeared and returned with candles.

Philippa thought the candles made the room more bearable. At least she could look at herself in the mirrors without wincing.

"Are you hungry?" asked David. "This man wants to cook dinner for us, but if he does I think we might be rather sick tomorrow." He spoke rapidly as the old man seemed to understand some English.

"I have some cheese and crackers tucked away," said Philippa, ever resourceful. "We can have that, and perhaps he has some fruit. Frankly, I'm so exhausted I can't wait for him to fix dinner."

"We have our own food," said David. The old man looked relieved. "Bring us some boiled drinking water and a mango or two." He remembered there had been a mango orchard nearby.

The old man nodded and soon returned with a battered thermos full of water. Philippa got out the cheese and crackers. The cheese tasted like processed latex. Soon a bowl of mangoes and two buckets of hot water materialized, and the man asked if sahib would require anything more before he took his leave. David thanked him and gave him a tip. The old man smirked and shuffled wearily out.

"What was that all about?" A wry expression flickered at the corners of Philippa's mouth. "Does he think I'm some tart you've picked up?"

"Possibly." David sighed.

She undid her hair and collapsed on the bed, her cheeks flushed. "Is there any reason why we can't leave tomorrow?" she said, staring at the ceiling. "It seems so pointless to put ourselves through all this nonsense. Not your fault, of course, I'm not blaming you, but you must admit things have changed since you were last here, and we're not going to have the sort of holiday we expected. There's that lovely hotel in Portofino, the Splendido; and we have so many friends nearby. Let's just admit we made a mistake and leave. We could be in Italy in two days—what are you doing?"

David was looking at a letter he had received fifteen years ago containing a photograph of himself and Madho Dev on an elephant. It was the last letter he had received from Madho Dev. He handed the picture to Philippa.

"Dashing young bucks, weren't you?" She smiled wanly.

"He was such a good friend. Saved my life once. I've come all this way to see him, I can't turn back now."

"I suppose you can't." She sighed, wondering how she would survive without a hairdresser. "Promise we won't have to stay too long, though."

"Promise. Only you have to give it a try, you know." He read the letter again and spoke to her, but she was already asleep. Blowing out the candles, he paced back and forth in the darkened room and found it difficult to think of sleeping in that bed again. That bed! How could he have deceived himself so? Years ago, in this very room, his life could have taken a different course if he had let it. If she had let it: Kamala Devi, the girl he left behind. First, he had convinced himself he was depressed about his life and needed a change. Then it was the idea of meeting Madho Dev again. Now the truth: Kamala. The memory of her swept over him like an avalanche. Here in this room of lost chances, something in him had lived and died and was gone forever.

An old-fashioned train whistle sounded in the distance, and he remembered another night long ago. From Madho Dev's suite of rooms the sound of Glenn Miller and his band had echoed through the house. Madho Dev had introduced him to Kamala the previous year. She was a so-called "liberated" young woman, a Rajput princess working for the Red Cross. He was twenty, she was eighteen. They fell madly in love but knew from the beginning it was impossible. No, that was wrong. From his point of view it had not been impossible, and he had begged her to come back to England with him. From her father's point of view, however, it had been out of the question. Ah, yes, the old despot, he was the culprit.

Although they hadn't known it then, it was to be their last night together. The scent of tuberoses had filled the room. The fact that Madho Dev was enjoying his bride in another part of the house made them feel it was their honeymoon too.

And what a splendid wedding it had been! A cherished elephant transporting Madho Dev to the palace of Devika's father, the plaintive wailing of the shehnai from within, the state band on the lawn, a dowry room filled with gold and jewels, Rolls Royces crowding the drive. The next day they had gone off to Ooty in the Nilgiri Hills, a big party of them. Two weeks in a lodge kept by Madho Dev's father, trying in vain to outwit the chaperones sent along to watch Kamala. Then back to Kotagarh, where there had been a grand reception, more processions, ceremonies, parties, and then this room he had crept into, after she had given her nurse a sleeping potion. Divine madness. But now, like the pathetic wedding procession they had passed earlier that evening, he felt decrepit, wasted.

He remembered creeping barefoot into this room, unbelievably tense, for although they had known each other for over a year and had been together constantly for two weeks, nothing had happened between them. She had changed into a transparent caftan and let her hair down, long black hair that fell to her waist. Even now he could feel her glorious warmth as they embraced, and she had worshiped him guiltlessly and explored his body until he lay trembling. No other woman since had treated him like that, aroused the same passions. A true marriage; he had been a fool to let her go. How could he have put that night so completely out of his mind? She had let loose a torrent inside him, then disappeared, and he had followed the commandments of his tribe, rigidly conditioned natives from a faraway island, and gone "home"—the word stuck in his throat. Some of that conditioning had slipped away, but not enough; he had tried to impose it on his son and daughter with disastrous results. The same conditioning had no doubt made him believe he was coming back to India to find Madho Dev.

Without warning, her eyes were there now in the darkened room, eyes that had devoured him that night. How different his love for Philippa was. As different as the scarlet lotus from the bluebells that lined the brook at Dunwell. But did he actually believe the girl he left behind would even faintly resemble the woman he might find again here in India? The thought of meeting her sent his heart to his throat. Yes, Philippa was right as usual, they must leave in the morning before Madho Dev found out. Ah, but this was India. Wouldn't Madho Dev already know? During the fighting in Burma they had been as close as two men can be and still be men.

He opened the glass doors that faced the veranda. Somewhere in the heavily scented closeness a nightingale sang, and far off he could hear the roll of thunder. What a dangerous place, this India, for an Englishman. So infused and fortified with powerful dream waves and visions, its very soil the dust of millions who had come and gone before. That he had been born here, stayed until he was eight, and returned during the war was considered auspicious. When Madho Dev had first learned of it, his whole attitude had changed.

"What are you doing?" It was Philippa's voice from the bed. "Is there something outside?"

"Just letting in some fresh air," he replied.

"I had the most frightful dream," she whispered. "There was this enormous monkey, perhaps it was an ape, absolutely huge and smelly. He reeked. And in my dream I thought, How can I be dreaming this because things don't smell in dreams, do they? But he was coming into this room, right through those doors. Then I woke up and saw you standing there." She sighed. Lightning illuminated the room.

He leaned over and kissed her. "Try and get some sleep. Tomorrow is certain to be a day full of surprises."

# 2

THE SUN was already shining brightly when a young boy shuffled in with two cups, a small bowl of coarsely milled sugar, some powdered milk, and a teapot shrouded in a frayed cozy.

Philippa shook her blond mane, yawned, and sat up. "You'd think with all the cows here. . . ." Her voice trailed off as she spooned milk powder into her tea.

David peered from under the sheets and opened one eye. Her ability to look reborn each morning always amazed him.

"The best milk comes from those big black buffaloes you saw last night on the road," he said.

"The ones with the big, wet, black noses." She smiled. "They're so sweet."

"You wouldn't think so if you had to milk one," he said, getting out of bed.

"How about another piece of that rubbery cheese?" She laughed, surveying the room as she unwrapped the foil-covered squares. "Actually, it could be rather attractive. In London these pieces would fetch a handsome sum—Art Deco. Very 'in' these days."

"It was once very grand," said David, looking about sadly. "Photographs in gold frames, great bowls of flowers. The furniture came from Paris, rare inlaid woods; some fool has painted it. Madho Dev's mother did it up. She was very proud of the guesthouse."

"How sad. And the government took it away from them?"

"Afraid they did, after we left."

"But I thought the government promised the princes. . . ."

"Promised them everything, then conveniently changed its mind."

"Like all governments." She nodded.

"Mind you, they didn't kill them like some revolutionary governments, just strangled them slowly. You know, expropriation."

"But didn't you say Madho Dev's father and mother were killed? Surely not by Mr. Nehru's government?"

"No one quite knows. It happened a year after he married Devika. Dev was sent off to Kashmir. Many of his father's servants had quit because there was no money to pay them. One night armed men came, tortured Dev's mother in front of his father until he told them where he'd hidden his treasure, then axed them both to death. Devika escaped by hiding in a secret passage. Financially they were finished. Even Devika's dowry was gone. Dev had just enough left to get to Bombay with two of his father's cars. He started a taxi company, made a lot of money, and then came back here and took up farming."

"What a ghastly story." Philippa stared into space. "Imagine living with a memory like that. Poor Devika."

The old man brought warm water, and after they had bathed and dressed, they climbed a staircase that led to the roof.

"If we'd got up a bit earlier, I'd say we could walk it," David said, shading his eyes. "From what the stationmaster told me, it should be just down the road."

"What do you think that is?" asked Philippa, pointing toward Kotagarh, where a huge stack belched clouds of smoke.

"Factory of some sort. Certainly wasn't here before."

As they watched, emissions from the giant puffing stack blanketed Kotagarh: yellow, black, then white. From below, the old caretaker shouted up to ask if they would like a lift anywhere. A taxi had brought someone and was about to leave.

In the driveway they found a battered old British Ford with peeling paint. The driver, a barefoot teenage boy in a soiled white dhoti and crimson turban, saluted and opened the door for their inspection. The interior was upholstered in pink plastic with swastikas embossed in gold. There were machine-made lace curtains on the windows, and mounted on the rear window shelf were a plastic god and goddess performing coitus. David looked dubiously at the car and wondered if the boy could really drive. As the engine started, clouds of black smoke exploded from the exhaust pipe.

"Converted to diesel, sir, no problem," yelled the young driver, desperately pumping the gas pedal.

David looked doubtful.

The caretaker clucked reassuringly. "This boy is owner's son. Him very good driver."

They got in the car and lifted the doors back in place. Philippa noticed the boy's lips and tongue were bright red.

"He's chewing betel nut," David explained. "Gives you a rush, a bit like cocaine."

Philippa reached for the door handle. David restrained her. "He'll do all right, you'll see. Just don't look at the oncoming traffic."

Philippa glanced at the dashboard where a LOVE IS GOD sign was pasted. "What do you think it means?" she said. "I saw that yesterday too."

"Love is *a* god, not God is love," he laughed.

"Really, darling!" She looked askance at him. "Can't you be serious?"

They turned out the drive and she had the impression the driver, who sat far back in his seat and gripped the wheel at arm's length, hadn't the faintest notion what he was doing. The main road was crowded with trucks, bullock carts, bicycles, rickshaws, and tongas— open horse-drawn two-wheeled carriages. The driver careened along, honking furiously, as if all traffic must give way before him.

"For God's sake, ask him to slow down," Philippa shouted.

"Dheri, dheri!" cried David. She looked alarmed. "It means slow down," he yelled, "not what you're thinking."

A few seconds later a truck in front of them jammed on its brakes and crashed into something ahead. At the same time, another truck lumbering toward them from the opposite direction was forced onto the shoulder of the road and hit several cyclists. The brakes on their car failed. The boy swerved into a ditch and slid to a halt at a forty-five-degree angle. Suddenly everything was very still.

"Are you all right?" David asked. "It happened so fast."

"I'm fine, but look at him." She shook her head. "Still chewing that stuff as if nothing had happened—and grinning."

Screams and high-pitched wails of women broke the silence.

"Someone's been hurt. I'd best go see if I can help. You stay here."

"I don't think I really want to see what's out there," Philippa said. She pulled the curtains across the windows, slumped low in the seat, and closed her eyes.

David wrenched open the door and ran down the road to where a large crowd had gathered around the mashed cyclists. Two men and a young woman lay inside the twisted bicycle frames, pools of blood oozing from under them. David ran ahead between the two trucks to where some men were trying to lift a tonga that had turned over on top of its passengers. What looked like an entire family lay under the wreckage. A pink substance he supposed was brains was splattered across the pavement. The horse that had been pulling the tonga lay dying. David put his shoulder to one of the wheels, and they managed to lift it until it fell the other way. Ten people and a baby were crushed under it. Most of them looked dead, but the baby was miraculously alive and screaming. A woman with a ravaged face ran forward, caught up the baby, and began wrapping it with pieces of cloth which she tore from her voluminous petticoat. A young man yelled at her that she should touch nothing until the arrival of the police. She called him an asshole and told him to go to hell.

While they had been raising the tonga, David had been watching a man with a short gray beard wearing a carelessly tied pink turban and white pajamas who stood conversing in angry tones with the driver of the truck. The surly driver lounged defiantly against the vehicle's door, disclaiming any responsibility for the accident. Hadn't he blown his horn at the bloody tonga? Yes. Had it moved over? No. And when he started to pass it, hadn't the truck in the other lane veered toward him without warning? It was certainly the fault of the tonga driver, as he had heard the horn and had plenty of time to get out of the way.

"So you just ran them down, you sisterfucker," yelled the man in the pink turban.

"What else to do?" whined the driver. "Do you think I am such a fool as to let a truck twice as big as mine hit me? I would be dead."

Suddenly David realized the man in the turban was Madho Dev. During his heated argument with the truck driver, he had looked over sharply several times. He was heavier than David remembered. The voice had deepened, the beard and the turban made him look very different, but there could be no mistaking those leonine eyes. Realizing how unlucky a meeting under such circumstances might seem, David started back to the taxi.

"David?" the man called after him uncertainly. "David Bruce, is it you?" David stopped and turned. The man strode up and extended his hand. "It *is* you! The chap at the station phoned this morning. I couldn't believe it." They fell into each other's arms. Madho Dev's eyes filled with tears.

David held him at arm's length. "I thought I recognized you but wasn't sure. Seems we're destined to meet among dead bodies, eh?"

Madho Dev kissed him on both cheeks. "Come," he said and led him through the crowd to where the emaciated tonga pony lay dying. A good-looking man in khaki shorts with serious dark eyes and a black mustache was squatting beside it. "Arjun," said Madho Dev, "I want you to meet someone. This is Captain David Bruce; you've heard me speak of him many times. He has appeared out of the blue. David, my son Arjun."

Arjun stood up, stared steadily at David, and flashed a dazzling smile. "The gods speak in many ways," he said huskily as they shook hands.

"You look a lot like your father—as I remember him," said David. They all laughed.

"Another bull of Bharat, eh, David?" Madho Dev smiled proudly.

"I say, we're stuck in the ditch behind that truck. Philippa, my wife, is rather shaken up. Wouldn't it be easier if we went back to the guesthouse and came to see you after lunch? No telling when they'll clear this mess." It wasn't at all the kind of meeting David had imagined. Damned unlucky. He wanted to go back to square one and start over.

"No problem," said Madho Dev. "Happens all the time. Arjun will organize everything."

"You must be in Ram Singh's famous taxi." Arjun laughed. "Wait here, I'll take care of everything."

"Awful, eh?" said Madho Dev, wiping his broad unlined forehead with the end of his turban. "Most of these drivers should be jailed; no business behind a wheel. Do it to get out of their villages, smell of petrol means freedom, think it's glamorous. No doubt this fellow bought his license for a few rupees, and when this little drama is over, for a few more the police will let him go scot-free. That is the condition you find us in, my friend." He clapped his hand on David's shoulder. "In India these days you can buy anyone."

"Wasn't it always like that?" said David.

Madho Dev glanced at him and nodded sardonically.

Just then the taxi, with Philippa inside it, borne on the shoulders of a dozen men commanded by Arjun, came gliding over the crowd like some ship of state. David was impressed. "We no longer rule here," observed Madho Dev, "but these chaps still like us and help us—now and then."

At the rescued taxi they found Arjun talking to a smiling Philippa through an open window. She seemed considerably brighter than

David had seen her since their arrival in India. He introduced her to Madho Dev.

"Your son is a hero," she said, beaming at Arjun, who beamed back. "Most ingenious. It was really worth the trip just to be picked up and carried like that."

Madho Dev caught her laughing eyes and held them. What a beautiful woman! David always did have good luck. "We mustn't stay here." He smiled. "It's too hot, you'll have sunstroke. Come, our place is just down the road." He helped her out of the taxi, they crowded into Arjun's jeep, and a few minutes later pulled in through a gate in a high wall on a drive bordered by a series of whitewashed buildings decorated with stylized paintings of peacocks and flowers in dark red. Through a second gate could be seen a farmyard in which several young camels lay dozing in the shade. Entering the largest of the buildings through massive teakwood doors, they removed their shoes in a cool hall that looked out over an inner courtyard shaded by an enormous pipal tree. Arjun excused himself. Madho Dev made David and Philippa comfortable on low divans and shouted for the servants.

"Not like the old days, eh, Davidji?" He shook his head, lit a pipe, and smiled at Philippa. "Then there would have been twenty people standing around fanning us, waiting on us hand and foot."

"I rather like it this way." Philippa smiled back. "It's more relaxing."

Madho Dev liked her look: intriguing physical specimen, rather different from other Englishwomen he'd known.

"What happened to your father's place?" asked David.

"As you know, my father and mother were murdered while I was in Kashmir; everything was stolen. I went to Bombay and tried my luck at organizing a fleet of taxis, did quite well at it, but hated Bombay. When we returned here, Father's place was a mess, like everything else in Kotagarh—gutted. I tore it down and used many of the materials to build this farm. It's been difficult. Neither Devika nor I knew what we were getting into but Bombay was no place for our children—we knew that. The rich families didn't suffer as we have but we were a small state, no privy purse to speak of. . . ." He looked at David. "We corresponded for nearly twenty years, old man; then what happened?"

"I wrote a number of times," protested David. "Never an answer."

"Like everything else, our postal system went down the drain." Madho Dev sighed. "Government of fools, that's what it's been, blind leading the blind. So different from what anyone expected."

Just then a tall woman, her thick black hair in a braid to the waist, came in from the sun-dappled courtyard and walked purposefully toward them. Gold anklets jangled beneath the border of her dark blue sari, and a large diamond sparkled in her aquiline nose. Philippa thought of the women in the Rajput paintings her grandfather had collected. Her large almond-shaped eyes were outlined in kohl, her gestures were courtly, restrained. David got up and extended his hands to greet her. She smiled helplessly at Madho Dev.

"Devika, this is David Bruce. You remember him, don't you?"

Her Buddha-like smile revealed nothing.

"It's been nearly a lifetime, if you think about it; I'm not sure she does." David grinned awkwardly. "Must say I'm not surprised."

Philippa got up, and Madho Dev introduced them. She sensed that Devika was upset about something.

"The P.M. has sent the army into the Golden Temple," said Devika nervously. "It's just been announced."

"You must forgive us," said Madho Dev. "The politicians are making a mess of things again. We're rather worried about it; last resort of that woman's bankrupt policies. But of course you haven't been following the latest idiocies here."

Devika frowned at her husband. "You mustn't pay too much attention to his political views," she said. "He doesn't like the Congress Party."

"We heard a speech Mrs. Gandhi gave the other night," said David. "Everyone in the train seemed to be listening. Something about the Punjab."

"She's trying to do in the Sikhs," said Madho Dev, "just as she tried to destroy us. But she'll discover they aren't that easily controlled. Lions are patient creatures, slow to anger; irritate them, however, and they become dangerous."

"I met your Mrs. Gandhi once at Windsor," said Philippa. "Charming woman, incredibly energetic. Has she changed?"

Devika eyed her husband warily. "She's set a wonderful example for us Indian women. The men are all afraid of her."

"Bah!" said Madho Dev and changed the subject. "There was a bad accident up the road. We found David and Philippa in a ditch."

"So I heard," said Devika, glancing at them. "These days the roads are unsafe. Are you all right? Would you like to have hot baths?"

"It was a family from across the river," said Madho Dev. "Squashed like bugs."

David studied Devika. He felt strange meeting her. Physically she was remarkably unchanged, not a line on her face, yet beneath the surface he felt she had undergone a radical transformation.

"Where's Gayatri?" asked Madho Dev.

"In the barn, dealing with Nadina; she's having trouble giving birth."

"Nadina is a cow," explained Madho Dev.

"My daughter-in-law, Gayatri, is something of a veterinarian," said Devika almost apologetically. "Very good with animals."

"But not strong enough to birth a calf," said Madho Dev.

"She's supervising. The new vet is young, not too experienced. But enough of this. I'm sure Mrs. Bruce would like to freshen up." She took Philippa's hand. "Come, let us leave these men. I'll show you where we women spend most of our time. Dev, why don't you fix Captain Bruce a drink? I'm sure you both need one and have a lot to catch up on. Lunch will be ready in about an hour."

MADHO DEV led David into a book-lined room filled with East India Company furniture. "My study." He waved his hand. "Spend most of my time in here." The room was dark and cool. "Gin?" he asked. "If I remember, you always took gin before lunch."

A barefoot servant boy appeared with ice.

"Ice! That's something new, isn't it?" said David.

"But my father had refrigerators," replied Madho Dev. "We had our own generators."

"Funny, I don't remember ice in your house."

Madho Dev looked him squarely in the eyes and paused, "It's been a long time, hasn't it? I don't know how to act with you."

"Nor I," said David awkwardly, convinced he should never have come. "Wrong to dig up the past like this, I suppose. Painful."

"Painful?"

"Well, you know, passage of time, change, all that sort of thing. Last night we landed up in the same bedroom where I slept with Kamala all those years ago. It was quite a shock."

Madho Dev observed him thoughtfully. His mustache twitched. "You still remember her, eh?"

"You must be joking. Of course I do. Is she still—"

"You don't know whether she's dead or alive, do you?" He smiled. "Well, she's alive and well and spends most of her time in Terripur these days."

"The hill station?"

"Yes."

"The place the four of us went on holiday that time?"

"You remember, then?"

"I remember everything. Whatever should best be forgotten, I remember. The older I get, the more things come back."

Madho Dev unwound his turban. His graying hair was long and curly. "After you left, I lost track of her; that's really the truth. I wasn't keeping anything from you. Found out later she'd gone off and married a Sikh: love marriage. He died piloting his own plane and she married again, some Punjabi millionaire who lived in Europe. He also died, left her some property in Paris; she still spends time there. Had one child with each husband, a boy and a girl. Then her father died and she inherited everything. She's extremely rich, I gather, but drinks too much."

"She goes to Paris?" said David. "How very odd. Philippa and I are often there."

Madho Dev nodded. "Avenue Montagne. It's just as well you never met. I think she hoped to forget you."

"I'm sure," said David. "Does she live alone?"

Madho Dev shrugged his shoulders. "Haven't seen her for some time. Hear about her second-hand from the few friends we still have in common. Most of our old crowd dropped us, you know: can't understand Devika and me living like this; guess they expected me to go into business, something respectable. After Independence, being a prince meant nothing if you didn't have the money to go with it. We never dreamed, when we supported them, the Congress would mean the end of us. We thought we'd have a role to play."

"But your family was so illustrious. Unbroken succession without adoption for nine hundred years, wasn't it?"

"Was and is." Madho Dev smiled. "I have three grandsons to keep it going. But it means nothing to this trash who are running things. Slowly they have squeezed us dry."

"But why should they have done that? The princes were the most educated group. I should think the Congress would have needed every intelligent person they could find."

"Jealousy, I suspect—our great Indian defect. Some of us were all right, but a great many were drunken sots." He sighed. "What's done is done. By now you must have seen the results of this social tinkering."

"Chaos," said David, shaking his head.

"We call it Kali Yug, the end of the world. But what about you, my friend? You seem prosperous and happy; a beautiful wife."

"We still have our land, they haven't taken that or our house, but we have high taxes and death duties. Unless I make my property over to my son ten years before my death, it will all go in taxes."

"Tell me about your son."

"Edward"—David cleared his throat—"is a drug addict, got into it at Eton. By the time I found out it was too late. Terribly upsetting, really, one of the reasons I decided to come out here—to get away, give myself some perspective."

"And your daughter?"

"Remarkable girl, in the throes of her third divorce."

Madho Dev rolled his large eyes. "So it's like that?"

"Afraid so, and the worst part is one can't put one's finger on the cause. Where is the heroin Edward takes actually coming from? Why is Belinda so restless, unresourceful, bored, and stubborn? I feel so useless. Why can't I do anything about it?"

"I'm sure you've tried, old chap."

"At least here you still seem to have a certain stability. Look at your son. You're a very lucky man."

Madho Dev's face lit up. "We call it karma, as you'll remember, or perhaps it's just luck. Stay here for a while, though, and you'll soon see we have the rot too. Perhaps it's different here, a kind of mind rot, but we have it. Too many people; not enough to go around. You must have noticed. Four hundred million more since you left."


PHILIPPA had followed Devika's graceful, measured stride out under the rustling leaves of the pipal tree to another wing of the house, where a cool wide hall tiled in black and white hexagonal designs offered relief from the heat of the courtyard. She was enchanted by the beauty and craftsmanship of the work and remarked about it to Devika. Intent upon her duties as a hostess, however, and guided only by her memories of her father's court, Devika nodded curtly. She had always detested the superior light in which the English memsahibs seemed to hold themselves. What did they, who had always been spoiled and pampered, know of the dangers and problems of life?

Several rooms opened off the hall, and into one of these she conducted her guest. The floor was covered with a priceless Moghul carpet. In one corner stood a carved and painted bed; in another, behind a magnificent teakwood screen of peacocks and lotuses, a music stand held two violins.

"What a lovely room!" said Philippa. "So restful. Do you play the violin?"

"For my pleasure only. I'm afraid I'm not terribly good at it, but now that my three daughters are gone, I have more time." She smiled tentatively. "My mother is still alive, she lives in the next room, and my daughter-in-law, Gayatri, and her five children are down the hall. Would you care to see their rooms?"

"I wouldn't want to disturb them."

"It doesn't matter," said Devika. She opened a door into a nearly identical room where a gaunt old woman in a white sari sat cross-legged on a large pillow, knitting.

"My mother," said Devika, her finely drawn eyebrows arched in an expression that betrayed a certain amused resignation. The old woman nodded but did not get up or attempt to speak. "My mother has taken a vow of silence for one year; that is why she does not speak to you. Otherwise, she would be babbling away." The old woman smiled mischievously.

The walls of the room were hung with old photographs. Handsome men in turbans with huge coiffed mustaches, ropes of pearls and diamonds around their necks glared out of elaborately carved frames, while jewel-covered maidens in elaborate costumes posed stiffly against painted backgrounds of romantic English gardens.

"My ancestors," said Devika with a diffident wave of her hand.

A servant brought in a lunch tray, knelt beside the old woman, and proceeded to feed her.

"Come," said Devika. "I will show you the bath, and then we'll visit my daughter-in-law."

After washing and repairing her face and hair in a large, well-appointed room with a white marble tub set in the floor and an elaborately carved washbasin, Philippa followed Devika down a long corridor to a pair of teakwood doors. Devika knocked, opened the door a crack, and said something in Hindi.

"Aiyiay, aiyiay; come in," said a high-pitched voice on the other side, and a young woman with fair skin and striking emerald green eyes, her dark hair hanging loosely to her waist, pressed her palms together in the Hindu fashion. "You must forgive my appearance," she said in halting English. "I have just come from the barn."

"My daughter-in-law, Gayatri," said Devika formally. "Gayatri, this is Mrs. Bruce. The Bruces just arrived from England. You may remember Arjun's father speaking many times of his old friend, Captain David Bruce?"

The young woman nodded cautiously. A frightened doe, thought Philippa.

"I am showing Mrs. Bruce our women's quarters, so she won't get the impression we are kept in closets."

Although she'd married David when she was eighteen, Philippa had not been untouched by the lives of her friends who had rebelled against the accepted standards of conventional English womanhood. Now she wondered how these obviously strong women could continue to permit themselves to be segregated, told where and how they must live, whom they should meet? It was positively medieval.

Except for a television set, the furnishings of the room duplicated the others. The only difference was a magnificent collection of animal prints and paintings that hung on the wall.

"More illustrious ancestors." Devika smiled.

It broke the ice and they all laughed.

"I like animals too," said Philippa. "On our farm in England I raise horses, and we have cattle, pigs, goats, sheep, dogs, and a variety of chickens and other fowl. But your animals seem almost human. Or am I just imagining this?"

"Perhaps, as they have no fear of being eaten, they are more secure and able to develop to higher states," replied Gayatri.

Philippa felt the floor open beneath her. "Well, naturally we don't eat our dogs or horses," she said defensively.

"My daughter-in-law is a strict vegetarian," said Devika. "You must forgive her. Her own husband, my son, eats wild pig and venison."

As she suddenly realized the great gulf of cultural differences that separated them, Philippa's mind went blank. One awkward moment followed another.

"It's time for the news," cried Gayatri finally and turned on an old radio set.

"You delivered the calf?" asked Devika.

The young woman nodded. "Unfortunately a bullock. Now Father will want to sell it immediately." She turned up the sound, and they listened while the news was read in Hindi.

Devika's face became troubled. She twisted the end of her sari in her hands and turned to leave. "Lunch will be ready soon," she said. "Where are the children?"

"In the kitchen bothering the cook." Gayatri laughed. "I'll just change and join you after they've been fed."


IN THE large dining room, two ceiling fans whirred above a long low mahogany table, surrounded by cushions, that stretched the length of the room. Three massive jardinieres of export porcelain filled with scarlet geraniums stood silhouetted against doors overlooking a jasmine-covered veranda. The only other objects in the room were two barefoot servant boys, who stood motionless on the cool indigo tiles, waiting.

Everyone sat down on the cushions and crossed their legs. Arjun's dark eyes flashed mischievously as Philippa struggled to get her knees under the table and finally gave up. Madho Dev said he hoped the Bruces wouldn't mind eating on the floor, Indian fashion. In the old days, of course, they had chairs and dined off tables using silver utensils. But when they returned to Kotagarh and built this farmhouse, he and Devika decided to follow the customs of the local people. Eaten with one's fingers, the food tasted better, and sitting on the floor kept them all fit.

The two servant boys now came and went bearing steaming plates of rice and curried vegetables. Devika stared impassively down the table at Madho Dev. That her husband felt he must apologize to these people seemed inconceivable to her. And why must he talk so much? Eating was a biological function, not an occasion for social intercourse. She had always found the European custom of engaging in conversation while putting food into one's mouth, barbaric.

Madho Dev continued on bravely. What did David think of Mrs. Thatcher's government? Why had the British issued second-class passports to Indians and Pakistanis living in England? And so on. When he ran out of questions, he turned to the subject of the newborn calf.

Out of the corner of his eye, David watched as Philippa strove valiantly to transfer rice and curry from her plate to her mouth with her fingers.

"In my father's day, a young bull calf like that would be used for baiting tigers," said Madho Dev gruffly.

"Happily those days are gone," said Arjun.

"You'll see, we'll get a good price for him in a year, really," Gayatri pleaded.

The family knew that Gayatri became attached to young animals and tended to spoil them until they became disobedient.

"Enough to pay for his fodder, I hope," said Madho Dev. "Really, we should sell him right now."

"Do you still shoot, Dev?" asked David.

"A bit now and then, but not for sport," replied Madho Dev. "As you know, I never liked it all that much. But in my father's day one wasn't considered a man unless one hunted. Killed my first tiger when I was fourteen, over in Gwalior; old Scindia was a friend of Father's, admired him because he was such a great shot."

"We have over three hundred tigers in the game preserve now," put in Arjun.

"Arjun is in charge of our local game park," explained Madho Dev.

"I'd very much like to go there with you," said David. "I'm sure Philippa would enjoy it too."

"You are in the park here, more or less," said Arjun. "An arm of it comes down and meets the river a few furlongs away."

"Officially, it's part of the park," said Madho Dev. "But we have trouble keeping these nomadic people out of it, so the groundcover is pretty well eaten away by their livestock."

"The desert follows the tail of the goat," said Arjun. "If these people and their animals aren't controlled soon, the whole of Rajasthan will turn into a desert. We have over a hundred guards on the borders of the park, and still the edges are being slowly eaten away."

"Too much freedom in India," said Madho Dev. "We Indians are too easygoing, refuse to discipline ourselves. That's why we admired you." He smiled at David. "You British have this concept of self-discipline."

"There is more news of the Golden Temple," announced Gayatri. "They say heavy fighting is going on, but the Temple itself has not been damaged."

Arjun shrugged his square shoulders. "You believe everything you hear on the radio. How do you know what is really happening?"

Philippa resented the tone he used with his wife, as if any information from her was not to be taken seriously.

"It's a great mistake to have gone into their Temple," said Madho Dev.

"But how can you let terrorists take over a holy place, use it for a fortress?" asked David.

Madho Dev pulled at his mustache. "The question is, who are the real terrorists, the Sikhs or the government of India? The whole mess is a creation of Indira Gandhi and the politicians. This fellow Bhindranwale was only an illiterate village preacher; they cultivated him, thought he was some kind of fool who could be manipulated to split the Sikh vote in Punjab. Now he's decided he's a warrior saint, Saint Jarnail Singh from the village of Bhindran." Madho Dev held up his hands in a gesture of hopelessness. "But if I remember my English history correctly, your Henry II had the same problem with someone called Thomas à Becket. The Congress Party is getting back the results of all their wrong actions, their treachery, thirty-seven years of broken promises. And now the whole country will suffer."

"Let's not get started on the broken promises, Father." Arjun grinned. "I'm sure Captain Bruce is not interested in our politics."

"Please do call me David," said David. "Enough of these formalities. And I am interested in your politics, passionately!"

"I'll call you Uncle," said Arjun. "It would not be proper for me to call you David; that's for Father. When would you like to visit the park?" Arjun gave David a quick searching look whose intensity caught him off guard.

"We've absolutely no schedule," said David, glancing toward Philippa. "I've arranged everything at home so we can be away for six months if we choose. Thought we might visit one of the hill stations for a while and of course Calcutta and Agra . . . so whenever it's convenient for you, we'd love to come along."

"I go for a week at a time. Could you rough it that long? We'd pack in supplies and live in one of the park guesthouses."

"That sounds splendid," said David.

A beautiful young boy of five or six, eyes heavily outlined in kohl, long hair curled over his shoulders, suddenly burst into the room, trailed by a servant, and jumped into Gayatri's lap.

"My youngest grandson," said Madho Dev proudly. "Come here, Sona, I want you to meet my old friend from England, Captain Bruce, and Mrs. Bruce."

Released from Gayatri's arms, Sona skipped around the table and shook hands with David and Philippa. David noticed he had green eyes like his mother and reminded himself to ask Madho Dev about her background.

The servants removed the lunch dishes and brought in rasmalai, sweet dumplings made from milk solids floating in almond-flavored cream.

Just then there was a commotion in the hallway and a craggy old patriarch with a white beard and blue turban limped in on a cane, accompanied by a heavyset young man who halted in the door. The old man was agitated and obviously anxious to unburden himself. Seeing Philippa and David, however, he turned back.

"Baithiyay; sit, Harbinder Singh," said Madho Dev, waving to a cushion hastily drawn up by Gayatri. "And your son; let Harpal come in too. Why does he hesitate like some stranger?"

The old man said something in Punjabi. Removing his sandals, the son loped in and squatted behind him. Madho Dev introduced everyone in Punjabi and English: Harbinder Singh was the neighbor whose lands bordered his, with whom he cooperated in sharing farm equipment. His elder son, Harpal, had grown up with Arjun. Harbinder Singh had come to Kotagarh from Lahore in 1947. He had been a major in the army of the Punjab, a member of the landed aristocracy, but at Partition all their lands had become part of Pakistan and Harbinder Singh had started over again here on a small farm granted by the government. Harbinder Singh's younger brother had been a classmate of Madho Dev's at Mayo College.

"Have you heard the news?" cried the old man in a mixture of Hindi and English. "That woman has sent her low-caste *jawans*— soldiers—into Harminder Sahib, the Golden Temple. It is not to be believed. Do you have any idea how that makes us feel? It is the beginning of civil war. We Sikhs will not stand for it."

"We have heard," replied Madho Dev grimly. "Devika and Gayatri have been listening to All-India Radio. They have told us everything."

"But you haven't heard all. We have just received a telephone call from my wife's family in Punjab. Hearing that the army had gone into the Temple, all the men from the surrounding villages gathered and began marching toward Amritsar, but the authorities brought in helicopters and are gassing them. That is what is going on now. They are dropping poison gas on the countryside all around Amritsar, while inside the Temple a fierce battle wages, hand to hand. They say Saint Bhindranwale is putting up a good fight. And some Sikh in England has just offered a large reward for that Gandhi woman's life over BBC." The old man's eyes were sparkling with suppressed tears. "What will become of us now? Harpal wants to get on his motorcycle and set out at once for Amritsar. If I were younger I would go myself, but if he goes, I know I will never see him alive again and he is my eldest son."

David wondered what had got into the BBC, letting someone offer a reward for Mrs. Gandhi's life. It could endanger every British person in India. He looked glumly at Madho Dev.

Madho Dev held up his hand. "None of us has enough information to say what is happening. I'm sure the P.M. is doing the only thing she can do under the circumstances. After all, Saint Bhindranwale has given orders for the killing of many Hindus, and people are upset. But Harpal must not go to Amritsar. Harpal, you are needed here. Chances are they closed all roads and sealed the borders before attacking."

"That is true," said Devika. "That was one of the first announcements."

"So, you see, you couldn't get there, Harpalji. You must go about your daily work; that is the most important thing. You are your father's right arm. It is your duty to remain here."

The pugnacious Harpal looked as though he wanted to punch someone. "You didn't talk to my cousins. I did. They say it is time for Sikhs to take up arms. They say thousands of women and children are being massacred inside the Temple." He cracked his knuckles. "She

has sent in her bhangi"—shit-carrier—"and chamar"—shoemaker—
"troops into the Temple on purpose to pollute it."

In his heart, Madho Dev felt sure Harpal was right. Indira Gandhi
could be vindictive. In Rajasthan, during her so-called Emergency,
she had done the same thing to the Jaipur family: sent in soldiers of the
lowest caste to search the Jaipur palace and treasury. But he did not
want to seem unpatriotic in front of Harbinder Singh. Gossip traveled
fast. One's friend one day might be an enemy the next, or he might be
arrested, tortured, and made to say something against you. It was
dangerous to be too candid.

"Sikhs aren't supposed to believe in caste," he said. "You must listen
to reason, Harpal, your father's and mine. I have known you since you
were born; I think of you as my own. If you try to go, I shall try to
stop you."

Harpal turned his face away and stared moodily into space.

"Fifty years ago the odds might have been even." Madho Dev
pressed his point. "But today men armed with handguns are no match
for the weapons of a modern army. With the government controlling
the food supply of an army of three million, civil war is not possible.
Mistakes have been made on both sides—criminal mistakes, that is
true—but think, Harpal, if it weren't that your father got a telephone
two years ago and television last year, you would not even know about
it. So be happy you are in Kotagarh instead of Punjab."

The servant brought small cups of coffee and a tray of crushed betel
nuts wrapped in pan leaves. Although pressed to try some by Devika,
Philippa remembered the red drool that oozed from the taxi driver's
mouth, and declined. David could see Devika felt rebuffed. It was
considered a social slight to turn down pan offered by one's host or
hostess, and although the stuff upset his stomach, David dutifully
popped one into his mouth. The pan chewing seemed to calm Harpal
Singh. Devika pursed her lips, and she and Gayatri excused themselves, taking Sona with them; Philippa was left with the men, and
Madho Dev wondered what to do with her.

He sighed, fanned himself with his napkin, and glanced at David.
"Oppressive, this heat, just before the rains; keeps everyone on edge.
You must both be tired. You'll find the room off my study quite
comfortable. After lunch, a nap, eh, David? I think you must remember that much from the old days, except now we have electric
fans."

David nodded and helped Philippa to her feet. "Considering what
Harbinder Singh has told us about this death threat to Mrs. Gandhi
on the BBC, shouldn't I attempt to call the British High Commission

in Delhi?" Unbelievable as it seemed to him, it looked as though the British were interfering in a serious way.

"You're welcome to try if you like," said Madho Dev, "but I can assure you it will take hours. First of all, it's just after lunch, and if any operators are actually in the exchange, they'll be so sleepy they won't answer, or if they do they won't keep trying your call, which is necessary if you want to get through. Please remember where you are, my friend, and try to relax. Nothing much is going to happen here in Kotagarh. It never has and it won't now. And if worse came to worst, we could hide you in the game preserve for years."

Arjun led David and Philippa to a cool dark room in a connecting wing between the men's quarters and those of the women. There were two low beds, teakwood tables, several old campaign chests, chairs, and a large bathroom beyond.

"I hope you'll be comfortable here," he said. "If you need anything, just press the button and a servant will come." He turned on the ceiling fan, stared at Philippa inquisitively, and left the room.

As it always had, the betel nut was making David dizzy and he excused himself to bathe. When he returned he found Philippa was still awake, staring into space.

"I think it's all going to be too much for me, David, really I do. I'm not interested in their involved politics, and they do things so very differently from us. If you don't behave exactly as they wish, they're upset—like Devika, just now, stalking off in a huff because I wouldn't try that betel nut. It's all too tiresome."

"How did it go when you were alone with her?"

"She was polite enough, I suppose. Rather bossy. It wasn't what she said, it was her attitude. I was the spoiled memsahib; she was the vastly superior Indian princess. I felt like a naughty child with a nanny—and for no reason; she doesn't even know me. Damn rude, if you ask me!"

"Unfortunately, most women of our race she's dealt with have been rather spoiled. She used to tell me how she hated the wife of the British Resident attached to her father's court: putting on airs, ordering everyone about. You see, we didn't bother the twenty-one- and nineteen-gun-salute states—too much money and power—but we harassed the smaller nobility, and except for a few rare cases, the British mems were really impolite to Indian women."

"Residents? You mean our civil servants?"

"Not the old boys like your great-grandfather, of course, but his flunkies and their wives, the ones we sent out to do our dirty work."

"But I'm not like them. Not only is this 1984, nearly a hundred years later, but I'm half American. I don't even think the same way."

"Devika doesn't know that. You must give her a chance."

Philippa sighed. "It's not just that, it's everything. All this living on the floor, getting up and down, watching them eat with their hands—frankly, I was nauseated, especially as I notice there's no paper in any of the loos."

"The heat's getting to you, darling," said David gently. "You'll feel completely different when the monsoon breaks; it's a beautiful time of year. The temperature will drop twenty degrees."

"When will that happen?" Philippa asked doubtfully.

"A week, two at the most. It ought to start any time. Please try, for my sake. I agree it's a big change, physically and every other way, but perhaps all this getting up and down is good for us."

"I suppose so"—she pouted, gaminelike—"but I loathe it. And all these male servants. I miss my maid."

"Philippa, really!"

"Well, I do."

"What you need," declared David firmly, "is to get some exercise, get out on a horse. If I know Madho Dev, he'll have some good horses here. When Devika sees how well you ride, she'll think quite differently about you."

"Is she good with horses?"

"First class. She used to play polo; wasn't allowed in any matches, of course: pity. She's a terrific shot too; used to hit a moving target at a hundred yards, riding at a full gallop. Do try and relax, darling. This means so very much to me."


TOWARD evening the muffled beat of drums awakened David from his nap: drums, the immemorial sound of India. He'd been dreaming of Bengal; a boy again, he was lying in a cool room of his uncle's house, staring into the darkness, waking from his hated daily nap, thinking of his mother and father who had died of typhoid the previous year within the space of a few months. He disliked his uncle and missed his parents horribly.

But this was certainly not Bengal, he realized with a start as he became aware of the ceiling fan. In his uncle's house there had been a punkah on the ceiling, manipulated by a string that went through a hole in the wall to an anteroom, where it was tied to the big toe of a boy called Hari, who sat half dazed, wagging his foot back and forth.

In fact, the amazing thing about Hari was that he could really sleep and keep working those fans.

His mind cleared. Across the room Philippa was still asleep. He got up and splashed himself with cool water. When he returned, she was awake.

"God, it's hot." She sighed.

"Have a cool bath, you'll feel revived." He stumbled around the dark room, trying to find his clothes.

"Is that drumming I hear?"

"And a harmonium. Seems to be coming from the courtyard."

They dressed and went out on the veranda. The sun was just setting. A large crowd had gathered in the courtyard, and there was Madho Dev, playing a harmonium, seated in front of a fire which burned brightly in a round pit. Arjun sat beside him, beating on a large oblong drum, while a white-haired old man with a mustache that fanned out like the wings of a luna moth played a wind instrument.

When Madho Dev saw them, he motioned them forward to sit beside him—David on his right with the men, Philippa on his left with the women. Philippa found this constant separation of scxcs hard to understand. Not that she really minded it, but what was the point? Devika handed her a pair of cymbals and showed her how to use them. She felt awkward and let them rest in her lap. On a floor cushion again, her knees beginning to ache, she found herself longing for the comfortable chairs of her drawing room in England, where about this time of day she would be sipping a whiskey sour, scanning *Vogue* or *Town and Country* and waiting for David to dress for dinner. Looking around through half-closed eyes, she caught glimpses of eager faces—young and old—scrutinizing her. Why did they have to stare so? It made her feel freakish.

After repeating a few chords on his instrument, Madho Dev began a long introduction to a song; she was surprised by the sweet quality of his voice, which traversed the scale in a series of tremulous notes from high falsetto to lowest base. The wind instrument played by the old man mimicked Madho Dev's voice and cleverly improvised on the melody set forth in the first few bars. Then Arjun picked up the beat and Madho Dev broke into song, punctuated by dramatic gestures. As he pointed to the sky, Philippa caught the words "Krishna, Krishna," and everyone followed his gaze, as if Krishna were out there, lurking in the night. She didn't know much about the Indian gods and had always associated Krishna with those sickly pale-faced young people who shaved their heads and begged in airports and train stations. The women around her were singing and clapping their hands. How did they manage to reach those peculiar high-pitched birdlike notes which sounded so inhuman? But then she supposed Wagner would sound just as strange to them. Everyone in the courtyard was now swaying together. The song reached a crescendo and then stopped.

Madho Dev turned and spoke quietly to her. "When my father was ruler here he had evening receptions, called durbars, open to everyone. Light for the house would be brought from a fire that had burned continually in front of the family gods in the palace temple for hundreds of years. At that time anyone could come and speak with him and tell him their problems. There was singing of devotional songs like this and general discussion. The old man you see with the flute was the court bard, a hereditary position. After Father died, while I was away in Bombay, he kept the fire going in the temple, he and a Brahmin priest, and when we came back he urged me to continue the practice. So we moved the fire here, where it's been burning now for twenty-five years. The people were lost without a focus. Slowly we began to have these gatherings again and now, even though I have no power, I try to help them with their problems. The politicians despise me for it; they're a greedy lot, only out to cheat these poor folk. But I know the law; I tell them their rights. For that I'm seen as a dangerous element."

All this was said sotto voce in English so that no one but Philippa and David should hear Madho Dev. Several people in the crowd now addressed him, and for the next hour he sat listening to complaints and problems. Then he solemnly waved sticks of incense in front of a small plaster image of a goddess whose shrine nestled in the roots of the pipal tree, poured libations onto the fire from various small silver bowls placed in front of him by Devika, and repeated a long prayer.

Sitting in the courtyard, which seemed all the more quiet for the number of people gathered there, David realized his friend had changed profoundly. From the genial, hard-drinking young playboy prince and war hero he'd known, a new person had evolved: compassionate, wise. Like a moth from a chrysalis, the transformation was so complete, hardly a trace of the original remained. How had he done it?

The old bard had begun another song. Madho Dev accompanied him, translating for them as he went. "He is telling the story of one of the great battles of our clan. How when everything seemed lost, the warriors all slain, the wives preparing to immolate themselves on a pyre they'd built, the maharaja's first wife put on men's clothes and armor and, with other brave wives, rode forth through the gate, slew the leader of the attacking forces, and turned the tide. It all happened nearly a thousand years ago, but to these people it might as well be yesterday."

Philippa exchanged glances with Devika. A moment of recognition seemed to pass between the two women.

"You are thinking that your old friend Dev has changed, aren't you, David?" Madho Dev whispered.

"You're reading my mind," David replied. "I was also thinking how I have *not* changed, but have been hanging on to the past, to youthful dreams, like a shipwrecked sailor. The past is gone, isn't it?"

"The past is always slipping away and yet is never gone," said Madho Dev. "The more fixed we are, the more things seem to change. You should have come back sooner, my friend. I was here waiting for you all this time."

The sky lit up above the rooftops, and a long roll of thunder sounded from the southwest. The old bard lifted his hands and uttered a salute.

"You have arrived just as the rains are coming," said Madho Dev. "That is auspicious. Within a few days, monsoon will be here. It's late this year."

The crowd in the courtyard began to disperse. Gayatri took the children off to bed, and Devika stood talking to a group of young peasant women.

"We must be getting back to the guesthouse," said David. "I'm afraid we've strained your hospitality."

Madho Dev looked pained. "There you go again, acting like an Englishman. You are in India now. My house is yours. Go back to the Tourist Bungalow if you must, but first have some food. We eat very lightly at night—a few puris, some fruit. Come."

In the dining room the conversation turned to the coming rains and whether the farm was prepared: there were some tiles missing on the roof of the granary, some fields still to be plowed. Arjun pointed out that if David and Philippa wanted to visit the game preserve and hoped to see tigers, they'd better do it immediately.

"Right now, except for a few spots, the waterholes are all dried up, but once the monsoon breaks and there is plenty of water, it becomes most difficult to find them."

"Quite right." Madho Dev nodded.

"My suggestion is that you come with me tomorrow," Arjun said eagerly. "I'm going in for five days. I'll be touring around, but we've built a very nice cottage overlooking one of the best waterholes, where you'll be able to sit and watch everything. It has a jeep that goes with it. You can drive around the park if you like. Best not to walk, though; our tigers aren't afraid of jeeps but they're wary of people. And you'll have an interesting neighbor not too far away."

The whole family laughed. David and Philippa looked bewildered.

"A holy man." Devika smiled. "It's our little secret. We are laughing because he is not supposed to be there but we are hiding him."

"A great sage," said Madho Dev. "He's been living there as long as anyone can remember."

"Claims he's the lord of the universe," said Arjun. "We let him stay; after all, he was there before the park. I make sure none of the bosses see him. Our only problem is that villagers nearby know about him and walk through the forest to see him. Several of them have been badly mauled by tigers, one even eaten."

"But how does he live?" asked Philippa.

"That's just it," replied Devika animatedly. "We don't know."

"He lives on roots and leaves from the forest," Madho Dev said, "and he has a cow."

"Don't the tigers go after the cow?" asked David.

"That is another strange thing," said Devika. "He takes the cow out to graze, and it is said the tigers have been seen walking with them. We call him Durga Baba after the goddess Durga, who rides a tiger. She is one of our principal deities. In olden times, before a battle, we Rajputs always prayed to Durga. She's very ferocious."

"Perhaps you'll meet him," said Madho Dev, "although he's very shy."

"When do we leave?" asked David.

"Could you be ready by nine in the morning?" asked Arjun. His dark eyes darted toward Philippa. "You can store your extra luggage here. We'll reach park headquarters by midday, have lunch, and drive in the rest of the way when it cools. The roads aren't very good, but we should arrive in time to unpack and have dinner before it gets too dark."

David glanced at Philippa.

"Sounds marvelous to me," she said, and smiled at Gayatri. "Won't you come too? It would be nice to have some female companionship."

Gayatri blushed, glancing at Arjun. His handsome face revealed nothing. "I . . . ah . . . think I should remain here with the children," she said shyly, "but Mother could go."

"I'm afraid I can't," Devika said reluctantly. "If it were any other time, I would. I'd love seeing Durga Baba, but there is too much for me to do here before the rains begin."

Madho Dev shrugged his shoulders. "Go if you like. We can manage."

"I think it's best I stay here," she concluded. "During the rainy season, when the flowers come out, then I'll go. The jungle flowers are so beautiful."

"You must come to England for a visit. I have a beautiful garden," Philippa said impulsively. "I spend half my time working in it."

"You work in it yourself?" asked Devika, surprised.

"Why, of course," replied Philippa.

Devika glanced at her husband. "I would like to do that, but Dev won't allow it; says the servants would think it wasn't fitting."

Devika had relaxed a bit: at some point during the singing, or perhaps when Madho Dev told the story about the queen who had saved her husband. Philippa was relieved. If she could somehow really get to know such a woman, India might prove less daunting.

# 3

THE FOLLOWING MORNING Philippa was up early, and by the time David had awakened from another bout of dreaming, there was a steaming cup of tea in front of him. "Come on, darling, it's not a morning to lie in bed," she said brightly. "See what a splendid day it is. That dreadful dust is gone. You'd better get up and get ready. Arjun will be here any moment."

David bathed, dressed, and stood on the veranda inhaling the sweet fresh air. It was reassuring to see Philippa in good form again. When she was happy, the world seemed filled with energy, and you felt everything was going to turn out right; when she was not, she could put you in hell.

Just then Arjun drove up and jumped out of his jeep. "Morning, sahib." He grinned. "Kind of morning one feels really young again, eh?"

David laughed. "I'll have you know I'm not a sahib and refuse to be made into one."

"You are a very pukka sahib, Uncleji"—Arjun smiled—"and that's a compliment. But if you prefer not to be called that, I'll refrain, except in front of servants. They wouldn't understand you any other way."

David put his arm around Arjun's shoulder. "Call me anything you want. I have an Indian name too."

"You do?"

"Yes, of course. After all, I was born here. Your father never mentioned it?"

"You were born in India?"

"Yes, on a Sunday. It was full moon, so I was called Raviwar-chandra, shortened to Ravi by my ayah. You may call me that if you like."

"I'll try, but it will probably turn out Uncle." Arjun laughed merrily.

They loaded their bags onto the jeep and, after depositing the ones they wouldn't need with Madho Dev, were soon bouncing along the country road that bordered the park.

Cutting through the dry scrub of the foothills, they reached a narrow canyon, which they followed for several miles. Soon the jungle became thick and lush. A sparkling river fell over huge boulders where herons, egrets, and indigo kingfishers with scarlet beaks hunted fish. The transparent atmosphere was alive with birdcalls and the chatter of monkeys. They climbed a steep hill and stopped. Arjun explained they had reached the top of a three-hundred-foot dam constructed centuries ago by his forebears.

Starting up again, he pointed out marshland formed as a result of the slow filling of silt behind the dam. "The perfect habitat for tigers. That is why the entire three thousand square kilometers has been protected for years as a shooting area by the rulers whose lands bordered it. They were strong conservationists; knew that game was limited and killed only what they considered surplus. The average tiger needs ten square kilometers to hunt in and feed itself. If the tiger population exceeds that, the dominant males begin to fight each other. Those who become incapacitated and unable to hunt turn into man-eaters. When that happens, you know your tiger population must be thinned out. But I'm beginning to sound like a tour guide. Sorry."

"It's fascinating," declared Philippa. "Do go on. What's going to happen now?"

"Fortunately there's so much natural food here—plenty of deer, antelope, black buck, and nilgai for the tigers to feed on—our ratio could probably drop to eight square kilometers per tiger. We are just now finding evidence that the males are beginning to fight. Some of them have to be moved to other sanctuaries or shot. We don't like to start shooting, because the tigers are becoming quite used to us. It would be a shame to change that."

As they went on, crenelated battlements and ruined temples came into view. Driving under an arch, they arrived at a beautiful recon-structed pavilion overlooking a lake, where servants and conservation workers greeted them, and soon lunch was served under an enormous banyan tree while peacocks tame as dogs walked around, begging food. From the terrace of the pavilion, they looked out over a vast expanse of marshland where blue and scarlet lotuses bloomed against a background of mauve-colored water hyacinths. Arjun pointed out what looked like logs on the shore—really crocodiles—and birds which stood on their backs and pecked at parasites. Large herds of spotted deer stood motionless at the water's edge, watching the big mooselike black bucks swimming in a group to the other side.

"What a romantic place!" Philippa beamed. "The lost jungle king-dom!"

Arjun smiled. "Yes, from here it is very romantic. But for the animals out there it is quite another. Also for us. You must absolutely never go walking about. The tigers won't attack a jeep as long as everyone sits very still, but never forget they are our hereditary enemies. It's in their genes. From here it's quite dangerous to go more than fifty meters on foot. A tiger has great patience. It will sit stock-still for hours, and you will never see it until it's too late. One of our servants was picked off by an old female a week ago. He'd gone out in the high grass to perform his morning ablutions, and that was the end of him."

"How awful," said Philippa and looked at the peaceful scene before her in a different light.

The sun burned mercilessly in the sky and the dry reeds of the lakeshore rattled in the wind. They retired for the midday nap and David slept dreamlessly for the first time since he'd arrived in India.

After tea they set out again, driving through grass higher than a man, skirting lakes, and finally climbing over a long plateau of dry brush to drop down into dense jungle interspersed with thickets of cane and palm along a dried-up streambed.

Ever on the lookout, Arjun suddenly stopped, jumped out, and inspected the dusty road ahead. "Look sharp," he said softly. "We have a big one nearby, crossed here less than an hour ago."

Driving cautiously now, he stopped again. The tiger had come back onto the road and walked down it. David was impressed with Arjun's tracking skills and got out to look.

"See here." Arjun pointed. David saw there were now human

footprints alongside those of the tiger. "Our holy man," explained Arjun. "We've never seen them together, but we know he's friendly with the tigers because we see these prints."

Returning to the jeep, they followed the two pairs of tracks until they left the road. "Ah," said Arjun, "you see? That is the path to his kuti, his habitation. Actually, he has taken a cave and blocked up the front of it with stone to form a hut of sorts."

They went on a short distance, and Arjun pointed to the base of a cliff visible through the majestic jungle trees, where a tall man with white hair to his knees stood in the setting sun.

"Why, he's stark naked," observed Philippa, looking through her binoculars. "How extraordinary. Here, see."

"He looks very robust," said David. "How old did you say he was?"

Arjun laughed. "That's just it. The oldest person I know—a villager who must be near eighty—says he's always looked that way. No one really knows."

"Mind you, one doesn't see these fellows too often," said David. "Come to think of it, I haven't seen one since we arrived." He put down the binoculars. "Before, one saw them everywhere."

Arjun nodded. "What to do? The environment is changing. Nowadays these forest yogis are an endangered species. In the past they had a function: ministering to the people, healing the sick, bringing news. Now your Western magic has captured everyone's imagination. Men on the moon, that was a major blow; magic pills that seem to cure most diseases; strange voices on transistor radios and on television, the magic box. It's powerful stuff. These men are being neglected. The serious ones are all hiding in remote jungle areas like this. We have more at the southern border of the sanctuary, but Durga Baba is the only one in this area." He waved. The naked man responded with a taciturn gesture and disappeared.

"I certainly don't see any tiger up there," said Philippa, shading her eyes.

"Sher Khan is nearby," said Arjun. "You can count on that."

"How long did you say this chap has lived here?" asked David.

"As long as anyone can remember. When the area became a sanctuary, we had orders to evict him but didn't. The local District Magistrate finally came to throw him out, but the Baba cursed him—a regular Vedic curse in Sanskrit. All about what would happen to the D.M. and his descendants and the souls of his ancestors for seven generations back if he was forced to leave. The D.M. was scared to death and never pressed the issue. Later, word came down that Mrs.

Gandhi herself was interested in meeting the Baba, but he refused to go to Delhi. We've heard nothing since, so here he remains."

Starting up again, they drove along the edge of the valley beneath low-lying limestone cliffs until they reached an outcropping of rocks, shaded by tall trees overlooking a boulder-lined pond. Against the cliff, a modern rustic cabin with a balcony had been built on stilts. Under the cabin was another jeep. As they unloaded, Arjun explained that the waterhole was, in fact, one of the deeper parts of a river which in a month's time would be a raging torrent.

"Right now this pool is the only place within ten kilometers for the animals to drink. That's why I suggested you come now before the monsoon breaks."

The cottage had two bedrooms, a large main room divided from the kitchen by a bar, a sit toilet, and a hot shower. Philippa, who'd been preparing herself for a strenuous week of physical effort, was delighted. It was nearly dark. She busied herself stowing away food while Arjun and David unloaded the jeep and lit the Coleman lamps. After they had settled in, David made drinks and they stood out on a deck overlooking the pond. A nearly full moon rose out of the jungle, transforming it into a mysterious paradise of shimmering silver.

David went in to experiment with some dehydrated lobster Newburgh he'd purchased before leaving England. Arjun, free to scrutinize her for the first time, watched Philippa out of the corner of his eye: the first beautiful Western woman he'd ever seen outside the cinema and not half as frightening as he'd imagined. How he longed to touch her blond hair shining there in the moonlight, run his fingers through it, cover his face with it, kiss the skin of bare shoulders. But was there not something about her that was inconsistent with one so desirable, the look of a woman who hadn't been properly loved? He felt a deep masculine urge to arouse her. What would it be like? Would he be able to satisfy her? Just then she glanced at him. Her eyes told him she was reading his mind. Under the pretext of pointing out something at the waterhole, she touched his shoulder.

At the same moment, a thunderous roar pierced the still night.

"What was that?" cried Philippa, clutching his arm. "David, come quick. Did you hear that?"

Arjun knew the tiger's roar was an auspicious sign, for it had given her an excuse to hold on to him. Her fingertips were filled with longing. By the time David came out, she had withdrawn her hand, but not before glancing at him in what he thought was a very odd way.

They watched the waterhole in silence. The jungle trembled. Philippa took both their arms.

"Isn't it marvelous?" she exclaimed. "Really, what an amazing sound."

"A tigress in heat," murmured Arjun.

The tigress roared again, and then a big male suddenly appeared, silhouetted in the moonlight. The tigress approached fawningly. With a swift movement that seemed impossible for such a large animal, he was upon her, biting her neck. They rolled off the rock into some high grass, from which the ferocious sounds of their mating went on for some time.

Back in the cabin, Philippa felt limp with excitement. David produced the Newburgh while Arjun explained the routine they would follow for the next five days. She could barely eat. Each time Arjun's eyes met hers, something queer seemed to happen. And why was he constantly smiling, as if he knew a wonderful secret he was keeping to himself? Even when he was silent, his lips were fixed in a smile so intense she had to look away. She wondered if David noticed. Of course, he would not. He was so lost in his own world, poor dear, he rarely noticed anything. She walked out on the deck again, hoping to see the tigers, but they had gone. The moon sailed between puffs of fast-moving clouds. At last, the real India, she thought, the India she'd always imagined.

BY THE time they rose the following morning, Arjun had left on his round of duties. Philippa's sleep had been disturbed by his face, which had appeared on the body of a tiger. And David, despite his hope that a change of scene would put a stop to his nocturnal *recherches*, had dreamt again of Kamala, a shamelessly erotic dream that left him depressed about growing old. They sipped their coffee in silence and Philippa made scrambled eggs and toast, which they took out on the deck. Morning sun dappled the forest floor. Monkeys chattered in the tops of trees, and at the pond two herons fought fiercely over a fish. Suddenly, from nowhere, the naked hermit appeared and climbed up on a boulder near the pond. For a long time he sat with his legs crossed and seemed to be chanting something. In a lump of clay he had placed before himself, smoke curled from several joss sticks. Then he took off a necklace of large beads and, holding them in his right hand, slowly began to pass them through his fingers.

"Look," whispered Philippa, "he's saying his beads. It's a rosary."

"I believe they're called rudraksha beads," replied David. "Nuts off some tree that grows in the Himalayas."

They watched in silence as the Baba got up and, ambling to the edge of the pond, immersed himself three times, noisily venting water through his nose. Undisturbed by all this, a herd of deer on the other side had been drinking peacefully. Suddenly they raised their heads and bolted into the jungle. Seconds later a large female tiger walked calmly out onto the rock where the Baba had been sitting, flopped down, and put one of her huge paws on his beads. Turning around, he saluted her, bowing three times. David froze, his coffee cup suspended in midair. The Baba nonchalantly shook the water from his matted white locks, waded back to the boulder, sat down beside the tigress, pulled the beads out from under her paw, and resumed his chanting. The tigress let out an indescribable sound, half hiss, half cavernous mew, leisurely circled the pond, and strolled off into the jungle in the wake of the fleeing deer. Philippa was about to clear the breakfast dishes when the Baba turned and beckoned to them.

"Could he be signaling us to come down there?"

"Appears to be," said David.

"Didn't Arjun say we mustn't go outside the cottage except in the jeep?"

"Did he say that?" replied David absently, his eyes focused on the hermit. "I say let's go down; it's just a few steps."

Descending the stairs that led under the cabin, they walked the short distance to the pond. The hermit, who towered over them, greeted them with a raised right hand. Except for his matted white hair, he looked ageless. His sinewy muscles were firm and hard; his broad face, with its long nose, clear eyes, and large ears, from which hung gold earrings, was unlined.

"Wonder if he knows any English?" said David. "English hai?" he asked.

"English tora tora," the yogi answered. "Hindi?"

David nodded. "Tora tora; little little."

The Baba motioned them to sit down.

"We're going to be sitting here on this rock when one of those monsters comes out, I know it," Philippa whispered. "Couldn't we invite him up to the cottage for a bite to eat? He's so big, he must eat a lot."

David tried to convey the idea that they would like him to come up and eat with them. Gesturing to the cottage, he repeated the Hindi word for food, khanna, but the Baba only laughed, rocked back and forth, and patted the rock. They sat down and were just beginning to relax when the Baba uttered a strange cry.

Philippa gasped. "He's calling that tiger, David. Good God! Let's get out of here!"

"Bit too late, I'd say. Look." David nodded toward the opposite end of the pond.

Philippa's heart jumped into her throat. The tigress waded into the water and swam toward them. The Baba stretched out his right arm protectively.

"Let's hope she understands," Philippa whispered, hypnotized by the beast's outrageous beauty.

Then the tigress was up on the rock beside them and they could feel her warm breath. The stench was awful. With her enormous eyes, she gazed down at them, gave a deafening roar, ending in a guttural purr, and plopped down like a huge house cat, her back rubbing against their knees. The Baba sat very still, muttering some incantation. After a few minutes, two half-grown cubs not quite old enough to be out on their own paddled across the pond, shook themselves, and stood there. On her haunches now, the tigress trembled, cuffed them playfully, and sent one rolling back into the water. The grace and swiftness of her movements were amazing.

"Now it's even," muttered David pessimistically. "Three against three."

While their mother swam around in the pool with one cub, the other put its head between its paws and gazed at the Baba. With his left hand he reached out, scratched it under its chin, blew his breath into its nose, and began singing to it. The cub's whiskers twitched, and its eyes closed. Philippa remembered how the manager of their dairy in England would play Mozart and Vivaldi on an old gramophone at milking time. For a moment she was there, walking in her gardens; her famous peony beds would be in full bloom now—what on earth was she doing risking her life here?

Again the tigress approached them across the rocky basin, shook herself, and hissed at her cubs. They hissed back and she spat and growled, baring tusklike teeth; then, as suddenly as she had come, she bounded away. The cubs followed and disappeared into the tall grass. David and Philippa sat quietly, their hearts pounding. David wondered whether to invite the Baba for tea again. Considering he was stark naked, perhaps he wouldn't come. Then he remembered that in India members of certain religious sects attended Parliament and gave speeches in the nude.

"Please join us at the cottage for tea—chaya, chaya." He managed with appropriate gestures. But the Baba only smiled enigmatically and strode off down the forest road. In a daze, David and Philippa scuttled up the path, climbed the steps to the cabin, and fell asleep, exhausted.

LATER that afternoon Arjun appeared, and when they told him what had happened, he stared at them as if they were mad. Although it was obvious from the footprints that the Baba was on intimate terms with tigers, certainly he had never shown such powers to anyone before.

"It must have been very exciting. But didn't I caution you never to go out except in the jeep?"

"He doesn't believe us." Philippa laughed merrily. "But Arjun, it actually happened."

"A great yogi can create illusions, you know, make you think you're seeing things."

"Come, come," cried David, "in broad daylight? Mind you, if that were true it would be even more incredible than what we actually saw. Look here, if you don't believe us, you must stay here tomorrow and see for yourself. Surely he'll come back. He indicated as much."

"Afraid that's impossible, Uncle. Tomorrow I must go to a village on the far side of the sanctuary. And I'm sure he won't come if I am here. He tolerates me because he knows I am on his side, but he stays clear of me as an official."

"But how could he have known you wouldn't be here today?" asked Philippa.

"He knew," declared Arjun. "Perhaps he is what you call clairvoyant—is that the word? Or perhaps he can smell me."

"Now you're poking fun at us." Philippa smiled. "Well, believe what you want. It was a totally unforgettable experience, and I'm a wreck."

"Time for a drink," suggested Arjun. "The usual, Uncle?"

"Uh—yes, I guess so," said David. He was staring at the pond, amazed that he had really been sitting there with three tigers. Arjun went into the kitchen, and Philippa followed him.

"Let me heat some water," she said. "I'd like a hot rum and lemon. Afraid I'm rather drained from all the excitement."

She busied herself cutting and squeezing lemons. He brushed against her several times. She wondered whether he was trying to signal her. Frivolous thoughts of an older woman, she thought, and put it out of mind. They took their drinks to the deck. The moon rose gold through the trees.

"When the rains begin," Arjun said, "centipedes a foot long come out of the ground. Some of the tribals even eat them; great delicacy, they say."

The talk turned to dangerous jungle experiences, then to pigsticking, and David related several stories in which he and Madho Dev had almost been gored, but he concluded that for sheer suspense and excitement nothing in his experience had equaled today's encounter.

Arjun cautioned them again not to make the mistake of going for a walk, either along the road or just to the waterhole.

"It may well be that Durga Baba has learned to control tigers; that does not mean you or I would have the same luck. And even if you use the extra jeep, don't stand up in it. You might find a tiger jumping over your windshield."

After dinner, Philippa excused herself and, to calm her nerves, got into bed with one of the light novels she always carried with her. Arjun sat with David on the deck, watching the moon climb through the vines and towering trees.

"It's so beautiful here, one forgets the rest of India exists," observed David.

"Ah, but it does, Uncle, it does. What would you say if I told you I plan to leave?"

David took out his tobacco, lit his pipe, and puffed slowly.

Arjun continued. "I feel like someone trapped in an insane asylum by mistake."

David liked that image and chuckled. "Well, it is rather that at times, I grant you: open-air madhouse, what? On the other hand, you might miss it very much. I know I did; first when I left as a boy and again in '47. The rest of the world is not as marvelous as you might think."

"That's just it, Uncle." Arjun leaned forward intently. "How can I make any judgments? I must go and see for myself. Father has brought us up in a fantasy world of English traditions. I must go out. I must make up my own mind."

"But your father has changed completely. I didn't see any English traditions."

"You mean he's gone native." Arjun laughed. "That's exactly what he has tried to do, but underneath he is still living in the days of the British Raj."

"You're right about calling it a fantasy." David nodded. "I can tell you England isn't very pleasant these days. Hopeless deterioration of standards and values. I call it the rot."

"Ah, but Uncle, here it is much worse. Here you can see it happening day by day, like mold destroying a plant. The people do not come to us for food anymore, they come for help with their bank loans. In that sense things are better, but the jealousy, the heartlessness: sometimes I feel I'm being eaten alive."

"Man-eaters."

"Exactly. Just as one would never trust a tiger, one cannot trust people here. They will always let you down, go back on their word, amend the laws, even the constitution if it suits them. In forty years our constitution has been amended over sixty times!"

"And yet there's still tremendous freedom here," observed David, "and things seem relatively peaceful."

"There is freedom only at the top," replied Arjun, "and things are calm because people are underfed and communication is kept expensive and erratic. The government controls the price of food, so the average person must work all day just to eat. Nothing is left over. It's impossible to plan ahead more than two or three days."

"And yet one sees so many rich people about," said David. "In Bombay, for example."

"That is true, there are many rich people in India. If my grandfather had not been robbed and killed, we would be among them. But the rich here are very selfish and determined to keep the poor down at all costs."

"Do you think it's different anywhere else, my boy? Not much, I think."

"Listen, Uncle, in this country certain castes lend money at interest rates so high an average man becomes permanently indebted—a bonded laborer. You certainly don't have that in Britain."

"Are you really worried about this average man?" asked David seriously.

"Yes, of course, but not for the reason you think. It is these poor who have multiplied like rabbits, not us. And we have been unable or unwilling to educate them. Now they are unemployable, without values of any kind, and going out of control. In former times, religion was the glue that held India together and kept each person in place. This faith has been shaken. In the near future you will see these people taking things into their own hands. It will be the end of even small landowners like ourselves."

"My dear boy, what you are saying is happening all over the world."

Arjun wished Captain David Bruce would stop calling him his dear boy. Didn't he realize how condescending he sounded?

"Technology is seen as the cure-all"—David droned on—"and the final returns are not in on that. Things have changed so fast. One wonders whether the improvements are real or just so many poultices applied from without when what is needed is a systemic cure. Which is why I've always admired your Indian philosophy of nonaction, brutal as its effects may sometimes seem."

Ah, nonaction, thought Arjun, the universal Indian excuse for the laziness and indifference that infected everyone. How he hated it; it was the ruin of India. But how could he explain that to Captain Bruce, who sat there puffing his pipe, lost in his own version of the world, whatever it was? It was obvious he didn't want to think about helping anyone leave India.

DURING the night it rained again, and in the morning the air was fragrant with the scent of newly awakened herbs and flowers. Philippa got up early and was out on the deck in a dressing gown watching the sun rise when Arjun emerged sleepy-eyed from his room.

"Good morning," she said. "I was just about to make tea. Or would you prefer coffee?"

"Coffee, please," said Arjun. He followed her into the kitchen and stood beside her at the stove. "You went to bed early," he yawned.

"I was exhausted. That business with the tigers yesterday left me a wreck. It didn't really dawn on me how frightened I'd been till I got in bed."

Arjun paced about, running his hands through his thick black hair. Then, unexpectedly, he put his hands around her waist and held her at arm's length. "I didn't bring you out here to be turned into tiger food, you know. Perhaps you realize how careful you must be; I'm not sure Uncle does. I think he rather enjoys taking chances."

"So do I," said Philippa.

He searched her eyes for the meaning of what she had just said. It was obvious she was wearing little or nothing under her bathrobe. He knew from the expression that flickered across her lips that she was attracted to him. Morning had always been the time when his passions were most easily aroused. All his five children had been conceived in the early morning hours. One sign from her and he would do the rest. His bedroom was just there. It would be so simple. But she only smiled blandly with those impenetrable blue eyes which seemed to bounce back the signals he was sending.

"I see there's some porridge here," she said. "You'd better have something to eat before you go."

"I'll just shave and dress," he said, backing away.

Philippa poured powdered milk, water, sugar, and porridge into a pot and brought it to a boil. What an odd man, she thought, so provocatively good-looking, yet shy, almost naive. He returned and ate in silence.

Philippa sipped her tea. When he was ready to leave, she took his hands and held them. He looked confused and jerked his head away like one of her Thoroughbreds when she tried to adjust its bridle.

"When shall we expect you back?" she said.

"Late. Today I must drive to the other end of the park and check on a new dam. It's a long way and the road is nonexistent." He kissed her hands quickly and she released him. "Take care of yourselves," he said sternly. "Father would kill me if anything happened to you."

Philippa stood on the deck and waved as he drove off and the noise of the jeep was lost among the early morning sounds of the jungle. Attractive, too attractive, she thought, and settled down to write some letters.

David woke up a few hours later, and she had just made fresh tea when the Baba appeared, walking up the path from the pond.

"Strange how one never sees him until he's suddenly there," she whispered.

David leaned over the railing and waved. The Baba waved back and indicated he would like to come up. David went down and conducted him up the stairs. Philippa produced a cup of tea and the Baba sat down on the flooring of the deck to drink it. She found the appearance of a stark naked wild man at the cottage so ludicrous it was difficult to keep from laughing.

Smiling with satisfaction, the Baba slurped his tea. Then he got up and said in broken English, "Jeep, you come, me visit, now."

Was it an invitation or an order?

"Well, that solves the problem of how we'll spend the day," said David. "What do you say, shall we go?"

They changed into their hiking clothes, climbed into the spare jeep, and bounced off down the jungle road. At the path to his cave, the Baba jumped out and motioned them to follow him.

"I say, darling, we're not supposed to get out of this jeep," cautioned Philippa. "Those were Arjun's last words to me this morning."

"I'm sure he meant walking about on the roads," protested David. "Look, it's less than a hundred yards to his place; you can see it from here. Aren't you interested in seeing how he lives? It's the chance of a lifetime." He got out and followed Durga Baba.

Carefully looking around, Philippa climbed down and ran after them. She wasn't the least curious about how the Baba lived; on the other hand, she had no intention of sitting alone in a tiger-infested jungle. Climbing up a well-worn path between large lichen-covered boulders, they reached a spot where the cliff overhung its base and the Baba had ingeniously built up walls of mud and stone, creating several rooms apparently connected with a cave that lay beyond. They ducked in a low door, and a beautiful pearl-colored cow rose to its feet. The Baba patted its forehead and led them to a large alcove where two enormous logs smoldered in a square stone fire pit filled with pale gray ash. The inner limestone walls formed by the cliff were fine-grained, white, almost like marble, and in countless niches were set human skulls, various statues of gods, strings of beads, feathers, birds' nests, and faded photos. On one wall a crude image of the goddess Durga astride her tiger had been carved and colored bright red with some substance that looked to Philippa like lipstick.

Motioning them to sit down, Durga Baba brought the fire to life and placed a pot of water over it, into which he dropped pinches of this and that from small paper packets he withdrew from a red cloth pouch. Then he ground up some leaves on a flat stone and, reducing them to paste, spooned them into the pot, which bubbled like the proverbial witches' brew. When the concoction had steeped, he poured out four cups, scattered one reverently over the fire, causing a pungent steam to rise, passed two to David and Philippa, and kept one for himself. Philippa sniffed the air. The scent was familiar but elusive. Sassafras? Yes, it was the same sassafras she and her sister were given as children by their nanny—or was it?

They fell silent. Somewhere inside the rock David thought he could hear singing. In one corner he noticed a stream of clear water bubbling up out of a crack into a round pool. The fire crackled. He felt his mind slide a bit. Philippa began to feel a rush not unlike that produced by a few cocktails. It seemed to start in her stomach and was radiating out toward the tips of her fingers. She felt she had something of great importance to say to David, if only she could remember what it was. As soon as she opened her mouth to speak, however, she went blank. A very queer sensation, like Alice in Wonderland, she thought, and wondered if she were going to shrink or expand.

In fact, the Baba now seemed to be expanding. His body, enormously puffed up like a weight lifter's, glowed with a pulsating fuchsia-colored light, which floated over the surface of his skin and down the ropes of white hair that fell to the floor around him. She looked on in amazement as jets of blue light shot from his eyes. Turning toward David, she saw his eyes were fixed in a trancelike stare. What was he watching? Was someone talking to him? As her mind drifted, the Baba gestured, and suddenly there was a full-grown tiger standing in the low door. She wanted to get up and run but she couldn't move. The tiger was hesitating on the threshold. Between its black stripes the fur seemed on fire, and its huge eyes shifted about, generating green light rays.

"Tiger, tiger, burning bright!" Surely this had to be an illusion. She glanced again at David, still lost in his own world; then at Durga Baba. His arm outstretched, the Baba was beckoning the tiger to approach him. Or was he creating the tiger from the tips of his fingers? She was too enchanted to decide or care. Electric charges seemed to be pulsing from his fingertips toward the flared nostrils of the tiger. Finally, after a few hesitant steps, hugging the wall, it crept up to the Baba on its haunches, rolled over on its back, purred loudly, and threw its head back on the Baba's lap. His eyes like slits, Durga Baba scratched its chin and stomach and examined the pads of its enormous feet. Then David's eyes came into focus. He saw the tiger and cried out in terror. In one quick motion, the beast rolled over and crouched, poised to attack.

There was no way the Baba could physically stop the tiger from attacking them if it was determined to do so. But quite simply, as one would distract a cat by dangling a piece of yarn over it, the Baba took a long strand of his hair and tickled the tiger's back leg. With a grunt, the beast whined and playfully swatted the yogi's arm. Catching its paw, Durga Baba wrestled it to the floor and climbed on its back; they rolled over and over until the tiger had pinned him down. Huddled together now in the farthest corner near the cow, Philippa and David held their breath. The yogi lay perfectly still. One wrong move and the huge cat might maul them all. Suddenly it looked at Durga Baba and roared. The roar shook the walls and reverberated through the cave behind them. Then it stood up, shook itself, and flopped playfully down facing them, its head between its paws. Durga Baba got slowly to his knees, shook his mane, and stood up. His movements were not those of an ordinary human being, thought David; they were too sleek, too coordinated. The Baba now reached into a cloth bag and withdrew a can of tuna fish and an opener.

Philippa swallowed. Where on earth would he get those? The commonplace event seemed to confirm the fact that they were not just seeing things.

The tiger lifted its head, sniffed the tuna, and walked over to the Baba, who picked out pieces and placed them one by one on the tiger's tongue. It licked its chops, put its forehead against the Baba's shoulder, and nuzzled him. Then, as though perhaps it had forgotten something important, it turned and ambled out through the door.

Again silence. The Baba sat down and calmly stirred the fire, lit some incense, and waved it up and down over his own body, giving himself a fragrant smoke bath.

"From a cub you raised him up?" asked David in Hindi.

The Baba nodded gravely but said nothing. It was obvious he preferred not to talk. They sat in silence for a long time, until Philippa, coming to her senses at last, realized her legs had gone numb and managed to ask David if he thought they could leave. Still, it was very difficult for her to concentrate long enough to do anything. With great difficulty, she managed to drag herself to her feet. Rising after her, David put his hands together in the Hindu fashion and they backed out the door.

"I don't really think we should walk to the jeep with that cat around," Philippa whispered anxiously. But before David had a chance to answer, the Baba darted from the cave and shepherded them down the path.

David was so shaken he flooded the engine and they had to sit waiting in the jeep several minutes before it would start. Finally they lurched away down the road, waving goodbye to the Baba, who smiled benignly after them.

"What do you think that man put in the tea?" shouted Philippa over the sound of the motor.

"What makes you think he's a man?" yelled David.

"What else could he be? You mean he's not human?"

"I'm not sure, but I saw some very odd things."

"You mean that tiger; don't you think he was real?"

"Not the tiger. Of course he was real. Do you know the sculptures of Khajuraho?"

"Yes, naturally."

"Well, behind the Baba I was seeing all those jolly youths and maidens, alive and moving."

Philippa looked at him and frowned.

"You think I'm making it up, don't you, but they were unbelievably lifelike, until they turned into skeletons."

"Skeletons?"

"Yes, but skeletons that continued to make love and dance. What do you make of that?"

They drove on. The sun beat mercilessly down out of a colorless sky. Finally, David stopped.

"Think I made the wrong turn. We'll have to go back the way we came. Too much talking, I suspect." He wiped his forehead with a bandanna and laughed halfheartedly.

They backtracked for a while, came to a fork in the road, and stopped. The jungle looked the same in every direction. David lit his pipe and continued until they came to a stream.

"This certainly isn't the way we came," said Philippa.

The road dipped down and crossed the stream on a rocky base.

"I have to have some water or I'll die of thirst. Why didn't we bring some with us?"

"Because we never expected to get lost," said David.

They looked at each other, got cautiously down from the jeep, and splashed themselves. By now the sun had dropped behind the horizon. A warm wind blew through the tall grass and rustled the leaves of the trees overhanging the stream.

"Ah, we came up here from that fork in the road just by that reddish stone ruin," said David, pointing. "Look."

Philippa looked up and screamed.

"For God's sake, what's the matter?" cried David.

She was screaming and pointing to the base of a large tree on the opposite bank of the stream. At first nothing looked unusual. Then he saw what looked like a mass of roots, near the water. But they were moving. The Baba's tea, he thought.

"Snakes." Philippa groaned. "Can't you see?"

"I say, you're sure they aren't tree roots? They're too big to be snakes. And where are their heads?"

"There's one." She panted. "Look, it's got its jaws open." Her arm shook.

David took up his binoculars. "It's swallowing something: the other snake, I think."

"And look, there's the other head." She pointed to another huge snake's head, its jaws engaged around a writhing column. "Oh, God, I'm going to be sick."

Just then they heard a shout. Arjun drove up in his jeep and jumped out.

"Is everything all right? I heard a scream, thought you might be lost. Been following your tracks for almost an hour now." He waded through the shallow water to where they were standing.

"Look," said Philippa. She put her hand on his shoulder and pointed. Her teeth were chattering.

"Ah." He nodded. "Settling a long-standing grudge. Snakes have terrible tempers, you know, especially these old ones. They feud with each other. Once they start swallowing, they can't stop." He liked the feeling of her hand. Perhaps she would faint and he would have the pleasure of carrying her limp body back to the jeep. "Soon they will start digesting each other and die."

"Don't tell me any more, I'll faint," she said.

He walked through the water toward the snakes and Philippa screamed again. "No problem," he shouted. "Uncle, just give me a hand. I'd like to get them out on flat ground where I can measure them."

Philippa watched grimly as they wrestled and dragged the heavy writhing forms across the shallow crossing and untangled them into a circle. The snakes' eyes darted fiercely. Arjun got out a small tape measure.

"About three meters left to go and I'd say they've swallowed half of each other, so you could say they were each about six meters long." As they watched, they could see the body of each snake slipping inexorably into the mouth of the other. "I've heard of this but never seen it," said Arjun, pulling a flash camera out of his shoulder bag. "Lucky for us you stopped here."

"Actually, I believe we were lost," said Philippa.

"A little confused," added David. "Not really lost."

"We visited the Baba. He came to the cottage this morning and invited us to his place."

"Where he made us some herb tea," said David.

"And wrestled with an enormous male tiger," said Philippa.

Arjun stared at her, an amused expression hovering at the corners of his mouth. "And you two calmly sat there while he played with it?"

"Riveted," replied Philippa. "Absolutely riveted to the spot."

Arjun smiled. "Tell me, was it regular tea he gave you?"

"Definitely not," said David. "That's what I've been telling Philippa. I had the most extraordinary visions."

"Did you see the tiger too?"

David described in detail what he had seen.

"And how did he make the tea, did you watch him? What did it taste like?"

"He pulverized some herbs and roots on a flat stone," explained Philippa.

"And ground up some dried seeds and other things in a mortar," put in David, "and boiled them all together."

"It tasted sweet and spicy, with a bitter aftertaste," said Philippa.

Arjun looked at them and began to laugh. "He gave you bhang. I should have known by your eyes."

"Bhang?" asked David. "What on earth is that?"

"You mean you were born here and never had bhang?"

David looked blank.

"You must know it, it's a drink made with hemp."

"Do you mean marijuana?" asked Philippa.

"That and other things."

David laughed uproariously. "Philippa's been railing against marijuana use for years."

Philippa's lips pursed and broke into an embarrassed smile. "Are you saying you think there was no tiger? How could we have both seen it? And I'll tell you another thing: the Baba opened an ordinary can of tuna and fed it to him. One's mind certainly wouldn't invent tuna."

Arjun refused to take her seriously. "Bhang can make you see things that aren't there," he explained. "And I'm sure it made you lose your way. I shall have to reprimand the Baba. He shouldn't give his concoctions to foreigners."

"I rather enjoyed it," said Philippa, avoiding his gaze. "Until I saw those two." She pointed to the snakes. "Then I really thought I'd gone round the bend. Look at them, poor dears. Isn't there some way they can be saved?"

"If I could, I would," said Arjun. "They're very useful in keeping the rodent population down. But once they start swallowing they can't stop, and it would be impossible to save them now."

"What a way to go."

"It's what anger does," said Arjun. "We don't usually see it this clearly."

"Hadn't we better shoot them, put them out of their misery?" asked David.

"No, no." Arjun shook his head. "It's their karma. Somebody will have a good meal. Vultures will begin to eat them soon; perhaps one of the cubs will try its hand. They're supposed to be quite delicious. Come, it's getting late, we should head back."

"Lucky you came by," David said, when they had showered and settled down over Scotch and sodas.

"That's my job," said Arjun. "If I hear screams, I must go and see what is screaming."

They all laughed.

"Actually, these tigers seem so tame," said Philippa. "There is so much for them to eat here, why should they want us?"

"You're tasty," said Arjun, smiling boldly at her. "And tigers are extremely unpredictable. Some day they will eat Durga Baba. I am waiting for it."

"Mind you, he might like that," observed David.

"Ah, yes," said Arjun. "If you believe, as he does, that this world is an illusion, then it is best to get out of it as soon as possible. The catch is, according to his belief, you can't take your own life. So you live dangerously. Durga Baba's supreme moment would be to have a tiger eat him."

Philippa gulped. "Well, it's certainly not my idea of a supreme moment. I'd rather die in bed, thank you very much."

"What's the use of finishing yourself off if you just get reborn again?" asked David.

"The austerities and rituals he's been performing all these years are supposed to take him straight to heaven. There he'll be sitting with all the gods and goddesses, enjoying."

"Enjoying what?" asked Philippa.

"Just enjoying," said Arjun, shrugging his shoulders. "Feeling good. But that's the question, isn't it? My philosophy is to enjoy now, not later. One time I dreamt I had died and gone up or down, wherever, and found myself with Brahma, God of creation. Well, Arjun, he asked, are you happy to be here? Are you glad to be finished with earth? And in my dream I told him that although I was very happy to be sitting there beside him, I had also enjoyed earth very much and thought it was a nice place."

"And what did Brahma say to that?" asked Philippa.

"He was extremely pleased. Said he had worked very hard creating earth and was irritated when people called it illusion—maya—and the place of sorrows. When they felt that way, they had no respect for it, went about mucking it up and spoiling it. In fact, he was so delighted I liked his creation that he asked me if I would like to go back. I said yes. And he said that although he could not control what womb my soul would enter on its arrival, he could regulate the amount of intelligence I received and would give me double the usual amount so that however I was born, high or low, I would be bound to prosper."

"What an excellent dream!" said David. "Wish I had that kind. My dreams leave me exhausted." He yawned.

Philippa began fixing dinner. Arjun showed her how to prepare dal, a nutritious lentil. He liked her perfume and tried to stand as close to her as possible. They ate out on the deck. David could hardly stay awake.

"Effect of the bhang," said Arjun.

"But then why don't I feel it?" inquired Philippa.

"You're just an old drug addict at heart, my dear," said David.

"Really, darling," said Philippa, irritated, "if you're so tired, you ought to get some sleep. Up late last night, driving around all day."

"Exactly what I intend to do. I wonder if those snakes have expired yet?" He yawned again and ambled off to his room.

After doing up the dishes, Philippa and Arjun stood together at the railing of the deck, sipping coffee, listening to the night sounds of the jungle. Arjun was identifying as many as possible and Philippa tried to pay attention, but her mind was still wandering. If the Baba could look so different after a cup of whatever it was he'd given her, was there a part of reality she'd been missing? And, if so, was there a different Arjun behind the person who was talking to her? She certainly felt as though unseen waves were passing back and forth between them.

"And that is *Cicada indus*. Do you hear it?" he was saying.

"I do and I don't," she replied, gazing into his dark eyes.

"You don't like the sound of *Cicada indus*?" He smiled. "I don't think you've heard one word I've said."

"Oh, I have, I have." She felt like a fool. "*Cicada indus*, yes, I hear it. Very loud, isn't it? Does it make these sounds with its mouth or its wings?"

"With its legs," Arjun replied. Her nostrils had suddenly flared imperceptibly. He felt as though on another level they were engaged in an entirely different conversation. Had the moment come to stop talking and do something? But that was the problem, wasn't it: what to do? What did she expect, this strange blond goddess who stood before him? He had no experience in what these Westerners called lovemaking. In India many considered "love" to be a Western disease. Himself, he was of quite the opposite opinion and had experienced moments of rare pleasure while watching lovemaking in Western films at the cinema in Delhi. But his only real experience had been his dutiful performances with Gayatri and a few brief encounters with local prostitutes.

He took his coffee cup and put it on the deck floor. Then he put his arm around Philippa's waist and kissed her neck. She did not move, seemed to be pretending they were still listening to night sounds. What next? The idea that they were not in a darkened room, that she was not just lying there like a sack of rice waiting to be taken, alarmed him. Then he remembered his namesake, Arjuna, warrior prince at the battle of Kurukshetra, and what Krishna said to him: "Happy Kshatriya, O son of Pritha, find such a battle as this, come of itself, and open the door to heaven." With renewed courage he took her in his arms, kissed her, and stared into her wonderful blue eyes.

To his surprise, her lips searched out his tongue. Never before had he been kissed like this.

Philippa, afraid David might wake from one of his dreams and appear behind them, tried to watch the door onto the deck, but Arjun's imploring gaze and the unflagging pressure of his body against hers were too much. She longed to let herself go with him. Yet how could she? The situation was much too complicated. It could be explosive.

"Don't you think we'd better stop now while we still can?" she whispered, stroking his smooth cheek. "Listen to *Cicada indus?*"

"We can hear him in my bedroom. Come. If you want to listen to something, listen to my heart."

She put her ear to his chest. "You must have had many women. I can tell by the sound of your heart."

He traced the outline of her lips with his finger. "Ah, now you are joking with me, Mrs. Bruce. In my circumstances, it is impossible."

"Now you are joking," she smiled. "You're much too attractive, and I'm too old and wise to be fooled. Old enough to be your mother."

He held her tightly. "Don't be crazy. I am not as experienced as you think, and you are not so old either."

"I'm forty-seven, I was forty-seven last month."

"And I am thirty-eight, what is that?" He stroked her forehead. "And when you do that with your lips I know you do not want me to stop."

"You're making it very difficult," she murmured. "After all, I'm not a saint. But how can I relax with David there in the next room?"

"Do you love him?"

"That awful word." She sighed. "I hardly know what it means anymore. Once we were lovers; now you might say we're devoted friends. And you, do you love your Gayatri?"

"With us, what you call lovemaking is a new thing. Showing so much emotion makes Gayatri feel self-conscious; she does not understand it. I respect her as the mother of my children. I have known her from childhood. She was orphaned during the disturbances of '47 and brought up in our house. Between us it is not a question of love, it is duty. Duty to my father and mother, who decided we should marry.

Duty to the children we have had. Your kind of love is very new to me, I have only seen it at the cinema. It is something we have forgotten here in India—we had it, then we forgot it. Now I can only experience it with you, a Western woman." He kissed her again.

She felt herself caving in. "Do you really believe Western women are so different? After all, women are women the world over."

"Our women do not enjoy expressing themselves physically."

"That's nonsense. I have eyes, I can see. There are plenty of very expressive women here. In Bombay, for example. . . ."

Arjun felt trapped. How could he explain anything? It was all too complicated. "You asked if I loved my wife," he said impatiently. "I have explained that my feeling toward her is one of duty more than what you call love. Yes, we have friendship too, in the same way you and Captain Bruce have, but that does not mean I may not experience other women. As a man that is my right, even though I have not exercised it much."

"Oh, really." She smiled. "Is it your right to experience other women and not hers to experience other men?"

Her remark angered him. "She may if she likes, some women do, but I would never know it. My wife would think it very old-fashioned, but she would not be too surprised if I took another wife. In certain Indian communities a man does not sleep with a wife after she has had their first child. He goes on to another wife."

"That's sinf—" Philippa blurted out and caught herself.

"Ah, there you are, sin." He smiled triumphantly. "I was expecting it to come up sooner or later."

"I don't really believe in it," said Philippa.

"Aren't you a Christian?"

Philippa panicked. "I'm not sure. I'm supposed to be one."

He held her close and smiled. "Here we do not believe in that sin business. For us, sex is like eating. We enjoy it like a well-cooked meal, or because it feels good. Feeling, Mrs. Bruce, is very important. Life is short, so much of it is painful, we want to enjoy. We don't feel guilty about it."

"What about Gayatri? You say she does not like to express herself physically. Does she enjoy?"

"She has been touched by this Christian guilt. She gets it from my mother, who had a Scottish nanny. She does not enjoy."

"And what about the woman whose husband stops sleeping with her after her first child? Is she going to enjoy life?"

"Oh, yes, he must provide her with an establishment of her own and as many young men as it takes to satisfy her."

"No wonder Indian women don't trust men."

"Indian women are realistic, Mrs. Bruce. Men can never be trusted. Look at us: we kill, often for pleasure; we rape; we fight continually. You don't find many killers or rapists among women. Women are necessary for life. Men are superfluous. Except to provide food and protection for a while, we men are pretty useless; we don't have the responsibility of carrying a child inside us."

"And you think women find this irresponsibility exciting, is that it?"

"Correct." Arjun smiled, smoothing her forehead and kissing it. "Now you are on the right track. Feeling your excitement over my freedom excites me."

"What a self-centered attitude!"

"It is because we are worshipped as gods by our mothers. They make us that way."

"Yet they don't take you seriously," she countered.

"Don't take us seriously?"

"You said Indian women are realistic and know men cannot be trusted."

"From the point of view of continuing the human race on this planet, we are a necessary evil. So they put up with us. We are frivolous. We might blow it all up."

"And yet they worship you."

He gazed at her with an intensity that left her weak. "Even the gods are frivolous, Mrs. Bruce. Sometimes they create, sometimes they destroy. Women worship male beauty, male ecstasy, not male steadfastness. Our god Shiva destroys in order that creation may take place. He is represented by an erect penis entering the world through the vagina of Mother Earth. Lingam and yoni." He wanted to kiss her again. In his loins, a tremendous pressure had built up. "Enough of philosophy," he whispered.

She released him gently. "I'm very fond of you, but I must get some rest. You've given me a lot to think about."

"I have spoiled things by talking too much. I want you."

"But not under these circumstances. I can't."

"You think too much," he muttered petulantly. "Thinking destroys enjoying. You will never enjoy."

"Perhaps that's my fate." She picked up the coffee cups and took them to the kitchen.

He leaned on the railing of the deck and stared angrily out over the jungle.

# 4

IN THE MORNING David stumbled out on the deck, rubbing his eyes. "Had a ghastly night again," he muttered. "Can't think what's happening to me."

Philippa was already up, making tea. "Poor darling, you don't look well; and you went to bed so early. Are you sick?"

"Spent the night dreaming again. All night, one nightmare after another. Disgusting."

Just then Arjun came out of his room, his face a mask. He avoided looking at Philippa. "Did I hear you say you didn't sleep well, Uncle?"

"Bad dreams. I might as well have been awake all night."

"He's been having them ever since we arrived in India," said Philippa. "You never were bothered by dreams before. I wonder what it is."

"Would you like to return to Kotagarh today?" Arjun asked. "I have a meeting scheduled with my District Magistrate, slipped my mind until last night when I was falling asleep. Of course, you are welcome to stay here if you like, but since you've seen the Baba and the tigers and don't feel well, you might want to come along. Otherwise, you'd be here alone for three days before I could get back." He glanced triumphantly at Philippa.

David turned to Philippa. "What do you say, shall we stay or go?"

"It's up to you, darling." Behind David's back, Arjun's eyes flashed angrily at her.

"I wouldn't mind," said David. "What would we do here for three more days? Might find ourselves getting in deeper with that Baba fellow. Spent half the night dreaming about him."

PHILIPPA was disappointed. The jungle had agreed with her. They'd been traveling so much, she'd hoped to be able to sit still for a few days and relax. Really, she hadn't handled Arjun very cleverly. If she'd gone to bed with him, they would still be at that delightful cottage and not bumping along this interminable hot road. She didn't believe a word he'd said about a meeting with his District Magistrate. But why should she have given in to him so easily? It just wasn't done. Surely it would only have confirmed his worst ideas about Western women.

Arjun was angry: angry with Philippa but even angrier with himself for being so naive and inexperienced that he had been unable to handle her. It might have been the greatest evening of his life. And what must she think of him, all the worst stereotypes of nervous Indian men . . . ? Like that Aziz in *A Passage to India*, who knew nothing of the ways of the world, of love and clever seduction. He reminded himself to search for his father's edition of the *Kama Sutra*. Once, as a teenager, he had discovered it hidden behind some other books, vividly illustrated, but before he had a chance to memorize the positions, it had mysteriously disappeared. He made a point of rubbing against Philippa as he shifted gears, but she did not respond.

Exhausted and a bit bored by Arjun's constant banter, David's thoughts drifted. What was the meaning of the repellent dream he'd had? Why should he have found himself in the Baba's cave and looked down to see his body covered with vile-smelling ordure he was unable to wash off? The Baba had laughed gaily and told him a number of things about his life that no one could possibly have known. "Wrong!" he remembered saying at one point. "Wrong, wrong, wrong. Sorry, old boy, you're off the mark." But the Baba had just shaken his mane and smiled. He tried to remember what the Baba had told him that upset him so but couldn't. Why was he so happy the Baba had made a mistake? And why was he unable to clean himself?

As the road finally descended through the valley and came out onto the plain, Philippa ran through a number of scenarios in which she could be alone again with Arjun. They were all impossible. Yet she had to talk to him, apologize. But why? Obviously her confusion over this point meant she cared about him, yes. And now they were about to be separated by all these people, she would have to be very careful. No one must see her looking at him.

ARRIVING back at Madho Dev's they found the family and servants, together with crusty old Harbinder Singh and his two sons, gathered around the television, which had been moved into the courtyard. A newscast from the Golden Temple was in progress. The camera moved past rows of dead bodies, soldiers washing blood from the marble terraces surrounding the sacred tank, stacks of captured weapons. A Sikh general was interviewed. Sounds of intermittent gunfire could be heard in the background, and the General said terrorists were holed up in the minarets and would have to be starved out. The picture changed and there was Zail Singh, the President of India, wearing a red rose in the lapel of his white sherwani, inspecting the precincts of the Temple. There were close-ups of the puja in progress and Mrs. Gandhi coming to pray and give money. The demagogue Bhindranwale had been killed, along with most of his henchmen, and "the healing touch" was going to make everything all right again. Over and over the newscasters talked vaguely of the "healing touch," but no one seemed to know what it meant.

"Words, only words," said Harbinder Singh. "They are all lying." Hadn't he received a second telephone call from a nephew in Delhi just returned from Amritsar who had reported the Granth Sahib, the holy book of the Sikhs, had been hit by bullets, that one of the raggis, men who recite passages from the Granth Sahib, had been shot while singing, that the famous library had been reduced to ashes, the treasury looted, and scores of women, children, and pilgrims killed or raped by Indira Gandhi's troops?

"They say someone has gone on the BBC and offered a million pounds for her life," said Devika.

"We heard that before we left," said David. "I just can't believe it."

"It is too much for her, she isn't worth it," said Harpal Singh.

Just then the report was repeated, along with pictures of a well-rehearsed mob protesting outside the British High Commission in Delhi.

"Down with BBC!" they yelled in Hindi. "British go home!"

Madho Dev was sick at heart. For years, caste and community grievances had been exacerbated by Congress Party zealots, hawkers of second-hand ideas and political ideologies, posing as leaders. That his country should be represented by these beggars on horseback was not only an embarrassment, it was a national tragedy.

"You must have noticed they are not showing the Akal Tahk," said Harbinder Singh. "Why? Because it has been destroyed; that is what my nephew has said."

"What is the Akal Takh?" asked David.

"Throne of the Immortal God," said the old man. "It was built by our sixth guru, Har Gobind Singh, in 1600. It is the seat of the spiritual and temporal authority of the Sikhs, like your Westminster Abbey in London. And now they are secretly spreading the story that the women who were killed in the Temple were prostitutes and European hippies and that large numbers of condoms were found in the debris after the fighting, along with opium, heroin, and hashish.

It's a cheap attempt to justify their Operation Blue Star, but they cannot. You will see, these accusations are all lies."

"But there has been no firing between Hindu and Sikh civilians in Punjab or anywhere else," said Madho Dev.

"That is because, no matter what the politicians say, the average man knows we are brothers, Hindu-Sikh bhai-bhai." Harbinder Singh smiled. "Sikhs are the defenders of the Hindu faith. Our ninth guru was executed by the Muslim Moghuls; it was said he martyred himself to protect the Hindu's right to wear caste marks and sacred threads." He laughed bitterly.

"And who are the Sikhs defending the Hindus against now?" asked David.

"Against the Russians, of course," was Harbinder Singh's blunt reply. "Sikhs do not see the people of Pakistan as enemies, we see the godless Russians. This Nehru family invited them to India to shore up their position during the early sixties and again in 1975, during Mrs. Gandhi's Emergency. The Congress Party trades our cloth and grains for Russian planes that do not fly, Russian tanks and guns that can't shoot straight, Russian tractors that break down."

"I have such a tractor." Madho Dev nodded. "We've been waiting for six months for a spare part."

Hardev Singh laughed. "Just the other day we read of an American company making much money selling kits to repair Russian tanks and planes in Third World countries."

"The Americans are simpleminded," exclaimed Harbinder Singh. "Because they have never faced war and bloodshed by foreigners on their own soil, they are not serious. Look at them, keeping their deadly enemies alive by selling them wheat. Do you feed your enemy today that he may destroy you tomorrow?"

Philippa noticed how tense they had all become in just four days. Listening as she had for years to members of her family discussing India, Indian politics had become a blur to her and, she decided, a blur to most Indians as well. She glanced at Arjun. In the presence of his wife and mother he had grown silent and sat staring into his lap. A man in the prime of life, how he must hate all this! Was there not some way to save him, pluck him out of India, transport him far away? What a dangerous thought!

On the television screen, a young man wearing an idiotic white satin costume with high silver boots was now cavorting with a plump young lady who was running away and popping up behind flowering shrubs. The awestruck servants were now dismissed to prepare dinner. Madho Dev passed the long hoses of the hookah around and everyone smoked. Something serious was in the air, thought Philippa, something the servants were not supposed to know.

Just then Madho Dev turned to Arjun. "There's something I have to tell you. You may not have heard that a number of Sikh troops mutinied and deserted. Fifteen hundred in Bihar, at Poona in Maharashtra, and several places here in Rajasthan, all heading for Amritsar when word of the fighting there spread."

"So it's that bad," said David.

"It is said most of them have been rounded up. A Sikh general has ordered them to be shot if caught. Anyone who is found aiding them will, of course, be prosecuted or shot, whatever." He waved his hand and sighed. "The problem is, we have some of them here."

"Here?" cried Arjun, jumping up.

"Please lower your voice and sit down." said Madho Dev. "They came through Harbinder Singh's fields and landed up at his house quite by accident because they were going across country to avoid the highways. Thoughtless warrior heroes that they are, they imagined they could get to Amritsar, where they were told their Golden Temple had been destroyed. As you have seen on television, the army has been careful not to destroy it."

"The Golden Temple is the pavilion in the middle of the artificial lake?" asked David.

"Correct," said Madho Dev. "And on that misinformation these young boys deserted—over in Alwar someplace—became separated from their fellow deserters, and landed up, fortunately for them, at Harbinder Singh's farm. We have moved them here."

"I was against it," said Devika. "Why should we—"

"Silence!" hissed Madho Dev.

"Father, I agree." Arjun took up his mother's point. "Why should we protect terrorists?"

Harbinder Singh and his two sons stared at the floor.

"They're not terrorists. That is a word invented by the government about six months ago to describe anyone who disagrees with them. I am a Hindu. I have been shocked at the killings of innocent Hindus and so has Harbinder Singh. But this is India. How do we know who these so-called terrorists really are? They may be Congress Party workers, for all we know. These soldiers are pawns. They haven't killed anyone."

"Where are they?" asked Arjun.

"In the granary." Madho Dev sighed. "Harbinder Singh's place could be searched. There aren't many Sikhs living around here."

"And you think the police won't search our place? What are you intending to do with these jawans? How many are there?"

"Only three," said Madho Dev.

Arjun looked relieved. "At least that's something. I thought you had a whole platoon."

"My nephew in Delhi tells me several retired Sikh generals have written to Indira Gandhi to plead for leniency for the mutineers. If they can be hidden for some time, at least their lives may be spared," said Harbinder Singh. He turned to David. "I was in a caravan from Lahore to Amritsar in August 1947. I have seen too much senseless killing."

"Couldn't Harbinder Singh just keep them on, say they were relatives who have come from Punjab?" suggested David.

Madho Dev shook his head. "We can't hide them around here. The servants would put two and two together and realize they could make money by going to the police. Half the police are low caste, like the servants."

"I think our servants are loyal to us," said Devika softly.

"You think, but you don't really know," replied Madho Dev. "It's something we can't risk, and neither can Harbinder Singh."

"Is their hair long or short?" asked Arjun.

"Their hair is long and they have light beards and mustaches. They are young, all under twenty."

"They must cut their hair and shave before we can do anything for them," said Arjun.

"But they won't," said Madho Dev. "Harbinder Singh asked them; they refused."

"They are ready to die for their faith," explained Hardev.

"There is no reason for them to die unnecessarily," said Arjun. "Let me talk to them."

"Go out the side door then," said Madho Dev, grateful that Arjun was taking an interest. "And you might take Philippa along with you. That way, if the servants see you, they will think you are taking her to see the horses. Parade one of our stallions for her, then slip into the granary."

Philippa followed Arjun out into the farmyard. A maidservant and her daughter were squatting over their dinner by the kitchen door.

"They'll be watching us," said Arjun. "Laugh and smile, look interested. They don't know a word of English."

"I'm sorry about last night," cried Philippa, laughing merrily. "It was stupid of me. I'm afraid I've become awfully fond of you. Isn't that the funniest thing you've ever heard? Doesn't it just make you want to die laughing?"

Arjun's heart jumped into his throat. "I feel the same way," he replied gaily as they rounded a bend out of sight of the servant and her daughter. "Lucky these Sikh boys arrived, it gives us a moment alone. All day, I've been dying. You mustn't think, because I don't show it, I'm not feeling anything."

Philippa pressed his hand. They reached the stalls, paraded a magnificent stallion beyond the barn where the servants could see it, and walked back inside. In the dark, they fell into each other's arms.

"We have no time now, but I will make time," he murmured.

Philippa clung to him.

"The granary is attached to this building. Quick, follow me."

They ran through the stables up a few steps and ducked through a low door. Three irascible young faces stared out of the darkness.

"Memsahib came along to avert suspicion by the servants," Arjun told them in broken Punjabi. They smiled thinly. "I am Arjun, son of Madho Dev. If you agree to cut your hair and shave, we will help you. Otherwise you will have to leave this very night and will probably be killed."

"If we cut our hair and shave, how will anyone know we are Sikhs when we get to Amritsar?" they protested.

"There is no need to go to Amritsar. The Harminder Sahib—the Golden Temple—has not been touched, not even damaged. Kirtan is still being performed. You must disappear for a while."

"That is a lie. We have been told Harminder Sahib is destroyed. You are just trying to make us cut our hair; you Hindus are all the same."

"Don't, then." Arjun shrugged. "But you go tonight."

"We want you to drive us, we need transportation. We are grateful to you for hiding us but we have the guns to make you take us." One of them pointed a pistol at Arjun.

"That won't get you anywhere," Arjun replied coolly. "If you kill me, you'll be dead within the hour. If you see the Harminder Sahib on Doordarshan, will you believe what I say?"

"You are having the TV?" one asked.

"Yes. At nine-thirty I will come for one of you. You can see for yourself." The boy with the pistol put it away. "We must hurry now," said Arjun, "or the servants will become suspicious. I will return in three hours. One of you will watch Doordarshan and come back with food for the others. The fighting in Amritsar is finished. The army has captured the Temple, and Bhindranwale and his men are dead. Your problem is what to do now. There are 'shoot dead' orders for all deserters."

Arjun and Philippa walked quickly back to the house. The servant and her daughter were still sitting by the kitchen door, watching.

"They really believe the Golden Temple has been destroyed," said Arjun when they returned to the house. "They want to commandeer one of our vehicles and drive to Amritsar; they have guns."

"They threatened you?" asked Devika.

"Mildly."

"Then let them have one of Harbinder Singh's old vehicles," said Devika. "Let them go if that is their desire. When they are caught, we will say the vehicle was stolen." She flushed angrily and lowered her eyes.

"I also had the same thought, Mother," Arjun replied, "but no one would believe us. If they are caught with one of Harbinder Singh's vehicles or one of ours, it will cause endless problems. I have invited one of them in to watch the late news. Let us hope they again show pictures of the Golden Temple. That may convince them to cut their hair. There is no point in their going to the Punjab. If they agree, I will drive them into the sanctuary, to Durga Baba's place. I will tell Durga Baba they are young devotees who have heard about him. They can hide out there for a few weeks until things blow over."

Madho Dev puffed on the hookah. "You think you could get them there without anyone seeing you?"

"You know I often go at night. People around here wouldn't be surprised at hearing my jeep start up. I can pull down the canvas sides, no one will see them. There's a shortcut, an old forest road nobody uses. If I leave by midnight, I can be there by dawn."

Devika and Gayatri looked uneasy. Philippa tried not to look at Arjun.

"Do you think the Baba would take them in?" asked Madho Dev.

"He can't refuse." Arjun smiled. "An ascetic cannot refuse anyone who comes to his door in need."

"From what I've seen, he's capable of handling any situation," said David.

"Uncle claims he saw the Baba playing with tigers," said Arjun.

"I saw it too," said Philippa. "I saw him wrestling a tiger."

Madho Dev rolled his eyes condescendingly.

"I know what you're thinking," protested David. "I remember that skeptical look from long ago. But really, old man, we did see it."

"If Babaji can cause a relatively unimaginative Englishman to see him playing with tigers, I'm sure he can handle anything," said Madho Dev.

They all laughed.

"Now let us think about those three boys," Madho Dev went on. "There are two proposals. If they will not cut their hair, they may be allowed to steal a vehicle, which would end in certain arrest or death for them and trouble for all of us. If they can be persuaded to cut their hair, we will hide them in the forest."

"Why can't they cut their hair and be on their way?" asked David. "Why the forest?"

"They would be recognized; they don't speak Hindi. If they had to speak, they'd be instantly undone. Let us first see if they will shave and cut their hair. If they will do that, then there is either the forest or we drive them to Kotagarh and drop them."

Just before the nine-thirty news came on, Arjun slipped out to the granary. It was dark, the moon had not yet risen, and the servants were asleep. Taking no chances, however, he took a soiled lungi and turban cloth and had one of them, a boy called Amreek, put them on so that he looked like a field worker. Then he walked him nonchalantly back to the house.

"This is Amreek Singh," he said, introducing the ferociously handsome young man.

"Amreek, have you ever seen television, do you know about Doordarshan, the government news broadcast?" asked Harbinder Singh.

Amreek nodded his head quickly. The news was just being read. Pictures of Mrs. Gandhi at the Golden Temple praying and giving money flashed on the screen. Amreek stared in disbelief. If Mrs. Gandhi was there, it couldn't be staged, couldn't be an old film taken before Operation Blue Star.

"Will you cut your hair and shave now, Amreek?" asked Harbinder Singh. "We don't want young Sikhs killed uselessly. If you cut your hair, we will help you. If you insist on not cutting it, we will have to send you on your way. We can't risk hiding you here or pretending you stole a vehicle."

"How will you help us if we cut our hair?"

"There is a large game sanctuary nearby. Arjun is the head of it. In the sanctuary lives a holy man. You can stay with him, pretend you are his devotees."

"Is this holy man a Hindu?" asked Amreek.

Harbinder Singh glanced at Madho Dev. They both hated this

division between Sikhs and Hindus that had been put into the minds of young men like Amreek.

"He is not a Hindu swami, he is beyond all that. He is a naga, a naked one."

For some time Amreek remained silent. Then, asking to be taken back to the granary, he nodded curtly and left with Arjun.

Dinner was served and the family sat watching a taped rebroadcast of the motion picture Academy Award proceedings from Hollywood. Philippa found the contrast unbelievable. Why were these strange rites being shown in India? For most viewers, they might as well be taking place on the moon.

Soon Arjun reappeared with the news that Amreek and his companions would cut their hair, shave, and go to the forest. They would leave at midnight. Although David was tired, he dreaded his dreams more and refused to hear anything but that he should accompany Arjun. Madho Dev produced two revolvers with shoulder holsters, and they were about to lie down for an hour's nap when there was a loud knock at the front door. It was the District Superintendent of Police, an arrogant young tough, accompanied by the District Magistrate and two officers. Both officials were members of the local Rotary Club, which, in self-defense, Madho Dev had forced himself to join. Although they were on opposite sides of the political fence, he could address the D.M. with the familiar "ji."

"Ah, Sharmaji," he said. "What brings you out at this late hour? Come in."

"We will not bother you long, Devji," said the D.M. unctuously. "Just now we are out looking for mutinous Sikh terrorists and wanted to warn you that we have had reports of some in this neighborhood. About three o'clock this afternoon six were shot dead on the highway near town in a stolen truck. Three escaped and were seen running in this direction."

The D.S.P. stared past Madho Dev at Harbinder Singh. "I don't suppose you have seen them, Harbinder Singh?" he asked.

"Harbinder Singh and his two sons have been here with me since midday, helping me fix my tractor," said Madho Dev smoothly.

"And I have just returned from the game preserve with Captain and Mrs. Bruce, who are visiting us from England," said Arjun, introducing them to the D.S.P.

Rising to the occasion, David played the intimidating sahib as best he could, explaining that he and Madho Dev had been in Burma together and that he was soon off to Delhi to visit certain generals who

had been friends of theirs in '47. His military bearing and commanding presence quickly sent the policemen on their way.

"I am afraid we are endangering you, Dev," apologized Harbinder
Singh. "I am very sorry."

"You are and you should be," said Devika angrily.

"Don't be rude, Devika," said Madho Dev impatiently. "It isn't his
fault the boys showed up at his house. Please forgive her, Harbinderji.
We are all Indians; it is the government that is endangering us."

Philippa announced she would like to go back to the guesthouse but
Devika wouldn't hear of it. "It's been a very bad day," she declared.
"The first thing I saw this morning was a black crow in the east—
always a bad omen. Then Madho Dev's truck broke down, the cook
cut his finger slicing vegetables for lunch, and the maid's baby came
down with a fever. We must all be very careful. The next six months
are most inauspicious, especially for the rest of June and the last two
weeks of October."

Just our luck, thought Philippa, and noticed that for the first time
that evening Madho Dev was really listening to his wife.

"Devika's father kept a famous pundit," he explained. "He taught
her many things. What must we do?" he asked.

"We must keep the holy fire burning brightly in the courtyard and
offer it certain things which I will prepare. And the pandal that we
always put up to cover it during the monsoon must be finished by
tomorrow night, for in three days it is going to rain very hard. We
must also repeat certain mantras in the morning and evening. That
way our house will be protected. I have been watching the television
very carefully, and I agree they are not telling us what is really
happening. That is why I am somewhat sympathetic toward these
Sikh boys. Things are more serious than the government would like
us to think. Something else is brewing. Perhaps they are going to start
a war with Pakistan. Elections are coming. Without a war to unify the
people, the Congress Party will never win."

Philippa was upset by the thought of Arjun and David driving off
into the night with three crazed Sikhs. Devika's talk had depressed
her. How ghastly to be living in a country where your life was on the
line all the time. How wonderful it would be if she and David could
manage to get the whole family out of India. But how? And would
they survive such a change? Perhaps Devika, because she had been a
princess and knew Western ways, but what about Gayatri? Innocent
Gayatri, holding Arjun's youngest son in her lap. Watching her, Philippa felt a disconcerting twinge of conscience.

# 5

THE NIGHT AIR was soft and warm. With the excitement of the undertaking, David's fatigue had vanished. At midnight they spirited Amreek, Amarjit, and Tara Singh out of the granary into the back of the jeep. The young men had protested fiercely when they had taken their pistols and buried their daggers.

"You will all come to us someday," Tara Singh muttered. "We are the only natural ones, that is why we will win."

"Natural?" queried Arjun.

"As God created us," he said piously. "You Hindus cut your hair. Muslims and some of these ferenghis, they cut off their foreskins. Cut, cut, cut—you are all disfigured Sikhs. Now you have made us cut our hair and taken away our weapons, we feel naked. We should never have agreed to do it; it is not good, it is unlucky. The Hindu does not trust us."

"Right." Arjun had grinned.

"What is it these fellows really want?" asked David as they bumped along Arjun's shortcut.

"It's their priests," Arjun replied. "They are rich, with large incomes from their congregations—land, jewels, gold. They oppose all outside authority. These days their constituency is very young; the priests are mostly old. The Sikhs are the most affluent group in India. Their youth are being tempted by all the things prosperity can buy; expectations are raised. Their rebellion must be directed outward. The priests fear absorption by Hinduism. Didn't your Protestants fight the Roman Catholics? So the Sikh priests want their own theocratic state. But they are a quarrelsome, argumentative, self-defeating lot; rarely has their Sikh party ever won an election. Many of their own people won't even vote for them, so they brainwash these simpleminded fellows with fundamentalism and use the Hindus as scapegoats. The communist threat is part of the gag. There are so many youngsters. North India is suddenly awash with country-made heroin, called 'brown sugar.' Perhaps the government is promoting it to kill them off. The median age is now fourteen. That means four hundred million kids to control. Religious fervor is one way. There's also the cinema, sports, and, of course, poverty." He laughed cynically. "That's the best, especially as Gandhi proclaimed poverty holy. If you have to work all day just to feed yourself, you don't have time or energy to make trouble."

The old moon was just rising.

"On such a beautiful night, you're sounding very dispirited," said David. "The air is sweet, soft."

"It's the flowering trees," replied Arjun. "But you don't have to live here, Uncle, you don't have children growing up here."

"You said the other night you would like to leave India. If you could, would you really go?"

"Are you offering to take me?" Arjun grinned.

David looked away, embarrassed.

"You hadn't really thought of it, Uncle?"

"Quite frankly, no, I hadn't," admitted David. "You would really leave?"

"Have you any doubt? Look around, see what's happening. Fit the pieces together, you have disaster. Everywhere I look, I see death coming. I don't care, but I feel bad for my children. What future is there for them?"

"You think the West is safer?" asked David.

"Perhaps not, but it must be cleaner. Fifty-two percent of our population is now of the lowest caste. This has never happened before. Ninety percent are not toilet trained. They shit anywhere; the country is sinking in shit. Shit, pesticides, and petrol fumes. The result is disease and madness."

Soon they were descending a steep section of rutted road into the center of the park. David thought Arjun had certainly not exaggerated his shortcut's condition. Without warning, they hit a rock and almost fell into a deep ravine. Arjun stopped.

"We'd best remove the canvas from the back," he said. "In case we tip over, the boys can jump."

They unsnapped the canvas and stored it under the front seat. The three soldiers sat huddled together, their faces grim, unsmiling.

"They're saying this is my idea and anything that happens is my fault," Arjun told David.

"Would they have preferred to die?"

"They've been taught that death with honor is preferable to life with dishonor. They have dishonored themselves by cutting their hair and giving me their arms; that's why they're so sulky."

"In the old days, I knew so many Sikhs," said David. "Always liked them. Some were jolly good friends."

"That was another age," replied Arjun. "Education was good, food and health were better. The Sikhs your age are a different lot, extremely responsible and hard-working. Young ones like these are brain-damaged. Even physically they are less robust."

At last the road flattened out and they moved faster. Sunrise was not far away.

"You haven't answered my question," said Arjun, breaking the silence.

"What was that?"

"About helping me get out of here."

"I've been thinking about it. Of course I would. Haven't the faintest clue how to go about it, though."

Arjun searched David's face for a sign that he was sincere but saw nothing. Probably by tomorrow he would forget the whole conversation, he thought. That's how older people were.

They turned onto the main forest road and, after a few more minutes, arrived at the Baba's. The sun was just rising. The Baba was standing in front of his cave with his cow and walked down to meet them. The three Sikhs looked suspicious and frightened.

"I doubt they've ever seen a real yogi," Arjun said to David. "Their 'sants' are more like priests, hardly renunciates like this Baba. Of course, they've seen pictures of Shiva, but it's not like seeing the real thing."

Durga Baba smiled and beckoned them inside, built up his fire, and began making tea. The last part of the trip had been tiring, and David was glad to relax before the fire.

"I hope he's not going to make one of his special brews. Don't think I'm up to it, and who knows how these boys might react?"

Arjun addressed the Baba, who looked up, grinned, pointed at the young men and said, "Sardars?"

"How could he know they are Sikhs?" exclaimed David.

"He knows everything," replied Arjun. "Even though their hair has been cut, I'm afraid they still look like Sikhs. I've asked him to keep them here for a few weeks. My superior officer will not be in the park for months, nor will there be any foreign visitors during the rainy season. But I have asked him to be sure no one sees them. On Sundays when his devotees come from neighboring villages, he should hide them deep in the cave."

"What will they eat?"

"We'll pick up some rations at the cottage: rice, dal, and wheat. They'll have to cook their own food."

Durga Baba passed around brass mugs of steaming tea. The soldiers slurped noisily. Arjun looked at them with disgust. Durga Baba smiled benignly, stretched his arms above his head, and shook his shaggy mane of hair.

"His name?" asked Tara Singh, glancing at Arjun.

"Durga Baba," Arjun replied.

"How can we trust this naked fakir? He looks like a sorcerer," said Amreek Singh doubtfully.

"And what will we do here?" put in the third soldier.

"Although he does not speak Punjabi," Arjun said, "I must warn you he can read minds."

"We should never have cut our hair," moaned Tara Singh. "We should have followed our plan, taken your jeep, and gone to Amritsar; that is where we are needed."

"I told you," said Arjun patiently. "You'd have been shot before you got to Delhi. They're out looking for you. Besides, you have seen the President and P.M. at the Harminder Sahib. Bhindranwale is dead. It's all over there."

Tara Singh clenched his fists. "That is a lie. Certainly he has escaped. And as for Giani Zail Singh, President of so-called India, he is no longer a Sikh. How could a Sikh allow the army to enter the Golden Temple? You will see, they will all die now. All who have desecrated our holy places will die. We Sikhs will not forget."

The rising sun shone through the entrance to the hut. Durga Baba stood up and made them understand it was time to go for a bath. Arjun conveyed the information to the young soldiers, who grudgingly followed them down the path to the pond.

Durga Baba sat on his boulder and began saying his prayers. Inside the yogi's hut, the three youngsters seemed brave and cocky; now as they undressed, they looked frightened and peered cautiously around them.

Furtively concealing their pistols in their clothes, David and Arjun waded into the warm water. Cautious as they had been, suddenly there was Tara Singh, pistol in hand.

Arjun and David stood helplessly in the pond. Amarjit and Amreek stood behind their companion. On his rock, Durga Baba sat in the lotus pose, his eyes closed tightly.

"We are leaving," said Tara, waving the gun. "We have seen the second jeep under the guest house. Amreek is just now going to disable it. Then he is going to get your jeep and we'll be on our way. We cannot remain here with this rakshasa. I know you tried to help us, but you should have let us take your jeep to begin with."

"You won't get very far," said Arjun, "even if you get out of the park—which is not certain because one can easily lose one's way."

"We are soldiers. I have remembered each and every turn."

"But when you reach the plain, then what? Three jawans in a forestry jeep. What if the police stop you?"

"Our hair is cut. We will say the army has commandeered the jeep to search for Sikh terrorists." He grinned. "We will smoke cigarettes if necessary."

David had had enough. "Look here," he said, his face flushed with anger, and started to wade toward Tara Singh. A shot rang out. David felt a sharp pain as a bullet grazed his leg.

"Next time I will kill you, ferenghi," said Tara Singh, his eyes glittering. "Stay where you are."

Amreek had driven up with Arjun's jeep. Tara and Amrajit began backing slowly toward it. Just then, the two half-grown cubs that David and Philippa had seen streaked out of the undergrowth and leaped on the young men. Amarjit Singh, unarmed, fell first. Tara Singh fired but missed and was immediately brought down. Arjun and David watched with horror as the two soldiers wrestled with the cubs. Amreek Singh, afraid to shoot lest he kill his companions, retreated toward the jeep. Suddenly, with an earth-shaking roar, the cubs' mother leaped out of the underbrush and downed him. On the rock, Tara and Amarjit lay dying.

Statuelike, the Baba sat passing the beads of his rosary through his fingers, his lips set in a Buddha-like smile, his eyes still closed. David glanced at Arjun, who was shaking his head from side to side in disbelief.

"This is terrible," said David. "Can't we do anything?"

"Nothing," Arjun whispered hoarsely. "They're finished."

"It happened so quickly," said David. "I can't believe it."

"Our tigers are not man-eaters," said Arjun. "I am shocked they would have done such a thing. Unless . . ."

"Unless what?"

"Unless the Baba had something to do with it."

"They're the same ones he was playing with the other day," said David. "The ones you didn't believe we saw."

The cubs were ripping open the soldiers' stomachs, devouring their vital organs in huge gulps. Blood flowed down the rocks into the pool, where it attracted a school of fish that churned the water to red froth.

Crows swooped down over the grisly scene, cawing with excitement; high overhead vultures circled.

"The smell of blood brings the jungle to life," muttered Arjun. "Birds pick up the scent from miles away while we can't smell a thing." The female tiger was trying to drag Amreek Singh's corpse off into the jungle. "She'll eat some of it, try to cover the rest up with leaves, and spend the next few days sleeping on top until she's finished it off."

Although the water was warm, David found himself chilled and trembling. "I say, do you think we can get out? These fish are making me nervous. Are they piranhas?"

"A variety, but not the bad kind, don't worry. It would be best to wait till these two young ones take what remains of our jawans into the forest. Once they eat up the innards, they'll drag them away. It won't be much longer."

The morning sun filtered through the massive trees and fell in patches on the placid surface of the pond. At the edge, white herons stepped shyly between lavender water hyacinths, hunting for food. Bees buzzed among the orange-flowering ashoka trees.

"Such a beautiful morning," remarked David. "Nature is so powerful, so indifferent."

"Brahm is khanna and khanna is Brahm," said Arjun.

"God is food? I don't understand."

"Brahm is food. The Creator is food and food is the Creator. Everything is food for something else."

Growling at each other, the two cubs finally dragged the disemboweled bodies off in different directions. A few moments later, the Baba opened his eyes, got up and stretched, walked down to the edge of the pool, and splashed water on the rock, washing away the blood. Then he waded into the center of the pond, submerged himself three times, and came up smiling.

"According to ordinances, disturbing meditation of holy man is greatest sin," he said in Hindi. "Goddess not permitting. They nogood boys, try kill you, they follow bad peoples."

"You saved our lives," said Arjun.

The Baba shook his head. "It is Goddess's work. She very pleased you let me stay here." He nodded. "Not me save life, me nothing."

Arjun came out of the water, shook himself, and sat on the rock next to the Baba. "Someday I may join you here, Babaji. It feels good without clothes."

"They say it is penance." The Baba smiled. "But it is luxury life even king cannot buy. All Goddess's grace that you are being here. Blessings."

"I might join you too," said David, climbing out.

"Welcome," said Durga Baba. "I make you young again. Your body tired. Bad food, no exercise."

"You're right," agreed David. The fear that had attacked him after his dream of the Baba had disappeared. "Tell me," he asked, "how many children do I have?"

The Baba giggled, rolled his eyes as he had in the dream, and held up three fingers.

"You're absolutely sure?"

The Baba nodded. "Yes, yes, no question, I have told you in dream." He stared hard at David, got up, and started back up the road.

Arjun glanced curiously at David. "What was that all about?"

"He came to me in a dream the other night, most disturbing."

"And the children?"

"As far as I know, I have only two. But he can invade my dreams, and he claims I have three—can it be true?"

THEY slept in the Baba's hut till after midday, then started back. The road was hot and dusty, and they were attacked by swarms of flying insects.

"Why couldn't those youngsters understand we were trying to help them," said David, over the sound of the motor.

"National disease," yelled Arjun, navigating the difficult road. "If you try to help someone, they think you must be crazy or weak or that you want something. Even knowing this, if someone tries to help me, I will be suspicious of his motives."

"What about the Baba? You helped him; now he just saved our lives."

"Perhaps, but that story isn't over either."

They were driving on a part of the road where the land had slipped from above when suddenly they hit a rut, tilted precariously, and went over the side. There was no time to jump. David was thrown out. Something exploded behind his eyes, and he rolled over and over. The jeep plunged down a steep bank and came to rest against a thicket of thorny shrubs.

He came to slowly, looked about, and staggered down the hill to the jeep. Arjun was pinned beneath it. He looked dead. David knelt beside him. One side of the jeep was resting on his chest: his leg, caught between steering wheel shaft and clutch, was badly twisted. David searched for a pulse but couldn't find one. Suddenly he saw Madho Dev. In an instant, forty years dissolved and he was in Burma again, in that foxhole. Forgetting himself completely, he sat down and stared at the pale, still face. Time stood still. Finally Arjun's eyelids fluttered.

"Ah," said David. "Thank God, you're alive. Don't try to move; you gave me a bad scare. Now I have to get this bloody thing off you."

"Knocked the wind out of me," rasped Arjun.

"I couldn't find your pulse. Don't talk, your ribs may be broken. I'll just disentangle your leg here and find something to lift this machine. I need leverage." He tried to straighten Arjun's leg. Arjun whooped with pain. "There," said David. "It's free. Now hold on and I'll find a pole."

But there were no poles, nothing but trees and some underbrush. He would have to lift the jeep up and hope that Arjun could roll out. A few years ago it would have been nothing for him to lift a light jeep, but now he wasn't sure.

"Can you slide free?" he asked. "Don't try if it hurts, but when I lift, slide out if possible."

David spread his legs, braced himself, and lifted, wondering if his back would take it, but Arjun didn't move.

"I can't," he gasped.

There was no other solution than to lift the thing up all the way and roll it over. Hard going, because it was stuck in the bushes. Squatting beside the roll bar, he put his shoulder to it and lifted. If he lost control, it would slam back down again. He pushed until the jeep was standing on its side, but it would not turn over. Just as he thought he was going to have to let it go, Arjun yelled and rolled free, the jeep fell back down, and David collapsed beside him. The worst thing about getting old was that you didn't feel it mentally. His mind felt nineteen but his body felt ninety.

"I tried to jump," said Arjun. "Guess I was stunned."

"Your foot got caught. Can you breathe?" He unbuttoned Arjun's shirt and felt his ribs. "Breathe in and out."

Arjun breathed deeply. "Feels all right," he said, getting up on his elbows. "What are you smiling about?"

"Was I smiling? I was thinking how much you looked like your father, forty years ago. We were trapped in a foxhole together, only that time I was the one in trouble. He saved me."

"But he was only twenty then, Uncle. I'm thirty-seven."

"Ah, but you look the same. Wait until you reach my age, then you'll realize how young you still are."

"You look in good shape to me," said Arjun. "What about the way you lifted that jeep?"

"Just lucky you were able to roll out. I was almost ready to drop it."

Arjun began testing his legs. "Something is sprained or broken. I doubt I'll be able to walk."

"Hang on, then," said David. He grabbed Arjun under his arms and dragged him up the embankment. When they finally reached the top, Arjun was able to stand on one foot, and after a rest they set off down the road, Arjun, his arm around David's shoulder, hopping on one foot.

"Any tigers in this area?" asked David.

"Leopards, no tigers; not enough water. We have about eight kilometers to go, all downhill," Arjun explained. "We should be on the valley floor by dusk."

"I think you're exaggerating our abilities, young man."

"Once we make it down, don't worry. I'll find something to carry us."

The road was uneven. Arjun had to stop frequently. If only he had a pair of crutches. Why had he forgotten to bring his machete? David could have cut crutches from any of the numerous small forked saplings that grew near the road. Arjun could tell by his breathing that David was exhausted. They sat down again beside the road on an old log to rest. The sun was setting.

"We still aren't halfway." David sighed. "It'll be midnight before we get out of here."

"Now perhaps you'll realize the trouble that helping people can get you into," said Arjun.

As he was speaking, two half-naked tribals came sauntering up the road toward them. Arjun gestured, and they came over and inspected his leg, all smiles and nods.

"These fellows have machetes; they can make something for me to sit on. Between the two of them, they can quickly carry me the rest of the way."

He spoke to them in an unintelligible dialect and they disappeared into the forest, returning a few minutes later with vines and branches out of which they constructed a small litter with handles. When it was finally finished, Arjun sat down; they lifted him on their shoulders and trotted off down the road. David had to run to keep up with them. After his ordeal with the jeep, by the time they reached the flatland at the border of the park, he collapsed on the ground, exhausted. Nearby, a tribe of nomads was camped with their livestock. Arjun had himself carried there and bargained with a fierce-looking group of men huddled around the fire smoking charis, hashish, from a stemless pipe. It was obvious they had finished exerting themselves for the day and, even though Arjun was injured, were reluctant to put themselves out for him. Finally, when he produced a roll of rupee notes, they sighed and nodded, and one of the younger men got up and brought up two camels.

David grumbled. Arjun grinned. "What, Uncle, you mean you've never ridden a camel? Great fun. These chaps have offered to rent us their beasts. Come on, it's not much different from a horse."

"It's because I have ridden camels that I groaned," said David, getting up. "I hate the bloody beasts."

Furious that their sleep had been interrupted, the angry camels rolled their eyes malevolently, growled, and spit as the men saddled them. Finally, on command, they knelt. With difficulty, Arjun was hoisted up on one, David wearily climbed aboard the other, and they ambled off down the road. The cloudbank which, during the late afternoon, had hung in the west was now moving in. Low thunder and bursts of lightning punctuated the still air.

"These creatures will go mad in a storm. We should make a dash. Think you're up to it?" yelled David.

"I'm fine!" Arjun yelled back. "Jeldi, jeldi!"

"Be careful of that leg."

# 6

AFTER ARJUN and David left, Devika went twice during the night to her husband's room, fretting about them. What a foolish idea it had been, taking those jawans into the jungle; no good would come of it. They should have been sent on their way; they were not to be trusted.

"If Gayatri's not worried, why should you be so upset?" Madho Dev had asked her.

"I'm Arjun's mother, she's only his wife," came the curt reply, old as India itself. "Think of all the innocent Hindus these terrorists have killed."

"Those boys are not terrorists." Madho Dev fumed. "If you'd been in the army you'd understand their feelings. It's two in the morning. There's nothing to be done about it. Now go to bed, say one of your mantras if you're so worried, but let me get some sleep."

Devika had given him one of her earth-scorching glances and left. He looked at the thermometer, which registered 39 degrees Celsius— 102 degrees Fahrenheit. Couldn't she understand he might be as worried as she? Why was he always cast in the role of the imperturbable father and husband who must absorb her frantic vibrations? He took a cool bath and tried to sleep but his mind turned to Philippa alone in the guestroom: unsettling creature, to say the least. David always did have good taste in women. He wondered if she knew about Kamala.

By eleven the next morning the temperature had soared. One of the hottest days recorded in a decade. Over breakfast, Philippa sensed Devika's concern and tried to reassure her that the worst was not going to happen. After all, David and Arjun were both grown men; they were armed and could certainly take care of themselves. But everyone's nerves were on edge.

"It's always like this before the monsoon breaks." Devika sighed, wringing her hands. "The very worst time of year. People go crazy. In former times in my father's state even murders were forgiven during this season. That's why I'm so worried about Arjun and your husband."

By lunchtime the wind had risen and the sun, now a copper disk, shone sullenly through clouds of blowing sand and dust. All the windows and doors were closed but despite the fans, which continued to function under power from Madho Dev's own generator, it was so hot no one could eat. The children were put away to nap in the farthest reaches of the women's quarters, everyone else retired, and except for the rustling leaves of the pipal tree in the courtyard, the house slumbered.

Irritated beyond reason by Devika's constant remonstrances and the weather, Madho Dev found his mind whirring like the fan above him. Just before lunch the D.S.P. had called, asking if he thought Harbinder Singh could be trusted, or might he be hiding the three escaped Sikh jawans, who, as he put it, had disappeared completely from the face of the earth. The last straw. He'd had to restrain himself from telling the thug to fuck off and mind his own business, but the conversation unnerved him, brought him face-to-face with all the frightening changes he had tried so long to ignore. In public he blamed the politicians for all that had gone wrong, everyone did, but privately he knew things were more complicated. People got what they deserved. The Indian people too, so how could anyone complain? The sadistic young D.S.P., the bribe-taking District Magistrate, weren't they only reflections of the hypocrisy and corruption that were afflicting them all?

In his white cotton pajamas, he paced back and forth and tried to calm himself by thinking of something pleasant. His mind returned to Philippa. He'd never cared much for Englishwomen, but this one was different, not fussy or priggish like most of them. None of that tittering false modesty. Against all common sense, he padded out of his room along the veranda to the guestroom, knocked on the door, and, without waiting for an answer, opened it and went in. She was in bed; she woke with a start and covered her breasts with a thin cotton sheet.

"Oh, Madho Dev." She sighed. "You frightened me. I was fast asleep. Has something happened?"

Seeing her like that, he felt an irrational urge to pull the sheet away. That's what his crazy grandfather would have done. His grandfather, who had over a dozen wives and ninety concubines, had been famous for the prodigious size of his sexual organ, immortalized in certain miniature paintings, for which it was said there had been fierce competition, even among certain aristocratic English ladies. Wearing only a pajama top, the sybaritic hero would parade through his women's quarters at will and, when the urge seized him, take any one of them on the spot with the others looking on. His prowess had always been a source of inspiration for Madho Dev, but times had changed. Unable to meet Philippa's steady gaze, he sat down gloomily on the edge of the bed.

"I couldn't sleep," he said. "Generally I have no problem napping after lunch, but today Devika has upset me with her constant worrying."

"You spent half the morning trying to calm her down," Philippa said soothingly.

"With the result that her anxiety has rubbed off on me." He pulled at his mustache, unable to take his eyes off the provocative outlines of her barely concealed body.

"You're mad," she said, her eyes laughing.

"Perhaps." He nodded. "Right now I'm having great difficulty remembering what I wanted to ask you. As the Urdu poets would say, I am seized with jazbah."

"What a marvelous word. Does it mean what I think it does?"

"Precisely."

"I think this heat has affected you. I'm told it drives the best of men crazy."

"It does," he said, and put his hand on her thigh.

"You're being impossible," she said. "Please."

Furious, he got up and resumed his pacing. "Actually I came to see you because I wanted to straighten something out. Has David ever mentioned a cousin of mine, Princess Kamala Devi?"

"Not that I recall."

"I thought he probably wouldn't have. Perhaps you'll think it's important, perhaps not, but as you are in India and may very well meet her, I thought it only fair that you should know. They were once very much in love."

Philippa shrugged. What had got into him? Had she completely misjudged him? "That was a very long time ago, long before I came into the picture. I'm sure it was something David felt I didn't need to know. Why are you being so vindictive?"

"They had a child together." Madho Dev blundered on. "Before he left India, Kamala disappeared. David went berserk trying to find her, but when the day came for him to ship out, he gave up and left. She was pregnant and hadn't wanted to complicate his life. He could have stayed on and eventually found her but he didn't. She had the child, a girl. She was raised by an old nurse for three years and then was given to Devika and me. We gave her our name, brought her up, and now she's married to Arjun. Arjun's children are David's grandchildren."

"Are you telling me all this to hurt me?"

"No, of course not," he muttered. "As you say, it happened long ago." He stopped pacing and stood facing her. "You're a very lovely woman. The last thing I would want to do is to hurt you."

"Does Arjun know David is Gayatri's father? Does David know?"

Madho Dev shook his head. "Only Kamala and I know, and now you."

She stared at him. He began to feel terribly awkward. What had got into him, blurting out all this? "There are certain things you can't possibly understand," he said. "Gayatri, Arjun, and the children would suffer greatly if this were to get out. I think it's important David see Kamala."

"Your secret is safe with me," she said coolly. "Where does this Princess Kamala live?"

"In a hill station northeast of Delhi, called Terripur: lovely cool spot. She has a showplace there, inherited great wealth from her father. He was my mother's brother by a different wife."

"Did she ever marry?"

"Twice. Both marriages soured, both husbands are dead. She had a child with each of them, a boy and a girl, grown now. One hears about them occasionally."

"I suppose we'll be visiting this . . . what did you call it?"

"Terripur. I'm sure you'll enjoy yourself there, fine views of the Himalayas."

"Of course."

"You're a very understanding woman," he said, sitting down on the bed again. "But I feel there is a wall between us, I want to get to know you better." He took her hand gently in his.

"There is no wall on my part, I assure you." She smiled. "But I'm afraid I may have to build one unless you stop."

"You're very beautiful. It would be unnatural if I were not attracted to you."

"I think you had better go, for both our sakes. I'm sorry."

His irascible Rajput ancestors stood up in heaven and cursed her. "You're not sorry," he muttered. "I think you may be incapable of feeling that emotion." The ceiling fan rattled in its socket. He got up and stalked out of the room.

She closed the door and lay down. What on earth could have gotten into him? As Devika said, the heat did strange things to people. But what a stroke of luck! When David found out, wouldn't he be eager to get his new-found grandchildren and their parents out of this awful place? Arjun would come to England, and no one need ever know there was anything between them.


By EARLY evening, when David and Arjun had still not returned. Devika paced back and forth in the courtyard, stopping every few minutes at the shrine in the pipal tree to pray. As usual, a number of people were gathered there, smoking hookah and singing bhajans— hymns. At eight-thirty the TV was brought out and they all watched the news, more "healing touch," "helping hand" platitudes and testi- monials by prominent Sikhs in support of the government's action. Afterward, Devika pleaded with Madho Dev to send out a search party—something had happened to them, some foul play—but he refused to get upset.

The family ate in silence. After dinner Harbinder Singh and his sons came over to inquire whether Arjun had returned. The house- hold had retired and Madho Dev sat alone with his old neighbor, impatient for him to go home. Though he sympathized with Sikhs like Harbinder Singh, who'd lost everything in 1947 as he himself had at Kotagarh, at the same time their obdurateness irritated him and the idea galled him that they alone among the warrior castes of India had special rights, especially as they had so often sided with the British.

The first drops of rain had begun to fall, and Harbinder Singh was getting ready to leave, when they heard hoofbeats in the farmyard. Running out, they found Arjun and David struggling down from their camels. Devika and Philippa dashed out of the house in their nightclothes, followed by Gayatri and the children. A sudden downpour cut their greetings short, and they followed a limping Arjun inside, where Devika roused the servants and food was soon set before them.

After they had eaten, the children put back to bed, and the servants sent off, Arjun told them what had happened. As he spoke, Madho Dev realized that Harbinder Singh and his sons did not believe a word Arjun was saying.

"You don't believe him, do you?" he said.

"The part about the tigers? You expect us to believe that?" scoffed Harpal Singh.

"I can believe the jawans gave Arjun trouble and he shot them," said Harbinder Singh, "but not that some yogi caused tigers to attack them. Why didn't they shoot the beasts?"

"They moved too fast, Harbinder Singh," replied Arjun. "That is the truth."

Harpal stared angrily at him. "After cutting their hair and all—"

"And all, and all. It is I who had *all* the trouble, and now you are blaming me." Arjun trembled with anger.

"We should have let them go off as they wished," said Harbinder Singh.

"Get out," cried Madho Dev dramatically. "Go home and go to bed. We are all hot and tired. I don't want to hear any more of this tonight. We did what we thought best. We tried to help."

Without a backward glance, Harbinder Singh and his sons got up and walked out.

"You see, Uncle?" Arjun said. "Just what we were talking about. Did I not tell you there is no point in trying to help people in this country? That it always causes problems; that nobody will ever thank you for helping them; in fact, will think you're a fool?"

"Everyone knows that," said Devika. "That was my position all along. It's you sentimental men who can't face the truth, always taking action against your own interests. People only admire force and strength. When you say no, they think, Ah, he is shrewd; if you say yes, they think you are weak and stupid. In India, might is right. It always has been and it always will be."

"You agree with Indira Gandhi, then?" said Madho Dev.

"What else could she do?" replied Devika. "Those terrorists were making a fool of her."

"But she hobnobs with terrorists!" Madho Dev exploded. "Muslim terrorists like Yassir Arafat and that Khadafi. 'Yatha Raja, tatha praja.' She's the ruler; she sets the example for others to follow. If you run with terrorists, how can you criticize the Sikhs unless you are a hypocrite?"

"I don't know what you're talking about. I only know Bhindran-wale's men were killing and torturing innocent people and had to be punished."

"And by doing so, by punishing the man she herself set up, she has united the Sikhs against her," declared Arjun. "You will see, there will be more trouble and violence."

"The Sikhs have to realize they are a minority," said Devika. "Just like we Rajputs, they have to swallow the idea that India is made up of hundreds of minorities who must live together in peace. Otherwise, the country will again be ruled by foreigners."

Madho Dev glanced at Arjun. "How is your ankle?" Arjun would not admit he felt anything. "Let me feel it. It doesn't look fractured, but you should have an X ray. Is it painful?"

Tight-lipped and angry, Arjun got up and hobbled off, trailed by Devika and Gayatri talking about cold packs. Philippa excused herself and went back to bed.

Touched by Madho Dev's concern, David wondered aloud why sons refused to let their fathers help them. He was thinking of Edward, far away in London, so stubborn he would never take advice, never let anyone help him, never come home except for money, then run away.

"First thing in the morning, we'll go see Dr. Sahib!" Madho Dev shouted after Arjun. He turned to David. "What to do? After a certain point, they don't need you. No one needs you. Sometimes I feel quite useless." He sighed and stared at David. "My old friend. Now that you've returned, I feel less useless, because at least you felt interested enough to come back and look me up." He reached out and took David's hand. "Your love and friendship mean more to me than you can imagine. I only wish we were young again." He sat contentedly back in his chair. "Will you go see Kamala?"

"Do you think she's in Terripur now?"

"She spends most of her time there. Remember that weekend we had there, was it at the Ritz? Boiled for three days? You ran naked in the rain to sober up and frightened some missionaries half to death."

"And you hired those musicians and dancing girls."

"Right," said Madho Dev. "And my friend Deepak got angry and started throwing champagne glasses at them."

"Dare I go back there?" asked David.

"Why not? Those people are all dead and gone. If Kamala can live there, you can certainly go for a visit."

"Why didn't you let me know where she was? I wanted to write her."

"I didn't know where she was till after you stopped writing. Lost track of her while I was in Bombay; then she was always in Paris with those husbands of hers. It's only recently she's more or less settled down."

"I was so in love with her," said David thoughtfully.

"Have you ever told Philippa?"

"No."

"If you were so in love, why didn't you stay on and marry her?"

"You know her father would never have given his permission."

"You could have run off—it would have blown over."

"If she hadn't disappeared those last months. . . . I still don't understand what got into her. I had land in Bengal at the time; we could have lived there."

"I don't think you looked very hard for her."

"That's not true." David stared into space. "You said she had children. Tell me about them."

"There's a boy by her first marriage, must be about thirty now, called Sonny, lives with a Punjabi truck driver: set the fellow up with a fleet of trucks. Kamala was furious with him at the time, but now they're making a fortune in the transport business she feels better. Then there is a daughter, Sumitra, in her early twenties, very attractive, but the last time I heard from Kamala she was complaining the girl was driving her crazy, having an affair with some fortune hunter in Paris."

David sighed. "Strange, isn't it? My children are disappointments too. You don't know how lucky you are."

"I wouldn't say Kamala is disappointed. I would say her feelings verge on the murderous. She's very much a survivor, you know. But not to worry; if you're as rich as she is, it's quite easy to get rid of people who become troublesome. They just disappear. It gets blamed on some terrorist."

"You make her sound awfully ruthless."

"Desperate is more the word. A woman alone in this country, especially a rich one, must be tough."

"I must go see her."

"By all means," said Madho Dev. "Go up to Terripur. You can easily rent a house, and it will be much better for Philippa up there in the hills during the rainy season. Staying healthy on the plains is becoming very difficult, especially if you're traveling. Malaria is coming back in a big way, all sorts of mysterious intestinal things too. Really. But do wait until Teej is over, especially for Philippa's sake. Devika would be disappointed if she missed that."

"Don't think I remember Teej."

"It's the first festival of the New Year, just next week with the coming of the rains. It's a woman's festival, very colorful—swings, games, that sort of thing. My daughters will be coming. Stay for that, then go to Terripur if you like. I might even come for a visit once you find a house—we can have another one of those drunken weekends. And I'm sure there are still plenty of missionaries there for you to scare."

THE next morning dawned so hot people woke up feeling they had had no sleep at all. Arjun hobbled in to breakfast, wincing at each step.

"So you'll admit now you should go see Dr. Sahib?" said Madho Dev.

Arjun grunted. "If Davidji will come along, I'll go. I want him to see just what we have to contend with."

"I'd rather like to come too," said Philippa.

"No, you wouldn't," said Madho Dev firmly. "It will be too hot for you. You'd best stay here with Devika and Gayatri, help with the preparations for Teej."

"What is Teej?" she asked, suppressing a frown. She was not accustomed to being told where she could and could not go.

"The first festival of the New Year. It's great fun." Gayatri smiled. "Our New Year begins with the coming of the rains."

"Teej is a festival for married women," Devika explained, "when daughters return to visit their families."

"Gives us all one more excuse not to work," said Madho Dev.

Watching Gayatri, whom she now knew was David's daughter as much as Belinda, Philippa was struck by the arbitrariness of life. Gayatri was a few years older than Belinda. In any Western country she would be considered a beautiful young woman, have memberships in the best clubs, an active social life, play sports, and perhaps even have a job. Here, even though in her youth her adopted mother had briefly experienced such freedoms, Gayatri had been brought up in the traditional Hindu way and already had five children. Rarely did anyone address her directly; even more rarely did she venture an opinion on anything in front of the male members of her family. Yet she was very bright. It could be even more important to get her out of India than Arjun. And yet perhaps ignorance was bliss, for Gayatri seemed happy while Belinda was certainly not.

In the farmyard, the camels from the night before were being fed by a group of servant children.

"Forgot all about them," said Arjun. "How do we get them back?"

"We'll keep them until their owners come along for them," said Madho Dev.

They climbed into the jeep and set off to Kotagarh. In the bottom-land, the first paddy was sprouting emerald green.

"What is that factory over there," asked David, "the one giving off all that smoke? Lucky it doesn't come your way."

"Chemical plant," replied Madho Dev. "Makes pesticides. Sometimes it fills the air with ash. You must have seen it. Cleverly positioned so it covers the town with gray soot. Everyone told them this would happen, but as some politician had bought the land on purpose to sell it to the government, it was put there."

"I should think they'd have wanted it as far away as possible. In England—"

"This is India," said Arjun. "When a factory goes up here, land prices increase tenfold; the owners are able to sell it off by the foot to workers who want to live as close as possible."

"Don't they understand it's bad for their health?" said David, staring in disbelief at a vast slum of tin-roofed shacks that spread out on all sides from the factory.

They reached Kotagarh and pulled in the weed-choked driveway of a crumbling old Edwardian structure. On the veranda, an emaciated dark-skinned girl, her face hidden by a torn sari, was throwing hand-fuls of white powder from a large flat wicker basket. The powder landed in puffs and blew about in the breeze.

"Is that more DDT?" asked David. "We saw the same thing at the station."

"Ah," said Arjun, his voice filled with irony. "I'm glad you are aware of it. It's one of the reasons I wanted you to come. She belongs to one of our Scheduled Castes who have been liberated from carrying shit on their heads only to be put to work distributing DDT." He laughed bitterly. "See, there in the back, those children playing in it? We have repeatedly written to the Health Minister, told him that

DDT is banned even in his precious USSR. According to tests some young doctors have made, Indian people have twenty-six times the allowable maximum DDT residue in their bone marrow and blood."

"Soon they'll start producing deformed babies, even monsters," said Madho Dev.

"But how awful!" said David. "Can't something be done?"

"You tell me why, Uncle," Arjun said.

David thought for a moment. "I haven't a clue."

"The World Health Organization backs up the chemical companies, says the stuff is saving more lives than it's killing; says in a monsoon climate it will all wash away! Do they think we are idiots?"

"Can't you form an action committee?"

Arjun and his father guffawed. "You can't be serious. Could you form an action group with a tribe of monkeys? Monkey brains, monkey manners, monkey values. Most of our intelligent people have fled or are trying to. We're giving you the true picture."

They stepped inside a dark room with a concrete floor and grimy plastic furniture on which sat a number of very sick-looking people. Across one corner was a table stacked with papers, some half-used bottles of vaccine, a tray of used hypodermic needles, a box of cotton pads, and an old sterilizer. Behind the table, presiding over this collection of junk, sat a moronic-looking young woman, her breasts bursting out of a low-cut sari blouse. The smell of insecticide was overpowering. With lowered eyes, the men surreptitiously ogled the saturnine receptionist. Women with chronically congested lungs spat on the floor; children wailed and were pinched brutally to keep them quiet; the ceiling fan squeaked and ruffled the inevitable calendar with the ubiquitous smiling face of Indira Gandhi. The only incongruous element in the setting was a faded picture of young John F. Kennedy in a cheap gilt frame. Now and then, two skinny young men in soiled white pajamas with sweat-stained crotches and pink plastic sandals shuffled in and out, conducting patients to waiting rooms beyond.

"I say, this can't really be a doctor's office," whispered David.

"The only private doctor's office in Kotagarh." Madho Dev nodded. "Of course, there's the hospital my father donated, but it's even worse. If I were really sick I wouldn't come here. Even healthy, I don't relish coming because I think I might get sick. However, this man has an X-ray machine, an old one, but it works. Otherwise, if we need medical help, we go to Delhi."

"Which is not much better," commented Arjun.

"But in our time it was not like this," said David. "I remember coming to Kotagarh with you: there were several doctors, the offices were spotless, and, of course, a first-rate hospital."

"What you are seeing is the result of thirty-seven years of neglect," said Madho Dev. "My father's hospital is still here, run down like this, staffed by incompetents; all the good people have left. Our government imposes a huge duty on medical equipment in order, they say, to encourage indigenous production. I think they hope people will die. I do myself."

The desperate reality filled David with gloom. "And you say this is one of the better places?"

"My dear chap"—Madho Dev grinned—"this is luxury class."

Just then a tall dark man with glasses, a white shirt, and fraying brown pants slung low on his hips, opened the door and beckoned them effusively to come in. He had the look of a harassed school teacher.

"Ah, Raja-sahibji," he shouted in English so the other patients would understand the importance of his visitor. "To what do I owe this honor? Bring in some chairs and tea," he crossly barked in Hindi to one of his sullen minions. "Just now I am hearing on my telephone that you are in town and—" He glanced at Arjun. "Oh, I see, your son has had a mishap, isn't it?"

"You owe our visit to chance," said Madho Dev, "to the goddess of chance, whoever she may be. His jeep turned over, Dr. Sahib; we need an X ray." The doctor looked curiously at David. "Sorry, let me introduce you to my friend. This is Captain David Bruce; we were in Burma together. After forty years, he is visiting me. David, this is Dr. Kapoor."

"You must be seeing a lot of changes," shouted the doctor optimistically. "Ever since your people have left us we have really progressed, isn't it?"

David was dumbstruck. The tea arrived in cracked cups; betel-nut pan was offered. Kapoor chatted on about the wonders of irrigation, chemical factories right here in Kotagarh, and the Green Revolution. Finally Madho Dev ventured to set him back on course.

"Ah, yes." The doctor smiled. "Certainly, we must have a look at your son's leg. Can you pull up your pant?"

"I think we should have an X ray, Dr. Sahib," said Madho Dev.

"Ah, well, that is the problem, Raja-sahibji. You see, just this morning our machine seems to be going on the blink. I think the voltage is less today, but by this afternoon I am sure it will be all right. Here, let me have a look. I can tell a lot by feeling it." The doctor felt Arjun's leg and ankle with his large hands.

"I do not think it is broken. It is a sprain, a torn ligament or two. I will wrap it in an elastic bandage and then, gentlemen, you must do me the honor of coming to my house for lunch. After lunch, I am sure my X ray will be working."

David could see the doctor was delighted his machine wasn't working so he could invite them to his house. It would be a triumph for him, something that would raise his social prestige in Kotagarh for months. While Arjun's leg was being bandaged, Madho Dev and David excused themselves and went outside.

"I say, can't we get out of this lunch? Tell him we're due back at your place or go to a quiet restaurant?"

Madho Dev shook his head. "Afraid that having lunch at his house may be the price of the X ray. As for a quiet restaurant, you must remember where you are. This is not Paris, after all."

Dr. Kapoor's house stood on a side street in the old Cantonment section of Kotagarh. In the days of the British Raj, it would have belonged to some official. It had gabled roofs, two wings, a reception room connecting them, and a courtyard. A riot of flowers was blooming in several fenced-in gardens. Though much of the Victorian gingerbread had fallen off, what was still left was freshly painted.

How exactly had the idea for all this cuteness come about? David wondered. Just where on earth had his countrymen imagined they were living, in some fairyland? Forty years ago he'd never noticed it, but now, compared with the simple majestic construction of Madho Dev's house, this hideosity seemed preposterous. Much to his surprise, however, for he had expected something like the doctor's office, the cool interior was neat and clean. It seemed Kapoor cared more for his home than his place of business. The floor of decorative tiles was polished. In one corner an old desk covered with stacks of books was a real relic of the Raj. The rest of the room was lined with 1950s furniture upholstered in pink and green plastic covered with crocheted doilies. There were potted ferns, family portraits, a religious picture of the monkey god Hanuman tearing open his chest to reveal a throbbing heart, and a framed print of Rama returning to Ayodhya from his victory over the forces of darkness. The sitting room was obviously the work of a woman, and soon Mrs. Kapoor appeared, a very small, plump, jolly soul with a buck-toothed smiling face, wearing a pink sari. A servant brought fresh sweet lime juice, and Mrs. Kapoor disappeared. The conversation quickly turned to politics and the pros and cons of Operation Blue Star. Dr. Kapoor was outspoken in his hatred of the government but full of approval for the way in which the army had at last been sent to destroy the terrorist nest.

Hindus were too passive; they were always letting people step all over them. That had been the problem all along. They had been too tolerant, with the Muslims, the British; now the time had come to stand up for their rights! The Sikhs were good people, but everyone knew they were really just Hindus with long hair and they had to realize they were less than two percent of the population. Of course, the main problem was the bureaucracy. It was so corrupt, so lazy and sycophantic, who could blame the Sikhs for not wanting to be part of India? Look at us doctors, how these government officials harass us with taxes and duties on equipment. "Come." He motioned them to follow him out through a gate in a wall to a vacant lot.

"What is this?" cried Madho Dev, gesturing at a pile of wreckage in the weed-grown lot.

"What does it look like?" said the doctor.

"Looks a bit like the remains of an airplane," said David.

"Absolutely correct, sir," said Kapoor. "It is the skeleton of a B-29, the second one I have been able to get my hands on." Madho Dev stared in disbelief.

"But what on earth for?" asked David, bewildered.

"Ah, gentlemen, it seems crazy, doesn't it, having a wreck like this in one's backyard. But from this junk we are making all kinds of things. The metal from it is very good. I make instruments for my practice, parts for people's broken-down machines, I've even made audio equipment, speakers, amplifiers. And why? Because we are forbidden to get anything from outside. In my office I spoke to you of how progressive we have become; that was for public consumption, in case one of those idiots should understand our conversation. Privately I am telling you, the gas chambers of the Nazis are too good for these bureaucrats and politicians. Formerly I used to say that about Mrs. Gandhi too, but just now I must support her because she is putting an end to the killing of Hindus in Punjab. And the cost has not been that high. Already we have seen on television how careful the army has been not to destroy their Golden Temple."

"You believe the television?" asked Madho Dev.

"I see with my own eyes," said Dr. Kapoor. "Their Golden Temple is still there, gleaming in the sun, is it not? No one has taken away the gold. And did you not see the piles of weapons they had? They even had antitank guns."

"Only three," put in Arjun. "And we have heard the army killed many more people than they are willing to admit."

"Of course, you have those Sikh neighbors," said Kapoor disparagingly. "Yes, I suppose that Harbinder Singh would be saying he has inside information." He gestured again to the wrecked B-29. "You see, sir, what we poor Indian doctors are up against. If I had been smart, I would have left years ago like my classmates who now have prosperity in U.K. and California, U.S.A. But we are having four children, two girls and two boys, and we hear it is hard to bring them up correctly in Western countries. My wife is not wanting to leave, she is very traditional, attached to her family, and has her mother and sister living with us too. So here we are. My two young sons are helping me in our machine shop, we are in the fix-it business. Between us, we fix anything—people, animals, cars, tractors, radios. A very good business, since everything is always breaking down."

In spite of Kapoor's bumptiousness, David thought him quite a delightful eccentric.

Lunch was served under a canopy of bougainvillea in one corner of the courtyard. They sat on mats and were served mounds of steaming white rice, dal, and some delicious fried vegetables by Mrs. Kapoor. They ate in silence with their hands and after the meal were shown to a room where three mattresses covered with spotless white sheets had been placed on the floor.

"Now, gentlemen, you must take your rest," said the doctor, wringing his hands. "After that, we will have tea and see about the X ray. If Arjunji will just lie down, I have something that should help his sprain." Producing some large furry leaves, Dr. Kapoor unfastened Arjun's bandage, placed them on his sore leg and ankle, and slowly rewound the bandage. "Let us see if they work." He smiled. "An old remedy we always use on sprains."

AT THREE precisely, a servant shuffled into the room with tea and sweets on a tray, followed in ten minutes by the doctor.

"Would Raja-sahibji be wanting a refreshing bath?" he asked. He turned to Arjun, who had stood up. "How does your ankle feel now?"

"As a matter of fact, it feels better," Arjun replied, taking a few tentative steps. "Really, it seems much better."

"Ah," said Dr. Kapoor. "I am glad to hear it. My experience is there must be a sympathetic reaction between patient and medicine, except for these allopathic remedies like tetracycline and penicillin. But then, they don't cure, they are only suppressing."

After a quick bath, they set out for Dr. Kapoor's office. The carnal-looking secretary was reading a film magazine and the waiting room was again filled with half-dead patients. Nevertheless, the electricity was on and the X-ray machine, after Dr. Kapoor had tinkered with it for a few minutes, actually worked.

"What an extraordinary character," said David as they drove away.

"Something of a genius, eh?" said Madho Dev.


WITH his leg propped up on cushions, Arjun tried to concentrate on a mountain of idiotic paperwork that had accumulated in connection with his job, but his mind wandered and he caught himself staring vacantly into space, thinking of Philippa. Those brief moments with her on the deck at the cottage and her declaration on the way to the granary had undone him. And though he hated losing control of himself, part of him was enjoying this new sensation. Being "in love"! Dangerous territory. The promise of her kisses. The ache in his loins. He'd set out to mesmerize her that she might help him to leave India, but now the very thought of her was bringing him to his knees. And unless something happened before she left, unless he had an opportunity to continue what had barely been begun, she would certainly forget all about him.

And so it was with frustration and anger that he sat there watching, waiting for her to acknowledge him. The preparations for the Teej festival went forward, his sisters arrived, the house, decorated with festive garlands, filled up with screaming children. Never in his life had he felt so trapped. The rains came more often, the weather grew cooler, and soon the world outside turned into a sensuous green paradise. The day of the festival arrived and was celebrated with traditional fasts and prayers. The women and children had a wonderful time on special swings, festooned with jasmine and hibiscus, hung from the low branches of the old pipal tree, and Philippa joined in with such enthusiasm and became so friendly with his mother and Gayatri, he became convinced she'd decided to put him out of her mind.

Then came the day he had dreaded, when David announced over breakfast that he and Philippa would be leaving soon for Terripur. She glanced quickly at him, a glance of desperation that made his heart stop. What was he to do? His brain clouded over with thoughts, dark as water buffaloes' eyes. But that night, as he lay restlessly awake contending with the physical manifestations of his desire, a solution came to him. Certainly David could not leave without seeing the ruins of a famous fort that lay not twenty kilometers away. The next morning he would whet his imagination with stories about the brave defenders, the buried treasure, the largest cannon in India, and suggest an outing. Yes, a regular English "picnic"—and perhaps, if the gods favored him, he could spirit Philippa away into the labyrinth of subterranean passages that he had known by heart since childhood.

Miraculously, the next morning his suggestion met with unanimous approval. Everyone was sick of being cooped up in the house and welcomed a chance for a farewell outing. A lunch was packed and they took the jeep and the Ambassador car. By noon they were climbing the steps to the fort with his father and Philippa in the lead. He was so excited by the movements of her hips beneath her clothes that he could barely walk. While his mother, Gayatri, and two of his sisters unpacked the lunch and were preoccupied with their children, he led the way on a tour and, when his father and David went off to inspect the battlements, managed to drop behind and spirit Philippa away into an underground passage, where he took her in his arms, opened her blouse, and kissed her breasts. He was afraid he might rape her if she did not submit, but she kissed him eagerly with a hunger as great as his own. Tearing at each other's clothes, they moved farther along the labyrinth, where they embraced again and again.

Philippa was nearly paralyzed with fear and excitement. He was warm, sleek, and incredibly strong. Her teeth began chattering, but he covered her mouth with kisses and the tremors descended through her throat and spine to her thighs. He groaned and she opened her eyes to find him staring at her, tears streaming down his cheeks. Just then, David's voice came echoing down the tunnel. They froze but, like a raft propelled toward a rapids by an irresistible force, they had gone too far to stop. As she started to scream, he blocked her mouth with a long kiss. She ran her hands down his back and held him. Now Madho Dev's powerful voice echoed down the corridors, disturbing a pack of large bats, which fluttered nervously about them.

Arjun held her firmly. They were both trembling. "I love you. Say you love me." His large eyes fastened on her.

"I love you," she gasped.

"Say you will never forget me."

"How could I?" she said.

"Say it!" He shook her.

"I'll never forget you."

"One way or another I'll come to you in Terripur," he said breathlessly. "Now listen, I am going to go out first. I'll say I've been looking for you and lead them away. There's another exit just behind us. When you have tidied up, come out that back way and wander over to the picnic place; it's a shortcut. Say you've been exploring, pick some flowers, collect some stones, anything. I'm sorry we haven't more time, but I will make more time later."

Wiping his forehead with his shirttail, he kissed her, straightened his clothes, and walked briskly away. After a few minutes, Philippa heard him talking to Madho Dev. What an actor he was. She wondered whether anyone would be fooled.

# 7

THE DAY OF DEPARTURE arrived. Madho Dev wanted Arjun to drive David and Philippa to Delhi, but Philippa thought Arjun might become unmanageable and do something crazy and persuaded Madho Dev to let them take the train. Of course, the train was late. It was unbearably hot again, and David became hostile. Why couldn't these new people with their pants and suits run things correctly when before a handful of Britons and barefoot natives wearing lungis managed everything efficiently?

"It's what they call socialism." Madho Dev chuckled. "To them it means no one has to work."

Philippa sat down on their luggage and buried herself in a book. She hated it when David got like this, and she couldn't bear to watch Arjun pacing up and down like a caged beast.

The platform was littered with refuse. David ranted on. The lunchroom was rank. Where were the sweepers? He knew how his countrymen had ill-used India—land taxed into barrenness, ruthless licensing policies, monolithic Indian civil service—but, objectively, could one say this was better? Forty years ago people died quickly but lived happy lives. Now it seemed they existed in a sort of living death.

Madho Dev sighed. "There is no answer. Basically we're an undisciplined lot, that's our charm, of course. India will be the place where all these ideas of progress will finally fail. We'll simply gum up the works with human bodies. In the back of my mind there is always the nagging feeling that things have come out right for the wrong reasons."

"Muddling through, I think we used to call it," said David.

"And then I have to remind myself I'm sixty years old and remember my grandfather complaining in the same way," said Madho Dev.

"Jaundiced eye of sixty." David smiled grimly.

Arjun waved from the end of the crowded platform. A whistle sounded down the track. Philippa got up joyfully and walked off down the platform. Madho Dev and David caught up with her.

"At last I can stop listening to your depressing conversation," she said. "Really, it just makes things worse." She thought of herself as an optimistic person and became terribly depressed by David's "end of the world talk," as she called it. She'd always lived in the present. What was the point in thinking of the future? It was too frightening.

The train pulled in. They all hugged each other and promised to be in touch soon. Arjun saluted with smoldering eyes. David and Philippa stood at the door waving until the train rounded a curve, then made their way down the corridor to their compartment.

The realities of travel are always unexpected. Often it is necessary for one's sanity to sit back and see the whole thing as a fantastic joke. The messy compartment into which they were now ushered by the conductor was no exception. At first the three children of various ages, the plump blond woman in a tight-fitting pink polyester suit, and the rather handsome man whose manner, after closer inspection, seemed to betray a certain sleaziness seemed innocuous enough. They were Americans.

Philippa settled herself and gazed out the window at the gorgeous shades of green, the ruddy earth: a landscape alive with white-clad farmers, animals, and children. These placid scenes did not seem to draw the attention of the American family, however, who busily occupied themselves eating and arguing over their food. David took up an anthology of Somerset Maugham and began one of his favorite stories, "Rain."

The father stopped chewing his sandwich. "So you're a reader of Maugham," he said. David looked over his glasses to see if he was being addressed. The man was wiping his mouth with a paper napkin and brushing crumbs vigorously from his lap to the floor. "Hi, I'm Stan Nelson and this is my wife, Jessie." He stuck out his hand.

David nodded politely but kept his hand to himself. "I'm very fond of Maugham, often reread him," he said. "Do you like his stories?"

"I should hope not," declared the woman. "Downright filthy-minded, if you ask me. Take that story of his, 'Rain,' for instance."

David closed his book. Could this mildly sexy blonde be clairvoyant? "How very odd," he said. "I just happened to be reading

'Rain.' But there must be some of his stories you like? 'The Razor's Edge'?"

"We've never bothered to read him," said the woman, "so we haven't read 'Rain.'"

"But we know all about it," said her husband.

"I see," said David. "Someone has told you to beware of 'Rain,' is that it?"

"It's on the blacklist put out by our mission in Little Rock," said Stan Nelson.

"Little Rock, what is that?" asked David, eyebrow arching.

"You must be English," Mrs. Nelson said. "Little Rock is a city in the United States, in the state of Arkansas."

"Of course." David nodded. "Little Rock. Isn't that where they had those race riots?"

"That's when we left," said Mr. Nelson. "When those niggers won. We've been in India ever since. Our church has a mission here."

David smiled. "Oh, you're missionaries. I can see why you wouldn't like 'Rain.' Excellent story, though, quite well written. What is your church? It must be very rich to send you first class." He was annoyed to have been drawn into this conversation.

"That was in the old days," chirped Mrs. Nelson. "Nowadays you get robbed blind if you go any other way. Tried it recently?"

The train had pulled into a large town and was stalled some distance from the station. Outside the tinted glass windows, a number of men could be seen squatting on the tracks, relieving themselves. The power had gone off, the compartment was stuffy, and the children were opening and closing the door, letting in more hot air.

"Just sightseein'?" Nelson asked.

"I've come back to see old friends after forty years," said David. "Actually, I was born here. Served in the Indian Army in '44 and '45."

"If you ask me," said Nelson, "you guys never shoulda left. These heathen can't control themselves; they got no discipline. Look what's happenin'."

"Perhaps we should never have come here to begin with," replied David coolly. "I have many friends among the people you call 'heathen,' and they are all perfectly well disciplined."

"Are you for Christ?" asked Mrs. Nelson, her ample breasts quivering with emotion.

"We are Church of England," replied Philippa. "But we don't believe that people who worship other gods are heathens."

"Idol worshipers," grumbled Nelson, "headed straight for Hell unless they come to Jesus."

"I say, with what church are you connected?" David inquired.

"Christian Church of the South. We're an affiliate."

"When I was in the army here," said David, "I had a Christian servant called James, Indian fellow. One night he came to me in tears, poor chap, said some mission had given him forty rupees to become a Christian, but when his baby died they wanted eighty rupees to bury it. So you see, every story has two sides."

"Sure he wasn't connin' you? These heathens are real tricky. Never heard of Christians chargin' for burial over and above what it cost."

"And we don't offer money to people to come to Jesus. Jesus is all-powerful, he doesn't need to bribe anyone," crooned Mrs. Nelson. "I'm sure you'd understand if you'd just open your heart."

"My heart is very open," said Philippa, "and I find it extremely rude of you, a guest in this country, to criticize people just because they don't happen to agree with your point of view."

"You think we want to be here?" cried Mrs. Nelson. "This is penance for us, for our sins. India is the cross we're carrying on our shoulders for Jesus."

"Hypocritical nonsense," muttered David. "You live like kings here, everyone knows that. You have servants you could never afford in Little Rock; your food costs nothing. When your ancestors were living in caves, people here were civilized. What gives you the idea your religious experiences are so superior?"

"It's people like them," said Nelson to his wide-eyed son, "who are draggin' Christ's name in the dirt." He turned back to David, and his voice took on the saccharine whine of an insurance salesman. "Brother, I can see you really want to come to Christ."

"All who come to Christ are born again," chimed in Mrs. Nelson. Her tight pink skirt slipped up above her knees, revealing the beginning of a thigh that evoked a love object rather than a modest missionary.

"That's what the Hari Krishnas believe too," said Philippa. "Born again with Krishna."

"We don't beg, we give," said Mrs. Nelson pompously. "I can see you're both deep in sin."

"Cheeky!" exclaimed Philippa.

"Pardon me?" said Mrs. Nelson.

"In America I think you say 'fresh.' You have a perfect right to believe what you wish, but you must keep your opinions to yourselves and be tolerant of the beliefs of others."

"Tolerance of sin is an abomination. If we see people who are sunk in it, it's our Christian duty to help 'em," intoned Nelson.

Philippa bunched up a sweater, slumped against the compartment wall, and stared out at the twilight landscape as it rolled past. People were coming home from the fields, youths bicycled down country lanes, groups of men sat smoking under enormous old trees with tangled roots. A little boy was tugging at a rope tied to the nose ring of a stubborn water buffalo. The smoke of cooking fires drifted over the fields in gray wisps. If God is still anywhere on earth, she thought, He is here in India and His children are not steeped in sin. Why were these missionaries so caught up in it, so obsessed? Obviously, they felt sinful themselves or had been made to think they were.

The sun set. Finally the grim industrial suburbs of Delhi flashed by. Goblinlike figures materialized and disintegrated in the murky gloom. It looked like a stage set for the end of the world. Surely this was not a Hindu way of life, thought David; that a whole culture had been led to believe in industrialization seemed a cruel joke, a preposterous mistake. And missionaries had been the advance troops. He knew it all too well. Hadn't his own family been deeply involved? In India, Burma, Malaysia, China: first came the missionaries, who told people they were sinful, then the industrialists with their tinsel baubles, who built factories and put people to work. When Adam got thrown out of the Garden of Eden for "sin," he had to work. David had to smile. He felt better about things not working well in India. These people really didn't buy that message. They could almost remember the days of Eden and didn't want this new industrial hell.

# 8

I N A W A Y," ventured Philippa after they had collected their bags, settled themselves into a moribund taxi and were bumping through the streets of Delhi to their hotel, "in a way, that was good for us. Perhaps we won't complain so much, and you'll stop talking about how decadent it all seems."

The taxi pulled up beneath a portico of red sandstone and white marble. The door was opened by a tall liveried doorman, who bid them good evening and escorted them into a vast, white marble lobby where cool fountains played.

David blinked. "I say, a raja's palace. Delhi has definitely changed."

"A people's palace." Philippa smiled, considerably cheered up. "I think it's lovely. I'm going to take a long hot bath in a big tub, order room service, and have my hair done."

They checked in and were escorted to their room by a young man who spoke perfect English and told them he was a graduate of Delhi University.

"Most of the staff here are college graduates," he said. "Jobs are very difficult to find nowadays, and this pays better than most. Are you coming from America?"

"From England," said David.

"Oh, I see," said the young man. His smile disappeared.

"What's the matter?"

"It's just this BBC business, sir. An exiled Sikh on the BBC offered a million pounds for our Prime Minister's life. You must not have heard due to traveling."

"Actually, we did hear but we didn't take it seriously."

"Oh, it is very serious, sir. There are huge crowds outside the British High Commission. The government is very angry. Every night it is shown on our television."

"I saw that too," said David. "The BBC made a great mistake letting that fellow on, but you must realize our British government doesn't have that much control over the news media."

The young man looked gloomy. "Not like India, I suppose. If you speak your mind here these days, you will be watched and followed and soon they will be calling you a conspirator or a terrorist."

The young man left and David flopped down on one of the comfortable beds with the newspaper. "I say, listen to these headlines, will you? HUSBAND CHOPS OFF WIFE'S NOSE IN QUARREL; HARIJANS BLINDED BY POLICE; P.M. CAUTIONS OF 'FOREIGN HAND' DESTABILIZING THE NATION; WIFE DOUSED WITH KEROSENE BY HUSBAND'S RELATIVES AND BURNED TO DEATH. What do you make of that? There's that bloody 'foreign hand' again, you'd think they could come up with something new." He threw down the paper in disgust and headed for the bath. India, the human hive, he thought, except it was the opposite of a hive; a hive of bees was organized.

Rising early the next morning, he left Philippa to sleep and embarked on an exploratory walk, only to find the streets he remembered had changed beyond recognition. He had hoped to locate the house of Madho Dev's father near the Gymkhana Club, a place where he'd spent many happy days and nights, but the landmarks had somehow vanished and the rush-hour traffic was so oppressive he lost all sense of direction. Diesel vehicles puffing black smoke had replaced the stately white cows that once leisurely roamed the streets. He rubbed his smarting eyes and, after asking directions from an old man on a bicycle, discovered at last, hidden away behind vine-covered crumbling walls, the house he remembered so well. Just as he was peering tentatively in at the gate, however, he was suddenly surrounded by men armed with Sten guns who jumped out of the bushes and pushed him toward a sentry box. "Didn't he know this was the residence of a Minister of State? Ah, an Englishman." They searched him for God knows what.

"Banana republic," David kept repeating to himself as he waited while they verified his identity with the hotel; "bloody banana republic." Then, inexplicably, he was escorted up the drive and ushered into an enormous room where a tired-looking little man, sitting behind a massive desk piled high with papers, received him. It was the Minister, looking for all the world like one of Tenniel's drawings for *Alice in Wonderland*. He gestured for David to be seated.

"Your name is David Bruce, British national," he said laconically. "What is the purpose of your visit to India?"

David was nonplused; this was the sort of question one expected from a customs clerk, not a minister of state.

"I was born in India," he explained, "I served in the Indian Army in '44 and '45 in Burma. I've come back to visit old friends and revisit the places I once knew. Like this house"—he gestured at the depressing room with its peeling plaster, worn rugs, and huge photographs of the Nehru family. "It once belonged to a good friend of mine. I spent many happy hours here."

The Minister was not impressed. "Are you aware that certain foreign elements are active in trying to destabilize this country? Are you aware that the BBC has—"

"Yes, yes," interrupted David. "I have heard about it. But you can't be implying that I am somehow connected to any of that?"

The Minister, who was obviously not accustomed to being interrupted, narrowed his eyes and gazed steadily at David for some time. "And what is your opinion of us after forty years, Captain Bruce?" he said finally.

"I think you're going down the drain unless something is done soon," said David.

The Minister shuffled his papers. "At least you're honest," he said. A sardonic smile lingered on his lips. "Shall I tell you what is happening? We are sinking into lawlessness, yes. It seems we are incapable of regulating ourselves. We would like to think it is being caused by outsiders, some unseen hand, but regretfully I can tell you it is not; it is us. We should face up to it, but no one will."

"When I was twenty years old," said David, "we used to dance all night in this room."

"I would have been ten then," said the Minister, "in my father's house in Bangalore. My father was a doctor from Travancore, now Kerala. He was an ardent supporter of Gandhiji. I remember sitting on Gandhi's lap, but of course he was assassinated before I was old enough to appreciate him."

"Thank you for allowing me to disturb your busy day," said David. "I really can't imagine any other country in the world where someone of your rank would take this much time to chat with me."

The Minister nodded. "Things may look bad, but they've always been that way here, haven't they, and foreigners have always been predicting India will, as you say, go down the drain, but we haven't. And now there are too many of us; we'd stop up any drain." He smiled at his own joke.

"I'm glad to hear you say that," said David, getting up. "I've always been very fond of the Indian people."

"Ah, most heartening." The Minister nodded again. "Have a good stay, Captain Bruce. Welcome to Delhi."

As he left the old house, the feeling of living in an illusion, of being haunted by ghosts, attacked him again. What a mistake to return to a city you had once loved, only to find there was no place left in it for you.

He checked his watch. Late for lunch. But then Philippa would be spending the day pulling herself together, as she called it, so why not risk one more disillusionment and walk to Humayun's tomb, a place he had often visited with Kamala. It began to rain. He stopped at a small shop, bought an umbrella, and set out on foot. For almost forty years he had thought of Delhi as one of the most romantic places on earth, dreamed of returning to its horse-drawn carriages with their tinkling bells, the wonderful multiplicity of its bird and animal life which had so beautifully coexisted here with man; to the lazy days of flower gardens, cricket, tennis, and polo, walks along the great Mall from Lutyens's Parliament House to India Gate.

If only his countrymen could have forgotten the color of people's skin, would they not still be here? Perhaps, as they had made rather efficient managers, but, no, they would never have forgotten and neither would Hindustan. That was the whole problem, wasn't it?

The problem that had destroyed his chances with Kamala. His jaw set, he struck off down one of the tree-lined avenues and came to an area he thought he recognized, but it was now so crisscrossed with highways and overpasses, he became confused. Just then two lepers came rolling along on their makeshift skateboards, all mindless grins and oozing stumps, and cheerfully directed him down a small road, through a gate, and there it was, the tomb, unchanged, its Persian dome floating above the great sandstone and white marble alcoves. Here were the octagonal rooms he had explored with Kamala so long ago, their vaulted ceilings, perforated marble screens, and dizzying geometrical floors. All here, unchanged. He was glad he'd come. He stood in the rain on the grand terrace near the grave of the ill-fated Dara Shikoh, lost in thought. Finally he sat down in a niche, and must have dozed, for it was almost dark when an old caretaker quietly prodded him awake, and he made his way down the red gravel path out into the din of Delhi's rush hour.

BACK at the hotel, he discovered Philippa in high spirits. She'd had a terrific time: steam bath, massage, manicure, shampoo, and set. He tried to tell her about his day, his sense of loss and frustration, but she was in another world. Why did he want to roam around outside in that polluted air when he could be in a nice, air-conditioned room?

"So you feel better about India now, that's good." He sighed, collapsing into a chair. "Two weeks ago you were ready to leave."

"Well, I guess I'm getting used to it. You'll have to admit, it's rather a big adjustment for someone who's never been here. Your problem is you're constantly looking back, comparing; I'm seeing things fresh, and it's not all that bad." She smiled contentedly. "And they really know how to take care of you here. I feel totally rejuvenated."

She added that a secretary to some official or other had rung up to invite them to something at nine-thirty that evening. He looked at the address she'd taken down, told her about going to look for Madho Dev's old house and his encounter with the Minister, and thought it strange that such a brief meeting should warrant an invitation. But she was excited at the prospect of an adventure and begged him to go.

Just then, the phone rang. It was Arjun calling to see if they'd arrived safely. The connection was bad and Philippa yelled into the phone, waving her hands, obviously happy to hear from him. It was good to see her so carefree, thought David. How odd it was that India, which he loved so much, was having the very opposite effect on him.

"What do you think I ought to wear to this affair?" she asked after he'd talked to Arjun and rung off. "What about one of those outfits with the pants and long tunics that hang to the knees?"

"You mean salwar-kameez?"

"Yes, that's the name Devika gave me," she replied. "They've some marvelous-looking ones in a shop downstairs. What are you going to wear?"

"I'll stick to my native costume"—David smiled—"tropical worsted. But by all means go down and see if anything appeals to you."

IN THE lift, Philippa wondered how she'd sounded with Arjun. Phones were such monstrous things. Had she sounded too diffident? Certainly he must have understood she couldn't say what she really felt with David sitting right there. Poor Arjun, he sounded so desolate, so far away.

A tall, rugged-looking man in the uniform of an army officer with a turban and too many decorations got into the elevator and by the time they'd reached the lobby was making stabs at conversation.

"You think we've met before?" She smiled. "Where could that have been? Geneva, perhaps?"

"Geneva I have never been to, madam," he said, his voice resonant with meretricious charm, and began asking the standard questions: how long had she been in India, was she traveling alone, and how did she like the country?

"I love it," she answered. "Mind you, I've only been here about a month, but I find it utterly fascinating. I'm with my husband, who is up in our room."

"And where are you going now?"

"Shopping for one of your salwar-kameezes."

"After you've purchased your salwar-kameez, why don't you have a drink with me?"

Philippa smiled and walked across the white marble lobby. The man followed her.

"I didn't mean to offend you," he said.

"You didn't. It's very flattering to be asked for a drink by a handsome army officer, but I'm afraid it's impossible now. How about tomorrow?"

"Tomorrow who knows what will happen? In India you must learn to seize the moment. There is a mini bar in my room. Come, your husband will never know the difference."

"If we could spend a week together, I'd say yes," she whispered, her ingenuous blue eyes gazing steadily at him. "I'm sure a week with you would be memorable. However, I can't, and I do loathe fast fucks."

The officer's jaw went slack. She left him standing, open-mouthed, in the vast lobby. It was awfully naughty of her, she supposed, but she didn't care. Her affair with Arjun had done wonders for her flagging ego. She felt young, powerful, and carefree.

When she returned to their room, David was already dressed. Opening her package, Philippa said, "I couldn't decide so I bought them both. What do you think?"

David said he preferred the white silk, and when she appeared in it a few minutes later, he smiled approvingly.

"It feels rather odd to be all dressed up going to a party given by someone one doesn't even know," she said. "Do you really think we should?"

"The fellow is from the south," David replied. "Perhaps he wants people here in Delhi to see he mixes with foreigners. Who knows, he could have been impressed that I'd served in the army. Actually, I rather liked him: sensitive chap, world-weary. And mind you, one oughtn't to turn fate away, especially in India."

A short time later, their taxi was motioned under the portico of Madho Dev's father's old house, its pillars twined with jasmine and clematis. The armed guards were not visible. Instead, a uniformed major domo saluted and gestured grandly for them to enter. A red carpet had been laid down.

"It's a big party."

"Thank God," Philippa whispered.

"Quite," replied David. "I was rather worried we'd be trapped at a dinner table making conversation."

The Minister and his wife were standing in the hall greeting their guests. He wore the usual white suit with a high Nehru collar. His wife was dressed in a lime chiffon sari, elaborately embroidered with gold threads and sequins.

"Forgive me for what you must have thought was a very strange invitation," said the Minister after David had introduced Philippa. "But I was telling my wife, Sarojini, how Captain Bruce had visited as a young man in this very house and she insisted we ring you up. Hope you don't mind. She thought you'd probably lost touch with everyone, might just be sitting in your hotel reading the newspapers. Who knows, you might run into some old friends."

"How very thoughtful of you." Philippa smiled.

David liked the Minister's wife immediately. She was a large, jolly woman, outgoing and forthright. Her shining hair was combed back severely, her eyes made up dramatically with lavender and gold eye shadow. Gold bracelets jangled on her arms.

"We're south Indians," she confided. "We don't stand on formalities the way our north Indian friends do. Come, I'll show you to the bar; it's at the end of the house in a tent. We're announcing our daughter's engagement tonight, so we thought we'd repay a few of our social debts as well." She laughed heartily, shaking an emerald necklace that glittered on her ample bosom, and conducted them down a long hall. "So, Captain Bruce, you spent your salad days in this house." She paused at the door of one of the larger rooms. "Of course, you must remember this room, it was once the drawing room."

David looked around. The room had been whitewashed many times. It was furnished with the same 1940s chairs and sofas upholstered in plastic that he had seen at Dr. Kapoor's house in Kotagarh. Instead of the crocheted doilies that Dr. Kapoor's wife had fastened on her furniture, however, a dark streak in a line around the whole room stained the backs of the pea-green chairs and sofas. Large blown-up photographs of Gandhi, Nehru, Mrs. Gandhi, and her dead son Sanjay were festooned with garlands of marigolds. The Minister's wife followed their startled eyes.

"It is now a waiting room for the many people who come to see my husband," she explained. "That dark line Mrs. Bruce is looking at is hair oil from the heads of the men who've had to wait here. I call the style of this room Bureaucratic Modern; it's supposed to suggest that we're a poor country. The ring of hair oil, I think, tells the whole story. I have a lovely old house in Kerala; that is why I've never been able to get very excited about this place. First of all, it's so big; then, as a government servant, one isn't supposed to care about one's surroundings; and, of course, one never knows how long one will be here, times are so uncertain. Tell me, Captain Bruce, was it very much different in your day?"

David found her most refreshing. "Indeed it was," he said. "Chippendale furniture, crystal chandeliers, Turkish carpets."

"Ah, yes, I thought so," replied the Minister's wife. "It must have been charming. My father-in-law's house in Bangalore is like that. Here, however, one must not show any wealth: bad form, you know."

"So you come from Kerala too?" asked David.

"Yes, but I went to school in California: UCLA, that was my undoing. You mustn't tell anyone, but it's hard for me to take all this too seriously. I'm supposed to be a tough intellectual; people are meant to be very frightened of me."

As if to confirm her statement, two young girls came up and reverently touched her feet.

"My daughter's friends," she said. "Come, I was taking you to the garden. You'll find it cooler out there. I'll introduce you to a few people, then I must join my husband at the door. The groom's party is due any moment, and the President and Prime Minister are dropping by. They'll probably have to sit in that waiting room; it's the only room with much furniture." Her large eyes laughed mischievously.

At the end of the hall, down a few steps, a brilliant gathering of people stood sipping soft drinks and eating hors d'oeuvres beneath gaily colored tenting.

"Ah," said the Minister's wife, "there is someone you must meet, one of the most attractive men in Delhi. Bobby!" She waved. "Oh, Bobby!"

Philippa swallowed hard. It was the army officer who'd tried to pick her up at the hotel. From behind her, David's hand shot out.

"I say, Bobby, is that you? David Bruce here, do you remember me?"

"What a wonderful coincidence you know each other," cried the Minister's wife. "I'll leave you in good hands then." She winked at Philippa. "When the P.M. comes, I'll send word; you must meet her."

"Darling," said David, "I want you to meet an old friend of mine, Bobby Singh. If I read his insignia correctly, it's now General Singh."

"Almost retired." The general smiled.

"Bobby, this is my wife, Philippa."

Philippa let him take her hand and kiss it. She was about to mention that they'd met in the hotel but decided to leave that revelation to the general. When he said nothing, she was amused.

"But certainly Bobby isn't your real name?" she said, smiling.

"Bhupinder is my real name." He grinned. "Much too hard to say."

"Everyone called him Bobby," added David. "We were in Burma together with Madho Dev."

"We've just come from his place," said Philippa.

"From Madho Dev?" said Bobby, obviously surprised. "Haven't heard of him in ages—well, since the fifties."

"We corresponded for twenty years," explained David. "Then lost touch. Thought I'd come back and find him. He lives in Rajasthan, not far from his father's old place."

"Did you know this was once his father's house in Delhi?" asked Bobby.

"That's how we happened to be here." David explained how he and Philippa came to be invited to the party.

"How lucky for me." He smiled. His eyes rested on Philippa. A waiter brought drinks. "Do you know about our host, Natarajan?" David shook his head. "Powerful chap, very sympathetic, all the key portfolios at one time or another. His father was a famous doctor in the south, sent Nata to Cambridge. They're from one of those peculiar tribes down there, out of caste but too rich to get in on the Scheduled lists."

"I like his wife," observed David.

"Ah, Sarojini, yes, she's everyone's favorite. Most outspoken, clever. Madam is quite fond of her."

"Madam?" queried Philippa.

"The Prime Minister," replied Bobby. "She's called Madam these days."

"I met her years ago at Windsor, some garden party."

"Then you must meet her again. She's due to show up at some point."

"Tell me about yourself, Bobby," David said. "Did you ever marry that stunning girl—Rita, wasn't that her name?"

"Rita? No." Bobby sighed. "She got away. In fact, they all get away. I'm a bachelor."

"Can't believe it," exclaimed David and turned to Philippa. "Bobby was our regimental ladies' man, had all the girls after him. Last person on earth to end up a bachelor."

They were interrupted by the appearance of a very large old man in a voluminous dhoti, with long white hair, a long Druid nose, and a gold earring. Merry deep-set eyes peered out from beneath bushy white eyebrows.

"Punditji," said General Bobby, deferentially stepping back so he could touch the venerable person's feet. "Very good to see you. How are you keeping these days?"

"Very well, thank you." The old man nodded.

"Punditji, I'd like you to meet Captain and Mrs. Bruce from England. David was a captain in the army here; we were in Burma together."

"You must have been children," said the old man.

"Nineteen, twenty," said David.

"Punditji is one of our Freedom Fighters, a disciple of Gandhiji's, spent half his life in jail."

"All life is a prison, one way or another, as long as we are in this body." The old man sighed, glancing about. "Have you seen any of my family, my son or grandsons? They're supposed to be here, and I'd like one of their drivers to take me home. I've had a long day and must do my puja before retiring."

"I hear Madam does puja with you from time to time," said the general.

"Yes," replied the old man. "These days she's becoming more devout. It is very good. I have known her since she was born. She's the only world leader I know who prays for at least an hour or two every morning, no matter how late she's worked the night before. But I'm worried about her at the moment; her astrological position is not favorable—" He broke off. "I see my son over there. I must go. Give my regards to your brother when you see him. Tell him I think he's a brave man."

The venerable soul shuffled unsteadily through the crowd. Many people stooped to touch his feet.

"Who was that?" asked David. "Impressive old boy."

"That's Probhackar Chatruvedi, a disciple of Gandhi's from the time he was a teenager. Grand old man of the Congress Party, one of our genuine sages. I'm amazed to see him here, he's never been that friendly with Natarajan. Wonder what it means."

"And your brother? Didn't know you had a brother."

"Hmm, yes, I do, one younger brother. He's a major general now; they called him up for this Operation Blue Star. Bad business, especially for us army Sikhs. He's taking a lot of flak."

"I shan't ask what you think of all this trouble, being a Sikh yourself," said David. "But it seems the country is firmly behind the Prime Minister."

"I'd prefer not to comment," said Bobby, looking grim. "All I can say is the situation is far worse than the politicians realize. We almost had a mutiny on our hands, the army is completely demoralized, and no one in the government wants to go out into the countryside and see what's actually happening. It's too dangerous."

"Some of the mutineers appeared at Madho Dev's place," said David. "He tried to help them."

"He would," said Bobby. "Always the maverick. Remember the night he pummeled the C.O.'s ADC at that banquet?"

"How could I forget?"

"If he hadn't lost his temper then, he'd be a general today."

"I think he's happier where he is," put in Philippa. "He has a fine son, three daughters, and numerous grandchildren."

"And how does he live?" asked Bobby.

"He's become a farmer," replied David. "Farming some of his

father's land, making a go of it too, seems quite respected in the community."

"I envy him." Bobby sighed. "Army's not what it used to be, neither is Delhi, you must have noticed. Foul place, quite changed, though most people aren't aware of it."

There was a sudden stir and Rajiv Gandhi, son of the Prime Minister, and his Italian wife entered.

"I'd never have guessed he was so tall," whispered Philippa. "And good-looking too."

General Bobby gazed around the room. "If I told you how many of these people are security men, you'd never believe me. Sarojini is really outrageous, inviting you here. I know why she did it, though. This is hate-the-British week."

David nodded. "We heard something about that. Really bad, eh?"

"Bad enough so that all of you will have to have visas soon, I wager. Up till now, as you know, no one in the Commonwealth has needed them."

"How could the BBC be so stupid!" Philippa exclaimed.

"It wasn't aired internationally," said Bobby, "only a local interview in England. Some fellow who claims he's the head of Khalistan in exile, all rot, offered money for Madam's life."

"Inexcusable," said Philippa.

"But here they're exaggerating the whole thing as usual. Who would have known anything about it if they hadn't overreacted? That's why Sarojini asked you on the spur of the moment. Out-of-caste people are sensitive about other people being squashed. She's very determined in that direction. Tomorrow you can be sure someone will phone and ask a lot of questions. Hope you're not in British Intelligence?"

"My dear chap." David laughed. "Me in MI-5? I'm far too old."

"That's the wrong answer. They send many retired people out these days, it's a new angle. The Americans do it too."

"But why on earth would anyone be spying in India?" asked Philippa.

"You mean, who would want us"—Bobby grinned—"eight hundred million people who can barely feed themselves? Mostly it's foreign governments spying on each other, trying to find out what the others are up to, like Casablanca during the war. Now you must excuse me for a few minutes." He nodded. "I must pay my respects to the Crown Prince. Want to meet him?"

"Not particularly," said David. "Might cause problems for everyone. You go ahead, we're fine."

Philippa and David watched as the general slipped through the crowd to pay his respects to Mrs. Gandhi's son. Philippa was amazed at all the bowing, scraping, and foot touching.

"Even the Queen doesn't get that. How can he bear it?"

"His wife appears to like it. Mind you, it's the Indian people themselves, they enjoy making gods out of ordinary mortals; it's in their blood."

"I think it's disgusting," said Philippa, turning away.

Soon General Bobby returned with an exotic young woman on his arm whom he introduced as Primula, a society columnist for one of India's fortnightly magazines.

"I noticed you when you first came in," Primula breathed, tossing a magnificent mane of henna-colored hair over her bare shoulders. "One sees so few foreigners at parties these days—except Russians, of course. Are you in Delhi for long?" She clung to General Bobby's arm.

"Two or three days," said David.

"I become so exhausted going to all these parties, especially in this heat. But if I don't show up, people become angry with me for not reporting their functions. I can't afford that. At least Bobby is here." She sighed. "That is some comfort. He knows everyone, such a font of information." She smiled brilliantly at Philippa. "You must tell me some of your impressions of India, Mrs. Bruce. What do you think of our Indian men, for example?"

Philippa paused. "Oh, I find them quite attractive; rather spoiled, of course, but most attractive."

"Better watch out, Captain Bruce, you might lose her. And Indian women, Captain?"

"My first real friend was an Indian woman named Savitri. She was my nurse."

"Clever man," purred Primula. "You'd make a good politician."

"Actually," he went on, "I've known many Indian women, think they're a formidable lot."

"But you've hit the nail on the head, Captain," Primula gushed, "*Formidable!*" She used the French pronunciation. "Most of the world thinks we Indian women go around like timid, obedient sheep, constantly having babies. But tell me, Bobby says you once lived in this house, is it so?"

"It belonged to a friend's father, and I stayed here many times. We used to dance in the Minister's office. Bobby came to some of those parties too."

"But how marvelous! What a delightful tidbit for my write-up."

Bobby was distracted by a flurry of activity at the entrance of the tent. Several men who resembled doormen at a hotel had come down the steps. They were followed by a portly man in a white achkan and matching turban. His skin was slightly pockmarked, and a long cucumber nose on an otherwise sad face suggested a strong sensual nature. Philippa thought she recognized him.

"The President," said Bobby out of the side of his mouth and shoved his way through the crowd to greet him.

"Poor man," whispered Primula. "Do you know, they didn't even tell him they were sending the army into the Golden Temple, not a word until they were already inside? And he's a Sikh, can you imagine how he felt? I've heard it's really broken him."

"But I'm told he's Mrs. Gandhi's creation," said David. "A manageable pawn?"

"Perhaps," murmured Primula. "But he's also a very clever politician."

He reminded Philippa of a water buffalo. She loved the way they seemed to see through their noses, very much the way the President now appeared to be sniffing his way through the crowd.

"They say he's a great connoisseur of women," said Primula. "Look, Bobby is bringing him this way."

"Sir! May I present Captain and Mrs. David Bruce," said General Bobby in official-sounding Hindi. "Captain Bruce, Mrs. Bruce, the President of India—Giani Zail Singh."

The President extended a limp hand, almost, Philippa thought, as though he expected her to kneel down and kiss it. His manner was listless and sybaritic. Nodding like a mechanical doll, he was propelled in a different direction by his attendants. General Bobby's skin tightened disdainfully around his eyes as he followed the President's progress.

"Well," said Primula, "if Zail Singh is here, can Madam be far behind? You must excuse me, I have to go inside now so I won't miss anything. But let's have lunch tomorrow, I want to know you better. You'll be my guests. I'll ring you in the morning." She swam through the crowd and disappeared.

"Stunning girl," said David.

The cloud still hung over Bobby's brow. "Hmm," he said. "If you have lunch with her, be careful what you say. She doesn't know when to keep her mouth shut, quite a gossip."

"Thanks for the warning. You look worried; is anything the matter?"

"No, no." Bobby sighed. "There's just so much one has to live through here in Delhi if you want to survive. I'm sure you see how things are. In many ways I admire Madho Dev. He got drummed out, but he's a free man. I'm ready to retire, just waiting for the day. I've a nice bungalow in Terripur, intend to fade away like a good general should."

"We're on our way there now," said David. "As I remember, it's a charming spot. Thought it might be wise to get Philippa out of the plains during the rainy season. Your place wouldn't be available, would it?"

Bobby came back to life. "Of course it is, standing empty, fully equipped. What luck, it's yours for as long as you like."

"But naturally I'll pay rent."

"Nonsense, glad to have it occupied. You can pay the caretaker if you like, stock the bar, and I'll come up for a visit. It has four bedrooms." Philippa saw the plot thickening. "Come," he said. "Madam will be arriving. I should show my face and you might like to meet her. At the least, you can see her."

They made their way to the spartan waiting room where the bride- and groom-to-be were now seated.

"As you know, they don't generally meet before the marriage," murmured Bobby, "but these two have known each other since they were children. Sarojini has quite modern ideas."

Surveying the people gathered in the crowded room, Philippa could not help but admire their apparent detachment. Beautifully dressed and groomed, they seemed completely disinterested in their surroundings. Or were they lost in some strange state of self-absorption she could not understand? But if they could wear fortunes in jewelry and be content to sit on plastic chairs stained with hair oil, they must also be oblivious to other things, like air pollution, which was so bad that evening she could barely breathe.

General Bobby glanced at the door. "Ah, her chief secretary is here. That means Madam is coming."

A number of men dressed casually in white cotton pajamas had sauntered in. No doubt her bodyguards, thought David. Then Natarajan arrived, leading Mrs. Gandhi, followed by Sarojini. Flash-bulbs popped, and someone from the groom's family began recording the moment with a videotape camera. As Mrs. Gandhi entered, a crush of people followed in her wake. She sat down and immediately made the young couple at ease with a remark that had them laughing gaily. A number of other young people sat on the floor at her feet, and Sarojini propelled David and Philippa into the circle and introduced them. Philippa noticed that even though Mrs. Gandhi looked exhausted, her eyes were alert and darted around the room, taking in everything. She waved to General Bobby, who dashed to her side and touched her feet. Was he an old lover? Did a woman like Mrs. Gandhi have lovers? After the first round of introductions, she asked Philippa to sit down beside her. It was well known she enjoyed meeting foreigners and always treated them with great deference.

"How do you keep so fit?" asked Philippa. "It must be extremely difficult with all the pressures you face."

The great lady smiled. "When one reaches fifty, one should never eat regular meals. I only eat when I'm hungry. Never more than just enough to kill my appetite, and, of course, I do yoga." She paused and looked intently at Philippa. "You look familiar. Have we met somewhere?"

"I believe we met at Windsor once, back in the fifties."

"Ah, yes, of course," said Mrs. Gandhi. "I was being presented to the Queen, you were waiting upon her, and we had tea together."

"That's correct." Philippa smiled. "What a remarkable memory you have!"

"Necessary in my job." The Prime Minister smiled too. "But you haven't changed that much, what's your secret?"

"I ride a lot and also don't eat much."

"And what brings you to India?"

"My husband, David, was in the army here. We've come back to look up old friends."

"How nice," said Mrs. Gandhi, a twinkle in her eye. "I hope you're having a reasonably good time. If there's anything you need done, just call me. That is"—she laughed—"if your phone works. Sometimes I can cut through some of our red tape."

Other people were brought forward; more oriental bowing and scraping. But Mrs. Gandhi remained relaxed, interested in everyone's questions and able to carry on several conversations at once. Then she presented something to the future bride and groom wrapped in a brown paper bag and, after a few more moments of light conversation, got up and, smoothing down her crisp cotton sari, managed to leave. Beckoning to General Bobby, the diminutive Prime Minister had a brief word with him at the door, got into her car, and was driven off. The crowd dispersed.

Primula sidled up to Philippa. "What do you think was in that brown paper bag?" she whispered.

"Haven't a clue," replied Philippa. "It was tied up and no one opened it."

"It was money," hissed Primula. "Plenty of it, too, by the size of it.

The whole purpose of this party was that package. It's hard to believe, but it's true. You have no idea how much money flows into her office from people wanting favors. She just threw a few days' take into a paper bag and tied it up. Enough to pay for their entire wedding and a trip around the world."

"Good heavens!" exclaimed Philippa, who'd been very favorably impressed with Mrs. Gandhi and didn't want to hear anything against her. "I really can't believe that. How do you know it isn't just a gorgeous sari?"

"I know what you're thinking, Mrs. Bruce. Yes, she's very charming, many people are taken in by her, but she has another side, which you didn't see tonight, a dark side. People say she's a dangerous witch." Primula's eyes glittered.

Philippa frowned. She found the columnist's conversation disconcerting. Why would she be talking this way about her country's leader to a perfect stranger?

Just then David came up with Bobby. "Bobby has to go now, but we're having dinner with him tomorrow night."

"Until tomorrow then," said Bobby, kissing Philippa's hand. He took Primula in tow and guided her away.

Sarojini came bustling through the crowd. She looked relieved. "Finished and all went well." She sighed. "Such a dear woman, so progressive and enlightened, but she makes me so nervous. All the threats against her life, and she doesn't seem to really care. She's supposed to wear one of those bulletproof vests but how can she, poor thing, when it's so hot? Whenever she comes here I always think, My God, what if someone shot her in my house, what would I do? What would become of us? Actually, we had an ambulance on hand behind the house all the time she was here."

Philippa was horrified. How could people live in such circumstances? What kind of life must it be? Then she tried to imagine the kind of personality, the ego, that presumed itself capable of ruling eight hundred million people and thought again about what Primula had said.

AT NINE the next morning, David was awakened by the hotel travel agent, who announced he had not received their train tickets for the following evening. If the captain expected to leave on schedule, he would have to go himself with his passport to the Baroda House railway reservation office and see what had happened. It was raining and David longed to spend the morning in bed. Nevertheless, he dragged himself to the shower and dressed.

"If that columnist calls," he said at the door, "say we're both ill. I shouldn't be long; see you for lunch."

Philippa looked at her watch and went back to sleep. A few minutes later the phone rang. Positive it was Primula on the other end, she answered in her sleepiest voice. But it was not Primula, it was General Bhupinder Singh.

"Hello, Bobby here. I'm calling to confirm our dinner engagement this evening."

"Confirmed," said Philippa.

"I hope I didn't wake you. Is David there?"

"He's just gone out to get our train tickets, some misunderstanding."

"He needn't have done that, I could have sent one of my boys over." He lowered his voice. "All last night I dreamt of making love to you. Let me come up now, I'm just a few floors below."

Philippa wondered if he had seen David go out. "You keep a room here, I take it?"

"My hideout. No one can find me. May I come up?"

"We're going to see each other this evening," she said. "It's not even ten-thirty. I'm half asleep."

"The perfect time," said the husky voice. "Let me come wake you up."

"What about your old friend David, my husband?"

"Come, come, Mrs. Bruce, anyone with half an eye can see that isn't a problem for either of you."

"Really, how presumptuous!"

"You mean observant," said the general seriously. "I too am in bed. What a waste, two people like us, alone in our separate beds on such a wonderful wet morning. Tell me, what have you got on?"

He was beginning to sound like one of those anonymous callers, the type that breathe at you over the phone.

"Certainly you have other possibilities," she said. "An attractive man like you."

"I'd like to bite the back of that lovely neck of yours."

Philippa laughed. "I think you're getting yourself too worked up."

"What you said yesterday in the lobby would work up any man. You should see how worked up I am right now, then perhaps you wouldn't sound so unfeeling."

"I can't really remember what I said, but I'm sure I didn't mean it. I very much want us to be friends. David is quite fond of you, but if you go on like this . . ."

"Is it being friendly to let me lie here alone? I'm coming up right now. I'll get in somehow." The phone clicked off.

Philippa panicked. Dressing as quickly as she could, without stopping to brush her hair, she grabbed her purse and umbrella, fled down the nearest stairway, hurried through the lobby, and found a cab.

"And where will madam be wanting to go?" the driver asked.

She hadn't the faintest idea where she wanted to go. First she had to brush her hair and put on her makeup. "Just drive around and let me think," she said. "I'll tell you in a moment."

The confused man drove out onto the busy street. Philippa fixed her face and brushed her hair. Then she remembered David had mentioned he wanted to take her to see a famous fort in old Delhi. It was the only place she could think of.

"Take me to the fort," she told the driver.

"Which one?" he asked. "Could you be meaning the Red Fort?"

"That's it, yes, of course."

The traffic was frightful. Hot rain fell in torrents. Half-naked people wrapped in pieces of plastic rode bicycles. Vehicles of every description honking incessantly jammed the road. Finally, the driver pulled into a parking lot beneath a massive wall and stopped in a sea of red mud.

"I shall wait for you, madam," the driver announced.

"I don't think that will be necessary. I might be some time," she said.

"With the rain you may not be getting a taxi so easily. I will wait," he said firmly.

"As you like," she said, wondering why Indian men were so consistently bossy. She opened her umbrella, purchased a ticket, and descended a ramp through a grim portal.

On all sides towered the monolithic rose-pink battlements that once guarded the Moghul emperors. She walked gingerly through the forecourt, skirting huge puddles, and came to a vaulted passageway under the great wall, large enough for several elephants to pass. The Meena Bazaar, where ladies of the court once bought silk and jewels, was now lined with dingy shops where listless shifty-eyed shopkeepers sat sipping tea. She inquired where she might buy a guidebook, but no one seemed interested in making the effort to sell her one. A pack of lepers careened toward her, oozing stumps stretched out, demanding money. And when she gladly gave it, others materialized out of nowhere and began hounding her. Just as she was about to turn in desperation and head for the taxi, a tall clean-shaven man in a shabby suit, with a kindly face and prematurely white hair, came up and shooed them away.

"It's odd weather to come sightseeing, or are you here to change money?" he asked in excellent English.

"Change money?"

"The fellows in these shops give very good rates."

"Actually, I've been trying to buy a guidebook," said Philippa. "No one seems interested in selling me one."

"I will guide you." The man smiled. "I am Professor Junius Zafeed." Philippa glanced at him. "I see you look surprised. Yes, I am a full Doctor of Philosophy—unemployed."

She smiled sympathetically. "I know a number of Ph.D.s in England who are unemployed these days," she said.

"I didn't lose my job, I left it," said the professor.

"Really?"

"Yes. The students in my college went on strike, God knows for what reasons, and closed down the college for three months. Then the mullahs, our Muslim priests, began harassing me to teach this fundamentalism, to 'reinterpret' the Sharia, our Muslim law. Since this man Khomeini has come to power in Persia, they are pushing very hard, and those of us who won't distort the truth are persecuted."

"How awful. You refused, of course."

"Naturally. But they made it very difficult for me, and when my college reopened, I found the students were taking this drug called heroin. Opium is not new to us, we know how to handle it, but this heroin is very bad. The college became flooded with it. Most of my students were asleep in the classrooms, and when they were not, they assaulted us teachers. I have lived in my college for years, but a few weeks ago I was robbed at gunpoint. So I resigned and am doing odd jobs, like this, and hoping to get some translations published. May I show you around?"

"Of course," replied Philippa.

"Come then." He nodded. "You have entered by what was known as the Lahore gate. From here the road went north to Lahore, which is now part of Pakistan. The fort was the work of the great emperor Shah Jahan, builder of the Taj Mahal in Agra. He intended to move his city here from Agra and commenced construction of this fort in 1638. It was finished just ten years later but he never completed the move, because his youngest son, Aurangzeb, usurped the kingdom and imprisoned him at Agra, where he died seven years later."

The rain had stopped. The sun burst through the clouds.

"Come," he said, crossing a level open space where flower gardens glistened and the sounds of the city gave way to birdcalls and the chatter of monkeys. "You are lucky today, The rain has kept people away." He stopped before an impressive marble pavilion. "Here we are at the Diwan-i-Am, Hall of Public Audiences. It was here the emperors sat listening to complaints and petitions of their subjects and received offerings and foreign emissaries. It is made of our famous red sandstone and white marble and was set with precious stones. They were removed by the Sikhs and the British during the looting that followed the Mutiny of 1857, when the last Moghul emperor was deposed."

Philippa stood silently in front of the vast pillared hall and imagined the richly clothed courtiers standing before their emperor, offering gold—even their wives and daughters—that they might be heard. She thought of Primula's story of the money that flowed into Mrs. Gandhi's office and thought times might not have changed that much.

"If you will notice," went on the professor, "the pillars are arranged to preserve the sight lines toward the emperor's throne so that everyone in the hall could see him—most ingenious. Now, we will go on to the Diwan-i-Khas, the Hall of Private Audiences."

From a distance the white marble building seemed to float on the green lawns like a pleasure barge.

"Here, the intimate members of the court gathered: distinguished guests, poets, musicians, and scholars. The famous Peacock Throne stood in that alcove. It was solid gold; peacocks set with countless sapphires and emeralds formed its back, and between them, over the center, was a parrot carved from a single emerald. At the end of the chair's arms were two of the largest diamonds in the world, one of which was the Kohinoor, now in the Tower of London, property of your Queen. In 1739, when Delhi was sacked by Nadir Shah of Persia, most of the stones were removed and the throne itself, now in Teheran, was reconstructed from bits and pieces that were left. Would you not have enjoyed meeting the people responsible for this beautiful creation? To have conceived of these buildings, they must have been superior to our nowadays rulers who have no taste. Or were they just as foolish and ignorant but lucky enough to be able to afford advisers of intelligence? That is the question which is posed by these ruins, isn't it, madam?" Junius Zafeed stopped to catch his breath.

"Mmm," mused Philippa. "There was much unhappiness here, I feel it."

"So you know some of our history then?"

"Yes, I do. I was brought up on books and stories about the

Moghuls. Actually, my great-grandfather helped Lord Curzon restore many of these buildings."

"Really?" cried Dr. Zafeed. "Then you have a feeling for it: the awful irony, the terrible things that happened here in this beautiful setting. Have you ever heard of a saint called Sarmad?"

"You mean the one who was beheaded by the Emperor Aurangzeb?"

"Correct. Later, if you like, I shall show you his tomb. He is a very important saint. He was a Jew, you know."

"I didn't know that."

"Yes, a Jew who became a Sufi and was murdered by Aurangzeb's mullahs. I am a Muslim but I believe in the secular society where every religion can practice without interference. These mullahs, our priests, are always interfering, always wanting political power. Pardon me for going on about politics, madam, it is the bane of our existence. Here, look, speaking of vanity and irony, what is carved there on the wall: 'If there be a paradise on earth, it is this, it is this.' Think of how they were seduced by luxury!"

"Yes." Philippa nodded. "But think how lovely it must have been: the Jamuna River flowing there beyond the walls, the fragrant shrubs and trees, the gorgeous flowers, the birds and tame deer; in a way it was paradise."

"If you could forget the people. Man creates these beautiful places but doesn't know how to live in them. Come, now we will see the Hamam, the royal bath. Imagine, if you will, what must have gone on there. The walls were mirrored, madam, and the ceilings too. The water was perfumed with attar of roses, a process discovered by Emperor Jahangir's wife. Imagine all the ladies frolicking here."

"Do you think they wore bathing suits?" Philippa smiled.

"Who knows, madam," said the professor, blushing crimson. "Look. Just beyond is the special mosque built by Aurangzeb."

"To pray in after his orgies, I suppose."

"Madam, you are toying with me. Aurangzeb was a terrible puritan."

"That's what his historians would like us to think," Philippa said. "But I've always doubted it, and he certainly had no scruples about murdering people."

"Yes, madam, that is true, but it was the custom in those days. Consider what people were like then."

"Consider what people are like now," retorted Philippa.

Dr. Junius Zafeed rolled his big, sad eyes. The surfeit of white marble depressed her. She remembered portraits of Aurangzeb in her grandfather's collection, a petulant, obscene-looking little man. She could see him now, sitting here before his Moti Masjid, praying. The archetypical hypocrite: murderer of his brothers and young nephews, poisoner of his aged father, corruptor of his sisters. There was something almost indecent about the place.

"What an awful man," she shuddered.

"You can feel him here, can't you?" said Dr. Zafeed.

"Yes, I can," said Philippa. "I think I'd like to leave."

They turned and walked away. "Shall I show you Sarmad's tomb?" asked the professor. "It is just by the Jama Masjid."

Philippa looked at her watch. It was twelve o'clock. She didn't want to return to the hotel before David. "Yes, of course, why not?"

"Come then. I'll have your driver meet us there. Meanwhile we'll walk around to the Delhi gate and follow the route Sarmad took to his death."

He shooed away a gaggle of vendors and rickshaw drivers, and they walked across a vast open area at the edge of the moat surrounding the fort. Cows were grazing in the moat.

"In former times the Jamuna River was higher, and a moat was filled with water," he explained.

"And hungry crocodiles?"

"Possibly, madam." He grinned. "Very possibly. See, over there, the Delhi gate, we are intersecting the former road just here. It leads straight to the Jama Masjid, the largest mosque in India."

As they walked the mile or so separating the two great structures, the professor told her the story of the Sufi saint, Sarmad. "In 1631," he said, "Sarmad arrived at the port of Tata near the present city of Karachi, Pakistan. He was a youth of twenty-two. It was not unusual he should travel to India. He was born in Kashan in Persia, and for years members of his family had moved freely as traders between the two countries. The Jews had been in India for centuries, the Ben Israelis in Bombay and the White and Black Jews in Cochin for as long as anyone could remember. The Moghul emperor Akbar, dead only a few years at the time, a very great and liberal ruler, had ordered synagogues built at his own expense in the Jewish enclaves throughout India.

"In Tata it is said that Sarmad became infatuated with a Hindu boy called Abhai Chand, son of a warrior landlord. Today, madam, people snigger and say that Sarmad was a homosexual. This is a complete misunderstanding of the kind of idealistic love that prevailed between men at that time and even today. Sarmad never could have attained the yogic powers he possessed if he was spilling his semen with young boys." The professor peered nervously at Philippa out of the corner of his eye. "Any yogi will verify that.

"When he first saw Abhai Chand, Sarmad said he was seized with jazbah—rapture. And though his feelings may have been physical, he must have sublimated them, for he wrote soon after: 'In this great monastery old and round'—by which he meant the earth—'is Abhai Chand my God? Whom have I found?' For Sufi mystics, beauty in any form constituted the transcendent embodiment of God, and for Sarmad, Abhai Chand became God."

They had reached a busy thoroughfare that separated the grounds of the Red Fort from the bazaar of the great mosque.

"Am I boring you?" the professor yelled over the noise of the traffic.

"No, not at all," cried Philippa, gasping for breath in the exhaust fumes. "Please go on."

"Abhai Chand's father was very conventional," shouted the professor. "Fearing a scandal, he reported the affair to the military commander of Tata, one Muhammad Bey, and sent his son into retreat."

"What was that?" Philippa yelled.

"Retreat: sent him away, exiled him."

The traffic stopped and Philippa dodged through the vehicles to the opposite side of the road. "Ah, this is better," she said. "Let's sit down in a tea shop and catch our breath."

Tea was brought and the professor continued. "The removal of Abhai Chand had a profound effect on Sarmad, who abruptly gave away all his possessions, including his clothes, and began wandering the streets naked. Mind you, he was not mad but a well-educated young man, proficient in a number of languages. Far from being judged insane, removing one's clothes was considered a penance, and Sarmad soon began to be viewed as a saint."

"How extraordinary," murmured Philippa.

"Not in those days, madam; people were cultured. Sarmad's love for Abhai Chand finally touched the father, who now believed beyond a doubt in Sarmad's earnestness, brought the boy back from exile, and began an historic pilgrimage with Sarmad through India.

"During those years, reciting his teachings extemporaneously in rhymed Persian couplets, Sarmad attracted a large following. On the recommendation of the ruler of Golconda, one Qutub Shah, he was introduced into the court of Shah Jahan. Now it happened that Shah Jahan had four sons, of whom his favorite was the first-born, Crown Prince Dara Shikoh. Dara had always been interested in mysticism and was a devotee of a Sufi mystic in Lahore. It was there that Dara first met Sarmad. He wrote, 'I found him naked, covered with thick crisped hair all over his body and with long fingernails, yet he is a handsome man with dark burning eyes and an aristocratic countenance, and he spoke and sang to me in most correct Persian.' By this time, Sarmad had attained the full powers of a yogic siddha: clairvoyance, manifestation of objects, mind control, and healing. His entry into Delhi was like the entry of a great prince. Walking naked, followed by a great throng of people, he arrived at the invitation of Dara Shikoh here at the Red Fort.

"You can imagine what jealousies the otherworldly Dara had stirred up. From the point of view of the mullahs from Mecca, since the time of Shah Jahan's grandfather, Akbar, the Moghuls had been slipping into apostasy. The mullahs circulated a sarcastic couplet that went: 'Sarmad's miracles work by fits and starts; the only revelation is of his private parts.' You see, it is perfectly natural for Hindu and Jain yogis to go naked, but for one of us Muslims it was—and still is—anathema."

Out of breath, the professor stopped and sipped his tea. Philippa was deeply touched by his enthusiasm and utter devotion for this mad mystic who had lived so long ago.

Junius Zafeed wiped his glasses and stared off into space. "Nevertheless, Dara Shikoh finally persuaded his father, the Emperor Shah Jahan, to invite Sarmad to court. To everyone's relief, he arrived wearing a loincloth. Shah Jahan's wife Mumtaz, for whom the Taj Mahal in Agra was built, was long dead, but all the emperor's children, the four brothers and two of his sisters, were present. Sarmad stunned them by predicting the horrible events that were soon to engulf the family, brought on by Aurangzeb's insane hatred of his father and older brothers. Dara and Sarmad became inseparable friends. At that very moment, madam, Dara was helping with a translation of the *Bhagavad-Gita* from Sanskrit into Persian. It was this version that finally reached the West. He was constantly in the society of Brahmins and sannyasins. The mullahs, fearing a continuation of the synthesis of Islam and Hinduism that had begun with Akbar, manipulated the jealous Aurangzeb into attacking his father's army. Dara led that army but, owing to the treachery of certain Rajput princes, was defeated at the battle of Samugarh, eight miles from Agra. Dara's army dissolved around him. He fled to Delhi with his wife and sons, raised another army, and marched to Lahore. Hounded in retreat, he was betrayed and finally captured with his two sons near Dahar in what is now western Pakistan. Dara and his fourteen-year-old son, Sipiher, were brought to Delhi in chains, arriving just after Aurangzeb had imprisoned their father in the Agra fort and was celebrating his illegal accession to the Moghul throne. Dara, the ideal enlightened prince, and his young son were then paraded naked down this very road on a miserable old elephant. The scene was so excruciatingly cruel, it caused rioting throughout the city. That evening, on Aurangzeb's orders, Dara's son was brutally murdered before his father's eyes; then Dara's head was severed. Can you guess what became of the head of Dara Shikoh, Crown Prince of the Moghul Empire?"

"I've read that Aurangzeb had it taken down to Agra by runners and served at breakfast in a covered dish to his father, Shah Jahan."

"Correct," said the professor. "You know your history well, madam."

"That is why I was shuddering back there at the mosque Aurangzeb built. What a monster!"

"No worse, madam, than Idi Amin, who is alive and well in Saudi Arabia, or the Ayatollah Khomeini, son of a shoemaker from Lucknow, India. All these tyrants are the same. Yet there is more you might not know. With Dara gone, a wholesale crushing of Sufi mystics took place; thousands were killed. Islamic philosophy has never recovered. Sarmad was brought before Aurangzeb in the Diwan-i-Khas, that paradise on earth we have just seen, and asked to answer formal charges of heresy. First, that against the Islamic law he went naked; second, that in reciting the Kalima, which goes 'There is no God but Allah, and Muhammad is his Prophet,' he never went beyond the phrase 'There is no God'; and, thirdly, that he denied the bodily ascension of the Prophet Muhammad."

"What happened then?" asked Philippa.

"Sarmad presented a brilliant verbal defense. First he observed that the prophet Isaiah, whom we of Islam also venerate, had gone about naked in his old age. On the subject of stopping short on the Kalima, he said, 'Why should I tell a lie? I am still uncertain of God's existence; hence "there is no God" is as far as I have got.' And to the charge that he claimed Muhammad had not ascended to heaven in the flesh, his answer was the question 'Why should the Prophet have to rise to heaven in order to see God, who exists everywhere without limitations of time and space?' Aurangzeb himself guided the ecclesiastical inquisition and reminded the jury of mullahs that a man was not liable for execution for nudity but that he should be required to pronounce the whole of the Islamic creed. Now at this point I believe we have to deduce that Sarmad was so shaken by what had occurred that he no longer wished to live, for he could have saved himself by disclosing that he was a Jew, which he did not, or by repeating the Kalima. He refused and was sentenced to death.

"And now, madam, let us walk to the foot of the steps of the east gate of the Jama Masjid, for it was there he was executed."

They left the tea shop and walked toward the massive sandstone steps of the mosque.

"He was paraded naked on this very path. From the account of Europeans who were present, more than seventy-five thousand people gathered here, for in Delhi Sarmad was considered a great saint. A platform was erected over there to the left, near that tree, where a temple to him now stands and where he is buried. Reciting a series of beautiful quatrains in Persian, he was passed by armed soldiers through a crowd so dense it took over an hour for him to go the distance that we have just covered in ten minutes."

They came to the place where the martyr was executed and buried. An ancient tree spread its branches protectively over a small tomb in which candles burned over a flower-decked stone sarcophagus.

"When he reached this spot," Dr. Zafeed continued, "the executioner approached Sarmad with an unsheathed sword and proposed to cover his face. Sarmad addressed him in verse: 'My sweetheart is here and his sword is bare, I know him whatever disguise he may wear. We opened our eyes from eternal sleep, awakened by the din, but it was still evil night and so we sleep again.' The crowd became hysterical. In the moment before execution, Abhai Chand rushed to the platform with one Shah Asadullah. 'Do escape this hopeless tribulation,' he was heard to plea. 'Cover your nakedness and repeat the whole of the Kalima.' Sarmad replied, 'How many Sufi martyrs linger on people's breath? Let me remind the world of these instruments of death.' " The professor paused and gazed up the steps to the east gate of the mosque. "And then, dear lady, took place one of the strangest events in all Indian history. As the great saint's head rolled from the block in front of the vast crowd, in front of Bernier, Ambassador from the court of Louis XV of France, the lips opened and recited the whole of the Kalima. Even more amazing, the headless saint now got to his feet, picked up his own head, and, holding it aloft, carried it up these very steps into the mosque, the head all the time crying out, 'I am God, I am God!' "

Shaken by the professor's tale, Philippa stood quietly and looked up the steps toward the mosque.

"Would you like to go in?" he asked.

She shook her head. "Not really, but I would like to see where he is buried."

In the shrine she left an offering of money, and they went out again.

"You've left me spellbound, professor." She smiled. "My knees are weak."

"It's a sad story, madam," he replied, "but I am afraid the belief that might is right is still very much with us. Everywhere I look I see the strong and powerful crushing the weak. I see people constantly mistreating one another. I see monsters posing as spiritual leaders. I see politicians feigning spirituality. Above all, I see hypocrisy, the scourge of modern times."

"How can I thank you?" said Philippa.

"The guide fee is ten rupees," replied Junius Zafeed modestly.

"But that's ridiculous, not even one pound, and you've spent hours with me." She held out several hundred-rupee notes.

The professor shook his head. "I cannot take them, madam, and I will not."

"Then what can I do for you?" asked Philippa. "There must be something. Please."

"You can tell this story to others," he answered, "You can tell them that a Jew became a Sufi saint and is worshiped by millions of Muslims and Hindus in India. You can tell them Islam is not all blood and the despicable human sacrifice that is just now going on. Islam is peace and beauty and the unity of a God who is in everything and everywhere at the same time. History is told so that it may not have to be repeated, but it is never told enough."

As the taxi driver transported her back to the hotel, images of the professor's tale possessed her mind so completely that by the time she reached the hotel and David asked her where she'd been, Philippa threw up her hands and cried.

"Silly of me," she sobbed, collapsing on the bed. "Yesterday I thought I was all right, but really, I think this place may be too much for me. That sweet professor, so self-effacing, he made it all so real. Actually, it comes down to the fact that I'm basically terrified here. These people are so frighteningly . . . intense. I want to go home."

David could not understand what had happened and chalked it up to a combination of monsoon jitters and female nervousness. Why hadn't she just stayed in bed? Why had she suddenly decided to visit the Red Fort, of all places, without him and exhaust herself walking around in the heat?

She let him rant on, said nothing about General Bobby's call; and slowly, as he told her about his disastrous morning, her sense of humor returned.

His taxi had developed engine problems in the rain and had taken one hour getting to Baroda House. At Baroda House he had gone to several wrong rooms before he found the one for reservations. There he was told to fill out endless forms while clerks read them and pointed out small mistakes that had to be done over, until he felt certain that if Kafka were alive he would have recognized in the Indian bureaucracy the culmination of his visionary nightmares. No wonder Madho Dev was slowly going mad; no wonder Arjun was desperate to leave and Dr. Kapoor felt all bureaucrats should be gassed!

"Well, there's a positive side to it all," said Philippa, blowing her nose. "We missed that reporter, Primula. There's a message she called while we were out, lucky us."

"I bumped into Bobby downstairs," said David. "We're to meet him at his flat around eight tonight."

Philippa had forgotten about the general. How could she possibly go through a dinner party with him after their telephone conversation that morning? "I'm not sure I'm up to it," she said.

"Perhaps after a nap you'll feel better."

"I'll see," she replied. "I feel as though I might be coming down with something, but there's no reason you shouldn't go."


WHEN he arrived at General Bobby's apartment alone that evening, David was surprised to find his old friend in cotton pajamas, his long hair tied in a bun.

"Ah, my friend," said Bobby, hugging him. "Welcome. Take off your shoes and be comfortable. Have to let one's hair down occasionally. Pity Philippa couldn't make it; you say she's sick?"

"Bit of a bad stomach," said David.

"In that case, I thought we'd be informal. What will you have? Scotch, gin? Weren't you a rum drinker?"

"Of course, that great rum—what was it called?"

"Hercules, my man; best rum in the world, don't tell me you've forgotten. Those were the days, weren't they?" Bobby busied himself at the bar. "How's your sex life, old boy? Perhaps I shouldn't ask that, but you were quite a Romeo."

The sudden question caught David off guard. "After one's been married for thirty years, it's not a subject one thinks much about."

"Come, come, I can't believe that. You were always much too sly not to have something going. Besides, your wife is damn attractive."

"A good deal younger than I am. Afraid she finds me rather boring these days."

"Nonsense." Bobby grinned and handed him a glass. "Here's to old times. Splendid to see you after all these years. How long are you here for?"

"Till late autumn, most likely. We should be home by Christmas, not that it means much anymore. Our children don't celebrate it with us, always taking off for some tropical island with their friends. But we've a lot of people on our place who depend upon us being there."

Just then a beautiful young girl came through the door bearing a tray of hot hors d'oeuvres: long black hair over cream-colored shoulders, a chiffon sari that hugged her voluptuous hips. David felt his blood rise.

"This is Anandi," said Bobby. "She helps me out sometimes. Anandi," he said in Hindi, "see if you can find something comfortable for the sahib. We're about the same size, aren't we, David? You can't possibly relax in that suit. Do change."

Anandi returned, holding up a pair of white silk pajamas. "Come, take off your uniform, old boy. Show him where to change, Anandi."

David followed the girl into a bedroom and expected her to leave but she stood silently waiting. He felt awkward but remembered how his nurse in Bengal always helped him change his clothes and realized he was still a sahib.

"Ah, now you must be feeling better," Bobby said when he returned. "Have another drink. Some friends of mine are due by any minute now."

Anandi came in with another tray of snacks. David's eyes followed her.

"Quite a piece, eh?" Bobby grinned. "Don't worry, she doesn't understand English."

"You're having an affair with her?"

Bobby roared with laughter. "No, no, she's just around. This is India, old man, remember? One keeps them like a string of polo ponies. This one gives an unusual massage. Would you like to try her?" He switched to Hindi. "Hey, Anandi, would you like to show sahib here what you can do?" The girl smiled mischievously.

"Another time," said David. "That is, if you want me to stay awake."

"She'd wake you up, old chap. No matter, there will be others soon. Tonight is your night. As Philippa was unable to come, I've organized a little entertainment."

"You must have the pick of the crop," observed David.

"It's one of the perks that goes with this awful job I've got. But there are others who do better. Politicians, for example: corrupt buggers, money to burn these days."

"In Britain the press savages them."

"That's your problem," said Bobby, refilling their glasses. "It's why in the end you English bored us: because you refused to have any fun. Once we decide we want something, we don't waste time feeling guilty."

"By we, you mean Sikhs?" David laughed.

"These Hindus like to think of us as sex maniacs; must say we have the tradition to back it up. When our prick's in heaven, we feel close to God."

"Love is God?"

"You've seen that slogan then; it says it all."

The doorbell rang, and presently Anandi ushered in two young men in army uniform, a beautiful woman whom David judged to be in her thirties, and four young girls.

"This is Rena," said Bobby. "She's the only one who speaks any English. Powerful lady, believe me; knows everybody's secrets."

Rena settled herself voluptuously on a large cushion.

"Who are the two young men?" asked David.

Bobby laughed. "These boys? Gunmen, bodyguards. They owe me everything. Where I am, they're sure to follow. Precautionary measure to keep these girls in line tonight and add a little life to the party. They're brothers, actually relations."

"Your brothers?"

"I have only one brother. These are sons of concubines, born a few years before my father died. There were quite a number of them; they have no rights. I found places for these two in the army. They're my servants really, jolly good ones too. As kids they used to sleep on the bottom of my bed to keep my feet warm. They'll do anything I ask."

He downed his drink.

"Rena started life as an airline hostess. She's a Goan: famous beauties, the Goan girls. As an air hostess, she came to the attention of certain—er, important people. Now she's in business."

Rena smiled at David. Her face, though wise, was unlined, almost innocent. Her beautiful, large doe eyes, long eyelashes, and pouting lips set in a lubricious smile betrayed no thoughts, no problems, no romance. Anandi brought in a drink, squatted down to serve Rena, and touched her feet.

Bobby said something in Punjabi. One of the young men put a tape in the elaborate hi-fi system, and soft disco music filled the room.

"Tell me what it's like, living in England," said Bobby. "Do you think I should retire there?"

"Thought you were going to retire up in Terripur."

"What if I decided not to? You know, they offered me a British passport in '47."

"Did you take it?"

"Of course not, but wouldn't it make things easier? Would you give me a job on your farm, in your stables? I know horses." He rolled his eyes and clapped David's knee.

David realized Bobby was getting drunk. "That would be a fine thing," he answered. "I wouldn't think of it, you'd be my guest. Our house is virtually empty. Some of the rooms haven't been used for fifty years."

"But on my pension, I'd need work. You don't realize, my friend, the kind of retirement money they give us. Barely enough to eat and then they wonder why we aren't happy and have to do things on the side."

Anandi passed the snack tray around again, and Rena fed a hot cheese puff to Bobby. Bobby said something in Punjabi. She rose languidly and ambled off into one of the bedrooms.

"Wait till you see these girls dance," Bobby declared. "Hey, Kuljit." He addressed one of his gunmen. The strapping youth sauntered over and squatted attentively beside him. "This is my old friend, Captain David. He is good-time fellow, first class. Many years ago we are lads together in army; he is army man like us. I want you show him how you make these girls dance. Are you feeling good?"

"Very good, sahib."

"Anandi, give the boys more whiskey and another rum for Captain David."

Anandi filled David's glass and produced two full glasses of whiskey, one for Kuljit and one for the other young soldier, whose name was Kulwant.

"Drink, drink," said Bobby expansively. "Then we two old men will watch you dance. Hey, David, you like this disco music? I got it in Kuwait; you should see the women there! Anandi, turn up the volume. Kulwant, clear the deck. That's a good fellow, we want to see some action. I take these boys everywhere. Last year I took them to Paris. We were buying helicopters and fighter planes from the French. In Paris they learned this break dancing. Ah, if we were only young again, eh, David? In our days it was the fox-trot, right?"

Rena appeared with two girls in voluminous silk pants cut below the navel, a film of chiffon covered their ample breasts. They began grinding and bumping to the music. Silver anklets jangled. Kulwant and Kuljit executed athletic splits and falls. The music stopped and Bobby yelled for more.

" 'Money, Money, Money,' play that one," Bobby shouted. "And Prince, play him too. Have you seen 'Purple Rain'? I have the video. Videos keep us from going crazy. Anandi," he yelled again, "put on a video. You know the one I like."

Anandi fumbled with the machine. Suddenly the screen lit up and there were a young man and a girl in a bed together. The two girls stopped dancing and stared at the video.

"Keep dancing, you sluts," snapped Rena in the coarsest Hindi. "The sahibs don't have you here to watch videos, you daughters of whores."

The girls recommenced their jiggling. David's mind raced back years to Lucknow, on leave with Bobby and Madho Dev: hired dancers, a drunken orgy lasting three days during which a succession of girls had to be brought in to satisfy Bobby's insatiable appetite.

"Remember Lucknow?" Bobby roared, clapping his hands.

"I was just thinking of it," yelled David.

On the video screen the girl was coaxing a tumescent penis to erection.

"Like mine," shouted Bobby. "So big, it needs a lot of excitement to get it up."

Rena called the other two girls from the bedroom. They were wearing kinky Western lingerie. One slid down beside General Bobby and fondled him. He handed his empty glass to Anandi, who immediately refilled it. David was beginning to see double. Kuljit tore away the gauzy film covering the breasts of one of the girls and held on to her nipples as she danced in front of him. The penis on the video screen had finally become hard and was entering a vagina. Anandi, arms folded, watched matter-of-factly, as though it were a cooking lesson. The fourth girl lay down at David's feet and slipped her hand inside his pajamas. David wondered how, if Bobby had been doing this sort of thing steadily for forty years, there was anything left of him.

"Not sure I'm quite up to this," he said.

"Nonsense, have another drink. Hey, Anandi, you slut, see my boys have more whiskey."

Kulwant and Kuljit grinned like young satyrs. The general waved his hand; they dropped their pants and grabbed for the girls. Kulwant fell on the floor, caught hold of Kuljit's pants, and pulled them off. It was a Marx Brothers farce.

Kuljit jumped to his feet, and the two of them staggered about after the girls, holding their stiff penises like Sten guns. Just then, the phone rang. Everyone froze. David expected the scene to melt like film stuck in a projector. Anandi answered.

"General Bhupinder Singh's residence," she said in a low voice. "Who is speaking?" Her brows furrowed. She handed the phone to the general. "Madam," she whispered, covering the receiver. "Madam, hey."

Bobby grimaced and stayed Rena's hand, which was roaming about his chest. "Hanji . . . ah, yes, achcha." David could hear the strident voice of a woman on the other end. Bobby sighed, lay back on the pillows, rolled his eyes, took the receiver from his ear, and played with Rena's breasts, saying "hanji" agreeably at intervals. The video debauch had reached a fever pitch. The voice on the phone stopped, then David heard the caller ask if the general was there.

Bobby put the receiver to his ear. "Of course, I am, madam . . . What? Now? . . . Yes, yes, of course."

There was more conversation back and forth, too rapid for David to understand, then a click on the other end. Bobby made a wry face, handed the phone to Anandi, stood up, and tugged at David's sleeve. They staggered into a bedroom.

"She's psychic, absolutely, or this place is bugged. Third time in a row she's interrupted a little party of mine."

"Who?" asked David.

"I.G.," replied Bobby. "What time is it?"

"Eleven," said David, looking at his watch, "and who is I.G.?"

"I.G., my good friend, is Indira Gandhi, and this is the third time this month she's interrupted me. It's as if she knows when I'm having a good time. She gets these brainstorms at night, calls us all over to Safardjung Road. You should see the others, they come in looking like corpses. Ah, well, can't be helped. If only she would retire to one of those ashrams her yogi friends run and we could have a man in charge, everyone would breathe easier. Men are more sensitive, more understanding. This woman will be the death of us." The general growled like a dog and hauled his huge frame under the shower. "You carry on, old chap, enjoy; you'll have them all to yourself. Ask Anandi to put out a fresh uniform for me. And tell my boys to look sharp, pull themselves together. I have to take them with me."

David went back into the living room where Kuljit and Kulwant were already adjusting their turbans in front of a mirror. The video image was stuck. Like some fly-catching lizard, a tongue was poised to catch a drop of semen from a penis. David turned it off and told Anandi to attend to her boss. Rena was rounding up her girls, scolding them to clean up the room and watch they didn't take anything, because if they did, she'd see they were doused with petrol and set on fire. David went into the spare bedroom and changed into his suit. When Bobby reappeared from his bath, Rena and her girls had vanished and the two soldiers were slouched in chairs, reading comic books. Anandi appeared with hot coffee.

"This is terrible," exclaimed Bobby, looking very distinguished in his crisp uniform. "You aren't meant to be leaving. Where has Rena gone, where are the girls?"

He looked at Anandi, then at Kuljit and Kulwant. They stared back as if they hadn't the faintest idea what he was talking about, as if the last two hours had been a dream.

He burst out laughing. "You see, David, what good people I have? They've already forgotten everything. Very artful of them, wouldn't you say? You sister-fucking chootiyas, didn't I tell you my friend David-sahib was to be royally entertained? Why did you let those women go?"

"It was Rena, sahib," said Anandi calmly. "She didn't want to stay here without you. When you return, she will come back. She gave me the number."

"I have her number," roared Bobby, rolling his eyes furiously. "David, will you wait here with Anandi? Relax and let her give you a massage. She must be quite worked up by the goings on, insatiable appetite."

David begged off, explaining that Philippa would be waiting up.

"Oh, blast Philippa," cried Bobby, hugging David. "Can't you people ever forget your bloody duties? Damn her and damn this woman who takes me away from you, my old friend, before I see you well satisfied. This was to be our night of nights."

"Tomorrow we leave for Terripur. We'll get together up there," said David.

"Up there," scoffed Bobby, gulping his coffee. "In heaven, I suppose you mean. Eat, drink, and be merry, I say, for tomorrow we could all easily be dead."


AT THE hotel, David found Philippa asleep. Lighting his pipe, he opened the glass door of the sitting room and stepped out on the terrace. A gentle mist was falling and he thought regretfully of Anandi alone at Bobby's, her taut hips, pliant thighs. Why was it he could never seize the moment but stood back from life, watched it

flow around him? With Kamala he'd procrastinated when he should
have made an effort to find her. His marriage to Philippa had been
almost fortuitous; his relationship with his children one of a remote
observer. Philippa was smiling in her sleep. He was happy when she
was content. He'd always felt she'd got the bad end of the bargain
when she married him. His difficulty in connecting with reality; not
easy to live with. But that feeling of disconnection had vanished after
his encounter with that Baba and his tigers. Why? Should he throw
off his clothes, retire to the jungle? Ruminating on this, he suddenly
recalled something from his childhood. He'd been six or seven at the
time and, against all rules, had wandered off the grounds of his uncle's
tea estate. Beautiful day in May it had been, great white thunderheads
billowing up against radiantly green hills, sky filled with butterflies,
the air fragrant with a thousand flowers. Out the compound gate,
down a footpath past the servants' quarters into the jungle, he'd run.
First time in his life he'd ever done anything on his own. The path was
interrupted by a shallow river, where he'd stood transfixed by the
light of the sun sparkling on the rushing water. About to wade across,
he noticed a large mound of rocks on the other side and then, to his
astonishment, realized it was not a mound of rocks at all but a mound
of skulls: hundreds of empty eye sockets staring at him. He wanted to
escape but was rooted to the spot with fear. As he stood there trembling, a smiling youth appeared from an opening in the mound.
Copper-colored hair fell to his waist. Naked except for a scarlet
loincloth, he strode forward to the river's edge, his arms outstretched,
beckoning. A glowing blue light seemed to surround him, like Jesus
in his uncle's Bible, or Krishna on the calendars that hung in his ayah's
room. His fear melted away and was about to wade across the river
when a hand grabbed him from behind and dragged him off, the hand
of Savitri's husband, a surly fellow whom he hated for beating the
woman who was everything to him. He recalled looking back over his
shoulder as he was dragged away, but the radiant youth had vanished
and he was taken back to the servants' quarters, severely thrashed, and
confined to his room for weeks. What a strange thing to remember,
even stranger that he should have forgotten it so completely. Had it
really happened? Why were these pieces of his past rising to the
surface again, like so many dead fish floating in the sea?

# 9

FROM PHILIPPA'S POINT OF VIEW, one of her husband's greatest defects as a traveler was that he was always early, seemed incapable of arriving at a station or airport at a reasonable hour.

"Well, there you are, you've done it again," she said, shrugging her shoulders as they arrived the following evening at the New Delhi station a full hour ahead of schedule. Settling herself grumpily in one of the uncomfortable cane-back chairs of the first-class waiting room, she'd lost herself in an old copy of the *Times* of London when David came up with a rather crazed-looking young man.

"Prince Iqbal Muhammad Khan," he said with that expression of amused skepticism she knew so well. "He wants us to meet his mother, Princess Nawabzadi Sultan, the Begum of Allampur."

Philippa looked doubtful.

"Come," said the young prince ingratiatingly. "My esteemed mother would be very pleased to meet you, she is just down the way in the VIP waiting room." Philippa gave David one of her what-is-this-all-about? looks. "Ah, madam," said the young prince, who seemed to miss nothing, "what has befallen us is a very sad story. I try to meet as many foreigners as possible, especially distinguished-looking ones like yourselves, to publicize our plight."

David tipped a coolie to watch their luggage and they set off.

"You must have heard of the illustrious kingdom of Allampur," the prince said as they pushed their way through the crowds.

"You mean the licentious kingdom of Allampur." David smiled.

"Then you know of it," said Iqbal Mohammed, a wicked, unstated "why not?" manifesting itself on his dissolute young face.

"Didn't Allampur have something to do with the Mutiny?" asked Philippa.

"War of Liberation, please!" said the young man. "Allampur struck one of the first blows for Indian independence. Our family fought fiercely against the British and, although we were honorably defeated, we continued to live peacefully on our various properties until 1947, when we were evicted by the new government of India. In 1971 they burned us out of our last remaining palace." He narrowed his eyes and proclaimed indignantly, "Indira Gandhi, granddaughter of a British employee, she burned us out."

"Mind you, we are British," said Philippa. "My great-grandfather was a viceroy here."

"You misunderstand me, madam. We fought against you, true enough, and were defeated by you. But defeat in war is something different from humiliation at the hands of the servants of those who have defeated you. You British left us alone, allowed us to retain many of our properties. Who else was there to look after things?"

Remembering that Nehru had been jailed many times by the British authorities, Philippa thought the prince a bit confused. "I'm rather bewildered at what you're actually getting at."

"Ah," said the young man, leading them up a stairway. "What I am getting at is that since 1972, when my mother decided not to take such treatment lying down, we have been living here in protest in the VIP lounge. The Government of India absconded with our property; we are squatting on theirs and will stay here until we receive fair treatment."

Iqbal Muhammad opened the door to the VIP waiting room. A cabinet of madness met their eyes. Bare bulbs, covered with bits of cloth in shades of rose and burnt orange, produced an eerie effect; the walls had been hung with faded damask brocade. A bed of coals glowed in a large ornate brass brazier into which a striking looking woman was casting a handful of aromatic resins that perfumed the air. A haughty expression played over her ravaged face, and her dark, unkempt hair fell to her waist. On the floor of the large room, covered with priceless carpets, crouched twelve hungry-looking Dobermans. The dogs growled menacingly.

"Let me present my mother, Her Highness Begum Nawabzadi Sultan of Allampur, and my sister Princess Shenaz Sultan," said the young man grandly.

The girl standing in the shadows did not acknowledge the introduction. She wore a crimson shawl over faded blue jeans; her pinched face betrayed a bored, petulant nature.

The Begum nodded condescendingly and stared at them with angry red eyes. "I have been reduced to the status of a lady-in-waiting," she said in a well-rehearsed voice. "Twelve years ago, the government turned our only remaining palace into a pharmaceutical factory, so we are living here in humiliation. It is a great crime against our heroic family. Now the Railway Minister is talking of evicting us by force."

"The founder of our dynasty, Nawab Mansur Ali Khan, drank poison in 1757 to avoid dishonor," put in Prince Iqbal Muhammad. "Notice the silver cup at my mother's side; it is filled with poison, which she is ready to drink at a moment's notice if she is evicted. The ladies of Allampur have always been known for their bravery."

Princess Shenaz abruptly came to life. "Now Mrs. Gandhi's conscience is finally beginning to bother her. You may have noticed in the newspapers she is making arrangements at long last to find a suitable place for us to live." Her voice was indignant. "There are so many forts and old buildings lying deserted in Delhi that belonged to our family. There is no reason why the government can't give us one of our own properties."

Philippa looked around. "You've actually been living here in this room for twelve years, with these dogs?" she asked. "Where do the VIPs go?"

"How should I know?" The Begum shrugged. "They go somewhere. They are always coming and going. I do not concern myself with such creatures."

"I say, that takes guts," said Philippa quietly.

"Indeed it does, madam," said the sharp-eared Iqbal Muhammad.

"You are sympathetic," said the Begum. "Come sit and talk with me."

While his mother engaged Philippa in conversation, the young prince took David to a far corner of the room, where he uncovered an old trunk and withdrew a pair of ceremonial swords elaborately worked with gold, enamel, and what looked like priceless sapphires and diamonds.

"I wish to go to college abroad," Iqbal Muhammad informed David. "If you know of someone who might be interested in these gemstones, please let me know; they can easily be removed from their setting and smuggled out of the country. One or two would pay for my education."

"Who taught you English?" asked David.

"We had private tutors at home, and then I went to Mayo's."

"How do you live here?"

"We have some very valuable carpets. When we need money, we sell one."

"But these," asked David, holding up one of the swords, "they look like good stones."

"If the government knew of them," whispered the Prince, "they would be seized immediately. They were state treasures."

David admired the young man's ingenuity. "They look like very high-quality stones."

"Ultramarine, the deepest and most beautiful of the blues," he said proudly. "That is the reason for the dogs."

"I'll try to help," said David, touched by the scene. "I know several jewelers in London who should be quite interested."

The prince stared at him and smiled. "Many people have promised but nothing ever happens. Please, when you are back in London, remember me, Prince Iqbal Muhammad Khan of Allampur, living in the Delhi railway station. Remember that I wish to study abroad and send someone to save us."

After drinking a cup of tea and discussing the problems of looking after so many dogs, David and Philippa made their way back to the waiting room.

"Do you think they were real, or was it some sort of bogus ploy to get you to buy worthless jewelry?"

"Who knows?" David shrugged. "They seem quite mad, but I must say I was very touched."


AS THE train crawled north and east from Delhi and halted at bleak stations along the way, David stared out in amazement at the hordes of people huddled beneath rain-soaked rags. This was Uttar Pradesh, the Hindi heartland, an area the size of France with a population now greater than all of Western Europe.

When morning came at last, and they got down at Hardwar, a damp, gray, silent world greeted them. Behind the town rose mist-shrouded cliffs. The pilgrimage season was over and the narrow streets were deserted. As they made their way to the station where they would catch the bus to Terripur, they paused on the road above the famous ghats at Harki Puri and looked down at the Ganges in spate—a muddy flood plain as far as the eye could see. David explained how it had all looked forty years ago. Even during the monsoon, the river had been clear, dotted with grassy islands where elephants roamed. Below them, bare-chested priests were ringing bells and waving incense and flaming salvers of camphor out over the river. River as goddess Ganga, mother of them all. Without her, India was nothing.

The rickshaw driver stood up on his bicycle pedals and looked nervously at the sky, which seemed about to empty itself again. They moved on toward a crumbling ruin of a bus station. In lieu of tea or breakfast, which, judging from the look of the food shops that lined the area seemed not a wise idea, David bought some apples and bananas and they boarded the "luxury bus" that was to take them to Terripur. Two seats were found for them in the fourth row where, the young conductor assured them, they would have a good view of the video screen. No need to look out at the dull gray landscape, at the miles of stumps where forests once towered, at the factories puffing their black smoke, at the acres of cement cubicles put up to house the workers. Why think of those things when one could float away in the arms of film stars like Roshana or Amitabh Bachchan?

After a few miles, the bus stopped and they were told a bridge over a tributary to the Ganges had washed out. There would be a detour to another bridge. The detour turned into a rutted path in which vehicles of all descriptions were mired down. Never mind; the video played on and the passengers barely noticed while cars were lifted out of the mud or the bus itself was pushed through the worst patches by gangs of young men. The world could have ended, thought Philippa, and no one would have known the difference.

David was apologetic. "Now you are going to see the really beautiful part of India," he had told her. Not only had they not seen much, but in three hours the bus had not gone ten miles. The idea of spending another two or three hours in the nightmarish contraption was too much, so when they ground to a halt in sight of the second bridge, David corralled two young boys to carry their luggage, and they set out on foot.

A stone bridge they were to pass over was in danger of collapsing. Silt, washing down from eroding mountains, had raised the water to within a few feet of the top. At any moment the bridge might be inundated. It happened that way, the two boys said; all at once a wall of water would come thundering down the riverbed and sweep everything away. They could see this was true. Brown water boiled under the bridge and big boulders rolling along with the flood could be heard crashing against its foundations. At both ends, small streams had formed across the road.

"My God, do you think it will last until we get across?" Philippa gasped. "It's terrifying."

The boys carrying the luggage cocked their ears, listened for a wall of water, beckoned and joined crowds of people running toward the other side where taxis stood waiting. Safely across, Philippa and David headed toward one of the more respectable-looking vehicles, and soon they were on the road again, climbing through a mixture of fog and smoke up the twisting mountain road to Terripur.

The driver pointed ahead at great gashes in the mountainside. "Limestone quarries, highest quality for making steel." He grinned.

And indeed, as David sat up and rolled down the mud-spattered window, he could see the once-towering cliffs and pine-covered palisades below Terripur had been recycled into open pit mines, makeshift roads, and landslides where hordes of half-naked workers, hardly human, were engaged in hand-loading piles of crushed rock onto waiting trucks. They came to a sharp curve in the road and passed a series of oil drums painted red and green, each marked with a different letter spelling out S L O W  D E A T H. David yelled at the driver to slow down.

"What a disaster!" he cried. "Who could be responsible for this? Are they utterly mad? Destroying one of the most beautiful places in the world, equal to Delphi."

"Slow death." Philippa thought of the elegant men and women at Sarojini's "function," sitting on the stained plastic chairs. "People only see what they want to see."

As the tops of hills appeared in the distance, David pointed to a tiny group of buildings that straddled them. "Terripur," he said and mumbled something incoherent.

"What did you say, darling?"

"I was sitting here wondering what I really expected to find. Everything looks so depressing. All these years I've been thinking of it as paradise, but it's actually a paradise lost, isn't it? I suppose I identified it with my youth, which has—" He stopped. Philippa had plugged her ears with both fingers. "Now what are you doing? What's that supposed to mean?"

"You've been saying the same thing over and over," she cried. "I'm tired of hearing it. Can't you think of anything else to say?"

They were passing a series of signs advertising hotels in Terripur: Whispering Windows, The Connaught, Claridge's, and finally the Ritz—TERRIPUR'S LARGEST, MOST COMFORTABLE HOTEL, HOT AND COLD RUNNING WATER, VIEWS OF THE SNOWS.

"Ah, that's where we're staying for a few nights," said David. "Hope it hasn't changed."

"How can you think it hasn't when everything else has?" Philippa sighed.

He set his jaw and stared grimly out the window. They were high above the mists now, driving through forests of ancient oak trees whose limbs, except for those at the very top, had been mercilessly hacked off. Gangs of hill women roamed the hillsides with machetes looking for wood. Several large bungalows, little more than crumbling ruins, came into view, and soon they were passing newly constructed cement cubicles of uncertain design that seemed destined to slide down the mountain. Nearer the town more landslides and a great hollow flanked by squatters' hutments marked an area where the sewage of Terripur flowed out and the enterprising poor grew animal fodder on terraces irrigated by the effluent. The stench was overpowering. Arriving at the top, their taxi plunged into a confusion of buses, coolies, and owners of hand-pulled rickshaws.

"Drive on," commanded David as they came to a roadblock. "Quickly. We are going to the Ritz. Don't stop here."

"It is not permitted to go beyond the barrier," said the driver sullenly. "Three hundred rupees."

"But how are we to get there with this luggage?" yelled David angrily.

"You must rent two rickshaws, one for yourselves and one for your luggage," said the driver.

A gleaming white Mercedes, flying a small flag, throttled past them, stopped at the gate, and was allowed to pass.

"There, you see, a car has just gone through, sawar kay bacche— child of a pig," snapped David. "Drive to the gate and let me speak to the guards."

The driver sank back into his seat and drove up to the barrier.

"I say, we're on our way to the Ritz," said David to a phlegmatic-looking policeman. "Be a good fellow and let us pass."

"These days everyone is going to the Ritz," the young man shouted in Hindi to an audience of bystanders. "What makes him think he's so special? It is not permitted to drive car on Mall without a permit," he barked in English.

"I suppose they had a permit?" said David, gesturing at the vanishing Mercedes.

"But of course," replied the policeman. "That was Princess Kamala."

David caught his breath. By this time it was all too much for Philippa, and she was quietly giggling.

"What's wrong now?" David asked irritably. "I'm only trying to save you from getting bitten to death by fleas. Those rickshaws are crawling with them."

"Sorry, but it sounds so funny, talking about the Ritz in this place. I'm beginning to feel like I'm in a Fellini film. Why can't we ride one of those nags they seem to be hiring out?" She gestured to a line of half-starved horses with bells around their necks.

"More bugs," explained David glumly.

"Let's get out and walk, then," said Philippa. "Let some coolies bring the luggage. It can't be all that far."

David forestalled an argument by overtipping the driver. Soon the bags were unceremoniously dumped into the arms of three ragged coolies and they set off on foot.

The Mall, a wide thoroughfare the British had built as a promenade on a saddle connecting two higher peaks, was lined with shops, which, Philippa suspected, were supposed to remind one of Brighton or Blackpool. The Indian climate and the entrepreneurial instincts of the shopkeepers, however, had taken their toll and most of the buildings were barely visible beneath a clutter of signs, displays, and multiple layers of faded paint and whitewash.

Until 1947, David explained, the Indian people had not been permitted to walk on the Mall; it was reserved for the exercise of British memsahibs and their children. Now it was jammed with honeymoon couples, retired bureaucrats and army officers, tourists from Punjab, eccentric leftovers from the Raj, and students from nearby private academies. A pan-chewing crowd of vagrant men and youths gazed mindlessly at the passing scene as they waited for a film at the local cinema, the Picture Palace; next door an arcade of computer games had attracted a large crowd. The sickening smell of cheap incense and rancid mustard oil filled the air. At the far end stood the Christian church, a derelict eighteenth century relic with peeling paint, and opposite it David pointed out the library, which seemed to have been converted into more shops and eating stalls. In the center was the former bandstand, a fanciful Victorian example of cast ironwork that had been glassed in and now housed a fast-food joint called the Kwalitee where packs of young men in skin-tight jeans and longish hair stood at counters eating mutton burgers. These fresh examples of "progress" only increased the state of apprehension and shock in which David found himself.

"One would have thought that here, at least, they would have left things alone," he said sadly, as they walked past the superannuated library and climbed the steep lane to the Ritz. Like the rest of Terripur, it appeared, the Ritz had not escaped the ravages of time. The masonry and stucco walls enclosing its gardens and grounds were crumbling. Several pan shops, a shoemaker's stand, a tailor shop, and a newspaper stall had been built against them. Inside the compound, the drive was filled with potholes, the once magnificent gardens had gone to patches of grass and weeds, and a large part of the lawn had been given over to an unkempt parking lot in which used condoms floated in muddy pools. A warm fog had descended, smothering the place in a sepulchral gloom. Two old bearers, whom David was sure had been there in his youth, struggled to lift their bags off the coolies' backs, while a distraught-looking manager fiddled with keys in the reception room where they signed the register.

# Part Two

# 10

THE RITZ, built in the early part of the nineteenth century, faced the snow-covered Himalayas. Two medieval-like towers at either end of a U-shaped courtyard were connected by verandas, balconies, public rooms, and glassed-in solariums. They climbed up the circular stairs of one of the towers. The walls were covered with graffiti; the place seemed abandoned. Of course, it was the rainy season and the crush of summer people who came up from the sweltering plains would be gone; still, David wondered, when the bazaar was so crowded, why did there seem to be no guests?

The bearers showed them to a suite of rooms and deposited their luggage. A middle-aged barefoot servant in a tattered white uniform began listlessly batting at the furniture with an old rag. David thought he recognized him as a boy who had worked at the hotel years before, but he kept quiet. Clouds of dust filled the air and Philippa began coughing.

"Stop," ordered David in Hindi. The man stopped, his arms akimbo. David looked at his watch. "Lunch is at what time?" he asked sharply. "And is there hot water for the bath?"

"Lunch is served at one o'clock, sahib, and hot water comes for one half hour at nine-thirty and six-thirty."

"Then bring a bucket of hot water now, we've had a hard trip."

The man stared at David through clouded eyes. "Sahib has been to the Ritz before?" he asked tentatively. "It has been many years?"

"Yes, many many years," replied David, smiling.

The man's eyes watered and David thought the fellow was going to cry.

"I am thinking sahib was coming here with a young prince from Rajasthan, is it not so?"

David nodded. "Correct. My name is David Bruce. I remember you gave us massages every evening, best I've ever had. Your name is . . . Ravi."

A flash of recognition passed over Ravi's face. "Ah, sir, I am knowing you now. It has been many years. Welcome. But why have you come here, sahib? The Ritz is not as it was. The clientele has gone down, and I am afraid we have gone down with them." He wiped his eyes with his rag. "But I will try and get you some hot water, you must be wanting a wash. Don't look at these rooms too closely, sahib, memsahib, they are not very clean, but the staff is old and cannot work much. Nowadays the Ritz is just a good-time place, sir, and a retirement home for us boys who have always been here. Have you paid your money for the night?" David nodded. "Too bad," said Ravi, shaking his head.

"Actually, we're taking a bungalow belonging to a friend, but I wanted to see the Ritz again. One night here shouldn't kill us. Perhaps you could get leave and work for us. Is it the same owner here?"

"The same," said Ravi, "but she is very old now, over eighty. Sir, I will try to get the hot water now."

Overcome with emotion, Ravi left the room. The sahib had come back. Did that mean perhaps other sahibs might be coming and things would be as they were long ago? The English sahibs had been strict, but those who came to the Ritz had also been generous. Not like the rich scum who came nowadays, the heartless politicians who themselves lived on baksheesh, ordered him about mercilessly, and never tipped.

Philippa wandered through the suite, peered out through the diamond-paned Gothic windows. "Quite charming, really, like a seaside resort. Rather a wreck, though."

"I hope the beds don't have bugs," said David nervously. "You've never slept in a bed with Indian bugs. They can be vicious."

"See the walls?" She pointed. "What on earth are all those spots and stains?"

"Ravi said it's a good-time place now. People get excited, I suppose, throw things, spill drinks, ejaculate, how should I know?"

"Really, darling, I can see you're upset. Well, it's your own fault. If you'd listened to my advice, we would be in Italy right now, sitting around that lovely pool at the Splendido."

David grunted. "The old woman who owns this place was always very close to her servants; she's probably supporting all of them, which means giving out food, clothes, and medicine. I suspect there's no money left over for extras like painting walls, especially as most people must be too drunk to notice."

Ravi returned with hot water in a pink plastic bucket.

"Thank you, Ravi," said David. "That should be enough for a good splashoff till six-thirty, when we'll have proper baths."

"Sir," said Ravi. "Water heater is now electric. If electricity is coming, you will be having hot water. If it goes off, garam pani nahin. But do not worry, I will bring."

"Tell me now, honestly," asked David, "do these beds have bugs?"

Ravi looked downcast. "Who knows until they bite, sahib? Bugs live inside and crawl out at night. Shall I bring some bug powder?"

Philippa shook her head. "Absolutely not, the bug powder will be DDT. I'd rather take my chances. Can't we wrap them tightly in several sheets? Wouldn't that stop the bugs from coming out?"

Ravi seemed doubtful. "If they are inside, memsahib, they have to come out."

"And what time did you say lunch was served?" inquired David.

"Lunch from one to three, sir."

"And dinner?"

"Eight-thirty, sir, and tonight there is dancing, Hindustan TV Queen Ball, 1984."

Ravi helped them unpack. Seeing the sahib reminded him that forty years of his life had passed, something he had never thought of before.

"Anything else, sir?" he asked.

"Not just now." David smiled.

"Then I will take my leave, sir. Call if you need anything."

They took sponge baths and changed and went downstairs to the cavernous old dining room, where at least a hundred places were set for lunch, all unoccupied.

"Are we too early?" David asked the headwaiter, a tall stooped man with gray hair and trembling hands, who seated them.

"No, sahib," was the enigmatic reply. "There is buffet today; you may help yourselves."

"A real buffet," observed Philippa. "How very nice."

The old waiter conducted them to a sideboard set with silver chafing dishes, where numbers of other old waiters in tattered white uniforms and green turbans alternately wiped their noses and polished the plates and drinking glasses with the same cloths. One of them handed Philippa a plate which he had just wiped off with such a rag. Not noticing his performance, she helped herself to large portions of curry and other familiar-sounding dishes which, although they once might have resembled their originals, existed now in name only. Having noted the slovenly behavior of the waiters, David took a plate from the bottom of the pile, on the theory that its bacteria might have died of starvation, and limited himself to rice, yogurt, and fruit. The plates were borne ceremoniously to the table and they sat down. Still, no one else had appeared and David could see why. The setting was surrealistic, a painting by Magritte: an overpowering feeling of emptiness, of existing in a vacuum.

"But, darling, you're not eating," said Philippa, sampling the different concoctions she had put on her plate.

"Actually, it's not wise to eat a lot when you first come to this altitude," he said, not wanting to scare her. "One's digestion, you know—er . . . slows down. How's the curry?"

"Passable. I don't think it's lamb, though, tastes more like venison."

"Goat, I would say."

"Goat!" cried Philippa, taking a piece out of her mouth. "You can't mean it? People don't actually eat those smelly things?"

"Come, come," chided David. "You've been to Greece, they eat a lot of goat there."

"I certainly have never eaten goat in Greece! Lamb, but never goat." She put down her fork. "Why couldn't you have said it was venison? Now my lunch is spoiled."

"Try some of the chicken then," he suggested.

"It's too tough."

"Then you'll have to settle for the rice and dal and some yogurt. Here, I have a bowl of yogurt, and a mango to top it off."

"One would have expected something better than this." She looked around the room. "What I'd give for one decent meal."

"I suspect they're running on rote: cooking the same food for forty years. I'm sure they don't give it much thought."

"But who on earth eats it? There is still no one else here. It's frightening."

David chuckled. "Why, they eat it, of course. At three o'clock they will all sit down and fill up. Don't fret, it's only for one day. Tomorrow we'll move to Bobby's, have a cook, and eat what we want. I'm hoping the old lady will let Ravi work for us while we're here. As I remember, he made rather nice crepes."

All at once Philippa looked pale and put down her fork. "Would you mind?" she said faintly. "I don't think I can stand this room any longer. In fact, I think I'm going to be sick."

"Mmm," murmured David. "Let's go up to the room and lie down. When one first comes up from the plains one needs a nap." Leaving their half-eaten food, they got up to go. A waiter rushed over. "Sahib has not finished his meal," he protested. "There is pudding for dessert. Shall I bring?"

Philippa was staggering toward the foyer.

David shook his head. "Not just now. Memsahib is not feeling well."

"Too bad," said the old man solicitously. "Altitude. It happens to some when they first come here."

"You're right," agreed David.

"I should send tea or coffee to your room, sahib?" asked the old man.

"At four-thirty, yes, please do."


AT FOUR-THIRTY, however, it seemed to Philippa every cell in her body had declared war. Upon reaching the room, she had gone to bed and fallen asleep, only to be awakened later by an overwhelming necessity to throw up. In the other bed, David slept soundly. Outside, rain thundered down on the steel roof. Shaking with numb cold, she staggered to the bathroom and, bracing herself with one arm, hung her head over the toilet. No sooner had the foul onion-flavored bile risen from her stomach than explosions of gas and diarrhea began. Worst of all, when these finally subsided and she stood panting in her own filth, she discovered upon turning on the tap there was no water. Only a few cupfuls remained in the pink plastic bucket Ravi had brought. More than anything else, she needed to collapse into a hot tub. The cement bathroom was dark and cold. She pressed the light switch but no light came on. Somehow she removed her soiled clothes, struggled into a bathrobe, and got to the telephone but it was dead. She threw it across the room and burst into angry tears.

"For God's sake, what is happening?" cried David, suddenly waking.

"I'm madly sick," shouted Philippa, "there's no water in this awful place, the lights are out, and the phone doesn't work. I can't stand it a minute longer."

Jumping to his feet, David opened the door and began yelling for Ravi, but his voice was smothered by a drumming rain now turned to hail.

"I'll go find someone," he yelled and disappeared down the veranda.

A blast of wind blew the door shut and she sat shivering on her bed. Finally he returned with a serious-looking Ravi bearing two buckets of water, one steaming hot and one cold.

"Memsahib is suffering from Delhi belly," he pronounced.

"Delhi belly indeed," snorted David, helping Philippa to the bathroom. "You know very well it's the Ritz belly and nothing else. I watched those waiters wiping their noses on their cloths, what is that?"

"That is very bad, sir, but now there is no one to remind them not to do it, they forget."

David had got Philippa's robe off and was pouring cupfuls of warm water over her. "In my day they would have quickly remembered," he grumbled. "Here, take this bucket, get us more hot water, and bring some that has been boiled. How long does the cook boil the water for drinking?"

Ravi looked puzzled. "Boil water, sahib?"

"Yes, for drinking. The water must be boiled for twenty-five minutes at this altitude to purify it, otherwise we get sick."

"He is not boiling for twenty-five minutes, sir," said Ravi apologetically. "Maybe five, ten minutes boiling."

"Do you have any bottled mineral water?"

"Yes, sahib, I will bring." He backed quickly out of the room.

"First, bring more hot bath water," David shouted after him.

Philippa stood on the cement floor. David mixed more hot and cold water and poured it over her, washing her down with a cloth.

"What a mess," she groaned. "Awfully sorry, darling."

"It's my fault," he said, massaging her back. "This place is disgusting, we should have left immediately."

Ravi returned with more hot water and three bottles of mineral water. David finished bathing Philippa, dried her, and put her to bed.

"Ravi," he said, inspecting the bottles of mineral water, "did you open these bottles?"

"No, sahib," he replied, looking blankly at the bottles he had brought.

The bottles were secured with peel-away seals. The broken seals on each bottle had been cleverly reattached.

"I know most of your clients must be too drunk to notice the difference, but I am not," said David sternly. "These bottles have been opened. They are used bottles filled with ordinary tap water."

"Oh, sahib, I thought it was mineral water." Ravi peered tentatively at the bottles. "Someone has opened them."

"Indeed, someone has." David sighed. "Now be a good fellow, run and bring me three unopened bottles." Ravi retreated through the door and closed it as gently as he could. "They think I'm blind," David muttered, pacing the room. "Nothing has changed, nothing and everything. You have to watch yourself every minute or they'll best you."

"You mean, they sell the same bottle twice?" Philippa asked bleakly.

"As many times as they can. I'm sure to them water is water. They can't understand why anyone would buy it when it comes free out of the tap."

"Sir, there are no unopened bottles of water," said Ravi, returning. "But Cook says he fills the empties up with boiled water and it is just as good. I will go to bazaar and find real mineral water."

"First, bring tea," David ordered. "And please stand there and watch that the water has boiled for twenty-five minutes."

"Already boiling for fifteen, I am timing. Tea coming up, sahib."

"Very good. And, Ravi, do you think you could ask the desk clerk to call a doctor?"

"Telephone is not working, sir, I will get doctor and mineral water. First-class young doctor, very smart, he just nearby."

"Thanks, Ravi." David smiled. "Didn't mean to yell at you, but memsahib seems quite ill."

"No problem, captain-sahib." Ravi beamed. "I am understanding. Now I am getting tea."

Outside the rain and hail had stopped. David gazed out at shimmering Himalayan peaks lit by shafts of sunlight as they suddenly appeared through the clouds.

"How absolutely staggering," gasped Philippa, her teeth chattering. "I never dreamed they would be that big. It's almost worth being sick just to see them."

Ravi appeared with the tea tray and some glucose biscuits. Lifting a tattered cozy, he prepared the tea and served it. "I have brought lemon for memsahib, milk no good for bad stomach. Shall I fetch doctor now?"

"Please do." David nodded. "And ask him to bring a thermometer. I want to take memsahib's temperature."

David threw open the window and watched as Ravi left the hotel and plodded dutifully down the path under an old umbrella. Droplets of water glistened on the needles of the great fir trees, and from somewhere on the lower slopes the piercing sweet notes of a flute sounded. Soon, Ravi reappeared, one arm around several bottles of mineral water, the other holding his umbrella above a young man in a dark suit.

"Dr. Joshi, sahib," he announced as they arrived at the door. "He has brought his thermometer."

Dr. Joshi, who wore thick glasses over finely chiseled features, nodded politely, shook the thermometer, and put it under Philippa's tongue. "Don't worry," he said, "it's sterilized."

David was surprised at the young man's accent. "You have studied abroad?" he asked.

"Johns Hopkins," replied the young man.

"You look much too young to have done all that. May I ask why you returned to India?"

The young doctor smiled modestly. "I am married and have two small children. Emotionally, it's better here for our children; my family is here too. In America, family life is not respected, there is no peace of mind. Here there is peace of mind but no common sense. Indian people have their heads in the clouds and never see the realities about them. I hope to help my country see; at least I'll try for a while." He withdrew the thermometer from Philippa's mouth. "Your wife has a high fever. No doubt some form of gastroenteritis. I will have to give her an antibiotic. Fortunately, I have the proper ones from Germany. I'll just send a note to my house with your man and he can bring them. You will not find this particular medicine in the local chemist's shop. Even if you should, you must never trust Indian-made antibiotics."

"Why is that?" asked David.

The young man wrote out a note and gave it to Ravi. "There are too many vested interests here, ignorant old men who will do anything for money: unscrupulous, powerful, and because they set a bad example, the general population follows. Locally made antibiotics are untrustworthy because they are often adulterated to save money. To stay in business, manufacturers must obtain countless permits and clearances. Most of this paperwork consists of made-up regulations that are not necessary. A bottleneck is created that can only be cleared by the politician himself. In this way, the powers that be fill their own pockets and the coffers of their political party." He shrugged. "And so our medicines are diluted and the quality of our manufactured goods comes down."

"What do you think is going to happen here?" asked David.

"Those of us who know what is going on must do what we can.

Slowly these corrupt officials are dying out. We young people are more honest because we have experienced corruption at every turn and are sick of it."

"Will you have some tea?" inquired David.

"Yes, thank you very much. If your wife's fever goes too high, you must bathe her in cold water to bring it down. At this altitude, circulation slows down, antibodies don't work as well, and the bacteria win. Do you intend to stay in this place long?"

"We're moving into a house tomorrow," explained David. "General Bhupinder Singh's place."

"Ah." Dr. Joshi smiled. "General Bobby, quite a character. I am sometimes called there to treat him or one of his—" He broke off in an embarrassed chuckle.

"Tell me then," David asked. "Are you a general practitioner?"

"So many people are sick these days I seem to be drifting into it. Actually my field is toxicology."

"You mean poisons?"

"Yes, but mainly the effects of various chemicals like DDT."

Philippa came out of her stupor. "Ah, just the man I've been wanting to talk to," she whispered. "Why do you not ban DDT here?"

"Not only DDT, Mrs. Bruce. At least four other compounds banned everywhere else are permitted here."

"But isn't the government aware of the dangers?" asked Philippa.

"Again, it is vested interests," explained Dr. Joshi. "From the top to the bottom, everyone is being paid off. And as they think it is only the lowest castes who are suffering the effects of these poisons, no one cares. But, of course, everyone is suffering. I have investigated villages where not only the people but even snakes and lizards have developed a form of epilepsy brought on by exposure to DDT. You see, the pesticides are often stored in gunnysacks next to bags of wheat, flour, and sugar. They are very pervasive and the foods become adulterated. Also, because they fear the mosquito, people spray their houses constantly. But the mosquito has mutated and now we have resistant strains. For example, there is a new cerebral malaria."

"We were told the DDT levels here are twenty-six times the maximum amount considered safe by the World Health Organization," said Philippa.

"Can that be true?" said David.

"Yes, especially in the cities; that is established fact. But here in Terripur we have tricked them."

"How?"

"From the disastrous mining operations you have no doubt seen down below, we have managed to get quantities of limestone powder, which looks like DDT, and have persuaded the sweepers to use this harmless stuff, which they can get for a few paisa, and sell the DDT on the black market. The reality of India is that our people are capitalists. If you can think of a way they can make money out of something, it will work."

"Do you still think it's worthwhile living here when you could be making so much more abroad?"

"I am young, I enjoy a good fight, and I feel I must try to help my people. I also love my father and mother, sisters and brothers, and wish to be near them. Ah, here comes your servant. Let me see if he has brought the right thing." Dr. Joshi opened the bag and withdrew a bottle. "Yes, quite correct. This medicine contains sulfa but it is not dangerous. Only you must drink plenty of water, as it is hard on the kidneys."

Philippa nodded.

"Well, I must be going. If you need me anytime, please don't hesitate to call. Once you're settled in the general's house, I'll come by and try to interest you in our campaign to stop the mining operations down below. Is General Bobby coming up soon? I want him to be on our board of directors."

"Says he is," replied David. "I'll have him call you."

"It's good you're getting out of this dirty place," Dr. Joshi said, looking around the room. "Everyone feels sorry about it, but there is nothing to be done until Mrs. Kapoorchand dies. She refuses to change a thing."

"I stayed here several times about forty years ago. Those days it was very grand."

"Did you really, sir? It must be a disappointment for you to see it like this."

"Yes, but it's this way all over."

"That's because we are still in the process of destruction and haven't begun constructing yet. Forgive me, sir, no offense, but we must destroy your British traditions and develop our own lifestyles; our indigenous customs are complicated and very strong. For example, in India we assume that any kind of action is dangerous and will lead to unforeseen circumstances, and one must be extremely cautious. Everyone knows this, so things move slowly. Rather than taking action to destroy, we would rather let things fall apart. Benign neglect. And so this hotel has been left to its own metamorphosis, as you will presently see when the guests begin to arrive."

"You mean it will actually be filled up?"

"Oh, yes, tonight is a big night, the Hindustan TV Queen Ball. You and Mrs. Bruce may need a sleeping pill."

David stood at the bay window and watched the doctor disappear down the path. For the first time since he'd arrived in India, he felt optimistic. There were people who cared about their country, and they were young and intelligent. A scarf of mist twisted around the mountains, gold in the setting sun.

Philippa had fallen asleep and was breathing regularly. In the failing light David had not noticed Ravi, standing in the corner, hands behind his back, smiling benignly.

"Ah, Ravi, you are still here. What are you smiling at?"

"Meeting old friends after a long time is good, sir."

"Yes, it is." David nodded. "I see life has not been too unkind to you. Are you married?"

"After your peoples left, sir, then I am got married. My childrens all grown now. My wife returned to village, is happy. I have two sons, lorry drivers, and one girl, she is nurse. That is how I find out about this young doctor-sahib, he is good man, no? He says right, helps all. Just some two months back I am applying for loan granted by government of India. Part of loan government is taking back in interest before I get any. Another piece was eaten by the clerks at the bank who fill out the papers. They charge me five hundred rupees because I am too simple to understand. This Dr. Joshi, he helped straighten them out and got my money back. I have been indebted since forty years, sir."

"But you were so good at massage, I'm surprised you didn't go into that," said David.

"I still give, sir, make good money, but I have bad habits. Women and liquor, both expensive."

David laughed. "Now I see why you stay in Terripur."

"What to do, sir? There is not much else in life for me. Once I was wanting to travel but was unable, and now I am too old. So I satisfy myself here and see the world in Terripur. Would you like massage now, sir? I remember your friend, the Yuvaraj of Kotagarh, I give you both massage every evening before going out. Have you seen him?"

David told Ravi about Madho Dev and his family.

"In Terripur many rajas and ranis are still living, some very poor. Please lie down on your bed now, sir. I will give good massage and you will sleep."

\* \* \*

LATER that evening David awoke from a long dream in which he was dancing in some nightclub with Kamala. The dream had ended but the music had gone on. It was the sound of the band in the hotel ballroom, drifting up through the thick fog along with laughter, screams, and an occasional smashing glass.

For some time he lay there listening to cars grinding up the drive, doors slamming, high-pitched voices and giggles of women, grunts and yells of their men. Philippa slept soundly. He felt her forehead, which now seemed cool. It was already eleven, and he wondered whether he should bother going downstairs. Knowing he would not go back to sleep, however, and intrigued by the goings-on, he got up and stumbled into the bathroom. Miraculously, hot water came out of the tap. He took a bath, felt suddenly fit, and realized he was getting a kind of perverse satisfaction from reliving the past. With all the pain it brought, one thing had become very clear: he had romanticized everything and failed to live in the present, the reason, perhaps, for the feelings of unreality that plagued him. He wondered what Philippa would think if he announced he was going off to live in the jungle for a few years as a hermit.

Dressing quietly so as not to disturb her, he slipped out the door, stood for a moment on the balcony, and listened to the raucous *thump, thump, thump* of the band. Light from myriad panes of the glassed-in conservatory lit up the foggy night. Walking down the former grand staircase, he came to the vast dining room where they had tried to eat lunch. What a lovely room it had once been! The first time he had come here, he was six years old. For some reason, his uncle had brought them all on holiday. If his calculations were correct, that would have been 1930. At that time there had been a bronze plate on the gate which read NO DOGS, NO INDIANS. The hotel was owned by an Englishman, run for Englishmen. The second time he'd come to the Ritz had been in 1945, after he and Madho Dev had got out of Burma. Devika and Kamala had come up with their chaperones. Bobby Singh had been there too. The hotel had changed hands. Having seen the writing on the wall, the Englishman had sold it to a glamorous woman from Lahore, of mysterious origin, an object of great speculation among the British community. She had immediately opened the place to Indians; he remembered seeing Nehru and his daughter Indira playing tennis. Some international conference had been on and Muhammad Ali Jinnah, Chiang Kai-shek, and Haile Selassie were also guests. A vision of the dining room with its glittering Waterford chandeliers and wall sconces, its thick carpets, its mahogany dining chairs and tables, illuminated his mind's eye. He stood for a moment, trying to get his bearings. The place was a vast complex of separate buildings and cottages strung together by a labyrinth of verandas and covered passageways. A bearer directed him down a flight of stairs toward the old ballroom. The passageway was decorated with banners welcoming guests to the annual Hindustan TV Queen Ball. Arrogant-looking young policemen in khaki uniforms lounged outside the door, chewing pan. One of them demanded a ticket, but he relented when Ravi suddenly appeared and made it clear that Captain Bruce was a guest at the hotel—and, moreover, had been a guest before they were born.

The ballroom had been converted into a nightclub. Remnants of the Victorian furniture from the hotel were scattered about, but the gilt chairs he remembered were gone, along with the lighting fixtures, and the intricate wrought-iron railing of the balcony from which old ladies and children with their nurses had once watched the dancing below was painted silver and red. The room was decorated with tinsel, balloons, and satin banners advertising Hindustan Color TV and Hindustan TV Queen 1984. Under an incongruous 1930s mural of black-faced musicians in top hats, which had somehow survived, a group of young men in scarlet-sequined suits and a fat girl singer in silver lamé split to her thigh were improvising on Michael Jackson's "Beat It."

The dance floor was crowded with voluptuous women in saris, handsome men in dark suits, college students in jeans and sweaters, and beautiful girls in short sequined dancing dresses, all energetic, determined dancers. David stood thinking how dangerous the Lindy hop had seemed when he and Kamala had performed it on that same dance floor. Just then an enormously fat young man in a dark pin-striped suit grabbed his hand, led him to the dance floor, and started boogying. David was amused to see how many members of the same sex, both men and women, were dancing together. He thought he'd never seen Indian people looking so happy, and his heart lightened. Then the Master of Ceremonies interrupted the music.

"And now the Prince of Pokhara is going to give us a song," he yelled. "Let's have a big hand for Mr. Tashi. Come on, Tashi!"

The fat young man who'd led David to the dance floor climbed onto the banner-draped podium, and the M.C., a plump mustached Punjabi, threw his arms around him.

"What are you going to sing for us tonight, Tashi? We are all breathlessly waiting."

Mr. Tashi mumbled something inaudible to the audience, and the M.C. yelled over the din, "The Prince of Pokhara is going to give us his rendition of that great love song 'Anna Mé Core'! Strike up the band, Mr. Deadley."

Mr. Deadley, a young man sitting at a Roland synthesizer, played a chord; the Prince took up the crackling microphone and began to sing off-key. Other band members joined in. The drummer injected a disco beat, and soon the crowd was enthusiastically boogying as Tashi belted out his song.

Suddenly, through an opening between the dancers, David saw a ravaged facsimile of Mrs. Kapoorchand, the once-beautiful hotel owner. The gap closed. Could it have been an apparition? Elbowing his way across the floor, he saw her again. She wore large dark glasses and was beautifully dressed in a chiffon sari shot with gold, beneath which her skin glowed like old ivory. She said something to a tall thin man with a turban sitting next to her, who rose and quickly pushed his way toward David.

"Mrs. Kapoorchand would like you to sit down with her," he said over the music.

David followed him to her table.

"I think you have been here before?" She smiled when he sat down.

"Ah, yes," replied David, "forty years ago. I spent several of my leaves here. I recognized you at once, Mrs. Kapoorchand."

Drawn lips smiled under the impenetrable black disks. "I also recognized you, but I have forgotten your name." David introduced himself. "Of course." She nodded. "You were a friend of Princess Kamala's. Have you seen her? She is here tonight. Shall I call her over?"

Terrified, David glanced across the ballroom where a woman swathed in a sari the color of jacaranda blossoms, her back to them, was holding forth at a big table, surrounded by laughing men in dark suits.

"I have just arrived with my wife; we are staying in the hotel," said David. "I would prefer to meet her another time."

"I understand." Mrs. Kapoorchand smiled.

A young man from the crowd introduced as Mr. Kinkey now held forth on the stage with "Ebony and Ivory." Positioning himself so Kamala could not see him if she happened to turn around, David observed Mrs. Kapoorchand out of the corner of his eye. Though forty years had passed, he sensed that, for her, nothing had changed. A certain obstinacy in her frozen features revealed a fierce battle waged against the vicissitudes of time. The reality of the world about her must never have penetrated her dark glasses. How glamorous she had seemed when he was twenty, the mysterious older woman from Lahore who'd bought the Ritz and had the NO DOGS, NO INDIANS plaque removed! It was rumored she was very rich, a descendant of the famous Maharaja Ranjit Singh, and involved in several unconventional love affairs. "Life is for living" had been her motto, and it appeared she had not renounced it.

The dancing was interrupted by the M.C., now quite drunk, whom Mrs. Kapoorchand seemed to find most amusing.

"And now we are going to present to you a fine cabaret," he yelled, his plump face perspiring freely. "Yes, for your delight, for your benefit, ladies and gentlemen, the three lovely ladies Rika, Dipa, and Meeka."

The band struck up a brave fanfare, but the three beauties who dashed onto the floor, like the decadent elegance of the old hotel, were fat and frowsy. David stifled a sudden desire to laugh, for neither Mrs. Kapoorchand nor the rest of the audience seemed to find them funny. He recalled the beautiful nautch girls he'd seen dancing on the same floor years ago and wondered if these creatures might, like Ravi, have grown old with the hotel. One had a navel that seemed to have been tied off at birth with a rope, another an enormously fat belly whose two sides moved in tandem with each other. But no one in the audience cared, and wild applause followed the conclusion of their dance.

"You must be noticing many changes," Mrs. Kapoorchand said wistfully. "I have tried my best to keep this place exactly as it was. Why do you not wish to see Princess Kamala? Look, she is getting up to leave. Let me call her over."

"Please, I'll get in touch with her later. I plan to stay for some time. Bobby Singh has offered me his house; we hope to move in tomorrow or the next day and stay through monsoon." To David's relief, before Mrs. Kapoorchand could press her point, the floor became crowded again and Kamala disappeared.

"I hear Bobby's house is very nice," said the old lady. "I haven't been there myself, but he comes to the hotel quite often. Of course, you must be knowing him from the old days."

The M.C. was at it again: "And now, ladies and gentlemen, if you please, we are going to reveal—or, rather, the judges are going to give me an envelope containing the name, ladies and gentlemen—the name of the beautiful girl in this audience who has been selected as this year's Hindustan TV Queen!" A roar of applause greeted this announcement.

A drunken friend of the M.C. grabbed the microphone. "Envelope, pass the bloody envelope up." A white envelope appeared over the heads of the dancers. "Clear the floor, ladies and gentlemen, so those in the rear can see."

The dancers left the floor and were immediately replaced by a gaggle of photographers ready to snap pictures of the lucky girl. The M.C. fumbled with the envelope, struggled through a series of drunken jokes and finally announced the name: "Rakhi Sharma! Will Rakhi Sharma step forward, please?"

A girl of great beauty with a world-weary look, wearing a nearly transparent shirt, tight silk pants, and high heels, was escorted to the podium. She had come all the way from Jabalpur in Madhya Pradesh for the big event, and while three drunken men in dark suits stood holding a huge carton containing her prize, a new Hindustan color TV set, Rakhi was garlanded, crowned with a sparkling rhinestone tiara, and photographed. The M.C. interviewed her, asking if she was a Miss, a Mrs., or a Ms. Upon learning she was only seventeen and still a Miss, a roar of applause rose from the audience of hopeful males, and her father, a beaming man in tan polyester, rushed to the microphone to invite everyone to a "champanjee" breakfast he would host the following morning at the famous Aroma Hotel just down the hill. After all, one's daughter winning a beauty contest was not an everyday occurrence but a stroke of great good luck. It could lead to a profitable marriage or, if the gods but willed it, to a fabulous career in films.

The evening wore on. Mrs. Kapoorchand invited David to her cottage for a nightcap. As they left the ballroom, they had to pick their way through a sea of uprooted plants, broken pots, and overturned furniture, the result of a riot that had occurred when a number of rowdies without tickets had been refused entrance. Stepping gingerly through the mess in her gold slippers, Mrs. Kapoorchand acted as if nothing unusual had happened.

"Does this kind of thing take place often?" asked David. "What about the police? I saw them at the door."

"These days the police are useless," replied the old lady. "Recruited from the lowest sections of society, no discipline. It happens every year, sometimes twice a year now, nothing we can do about it."

They arrived at Mrs. Kapoorchand's well-kept cottage behind the hotel, another romantic Gothic bungalow with diamond-paned windows.

An old servant opened the door, and Mrs. Kapoorchand led David into the sitting room, where he was astounded to see a life-sized photographic cutout of a handsome, swarthy-looking man seated in a Victorian armchair. The cutout was garlanded with fresh roses.

"My late husband, Prem; he died twenty years ago," said Mrs. Kapoorchand, introducing David to the cutout with a gesture of despair. "I was very fond of him. Please sit down."

She ordered coffee and cognac. David found the staring eyes and fixed grin of Mr. Kapoorchand most disconcerting.

The old lady sighed. "He left this world in a motor accident. This picture was taken two days before that sad event. They say the good die young, and I wonder if it isn't true. Difficult thing, this growing old, outliving one's friends, even one's children."

"Do you have children?" asked David.

"I have outlived two sons but I have a daughter by Prem." She smiled at the cutout. "Now she is very ill. It is hard to bear. This place is a great burden for me. I would have sold it long ago except that the litigation that would follow among my relatives would consume all the profits of the sale. It's all I have left, and what with supporting these servants, many of whom I've known most of my life, and the expense of keeping this big place up, it's difficult to make ends meet. In fact, some months we are losing money, and, of course, one cannot trust one's managers these days. Most upsetting. I shudder to think what will happen when I become feeble. Really, I pray daily for the gods to strike me down so that I may not live to see those whom I've raised up turn against me."

"Will that really happen?"

"It already has." Mrs. Kapoorchand snorted. "My manager is pilfering. Minor to be sure, but I know it. I took him in as a boy and trained him, cared for him, but nowadays in India loyalties run thin where money enters in. I think he plans to own this hotel, and I wouldn't be surprised to see it happen. He's very determined."

"After all you've done for him, don't you think he'd take care of you? And certainly your daughter—"

"My daughter"—the old lady grimaced—"is a victim of her husband and his family. One of those love marriages. I knew it would never work out, their horoscopes were hopelessly mismatched, but you can't tell the young anything, and now her life is ruined and she is ill from it. However, I was once a very strong-headed girl myself." She smiled wanly.

"We were all in awe of you," said David.

She took off her dark glasses, revealing liverish splotches below weary eyes.

"You were the glamorous mystery woman, now don't deny it."

A slightly crazed expression passed over her otherwise calm features. "What fun we had, didn't we?" she said, her eyes glittering. "People don't seem to have fun anymore; they work so hard having a good time, there's no fun left."

"To begin with, there weren't that many people," said David.

"Ah, yes." The old lady sighed. "Breeding like rats, they are, and if you think U.P. is crowded, you should visit Bihar: millions of hungry naked rats." She shuddered and gathered her sari around her shoulders. "Something frightful is bound to happen. I hope I'm not around to see it, I've seen enough."

A young boy shuffled into the room unannounced, bowed, took off Mrs. Kapoorchand's shoes, and began rubbing her feet.

"You remember Ravi, of course?" she asked.

"We have just met again after all these years," replied David.

"This is Ravi's grandson, Hari; he comes every night and sleeps on the bottom of my bed to keep my feet warm. After Prem left his body, I slept with two dogs for some time—golden retrievers, very fine animals—but when they died Ravi suggested Hari and I must say he's just as good."

"Actually, I was going to ask if I could borrow Ravi while I'm here," said David.

"But, of course, my dear, do. One less salary I'll have to pay and one less mouth to feed. Take him back to England with you if you like."

"I'm not sure he'd be happy there. England has changed too."

"So I hear." Mrs. Kapoorchand nodded. "My sons spent most of their time there, drank themselves to death, seems it was the thing to do. But tell me about yourself. Do you have children?"

"A boy and a girl."

"You don't sound too happy about them."

"I'm not," admitted David. "The boy is a drug addict and the girl is on her third husband, no grandchildren. I can't seem to communicate with them at all."

"At least they're alive," said Mrs. Kapoorchand sadly, "and you must remember it is a much harder world than we had to face; the youth are very disillusioned. One must be understanding, try very hard to reach them. That's my regret; I was too busy with my own life to pay attention to my sons. I left them with servants, and by the time I wanted to know them, it was too late; they didn't want me or my advice. You say your daughter is on her third husband; what's so wrong with that? I've had four. Who knows, I may still have another, might marry my manager to keep him in line." She laughed a brittle laugh and finished her brandy. "You really must see Princess Kamala.

It might be difficult, but I believe you were very much in love with her."

"How did you know that?" David asked, surprised.

"I have eyes, don't I? Yes, yes, and now after all these years you've come back to . . . find her, isn't it?"

"I thought I came back to find my friend Madho Dev, but you're right; it is Kamala I came back for. Which is why I didn't want to meet her tonight, surrounded by all those people."

"Her son and his friends," said Mrs. Kapoorchand, rolling her eyes.

"I must see her alone for the first time."

"That shouldn't be too hard. Every afternoon before tea, when it's not raining, you'll find her working in her garden; it's her exercise. She has a very lovely garden, magnificent roses. Wish she would come and work in mine; my gardeners are hopeless."

The boy had washed Mrs. Kapoorchand's feet, rubbed them with a greenish oil, and encased them in stockings and a pair of embroidered velvet slippers.

"Now I think Hari is getting drowsy." Mrs. Kapoorchand sighed. "I'd best be getting to bed before he falls asleep." She held out a withered ring-covered hand. "Please bring your wife around to see me before you move into Bobby's house. It's quite a distance from here, I doubt I'll get there even if you invite me, but I would so much like to meet her."

"I will," replied David. "Thank you for a lovely evening, a very nostalgic one for me."

"Ah, yes, nostalgia, I hope it was not too depressing." She smiled. "And you have made me laugh. I had despaired of ever laughing again."

David let himself out of the cottage. A pale moon shone through a break in the heavy fog that now curled around the building and blew into the neglected gardens. Reaching the veranda outside his room, he paused, listening to the night sounds. The *paco, paco, paco* of the night birds, the distant drumming from the valleys below, the cry of jackals somewhere far off, a muffled groan of ecstasy from a room across the courtyard.

Then Ravi was beside him, dark, silent, compassionate. "Your evening was good, sir? I have been staying here in case memsahib called. She is asleep."

"I had some coffee with Mrs. Kapoorchand," David explained. "She remembered me from the old days and said you could help us out while we are here."

"That would be very good, sir." Ravi beamed.

Below the veranda, a thin bent-over form staggered out of the hotel, and down the drive.

"Poor chap, he's quite drunk," said David. "Hope he makes it, wherever he's going."

"Tommy Singh," said Ravi softly. "A young man but old beyond his years from drugs and drink."

"Tommy Singh?"

"Raja of Sind," said Ravi. "Last of his family."

"But I knew his father, Dickie Singh."

"So did I, sir," said Ravi. "A very fine gentleman, killed in action against Pakistan. The good days are gone forever."

# I I

THE FOLLOWING DAY after breakfast, David set off with Ravi to look for General Bobby's house, which they found at the opposite end of Terripur, nestled in the brow of a high hill, surrounded by ancient deodar trees. A toothless old woman came running through the mist from an outbuilding trailed by two yellow dogs, shook her fists, and told them to get out. Ravi explained she was the caretaker's wife and told her the general had given David the key. She followed them suspiciously through the house. Despite the dark, damp day it was bright and cheerful inside. Glassed-in verandas filled with plants surrounded the main rooms. The kitchen was modern, and there were baths with hot-water heaters.

"Well," said David, rubbing his hands, "everything seems absolutely pukka. Back to the hotel, then. The sooner I get memsahib out of the Ritz, the better."

That afternoon when David and Philippa drove up in a taxi with their luggage and groceries from the bazaar, Ravi greeted them at the door. The house had been swept and dusted and fires were burning brightly in the hearths.

"Your General Bobby has good taste, or someone he knows does," observed Philippa, looking around with approval at the handsome furniture, Chinese rugs, and comfortable sofas upholstered in white.

"There is fire in memsahib's bedroom," said Ravi, showing Philippa into a large oval room with a four-poster bed and a fire crackling in a large Queen Anne fireplace. "Bathroom is here," Ravi continued. "And next to that, sahib's bedroom joining. Memsahib should get into bed quickly, and I will bring hot lemon water. Moving about too much when sick not good."

"Ravi will unpack for you," said David. "I must say it's very kind of Bobby to lend us this place."

"Yes," murmured Philippa, rummaging through her suitcase. "Shows he has a decent side, after all."

"You didn't think he had?" said David. "Bobby's really all right."

"He's quite naughty," Philippa said. "He propositioned me, that morning you were out getting railway tickets. That's why I dashed off to see the Red Fort. He was absolutely crazy. Threatened to come up to our room and break down the door."

"Did he?" David laughed. "Doesn't surprise me at all. Actually I did think it odd, you running out like that. Not all that unflattering, though, eh?"

"Humph," sniffed Philippa and went to bed.


A few days later the rain stopped, the clouds dissolved, and the snowy Himalayan peaks shone with startling precision. The day was warm and clear. David sat on the veranda sipping tea, trying to find a metaphor that would encompass the view: mighty Himalayas, lingams of Shiva, abode of sorcerers, the gods' playground; vast, inaccessible, aloof, like the sea, beyond human reach. And yet on this pleasant morning, sitting at the edge of the beautiful garden that surrounded three sides of the house, with the heavy-headed dahlias bobbing in the sun, the world felt light and cheerful and the mountains looked for all the world like immense ice cubes in some cosmic cocktail.

Philippa appeared wrapped in a warm dressing gown. She looked pale but considerably improved, and they sat together in the soft breeze, listening to the hum of bees, the tinkling of cow bells, and the drums in the valley below.

"Drums for rain," said David, "for marriage, death, birth, fertility."

"It's so peaceful." Philippa sighed, stretching lazily. "This is the first time I've felt absolutely at home since we came to India."

A click on the gate at the bottom of the garden path, however, heralded a sudden intrusion as two angry-looking young men in police uniform headed up the path. Ravi strode out of the house, eyes narrowed, and blocked their way.

"What do you want?" he barked, as though addressing a pair of dogs.

They jerked their jaws toward David, telling Ravi their business was not for the likes of him.

"Mr. David Bruce?" asked one.

"I am David Bruce."

"And Mrs. David?" said the other.

"My wife," said David. Philippa nodded. "Ravi, bring these gentlemen some tea."

Ravi rolled his eyes and retreated into the kitchen.

"Passports," snapped one of the young men. "I must see your passports."

David went into the house, found the passports, and handed them to the more authoritative-sounding young man.

"May I ask who you are?" he said, reseating himself.

"We are police from the DSP, District Supervisor of Police, Sonagar," one answered, thumbing through the passports. "You are English; you must come to the Foreigners Registration Office and register immediately."

"Not today," said Philippa, dismayed. "I've been quite ill, really I can't move. Certainly tomorrow will do."

"But India is part of the Commonwealth," said David. "What is this all about? It's my understanding that Commonwealth members need not register."

"A new rule, all must register," was the stern reply. "Englishmen, Canadians, Australians, New Zealanders—all of you must now have visas."

"You were born in India?" asked the other officer.

"Yes, actually I was." David smiled, hoping the man's face would brighten.

"Then you should have some feeling for the situation. There have been threats against the P.M.'s life from your country. All must now register."

Ravi brought tea on a tray and the two officers stood, slurping loudly and staring suspiciously at David and Philippa.

"We will take your passports with us," they said, putting their cups back on the tray.

"Look here," said David in Hindi. "How do I know who you are?

You must show me your identification before I give you our passports."

The two young men produced identity cards in plastic cases. David committed their names to memory.

"Tomorrow when you come F.R.O., you will get these back," they said and, without changing their unsmiling manner, turned and marched down the path and out through the gate.

Philippa sighed. "So much for feeling at home here."

"Androids," muttered David.

"Perhaps we should call Mrs. Gandhi," suggested Philippa. "Don't you remember she told us if we needed anything to just ring her up?"

"I'm sure she wouldn't have the remotest idea who we are," said David grumpily.

"I'm quite certain she would. Didn't she remember me from years ago at Windsor?"

"Point taken." David shrugged. "But still, one doesn't just go ringing up the leader of eight hundred million people about minor nuisances. It isn't done."

"I wouldn't call impounding one's passport exactly a minor nuisance!" Philippa grumbled.

"I'm sure it was just their way of making sure we'd show up to register. You don't really have to go down to Sonagar. I can sign for you."

"Are you saying women don't count here?"

"More or less, and certainly not in their eyes." David patted her shoulder. "I say, let's forget about the bloody thing till tomorrow. Ravi can fetch a taxi in the morning, and if you're feeling well enough, we'll take a spin and see what it's all about. Otherwise, I'll go alone. Nothing serious, just more bureaucratic nonsense."


"I'D NEVER have believed it could be this hot," Philippa said with a sigh the following morning as their taxi approached Sonagar after a two-hour drive down the mountain.

"And we're still at three thousand feet," replied David, fanning himself with a newspaper.

Rice paddies and cane fields gave way to a jumble of suburban slums, and soon they were in the heart of the city. Once a showplace of prestigious schools and important Indian institutions with broad tree-lined streets and spacious parks, Sonagar was now a filthy decaying ruin choked with smoking vehicles of all kinds and smothered in gray smog from the factories that processed limestone from the mountains. Philippa recalled signs she had seen along the highway: VISIT BEAUTIFUL SONAGAR. HAVE A HAPPY VACATION. COMMUNE WITH NATURE.

Inside the Foreigners Registration Office, it was dark and steamy. A long table ran down one side of the room at which three barefoot toughs shuffled papers. At either end of the room, facing each other, sat two other men: one with a long comical face and feminine gestures who coughed constantly, the other tall, well built, and ruggedly good-looking. Between them was the line of inevitable plastic chairs uphol-stered in green. Two bare light bulbs flickered above, and high in the broken ceiling panels a pair of mynah birds were nesting. The scold-ing of the birds as they flew in and out of the window to their nest, the coughing of the sybaritic-looking head clerk, and the squeak of an old table fan were the only sounds.

Philippa sat down, while David was directed to a doorway covered with a tattered bamboo blind. Pushing it aside, he entered another dark room. Behind a desk at the far end sat a husky middle-aged official in uniform. Three other officers sprawled on chairs chewing pan were engaged in an animated conversation that broke off when David entered. His mouth so full that he could not speak properly, the officer behind the desk motioned David to sit down. Then he spat out the window and snapped, "You have broken the law. You should have registered immediately on your arrival in Bombay." The words gur-gled out through the pan juice.

"I know of no such law," said David quietly. "No one informed me, either in the High Commission in London or at airport customs."

The officers looked at each other. "Ignorance of the law is no excuse. In all countries one must register immediately."

"Nonsense!" shouted David authoritatively in Hindi. "In most countries one does not have to register at all."

Seeing their superior shouted at in their own language by a British sahib, broad smiles appeared on the faces of the three other men. What would happen now? The man behind the desk stared furiously at David.

"Give me a letter then," he croaked. "Write that you have broken the rules and plead for a variance."

"I cannot understand you," said David loudly in Hindi, his temper rising. "Take that disgusting cud out of your mouth and speak prop-erly."

The official rose from his chair, his fists clenched. One of his cronies jumped up and dragged David back to the first office, where he produced a blank piece of paper and pen.

"Write anything," he muttered. "No one will ever read it."

David wrote that he was sorry he had committed such a dreadful error and pleaded for mercy. The young officer snatched the paper from him, stamped it with a rubber stamp, initialed the stamp, and handed it to the consumptive head clerk with an expression of utmost contempt. David decided there was considerable infighting between the various departments of the Foreigners Registration Office.

Philippa, her head resting on the back of the plastic chair, stared at the ceiling where the mynah birds, unconcerned with affairs of state, were fluttering about, chattering to one another and feeding their young.

The consumptive clerk flipped slowly through the mound of papers on his desk, got up, shuffled over to an old green filing cabinet with a broken door, and returned with more papers and their passports.

"Complete these," he coughed, waving them at David. "Five copies each."

David took the papers and counted out five for Philippa. They were long and detailed, and for the next half hour they sat filling them out while the clerk wagged his knees back and forth, sighed, and rolled his eyes.

"Photos," he said languidly when they had finally completed them.

"Photos?" asked David.

"You must have five photos each."

"I don't have any."

"Ravindra," he snarled at one of the clerks sitting at the long table. "Take these people to Kwick Photo Shop."

The young man yawned, rose slowly, and ambled out the door. David and Philippa followed him through a maze of buildings to a congested road. It was lunchtime, and hundreds of skinny young clerks stood eating food sold by local vendors. The heat was intense, the air filled with the smoke of cooking fires mixed with the exhaust from auto rickshaws, an all-pervasive onion-flavored smog.

They were led to a small shop where they waited fifteen minutes for the electricity to come on and a young boy took their pictures. After another wait while the pictures were developed, they followed Ravindra back to the F.R.O. office, which was now vacant.

"Lunchtime." Ravindra grinned. "You will have to come back at three-thirty," he said, and disappeared.

David looked at Philippa, who appeared faint. "Think we'd better find a hotel where we can get out of this heat, take a bath, and have a cool drink."

They found their driver asleep. David pounded on the window and woke him up. Driving off through the blinding heat, the driver angrily honking his horn, they finally pulled up before an ugly concrete structure with balconies and rounded windows.

"Hotel Relax," the driver announced curtly.

In the dark lobby a number of businessmen carrying briefcases waited for rooms with attractive young women in chiffon saris. The clerk pretended not to understand what they wanted, but when David produced a rupee note of a substantial denomination, a room key was immediately forthcoming. Philippa collapsed on the bed while David tried the shower to see if there was any water. A malfunctioning air conditioner rattled at the window and spat gusts of musty air and chemicals across the room.

He lay down on the bed and yawned. "Unbelievable," he said. "Imagine what the average Indian has to put up with: a government that doesn't govern, stifling rules and regulations, castes who despise one another and do their best to thwart one another's hopes and prospects. I've been seeing it as a hallucination only because it's too incredible to believe."

"How do they expect tourists to come here?" asked Philippa. "All those glossy ads for exotic India."

"Tourists come in packages, darling. They're flown into luxury hotels and transported to the sights in air-conditioned buses. Not many tourists see what you've seen."

"Somehow I wish I hadn't seen this real India," said Philippa. "If you want to know the truth, I find it terrifying. Repressed desire, turning in on itself, a time bomb ticking away."

As she uttered the word "bomb," there was a crash and screams in the next room, followed by sounds of a whimpering woman and a man threatening her. From the room on the other side came raucous film music, ecstatic grunts, and cries.

"What on earth is happening?" she exclaimed.

"Oh, that." David smiled. "This is the recreational hour. Long lunches when you can safely escape from your wife, who is having lunch with the wives of your friends or presiding over a meeting of her favorite charity."

"Couldn't she be having a matinee with a hot-blooded young lover?"

"Difficult to arrange with so many neighbors and servants," David laughed. "Someone is always watching."

"Awful," murmured Philippa.

AT THREE-THIRTY they emerged from the Hotel Relax into the still-withering heat of the afternoon and made their way back to the Foreigners Registration Office, where coffee was being served. The mynah birds clucked softly overhead, crows cawed drolly at the windows, and the five clerks, now sprawled in different positions over the chairs and tables, made no pretense of straightening up when they came in.

The head clerk lifted his kurta, casually scratched his belly, and yawned. "You really should have registered in Delhi. Now it is going to cause problems."

Philippa found him terribly amusing.

"What is all this?" said David in Hindi. "Would you be so kind as to explain just what is happening?"

"Before, you were like us, like Indians." The clerk smiled cynically. "Now you are foreigners. Who knows what tomorrow may bring?"

A boy came in with a tray of pan. Everyone took one and started chewing. David and Philippa declined.

"Ah, but you should really take one, Mr. Bruce," said the good-looking clerk. "After all, you were born here."

"How can I take pan when you keep saying that now I am a foreigner? How do you think that makes me feel?"

The five clerks chewed silently.

"You see, BBC has offered a big reward for the P.M.'s life," said the head clerk, "and in Canada, Australia, and New Zealand too there have been problems with Sikhs. So now all must register. Government is very afraid terrorists will come in. That is the reason you are having this problem. You should lock up all the Sikhs in England."

"Do you really think we look like terrorists?" Philippa smiled sweetly at the head clerk, whose expression under the influence of the betel nut had grown slightly idiotic.

"Who can tell, madam," he replied, wagging his head. "That is not for us to say. We are only the humble servants of Madam's government."

The good-looking clerk guffawed loudly, and the others all tittered in unison.

David smiled and addressed the head clerk in a tone of confidence. "Come now, when are you going to give us back our passports?"

He got up, spat a stream of red juice out the door, and motioned David to follow him outside. "My difficulty is that the orders from government are not clear," he whispered. "Today this, tomorrow that.

What to do, Mr. Bruce? You give me donation; you stay up in Terripur as long as you like; I will take care of everything."

"How much will you require?" asked David.

"That is up to you, sir, as you wish. The more one gives, the more one gets, isn't it?" He looked around quickly to see if he was being watched.

David produced a wad of bills which the clerk pocketed without a glance, and they went back inside. The other clerks were all suddenly busy writing at their desks as though nothing unusual was going on. "You may collect your papers from him and the passports too," said the head clerk, pointing to the good-looking one at the other end of the room.

David accepted them and asked if they could leave.

"You can stay or leave as you like." The head clerk smiled. "We must sit here until seven P.M., so you also can sit with us as long as you wish. It is still very hot outside." He fanned himself with a paper. "Would you like another coffee?"

"I think we will go on," said David. "By the time we get home, it will be almost dark."

"You are staying at which place, Mr. Bruce?" asked the head clerk.

"General Singh's house, General Bhupinder Singh. He's lent us his place for a few months."

As David knew it would, this revelation had a profound effect. The head clerk rose to his feet, bowed, and extended his hand.

"Very good to have met you, sir," he said obsequiously. "Anytime we can be of help, just let us know."

"I shall indeed."

The good-looking clerk saluted and the three other clerks stood at attention. David and Philippa backed out the door. The mynah birds fluttered after them. The two officers who had visited them in Terripur were lounging against a tree.

"You got your passports back?" one asked.

The head clerk, who was standing at the door, shouted at the two policemen to come into the office at once.

Outside the compound wall, David put his hand on Philippa's arm. "Listen," he whispered.

The head clerk and the officers were engaged in heated conversation.

"He's telling them they are assholes and have made a terrible mistake," translated David. "It is all their sister-fucking fault; they should never have made us come down. He's saying that he asked me for money, some of which he is giving to them as agreed, but warning them that if anything happens it is their fault because Bruce-sahib can get them all canned."

"You gave him money?" Philippa whispered. "But that's bribery!"

David grinned. "Those fellows make eight hundred rupees a month. Try living on that and see where it gets you. When the system doesn't pay, the user must. It's a user's tax, there's no other way."

Philippa was amazed. "You don't mind?"

"Not at all. The price of admission. You must admit it was rather more amusing than calling Mrs. Gandhi's office."

Philippa giggled. "That clerk was terribly funny—so feminine, so sly."

"It's all theater," said David.

ALTHOUGH the break in the monsoon continued, Philippa had a relapse and spent several more feverish days in bed, drifting back and forth between consciousness and sleep. One thing was very clear. Living with tales of viceregal splendor had hardly prepared her for the reality of India. What conflict her great-grandparents must have experienced between their authoritarian role and their naturally eccentric natures! Or perhaps their eccentricities were a result of living in India. No doubt it was this whiff of nonconformism that had attracted her to David. Poor dear, had he been born ten years later, he might have been quite different. The mold was cracking then. He could have broken out of it. Most probably he would have been happier if he had stayed on in India to begin with. The way he kept reminding everyone he was born here certainly made one think that. Now he was terribly disappointed. She reminded herself to be more sympathetic about his romantic illusions. And what of Arjun? Was she being condescending in her attitude toward him? What must he really think of her; did he see her as the oppressor? Separated from his physical presence, she knew she could certainly live without him but would she feel that way if she saw him again? When she thought of him, her teeth began to chatter. They said the altitude slowed one's circulation, but she knew if Arjun were there it would speed up. Arjun could melt a glacier.

While Philippa convalesced, David spent his time exploring Terripur, hoping to find Kamala at work in her garden. One could hardly miss the sprawling, imitation villa set in the midst of lovely gardens behind a crumbling rose-covered wall. For two days he walked by the place, gathering his courage. Then on the third day, as he was passing one of the gates situated on a back lane, he caught his breath.

Although she was wearing baggy tweed pants and her beauty had been honed spare by the years, there was no mistaking the thrilling eyes that stared at him. She was cursing two men who were trimming rose canes and stopped in the middle of a sentence. A puzzled expression crossed her brow. The same inquiring furrow he'd always loved was still there. He walked on a few paces; above all he did not want to shock her. If she recognized him, well and good; if not, then their meeting was not meant to happen.

"David? David Bruce?" The lilting voice called after him. He stopped and turned around. She came out through the gate and walked toward him.

"Sorry," she faltered. "Thought I recognized someone I knew years ago."

"Don't be sorry, Kamala," he said. "It's me, David."

He took her hands in his and they stood gazing at each other. The muscles of her face went slack. She turned away self-consciously and brushed back her graying hair.

"I can't believe I'm seeing you. You haven't changed that much, but I have and it embarrasses me. When did you arrive? How did you know I was here?"

"Madho Dev," replied David.

"Ah," she said, "so you've been to Kotagarh? I haven't heard from them in ages. Are they all right?"

"Yes, fine. They're all there on the farm—Madho Dev, Devika, Arjun, his wife, and five children."

"Five children, is it? Last time I heard, it was three. I went to their wedding, you know. And Gayatri?"

"A sweet girl, quite shy. I liked her."

She scrutinized his face for a sign of what Madho Dev might have told him and sighed. It was too much. She'd thought about this moment for years, wondered if it would ever come, and now she felt helpless. "But why are we standing here in the road?" She smiled nervously. "You must come in. It's almost tea time. I'll just tell these malis to go home for the day. Gardeners! If I leave them alone, they'll cut down everything in sight." She turned away, trembling.

"Don't let me interrupt your work," said David. "I can come back another time."

"Nonsense," she said. "You don't think now that you've found me after all these years, I'm going to let you just wander off, do you?"

They walked up a path through the beautiful gardens. At the house, two servants were struggling with an obstinate cow that had strayed onto the veranda.

"Please sit down," she said. "Let me change out of my gardening things and order tea. I'm a mess."

She disappeared inside. David seated himself in one of the wicker chairs and watched the performance with the cow. Just then a young woman appeared from around a corner. When she saw him, she stopped short. He stood up, barely able to believe his eyes. It was as if one Kamala had gone in and another, the one he remembered, had come out. She cursed the servants and dismissed them.

"Sorry," she said. "Afraid I abused them badly. Hope you don't mind. But they wouldn't understand anything else. Who are you?"

"David Bruce," he replied, "an old friend of Princess Kamala's. And who might you be?"

"I'm Sumi, short for Sumitra. I'm her daughter. Where is Mummy, anyhow?"

"She went in to change and order some tea."

The girl leaned against a pillar and stared boldly at him. She wore cut-off shorts and a flimsy shirt that barely covered her magnificent unsupported breasts.

"I must say Mummy has good taste." She smiled. "Why haven't I seen you before? When did you know her?"

"Here in India, many years ago."

"And now you've come back, after such a long time?"

"Yes, we met by chance, just now on the road."

"How romantic," she said with a breath of cynicism. "You must have been rather shocked. Mummy isn't exactly the beauty she once was."

"That's a rather unkind thing to say about one's mother," he observed, put off by her bluntness. "Has anyone mentioned you're very much like her?"

"I've seen pictures, naturally one can hardly avoid them, they're all over the place. In fact, I might have seen a snap or two of you in one of her albums. You're the sexy Englishman in the uniform, I'll bet. I've asked about you."

David smiled. "And what did she tell you?"

"Oh, something about a war, how you were good friends. But I think you're better looking now, your gray hair is much more attractive."

"You've made my day," said David.

Sumitra gazed at him, her full red lips in a pout. David had the feeling she was restless and bored.

"Do you live here with your mother?" he asked.

"Off and on," she replied, tapping her foot. "When I'm not in Paris or Saint-Tropez—I prefer France. People here are so old-fashioned about things. One must put on these wretched saris and churidars. I hate clothes; the fewer I have to wear, the better. In France, one can wear anything."

"Or nothing," said David.

A servant bearing a silver tea service appeared, vanished, and reappeared with a plate of sandwiches. Then Kamala sauntered out in a chiffon sari, freshly made up, her defenses repaired. When she saw her daughter she paused. David guessed they might not be getting on.

"So you've met Captain Bruce," she said, settling herself in a chair.

"I recognized him from the photos in your album," Sumitra replied coolly.

"She thinks I look better now than then." David laughed.

Kamala shot a piercing glance at Sumitra. "Don't you have a tennis engagement with Ajit?"

Sumitra smiled wickedly. "Mummy wants to get rid of me so she can have you all to herself. I don't blame her. I'll go along then. Not even a crust of bread or a cup of chai for poor Sumi, Mummy darling?"

"One should not stuff oneself or drink tea before tennis. I'm sure you'll see Captain Bruce again."

"See you later, Captain." She waved flirtatiously and ambled off.

Kamala rolled her eyes. "I'm having such problems with her," she said, flicking imaginary bits of dust from her lap with the tips of her long fingers. "Her father is dead, left everything to her; however, I'm the administrator of her estate. It makes for considerable tension between us, which, of course, was what he intended."

"Ruling from the grave," said David.

"Exactly." Kamala sighed. "So she spites me and disagrees about everything, tries to upset me by going around half naked, frightening the servants, having affairs with riffraff. She even had a fling with my chauffeur, can you imagine? That shows you the value of a foreign education."

"She's been going to school abroad?"

"In Switzerland, needed the rough edges taken off. They do it so beautifully there, you know, or did. Nowadays I think they teach them to be good whores." She laughed caustically. "But how are you after all these years? I was counting them up in my bedroom, thirty-eight, nearly a lifetime. I must say Sumi is right, though, you're better looking than ever, if that's possible." She poured tea. "I suppose you are or have been married and have children?" she inquired, handing him a cup.

"Yes." David nodded. "I married about eight or nine years after leaving India; have a son and daughter. Not too pleased with the way they've turned out, but I've done my duty. Actually, one of the reasons we came out was I've been depressed about them. That and the fact I've just turned sixty. Decided it was now or never."

"You say 'we.' Is your wife with you?"

"Yes, we're staying at Bobby Singh's place. She's been ill, caught something at the Ritz. In fact, I saw you there the other night, you were surrounded."

"That ghastly place! One goes there occasionally out of boredom. But Bobby's house is lovely. Too bad one cannot say the same for him."

They sipped their tea in silence and listened to the wind in the large oaks at the side of the house.

Finally David spoke. "Kamala, I must ask you something."

"Go ahead. I know what it is." She looked sad.

"What?"

"You want to ask why I never got in touch with you, why I let you leave India without saying goodbye, why I disappeared."

"Yes. One of the reasons I've come back is to get the answer to that question. You see, if you hadn't vanished, I'd have stayed on. I loved you very much, dreamt about you for years."

"Disturbed your dreams, did I?" She smiled nervously. "That's most flattering."

"Come, be serious."

"It's too depressing."

"You haven't answered my question. Why did you vanish?"

"Because it would never have worked, never—even if my father had permitted it, which is doubtful."

"But we could have lived in England. As my wife you would have been welcome there."

"Me, live in England?" She snorted. "That's the last place I'd ever live. Freezing cold and dreadful food!" She shrugged. "Paris, perhaps, but England? My mother's father died there on a state visit: food poisoning. No, my dear, I saved you from a fate worse than death. To stand by and see one's way of life dying as I have here is not a pleasant thing. And ours would have been a mixed marriage, you would have always been the 'foreign husband.' No doubt you've sensed the provincialism, the chauvinism this country has fallen into, how foreigners, thanks to the powers that be, are thought of nowadays? 'The foreign hand'? All that nonsense? We've always welcomed foreigners;

now they're all supposed to be agents and spies plotting our down-fall—except for the Russians." She laughed. "Just tell me, who in their right mind would want us?"

David chuckled. "Philippa and I had to visit the Foreigners Regis-tration Office the other day, quite an experience. Seems we must have visas now."

"Ah, you've seen it then, the hypocrisy, dishonesty. What it comes down to is they're so damned patriotic any spy can buy a visa for a few hundred rupees. And now that some Sikh in England has offered money for Indira's life, you will all have endless problems. I've seen the staged demonstrations on TV but I can tell you privately, there are masses of people here, my dear, masses who are praying someone will take that man up on his offer."

"All this has nothing to do with us," said David softly and took her hand.

"Indeed it does," she said good-naturedly. "If you'd stayed, you'd have had to live through it and be crazy like me."

David smiled. "You don't look crazy."

"Thank you, darling, but I disagree. Perhaps outwardly it's not obvious, but when I look inside myself, I know I'm quite gone." She squeezed his hand. "But I've often thought of you, even dreamt of you. Perhaps we've met in each other's dreams? It is possible, you know; our holy men tell us so."

"In Kotagarh, Philippa and I spent our first night in the state guesthouse. It's called a Government Rest House now. Do you remember it?"

"In the same bedroom, I suppose?"

David nodded. "Yes, on the same bed."

Kamala sighed. "You and your wife were there together?"

"Yes."

"Does she know about us? I mean, the us of long ago: have you ever told her?"

"No."

"Why not?"

"Expect I wanted to keep it to myself, something sacred, jealously guarded. Suppose you think I'm a sentimental old fool?"

"Not at all." She smiled. "I too have cherished the memory of that night. But it's one of your English staples, you know, this sentimen-tality—very sweet but a luxury. Here in India we aren't sentimental-ists. Emotional, yes, but we can't afford to be sentimental. Life here is much too"—she shrugged expressively—"capricious. Things happen so suddenly, so brutally, and these days there is such an utter disregard for human life. How can one be sentimental under such circumstances?" She gazed at him intently. "But I loved you, yes, very much. We were very young, weren't we? I think I loved your body, though, more than your soul. Yes, I have to admit it. And many times since, through two utterly inept husbands pawing and groaning over me, I often closed my eyes and thought of you, dear David. Now I see you, how I wish I could feel the same way, but the flesh is weak, desire fades; you are not the same man, I am not the same woman. The cells that once made love have long since died away and been replaced by new ones—except in the brain, of course. Ah, that's the rub, isn't it, the bloody brain? If one could only stop thinking, stop remembering. The body ages, but the brain is always young."

They sat quietly watching puffs of cloud skid across the brow of the hill.

"Has it really been that bad here for you?" he asked. "I know many things have changed for the worse, but you aren't destitute."

Kamala exhaled. "My dear, if what happened here had happened to you in England, there would have been war. We had solemn agreements with your government; we then made solemn agreements with the new government of India. All have been broken. I suppose we should be grateful they didn't murder us like the French or the Russians did in their revolutions, but Hindus don't believe in killing. No, we go in for slow strangulation, suffocation, starvation, benign neglect. Neglect of duty, neglect of holy places, neglect of the people and the environment. In 1948 I stood here with one of my father's tiger guns to keep the servants from cutting down these trees. Nothing is done today that can be put off till tomorrow, and it is fervently hoped that when tomorrow comes it won't be necessary to do anything then either. This principle has been enshrined in our institutions by our politicians. The world's largest democracy? What rot! The elections here are purchased, and many at the point of a gun."

"You sound like Madho Dev," said David.

Her features, full of troubled arrogance and reserve, became taut. "That is because we both come from a vanishing race. There is so much intrigue. It has been so difficult, especially with that woman in power and her private vendetta against us. If I were a man I would be a terrorist. I don't see why some of our Rajput princes have not killed her, except so many of them are sots. The only one who stood up to her was the Rajmata of Jaipur, Gayatri Devi, and look what happened."

"I heard something . . ." began David.

"Indira hates her: old jealousies. In 1975 she sent her secret police to Jaipur, locked everyone up—even the Rajmata's houseguests, members of your British peerage—and spent days searching for gold, which they eventually found under some floor tiles. For this 'crime,' about which she knew nothing, the poor thing was sent to jail—and not the normal kind of house arrest one would grant a princess; no, she was thrown in with prostitutes, told she deserved it! And all that time, the Nehru woman was ruling illegally under emergency powers which she grabbed when she was found guilty of election tampering by the Supreme Court. It was at that time she called on the Russians for advice. KGB people flew in to help her manage her 'Emergency,' and they are still here. Still here, which is the reason for the present so-called terrorism. Indira Gandhi deserves everything that is going to happen to her, everything! How dare she talk about the evils of terrorism when she is hand in glove with terrorists on public platforms all over the world? Her own party has always used terror as a weapon, that and caste division. It is the Congress Party which exploits caste differences, keeps everyone fighting."

"I tend to agree with you, but we met Mrs. Gandhi the other night in Delhi—actually Philippa had met her in England years ago and the Prime Minister remembered her. I was pleasantly surprised, found her very bright, quite delightful."

"Ah, you saw her other side, the bright and good side. She's crazy too, like all of us, what you call schizophrenic. Our society makes us so. One side is charming, intelligent, sympathetic. The other is this hag with a withered heart, would-be sorceress, doctrinaire ego-driven politician: rationalizing all her mistakes, all her compulsive vindictiveness, by saying it's for the good of India. What rot! She's a nonentity, and I tell you when she leaves the scene, however it happens, within a year or two no one will remember her." Kamala heaved a big sigh. "I despise politics, a livelihood for third-class minds. Politicians are dirt. But here, to survive, you have to be aware of them."

"Why haven't you left?"

She shrugged. "Pride. I must confess it. My ancestors have lived and died here for thousands of years, I do not wish to die on foreign soil."

David sighed. From the carefree "modern" girl he'd once known, it was plain to see Kamala had become as Madho Dev had described her, a tough survivor. Yet in the movement of her exquisite hands that had once caressed and aroused in him a great passion, he sensed a longing to reach out and touch, to hold, to feel again.

A bronze thunderhead had formed over the mountains above Hardwar and Rishikesh, bright rainbows descending beneath it; far away to the west, the silver ribbon of the Jamuna unwound its way to the plains. A handsome English setter padded out of the house and laid its muzzle in her lap.

She stroked its head. "This is Winston. Yes, Winston, Captain Bruce is still very handsome, isn't he?" Winston looked over his shoulder briefly, then nuzzled deeper into Kamala's lap. "Now tell me, David, what have you been doing with yourself all these years?"

"Business mostly, trying to make enough money to hang on to our place, pay the heavy taxes they keep levying on us."

"At least they didn't take your land away," replied Kamala, "redistribute it, only to find the poor to whom it was given couldn't hang on to it, lost it to moneylenders. Here, the moneylenders have become rich on our properties. The benefit has not been to the poor; they are even poorer. At least in the old days we could take care of them."

"There are so many more of them—it's a shock."

"Ah, because the politicians eat up the money given for modernization, electrification, and so on. The moment you have electric lights in a village, the birthrate goes down. Now half our population is fifteen years and younger. It is they who will finally destroy the present establishment, but God help us when they do. Hope I'm not around." She laughed bitterly. "So you've been in business. What have you learned?"

"That I'm not very good at it. With what I had to start with, others have made millions. Even doing as well as I did, I neglected my children, with the result that my son is a drug addict and my daughter is a . . . well, she's ready to end her third marriage. In fact, I'm amazed she bothers."

"Do you think we are totally responsible for the way our children turn out?" asked Kamala seriously.

"I hope not," returned David.

"I hope not too. You see, I have a son whom you haven't met. In a way it gives me some satisfaction that yours is on drugs because mine is a pansy."

"The new word is 'gay,' my dear," said David with a rueful smile.

"I'm aware of that word, but I wasn't sure you were."

"In many ways, I think it's good for people to come to terms with that side of life."

"Perhaps in your society," retorted Kamala, "but not in ours. Here one gets taken advantage of terribly. My son is in love with a Punjabi truck driver, if you please."

"Perhaps it's worth it if he's happy."

"Sonny happy?" She sniffed. "The problem is his friend has made a great amount of money with what Sonny has given him, hand over foot as you would say, but keeps him dangling on a string with stories of other lovers he has or could have. Sonny gets very upset. I'm at my wits' end."

"Why don't you send him abroad? Don't you have a place in Paris?"

"I need him here, there's too much at stake, and, of course, he doesn't really want to leave this boyfriend. I must say the fellow is good-looking and very protective when it comes to Sonny, but I hate having him made a laughingstock, he was such a bright, happy child."

"My son too," said David sadly. "Then something happened, I don't know what."

A warm wind was rising, the sun had set in an amber band far out over the plains, and in the northeast, the dissolving clouds revealed the Himalayas, gold and pink.

"I must be going," said David, rising. "I'll come again."

"I'm delighted you've come back," said Kamala. A melancholy look spread over her fine features. "Words can't express how good it is to see you."

David took her hands in his, lifted her up, and held her in his arms.

"Give me a few days," she whispered. "I'll organize something and send you and your wife an invitation." She held him at arm's length. "Of course, I'm dying to meet her. I'll say I heard you were here through Bobby and that he asked me to have you round. It will all seem quite casual." She raised one eyebrow.

"That would be splendid," said David. "I'm sure you'll both get on."

"Don't be too sure, darling," said Kamala. "We women are a jealous lot."


SHE stood in the russet afterglow and watched him stride down the path. What would it have been like if she had not run away from those strong, uncomplicated arms? Suppose they had gone off together to Nepal or divided their time between India and Paris? What a fine-looking man he still was, what a kind face too. Yes, a kind man, and deserved more than life had given him. But don't we all, she thought, or do we get just what we really deserve? She wondered if it could still happen between them? Was he tired of his wife? Possibly. Perhaps she was one of those domineering memsahibs with a bossy masculine voice: big-boned cave woman, pale skin, blue-veined legs, and a condescending manner. If he were to learn that he had a daughter and grandchildren in India—his only grandchildren—what would his reaction be? Obviously, Madho Dev had not told him or he would have behaved quite differently. She thought of trying to call Madho Dev to make sure, but the prospect of screaming something so intimate over the telephone was too daunting. She sighed. What would happen would happen. At the appropriate time she would tell him; or perhaps she wouldn't.

A white Mercedes pulled up the drive and two young men got out: one, tall and burly, wearing a black turban, white shirt, and tight black pants; the other, slight and slim, in white kurta pajamas. Ignoring their arrival, Kamala turned to go into the house.

"And who was that good-looking fellow we just saw coming out at the gate?" shouted the young man in the kurta pajamas. It was Sonny and his Punjabi friend, Kirpan. She wanted to disappear, but it was too late.

"Mummy, I think you are keeping things from me."

Kamala stared past him toward Kirpan. "And since when are you wearing the black turban?" she asked.

"Just a piece of cloth, Highness," he replied, smiling blankly. Rows of white teeth gleamed like pearls in his black beard.

"Just a piece of cloth," mocked Kamala. "We all know what it means. Have you decided to become a terrorist?"

"Of course not, Highness," said Kirpan. "But it is better for me with my drivers if my turban is black. These days they are all upset about Operation Blue Star and are wearing the black turban."

"It is all right for them but not for you," said Kamala firmly. "It doesn't do to advertise one's views. Most unwise, especially as you are connected"—she glared at Sonny—"with this family and especially here in Terripur. There are too many eyes."

"I always thought you looked better in blue anyhow, Kirpanji," said Sonny facetiously. "Now be a good fellow and do what Mummy says."

Kirpan glared and swaggered to the car, where he rummaged in a bag and produced a long pale-blue cloth. As he removed his turban, his thick black hair fell down over his shoulders.

Doesn't even tie his hair up like a proper Sikh, thought Kamala, but she had to admit that Sonny had good taste. Kirpan was a fine specimen. She looked on with satisfaction as he obediently bound up his hair in the blue turban.

"That's better, thank you." She nodded unsmilingly and addressed herself to her son. "What brings you here? I thought you were in Delhi."

"Two of our trucks broke down near Hardwar, we drove out this morning. Kirpan had to fire the drivers: they were selling parts off the new trucks, replacing them with old ones, the usual story. So we thought we'd come up and pay you a visit. It's too hot in Delhi just now. Who was that man?"

"An old friend of mine," said Kamala, averting her eyes. "Captain in the British army, staying at Bobby Singh's place."

"Good-looking chap," said Sonny. "Looks like a film star, can't remember which one. . . ."

"James Fox," muttered Kirpan, who spent a lot of time keeping up with Western films.

"Ah, quite right," exclaimed Sonny. "Will we be seeing him again? Was he an old flame of yours, Mummy? You know you can't hide anything from me."

It was true, thought Kamala; since childhood Sonny had always been clairvoyant, would often tell her what she was going to do or what she might be keeping from him.

"We were friendly during the war years," she said coolly.

"You mean when you were playing Red Cross angel?" Sonny grinned. "You must have been very close for him to look you up after all these years."

Kamala ignored him. "Your rooms must be swept and made up. I'll go and find a servant."

"Ha ha, you are escaping, Mummy dear, that means it's serious. Undoubtedly we will see this handsome Fox again."

# 12

THE MONSOON continued to pause, the sun shone through rising mists, and in a few days Philippa was up and about again, weeding the garden and planning meals with Ravi. But David seemed distracted and irritable and she was certain he'd been to see Kamala. One didn't live with someone for almost thirty years without acquiring a certain dogged instinct about them. Ravi shuffled out with a tray of tea and biscuits and David followed from a nap, stretching.

"Seems all I can do here is sleep." He yawned. "Meant to go to the bazaar this afternoon, now it's too late."

Philippa poured the tea and they stared at the mountains in silence. The front gate squeaked and a young boy came up the path between the shoulder-high cosmos, bearing an envelope. David came awake.

Ah, she thought, this is what he's been waiting for.

The envelope was sealed. In one corner it bore a small coat of arms and was addressed to Captain and Mrs. David Bruce, Snow View Cottage. Putting on a show of bewilderment, David turned it over in his hand. Ravi brought a letter opener and stood smiling while he opened it.

" 'Dear Captain and Mrs. Bruce,' " he read aloud. " 'My friend General Bhupinder Singh has written me that you are in Terripur at Snow View. I've arranged a little dinner party for the day after tomorrow and hope you will be able to come. Informal, about eight-thirty. RSVP this boy. Signed Kamala Devi, Prospect Point.' "

"Where is Prospect Point?" David asked Ravi.

"Just on the other side of the mountain, Sahib, past the English graveyard, a few kilometers. You can take a taxi."

"Feel up to it?" David asked.

"Who do you suppose Kamala Devi is?" said Philippa. "Someone you knew in the old days?"

"A friend of Bobby's, I suppose." He shrugged. "I did know a girl once called Kamala, it's not an uncommon name, but the Kamala I knew was in the Red Cross during the war: friend of Devika's, as I recall. Shall I tell this boy we'll go?"

Philippa was relieved he hadn't lied totally to her. "Why not? It might be fun, get us out of the house, meet some people. You'd better write something back."

He went in the house and returned a few minutes later with a small sealed envelope which he gave to the boy. The boy did not move.

Ravi reached into his pocket and handed him a coin. "Now go," he commanded. "Tell your memsahib that Captain-sahib and Mrs. Bruce will come."

The boy shambled back down the path and disappeared. Ravi wondered why the sahib had pretended about Princess Kamala. All the servants knew he had been to see her and had tea there last week. But the ways of sahibs were mysterious and not to be questioned by the likes of him.

David sat drumming softly on the table, gazing out toward the snowy Himalayas while Philippa concentrated on finishing E. M. Forster's account of the trials and tribulations of the unfortunate ruler of Dewas Senior. He was drumming because he was angry with himself. Angry at the passage of time; furious that he'd wasted his life in day-to-day dealings of the most insignificant sort, transactions of a shopkeeper-dragon. Yes, some foul, scaly dragon sprawled in a Bond Street cave, guarding piles of gold, puffing smoke. Hanging on. And out there were those astonishing mountains that made him feel like a cosmic afterthought. Seeing Kamala after forty years had had a similar effect. He had walked away from her through the bazaar, along the Mall, past the British cemetery with its wizened deodars, its ivy-grown tombstones, and felt dazed. He had romanticized her memory beyond belief; been completely overwhelmed by the reality of meeting her again. If he had not met Sumitra. . . . Yes, that was it! Mother and daughter, mirror images separated by forty years. Yet the daughter was even more disturbing than her mother had been: standing there, lolling against the pillar of the veranda, telling him she hated to wear clothes, tantalizing him with her eyes, she had excited and confused him. Would he see her again? Part of him hoped he would not. But there was another side, wild and uncivilized, that was already inventing stratagems to get her alone somewhere: he and Sumi, alone and free.

He stopped drumming and went into the house. Seize the moment. Hadn't he been telling himself that's what he must do? By God, if she flirted with him again, why not? Gazing at himself in a mirror, he pulled at his mustache. Should he shave it off, give himself a younger look? Or would it? Better not to change things too much or Philippa and Kamala would become suspicious. He was surrounded by shrewd women. Perhaps they would hate each other on sight. Who could tell? It might be better than their becoming friends and conspiring against him.


COMPLETED in 1880 by a Francophile great-uncle of Kamala Devi's, Prospect Point was a fanciful re-creation on a larger scale of Gabriel's Petit Trianon and was considered one of Terripur's showplaces. Already in ruin when it had been given to Kamala as a present at her first marriage, successive layers of whitewash and stucco had obscured most of the original details, and, though still impressive, it was difficult to connect with the original.

On the evening of Kamala's party, the drive had been swept clean and, except for Sonny's Mercedes, was now crowded with various derelict vehicles not usually found in front of a French château. There was a secondhand Vespa belonging to a young American couple, Ron and Sherri, rumored to be the heirs to a vast fortune in steel, who affected Indian dress and were "on the spiritual path." According to

Kuldip Singh, Kamala's diminutive middle-aged raja friend who swallowed his words in a thick Oxford accent, Tom and Jerry—as he called them—were looking for "peace of mind." Raja Kuldip Singh was an avid fan of *Dallas* and *Dynasty*, which he had taped for him by his nephew in Los Angeles and flown weekly to India. He wept at the way the protagonists of these dramas unnecessarily complicated their lives and said people should admire Tom and Jerry for rejecting all that. Kamala had met them one day while chasing a pet tiger cub who'd managed to escape her menagerie. Delighted at the unusual sight of a young tiger romping through their yard followed by two breathless retainers, they had invited Kamala to tea and soon became fast friends.

At thirty-four, with a handsome head of mahogany-colored hair and a deep tan, Ron had a history in India of doing crazy things. A decade earlier, he'd become famous for speeding about to various religious sites in a white Rolls convertible filled with holy men. The spectacle of Ron in white suit and long flowing hair, the sadhus in scarlet loincloths with their tridents and chimtahs, their flags fluttering in the breeze, had caused a sensation. Another time, giving up clothes altogether, he caused a near riot in the main bazaar of a famous hill station and later was almost killed by a mob for accidentally striking an old missionary from Nebraska when she inadvertently interrupted an acid trip on which he felt he was finally being released from Samsara. For this he was politely asked to leave the country, but finally his misdeeds had been forgotten and he had returned with Sherri, a born-again dancer whom he'd met hitchhiking her way out of Las Vegas. By the time they'd reached Los Angeles, he'd converted her to Raj Yoga, married her, and they had now been living quietly in Terripur for almost a year. Sherri's satin skin, amazing breasts, and lithe hips undulating under thin silk pajamas caused old Kuldip Singh to purse his lips and make sucking sounds under his twitching mustache.

Another vehicle in the drive at Prospect Point that evening was a cream-colored Ambassador belonging to Shri Ramakrishna Rao, a Chief Secretary in the Government of India. The son of one of Kamala's father's diwans, Rao, as a young boy, had displayed signs of extraordinary intelligence and was sent abroad to Harrow and Cambridge. It was a farseeing move, for when he later returned to join Nehru's Congress Party, he remained loyal to Kamala's father and was now the family's main connection with the court of Indira Gandhi. A tall, imposing man with a hawklike nose, sensual lips, and an implacable poker face, his head was securely fastened to his body by a thick brontosaurian neck. His wife, Saraswati, a large Iyer Brahmin woman from Madras with steel-gray hair, had attended Radcliffe College and preferred living in Washington, where Rao had been with the World Bank. Although they didn't grumble about being back in India, they hinted privately to Kamala they believed the country was falling apart and advised her to buy more property abroad, preferably in Italy, where they had just acquired an apartment house.

Perhaps the most unlikely conveyance to be found in the gravel drive that night was the hand-pulled rickshaw that had transported young Hari Marwari, the Bombay billionaire, and his wife, Nita, from the Ritz to Prospect Point. Although the Ritz was a short walk, it was too far for Hari, who weighed nearly three hundred pounds. In fact, it was rumored that in the bedroom of his Bombay penthouse a special sling or harness suspended from the ceiling had been devised so he could copulate without crushing his partners. He appeared dressed in dark-blue polyester pants, a white shirt open at the neck, white socks, and cheap black heavy-soled Indian shoes. His almost featureless head sat on a bull neck, and, as he talked, surprisingly delicate hands fluttered before him. Although most of his conversation was about money, Kamala liked Hari because he refused to be serious in a world of grim happenings and was notoriously generous.

Nita, his wife, had just given birth to a baby boy, which pleased Hari immensely, not only because he now had a son and heir but because, according to the custom of his community, which permitted only one child to be fathered on each wife, she could now be set up in a separate establishment with hired lovers to please her, freeing Hari for his next marriage. No doubt, Nita would be relieved to get all that weight off her chest and go on to more interesting liaisons, or so the gossips said. As much of Kamala's wealth was in real estate, objets d'art, and jewels, which sometimes had to wait to be sold to an appropriate buyer, Hari came in handy as a source of ready cash. And though she'd been initially horrified by his appearance (even Sonny's friend Kirpan was more presentable), she had soon come to enjoy Hari and delighted in introducing him to stuffy people like the Raos, who looked down on the Marwari community as a pack of thieving gypsies.

Next to the rickshaw, and the sleeping wallahs who pulled it, were parked two Harley-Davidson motorcycles which belonged to Rez-wand Bey, prince of a former Muslim state, and his husky friend Chuck Davis from Vancouver, British Columbia. Rezwand Bey, tall, swarthy, with hard eyes, a haughty Persian nose, and a cruel mouth, had attended the same schools as Sanjay Gandhi and was credited with leading him astray into the sybaritic world of criminal types with whom he'd surrounded himself before his untimely death. It was said the Canadian was either his accomplice, flunky, or sometime lover. Rezwand's mother had been a close friend of Kamala's, and he was there because she knew if ever she found herself in desperate straits, needed to threaten anyone or have him removed, Rezwand would know how to do it.

Yet another car, with discreet maroon curtains and license plates indicating it belonged to a Minister of State, glided up the drive. The occupant who emerged from it and lumbered up the steps attired in cream-colored silk kurta pajamas and velvet slippers was none other than Anand, the great Indian film hero. Kamala had known him since the war years when his father, a Tamil cameraman, was in charge of a newsreel crew and Anand was a child of ten or eleven. By fifteen he was playing the boy Krishna in his father's postwar religious epics, which caught the imagination of the devout and catapulted Anand into national prominence. Since then he had played Rama, Brahma, Vishnu, and Shiva, and whole sections of the populace were certain he was actually a god. When he visited a temple, villagers from miles around would come to glimpse him, and women, hoping to attract his attention, would swoon, roll in the dust, and pretend to have, or really have, ecstatic religious experiences. As he grew too old and fat for hero roles, instead of retiring or taking minor parts, he entered politics and immediately became a force to reckon with. Like the American film personality Ronald Reagan, Anand appealed to fundamentalists and religious fanatics, who were making a big comeback in Hindu India. Struck by the size of his constituency, which included not only templegoers but millions of film fans, the ruling party had managed to neutralize him by appealing to his vanity and creating a cabinet post he could not refuse.

"How clever," drawled Raja Kuldip Singh, standing with Kamala as Anand entered the drawing room.

Kamala loved to stand back and watch people who'd heard about each other, but never met, meet face to face. She was especially amused by the reaction of Kuldip's wife, Sylvia, a good head taller than her husband, who now stretched and preened, hoping to attract the attention of Anand. Raja Kuldip had had a long succession of Sylvias (beginning in Oxford) and, fancying himself a photographer, had taken romantic pictures of them, all in various stages of undress, which hung in the Louis XVI dressing room of his Terripur villa. As he was quite blind without his glasses, which he rarely wore, the Rani was able to flirt openly, which she did now with Anand, parting her truly carnal lips, moistening them with her tongue as she spoke, and gazing hotly into his famous dark eyes. Kamala was highly amused.

Now an old MG arrived, driven by a thin young woman in a lemon-yellow sari. Haltingly, it jerked and rattled up the drive and coughed to a stop. Accompanied by a fat young man in white kurta pajamas carrying a long white scarf with a gold design worked into it, the young woman climbed out and ascended the steps. The man was the famous Urdu poet Akbar, who had lived most of his life in Paris, where he was considered a genius by French literati. The young woman, her features set in a permanent expression of desperation, was attempting to repair a life savaged by a sadistic husband. Eira was her name, a princess from Bengal, poetess of sorts and graduate of Shantiniketan. Her arranged marriage had not worked out and she had run away to an ashram near Hardwar, which did charitable work among the hill women of the area. Kamala had met her while raising money for the same organization and, sharing a mutual concern for the plight of hill women and the ecological decimation of the Himalayas, they had become close friends.

If the façade of Prospect Point looked as though it had seen better days, in contrast the interior was well preserved. Polished marble and parquet floors reflected the glitter of carved ceilings encrusted with gold. Rare porcelains were displayed in lighted niches, the ceilings were painted with frescoes à la Fragonard, and original Louis XV furniture covered with glorious petit-point tapestry—sky blue, pea green, cream, pink, and mauve—matched the tones in the Aubusson carpets. There were six-foot-high Sèvres urns on pedestals of gesso and gilt, marble busts of Kamala's ancestors, and magnificent marquetry cabinets with gold ormolu fittings. The main drawing room was dominated by an enormous fireplace with a mantel of gilded bronze containing the family crest and cupids astride elephants whose golden trunks arched gracefully into a mirror above.


IT WAS toward this setting, then, that David and Philippa, last of the guests to arrive, now made their way, past the collection of vehicles and lounging drivers to the upper terrace.

Feeling they needed the exercise, they had walked over from General Bobby's house. A light mist had begun to fall and they had worn their tweeds, Burberry raincoats, and walking shoes. A servant opened the door for them, and two liveried footmen showed them through the marble foyer toward the drawing room.

"You should have told me it would be this sort of evening," whispered Philippa. "I feel like an old sheepdog."

David, in his baggiest tweed suit, coughed and looked around. "Doesn't look that fancy to me," he muttered. "The invitation said 'informal.'"

Just then, Kamala appeared at the drawing-room door. Extending both her hands, she betrayed no sign that she had ever seen David before. "You must be Captain and Mrs. Bruce." She smiled. "I was beginning to think you might have lost your way."

"We walked over," said Philippa, shaking the dew from her blond mane. "I'm afraid we didn't dress."

"Nonsense, my son is wearing jeans." Kamala laughed. "These days we don't worry about those things."

Sumitra made her way across the room, and Kamala quickly introduced them. David was terrified Sumitra would let on they'd already met, but accustomed by now to her mother's intrigues, Sumitra was charmingly poker-faced and, after a few pleasantries, excused herself to make sure her brother did not mess things up. Obviously, the attractive blond wife was not supposed to know her husband had been round earlier. Whatever it was Mummy was hiding, it would certainly be better not to make waves, not now anyhow. Was Mummy interested in Captain David Bruce? She couldn't blame her. An older man in good condition was hard to find. But the wife looked as though she could put up a good fight. Perhaps while Mummy and Mrs. Bruce were dueling, she would move in. Sonny was right, he did look like what's his name . . . Fox.

"You mustn't let on you've seen Captain Bruce before," she murmured to her brother. "That's them over there. For some reason, Mummy's pretending she's never met him."

"Ah, you mean Foxy James? Yes, yes. Do you think they're old lovers and don't want the wife to know? Damned beautiful woman except for the clothes and those awful shoes. Gawd!" Sonny arched his eyebrows.

Sumitra drifted back to her mother and the Bruces.

"Captain Bruce, you may not remember but we have met before," Kamala was saying.

This remark caught David by surprise. "Really? When could that have been?" he said blandly. "Do you often get to England?"

"I'm afraid it was a very long time ago, but we were at a wedding together. You were in the groom's party, I was with the bride. Madho Dev Singh was the groom."

"Ah," exclaimed David, striking his forehead. "Of course, what an odd coincidence." Why was she going on like this? he wondered, hoping the worst was over.

A waiter came with drinks. Philippa was amused the two of them felt it necessary to carry on this little deception. Poor things, they must have been very much in love. Had Kamala told David about their daughter? Obviously not. Her estimate of Kamala rose.

Sonny sidled over with Anand in tow. "Anandji," he drawled before his mother could introduce them, "I want you to meet Mr. James Fox, I'm sure you've seen his films. Mr. Fox, Anandji is probably our most well-known, well-loved Indian film star."

Anand extended a limp ministerial hand. "You have just finished shooting *Passage to India* in Kashmir, I believe; hope all is going well with the film. If there's anything I can do to help, just ring me up."

"Sonny," cried Kamala, "you're being very naughty. Anandji, Sonny is a bad boy. This is not James Fox, this is Captain and Mrs. Bruce. They are friends of General Bhupinder Singh and staying at his house here."

"Mmm," said Anand, grinning mirthlessly at Sonny. "But he's right, sir, you could stand in for Mr. Fox. You ought to ask David Lean for a job."

"I'll do that." David smiled. "Sounds amusing. By the way, I've seen several of your films, liked them very much."

Anand brightened and puffed out his chest. "Films aren't what they once were, too much violence; these days the public is only interested in stories about dacoits and rickshaw wallahs."

"But you gods are immortal!" cried Kamala. Anand smiled slyly at her. "And here are two people who certainly appreciate the gods." She introduced Ron and Sherri, who were hovering nearby. Having learned it paid to be remembered by powerful politicians, Ron bowed low and touched Anand's feet. The great star pretended to be embarrassed. Kamala told everyone how she'd met Ron and Sherri when one of her tiger cubs escaped. Anand related some of his experiences with tigers in movie making, and Kuldip Singh, a famous hunter of the old school, added a few tales of his own. Philippa was tempted to tell them about Durga Baba and his tigers but realized no one would believe her.

Ramakrishna Rao and his wife now edged into the group, and Kamala introduced them to Philippa and David.

"Well, sir, and what is your opinion of India after forty years?" asked Rao in the kind of pompous parliamentary voice Kamala despised.

"Actually, I haven't formed any opinion yet; just arrived, you might say. But it's nice to be back. Generally things don't seem to have changed that much." David realized instantly it was the wrong thing to have said, for Ramakrishna Rao's lips tightened, his chin jutted forward, and he rattled off a stream of statistics about life expectancy, literacy, and manufacturing accompanied by a monologue from his wife on how taxation by the British Raj had ruined India economically, a plight from which the country was just now recovering. A number of allusions were made to Cambridge, Radcliffe, and Harvard, so that there should be no doubt in anyone's mind that the bona fides of the Raos were of the highest order, their opinions not to be disputed.

"Mrs. Bruce is the one whose impressions you should get, Raoji," broke in Kamala. "She has an absolutely fresh eye."

Everyone looked expectantly at Philippa. She panicked. Her impressions of India would finish her with these people. She smiled vaguely. "I thought there would be more elephants," she said. "Actually I've seen only two."

Rao and his wife greeted her observation with stony-faced silence, and Kamala was momentarily nonplused. Was this woman stupid or just putting them on?

Kuldip Singh's mustache quivered and his little eyes twinkled. "I say, quite right, quite right. I think you're marvelous; that's exactly what I miss too." He took Philippa's arm and spirited her away. "Do you really like tuskers? I'm mad for them."

"Adore them," replied Philippa. "Most wonderful creatures."

"Would you like to see some? There are about twenty-five of them in the forests just below here. We could go in my jeep." He looked urgently up at her. "I think you're smashing. Say yes and you won't regret it."

"You mean safari," said Philippa in her most innocent voice. "That sounds like great fun."

"Ah, yes, it would be fun," whispered Kuldip conspiratorially. "I'd make sure of that." He winked. "I'll show you things about elephants you won't believe." And he launched into a monologue about elephants he had known.

Half listening, Philippa surveyed the room and, following her gaze, Kuldip broke off his discourse.

"You'd better watch that husband of yours. These women are cutthroats." He giggled. "Absolute budmahshes when it comes to men. I ought to know, one of them's mine."

A voice with a French accent interrupted him. It was the poet, Akbar. "Kuldip, *mon vieux*, you are monopolizing this lovely lady. I insist you present me." He flashed a smile at Philippa. "Don't believe a word he tells you, madame; he's one of our naughtiest princes, aren't you, Kuldip?"

"You must not listen to him," protested Kuldip. "I should not introduce you to this man; he's extremely subversive: calls himself an Indian and doesn't even live here." They both laughed. "May I present Akbar, my dear Mrs. Bruce." Akbar nodded genially. "I'm told he's a great poet. I wouldn't know, gave up reading that stuff years ago. Now I only read books about animals."

"Brain-damaged," replied Akbar, shaking his head. "Mrs. Bruce, I should like you to meet Eira Kumari from Calcutta." Philippa liked Eira's look and thought she seemed to radiate an unusual quality of calmness—or was it tension? "I've persuaded Eira to come to Terripur," went on the poet, "so that she can see with her own eyes the destruction going on with this dreadful mining business. Doesn't the government know one of the most beautiful spots in India is being ruined?"

"My dear fellow." Kuldip Singh laughed. "The government doesn't know anything. What government? If you'd spent any time in your own country, you'd know that."

"But really, Kuldip," Akbar went on, "you live here; why aren't you involved in stopping it? That's why I brought Eira along tonight. She's at an ashram near Hardwar, deeply involved in the ecology movement."

"But that's marvelous!" cried Philippa. "So you actually have an ecological group going?"

"Yes, yes," cried the neurasthenic Eira. "Akbar is too modest, he's one of the organizing hands behind it: the first person to make me aware of what is going on. I hadn't the faintest idea until he pointed out how the forests are being cut down before our very eyes, the Ganga polluted. Now I'm almost afraid to use a match—and as for paper, I'm ashamed to even think of it!"

Rezwand Bey and his friend Chuck, guided by Kamala, now joined the ecological discussion. Like a crustacean which, after extending its tender body, suddenly retreats, Eira, who knew the history of every prince in India, withdrew behind a masklike smile.

"The basic damage was actually done in British times," observed Kuldip Singh. "I am old enough to remember it. There were lumber contractors, British fellows, who paid off the local rajas and landowners, cut the trees, and floated them down the rivers during the rainy season."

"Who's that chap that looks like a film star?" asked Eira, changing the subject.

"That is Captain David Bruce, this charming lady's husband," purred Kamala. "I'm not sure whether she'd let me introduce you to him."

Eira looked nervously at Philippa.

"On the contrary, it's flattering when others are attracted to one's mate, don't you agree?" Philippa focused on Kamala.

What exactly was she saying? Kamala wondered. Was Philippa aware of her relationship with David? She looked across the room to where David was still talking with Sylvia Singh. But now Sumitra had her hand on his shoulder, hanging on every word. Kamala tried to remain calm, but seeing her daughter make a spectacle of herself was too infuriating. She was thinking of an excuse to divert Sumitra when suddenly the lights began to flicker and abruptly went out.

David had been discussing hotels in Switzerland with Sylvia Singh, aware of Sumitra's hand resting lightly on his shoulder and wondering what to do about it, when the lights went out. In the moment of absolute blackness that followed, soft lips pressed against his neck. Then someone lit a match, the lips were gone, and soon the servants brought in candles. He wished a wind would come up and blow them out again.

He smiled at Sumitra. "Does the voltage vary a lot here?" he asked.

"A lot," she said mischievously. "Every evening at eight o'clock the coolies fall off the treadmill." He watched her lips move and wanted to kiss them.

A servant with a mauve turban announced dinner, and Kamala led the way into the Chinese dining room with its purple-silk walls and Chippendale furniture. Why do rich English women wear such baggy clothes? she wondered, glancing down the table at Philippa as she sat down between Cabinet Minister Anand and the American new-age seeker, Ron.

Opposite them, Sonny sat morosely sipping the wine that had been served with the soup. His mother had placed him between pretentious Sylvia Singh and dreary Saraswati Rao. No doubt Mummy's idea had been to isolate him from foxy David Bruce. In fact, as he was on the same side of the table at the opposite end, he couldn't even see the handsome captain, whereas his nymphomaniacal sister, seated next to that tiresome American, Ron, could see David Bruce very well, hadn't taken her big cow eyes off him.

Mrs. Rao made some remark to him about how good the wine was and asked whether it was the same Chardonnay she got in Delhi for two hundred rupees on the black market. Sonny glanced at her disdainfully. What a primitive! To think that women like that, a pack of female chimpanzees, were ruling the country through their useless husbands. His mind shifted to getting out of India. Perhaps Kirpan was right and they should sell the trucking business and leave—which brought him to the subject that was really driving him berserk: Kirpan was not at the dinner table. Mummy flatly refused to have him there because he made so much noise eating. It was too cruel. He liked Kirpan's noises, especially when he yelled Punjabi obscenities in bed. Sonny swallowed a spoonful of soup, the same tasteless gruel he'd been eating now for years, and put down his spoon. If only he had the nerve to throw his soup at his sister, that would stop her roving eyes.

He scorched her with a sidelong glance and turned his attention to Mrs. Bruce across the table. She reminded him of some blonde he'd seen at the British Consul Library's old film show several years back. Poor Mrs. Bruce looked as bored as he was. All the interesting people—Rezwand Bey, Chuck, David Bruce—were on his side of the table and miles away where he couldn't see them.

One of the servants standing against the wall winked at him, a good-looking boy called Srini, bastard son of one of the maids, who had just spent three years as an assistant cook in the army. They'd grown up together, and when Srini finished his army service he'd returned to work for them. Sonny thought Srini was cute and winked back.


ACROSS the table, Akbar thought the wink was meant for him and directed his coldest stare toward Sonny. Just because the boy was royal, he felt he had the right to behave outrageously, always throwing out shards of gossip about one's private life. Akbar glanced over at Saraswati Rao's fat little hands. Why had Kamala invited this intolerably boring woman and her husband? Just because she'd gone to an American university and lived in Washington didn't mean she was important. And all the time, mouthing that socialist jargon—Marx and Engels—which she'd obviously committed to memory and rattled off like a mockingbird when the occasion arose. Even the Russians no longer believed it. But people thought her a great intellectual. He, Akbar, thought her a contemptible fake. If she believed all this socialist slop, why did she never journey to the villages that suffered under her husband's administration? Even Eira was more liberal than this parrot, and Eira was a princess. . . . Princess Renunciate, something to write poetry about.

He turned to Sumitra. "And how is Paris these days?" he asked her.

"Awesome," she replied. "I've just taken a small studio on the far side of Montmartre and started painting. You must come visit me sometime. I have a new French boyfriend. French men are such fantastic lovers."

"I think your mother should find you a husband soon," said Akbar.

Sumitra giggled. "You think I'd let Mummy choose a husband for me? You must be mad. She's very unlucky with men, no sense at all."

"You're looking for a love marriage then?" asked Akbar.

"I'm looking for ecstasy." Sumitra sighed. "Love is a worn-out word. I want something more."

Ugh! thought Akbar.

The fish course had come and gone, a chicken course had been served, and now a roast was being brought in; red wine was poured into fresh glasses.

"And there I was, waiting on my elephant," Kamala was saying. "The tiger was wounded, you see, and my mahout was nervous. Suddenly the beast leapt out of the bamboo thicket, straightaway onto my mount's trunk, which it raked with its huge claws. My elephant reared; its scream was deafening. Mind you, I had never shot a tiger before; I was just sixteen. 'Shoot, shoot!' yelled my father. The tiger was not three meters away. I pulled the trigger, and . . ."

Akbar had heard this story over and over, in every princely drawing room across India. Obviously Kamala was making conversation to impress the Englishman. Why were they so keen on shooting harmless wild animals? Sex frustration, no doubt. If he shot anything, it would be people, the worst animals of all.


KAMALA finished her story and had even Ramakrishna Rao laughing—or at least smiling, for of course, as a Brahmin, hunting was not for him. Brahmins were above all that. For years Rao had watched his father contend with the antics of Kamala's domineering father. As last diwan of the state, his father's role had been to mediate between the British Resident and the Raja, and he had profited by keeping the Raja weakened by whatever means necessary; liquor, drugs, young boys and girls. And when the British left, the Congress Party became the Raj. Except for the habits of a people to whom democracy was foreign, if not distasteful and downright common, he doubted this

would have happened. Yes, it was the people of India who had made
the Congress Party into an autocratic organization.

KAMALA gazed down the table to where Anand was holding forth
with Philippa, and her mind wandered. What lay beneath the com-
posed expression of this beautiful Englishwoman? Somewhere inside
she sensed a certain duplicity: the slightly petulant expression at the
corners of the mouth, a certain suppression of natural feeling. One
tended to take these blue-eyed blondes at face value, but she had
learned that might be a mistake. Her innocent-looking English gov-
erness, for example: prim and correct, whom no one ever suspected of
having an illicit thought in her pretty golden head, until she became
pregnant and it came out that for years she had been having an affair
with a neighboring raja. Since then, she'd never really trusted blond
women. On the other hand, blond men might be different. Although
she'd been carrying on an animated conversation with him all through
dinner, she hadn't really looked at David so much as felt his nearness.
Emotions that had been buried for years had surfaced and were
oscillating back and forth between her heart and mind. What a cata-
logue of self-deceptions! Could a new relationship start up between
them, and at what cost? Until last week she thought she was finished
with love and had reached a calm plateau that would extend into old
age. Now she wondered. Was marriage for companionship still a
possibility? Certainly not for any other reason. And the man should
be amusing. People who could see the amusing side of life, the bright
side, had become terribly important to her. But David was certainly
not what one would call amusing. Men who were physically attractive
rarely were. Like registered bulls, they were much too concerned
with their bodies and satisfying their own drives to see the diverting side of life. Akbar, for example, was diverting. How delightful
it was to spend lazy afternoons with him, sipping iced tea, playing
backgammon, and giggling over the latest indiscretions of their
friends.

WHILE Kamala observed her guests, Raja Kuldip Singh shouted
across her at David, trying to pin him down on a date for an outing to
the Siwalik Hills where they could observe a herd of elephants and the
raja might see more of Philippa. The dinner had ended with a superb
mango fool, a sort of zabaglione made from mangoes and egg whites,
and a brilliant Château d'Yquem. As he pretended to listen earnestly

to the old raja, David's knee brushed her thigh under the table. Kamala thought it very naughty of him and, feeling distracted and confused, rose, signaling the end of dinner, and led the ladies to the Persian retiring room, an exquisite chamber inlaid with colored glass and mirrors where they would have coffee and gossip before rejoining the men.

Assuming his dubious role as male head of the family, Sonny conducted the men to the Moroccan room, a large library designed by his great-uncle, its walls covered with scarlet leather embossed with gold crests, its furnishings of fine teak inlaid with ivory, enameled screens, and silver hookahs, all of which the late raja had brought back to India from Marrakesh on one of his famous shopping sprees. There were elephant tusks above the massive pink marble fireplace and priceless carpets on the floors; standing around the cavernous room, poised to attack, stuffed tigers, leopards, and other wild animals glared out of glass eyes.

And here was Kirpan, who had not been allowed at dinner, making excuses that he had got tied up with business on the phone. Never mind, thought Sonny, didn't the Christians say the meek would inherit the earth?

At the bar, Kirpan dispensed brandy and cigars and fiddled with the sound system, a new addition that he and Sonny had installed. Kirpan kept up with the latest music and liked David Bowie, Michael Jackson, Prince, Queen, and Cyndi Lauper, whose hit song "Money Changes Everything" now blasted forth from the 500-watt system he'd smuggled in from Hong Kong.

Kuldip Singh, distracted by the raucous rock queen, yelled over the music and cast dark looks in Kirpan's direction. He considered rock and roll barbaric and longed for the gentle strains of Paul Whiteman and his orchestra.

Hari Marwari joined them, rocking his three hundred pounds to the beat. "These Americans are so clever," he cried. "Imagine a song about money."

Raja Kuldip looked through him as though he did not exist. Ramakrishna Rao had pulled up a chair, interrupting Kuldip's chatter, and begun asking David about conditions in England.

"It's this music that drives them mad in the West, don't you agree?" shouted Rao.

"But you must listen to the words," yelled Hari, swaying back and forth.

"Can't understand a thing," croaked Rao. "These rockers have such ghastly accents."

"I will translate for you." Hari grinned. "This one is very simple. 'Money, money, money—money changes everything,'" he yelled maliciously, knowing full well it was what the Raos never had enough of, that in fact they had been borrowing heavily against their real estate in Delhi and Bombay.

"Rather cynical," shouted David. "I can think of a number of things money doesn't buy."

"For one thing," yelled Rao, "it can't make a silk purse out of a sow's ear."

But the hapless Hari, blissfully ignorant of the intended slur, danced across the room.

The double doors opened and Philippa followed Kamala into the library. In the Persian room Kamala had questioned her casually about Kotagarh, what Arjun's children looked like, and whether he and Gayatri were happy. A silly charade, thought Philippa, since she was certain Madho Dev and Kamala kept in touch.

"I'm not really qualified to comment," she had replied, "but from what I've seen I'd say their life was rather traditional."

"At one time Dev and Devika were quite modern," said Kamala. "Now it seems they've reverted."

"Protective coloring, perhaps," Philippa replied. "They keep a fire burning in a pit, and before each meal a plateful of food is tossed onto it."

"Sacrifice." Kamala nodded. "They must be expecting the worst."

Philippa told her about the three young Sikhs who had shown up at Madho Dev's and what had happened to them.

"More government bungling," said Kamala, wide-eyed. "People like Ramakrishna Rao will never understand the Sikhs. What is needed is better communication between the two sides. Communication, ha!" She laughed. "My phone has not worked for two weeks; can you imagine, in the twentieth century? I employ three young men who do nothing but run here and there with messages."

Sumitra and Sherri came giggling into the library and began dancing together. When Kirpan saw them, he turned the volume even higher. Sumitra admired Sherri's open frankness, her lack of bullshit. Bullshit was a word she'd picked up in Paris from her new boyfriend, Roland. It expressed perfectly her feelings about the hypocrisy of India, which she and her friends hated and blamed on the older generation of Victorian ladies—like Mrs. Ramakrishna Rao, whom she saw staring lugubriously at her from across the room. To Sumitra, Saraswati Rao was a perfect example of the bullshit that had engulfed India: her tiresome gold-bordered saris, her lumpy arms covered with gold bangles, her fat little feet that poked out from sandals she boasted she never wore twice.

Ron cut in to dance with Sherri, and Sumitra winked at Kirpan, who was now rather drunk. Kirpan's muscular body gyrated erotically in front of her. She writhed seductively up to him. With Eira in his arms, the former film star Anand fox-trotted out onto the floor, head raised high, his doglike jowls drooping. The emaciated Eira broke away from him and danced in her own space, twirling like some possessed dervish, her diamond necklace glittering.

"I just called to say I love you," crooned the inimitable Stevie Wonder.

Sumitra closed her eyes and was back in Régine's with Roland. How she loved the freedom of Paris, of Europe: running naked on the beach at Saint-Tropez, driving to Zurich at two hundred kilometers an hour while Roland called ahead on his new cellular phone for dinner reservations. There, now Captain Bruce was watching her; would he dance? Her mother's back was toward her. She winked at him, turned and worked her hips, spun round, and saw his eyes following her as she gyrated toward Kirpan. Then, unexpectedly, Captain and Mrs. Bruce were dancing together. They both knew the latest steps. He danced like Roland and Mrs. Bruce was even better, an interesting revelation. She noticed her mother gazing with veiled eyes at Captain Bruce and recognized her hungry look. Someone switched back to "Girls Just Want to Have Fun," and now they were all dancing in a circle. Anand paired off with Mrs. Bruce, everyone switched partners, and suddenly Sumitra found herself dancing opposite the captain. She reined herself in and danced as sedately as she could. He danced with his feet spread apart, his loins rocking against the push and thrust of his torso. Inside those baggy tweeds lurked an educated body. She could tell he wanted her. Ah, yes, and if the occasion arose, she would go for it. "Go for it," that was another of Roland's expressions. "Go for it, baby," he would whisper as they were approaching a climax together. If Roland were here now, would she be thinking of going for it with Captain David? How well had her mother known him? How close had they been? Why had he come to Terripur, and why were they deceiving Mrs. Bruce?

David wished someone would turn off the music. He hadn't danced like this in months and found it exhausting. And now Sumitra was licking her lips most provocatively so that he had to turn away before he lost control. Her hot pink mouth. That greedy little tongue . . . ah, the hunger there! "Girls just want to have fun, fun, fun." She twirled and bounced in front of him, her breasts churning above sumptuous hips. To be suddenly awakened by this youngster was too painful. The pitilessness of her stare frightened him. Yet what a magnificent animal! Like some priapic satyr, he longed to chase this voluptuous nymph out into the Indian night and ravish her.

Kirpan had turned the volume so high even Raja Kuldip Singh had been driven to dance and was attempting to spin Kamala around the room. "Born in the USAaaaaaaa." Kamala struggled in his arms and watched David. Where had he learned to dance like that? How antiquated it made her feel. The rest of the world changed but not India, no, never. In the West, women her age were still young, but not here: here where there had already been three hundred bride burnings this year in Delhi alone, wives doused with petrol and set on fire; here where husbands refused to let their women see doctors, where there were no gynecologists worth the name. No wonder most Indian women were finished at thirty-five. But look at Philippa: of course, she was much younger, but every man in the room was watching her.

The lights flickered and went out again. The music died, and there were sighs and giggles while they waited for the servants to come with the candles. David felt a panting body against his and realized Sumitra was clinging to him. She smelled of patchouli and perspiration. He reached down and brought her lips to his.

"Hasn't anyone a torch?" Kamala cried, "Sonny, are all the servants drunk? Do something!"

David felt Sumitra's hand slide around his waist.

"When will I see you again?" he whispered. "I must see you."

"It's very difficult," she said breathlessly. "Someone is always watching, but I'll think of something and send word."

A dim glow appeared in the corridor. Sumitra broke away and, when the candelabras came through the doorway, was talking with Eira.

Clever girl, thought David. He felt good about trusting her to arrange something. Outside, thunder was rolling and torrents of warm rain poured down. During the monsoon, he recalled, one was supposed to write poetry, make music, and exhaust oneself in making love. Volumes had been written about it. He had sweated profusely, his shirt was soaking wet, and now his loins were aching like a schoolboy's. Walking stiffly to Philippa's side, he made excuses about its having been a long day and suggested they leave.

Kamala observed Philippa, released smiling and flushed from the arms of the great Anand, her blue eyes sparkling, the pupils like ice picks, stabbing out at you, and envied and despised her. Envied, because she would be leaving in the arms of David, arms she had nestled in long before there had ever been a Philippa in his life; despised, because she felt Philippa had never had to cope with life's problems and was spoiled, willful, selfish, and hadn't really made David happy. But then, she asked herself, could any one woman have made such a man happy?

He extended his hand, caught hold of hers artfully, kissed it, and looked up just in time to catch her eyes smiling wistfully. "You must come dine with us very soon," he said. "We'll arrange something. We must see a lot of each other. It's been a smashing evening, haven't danced like that in years."

Kamala kissed both their cheeks. Ramakrishna Rao came up and offered them a lift home. Footmen with large umbrellas were dispatching the other guests. Kamala stood in the doorway with Sumitra beside her. Sumitra, her arms folded about herself as if she were frantically hanging on to something, looked as though she were going to be sick.

# 13

THE STORM THAT BEGAN after Princess Kamala's dinner party became a deluge. On the mountain above Terripur, General Bobby's house was engulfed in a hushed green shroud. Surprising ferns unfurled. Giant crimson-topped mushrooms shot up through the lawns, lavender wood orchids and blue datura plants burst into bloom, hedgerows of ganja seemed to materialize overnight, and the huge gray monkeys, usually so mischievous, crouched silently in the thickest trees. Mornings merged into afternoons which expired into evenings of sepulchral gloom that seemed neverending. Ravi brought pot after pot of tea, cooked, drew hot water for baths, and got up later each day. Philippa wrote letters and soon exhausted Bobby's scant supply of readable books; David, between massages from Ravi, went into hibernation.

Then came a morning when Ravi tiptoed into her room with the tea tray, pulled back the curtains, and the sun streamed in. Philippa was so astounded she jumped out of bed and, without waiting for her bath, dressed and ran to the front door. Mists rose from the valley below, where the sound of water cascading down the mountainsides echoed through the vastness; to the east the Himalayan peaks, dazzling with new snow, shimmered in a rain-washed sky.

"You think it will last?" she asked Ravi, who stood beside her with the tea tray.

"It might, madam, but who can tell?"

"I'm going to the bazaar," she announced impulsively. "If I don't get out of this house and stretch my legs, I'll go mad. I've masses of letters to post and I'd like to get some books from the library."

"You must find the librarian first," said Ravi dubiously. "Her name is Mrs. Patton, she lives near the library. Just ask anybody. And you'd best take an umbrella, no telling when it will start up again."

Philippa drank her tea standing up. "Is sahib awake?"

"No, ma'am, shall I wake him?"

"Let him sleep, he must be very tired. I've never seen anyone who could sleep so much. How long has this been going on?"

"Five, six days, ma'am, I'm not sure."

"I'm not sure either." Philippa smiled, putting on her raincoat. "Well, when he wakes up, tell him not to expect me for lunch. I'll be back this afternoon."

Ravi stood at the door, a quizzical smile on his lips, and watched her evaporate like a ghost into the sun-bright mist. Who in their right mind would want to be walking around in this kind of weather if they didn't have to?

Underfoot the ground was spongy, and Philippa walked slowly, skirting potholes in the road. As she rounded the mountain and descended toward the town, the disgusting odor of onions and bug spray drifted up in warm damp clouds. Halfway down, she came upon a crowd of people yelling and moaning. In the pervasive dampness, the walls of an ancient three-story building had collapsed. Women screamed while several youths stepped gingerly over the rubble, trying to locate victims trapped inside. Farther on, the gray forms of half-naked coolies, some mere children, huddled in corners under rain-soaked gunnysacks. Making her way around piles of refuse and puddles of mustard-colored excrement, past clutches of Tibetans squatting on the ground selling cheap machine-made polyester sweaters in ugly colors, she emerged at last from the labyrinthine maze of lanes onto the Mall. The library was at the other end, a long walk as she remembered, and she would have liked to sit down and rest, but where? The only places to sit were the grimy tea shops filled with staring men.

Rickshaw wallahs stood in wet cotton undershorts under pieces of plastic wrapped around their shoulders. Some pleaded softly, others yelled at her to command their services. But she could not bring herself to sit down in one of those conveyances and be pulled along by other human beings doing the work of animals. What was in the minds and hearts of the fat, haughty, overdressed men and women who rode in these conveyances with their equally fat piglike children? Even more interesting, what must have been the state of mind of her great-grandfather and his friends, who had not only been pulled by ancestors of these men but had dressed them up like trained monkeys in fancy clothes with epaulettes and plumed turbans in pastel shades? Was there something she was missing? There had to be something. Did these men think of themselves as human, did they have any form of self-consciousness at all? What was the reason for all this subservience?

"We are all blind in India," she remembered Eira Kumari saying at Kamala's dinner. "We live in the world of the unseen."

Finally reaching the end of the Mall, she looked around. About fifty coolies in rags were lounging against the famous gate, beyond which vehicular traffic was forbidden, smoking bidis or opium and waiting to carry luggage.

The three-story Victorian building David had pointed out as the library stood opposite a square, its wrought-iron porches and grill-work nearly hidden beneath a veneer of ugly painted signs in garish pinks, tomato reds, and sickly greens. At the top she could barely discern, embossed in the ironwork, the words TERRIPUR LIBRARY, 1872. But where was it? The ground-floor level was given over to shops selling foodstuffs, cheap cosmetics, and the inevitable betel nut. She wondered where the library itself might be and asked at one of the shops, but no one spoke English. Finally she found herself shouting the name of Mrs. Patton, the woman Ravi had mentioned, was waved in the direction of a small lane that branched off a few yards away, and soon arrived at a crumbling replica of an English seaside cottage. Perhaps this Mrs. Patton would ask her in for a cup of tea—she certainly could use one—and to sit down for a moment. She started to open the gate of the fenced-in yard and was immediately driven back by a pack of small, yapping mongrels.

"Who? What?" came a strident voice, and the liverish face of an old woman with small piglike eyes and a head of wildly disheveled orange-tinted hair peered out. "What is it?" she cried menacingly. "Who's there?" The door opened wide. Battered open-toed pumps and feet clad in pink ankle socks supported two skinny legs laced with varicose veins. Above them a soiled calico chemise covered a huge sagging body. The apparition left Philippa speechless. "Well?" screeched the woman over the din of yapping dogs. "What do you want?"

"I'm looking for a Mrs. Patton," Philippa shouted back. "I've been told to see the librarian. I want to visit the library and take out a few books. I'm here in Terripur for several months, and time weighs heavily in this weather."

"Not possible." The woman grunted and spat in a drain near the stoop.

"Not possible?" repeated Philippa incredulously.

"You must make an application and obtain references from three Terripur property owners. If you run off with the books, someone must be responsible."

"Well, I certainly shan't run off with any books, as you say. Are you sure it's not possible for me to just go inside the library and see if there are any books I might like to take out before going to all the trouble of making an application?"

It began to rain again, and Philippa struggled to open her umbrella. The dogs, excited by the sudden movement, began to jump up at her from behind the fence.

"Only by appointment," screeched the woman.

"What was that?" cried Philippa.

"Appointment, appointment!"

"Well then, may I make an appointment for later this afternoon, say two o'clock or half past? I've come all the way from General Bhupinder Singh's house. It's taken me three hours. Please, I'm really exhausted."

"Only on Tuesdays and Thursdays," the woman yelled. "This is Wednesday." A smug look of having won spread over her ravaged face. "You can call for an appointment. I will try and fit you in."

"My telephone is out of order," replied Philippa. "Can't we make an appointment now?"

"Your telephone is none of my affair." The woman sniffed. "Call for an appointment, that is the rule, or send your servant with a note."

Philippa couldn't believe she was actually talking to a librarian. Didn't librarians welcome people who liked to read? "Are you the librarian, Mrs. Patton?" she asked pointedly.

The woman stared at her implacably. "Yes, I am," she said and slammed the door.

Near tears, Philippa leaned on the fence. Why were the simplest things so difficult here? Turning away from the gloomy cottage, she walked slowly back to the library building and, near the cosmetic shop, discovered an entrance to the second floor. Climbing a dusty wooden staircase littered with contraceptives and empty bottles, she came to a dark hall. At the end was a door with a glass window secured by a massive lock. Cleaning a patch of glass with her hand-kerchief, she peered through at the remains of a once-grand library. Massive carved cases were piled helter-skelter with dusty books, and on tables covered in torn green felt more books were stacked. There was a frayed blue and red carpet and vintage light fixtures with lily-shaped glass shades. She closed her eyes. What a tragedy. How could it have come about? Didn't anyone care?

NOT long after Philippa had disappeared down the path, a young man whom Ravi recognized as one of Princess Kamala's drivers mate-rialized on the veranda.

"Nameste-ji," the young man said sarcastically. "Is memsahib here?"

Ravi replied curtly that memsahib was not there. She had gone to the bazaar and would not return until after lunch.

"Then you give this note to sahib, very important."

"Sahib asleep," said Ravi, "not to be disturbed."

The young driver stared at the ceiling of the veranda and tapped his foot impatiently. After all, he was in the service of the Princess Kamala; who was this old hotel wallah to be acting so high and mighty just because he happened to be working for a ferenghi sahib who had appeared from nowhere? "Wake him up," he commanded, handing Ravi a thick white envelope with a coat of arms on it. Scenting intrigue, Ravi turned it over several times and smiled. It was certainly not the usual kind of note. "Wake him up." The young man grinned. "He will want to read it."

Ravi shuffled to David's bedroom and knocked tentatively. David grunted. The door opened and Ravi handed him the note. He tore it open and withdrew the heavy notepaper on which a few lines were scrawled. *Have come to take you both to see the waterfalls. Waiting in car. Sumi.*

David's eyes opened wide. "Where is memsahib?"

"Memsahib gone bazaar," said Ravi. "Library. Coming back this afternoon."

"Is there someone waiting?"

"Yes, sahib. Princess Kamala's driver, sahib."

"Tell him I'll be ready in a few minutes. Give him a cup of tea."

Ravi disappeared. David rushed to the bathroom, splashed himself with cold water, toweled himself briskly, and dressed. What luck. Philippa had gone out; extraordinary timing. But where was Sumitra? He finished dressing and asked Ravi to bring the driver to him in the study.

"Will you come with me, sahib?" the young man said.

"Yes," said David, putting on his raincoat. "Where?"

"Just follow me, sir, not far."

"If memsahib returns, tell her I've gone for a walk," David told Ravi.

"Teek hai, sahib, teek hai." Ravi leered.

At the end of a path that ran up to the motor road the gray outline of a sleek limousine, its engine quietly throbbing, materialized in the bright mist. The young man opened the back door.

"Bonjour," drawled Sumitra's liquid voice from the plush gloom of the curtained interior. "Where is Philippa?"

"Gone out somewhere: library," replied David, climbing in next to her.

"Oh, too bad. This wretched weather is so boring. When it cleared this morning I thought you might both enjoy getting out. Couldn't get you on the phone so I took my chances. I've had them pack a picnic lunch." She opened the dark glass that separated them from the driver and said something in rapid Hindi. The car crawled forward. Sumitra drew the glass shut and pulled a curtain across it.

"Are there any roads worth driving on?" asked David. "Not much to see in this fog."

Sumitra lit a cigarette and sank back in the soft seat. "I've told him to drive us to the waterfall. It's on the other side of the mountain at a lower altitude, much warmer there, very beautiful just now, fantastic cavern underneath it, the perfect place for a picnic; pity Philippa couldn't come." She smiled her catlike smile and laid her hand on his knee.

"You knew she'd gone out, didn't you?" He sought to pin her down.

Her fingers contracted like cat's claws. "Word of mouth travels fast. You ought to know that, Captain, weren't you born in the mystic East?" Her long black hair fell down over a shawl and silk pajamas. She was laughing at him. "Let's have some champagne." She stubbed out her cigarette in a silver ashtray. "I filched some from Mummy's stash. It's in the fridge." She opened a cabinet door, withdrew two iced glasses and a bottle, pressed a button, and caused a small table to pop out. The glasses steamed.

"Afraid I haven't had breakfast," said David. "You caught me in bed."

"Just the thing to start the day." She uncorked the bottle and poured. "Cheers."

"Cheers," he said, smiling at her. There was something desperate about her gestures, as though she felt all her actions were mistakes, had lost her identity or never had one. Yet she was extremely intelligent and very beautiful.

"Tell me," she said. "What exactly is your relationship with my mother? The two of you put on an interesting little performance the other evening. Is there something between you that your wife is not supposed to know about?" She pursed her lips and sipped the champagne.

David stared out through the sheer curtained windows, wondered how much he should tell her, and cleared his throat. "We knew each other long ago during the war. My friend Madho Dev introduced us. We were good friends."

"Come, come, you were lovers. Admit it. Please don't be hypocritical like everyone else, you're too attractive."

"You said it, not I," he responded evasively.

"Do you think I'm going to blackmail you?" She giggled. "Lucky Mummy. You must have been quite a catch."

"Your mother was the catch, not I," he said quietly.

"I can imagine."

"You're her mirror image, you know, yet not at all Indian somehow."

She withdrew her hand and smiled thinly. "That's certainly a racist remark. I know the image you have in your mind: demure, dark-skinned beauties. You British are all alike. You make me sick!"

"Look here, I'm no racist. Daresay I've spent more time here than you."

"Right, and thank God! But that doesn't mean you're still not one underneath. I was born in Lausanne. Unfortunately, I have an Indian passport, which makes life difficult. Indians are mistrusted everywhere: no one likes us, no one wants us. Visas are a problem." She stared at him out of the corners of her large eyes.

The big car moved noiselessly past gangs of gaping hill folk, tending herds of goats.

"What did you think of my brother, Sonny?" she asked.

"Seemed like a nice young chap, a bit debauched perhaps, could stand to put on a few pounds. Didn't get much of a chance to chat with him. Why do you ask?"

She poured more champagne into his glass. "He's mad for you," she said slyly, her eyes glittering.

"Should I feel flattered?"

"You're a very good dancer. I enjoyed dancing with you the other night."

Her hand was resting on his thigh now and could not be ignored. The champagne was having its effect. They kissed and after a while, he noticed the car was no longer moving.

"We've stopped," he whispered. "What now?"

She pulled away, produced a mirror and lipstick, checked her makeup, and tapped on the curtained window. The driver opened the door. They were parked on the side of a road some hundred feet above a steaming gorge.

"Listen, do you hear the roar? The waterfalls are just around the corner."

"Sounds like thunder," observed David.

She took a picnic basket and led him up a path. The sun beamed through hot mist. Beyond a stand of immense teak and ancient twisted jungle oak, he saw the falls. She hadn't exaggerated. The water fell from two hundred feet and behind it—under the overhanging rock—there was probably enough space to shelter a small army. The scale was vast. He was impressed.

"What a shame Philippa couldn't have come," he said. "She would have loved this."

"What a shame, what a shame," she mocked mercilessly. "Come, we must get across this ledge and under the falls."

The precipitously narrow path led off through mint and lime-green ferns. Below, the young driver watched them, hands on hips, his mouth set in a cynical smile.

"This is the worst part," she said, negotiating a narrow ledge. "See, it opens up beyond. Come."

He was amazed how surefooted and fearless she was. The ledge, carved into the face of the massive cliff, was not more than a foot wide. One wrong move and I've had it, he thought, and tried to concentrate on his feet.

Behind the falls a huge low-ceilinged space the size of a football field sloped back into sandy alcoves. She led him to a patch of dry sand far from the spray and the din of falling water. It was dark and warm. She spread out a blanket from her basket, sat down, and began taking out containers of food.

David kicked off his battered sneakers and burrowed into the fine sand with his toes. In the car their sudden embrace had roused him from his monsoon torpor. But why in God's name was she setting out lunch? Did she really think he was hungry? One moment she was a woman, the next a child. Restless with desire and a little drunk from the champagne, he got up and walked barefoot in the sand, exploring the mossy alcoves, where he discovered traces of old fires and animal bones.

Sumitra watched him and wondered why she found this older man so fascinating. From the moment she'd seen him, she'd known they were going to have some kind of relationship. Call it a premonition, it was just that simple. He walked back, dropped to his knees beside her, took her in his arms, and caressed her breasts beneath her silk shirt. His hands were strong and warm. She asked him if he was hungry. "Not for food," he said, mocking her. She loved his pugnacious Roman nose, the way the nostrils flared with an instinctive, lustful reflex when he wanted something. Staring unblinkingly at him, she touched his lips with the tips of her fingers. "Why am I so attracted to you?" she asked out loud. He covered her eyes and lips with kisses.

"I'm much too old for you," he said. "I was your mother's lover. I could be your father."

Her hand wandered inside his shirt. "I never knew my father."

He stroked the nape of her neck, then her back, and her magnificent hips. She buried her head in his lap. He slipped her pajamas down, gently parted her thighs, and found her source. She groaned. As her excitement mounted she felt she was going to scream, but the thunder of the falling water muffled her cries. He stood up, and slipped out of his clothes. She sank to her knees before him.

He threw back his head and yelled.

She'd expected his body to look lumpy and knotted with age, but he was lean and hard and reminded her of one of those husky old warriors in a classical painting she'd once copied at the Louvre.

He helped her to her feet and tried to kiss her breasts, but she turned and ran. He ran after her but she was quick and agile and managed to escape. Finally, cornering her in one of the alcoves, he advanced playfully and caught her in his arms. The idea that no one could hear them was fantastically exciting.

She groaned, found his mouth, and sucked his tongue.

"Come," she whispered breathlessly, broke away, and ran toward the thundering water at the lip of the cave where rainbows flickered in the spray. He followed blindly. "Not there, silly, you'd be crushed," she cried, pulled him back from the edge and led him to a fern-covered crevice from which warm, pungent water flowed in a gentle stream.

They stood together under it, bathed each other, and played. She made a crown of ferns and placed it on his head.

"There," she said. "Now you look like Bacchus or Ulysses returned from his travels. You should grow long hair and a beard."

He lifted her in his arms. She wrapped her legs around his waist and covered him with kisses. Stepping out of the spray, he carried her back and gently lowered her onto the blanket. Their wet limbs slapped against each other in the warm darkness.

"Sand is not exactly my idea of the greatest place to make love in," she said at last.

He squatted beside her, and delicately brushed off her breasts.

"You look frosted," he said. "Very edible."

He was ready to start again but she held him at arm's length.

"Do you make love with Philippa?" she asked with sudden childlike simplicity.

"Nowadays, rarely." He smiled. "She has her affairs, I've had mine. But we're happy enough."

"Happy enough, can one ever be happy enough?" She drew his face down and kissed him passionately.

"It's not Philippa who would feel jealous, but your mother," he whispered. She turned away and muttered something incoherent. "You shouldn't be so hard on her," he went on. "She's lived through a lot. If you'd known her when she was your age, you'd feel differently about her. Her responsibilities—"

"What responsibilities?" murmured Sumitra.

"You, for one."

"You must be joking. I've never been a responsibility of hers. Sonny and I were raised by servants; she was always off racing horses, going to parties, having a good time. Responsibilities, *merde!*"

"But things can't have been easy for a woman in her position. Think of all she's lost. Wasn't she put in jail during the Emergency?"

"House arrest," Sumitra said, her mouth set. "And who's to say she didn't deserve it? Now she's insisting I marry here but the men she produces . . ." She rolled her eyes.

"You don't want to live in India?"

"It's not that," she said. "I'm frightened. Indian people are so blind. Living in the West wakes you up. When you come back here and see what's really happening. . . . It drives you crazy. And it's terribly depressing, because you don't feel at home anywhere else. Awful. I have friends who've gone quite mad when they returned. That's what I'm fighting." She sighed and wiped her eyes. "I'll be glad to get back to Paris. If I can work out my visa problems, I might stay there. But I'm often very lonely. The French are so condescending."

"I'm going to see that you aren't. When do you go back?"

"End of October." She brushed sand from his stomach and threw her arms around him. "You're really very beautiful. I'd like to paint you. I have a studio in the old part of Montmartre, just on the side of the hill. I've got a big bed there too, better than this sand."

"I'll look forward to that," he whispered. "As I am often in Paris on business, it should be a simple matter." He kissed her passionately.

"Come," she said. "We must really wash off and get back. The driver will be getting impatient; no telling what gossip he might spread."

"You must promise you won't let on to your mother or Philippa," he said firmly, as they walked to the car.

Sumitra tossed her head and smiled wickedly. "I won't promise anything of the sort. Who knows? I might liberate you from both of them. What would you say to that?"


CONTENT to rest awhile from the staring eyes in the streets below, Philippa had gazed, lost in thought, at what remained of the old library and then made her way back down the stairs. In the west, the sun had broken through voluminous black clouds and spotlighted the square. Standing in the confusion of tourists, rickshaw men, coolies, and frantic children, she realized she had not posted her letters, and there across the square was the post and telegraph office. Pushing her way through the crowd, she queued up in a long line and, when her turn came at last, gave her letters to the postal clerk, paid for the stamps, and turned to leave. It was now raining hard. Trying to keep her umbrella from collapsing, she leaned into the wind. Suddenly there was a honk.

"Philippa!" It was David's voice calling. "Philippa, over here." She saw David jump out of a car. "For God's sake, what are you doing wandering around in this beastly rain? You'll get sick again."

Closing her umbrella, Philippa slid into the car, slammed the door, and sighed gratefully.

"We've been looking all over for you," cried Sumitra. "I came to take you both to see the waterfall, spur-of-the-moment thing; thought you might be bored sitting up at General Bobby's in the rain. Have some brandy, you're wet and cold."

"Ah, Sumitra," Philippa said, "what luck you came along. I'd adore some." She dried her hair with her scarf.

"But what on earth are you doing all the way down here?" asked David.

"I wanted to find the library and I finally did, but I couldn't get in. There's a dragon lady called Mrs. Patton who thinks she owns it."

"Her!" exclaimed Sumitra. "Horrible Anglo-Indian witch. Her father was a British army sergeant; her mother was an Indian Christian. She and her brother were always talking about 'home,' meaning England, a place they'd only heard about. The brother eventually married an Englishwoman and went 'home,' but no one ever married the sister, so she's still here."

"Pretty much what I thought." Philippa nodded. "How sad."

"Life is what you make it," drawled Sumitra. "If Miss Patton were pleasant, people would like her and the library would be popular. Even when you finally get your card, she doesn't give you any peace but stands over you like an old buzzard, acting like you're taking too much of her time and you should tip her for being there. Disgusting. And the library has such wonderful old books, some quite valuable."

"What a pity," said Philippa, sipping her brandy.

The rain came down in sheets, obscuring the driver's vision. The car inched forward across the square and stopped suddenly.

"Good God, can't he watch where he's going?" cried Sumitra. "We must have hit someone." David started to get out. "No, no, let him handle it. If they see your face, it will be much worse." She leaned forward and opened the glass partition. "You sister-fucking animal," she barked in Hindi, "what have you done? If there's a scratch on this car I'll—"

Just then there was a pounding on the driver's window. A man was striking the glass.

"Roll down the window," ordered Sumitra. "I will talk to him."

The driver rolled down the window. "You'd better tell your driver to watch where he's going," yelled an angry voice.

"Arjun!" cried Philippa. "Why, it's Arjun!"

Sumitra looked at David. "You know this person?"

"Hello, hello!" Arjun grinned happily, rain streaming down his handsome face.

"Of course we know him," cried David. "Are you all right? Arjun, can you move your vehicle? Fancy bumping into you like this."

"I was in Delhi, had a few days to spare. Tried to ring up but couldn't get through. Thought I'd surprise you. Awful drive up that mountain—landslides." He shot a searching glance at Philippa, then at Sumitra.

"Let's get out of this rain," said David. "We'll lead the way up to the house."

"I'll just back up, Uncle. You go ahead, I'll follow." He ran to his jeep. The driver rolled up the window.

"What a coincidence," said David. "Lucky we did bump into him, it would have taken hours for him to find us."

"An old friend?" Sumitra asked Philippa.

"Rather a young one, I guess." Philippa laughed.

"He's the son of my friend Madho Dev Singh of Kotagarh," explained David. "Dev was—is—a good friend of your mother's; in fact, he introduced me to your mother."

"This person?"

"No, his father."

"Oh, I see. Quite an attractive chap." She winked mischievously at Philippa. "Now you'll have a houseguest to liven things up. It's always fun to have new people come, one gets so *bored* in the monsoon."

"You must come for dinner and bring your mother," said David. "Could you make it tomorrow night? I'm not sure we can communicate by phone."

"Let me see what Mummy's up to," said Sumitra. "She always organizes things."

"Tell her it's Madho Dev's son," urged David. "I'm sure she'll want to see him."

"I'll send a servant to let you know, and I'll have Mummy speak to someone about your phone. We'll try and get it working tomorrow. One has to bring pressure in these matters, you know."

# 14

E XHAUSTED FROM HER DAY in the bazaar, Philippa slept late but appeared for lunch. Afterward David and Arjun drove to the bazaar in Arjun's jeep to phone Madho Dev. By teatime, however, the sky was black with clouds, and at eight, when Kamala's car honked in the road above, it was raining hard again.

Unperturbed by the weather, Kamala entered the front hall wrapped in a priceless shawl, her famous rubies glowing, and extended her arms toward a radiant-looking Philippa, who, bent on dispelling the impression that she wore only baggy tweeds, had slipped into a black-sequined creation she'd picked up in Paris and fabulous pearls.

"Darling," cried Kamala, embracing her, "let me see if you're holding up in this ghastly deluge." She held Philippa at arm's length. "Yes, I believe you are; in fact, you look marvelous, Terripur must agree with you. Sumi, doesn't she look smashing? And, of course, you remember Akbar?"

Akbar bowed low.

"We'll have drinks in the study by the fire," said Philippa. "Come."

At the study door, they were greeted by David. "Of course, you know Princess Kamala," he said, introducing Arjun. Arjun bowed and kissed her hand.

"But you're even more handsome than I remembered." Kamala smiled, introduced Sumitra, and floated to one side.

Akbar and Arjun shook hands.

"What a lovely house and what a lovely room," said Kamala, smoothing her brocaded sari. "I haven't been here since Bobby first bought it. What a mess it was. I see he's done it up nicely, though, bright and comfortable."

Ravi served drinks while David and Arjun stood with their backs to the huge fireplace.

"Arjun dear, come over by me. I want to hear all the news about your family," said Kamala.

As was proper with a great princess, Arjun knelt on one knee in front of her. "Father is fine. I talked to him on the phone this afternoon; he sends you his warmest regards."

"And your mother? She's one of my oldest friends, you know." Her eyes flirted with him. She was positive he had no idea Gayatri was her daughter. "And that pretty bride of yours, how is she?"

"She is well and sends her regards along with Mother's. You gave us beautiful wedding presents, Auntie. We're all sorry you haven't come to Kotagarh again to see us."

"And how many children do you have now?"

Sitting nearby, Philippa was intrigued by Kamala's performance: going over everything again with Arjun, pretending she knew nothing about Gayatri or anyone else. What a complex woman, so attractive and intelligent, but grown devious with age and the wear and tear of life. What dreadful scenes she must have survived. Philippa was filled with admiration.

David was talking with Akbar and Sumitra, waiting for some small sign of yesterday's shared intimacy, but to his immense relief she affected a distant manner. There were too many shrewd eyes watching, too many alert sensibilities for her to risk looking at him. What a marvelous time they would have together in Paris; something to look forward to. How changed he felt.

Akbar was discoursing on famous holy places one could almost see on a clear day from Terripur. "One of the most beautiful," he said, "is Kedarnath."

"Shiva shrine, isn't it?" said David. "But what does the name mean?"

"Kedar is a Persian word meaning literally 'a swampy place in a meadow.'"

"But how can there be a swamp that high? Didn't you say it was fourteen thousand feet?"

"Glacial moraine, my dear fellow. Have you never been there?"

David shook his head and Kamala broke in. "But you must go; you both must go." Philippa looked blank. "To Kedarnath, my dear, the greatest and most ancient of our shrines. They say you get merit just thinking of going there. Naturally I went as a child with my father, but then I went again a few years ago. What a beautiful trek; nothing compares with it anywhere for mountain scenery. Kashmir, Switzerland, the Andes all pale before Kedarnath. It's fabulous."

"Did you ride or walk up?" asked Akbar peevishly.

"Believe it or not, my dear, I walked. Sumi went with me, didn't you, darling? She's my witness. She was only fourteen and rode a horse, but I walked and I'm proud of myself." She folded her hands in her lap and twisted an enormous diamond ring around one finger. "I have an idea," she said. "As soon as the weather breaks we'll make an expedition there. Captain and Mrs. Bruce have not been, nor has Akbar." She addressed herself to Arjun. "Have you been?"

He shook his head. "No, Auntie, I have been to Badrinath but never Kedarnath."

"Ah, then you must come too," Kamala said brightly. "Badrinath is nothing, you can drive there now; it's jammed with tourists."

"What a shame," said Arjun, fastening her with a limpid gaze that usually made women forget what they were saying.

But not Kamala. "You will come with us, won't you?"

"I'm supposed to be back in Kotagarh in a week, but as I just talked to my father this afternoon, I could probably extend it a few days."

"Then it's all settled. After all, it's September; the weather has to clear any day. We'll take two cars, one for us and one for the servants."

"But my dear Kamala," drawled Akbar, "it's not clearing. The weather is dreadful. Think of the landslides. Listen!" He pointed to the ceiling and they all listened. The rain was pounding ferociously on the roof.

"I shall send a message to my guru to stop the rain," said Kamala, smiling confidently.

"Really, Mummy!" exclaimed Sumitra, looking embarrassed.

"I know you aren't a believer, darling, but you'll see. Within two days the rain will stop. It has to, or Arjun won't have the time to come with us."

"To which guru do you pray, Auntie?" Arjun was curious.

"I don't pray *to* her, I pray *for* her. My guru, Ma, is a very old woman who lives near the source of the Ganga."

Akbar yawned.

"I know you disapprove," she said, "after all, you are a Muslim, but before you say anything, you must meet her. She has many devotees of your faith."

"Really?" drawled Akbar. "But darling, I'm just not interested in religion, even my own."

"Well, I wasn't either," declared Kamala. "But let me tell you a story. My mother was her devotee, not I. Every letter Mother wrote to me, she dusted with ash—verbuti—from Ma's fire. I always read her letters and shook the ash into the fireplace but never paid any attention at all. Then a few years ago I got in a real fix, something with the wretched government, as usual, but really a bad situation. There was this minister, charming fellow and we got along quite well, but he wouldn't budge, not one inch; even Rama Rao couldn't handle him. One morning I woke up and thought of Ma. I'd just received another letter from my mother with more ash. I woke up and said, 'Well, Ma, if you're really as good as Mother says you are, then do this work for me; remove this obstacle, this minister who is blocking me,' and I rubbed some of the ash on my forehead. Do you know"—Kamala paused dramatically, looking at Philippa with an enigmatic smile— "do you know that within two hours my work was done? Done, just like that! I received a phone call that the minister had unexpectedly changed his mind and the obstacle had been removed."

"Coincidence is not magic," said Akbar.

"You're so obstinate." Kamala laughed. "You know very well it was not coincidence. I will tell you more, Philippa, if I may call you that. I thought the same thing too, all coincidence, so the very next opportunity I asked again, and again within hours—I don't mean days— my problem was solved. Still, I was doubtful. So I began asking for frivolous things. One day I asked for rainbows. Can you believe that a cloud came up out of nowhere, it was the only cloud in the entire sky, right over Prospect Point? It sent down mist and the sky was filled with rainbows all day long, I swear it. Then I said to myself, 'Kamala, you must go visit your mother and have her take you to Ma's cave so you can see for yourself.' If you had known my mother, you would realize what an effort it was to go anywhere with her: formidable, my dear, positively, but I went. She took me to Ma's cave. It was a grueling trip but worth it, and I have gone many times since. The villagers for miles around are devoted to her." Kamala looked around and smiled at everyone. Ravi passed hors d'oeuvres. "How did we get onto Ma?"

"The trip to Kedarnath. You were going to ask her to stop the rain." Sumitra sighed.

"Ah, yes," said Kamala. "I shall ask and you shall see. Meanwhile, I will make plans for our journey. I hear there's a lovely young man there, one of the purohits; we'll be able to stay with him."

"Sounds like a strenuous undertaking," said David, glancing at Philippa. "Do you feel up to it, darling?"

"Of course I do. It's just what I need: some exercise, a change of scene."

"Good, then it's settled," declared Kamala. "Day after tomorrow. We should start early in the morning, as it's an all-day drive and there are a number of quaint places to stop along the way: shrines, tea shops, and so on. Are you coming, Akbar?"

Akbar smiled condescendingly, sure that the weather would not break so soon. "My dear, if you can stop this infernal rain, I'll go anywhere."

Kamala fanned the air with one graceful hand. "It is not I who will stop it, it is Ma. If she thinks we should go to Kedarnath, the rains will stop."

"I think you sound utterly batty," said Sumitra, embarrassed by her mother's excursions into the supernatural.

"Wait till you're a little older, darling, then you'll understand more," replied Kamala. "I might just retire to Ma's cave. It's quite comfortable once you get there."

"Is that a threat or a promise, Mummy?" Sumitra giggled.

"Take it any way you like, Sumi darling." Kamala smiled.

"I really don't think I can go," sighed Sumitra, "I have a tennis match."

"Nonsense," snapped Kamala. "Of course you're going. You'll just have to postpone the tennis."

The last thing Sumitra wanted was to go on an extended outing with such a group. It was bound to end in disaster.

"If *I* must go, you can bloody well come along too," said Akbar good-naturedly. "If you are not there, who will I make my snide remarks to?"

Sumitra had a sneaking suspicion her mother was trying to promote something between them. Although Akbar was witty and amusing, an international cultural figure, she just couldn't see herself living with all that fat, not to mention the other things that might be expected of her.

"Let's have no more negative talk," said Kamala firmly. "You can postpone your match. It's definitely settled. We're all going to Kedarnath."

Dinner was announced. David was having a problem not looking at Sumitra, who, in tight black velvet pants and top with a neckline plunging well below the usual level, was most provocative. In spite of himself, he wanted desperately to communicate with her, but each time he caught her eye, she looked away. It was Kamala Sumitra was afraid of. She had the antennae of a moth, or bat radar; not a nuance of feeling escaped her.

The conversation at dinner revolved around the latest political gossip. Kamala had heard that Mrs. Gandhi was thinking of a preemptive strike against Pakistan's nuclear installations.

"Politically she's finished," observed Akbar. "Look at the mess she's made in Andhra trying to manipulate things. The south hates the Congress Party, Bengal hates her, and now she's alienated the Sikhs."

"If only she would just stop," said Kamala. "Simply step down. Retire in favor of someone else and go to an ashram. If she did that, she'd become the Rajmata of Hindustan. Everyone would respect her, consult her, and take her advice, and she'd be well out of it."

"How can she possibly do something like that?" said Akbar. "There's too much at stake. She has to hand the power over to someone in the family, and Rajiv isn't ready yet. Furthermore, she's not in the least bit religious. What would she do in an ashram?"

"But I hear she does puja every morning," said Philippa.

"Wouldn't you if you'd sent an army into the Golden Temple?" Akbar chuckled. "I'd be down on my hands and knees praying for my life. It was all much worse than they let on. The army went in on some holy day; a number of innocent pilgrims were caught, and hundreds slaughtered. The Sikhs will never forgive her."

"Certainly they must be glad to be rid of that terrorist, Bhindrinwale," protested David.

Kamala shook her head. "You don't know them. Akbar is right; they'll never forgive her, and they have memories like elephants. I was married to a Sikh, Sonny's father: very glamorous man but so difficult and unforgiving!"

"After all, Bhindrinwale was invented by Mrs. Gandhi," observed Akbar. "He was a village preacher with an illiterate congregation. She patronized him, thought she could use him as a wedge to divide the Sikhs. Then he turned the tables on her, believed his own publicity, said God was telling him what to do. When fanatics begin to believe their own PR, things always get out of hand."

"Someone has to lead all these people." Sumitra shrugged. "If none of you intelligent ones go into politics, what do you expect? Look at most of the so-called world leaders: drunks, kinky womanizers, addicts, actors. You're quite lucky to have someone as straight as Mrs. Gandhi."

"I agree," said Philippa. "I think you're extremely fortunate."

"That's very patriotic of you, Sumi dear," said Kamala, "but you weren't arrested by her in 1975. You were with your father in France while I spent a year locked up in my house."

"When is this war supposed to take place?" asked David.

"The usual time." Kamala sighed. "November, December, the best time for battles here: monsoon over, cool weather. Our people are still living the *Mahabharata*, you know. A nice quick winter war, they think, over by the hot season in April. But this time they might be surprised."

As the table dissolved into general conversation and Akbar started a long joke about General Zia, Kamala leaned over and spoke to Arjun. "Tell me about your children, my dear. I want to know about each one of them."

"Well," began Arjun, "as you know, I have five. The boys are little rascals. . . ."

My grandchildren, she thought, as she listened. She liked him. He was damn attractive, perhaps too attractive. Was he faithful to Gayatri? she wondered. Come to think of it, would he have come all this way just to see David? David was very fond of him, that was obvious, but there had to be another reason. Could it be Philippa? She glanced speculatively at Philippa out of the corner of her eye and back to Arjun.

"You *will* come along to Kedarnath with us, won't you?" she whispered. "It's important to have a strong young man along. Akbar is so helpless."

"Of course, Auntie." He smiled. "I'm really looking forward to it."

Kamala sipped her wine. Pilgrimage trips were often very revealing. Perhaps the gods would stir up things to some purpose. She reminded herself to find some of Ma's ash and smear it on her forehead; perhaps also on that other place she was supposed to put it. Who could tell what she might discover?

LATE that night, oppressed by the thought of Philippa alone in a bed in the same house, Arjun got up and stole into her room. Except for a few furtive glances that revealed nothing she had given no sign that anything existed between them. The dying embers in the fireplace cast a warm glow. She was asleep, and he sat down on the edge of the old four-poster bed and gazed at her. Since she'd left Kotagarh, hardly an hour had passed that he hadn't regretted the scene at the old fort, raged at the impossibility of communicating: his terrible ineptness, his lack of affection—no better than an animal or some adolescent boy relieving an itch. And the moment the train carrying her away had left the station, he realized that what started as a challenge was much more than that. He began to see her as a goddess who had come to save him. With her, his soul seemed to lighten. She transmitted a kind of positive charge that he was sure could transform both their lives; as his energy was being stifled in Kotagarh, so hers was being lost and wasted with David. He bent over her sleeping form. Her lovely hair, spread out on the white pillow, gave off an evanescent glow. Hesitant to wake her, and noticing the door to the bath that connected with David's room was ajar, he got up and closed it and stood at the foot of her bed, uncertain whether to leave or stay.

She opened her eyes. He knelt down and took her hands in his. She smiled sleepily, drew his hands to her lips, and moved under the blankets.

She had been dreaming of him. The images had faded and in the half-consciousness that followed, she had been struggling vainly to recapture the lost thread. They had been together in a strange landscape of mists and trees and he had been carrying her somewhere. She felt warm and secure, like a doll in the stalwart arms of some strapping god. The sensations had been happy, delicious. Were these dream hands or were they real? She opened her eyes, drew the grave, handsome face toward her, and felt the warmth of his lips on hers. Closing her eyes again, she stroked the velvet skin of his neck and shoulders as he slipped in beside her. How she had longed to be held like this. How vital touch was, how healing. What an error it had been so proscribed by words thought up to keep people separated, afraid of each other: words like concupiscent, salacious, lascivious. No wonder people had difficulty believing they were part of one god, one soul.

She lay perfectly still, so still he could feel her heart beating in the veins of her neck against his cheek. He pulled the blankets up over their heads, and they lay in a warm cocoon. Would she ever believe how often he had thought of her? There didn't have to be a reason for loving this woman. Although getting out of India was important, there was something far more at stake, indefinable yet concrete. The word "bliss" came close to expressing it. If she were truly his he could achieve anything. She was his shelter. The sound of her voice was enough to lift his spirits and send them soaring. One glance from her was enough to make him happy for a week.

But these feelings he must keep to himself. Yes, it would not do to talk about them. If she knew how deeply he felt, it might scare her. She was, after all, not a schoolgirl. She had responsibilities. He had many duties and responsibilities too. She would only tell him how guilty his love made her feel. No, it would be best to worship her in silence.

"Am I disturbing you?" he whispered. "Forgive me. I'd best get back to bed."

She said nothing but held him more tightly. How much longer could he be expected to restrain himself? Her hands glided down his back and held him tightly. He stroked her forehead, kissed her closed eyes, and opened her mouth with his tongue. Each moment contained the seeds of eternity.

"I hope my coming hasn't complicated things," he said softly. "I couldn't stay away. I'm sorry about what happened before, at the fort, it was stupid of me."

She put her finger to his lips. "You aren't complicating anything. I've been waiting, praying for you to come. Everything is perfect."


ALL the next day, rain fell relentlessly from leaden skies, and by evening it seemed doubtful Kamala's guru had received her message. The following morning at five, however, Ravi awakened David to tell him it had cleared.

He jumped out of bed and ran to the veranda.

"See, sahib," said Ravi, handing him a cup of tea, "it is finished."

They stood in silence watching the sun rise behind the jagged silhouette of the Himalayas, turning the peaks silver and gold.

"Gongotri Ma." Ravi grinned.

David looked at him. "You heard the conversation?"

"The Ma lives near the village of Gongotri. The Princess is well-known devotee of the famous Ma," Ravi said earnestly. "She say she going to ask Ma to clear the skies."

"Which she seems to have done remarkably well," replied David, contemplatively slurping his tea in the Indian fashion. Whenever he was alone with Ravi, he found himself reverting to habits he'd picked up as a child from his ayah. It was a disturbing phenomenon. "Do you think monsoon is really over?" he asked.

"Yes, sir, finished. Wind has changed."

Just then the phone tinkled, the first time since they had arrived. It was Kamala.

"You see, David, not only is it a perfectly gorgeous day but your phone is working."

"I was having my tea with Ravi, watching the sunrise. He says the rain is finished."

"But naturally. Can you be ready to leave by eight-thirty?"

"Let's make it nine," said David.

"Perfect," said Kamala and rang off.

"Shall I pack, sir? Some utensils, some water?" Ravi was standing in the doorway. "Water in mountains very bad, sir, very septic. The general seems to have all good camping equipment here."

"Fine. And pack your own bedroll and something warm; you're coming too." Ravi looked surprised. "Didn't I tell you that?"

"You did, sahib, but your mind might change."

David laughed. Here, people didn't believe in the future; they believed in the past.

Ravi squinted at the mountains. "Tomorrow, sir, we will be there"—and he pointed. "The highest peak, that is Kedarnath; just below is the temple."

"Have you ever seen it?"

"No, sir, it is the chance of a lifetime. Very lucky for me, for you, for memsahib. All sins removed."

David smiled. "Very convenient. Then I can start sinning all over again, eh?"

"Sir?"

He repeated himself in Hindi.

"Ah, yes." Ravi smiled. "Clean slate, isn't it?"

David went into the house and knocked on Arjun's door. "Look out your window, my boy," he called. "The day is clear, fantastically beautiful. The princess rang up; we leave for Kedarnath at nine."

Arjun struggled out of bed and squinted toward the window. After making passionate love to Philippa again half the night, he had rather hoped it would still be raining. David knocked again, and he pulled himself together.

"Yes, yes, I see," he answered. "I'll just have a quick bath."

He examined himself in the mirror, looking for telltale signs of passion. Philippa had a habit of biting him on the neck. Except for the creases around his eyes, which usually disappeared after he had showered, he looked about the same as usual. Ravi appeared with a bucket of steaming hot water and glanced sharply at him before leaving the room. He knows, thought Arjun. The old bugger somehow knows what's going on.

# 15

GOOD MORNING," said Philippa, throwing open the door. "Seems Kamala's Mama or whatever she's called did the trick. What a gorgeous day!"

They sat down to breakfast. Arjun stood behind David's chair, gently pressed his shoulders, and gazed at Philippa.

"Ahhh, that feels good." David groaned. "Sit down and eat."

"Do you think there will be room for all of us in Kamala's car?" Philippa said. "Think of Akbar!"

"She's bringing a second car," said Arjun. "Couldn't he be squeezed in with the servants?"

"He'd loathe that," said Philippa.

"Perhaps I should take the jeep. It might come in handy if either car broke down; I have a reserve gas tank."

"Good thinking," said David. "People can take turns riding with you. Akbar can sit in the front of Kamala's car with the driver, plenty of room for him there, and three in back."

By the time Arjun and David had packed the jeep and Ravi was locking the house, Kamala's car, followed by the second car containing her cook, two bearers, food, and bedding, hove into sight.

"Hello, hello," cried Kamala. Her eyes twinkled with delight. "Isn't it a perfect day? See what Ma can do. You thought I was mad, didn't you?"

Akbar and Sumitra waved from inside the car.

"I say, what kind of flag is that?" inquired David. "Now I see it up close, it looks most peculiar."

Kamala laughed and looked embarrassed. A magenta flag embroidered with a golden coat of arms was mounted on a steel rod on the front fender. "Now don't make fun of us," she scolded. "It's really Sumi's idea. Naughty of her, but, you know, it actually works."

"Works?" asked David.

"Yes, gets us through almost anything. Of course, it's a complete hoax—Sumi found it in a Paris flea market—but people here don't know the difference. We put it on whenever we travel; if anyone tries anything, we just say 'Official business!' You'll see how handy it is."

"We're going to take Arjun's jeep," David said. "Gives us all more legroom, don't you think? Might come in handy if the roads are bad."

"What a good idea. I was going to suggest it." Her voice went to a whisper. "I hadn't realized till he got in, but Akbar takes up space for two or more. There's room in the servants' car, but naturally I can't put him in there."

"We're bringing Ravi too."

"Oh, then the jeep it is. We'll take turns riding with Arjun. I'll go first, I adore jeeps."

The caravan set out along the narrow mountain road toward the distant snow peaks. Villagers gaped and ran out of their houses, herds of cattle and goats blocked the way and had to be moved aside, occasional wandering holy men carrying spears and tridents saluted and blew their conch shells.

"I'm so happy everything worked out," cried Kamala. "So glad you could come along with us." Arjun looked thoughtful. "What's the matter, you don't look very happy. How can you look so dreary on a day like this?"

"I'm looking at these hillsides, Auntie, not a pretty sight." He slowed down and pointed to the erosion that had occurred during the monsoon.

"What to do?" said Kamala. "You have to think of the psychology of these people; they prefer grass to jungle. You don't remember, of course, but when I was young these forests were a threat: filled with leopards and tigers. The women who had to go out and gather grass for their cows were only too happy to have it cut down, no use whatsoever to them."

"It makes one feel so hopeless." He shrugged.

"Why hopeless?" Kamala asked. "You should see it as a challenge. You've been well educated, you've a marvelous job—out-of-door work, full of adventure and challenges—you can do something about all this." This was her son-in-law if he only knew it: handsome and moody like her second husband. What was he getting at?

He stared at her as if she must be mad. "Have you been down to the plains recently, Auntie? Oh, I don't mean driving through in your car with the curtains drawn, but have you been to any of the villages or towns, like Moradabad, Aligarh, Mathura, Agra, or Bharatpur, and seen what's happening? The hordes of poor people, gangs of lawless youngsters, dacoits at night, the filth, pollution, disease?"

Kamala observed his handsome face. "You must be brave about these things," she said. "We are Kshatriyas of noble blood living in a period of great decadence. It's not pleasant, but it's our karma. It's happening all over the world."

"That's what Captain Bruce says. But I ask you, what future is there here for my children?"

"Who knows? Perhaps there will be opportunities you hadn't counted on. Are they doing well in school?"

"Very well."

"Then?" She smiled. She was thinking of her will, how all her wealth was to go to this man's children, her grandchildren. If she could only tell him it would turn out all right. But wouldn't that mean telling him everything? How would he feel if he knew his wife was half British, that his father had known it all along? Wouldn't he feel tricked? Might he not even leave Gayatri for another woman? God knows, he was good-looking enough to get anyone he wanted.

The caravan sped along the treacherous roads, left the devastated hill country behind, and climbed toward the virgin forests at the base of the Himalayas. By the time they reached the small town where they were to stop for lunch, Kamala was exhausted.

"Congratulations, you're a first-class driver, but I think one has to have more of a padded bottom than I've got to survive these bumps."

The town was situated at the broad turn of a valley where green fields sloped down toward a river strewn with boulders, some as big as a four-story building. Under a large pipal tree in the town square they found a restaurant. The place was clean and prosperous-looking.

"What an absolutely glorious view!" cried Philippa, enthusiastically focusing her camera at the snowy peaks. "You're right, it *is* more impressive than Switzerland."

"At least in Switzerland the people are civilized," said Sumitra as she emerged from the big car hunched inside an embroidered shawl. "These people look positively neolithic."

"Nonsense," protested Akbar. "They look quite civilized to me, more than most places I've been."

"That's because you're a man," drawled Sumitra. "Just look around at these poor women: beasts of burden. I certainly don't call that civilized."

"Really, Sumi, must you spoil everything?" said Kamala. "We weren't talking about that. Please try and enjoy the natural beauty."

Sumitra smiled one of her young-witch smiles, shrugged, sipped some tea, looked past her mother, and giggled. "Just imagine if we were all one family," she said. "While David, Arjun, and Akbar played cards and lounged about like the men in this square, Philippa would be trapped in a kitchen all day long, and you and I, Mummy dear, would be out gathering fodder and firewood, sweeping and cowdunging everything in sight, and of course I would be having one child after another. Wouldn't you just love it? See that woman over there? That's what you'd look like." She pointed to a wizened old hag struggling under an enormous load of broken firewood.

"Sumi, really! Between you and Arjun's depressing talk about erosion, you're ruining my day."

"But it's the truth, Mummy. You never see anything around you."

Kamala rolled her eyes. "If I saw everything—which, mind you, I do—but if I let it affect me, I'd go mad. If you really feel for these women, don't go back to Paris. There are plenty of ashrams in these hills trying to help. I ought to know, I support half of them. You can go and live with Eira; that's what she's doing, and not so far away from here either."

A waiter arrived and Akbar ordered lunch.

"It's not a question of helping the women," Sumitra said, "it's a question of changing the men. Eira told me the men tie their women up to keep them from coming to her knitting school, where they are also taught to read. Until you change the men's attitudes, it's hopeless. They don't want intelligent, educated women, they want dumb workers and baby factories—male-baby factories, of course." Akbar glanced askance at her. "Yes, you too," she insisted. "You're just as bad as the rest."

"Oh, dear, this is what comes of sending our daughters over the waters to be educated."

"Because they've been outside the prison walls," cried Sumitra spiritedly.

"But women enjoy being dominated by men," said Arjun, slurping his tea. He thought she was right but enjoyed needling her.

"Hear, hear." David grinned. "Someone for our side." And he toasted Arjun with his cup of tea.

"Women are too powerful," said Arjun. "If they aren't directed, the world will go crazy."

"What a disgusting remark!" Sumitra said passionately. "It can't get much crazier than it is. Look how men are mucking things up—on the brink of blowing us all to pieces, really." He was too good-looking. She felt instinctively he was scheming about something. She'd never met an Indian man who wasn't scheming. "Look at you," she went on. "You've come on a vacation, a nice little outing. Where is your wife? may I ask; where are your five children? Did you think of bringing them along? Oh, no, they're at home, in prison, keeping it all together. You've been trained as an Indian man since birth to think only of yourself. Actually, Mummy, I agree with you; educating Indian women is important. Teach them first not to spoil their sons and suppress their daughters; that would be the first step."

"She thinks I've suppressed her." Kamala sighed.

"Well, now that you've blasted any notion we might have had that we'd stumbled upon some idyllic, pristine pastoral scene," said Akbar, "blasted our dreams about the simple folk leading the good life close to nature—"

"She's always doing that," said Kamala, "always deflating things. It's so boring."

To Arjun, Sumitra represented a challenge which, had he not been in love with Philippa, he would have gladly taken up. Her attitude bore all the marks of a young animal in heat. One moment she was laughing and smiling, full lips taut against white teeth, more a snarl than a smile; the next she was seducing you with her eyes.

"Well," he said when they had finished, "hadn't we better be moving along? Who will ride with me? Sumitra? You look as if you need some fresh air."

"Not me," said Sumitra, much to his relief. "I need a nap. Perhaps Philippa or David."

"I'd be happy to ride with Arjun," said Philippa. "It will give me a chance to get some good pictures."

"Next stop, Gaurikund," cried Kamala. "Better take a pillow, dear, that seat is awfully hard. We should arrive in three hours, lovely hot springs to bathe in. Drive carefully."

The cars sped away. Climbing a precipitous trail around a series of high hills, they descended into the valley of the Tungabhadra. Arjun slowed down and let the other cars speed ahead. The landscape, fed by the monsoon, was a luxuriant green. Far below, rice was ripening on terraced hillsides. Above and beyond, startlingly near yet even more unreal, loomed the frozen Himalayan heights.

"Are you all right?" he asked after they had ridden some time in silence. "We've had two rather late nights."

She smiled and patted his knee. "I'm fine."

"You look a bit pale."

"I must admit I feel rather like a worm coming out from under a water-soaked log." She laughed. "Frightful, all that rain."

"The weather will be fine from now on. Smell the air, isn't it wonderful?"

"What a mess my hair is," she said, examining herself in her compact mirror. She withdrew a scarf from her bag.

"You look beautiful to me," he said tenderly. He put his hand on her knee and drove with one hand.

She put her hand on his and sighed. "I love your hands," she said, pressing his long sturdy fingers. "I don't know much about hands, but yours look lucky."

"They are your hands now to do what you want with. I think they are lucky just to have touched you."

A series of potholes suddenly confronted them. He grabbed the steering wheel. Philippa let her hand rest on his thigh.

"Be careful, I'll have to fake a flat and take you off into the bushes."

"I'm afraid your eagle-eyed auntie would be backtracking in no time."

"You don't think she suspects anything? I wouldn't want her to think there's anything between us."

"She doesn't miss much. I wouldn't put it past her to have thought up this little trip just to see what happens to all of us, given enough rope."

"Ah, yes." Arjun nodded. "I suspect she's very clever. And Ravi is no fool either."

"Kamala had an affair with David, you know, years ago. I wouldn't be surprised if she were still interested in him."

He laughed. "Then that leaves us—"

"Where?" She smiled.

"I don't know," he said.

"Sumitra is madly after him too."

"You think so?" He looked surprised.

"I know so! Furthermore, I'm quite positive they've already made love. When you've lived with a man as long as I've lived with David, you can sense these things. Just wait."

"Our times alone seem so short," he said. "I want to be alone with you for a long time. If we could just run away and never be seen again. . . . We could, you know."

"You mustn't be impatient, it's unlucky. We British are meant to be the impatient ones; you're supposed to have the patience of Buddha."

"I have this feeling time is running out for us. What is your plan? To have David invite me to England? Why would he do that?"

"I'm not planning anything. You'll see, it will happen on its own."

Arjun set his eyes on the road. There was no reason David would ask him to come unless he wanted Philippa to take a lover. Was he that generous?

"As I told you before, for some time we've had an arrangement." She laughed. "Don't frown, it makes you look too handsome. He'll ask you, he'll arrange everything; neither you nor I need to do anything."

Did she think David was in love with him? He was appalled. "Am I to become your husband's lover then, is that what you're trying to say?"

"Silly." She giggled. "Sometimes you're utterly mad. Of course not. He isn't the slightest bit that way. Despite the fact that you've been flirting outrageously with him, I assure you—" He glared at her. She laughed again. "Oh, you can't help it, you flirt with everyone, I know you don't mean it." He shot her a resentful glance. "Anyhow, please relax, let things happen, and I am certain that by the time we get ready to leave India, you and your entire family will be leaving too."

"Are you some sort of soothsayer that you know this?"

"I feel it," Philippa said. "Don't you believe in a woman's intuition?"

He looked glum. "I think you're playing games with me. I think you're evading the issue."

"Think as you like, but I'm warning you not to show how you feel in front of Kamala."

IN THE Mercedes, sitting between Kamala and Sumitra, David felt most peculiar. At every turn, the thighs of one of them pressed imperceptibly against his. Sumitra, a pillow behind her head, feigned sleep, while under her shawl, mouselike, her fingers burrowed into his trousers pocket and scratched his groin. On the other side, Kamala held his hand.

"You're the same David." She smiled. "Back as stiff as a ramrod. Don't you ever relax?"

"Don't you?" he countered.

"Not any more." She sighed and began telling him of her feelings of doubt and angst. Suddenly her voice seemed to be coming from a great distance. Since meeting Durga Baba, he'd been having strange out-of-body episodes, and now they were occurring more often than he cared to think about. Was he seeing life as it really was, the emptiness, or was it a hallucination? Sumitra's touch brought him back.

"Philippa is most attractive. I like her very much; you're perfectly suited," Kamala was saying.

"We've been together a long time."

"Mmm, a mere inhalation for the gods, but for us a lifetime." She patted his hand nervously and stared out the window.

Inside his pocket, Sumitra had managed to excite him.

"And isn't Arjun a nice young man?" Kamala continued. "What a stroke of luck to have him with us. Akbar is incapable of doing anything."

They rode on in silence. Sumitra's tickling was driving him mad. It took all his concentration to breathe normally.

"How about a drink or something hot?" Kamala asked. "I can offer you either. "Sumi," she cooed, "time to wake up, dear. Chai, chai. We'll be in Gaurikund soon."

"Do you have any brandy?" David asked.

"Of course; that's what I'll have too. Good for the heart at these altitudes." She poured them both a drink. "Sumi darling, wake up, you're missing all the most beautiful scenery." Sumitra pretended to wake up. "See now, we're in a virgin forest, darling, isn't it fabulous? This is the way it all used to look."

Sumitra glanced wickedly at David. The car came to a sudden halt. Their drinks spilled.

"*Mon Dieu!*" cried Sumitra, opening the glass partition to curse the driver.

"It's not his fault," said Akbar. "There's been a landslide."

Kamala produced towels. The driver opened the door and they got out. Several cars had stopped ahead of them. The servants' car pulled up and Ravi got out, set up his portable stove, and began making tea while Kamala's cook made sandwiches. Arjun and Philippa drove up and Arjun walked to the landslide, discussed the problem with a local official, and gave some suggestions. One enormous rock still blocked the way. It was lucky for them the slide had happened early in the morning. Fifty men had worked all day with picks and shovels, to clear the way. Now only dynamiting the boulder remained. Cars had to be backed around the bend, each driver shouting at the car behind him, for there was now a long queue. After this maneuver had been completed, Ravi and the cook served tea. The occupants of the other vehicles gaped at the odd assortment of people gathered around the big white Mercedes with the strange flag. Philippa felt embarrassed and retreated behind the car, only to be surrounded by a group of half-starved hill children. She was about to get in the car when Kamala stopped her.

"Don't mistake their stares, my dear. In India everything is theater. You must realize this and bravely act your part."

"Life is a stage," said Akbar, devouring his fifth sandwich. "We're the actors. After a while you get used to these scenes."

"But the look in their eyes," said Philippa. "I feel like Marie Antoinette."

"You're misreading them," said Arjun. "It's not their kind of food. They are more interested in your shoes and clothes. They are admiring your good karma."

I wonder, thought Philippa.

The play went on. Arjun gestured theatrically, showing off his fine profile and explaining to everyone just where, geographically speaking, they were. Kamala and Sumitra argued loudly but artificially. Sumitra said the food was awful and Kamala retorted that she was lucky to have it and where did she think she was anyway, the Tour d'Argent? Akbar, sitting on the edge of the front seat, his legs stretched out the door, defended Sumitra against Kamala while Sunil, the driver, massaged his swollen feet.

"See, how well Akbar plays the raja." Kamala smiled wickedly. "Very good, my dear. Carry on. Pity you weren't born one."

"More snacks," Akbar commanded imperiously, going along with her. "It takes a lot of food to keep all this fat going."

Kamala clapped her hands, and a bearer appeared with a tray of sweets. Just as Akbar reached for one, however, an explosion shook the mountain. Ravi dropped the sweets into Akbar's lap and fled. Above them, they heard ominous rumblings, and a few small stones flew across the road like bullets.

"Back against the embankment, quick!" shouted Arjun, and everyone except Akbar and the driver managed to flatten themselves against the embankment on the opposite side of the road.

The thundering grew louder. A giant rock bounced down on the road, hit a car behind the jeep, and careened into the gorge below. Two cars went over the side. Kamala was down on her knees praying. Just then, a boulder as big as a house hurtled over their heads, grazed the top of the Mercedes, and shot out into the abyss. They waited, listening anxiously, but it was over. Three cars had been sent into the depths of the canyon, but no one was hurt. Kamala rushed to Akbar, whom she found stroking the forehead of Sunil, who lay beneath him.

Arjun strode ahead, shouted at the local engineer, pointed to the flag on the Mercedes, and reduced him to gestures of despair. People who had lost their cars begged rides with others.

"The Lord Shiva wants you to walk," declared a tall, serious-looking holy man who happened by. "I have been walking since Kanya Kumari; three years it has taken. Come, walk with me!"

Several people actually gave up asking for rides and fell in behind him. Kamala offered room in the servants' car to two old women, and Arjun took a couple in the jeep. Everyone got into their vehicles and crawled slowly forward.

Kamala looked puzzled. "Do you think that was auspicious or inauspicious?" she asked Akbar.

"Only time will tell," he replied, "but it frightened me to death."


BY THE time they reached Gaurikund, it was late afternoon and except for the giant fir trees on the cliff tops, the village—built near the bottom of a chasm—was plunged in shadow. Here, hot springs flowed out of the mountains into a rushing river. The town was warm and steamy. Mist hovered in the narrow medieval streets as they made their way through crowds of jostling pilgrims to the New Aroma Lodge, a modern cement structure perched precariously on the side of a hill. Although Kamala had cabled ahead for reservations, only two cement cubicles with mattresses on the floor awaited them.

"Three to a room: men in one, women in the other," barked the manager.

"I'm sorry, but I reserved four rooms," said Kamala firmly. "We are too many, we have four servants and a driver and"—pointing to Akbar—"his Highness must have his own room. My daughter and I must have one, Captain Bruce and Mrs. Bruce must have their own room, and Inspector Arjun Singh must have his also."

The manager cast a frightened glance at Arjun. "You are late, madam. Thinking you were not coming, I began renting your rooms."

"But they were prepaid. I sent a messenger with the money yesterday. How dare you rent prepaid rooms?"

"The town is very full, madam; many are without rooms altogether. But I shall give up mine for his Highness and the Inspector; surely they won't mind doubling up? And, of course, I will refund your money for the fourth room and send up mattresses for your servants, who can sleep on the balcony outside your doors. Will you go to the baths before your dinner, madam?"

Kamala was furious, but there was no point in arguing. A few minutes later she led them down damp stone steps to a large, steaming pool set between rock cliffs. A throng of pilgrims and holy men were gathered about it, bathing and saying prayers. Suddenly Philippa understood why Kamala had loaned her a sari, for though men stripped down to shorts or loincloths, women were expected to bathe fully clothed. She immersed herself in the warm sulfurous water, which gushed from a stone mouth carved in the rock. People gaped as Akbar, glittering with gold chains around his neck, arms, and waist, removed his white shawl and lungi and was helped in by Sunil, the smart young driver.

"I've been waiting for this all day," Akbar shouted to Kamala. "What a wonderful feeling! Do you think the water is clean? It smells peculiar."

"Herbs and minerals, my dear," said Kamala, splashing like a girl. "This water is better than Baden Baden; believe me, I've tried both."

In the warm water, David began to go out of his body again and was suddenly high above, looking down on all of them: Akbar floating on his back belly up resembled a huge dead fish; Sumitra, irritated by the weight of the clothes she was forced to wear, breast-stroked madly back and forth across the pool; Kamala, who couldn't swim, laughed with Philippa in one corner; while Arjun posed on the steps, the focus of countless female eyes. Watching them, he rose higher and higher until the town looked like a diamond embedded in the earth. The last rays of the setting sun lit up the distant snowy peaks, rosy pink with blue and purple shadows against the azure sky. How inconsequential it all looked, almost nonexistent. Then, abruptly, he was back in his body again, and someone was supporting his shoulders. He opened his eyes. It was Arjun.

"You fell asleep, Uncle, you were sinking."

"I wasn't asleep, and I was rising. Most peculiar. Since visiting your Baba, I've been going out of my body: flying around. All I have to do is think of him and I go out. Sometimes it happens without warning. What do you make of that?"

Arjun looked solemn to humor him. "To be able to go out of one's body is a great skill. Until now I had never believed it possible. Perhaps the Baba has given you a boon."

"Perhaps," said David, standing up. "I'm beginning to think this country is too powerful for me. In places like this, I realize I could quite easily flip out, as they say, and become a sadhu."

"You have thought of that, Uncle?"

"As a matter of fact, yes, ever since I was a boy. In Bengal there were many sadhus. One in particular, I recently remembered, lived in the jungle near my uncle's tea estate in a hut made of skulls. His hair reached to his waist, so that when he was squatting he could spread it out and look like a bush. I tried to go to him and got beaten for it."

"I can see why," said Arjun. "He was a tantric, could have been dangerous."

Suddenly embarrassed at revealing too much, David submerged himself and swam underwater to Kamala and Philippa.

"Well, I guess we all look our ages, don't we?" Kamala was saying.

"The bare truth." Philippa laughed. "There's certainly nothing flattering about these dripping clothes unless you're Sumitra."

"How do we get back to the hotel?" David asked. "When we get out of this warm water, we'll freeze to death."

"Not to worry. Sunil and Ravi are waiting with dressing gowns."

"Don't tell me you have one to fit Akbar." Philippa smiled. "Poor thing, just look at him."

"He needs some sun," replied Kamala. "He's much too pale. I shall take him to Aswan this winter and pass him off as a raja. Akbar-bhai," she cooed, "come, we are leaving now. Sumi, time to go."

Later in their room Arjun watched as an awkward hill boy, wearing a uniform embroidered with the name New Aroma, nervously poured tea. Akbar sat on his bed, one foot tucked under himself.

"What an odd name." He laughed. "New Aroma. He does have a rather pungent scent to him, or do my olfactory senses deceive me?"

"Aroma is a Punjabi word," said Arjun.

"Mmm," said Akbar. "But they should know it means smell and not use it. In fact, there is a most definite aroma in the loo, backed-up drains, I suppose. Be sure to keep the door closed."

Sunil found an old electric heater, plugged it in, and began massaging Akbar's neck and shoulders.

"Is there hot water?" asked Arjun. "I'd like to wash off that bath, don't quite trust it."

"Plenty, if you can stand the aroma in there."

Akbar sent Sunil off to complain about the smell. Why, he wondered wearily, did nothing ever work here? Switzerland was also an ancient mountain country, and everything worked there. He sighed. If India had all the money in the world, things still wouldn't work.

Why? Because people didn't care, they were too busy living in the spirit world, more concerned with ghosts and demons than improving the drains. He looked down at his enormous stomach and legs. There was something powerful about being fat, especially in a country where people worshiped it. In London or Paris he was considered a freak, but here in India his corpulence verged on godliness.

Arjun came out of the bath, toweled himself down, and dressed. "See you at dinner," he said, throwing a shawl over his shoulders. "I understand they have a table set up for us in the lounge."

"Lounge," drawled Akbar. "How poetic. But I think I'll skip it. I have my paunch to live on."

Sunil appeared at the door and said the management had sent for a sweeper, who would be unplugging the drain. Arjun slipped out and walked past the hotel office to the lounge, a small room, painted a bilious green with a messy assortment of furniture covered in powder-blue vinyl, stained cotton carpets, framed pictures of the gods, and photographs of the owner's family. In one corner near a wood stove, several mountain boys lay asleep. In another, a pink Formica table was set with plastic plates and cups. Arjun wondered what Kamala's reaction would be. When they had all gathered, however, he was surprised to see that she could easily have been in one of Delhi's five-star hotels for all the surroundings seemed to affect her. Which, of course, proved she was a real princess. Like the famous Draupadi, wife of the five Pandavas, it was well known a real princess should be able to endure all sorts of privations without complaint.

"Will you walk up the mountain tomorrow, ride, or be carried?" he asked her.

"Naturally, I shall walk." Kamala smiled. "At least I shall start off that way. Walking gives the most benefit."

Arjun nodded.

"Benefit?" Philippa asked.

"Points," explained Kamala. "Credit in heaven."

"Oh." Philippa laughed, "But in my heaven, we get points for hiring horses because it gives employment to the horse owners. I'll probably walk down, but I doubt I could actually make it up there on foot. It looks like a terrifying climb."

"I shall walk," David said.

"You'll have a heart attack, darling," said Philippa. "Altitude is not good for the heart, and we'll be going up to thirteen thousand feet; it says so in the guidebook."

"I shall hire a palanquin," said Sumitra. "That is the only way to go."

"Really, Sumi," said Kamala, "have you no shame? You might as well not go at all."

"If Mrs. Gandhi can go by helicopter, I can certainly take a palanquin," she said stubbornly.

"Look how much good it did her. Every day she gets herself in deeper trouble."

Arjun looked at Sumitra. "You really should walk."

Sumitra tossed her head and looked away. An indifferent soup arrived. Kamala tasted it and shouted for the waiter.

"Why are you serving us this Western food which you do not know how to make? Take it away, it tastes like bill poster's paste. Bring us Hindustani food. parathas, greens, dahi, curried potatoes, dal!"

The soup disappeared and there was a long wait. Finally the manager burst in. "We have prepared chicken especially for you, madam."

"That is not what we ordered," said Kamala. The manager looked frightened. "Very well"—she relented—"we will try your chicken, but bring Hindustani food too. Quickly, though, we are tired and must go early tomorrow morning to visit the Lord Shiva."

"Did you bring your climbing shoes, Mummy?" asked Sumitra wickedly.

"You will be surprised to learn, Sumi, that I am completely prepared. Your old Indian mother bought her kit in Switzerland. Not only do I have Nike climbing shoes, fully waterproof, I also have a white nylon jumpsuit, goggles, and a ski hat."

"But you must absolutely go barefooted to get the full benefit, isn't that true?" Sumitra looked to Arjun for confirmation.

"That's what they say, Auntie." Arjun winked.

Kamala protested. "Then why did you ask if I had brought hiking shoes, naughty child! I've seen many sadhus walking up these pilgrim trails wearing sandals with four-inch wooden soles, and my shoes are totally synthetic, not one bit of leather."

"That's the problem, Auntie, the synthetic materials block the auspicious waves of the earth. At least, wear wooden sandals and a sari."

Kamala gritted her teeth; she knew she looked ten years younger in her white jumpsuit. "Now you are making fun of me." She smiled. "Lord Shiva is a very advanced god; I don't think he will mind me looking my best for him."

"Then we three shall start out walking," said David, "and Philippa and Sumitra will be transported."

"And what about Akbar?" put in Arjun.

"*Mon Dieu!*" exclaimed Kamala. "I'd forgotten all about him."

David grinned. "Akbar presents huge problems."

"A big palanquin," said Arjun, "that's the answer. After dinner I will go out and scout around. They must have had fat people here before; they'll have something."

THE next morning, Akbar lay on his bed in a daze.

"Get up, we're going," Arjun shouted jovially. "I have ordered a special palanquin; you are to be carried up by eight strong men."

"What about Sunil?" Akbar asked gloomily, nodding with drooping eyelids toward the driver, who slept at the foot of his bed.

"Surely he can walk?"

"He says he can't stand heights, especially after yesterday. He has heard the path is extremely dangerous; many people fall to their deaths."

"Then walking will teach him courage."

"But he is afraid of high places, vertigo," protested Akbar. "We must engage a closed palanquin for him."

Arjun was furious. "He's Princess Kamala's driver. Let her decide what he should do."

"Are the other servants walking?"

"Of course, and with two horses for provisions and luggage. Princess Kamala herself is walking, so obviously Sunil *must* walk. Who does he think he is?"

"You must walk," Akbar said, nudging Sunil awake with his foot.

The driver hung his head moodily. That was the trouble with going too far with servants, Arjun thought.

"It will be good for you to walk," said Akbar consolingly. "You must learn to conquer fear. You aren't afraid of driving around on these dangerous roads. Why should you be afraid of a path traversed for centuries by thousands of pilgrims?"

"There are spirits that come and push people off," stammered the driver. "If Lord Shiva does not want you there, he will send them."

"Correct." Akbar nodded. "But I am certain Lord Shiva wants you to reach his shrine and come back safely, otherwise he would have sent both of us to oblivion yesterday."

Sunil's eyes were wide with fear.

"No argument," said Akbar, "you must walk! Princess Kamala is walking, Arjun-sahib is walking, so is the English sahib. Obviously I cannot, but you may walk beside me. I will hold your hand and prevent any spirits from attacking you." Akbar winked gleefully at Arjun. "Now let us get ready to go down before we miss breakfast. We are late."


THEY were eating rubbery omelets and hard toast when Sumitra appeared in a scarlet sari. Kamala, in her jumpsuit, looked stunned.

"What are you gaping at, Mummy dear?"

"You are wearing a sari, I can't believe it."

"For the Lord Shiva, Mummy. I put it on for him." She smiled deviously.

Kamala was speechless. Arjun tried to focus on his omelet. Overnight Sumitra had changed herself from a pouting young punk to a mysteriously beautiful Indian woman.

"I think she looks damn attractive," said David, trying to sound like an old uncle. The thought that in a few short weeks he'd be with her in Paris made him feel light-headed. What a formidable young woman she was! Would it really be possible to have a relationship with such a creature?

Arjun was studiously not looking at her, but he sensed a current passing between them and felt waves of lust welling up inside himself.

To Akbar, sitting at the head of the table, stuffing himself with chapattis, Arjun and David bore all the signs of two male dogs about to quarrel over a bitch in heat. The older dog, though trim, was not what he'd once been. Any day now he would wake up and realize he was finished. The young dog knew this. The time would come when he could easily overpower the old dog. Aware of this, the old dog would strike first; after all, he wasn't an old dog for nothing. Akbar often wished he could stop seeing people as animals. But in India, where the line between them was so blurred, it became a habit. It was very clear, for example, that some people were really monkeys, some goats, and of course there were the rarer and more important tiger, leopard, and elephant types. Elephant people were usually large and fat; he himself was one of their tribe. The elephant was the metaphor for the god of wisdom, craftiness, and, if necessary, brute force. Was he wise? In many ways he thought he was, except for his trunk, which depended, unfortunately, not from his head but from his loins. Except for that, he thought he might have been a very wise man.


AS SOON as breakfast was over, the servants assembled with Ravi and Sunil and the party made its way through the crowded narrow lanes of the bazaar to the staging area where the pilgrim trail began. On the hills above, the first rays of the rising sun were lighting up the forests. The smoke of cooking fires lay in wisps across the opening of the gorge, where a turbulent river whipped its way around huge boulders. Bells on the harnesses of the mountain ponies tinkled as they shook themselves in readiness for the nine-mile climb.

Arjun found the headman, with whom he had made arrangements the previous evening, and an oversized palanquin was brought out for Akbar. After certain adjustments were made, Akbar got in and lay down on the velvet-covered cushions. Eight sturdy young men groaned and lifted, Akbar raised one hand in an imperial wave, held on to Sunil with the other, and glided away. Philippa was provided with a good sturdy pony and a syce—a groom—and as Sumitra had announced at the last moment she would also walk, they set off.

Around a cliff, some five hundred yards ahead, the path began to climb abruptly, and by the time they reached the first resting place, Akbar, the servants, and Philippa were out of sight ahead. Badly winded, Kamala and David negotiated horses for themselves. As they waved goodbye, leaving Sumitra alone with Arjun, David felt totally defeated.

Arjun and Sumitra finished their tea and walked on in silence. He was surprised she was in such good condition. When he remarked on this, she laughed.

"But I practice yoga, play tennis, and do the Jane Fonda workout course. It's Mummy who makes me lazy, wanting me to be a model Indian maiden one day; a French debutante the next."

The path, paved with stones polished smooth by the feet of countless pilgrims, ascended the valley relentlessly and was mobbed with people: there were families of tall Rajasthani peasants in scarlet turbans and voluminous dhotis carrying bedding, cooking pots, and even firewood; a young, blond man in a loincloth with swollen bare feet passed them, leading a horse on which rode a fat orange-robed swami with a long greasy beard.

"See how we dupe these gullible Westerners," observed Arjun. "What cunning. Any one of us could put on holy robes—even Ravi— and do the same."

Hundreds of old people, some in rags and barely able to crawl, others so sick and crippled they had to be carried in baskets on the backs of coolies, advanced up the trail. A group of young Sikhs, dressed in trendy European ski clothes with climbing gear and modern camping equipment, passed them.

Soon they were high above the river, walking through thick oak forests. At intervals along the trail in makeshift huts and caves, holy men—hoping to attract pilgrims who would give them money—sat in meditation before smoldering fires. They came to a mountain stream tumbling down a small valley in a series of cataracts and pools. Climbing up, out of sight of the trail, they splashed their faces and rested.

"What a secluded spot," Sumitra said. "Could we bathe? I'm so hot."

Arjun smiled. "It is not good to bathe when one is overheated."

"You are in love with Philippa Bruce, aren't you?" she suddenly said.

"What makes you think that?" he said, drying his face with a cloth.

"I've been watching you. It's pretty obvious."

"Don't be silly, she is far too old for me."

"Then?" she said, staring at him provocatively.

"It's a long way to the top," he said. "We should save our strength."

She slipped her arms around his waist and pressed against him. His blood rose. Perhaps he should take her into the jungle and satisfy her, allay her suspicions about his feelings toward Philippa. She was obviously what the Muslims called a kus marani, a woman who could not get enough, but once he yielded, wouldn't she make trouble? He kissed her on the forehead.

"I am a married man," he said. "It wouldn't be right. As you have said, I must think of my wife and five children."

She slapped him across the face, spun about, and marched angrily away, her hips undulating. Cursing himself for not acting more authoritatively, he followed doggedly and caught up with her at the next resting place.

"We had better get horses," he muttered as they sat sipping tea. "We are above three thousand meters now, and you will be feeling the altitude."

She agreed sulkily, and after mounting two ponies they continued up the precipitous path, soon passing the young Sikhs with the camping equipment, and caught up with Kamala, David, and Philippa just as the gigantic peaks above Kedarnath loomed into view. After crossing a vast flower-strewn meadow, they joined Akbar and the servants, who were waiting for them at a bridge spanning one of the rivers which flowed from the base of the glacier. Behind the medieval town with its low stone and wooden buildings loomed mile-high vertical slabs of ice and snow.

They crossed the bridge and walked up a cobblestone street toward the temple. A few blocks away they halted in front of a small stone and elaborately carved timber house. On the ground floor, an open door led into a dark low-ceilinged room with a carpeted platform on which lounged a dhoti-clad young Brahmin. His forehead was plastered with sandalwood paste, and he was smoking a hookah.

"I received your very kind message, madam," he said in perfect English. "As you know, my accommodations are limited but they are clean. Three rooms, isn't it?"

"Yes." Kamala nodded.

They stood hesitantly at the door. The young man, who was called a purohit, stood up. Purohits, although affiliated with temples, are not necessarily presiding priests. Long ago, the ancestors of this particular young man had been tantric wizards presiding over the famous Shiva shrine. Exiled from those duties centuries ago, they still kept the ancient birth and death records of certain families, conducted private pujas, and were often considered to have magical powers.

Philippa realized with surprise that she had never seen a face like his before: savagely handsome, aristocratic, a face from the past. Yet his gestures and speech were those of an Oxford don—which, as it turned out, was not too surprising, for although he himself had not been farther than Delhi, his two uncles had been educated at Cambridge. When he stood up, Philippa saw he was a giant. Stooping low, he came out and led them up a steep narrow stairway to the floor above, where he showed them three small rooms with polished teak plank floors, straw mats, and mattresses.

Akbar squeezed up the small staircase but got stuck. The giant looked quizzically at him and said "Salaam," indicating that he knew Akbar was a Muslim. Out of breath, the poet glanced sharply at the purohit. It was obvious his raja cover would not work here.

"The Lord Shiva welcomes all religions, races, and castes, is it not so?" he asked in perfect Sanskrit.

The purohit seemed impressed and asked Akbar to wait downstairs. He backed down and waddled into the purohit's room. Soon the young man entered and sat down. On the wall hung a photograph of a compassionate-looking old man with matted gray hair to his waist.

Akbar gestured. "Your father?"

"Yes." The giant nodded. "He was sixty-first and I am sixty-second in an unbroken line. That places us here about the year 200 of the Christian era."

"You live here the year round?" asked Akbar. "It must get very cold."

"Our native place is a small village below Gaurikund; you passed through it. We are here six months of the year, six months down there. Two or three yogis stay here through the winter, that is all. But we are the oldest lineage. Those who serve in the temple nowadays were brought here over the last few hundred years. They are from south India.

"Many years ago we were accused of doing bad things—I do not know, we were only following the old religion, Sanatam Dharm—but out there"—he waved toward the plains—"religion changed and suddenly we were called witches and sorcerers. When you go to the temple, you will see where statues have been knocked off. This was done by the new Government of India in 1947. They said the statues of Shiva were erotic and sinful. If government can do that, it can do anything." He smiled. "But governments come and go and we remain."

"What of all these photographs of politicians?" said Akbar, pointing to the wall.

"They come here on yatras—pilgrimages—to worship and also spy on us. Most of them are arch-criminals; however, the gods of India will take care of them. Now they have gone into the Golden Temple at Amritsar, one more antireligious act, and the Sikhs will never forgive them. In twenty years there will be no Nehru family left in India. This is what I told Indira Gandhi, who recently visited us; there she is in that photo. It is written: the end is to begin here in India; two thirds of the world's population will disappear in a flash of light, struck by the divine weapon granted to Arjuna by Indra."

"But it is not supposed to be used," protested Akbar.

"Ah, I see you know our *Mahabharata*; most Mussalmen do not. Tell me, why are you coming to visit Lord Shiva?"

"My friends invited me. They said that making this pilgrimage absolved one of all sin."

"Sin is a Christian word; we prefer the word 'mistake.' But you do not look like a bad person."

The giant's mouth was set in a perpetual grin. Akbar found it most disconcerting; perfect rows of barred white teeth, so that after a while his expression was not felicitous but threatening.

"You are a great poet, or you could be." He nodded his head thoughtfully. "Your problems arise because at birth your body was invaded by a powerful female demon. She is still hanging on to you. That which you think is sinful are her thoughts, her desires. They are not bad; they only seem so because they are hers, not yours. She was very beautiful, yes, and is most unhappy to be in this body of yours. She finds it offensive, but it is better for her than no body at all. It is this conflict that is causing you to overeat. There is nothing wrong with you except you eat too much." The giant laughed and slapped Akbar's knee. "Let me see your hand."

Akbar gave his hand to the purohit, whose own hands were very hot. He pushed and poked at Akbar's fleshy palm.

"You have heard of Jhansi? I am getting that name. The female demon who invaded you came from there. She had many lovers but they never satisfied her. She is still not satisfied; this is why you find yourself wishing for the same, but as a man it is a problem for you."

Akbar was trembling. "I was actually born in Jhansi by mistake. My parents were traveling at the time."

"Koi Bad nahi hai, it does not matter," said the giant gently. "I will give you one mantra. With that you will worship the lingam of the Lord Shiva. I will write out certain instructions for you to follow and everything will change."

"But I am a Muslim, sir, and—"

"You may call me Pandu. It doesn't matter to me what you are. Go to one of your Pirs if you like, he will tell you the same. Mantras work for Mussalmen and Hindus alike, whether you believe them or not."

Kamala peered in through the door. "We are going to the temple for the evening puja, Akbar dear, are you coming?"

Akbar tried to withdraw his hand but Pandu held it tightly.

"Sit down, madam, the puja is not for one hour. Let me see your hand."

Somewhat irritated at being ordered about, Kamala sank to the floor and gave her hand to Pandu, who squeezed and kneaded it, spread it out, and squeezed again. "Left hand, please," he murmured, looking somewhat perplexed. Then he closed his eyes, sat silently for a few minutes, and opened them. "You have made some mistake in your life, one very great mistake. Tell me, have you had two or three husbands?"

"Two," stated Kamala, glancing at Akbar. "Everyone knows that."

"Ah, yes, madam, but I see three."

Kamala was furious that she'd allowed herself to become trapped, and with Akbar of all people. She smiled blandly. "I'm very sorry, but you are wrong. I have had only two husbands, and both are dead."

"But I see another and he is very much alive. Well, it shows one is not infallible. How many children do you have, madam?"

"Two," she replied.

"I see three." The purohit smiled. "One boy, two girls. One girl is married, has five children. It is all here in your hand"—he pointed—"where these lines come together."

Akbar stared skeptically at Kamala. She felt dizzy and took deep breaths to keep from fainting.

"Is something wrong?" asked Pandu.

"It must be the altitude. I feel faint."

"Of course," he said and clapped his huge hands. A boy appeared and tea was ordered. "Lie down here by me," he commanded. "You will be all right in a few minutes. You will please call me Pandu; that is my first name."

Kamala collapsed on the soft carpets, her head on a pillow against Pandu's thigh. Sumitra appeared at the door and giggled.

"What on earth are you doing, Mummy? Get up, we're going to the temple."

"Your mother is resting, she felt dizzy. Tea is coming. Please be seated." Sumitra looked sulkily around and sank to her knees. "You have been enjoying your walk today, yes?" Pandu looked keenly at her. "It is very good that you walked, at least part of the way. Rest now and take some tea."

Sumitra was exhausted; her mother was insisting they all go to the temple, and she wanted to get it over with and go to bed. "But the puja," she said in her slurred Mayfair accent. "We will surely miss it."

"It is too early. Have tea and rest." Pandu beckoned to the crouching hookah-maker to prepare a fresh pipe.

David, Philippa, and Arjun now poked their heads through the low door. They all stared at Kamala.

"Has something happened, are you all right?" exclaimed David.

Kamala raised herself on one arm. "The altitude . . . I had a slight dizzy spell."

"Sit down." Pandu grinned.

The hookah was passed around, and soon Pandu had Arjun's hands in his.

"Well, what do you see?" asked Arjun.

Pandu kept silent and examined David's hand, then Philippa's. Akbar thought he didn't really look at people's hands but was receiving information from a source for which hands were merely instruments.

"I am trying to determine why you are all here together," he said at last. "Your relationships are most complicated." He gazed inscrutably at Kamala and scribbled a note on a pad. "Now you had better all go to the temple. Give this to one of the priests, and he will take care of you."

Everyone except Akbar got up to go.

"You are not coming?" Kamala asked.

Akbar shook his head. "After all, I am Muslim."

"But this is a Shiva temple, they make no distinctions here."

"Still, I prefer to stay. Perhaps I will go in the morning."

"As you like." Kamala shrugged and followed the others out through the low door.

"You don't wish to go to the temple?" asked the purohit.

"I feel the real Shiva is here. Why should I go to the temple?"

Pandu smiled and beckoned for the hookah.

"What did you see in their hands?" asked Akbar. "You looked perplexed."

"I saw a mystery. The Princess Kamala says she has only two children, but I see three and also five grandchildren. How many children has Mr. Bruce?"

"Two, I believe."

"Again, I see three and five grandchildren in Mr. Bruce's hand. Is there some relationship between him and the princess?"

"It would have to be a long time back," said Akbar.

"There is also some peculiar relationship between this Englishman and Arjun Singh."

"Peculiar?"

"Not what you think, O demoness." Pandu laughed. "No, no, it is quite different from that. Their fates are entwined." He shook his head. "If I had the time, I could fit the pieces together. I doubt they will be alive in three months."

"Accident?" asked Akbar.

"Possibly, it is hard to say. But you must not repeat any of this to them."


AT THE temple there was a long queue. Arjun handed Pandu's note to a priest, and they were conducted through a side door to the inner sanctum. The ritual consisted of worshiping a stone, which was supposed to represent part of Shiva's body. First it was worshiped covered with expensive cloths and jewels, then the jewels were removed and the stone, which looked like a miniature quartz mountain, was worshiped with offerings and libations that were poured over it.

David found it difficult to pay much attention to what was going on. Since the trip began, he felt Sumitra had been flirting with Arjun. As the priests droned on, he remembered the softness of her skin, her youthful thighs. Had the events at the waterfall meant nothing? He pressed his knee against hers and felt her press back.

When they came out of the temple, the sun had set but the moon had not yet risen above the amphitheater of gray mountains. Below the temple twinkled fires of the sadhus and their glowing pipes. A warm breeze blowing up from the valley carried the pungent smoke through the streets. The others went on ahead, and he walked into town with Sumitra, past lamp-lit shops selling souvenirs, food, and offerings. Far above, snow was falling, the snow of winter and death, and he was suddenly overcome by a feeling of sadness for all the things he'd botched, especially his relationship with his daughter, Belinda. Getting to know Sumitra, he realized how harsh he had been on her. Mrs. Kapoorchand was right. Why shouldn't she have three husbands, or more if she liked? Perhaps it was because he'd been so strict that she'd revolted. He'd only meant to help her avoid the unhappiness his own promiscuity had brought him.

"Lost in thought?" Sumitra asked, clutching his arm. She was unaccustomed to wearing a sari and was having difficulty negotiating the uneven stones of the street.

"The gray landscape reminded me of England. See, it's snowing up there."

"It's like the end of the world here." She shuddered. "I find it rather frightening."

"I find you frightening," he muttered. "What you do to me, I find that frightening."

She squeezed his hand. "The waterfall was nice, wasn't it? Paris will be better."

"What were you doing with Arjun all day? I'm afraid I'm quite jealous. Don't be surprised if I come visit you in the middle of the night."

"You're very naughty; you mustn't try. Mummy is such a light sleeper."

"We could meet outside later. It will be full moon."

"David, really! See, here we are at the purohit's house. You must promise to behave."

They crowded into Pandu's room, where a statue of Shiva, a necklace of skulls around his neck, his left foot resting on a prostrate man, was illuminated by oil lamps. The purohit had just finished his puja. Like an enormous Buddha, Akbar sat in the shadows. Through a curtain was another room where dinner had been laid out. Subdued by puja and the mysterious ambiance of Kedarnath itself, they ate in silence.

Though he focused on his plate, David watched Arjun out of the corner of his eye and several times caught him looking at Sumitra.

Philippa, who had been watching Arjun too, wondered what had passed between them and began to think the whole trip was a ridiculous waste of time. Although the scenery had been most extraordinary, she would have preferred Terripur, where she could have had more time alone with him.

"Tomorrow," Kamala said, "Pandu has promised to take us to a hidden valley filled with flowers."

"That sounds marvelous," said Philippa.

"You will get some very good snapshots. The flowers just after the monsoon are truly remarkable."

The women retired and Arjun and David joined the purohit and Akbar for a hookah. The young giant's face was somber, his eyes unblinking. Before him, coals glowed in a brazier where, bare to the waist, he warmed his arms. So certain was he of what he had seen earlier, it was difficult for him to look at David and Arjun, whom he now saw as living corpses. His eyes narrowed to slits.

"Princess Kamala says you will take us to a hidden valley tomorrow," ventured Arjun.

The purohit nodded but did not speak, which made Arjun uncomfortable; could the giant be trying to read his mind? He began repeating a mantra Durga Baba had given him that was supposed to cut intrusive thought waves. After the hookah was finished, David excused himself and went upstairs.

"I shall go too." Arjun yawned. "Come, Akbar." He extended his hand.

"You forget I can't make it, old boy." Akbar grunted. "You'll have to survive without me. With Purohitji's permission, I think I shall sleep right here."

Pandu nodded. "Stay where you are. I sleep in my father's room in another part of the house. I shall have more pillows and blankets brought for you."

AROUND midnight Akbar was wakened from a profound sleep by a slight metallic noise. He opened his eyes and blinked. The light of the full moon cast a bar of silver across the carpet to the statue of Shiva. Then he saw that Kamala was sitting beside him, tossing coals into the brazier.

"I couldn't sleep," she muttered, seeing him come awake. "What the purohit said upset me so, I've been tossing and turning." She poked at the fire with a pair of tongs, turning over in her mind the horrible dream that had awakened her in which Sumitra was making love to a number of masked men, and shuddered. "I have to confide in some-one," she said softly. "You are always watching. Is something going on between Sumi and Arjun?"

Akbar rubbed his eyes. "Arjun is a married man," he said, realizing at once the stupidity of his remark. Nevertheless it gave him time to collect his thoughts and recover his customary poise. He cleared his throat. "He has just met your daughter, but as far as something between them . . . why do you ask?"

"I worry unnecessarily about her, I suppose, but today they fell far behind and were alone for hours. I'm no fool; I know the way men look at women, and I know Sumi. Arjun's father is a close friend. I wouldn't want Sumi breaking up his son's marriage."

"Like you, my dear, your daughter is most attractive and one cannot help noticing her, but I assure you I've detected nothing serious between them. But Arjun is not the only one who is watching her."

Kamala gazed at him. "I was afraid you were going to say that."

"All men notice your daughter, even David Bruce."

There it was, thought Kamala, what she had most feared. She'd been sure that one of the masked men in her dream had been David. How could he do it? It was too painful.

"But Captain Bruce is also married."

"Of course, but there is quite a difference between the two kinds of marriage." Akbar smiled.

Outside the window, the jagged peaks of Kedarnath glowed eerily in the moonlight. Off the highest one, a cloud of snow blown by the wind spewed out into the starry sky. The moon's ray caught the large diamond Kamala wore on her left hand, sending rainbow lights across Akbar's face. She glanced down at her hands, which looked suddenly wrinkled and old, and drew them under her sari.

"The party is over," she muttered to herself in Hindi. "The party is really over, and what is there left for me?"

"What party?" he asked her. "What are you mumbling about?"

"Although you are extremely wise, my dear, you are too young; you wouldn't understand."

"I think the moonlight has cast a spell on you."

"Moonlight is truth serum," she replied. "One says things under the influence of the moon that one could not say in the light of day. My mind is burdened by falsehoods, lies, insincerity . . . a lifetime of them. I long to break through this bag of flesh and bones and come face to face with another soul. I think I'm getting ready to die. I want to get out of my body."

"You believe in the soul, then?"

"Why, of course," she said, looking startled. "Don't you?"

"I'm not sure. If souls migrate from body to body, where are all the new souls coming from? Three hundred million new people here since I was born."

"From animals, of course," said Kamala, as though it were an obvious fact. "Can't you see? Look at the masses of newly born people; most of them are not much better than animals. As the wild animals of the forests are killed and become extinct, their souls take human bodies. Soon there will be few animals left and that will be the end. Then the process will reverse: many people will die and their souls will again go back into animals. The gods always balance the scales."

"I thought that once you got a human body, you didn't go back."

"That's all Buddhist rot," said Kamala. "It's not scientific, our ancient wisdom is."

"Why do you worry so much about Sumi?" he asked, changing the subject. "She's old enough to take care of herself."

"Because I've failed so miserably with my son."

"Sonny seems quite happy to me. Kirpan looks after him very well, good husband for him."

She winced. "You're so naughty. But you're right. Sonny is not really a man, is he? And he's so unhappy."

"You are the unhappy one, my dear. I submit that Sonny is quite happy."

"Well, the point is that Sonny is never going to get married and have children, assume his family responsibilities. That is why I am concentrating on Sumi. She is an Indian woman; nothing can change that. I want her to understand her country. But now, because she has lived abroad, she is neither this nor that. The men she meets here she finds lacking. Either they are oversexed or so shy they are useless drunks or perverted." She shivered. Her teeth chattered. "That hookah must have had opium in it, that's why I was having such strange dreams. Whenever I take opium, I have nightmares." She fiddled with her ring again. "You're a very nice young man. I enjoy talking to you."

For a moment Akbar thought she might crawl under the blanket with him, so desperate seemed her need for human warmth. To his surprise, however, she got up, pulled her shawl tightly about her, and stood silhouetted at the window, gazing at the moon.

"Moonlight glistening on snow drives me mad," she whispered. "I remember moonlit nights at St. Moritz. Sumitra's father died there in the snowy moonlight. It drives my tropical soul mad. We were bob-sledding down the side of a steep mountain. We'd been drinking, of course; Prem was in front; I became frightened and rolled off. The bobsled sped down the mountain and hit a tree. He was killed instantly; the couple behind me were in hospital for six months. It all happened in the bloody moonlight." She stared out the window.

"It must have been a terrible shock. I heard he was quite a man."

A look of distaste lingered at the corners of her mouth. "The odd part was I had decided to divorce him—or at least leave him. He was very handsome, all six feet four of him. Wherever we went, women lined up to get at him. But he was a tin soldier: nothing inside. So much outside; absolutely nothing inside . . . empty."

"Isn't that rather yogic?" Akbar tried to sound soothing.

"It was not that kind of nothing." She smiled. "There are different kinds, you know. Inside, Prem was a strange sort of imitation Englishman. Now I see that most of the people I know here are like that. At night he would sit reading the kind of comic books and magazines you find in military barracks, ones the noncommissioned officers read; that was the level of his mind. And he adored dirty jokes, spent hours telling them. On the surface he looked like Rama, or perhaps Bhima—magnificent physique, perfect face, unlined brow, sensuous lips, unblinking eyes like dark black pools—but he had no soul." She sat down on the carpet and sighed.

"What is your opinion of the purohit?" asked Akbar. "I think he is something other than he appears to be."

"Why do you think I fainted?"

"Did he tell you something that was true?"

"Yes, that is what really upset me, why I am sitting here. I have to tell someone." She paused and stared at him as if uncertain whether to go on. "The only man I have ever loved in my entire life is David Bruce." Akbar pushed himself up slowly until he was sitting upright. She said softly, "If I tell you more, will you promise never to betray my confidence?"

"Of course."

"Swear it," she said sternly.

"I swear it."

"And I am cursing you in advance if you tell any living soul. If you break your word, you will die and be reborn a one-eyed dog in Moradabad."

"Can't think of anything worse, my dear. Go on."

"I'm dead serious."

"But so am I. I have been to Moradabad, disgusting place. I can't think of anything more frightening than being a dog there, even for one minute."

"David Bruce and I were in love during the war. Arjun's father introduced us. I was only eighteen; David must have been about twenty. We saw a lot of each other during the war period in Delhi, Calcutta, Terripur. I was a close friend of Arjun's mother, Devika. The night of the groom's reception in Kotagarh, the last night of Devika's marriage festivities, David and I consummated our love. Captain Bruce may look like an Englishman, but his soul is Indian. He wanted to marry me but I was sure it wouldn't work out. You've heard stories of how proud and difficult my father was; well, he wouldn't have permitted it, especially as I was his only child. When I discovered I was pregnant, I vanished, went into hiding, never saw David again. He left India without finding me or knowing anything. The child was a daughter and stayed with a nurse for a few years; then I gave her to Madho Dev and Devika. My little girl, Gayatri, and Arjun grew up together and finally got married; that was Madho Dev's doing, not mine. I am Arjun's mother-in-law." She grimaced helplessly. "There, I've told you. I saw you watching when the pur- ohit read my hands and I knew you suspected something. But you must tell no one. My entire personal estate is going to those five grandchildren. The only other person who knows is Ramakrishna Rao. Sonny and Sumi have been well taken care of by their own fathers. It could be difficult for Gayatri if it got out. Arjun might leave her. All these years I've been protecting her from that stigma. Do you think me hateful?" She began to weep.

"Dear lady, not at all," Akbar said steadily.

"You don't think Arjun and Gayatri would feel tricked if they knew?"

"Undoubtedly Arjun's first concern would be having you for a mother-in-law."

"You are impossible," she said, patting her eyes with a scarf. "Be serious."

"I am. Actually, being a high-caste Anglo-Indian isn't that terrible anymore. On the other hand, I presume Gayatri's been brought up in a traditional way; she lives in a traditional environment. I can't imag- ine what she would think if she knew. I assume she doesn't?"

"Of course not."

"Are you sure Captain Bruce knows nothing of this?"

"Positive," said Kamala. "Only Madho Dev, Ramakrishna Rao, and now you know."

"Will you ever tell Captain Bruce?"

"If I can avoid it, no. He wouldn't be able to resist running to Kotagarh to reveal himself to Gayatri. The mother thinks of the child first, the father always of himself. Not only is Gayatri his daughter but she has three boys, his only grandsons. Of course he would blurt it all out to her. I will not have her bear that burden; it would devastate her, she could destroy her children." She stared gloomily at Akbar.

"The purohit is clairvoyant, isn't he? Rare in one so young. Must be a natural gift."

"Indeed, it's frightening."

# 16

THE NEXT MORNING, bundled in shawls and coats, everyone, including Akbar, crowded the inner sanctum of the temple, to attend puja, and, after a quick breakfast of puris, set out with the purohit on the trail to his secret valley. Crossing a river, they ascended the side of a barren plateau and came to a windblown moor where a scattered collection of stone huts and cairns marked the spot where the god Shiva in his world-destroying aspect was worshiped. Frightened, Kamala wrapped her shawl tightly around her while Pandu explained how three naked ascetics sat there meditating for the benefit of mankind, even through the winter months when snow piled up in drifts over twenty feet high. One of the hermits, a big robust man in his forties, came out and greeted them. Arjun asked him how, without firewood or clothes, he kept warm.

"Stay with me and I will teach you the secret," he said, laughing heartily.

"Someday I will." Arjun laughed back.

"Now," urged the yogi. "There is no other time. I can see you will never return this way again."

Kamala glanced at Akbar in his palanquin and rolled her eyes. They bowed to the yogi and hurried on between monumental cliffs, down into a grassy bowl some five miles wide where flower-strewn meadows bordered a deep blue lake.

Philippa, intent on photographing the exquisite flowers, began experimenting with various filters and fell behind. As the others wound their way across the vast landscape, through fields of shoulder-high dahlias and cosmos, Arjun dropped back and joined her.

"I haven't had a chance to tell you how much I love you," he said tenderly as she stooped down to get a new lens out of her carrying case.

She trembled. "I was beginning to wonder . . ."

"About what?" he whispered, crouching beside her, kissing her neck and cheeks. "There has been no opportunity."

"I know," said Philippa, "but when you fell so far behind yesterday with Sumitra—you could have taken a horse, you know. It was quite obvious she didn't change her mind till the last minute so she could be alone with you."

Arjun covered her mouth gently with his hand. "Listen," he said. "Sumitra is a hollow shell; she's nothing to me. I know what she wanted, but she didn't get it. I went along with her nonsense because I thought it would throw the others off the track." He kissed her again and held her in his arms.

When they got up and began walking along the path, the others were mere dots in the distance on the other side of the valley.

"How vast the scale is!" she exclaimed. "Look at the snow peaks. I can't believe this place exists. It's fantastic."

The purohit had followed a path around the perimeter of the valley to the opposite side. Near the edge of a forest of mighty firs, he stopped, and by the time Philippa and Arjun caught up, lunch had been spread out on cloths.

"Come, help yourselves," called Kamala, glancing suspiciously at Arjun. "Where have you two been?"

"I've been taking close-up shots of some of these gorgeous flowers," said Philippa. "I had to use different lenses and filters, which took quite a bit of time. Sorry."

Akbar and Sumitra were giggling over some piece of gossip and David was deep in conversation with Pandu.

"A few furlongs from here is a temple where a holy fire has burned without interruption for a thousand years, possibly more," he said.

"I would like to see that," said Arjun.

"But it is already afternoon, Purohitji," interrupted Kamala.

"You wouldn't come this far and not see a thousand-year-old fire, would you?" Akbar twitted. "It might bring us good luck."

"Unlike the rest of us, you are being carried, dear poet."

"Is it my fault that you choose to walk?"

"At the temple I will arrange for you to be carried back," said Pandu. "There are always some litters and men to carry them, no problem."

"Then we should not waste any more time dawdling over our lunch," said Kamala, staring pointedly at Sumitra.

"You know how I loathe gobbling my food," Sumitra replied. "And we haven't had coffee yet. No one is going to function without coffee, Mummy darling."

Kamala shouted to the cook to bring coffee and Ravi to clear away the lunch. Sumitra sighed, handed over her half-finished plate, got out her makeup, and repaired her face.

"You'd think she was lunching at Maxim's," said Kamala.

Sumitra glared at her. How beautiful she was, thought David, and remembered the same expression on Kamala's face when she used to rage at the ayahs and chaperones her father sent along to watch her.

They rose and followed Pandu along a path sparkling with mica through a forest of ancient fir trees. Far below could be heard the roar of a mighty river; across the valley, waterfalls of great height fell into green chasms. The sun on the pine needles caused a sweet scent to rise, and bees buzzed in profusion.

Rounding a corner, they came to a natural amphitheater protected by high cliffs. There stood a group of old, carved granite buildings, partly crumbling. Around them sat more ascetics, their ash-colored hair worn long or plaited in giant nests atop their heads. One of the biggest, a man of middle age in strong physical condition, came forward. The purohit saluted him with cool indifference. Kamala suspected there was some bone of contention between them.

"He doesn't like the idea of David or Philippa being here," explained Arjun, who understood Garwhali, "nor Akbar. He is saying they are non-Hindus and cannot enter; that this is not a public place but the property of an ancient sect of sadhus who have maintained it for thousands of years. In all that time, the fire has never gone out." Arjun turned to the purohit. "Tell them that Captain Bruce was born in India."

Pandu spoke. The naked yogi appraised David carefully and muttered something.

"He says," translated Arjun, "that it is most auspicious that Captain Bruce was born in India, but still he is not a Hindu. As he was born here, he could become one by renouncing the world and practicing austerities for some time, but, as he is already old, it is probably too late. His wife is most certainly not a Hindu, and the fat gentleman is obviously a Mussalman. They cannot enter."

"I am very sorry," apologized the purohit. "At Kedarnath, all are welcome, but here they have a right to their own rules. It never occurred to me this might happen. I am very sorry. Would you three mind waiting while I take the Princess, her daughter, and Sri Arjun inside?"

In his palanquin, Akbar sighed and lay back on the pillows.

"Really, I don't mind," said Philippa. "It's such a delightful spot. Would you ask if I could take a few pictures?"

Pandu petitioned the yogi but the reply was immediate. "No pictures."

"I am very disappointed in you," snapped Kamala in crisp Hindi. "These are my friends; they have come a long way to see this fire and should be allowed to enter. Ownership of this place is very debatable. I don't think you own it any more than I do."

"The ancient rules must be observed," said the yogi. "The fire must not be disturbed by the eye rays of nonbelievers or there will be universal disruption."

"I should have had him on my land when the government took it away," murmured Kamala. "Very well, then, let us go in."

"You must bathe first. There is a hot spring a short distance away. Take your bath and return."

Kamala nodded. "We won't take long. Come Sumi, Arjun, we must hurry."

"I am not going to bathe and I don't care about seeing some fire that's been burning for however many thousand years," pouted Sumitra. "Think of the wood, the forests, that fire has consumed."

"Look around you." Pandu smiled. "Do you see any signs of cutting?"

"No," admitted Sumitra.

"The yogis are not responsible for the decimation of our forests," said Pandu. "They are the best conservationists in India; they only burn dead wood, and they protect young trees."

Sumitra sighed. "I just don't feel like going to all the trouble of a bath right now, Mummy. If you must see the fire, you and Arjun go. I shall stay here."

Kamala threw up her hands in despair and disappeared with Arjun.

David looked at the sky, where clouds were piling up on top of the mountains. The yogis, some of whom had stood up while their preceptor spoke, resumed their duties and meditations.

"At Mount Athos in Greece women are not allowed, nor are non-Christians," observed David. He was happy to relax and watch the yogis and sadhus. It was not unlike a Greek monastery. From the first, the place had reminded him of Delphi, where a sacred fire had burned from within the earth and democracy was born among the tribes who had assembled there. How different, though, the Hindu mind was:

hermetic, authoritarian. But the fire at Delphi had gone out and this fire still burned. What did that mean?

THE sun had disappeared behind clouds and Kamala shivered as she stooped to enter the low door of the temple. Inside it was dark and warm, the air heavy with incense. Blinded by the sudden darkness, at first she failed to notice a wizened old man, sitting on deerskins in front of a fire contained in a square pit, frozen in a trance of ecstatic meditation, his arms raised. She thought he looked like a catatonic she had once seen in a Swiss asylum where she had visited a cousin recovering from a bout of hysteria. To the old man's right sat a young boy of twelve or thirteen, his eyes closed, hands folded in lap. Kamala touched the old man's feet.

"He is our mahant," said the middle-aged yogi. "I am his successor, and the boy is my successor. There are always three mahants; that way we have safeguarded our lineage. This fire is an oracle. It sends us messages, foretells the future, sees the past. We ask it questions; it answers them. We read it like a book."

Flames, first blue, then green, purple, turquoise, and scarlet tipped with gold, burst from between massive logs. Kamala gazed at the old man, whose long white hair reached his waist.

"He is ninety-four," said their guide. "I am fifty, the boy is thirteen."

Passing his hand over the fire, the old man placed his thumb on Kamala's forehead, then on Arjun's. The young boy handed him ash from the fire and he smeared their foreheads with it, mumbling Sanskrit phrases neither of them understood.

"You would like to ask something of the fire?" he inquired.

"I would like to communicate with my mother and father," said Kamala.

"Stare into the fire then."

She stared into the flames, felt drowsy, and closed her eyes. Without warning an inner vision unfolded and there were her mother and father. They were very young, younger than she had ever remembered them. The scene was so vivid she was overcome with joy. Her mother looked radiantly happy, her father strong and handsome. Her father was wearing a pink turban with a large emerald pin stuck into it, and her mother was dressed in a salmon-colored chiffon sari ruffled by a breeze from the bluest sky Kamala had ever seen. She was spellbound.

"I forgot what I was going to ask them," she said excitedly, opening her eyes. "It was them, I saw them; they were so lifelike I just forgot what I was going to say. I only wanted to run and embrace them. Oh, Arjun, you must try it; do as he says and stare at the fire."

Arjun couldn't think of anyone he particularly wanted to see but stared into the fire and thought of Gayatri and his children. Suddenly he was flying up away from the Himalayas over the Ganga toward Rajasthan. Far to the south he could see Agra, and to the north lay Delhi. Like a homing pigeon, he flew directly toward Kotagarh at a dizzying speed and was soon circling his house. He could see his mother and the children playing with a big red ball in the courtyard and Madho Dev helping with the repair of one of the tractors while Gayatri, at the kitchen door, supervised the washing and drying of some wheat. He wanted to alight and talk to them but could not control his flight and careened crazily around the courtyard upside down. Feeling disoriented and weak, he opened his eyes. The first thing he saw was the old mahant smiling and nodding at him.

"It takes much practice to control where one is going, even more to communicate, but it can be done. Would you care to go into the future?"

Kamala thought of the predictions of the purohit and did not think they were prepared to see what lay ahead.

"It might be too shocking."

"You are strong," said the old mahant, "only you don't know it." He said something in rapid Sanskrit to the middle-aged yogi, who then spoke.

"Why don't you stay with us, both of you, and let the others return. You are in some danger. We will seek to change your karma." He conferred again with the old man. "He says if you value your lives— and you should, because it is very difficult to attain a human body— you must stay with us for three months. By then the danger will have passed. The period commencing at the next dark of the moon is most inauspicious; the wise will not take action then. The fire has told us these things."

They are trying to capture me for a large donation, thought Kamala. All right, I can afford it and they deserve it. She decided to test them.

"I am very impressed, O noble sage." She addressed the old mahant. "That your people have protected this fire for so long is most commendable. I would like to settle a certain amount of money on you in a trust that will provide a monthly income."

"We thank you," replied the old man calmly, "but that does not change the fact that for your own safety you should stay here for the next three months. I am not trying to extract money from you. We are rich beyond measure."

"Do you know what is going to happen?" she asked. "Can you tell us?"

"Something is going to happen to Indira Gandhi, we do not know exactly what, but we know. There will be disturbances. It is there in the stars, in her horoscope, in the numbers, in the fire, in all the omens and portents. She knows. People have warned her; we have warned her. If she were to retire at once to an ashram and take ascetic vows, she might survive and become a great force for good in this world."

Kamala chuckled.

"You do not believe me?"

"I do believe you, holy one. Many people have advised her in this way. I am smiling because I am sure it is the very last thing she will do."

"It is not her fault," said the old man. "It is her karma; she is not capable of true wisdom in this lifetime. In her own small way she has tried to honor the gods. Unfortunately, her choice of preceptors has not been wise."

They stared silently into the crackling fire.

Kamala sighed. "Even though I might wish to remain here, O holy one, I cannot. Too many people depend on me. I am a Rajput. Is it not my duty to plunge into battle having no regard for heat or cold, pleasure or pain, detached from the fruit of my actions?"

The old man smiled. "Yes, that is your duty. You are a good woman."

"Am I also in danger, Holy Father?" asked Arjun.

The old man nodded. "Great danger. Greater danger than she is in."

"He also is a Rajput."

"That I can see by looking at him. However, unlike his namesake, Arjuna, his father is not a god, not Indra. Therefore, he is not invincible. Beware of stones," he muttered prophetically.

"Of what?" asked Kamala.

"Stones," said the old man, "stones in the sky. You must beware of those, and he must beware of fire." As the word "fire" left his lips, a violent clap of thunder sounded outside. "Megh Raj hare hare," he murmured.

Kamala shuddered. "We must be going. The purohit, our friends— they are all waiting."

The old man shook his head. "It is too late. You will not go from this place until tomorrow." He pointed upward. On cue, the thunder rolled again. "Your party will be comfortable," he went on. "We have dharamsalas for ladies and gentlemen. We will prepare your food here. Unaccustomed to this altitude, you could become ill if you were caught in a storm. Our people will take care of you." He smiled. "No problem."

"Please rest now," said the middle-aged yogi. "We will provide blankets and bedding. Come." And he gestured to the small door.

They touched the feet of the old mahant and backed out of the temple.

Outside, rain suddenly fell with great force. Sumitra, Akbar, David, and Philippa were nowhere in sight. Arjun and Kamala followed one of the monks across the courtyard to a long, low building. The building was divided in two equal halves. The floors were warm; the monk explained that hot water from the spring flowed under them.

"Spartan but warm and clean," said Philippa, in good spirits, as they entered the building. "They've been warning us not to go back this evening."

"The ladies may stay here and the gentlemen on the other side," said the monk.

"Now I shall have a bath," announced Sumitra.

"Now?" Kamala snorted. "Very well, if you must, but after that you should visit the great saint who is sitting inside the temple. He is ninety-four years old."

"That makes him a great saint?" said Sumitra.

Kamala looked disgusted. "Must you always be so negative?"

"Now I'm negative," cried Sumitra. "Just because I'm asking a simple question?" She appealed to Akbar.

"Don't look at me, I have no intention of getting between you two. Be an angel and take your bath; then you can decide what to do. I'm longing for one, and I'm sure the Bruces are too, so don't take forever."

Sumitra sniffed. "How much time am I allowed?"

"Twenty minutes," said Kamala. "That's quite enough. Or if you want to wait until everyone else is finished, you can stay all night. But you'll find the water highly sulfurous. Twenty minutes should be enough."

It grew dark. The monks brought in braziers filled with glowing coals, steaming pots of kedgeree, rotis, and hot milk. By ten they were all asleep, all but David, whose brief slumber was interrupted by explosive, crepitant sounds issuing from Akbar. The storm had passed. Moonlight streamed through the window. Arjun slept peacefully, his hands clasped behind his head. David went to the door and gazed out. A warm breeze from the lower regions had arisen. Beyond the stone terrace the forest was a fairyland of light and shadow. Akbar's noises were abominable; the room claustrophobic. He got up and stepped outside. Someone was sitting on a low bench in the shadows overlooking the moonlit valley. It was Sumitra.

"I woke up," he whispered.

"So did I," she said moodily. "It's the only time I have to myself, what with Mummy constantly at me. Isn't the moonlight beautiful? I was hoping you would wake up. Let's take a walk."

"I don't have my shoes," said David.

"Neither do I, but the pine needles will be soft."

"Someone will see us, one of the monks."

"I'm sure it won't be the first time. Come, stop fretting. See, there's a path up into the forest."

They crossed the terrace, climbed a path, and stood in the deep shadows of ancient gnarled fir trees overlooking the temple complex.

"Beautiful, isn't it?" murmured David.

"Too primitive for me." She shuddered. "I'll take Paris any day. Mind you, Mummy patronizes these places because deep down inside she's afraid. She believes in magic."

"Don't you?"

"No."

"I do. How do you account for that?"

"You were born here. I was born in Switzerland." She shrugged. "My father left India in 1946, clever man. Unfortunately, I never knew him."

They walked on around the mountain out of sight of the temple. Like quicksilver spilled by some careless god, radiant moonlight splashed the forest floor. He put his arm around her waist.

"What did you do with Arjun on the trail yesterday?" he asked. "He couldn't take his eyes off you last night."

She sighed and stared up into his dark blue eyes, the color of the asters in her mother's garden. Why did some men always have to find something to get angry about when they became excited?

"What do you think I did, take him off into the bushes? Can I help it if he stares at me?" She could see a relationship with this man was going to be difficult. She wasn't jealous of anyone; why was everyone always so jealous of her? "I guess I'll go back," she said and turned to leave.

He held her tightly in his arms and kissed her.

"I didn't do anything," she sighed, "but even if I had, what business is that of yours? The only important thing is what happens between us here, now. You can't own people, you know, that's a very old-fashioned attitude. There's nothing more boring than jealousy, it kills everything. You think too much."

She knew she was being brutal but it seemed the only way. Unbuttoning his shirt, she put her arms around him and kissed his chest. He spread out her shawl on the ground, unwound her sari, and sank to his knees. She loved the primitive feeling of being naked in the moonlight. They lay on their backs and listened to the night sounds.

"Just think," she said. "In a few weeks we'll be together in Paris and have all the time in the world."

He covered his face with strands of her long thick hair. How he loved the clean, young smell of it. It was true, of course, what she had said; what right did he have to lay claim to her? Yet now he had found her, not to be jealous was hardly human. She had given him life and hope again, something he thought was dead and gone. And yet the numbers were all wrong: old man, young girl. He knew himself too well. The moment she was out of his sight, he'd be wondering where she was, what she was doing, whom she might be going to bed with. She made him feel like the proverbial dirty old man. It wasn't her fault, of course, but there it was.

"It's your wanting things to last forever that makes you sad," she said, as if reading his mind. "Nothing lasts forever. You have to live for the moment; that's what I do. That's how people my age live because we have to. The world might end tonight, how do we know? Your generation has set it up that way."

She raised herself over him and kissed him passionately. He felt like a victim in the hands of some sacrificial priestess. Her disheveled hair hung down over his chest. If she had had a knife, he swore she could have carved his heart out. In fact, she had already done so, there under the waterfall. Now she was gyrating above him. A thousand tongues seemed to lick the root of his existence, a thousand arms and legs to caress and ensnare him. He pulled her down and took her like an animal. Just then an insane cry shattered the silence. For a moment he was confused and covered her mouth with his, but the call sounded again and was answered by others. The eerie, half-human screams seemed to excite her. She dug her nails into his back. Her body arched up, and they lay trembling together in the profound silence of the starry night. Above the valley, the icy peaks of the Himalayas floated in the moonlight like celestial beacons.

"If I never made love again it wouldn't matter," David said finally.

"Don't say things like that, it's unlucky," she murmured.

He'd begun to feel guilty, of course, as he always did after it was over. Post-coital tristesse. She was so young, younger than his own daughter, and there was Kamala, whom he'd come back to find, and what of Philippa?

"Why is it unlucky?" he asked.

"Because what you say often happens. I certainly wouldn't want to think this is the last time we're going to make love. It's only the beginning. We haven't really had a chance to be alone."

"Why do I feel guilty about what we've just done?" he asked her.

"Because you want to," she said sadly. "How do you think a remark like that makes me feel?"

"I don't want to," he said, "I loathe it."

"Well, something inside you does or you wouldn't. I thought it was beautiful, especially when those animals screamed. What were they?"

"Jackals."

"Whatever. I think they were watching us and became jealous. They screamed just when I wanted to." She giggled. "Stop looking so serious."

They dressed and stood together in each other's arms. He smoothed her forehead and braided her long hair.

"Let me go back first," she said. "If anyone is watching, I'll say I couldn't sleep and took a walk. You must stay here for some time before you come down. Mummy could be waiting for me."

He followed her back and stood in the shadows while she walked down the path to the dharamsala. Just as she reached the door, it opened and he saw Kamala step out.

"What are you doing out at this hour?" she hissed loudly. "I heard jackals and woke up and you weren't here. I became terrified. Where have you been?"

"Walking in the moonlight," whispered Sumitra. "In fact, it's warmer now than when we went to bed. Come out for a minute."

Kamala shook her head. "It's beautiful, but I'm too tired and we both need our rest."

Inside the room, Philippa lay sound asleep. Sumitra slipped into her bed but Kamala remained standing at the window.

"Mummy, I thought you were tired. Come to bed," whispered Sumitra, afraid David might appear before her mother left the window. "Mummy, come to bed. You'll be exhausted in the morning; we have a long walk back."

"I'm enjoying the moonlight from inside," said Kamala calmly. "As long as it doesn't shine directly on me, I love it." Soon she saw David descend the path, brush himself off, and go to his room. Her face was a mask. "You're right," she said, turning away. "I'll be exhausted tomorrow if I don't sleep. Good night, darling."

She slipped under her blankets, her heart pounding. Feelings of betrayal and anger welled up inside her. How dare Sumi make love with him, her lover, Gayatri's father, a grandfather? How dare David yield to her selfish, adolescent whims—slut that she was? How could she, Kamala Devi, have brought forth such an abomination? She pressed her mouth against her pillow to keep from sobbing. She would not break down; that's precisely what Sumi would love, to see her fall apart. No, she'd not give her that satisfaction; she'd remain calm and cool and send the little tart packing as soon as possible. The sight of her was a torment. And David, curse him! Now she would certainly have to confront him with the truth. Yes, it was high time someone held a mirror up and forced him to look into it.

THE next morning after worshiping the fire and distributing money, Kamala, driven by her anger, set a pace which was difficult to follow. They arrived back at Kedarnath for lunch and, after a rest and bath, as the setting sun turned the snowy peaks to gold, she went alone to the temple and, standing in front of the shrine of Lord Shiva, offered thanks to the god of destruction and generation for revealing to her here on his mountain the course of action she must follow.

That evening after the others had retired, she and Akbar sat talking with the purohit late into the night about the future of India.

"The rope is burnt out," Pandu said enigmatically, "but the twists won't go away."

"I've heard that expression before," replied Akbar. "What exactly does it mean? I've never understood."

"Have you never seen a burnt-out rope? The ash will retain the structure, but if you touch it—poof, it will be gone. That is India; that is you, me." He smiled disconsolately.

"But you certainly aren't burnt out," argued Kamala. "You have seven children; you are young."

"My place is in the temple, not here; our position has been usurped."

"But see these walls covered with photographs of your family's devotees. There you are standing with Ramakrishna Rao, my father's protégé, one of the most powerful men in India. And there you are wearing a Gandhi hat; were you just clowning or are you a secret member of the Congress Party?" Kamala laughed wickedly.

"Deception." The young giant smiled. "As you may know, our family is descended from the race of great snakes, the snake people of old. Snakes and jackals have a long history: both are very intelligent but snakes are older and wiser. In times of trouble they disappear deep inside the earth while the jackal runs here and there, always hungry, looking for food, deceiving his fellow animals. Snakes hibernate. Jackals are extremely clever; they have been known to defeat the tiger, the lion, the elephant . . . but rarely a snake. These days India is ruled by a tribe of clever jackals. Now they have challenged the sleeping lion of Punjab. After the two destroy each other, we snakes will show ourselves again."

"The old mahant said I should beware of stones in the sky. Do you know what he meant?" asked Kamala.

"A time of trouble is near at hand. He means what he says; for once we are in agreement."

"But stones in the sky? It doesn't make sense. Was he speaking in riddles?"

"That I cannot say, madam. He also invited you to stay with him for three months. You should respect his authority and accept his invitation. It was a great honor, one he would not bestow lightly. It is very safe there, difficult for paws and jaws of jackals to reach."

"You really believe it's that bad?"

"Very bad," said Pandu. "These days our rulers think like Kanika of old and follow his evil ways. Do you know of Kanika?" Kamala looked blank. "In *Mahabharat*, when King Dhritarashtra becomes jealous of the sons of Pandu, he calls Kanika, a wicked Brahmin versed in the ways of politics, to advise him."

Pandu recited the Sanskrit verses.

" 'What to do?' asks Dhritarashtra. 'Listen to me, O sinless king,' says Kanika. 'If your adversary be one of great prowess, one should watch for the hour of his disaster and then kill him without scruples. When a foe is in thy power, destroy him by every means open or secret. Do not show him any mercy although he seeketh thy protection. Carefully concealing thy own means, thou should always watch thy foes, seeking their flaws. By maintaining the perpetual fire, by sacrifices, by matted locks and hides of animals for thy bedding, shouldst thou at first gain the confidence of thy foes, and when thou hast gained it, thou shouldst then spring upon them like a wolf. For it hath been said that in the acquisition of wealth even the garb of holiness may be employed as a hooked staff to bend down a branch in order to pluck fruits that are ripe. The foe must never be let off, even though he addresseth thee most piteously. No pity shouldst thou show him but slay him at once. If thy son, friend, brother, or even spiritual preceptor becometh thy foe, thou shouldst, if desirous of prosperity, slay him without scruples. By curses and incantations, by gifts of wealth, by poison or by deception, the foe should be slain. He should never be neglected from disdain. Thou shouldst burn the house of that person whom thou punishest with death. Thou shouldst make thy teeth sharp to give a fatal bite. Thou shouldst never trust too much those that are faithful, for if those in whom thou confidest prove thy foes, thou art certain to be annihilated. Thou shouldst employ spies in thy kingdom and in the kingdoms of others. In speech thou shouldst ever be humble but let thy heart be ever sharp as a razor. And when engaged in doing even a very cruel and terrible act, thou shouldst talk with smiles on thy lips. He who trusteth in a foe who has been brought under subjection by force, summoneth his own death as a crab by her act of conception.'

"These are just a few of the poisonous thoughts let loose in the world by Kanika," said Pandu seriously. "Today, the jackals are all his followers. It was this thinking that led to the destruction of the Kauravas and Pandavas on the plain of Kurukshetra. Every jackal since has made Kanika his guru."

"You make things sound quite hopeless," said Kamala.

"In this world, dear lady, hope is an illusion. Even if a leader of unblemished character were found, he would inevitably be corrupted by the fawning jackals around him: corrupted, felled, and eaten."

"Then the whole country must change," declared Kamala.

Pandu laughed. "Of course, it will always be changing, but it will not get better. The universe is constantly in motion. It will destroy itself, then renew, then destroy, like that." He traced a spiral in the air with his forefinger.

"Is that what is about to happen—destruction?"

"The jackals will consume everything, finally each other. It has been foretold many times by sages of great ascetic merit. The end will start here in Bharat and will engulf the world."

"Where is one to go? What is one to do?"

Akbar guffawed. The purohit smiled. A look of perplexity crossed Kamala's features.

"What are you laughing about? I don't see anything funny."

"My dear Princess," Akbar said. "If the whole world is going to be engulfed, of course there is no place to go."

She looked thoughtful. "I could leave the country, but I won't! I have lived in Europe, America, Singapore, all very nice places, but I shall remain here, even if I should end my days begging in the streets."

"Perhaps you should try it," suggested Pandu and leaned forward eagerly. "I will tell you a story. One of my father's devotees was the president of a Calcutta bank. He became ill. Father told him to leave the bank and take up begging. Grudgingly he obeyed, took off his clothes, put on a gunny bag, and began to beg. It was very sad to see. I was about twelve at the time; we would see him here and there in these hills. He hated his new vocation and soon came to hate his fellowman. Several years passed. His worried family came to Father, who assured them he was alive and well. One November I was in Varanasi bathing at Dasaswamedh Ghat when whom should I see but this former bank president-cum-beggar. He looked ten years younger, his hunched back had become straight, his hair hung down over his shoulders, and, wearing only a loincloth, he glided through the crowd toward me, dancing with joy."

"Perhaps I should take up begging." Akbar grinned.

"And where is this man now?" asked Kamala.

"On the west coast, near the sea, sitting in a cave in the best of health. I get postcards from him. He made over his assets to his wife and children but kept one fixed deposit which pays him four hundred rupees a month." The purohit shuffled through some papers and produced a snapshot. "Here he is."

Kamala laughed. "He still looks like a banker: a naked banker."

"This calamity, whatever it's going to be, do you have an exact date?" asked Akbar.

"All signs point to the period just ahead. But what happens then, though seeming like the end, will in fact be only the beginning of something worse—corruption without end."

Kamala stared at the purohit, her eyes wide. "I am descended from women who burned themselves rather than be corrupted."

"Not all of them, my dear," Akbar drawled, "or you wouldn't be here."

"You know very well what I mean." She rattled her bracelets nervously. "Our family have been warriors in India for thousands of years, the men *and* the women. If I'm headed for destruction, then that is my fate, but I must do my duty."

"And what is your duty?" asked Akbar.

"To fulfill my obligations to those who depend upon me. What else? Do you think if I weren't watching over things these government jackals wouldn't do us in?" She sighed and touched Pandu's feet.

He smeared ash on her forehead. "I must thank you for all your kind attention," she murmured. "It is late now. I'd love to stay up talking, but tomorrow will be a long day and, as I remember, going down a mountain is harder on the legs than coming up. I must go to bed."

She excused herself and went up to her room. Sumi was asleep. At least she was not off with David. She said her prayers but lay awake oppressed by morbid thoughts. How old she felt, especially since last night. In fact, she'd recently had spells when she felt dead, looked about at her friends, family, and possessions, and speculated on how they would still be there when she had been reduced to ash. Horrible thoughts. Perhaps an evil spirit had taken possession of her through the jealous eye waves of an enemy. Perhaps the same demon had sent David and his wife to torment her. She reminded herself to try to see Ma. It was such a long trip. At the earliest possible moment, however, she must write to her and seek advice.


AFTER attending morning puja at the temple and saying their fare-wells to the purohit, they began their descent. With the young driver Sunil clutching his hand, Akbar in his palanquin led the way. Now the steep part had begun, he was terrified. Across the shoulders of the bearers, he could see nothing but space. One wrong move and he would go hurtling into the abyss. They might even become tired of carrying him and contrive an accident.

Sumitra, in jeans and sneakers, jumped from rock to rock, trying to keep up, while Arjun and Philippa followed close behind. Kamala and David brought up the rear.

"What a great natural treasure," Kamala was saying.

She paused and looked across the valley to where a waterfall coming from a glacier fell thousands of feet into the chasm below. The path had leveled out, and the others hurried on ahead. "David, I have to speak to you about something." She hesitated.

"We haven't had much time alone, have we?" He smiled.

She turned away, almost afraid to look at him, swallowed hard, and went on. "It's just this. . . . There is something you should know, something important."

He looked puzzled. "Go on," he said.

"That purohit is a very gifted young man," she said slowly. "I don't know how he does it, but he was right when he read your hand."

"About what?"

"You do have three children, and there are grandchildren."

David blinked. "Would you say that again, please? About a third child and grandchildren?"

"Yes, she is now a married woman and has five children."

"My child?" he asked.

"Yours and mine."

His heart leapt into his throat; he felt dizzy. "I think I'd better sit down for a moment," he said. "Why did you keep this from me all these years? When you knew I looked high and low for you?"

Her face was expressionless. "First of all, we could never have married; my father wouldn't have permitted it. Second, if you had acknowledged the child, she would have been branded an Anglo-Indian; I'm sure you're aware of the stigma attached to Anglo-Indians in our great new democracy. And then, as it turned out, I was able to arrange it so she was adopted by a distant relative of royal blood and married to a young man also of royal blood. The girl herself has no idea who her father or mother are. There is a vague story about her parents being drowned in a boat crossing the Ganga. One reason I've hesitated telling you this is that I don't want you running to her, disclosing yourself as her long-lost father, grandfather of her five children."

He sighed deeply, shook his head, and held her hand. "Strange, isn't it"—he smiled—"life, I mean. We each have a son and a daughter, they haven't turned out the way we would have liked, yet the daughter who never knew us is—"

"Happy? I'm not sure. Like all well-trained Rajput girls she has a strong sense of duty and she's very bright."

"Will I be able to meet her? If I promise not to say anything?"

"Ah, but that's the problem. You already have!"

He closed his eyes. Pain stabbed his chest. "Certainly not Sumitra, she's too young."

"No, not Sumi." Kamala laughed. "You needn't fear having committed incest."

Again a sharp pain. If she didn't stop, he thought he might have a heart attack. He swallowed. "I say, go easy on me, will you? I'm only a man, quite a simple one at that. If you had seduced my son I wouldn't mind; actually, it might be rather good for him. We were talking about our daughter."

"You haven't guessed who she is?"

He'd been racking his brain. Suddenly the vision of Gayatri and her five children illuminated everything. "So," he said slowly. "Arjun is our son-in-law."

"Precisely."

He got up stiffly and paced back and forth on the path. "I think we should consider ourselves very lucky."

"I'm glad to hear you say that; it's exactly how I feel. I've left my entire fortune to them. Most of it is in Switzerland."

"What can I do?" he asked.

"I want to get them out of here," she replied, "but it's difficult for me to arrange, if not dangerous. You're a rich man. I want you to buy their way into some other country, preferably not America or Britain. Australia or New Zealand, perhaps Singapore, would do nicely. There are good schools there. All you have to do is buy a business for them in one of those places: a ranch, a hotel, something like that. I've never asked you for anything. Now I am asking you to do this for me."

He put his arms around her and gazed up at the mountains. She seemed suddenly small and fragile. What a terrible injustice he'd committed with Sumitra. Somehow he'd make it up to her. They walked on hand in hand.

"Does Arjun know anything about this?"

"No, nothing. He only knows that Gayatri was adopted by his parents."

"But I thought you didn't approve of leaving India. Why don't we set them up here?"

"I can't leave, but they must. What I say in front of others is one thing. Now I'm telling you privately this ship is sinking. I shall go down with it, I'm too old and too much a part of it to leave. It will soon become a police state or destroyed in an atomic confrontation with Pakistan—perhaps both. With our population, there is no way out but destruction. We are not capable of regimenting ourselves like the Chinese. We are uncontrollable; we believe in fate and would rather die than plan ahead. I don't want our grandchildren to suffer. You must get them out. If you need help, Ramakrishna Rao will do anything that's required. He's the only person who knows everything about my affairs. He's become enormously rich doing my work. I want those children out soon. The income from my money abroad will take care of them and their children's children."

"If you don't mind my asking, how much do you have outside?"

"About a hundred million U.S. dollars—not that much these days compared to some others I could name, but there are also considerable amounts of jewelry and gemstones in safe deposit boxes. My father was farsighted. Sumi and Sonny have been generously taken care of by their fathers. I'm also leaving what I have in India to them: houses, land, and so on. But I doubt they will enjoy it. I foresee gangs of youths ravaging the countryside at the behest of the government.

That's the way it will begin, gangs of Congress-I youths, like Mao's Red Guards. Then the army will step in. But it will all be the same. We haven't had our Mao yet, but I suspect he will be young and handsome and will capture the nation through television. I see a dictatorship, what we have always had really, only the elite will be smaller and far less well educated. We are already on our way, but as the press of population becomes more unbearable, the elite and their stooges will become more repressive. We must give our grandchildren a chance."

"You're furious with me for letting myself go with Sumitra, aren't you?"

"I think you were having a last fling." She smiled. "Like beautiful women, handsome men must also have difficulties accepting age. But attempting to end desire by constantly satisfying it is like putting out a fire by pouring oil on it. No, I'm not furious; I love you, not because of the man you once were but because you're still rather mad and very sweet. We have a long tradition here of old rishis losing their heads over young maidens; perhaps you're one of them." She took a deep breath. It was taking considerable energy to express herself honestly. "Actually, I suppose I feel hurt and jealous. I certainly was jealous the other night when I saw you coming out of the forest. But then I thought, Of what should I be jealous? I had you when you were young and beautiful like Arjun, more beautiful and younger. You were a very naughty youth, always managing to spirit me away from the aunties and chaperones who were supposed to be keeping an eye on me, do you remember? And you gave me a dear child, not destroyers like Sonny and Sumi but a preserver."

They were now picking their way down a slippery shortcut. David swooped Kamala up and carried her.

"Thank you, that was lovely. I had a terrible time going to sleep, the night before last, I was so angry at you, but when I woke up my jealousy was gone. How can I be jealous, I asked myself, when he's given me so much? I hear from Devika from time to time; she tells me Gayatri is a good Hindu wife and the children are delightful."

"They are." David smiled. "Absolutely marvelous."

"And, although she is high-born, at least Gayatri has escaped the curse of princessdom, that's something. Madho Dev is extremely shrewd. Everything is going along smoothly at Kotagarh." She looked at him and stopped. "That is why you must never tell anyone about this. Neither Arjun nor Gayatri should know."

They came to more level ground and he put her down.

"Will Madho Dev want to leave India?" David asked.

"He might want to visit his grandchildren from time to time, but I doubt he'd ever leave permanently. He'll hold the fort here, and if it looks safe, one of the grandsons will probably be sent back to take over. After all, governments have come and gone but we of the lunar race have survived."

"Won't Madho Dev want to know why I am being so generous, helping them to get out?"

"He'll react negatively, of course, but Arjun will persuade him."

"Why?"

Kamala's eyes flashed mischievously. "Sit down, my dear, I have something else to tell you. This may come as a shock." Obediently, David collapsed on another rock and smiled up at her. "Arjun is having an affair with Philippa. Your Ravi has observed him going into Philippa's room late at night."

David clenched his fists.

"I know your pride is hurt but you must conquer it—as I have had to do," she said pointedly.

"It's not Philippa I mind, it's his treacherousness. We've become so close, he seems so open, so honest. I've become very fond of him."

Kamala laughed. "You just have to realize he's a bit more complex than you give him credit for. See him in a different light. He wants to be your friend. He also wants Philippa. As a Rajput, he's supposed to take what he wants."

"But what of Gayatri? I wouldn't want to see her hurt."

"As an Indian woman it wouldn't surprise her that much. But believe me, once out of India, Arjun's infatuation with Philippa will cool. There will be others." David looked bleakly out over the valley, his chin in his hands. "Cheer up, my dear." She smiled. "At least you won't have to do much. Arjun will take most of the action, and all you'll have to do is come forward at the proper moment and offer to pay."

"Odd, isn't it, how we think of wives as possessions?" said David. "Philippa and I have led separate lives for years, yet this affair upsets me."

"How do you think she feels about you and Sumi?"

"How on earth could she know about that?"

"I suppose because she's known you for thirty years." Kamala laughed. "But no one's to blame, it's Shri Kama Dev, the god of love, desire, and enjoyment; he has taken possession of you all and is shooting his arrows at random. You must all be excused. See what nice explanations we have for everything? Think of it that way and you'll feel happier. The gods are managing everything. You haven't got a thing to say about it."

"But that's fatalism," protested David. "That's totally irresponsible."

"Quite right; that's the way we are. It's ancient wisdom. You English think you can build this and that with your machines, predict this and that with your computers, but fate, in the form of desire, will always intervene; you'll see. Behind the apparently ordered façade are the messy personal lives of people. Because he desires beautiful women, a young man must have wealth, cars, liquor, good food, and jewels, so he does anything to make money: works on some engine of destruction, a new bomb, a new disease, a new chemical. He knows it may be used wrongly, but he continues. Why? Because of desire. The statesman's mistress leaves him for a younger man, he becomes despondent and starts a war; she discloses his corrupt practices and he's overthrown in a coup. Kama Dev is always there. Scorching one's desire through asceticism is one way of restraining fate, but something always happens; even monks are well known for slipping from celibacy."

David nodded. "I see what you're getting at. How does one know what course to follow?"

"Consult people who do—the rishis and the babas."

"And the Mas?" David smiled.

"Well, she stopped the rain, didn't she? And because of that you've learned you're a proud grandfather."

They laughed together. "I say, shall we carry on? Or are there further revelations I should sit down for?"

"No more revelations, darling."

"Promise?"

"Promise."


BACK in the lounge of the New Aroma Hotel, at the Formica table with its plastic plates and flowers, Philippa looked about and realized they had all subtly changed, especially David, who seemed suddenly serious and contemplative. Arjun looked younger, bursting with energy; Kamala more relaxed; Sumitra withdrawn, yet no longer tense. She smiled to herself at Kamala's cleverness in organizing such a trip.

As if reading her thoughts, Kamala leaned across the table, a hint of cynicism in her voice.

"Ah, Philippa, I believe you are seeing what I see."

"I was just thinking not one of us looks the same as when we last sat here. The frame's the same but the picture has changed."

"On celestial pilgrimages, one receives self-knowledge." Kamala smiled. "That is the point of making them. Only Akbar seems unchanged."

"That, my dear, is because I am the epitome of self-knowledge to begin with. I don't need any more, so more doesn't change me." The dark whiskers on his huge bearlike face twitched.

"Conceited wretch," muttered Sumitra, picking at her food.

"Quite true," said Akbar. "I am. Being enormously fat has something to do with it, I suppose. There is so much of me to think about, and every cell is filled with desire. However, being fat, one cannot move about too much and, not moving, one is forced into contemplation and desire fades. With fading desire comes wisdom. Lately I have begun to feel like a vegetable."

Sumitra giggled. "The reason nothing happened to you is that you were carried."

The proprietor had turned on the television set and there was Mrs. Gandhi again, speaking to a vast crowd of people, herded like cattle into wooden stockades as far as the eye could see. "Foreign hand . . . healing touch"—the hackneyed phrases resounded through loudspeakers.

"She's changed too," said Kamala, squinting at the tube through half-closed eyes. "She looks exhausted."

Akbar chuckled. "You can't repeat the same lies over and over again, lies even you can't believe, and not look tired."

"If this were Paris," observed Sumitra, "we could switch her off and get a good film."


DAVID and Philippa excused themselves early and went up to their room. Sensing he had undergone some change and there was something he wanted to tell her, Philippa sat propped up in bed, reading a novel. Just as she thought her intuition might have been wrong and was about to turn out her light, he crumpled up the newspaper and threw it across the floor.

"Absolutely nothing in it. Meanwhile the country is falling apart."

"You think so?"

"I'm afraid it's even worse than we think. Kamala is very concerned; wants me to help her get Madho Dev's family resettled somewhere else."

Ah, there it is, thought Philippa; she's told him! Concealing her interest, she finished the page she was reading and then asked him to repeat what he had said.

"I said, Kamala is worried about Madho Dev and his family. As you know, she and Devika are very close. Kamala's father got his wealth out of the country before Independence, but Madho Dev's father trusted the new government and lost everything. His grandchildren have no future here. She wants me to assist her in finding a place for them outside the country."

"How many would that be? As I remember, Arjun's sisters have about fifteen children between them."

"They have their own husbands. According to Hindu custom, they are part of their husband's family now. Kamala was thinking of Arjun and Gayatri, their children, and possibly Devika and Dev."

Philippa propped herself on one elbow. "But, darling, how marvelous; we could give them our stud farm, one more responsibility I'd be happy to be relieved of. What a good idea!"

Considering her supposed infatuation with Arjun, David was not surprised by her enthusiasm. "She doesn't want them sent to England or America. Anyhow, it could entail quite an expense."

"I thought Kamala was helping?"

"She'll help once they're out of the country, but they need to have an actual sponsor, committed to bribing all the right people here and initially franchising them abroad. She can't very well do that."

"In other words, a joint venture."

"Exactly."

Philippa picked up her book and pretended to read, but the words were a blur. Everything had happened so easily.

"Exhausting trek, didn't you think?" she said, breaking the silence.

"Mmm, but I wouldn't have missed it for the world; unforgettable, really. I say, what do you think of Kamala?"

"Fascinating woman. I love the way she tackles things. A woman alone in this country, dealing with all these men; I admire her." She sighed. "You were lovers once, weren't you?"

At a loss for words, David gazed into space, unable to look at her. "How did you find that out? Did she tell you?"

"Just a stab in the dark," she said gently. "After all, I've known you rather a long time. Your eyes change when you look at her."

He wondered if his eyes changed when he looked at Sumitra and whether she'd noticed that too. "A brief encounter," he murmured. "Met her a few years before I left India. As you know, she's a relation of Devika and Dev's, and we were often a foursome: quite difficult, me being British and all that."

"Brief but poignant," said Philippa. "I don't think you forgot her all that easily, did you? She must have been unbelievably beautiful."

"I had almost forgotten her; believe me, I didn't really plan to come to India to see her."

"David, be honest now."

"I am. Actually, I thought I was coming to find Madho Dev; once we got here, though, I realized it had been her all along."

"I'm not blaming you, darling, just wondering why you never told me."

"The whole affair was impossible. Why should you have to know about it?"

"Things like that stand between people."

"You think Kamala stood between us?"

"Something's been haunting you all these years. I've always felt there was another David, a shadow I didn't really understand. It made you mysteriously attractive, but rather distant and difficult to live with. You often seemed distracted. Rather explains why we've never been that close, doesn't it?"

"That's not the reason. It's deeper than that, and I think I've finally got it figured out. But as long as we're on the subject, there's more you ought to know." He glanced at her out of the corner of his eye. "Hope you don't find it too shattering, but Kamala had a child of mine—born after I left—a daughter."

She feigned surprise. "You didn't know about the child?"

"Not till today. No one ever told me. When she knew she was pregnant, Kamala disappeared. That's why I couldn't find her before I left; she'd absolutely vanished."

"And the child?"

"The child was adopted."

"Of course, you've never seen her. Does Kamala know where she is?"

"That's just it. I have seen her; you have too. She's married to Arjun."

Philippa dissembled. "Gayatri! You can't mean Gayatri?"

"Yes, and she must never know. Never, do you understand?" His expression was stern. "Nor should Arjun. He'd feel tricked. Gayatri's been brought up an upper-caste Hindu; she'd be utterly shattered. Please forget I said anything about it, but I wanted to be honest. After all, we're getting rather old to play games." He wondered whether she would now tell him about her relationship with Arjun.

"And so you have five grandchildren, don't you? That's more than Edward and Belinda have given you."

"But Edward and Belinda are my real children; I mean they're the ones I've known since they were born, the only ones I've ever loved and worried about. I don't even know Gayatri, probably never will."

She was relieved he'd told her, that it was finally all out.

"Arjun must return home," he said. "I think we should go back to Kotagarh with him. We must leave India in a few weeks. If Kamala's plans are to be carried out, there will be many decisions to be made."

"Of course. And Arjun tells me that after the monsoon Kotagarh is absolutely lovely, the best time of year there. We can ride every day."

Obviously, thought David, if she was having a relationship with Arjun she was not going to admit it, any more than he would mention Sumitra. It was a draw.

"How long do you think it would take you to get ready to leave India if you had the chance?" asked David as he rode in the jeep with Arjun the next day, on their way back to Terripur.

The sudden question caught Arjun off guard. Had Philippa said something? She'd seemed so certain that it would all just happen. He felt a spontaneous urge to hug this English gentleman. But wait! People were not usually kind and generous without reason. If anything was true, that was. There had to be some hidden motive. "About a week, I suppose," he replied. "Are you serious?"

"Yes, I am." David nodded. "Your father and I were very close. In my whole life I don't think I've had another friend like him. I don't know why we stopped communicating, but now we're back in touch, I don't intend to let him flounder."

"You think he's floundering?" said Arjun.

"No, not yet, but I agree with you; the future here looks rather bleak. He might be persuaded to leave if I can find the right place. Perhaps you'll help me convince him."

The brilliance and beauty of the landscape through which they were driving made it hard for David to think of India as a place from which escape was either necessary or desirable. Yet as Kamala had reminded him, less than a hundred miles away, in the plains of Uttar Pradesh, a population the size of Western Europe was facing irreversible poverty and decline. He produced hot tea from a thermos.

Arjun slowed down. "Where would we go?" he asked thoughtfully.

"Ever thought of Australia? Where would you like to go?"

"How would I know?" Arjun flashed a half-angry smile and shrugged. Didn't this man understand that the world outside India was a blank to him? Couldn't he realize this was the very reason he had to get out—because he felt so ignorant, so stupid? Yet faced with the reality of leaving, a certain panic seized him and he felt almost giddy. What could Philippa have said? Something about their affair? But of course, she hadn't done anything of the sort. It was out of the question; she wouldn't jeopardize everything.

David did not pursue the subject. The morning turned hot. At midday the caravan stopped at the junction of several rivers, and they sat under an old banyan tree while Akbar took off his slippers, dangled his perpetually swollen feet in the cool water and Sumitra fed the fish. After lunch, they rested on blankets in the shade, and when the sun had passed its zenith and the servants had eaten, cleaned up, and repacked everything, they set out once again for Terripur. This time Philippa rode in the jeep with Arjun, and they drove for some time in silence—like an old married couple, she thought.

Finally, Arjun turned to her. "This morning your husband spoke to me about leaving India. I didn't bring it up. He said he owed it to my father to try and get us out; just as you prophesied. What did you say to him?"

"Nothing, nothing at all," she said evasively. "It's Princess Kamala; when they were coming down the mountain yesterday, she spoke to him. She's impressed with you and wants to do something for your family. She asked David to help and he's agreed; he told me so last night."

"But why? Why should they do this?"

"Because they were all such close friends, I suspect. She's known your mother since they were girls; your father is her cousin. She wants to redress the misfortunes she feels he never deserved. She loves you all and wants to get you out of India, settle money on your children. She's asked David to help."

"You said nothing?"

"Nothing. I told you it would all work out."

Squinting against the sun, Arjun stared suspiciously at her. "I don't believe you," he said at last. "People don't give away money out of friendship. There are many friends and cousins who suffered more than my father; we are not that close to her. There is something else. Have you told him about us?"

"No."

"There has to be something."

"Nothing. There is nothing else."

He jammed on the brakes. The jeep veered to the side of the road, almost throwing her through the windshield.

"What are you doing?" she cried. "You're going to kill us. You've been telling me you want to leave; now it's happening, why are you acting so strangely? Is there something I don't understand?"

"There is something you are not telling." He gazed at her intently. "You may think I'm just a stupid Indian; you're right, I am stupid. This morning your husband mentioned Australia, and I am not even sure where Australia is. But I am not so stupid as you imagine. I know you are lying." He gripped her shoulders and shook her. "Why have you been telling me not to worry? You are concealing something. Tell me or I'll—"

Philippa stared at him. "You're too much like your father."

"What do you know about my father?"

"He has these childish temper tantrums too."

His grip tightened. "Now all of a sudden I am not supposed to touch you, is that it?"

"Not in anger."

"In anger, in love, what is the difference? You certainly haven't minded my hands before." He shook her again. "Tell me."

Tears streamed down her cheeks. He stared at her malevolently. "Arjun, please, I love you; I don't think you're stupid, far from it." She was convulsed by sobs.

An army truck came lumbering up the road behind them. Arjun abruptly let go of her, started up the jeep, and sped demonically ahead.

"For God's sake, slow down. You'll kill us both," she cried.

"What do I care?" he yelled. "If you keep lying to me, I will. You can lie to the rest of the world, but not to me. I'll drive faster and faster and go straight off the side." They rounded a bend on two wheels and were heading into a sharp curve. He stared straight ahead.

"In God's name, stop! I'll tell you, I'll tell you," she screamed, and burst into tears again.

Without changing expression, he braked the jeep and pulled over. The truck passed. He waved at the soldiers hanging out the back, then turned to her. "Well?"

"Turn off the engine," she said between sobs. "Is there some tea in your thermos? I'm about to collapse." He did as she asked, and after a few sips she took a deep breath. "Your father got angry at me one day and told me something I shouldn't have known. He thought he was going to hurt me. Anyhow, it's all rather ancient history and not that important. On the other hand, it's quite convenient for us."

"Tell me," he said firmly.

"It's Gayatri; she's Kamala's daughter."

The skin over his cheekbones tightened. "I had rather suspected that. I suppose you know who her father is?"

"Yes, it's David; she's David's daughter too. Your children are his grandchildren. That's why I knew your wish to leave India would come true. David never knew, but now someone has told him. I'd guess Kamala."

His eyes narrowed. He sat very still and stared straight ahead as if looking into the future. Then, slowly, he took up her hand and kissed it. "I'm sorry—not sorry that you have told me but that I treated you so badly. You know I love you more than anything else. Why did you not want to tell me?"

"First of all, after your father blurted it out, I think he made me promise not to. Then I thought you might feel tricked, hate them all—your wife, your parents, Kamala, David, even me. That would be a tragedy. At the time, I'm sure they did what they thought best. One has to forgive human frailty; after all, no one ever asked to be born."

"That means my wife is Anglo-Indian."

"Ah, you see, I knew that would be your first thought. What nonsense. That's one of the reasons I didn't tell you."

"My children are one-quarter English."

"Does that change the way you feel about them?"

"No, of course not." He bit his lower lip. "As you know, my relationship with Gayatri has always been one of duty. Naturally when we were youngsters, we had a romantic season. Like the Hindi films we saw in Kotagarh, we pursued each other through idyllic scenery. She hid behind bushes; I held flowers between my teeth and stared passionately at her. Seeing this, my father asked if I would like to marry her. She was a sister to me, so there was the added attraction of incest, of a shy young man not having to go too far afield, not having to deal with in-laws. Also, I was anxious to test my virility on something: anything. So we went from being brother and sister to man and wife. We never thought of questioning the idea.

"Our wedding was small. Come to think of it, Princess Kamala actually brought the pundit. We walked around the holy fire and that was that. But after flirting for so long, on the wedding night when we were finally alone, we found out we were completely ignorant. No one had ever bothered to tell either of us anything. Of course, she was a virgin and frightened. It was painful for her. I lost my head with desire. The whole performance was a clumsy mess. We both hated it. The next day, to our embarrassment, the bloody sheet was proudly exhibited. This episode turned Gayatri against sex, and since then we have only done it to have children. Until I found you, I hadn't realized it could be . . ."—he paused and glanced shyly at her—"beautiful. I thought it was a duty all women really hated. I told you I was quite stupid. So you see, nothing will change between us because there is nothing much to change. Does she have any idea who her parents are?"

"No, and she mustn't be told. I'm sure it would be a terrible shock. She might hate herself."

His eyes followed two enormous eagles as they sailed low over the jeep and out across the valley. "And so, my noble mother-in-law and English father-in-law have decided to do something for their daughter, is that it?"

"I'm not quite sure. Naturally, Kamala hasn't said anything to me. She told David she's ready to support you and your family, has money in Switzerland, asked David to sponsor your visas and buy you citizenship elsewhere."

"Can that really be done?"

Philippa nodded. "So I understand. One buys a business in your name, something productive that creates employment for the people in the country where you want to live."

"What if Father won't go?"

"David doesn't think your father will want to leave."

"I don't either," said Arjun.

"The idea is that your father and mother will stay on here; after all, your sisters and their families live in India. Perhaps after their schooling is finished, one or more of your sons could return. It all depends on the political situation."

Arjun looked gloomy. "Could I really leave my father and mother? It is my duty to look after them; I might feel lost without them. I suppose that is more of my Indian stupidity."

"Call it conditioning."

"The happy thing is this news relieves my guilt a little about loving you. My wife and my children are my duty; you are my enjoyment, my love. Performance of three duties is essential to happiness: first are religious duties and austerities, second is accumulation of wealth, and third is to enjoy. I have observed religious duties at home, my mother has seen to that; wealth I have created with five children; and now I am finally going to enjoy." He flashed one of his world-illuminating smiles.

"Love is God," said Philippa, smiling back, remembering the sticker on the taxi driver's window.

"Do you think David knows about us?"

"I would think his grandchildren are probably more important than anything else at this moment, wouldn't you? It seems the children I have given him are too selfish to have children of their own and aren't likely to."

"That doesn't answer my question."

"Oh, but it does. What I'm saying is, even if he were aware of us, the idea of having five grandchildren would more than compensate for any jealousy he might feel. After all, you're their father. . . . Just for that, he has to love you too."

He took her in his arms, held her head between his hands, and kissed her passionately. "We will enjoy, then."

"It won't do, you know, for us to be indiscreet. It would be inconsiderate. We mustn't hurt anyone. And Kamala would be furious. After all, you are her son-in-law."

He started up the jeep and they drove off. He drove fast, thinking of everything that had happened. As if by magic, his whole life had changed. How would his father react? Much would depend on that. And what about his mother and Gayatri? Gayatri, of course, would obey his wishes. More than that, she would probably even be enthusiastic. Whenever they went out driving together and stopped at a petrol pump, she would sniff the air and tell him how much she loved the smell of petrol. She was a girl with modern ideas and would quickly adapt. He felt layers of repressed desire leaving him like so many garlands floating on the waters of Mother Ganga. Philippa had awakened something powerful. He was beginning to feel like a real person, not just a spoke in the wheel of existence or a bullock yoked to a grinding mill, mindlessly traversing the same path. It would be a big shock at first to live away from his family, among strangers. Neither he nor Gayatri might be able to stand it, but it was worth a try. After all, if he didn't have the courage of his convictions, what kind of man was he?

They came to a small village where the caravan had pulled up in front of a tea shop. Arjun braked the jeep and parked behind the Mercedes. The whole village was staring at Kamala and her party debouching from her chariot. While everyone relaxed under a big tree, Ravi and Kamala's cook assisted the shop owner in preparing snacks. The late September sun was warm, the air filled with butterflies and buzzing bees.

"We thought we'd lost you!" exclaimed Kamala, sheathed in outrageously large dark glasses. "I was just going to send the driver back to look."

"My brakes came loose," said Arjun. "We had to stop and tighten them."

David stared at him thoughtfully over his pipe and looked away. Sumitra was watching him too, squinting against the sun, smiling a sarcastic, superior smile that made Arjun feel like a fool.

Akbar drummed softly on the table, sipped his tea, and thought of the impermanence of life, how it was always relentlessly changing. In a few weeks this small group of people communicating in tones that sounded more like the twitter of birds than animals would be dispersed far and wide. Things came together and vanished. Whence did they arise and whither did they go? Some said the source was the sun behind the sun, but was there such a thing? Often life seemed so ephemeral it was almost nonexistent, a chimera of sights and sounds signifying . . . ah, yes, nothing. No-thing. Then what?

"Tashkent," Kamala said. "Just think, in a few weeks Akbarji will be attending a poetry conference in Tashkent. How I envy him."

"Come along then," said Akbar goodnaturedly.

"No, thank you." She sighed. "I've dreamt of Tashkent all my life, I can't afford to be disillusioned."

Gazing out through the afternoon haze toward the plains, which he could see now shimmering through a gap in the mountains, David wondered about his attachment to India. It was not a place for the foreigner to grow old in. Yet if you went all the way and became a holy man, what then? To the country's great credit, many foreign sadhus were allowed to wander about. In the tea shop the plaintive music of the shehnai wailed out of an ancient radio. Certainly Sumitra would never join him if he took off his clothes and went to live in the jungle. The thought was so comical he almost laughed aloud. But she was very much in his mind at that moment: her warmth, the youth from which he could feel himself drawing strength. In a month he could be with her in Paris, wandering the lanes of Montmartre, strolling along the boulevards, making love to her on lazy autumnal afternoons. Yet what was that compared to the pleasures and joys of a newfound family? What indeed?

# Part Three

# 17

THE FEELING OF MELANCHOLY which often accompanied September in England was curiously absent, David thought, as the train from Delhi crawled toward Kotagarh through a vibrant landscape luxuriant with ripening crops.

There being no train reservation available, he and Philippa, accompanied by Ravi, had driven from Terripur to Delhi in one of Kamala's cars. Arjun had followed in his jeep, spent the night, and gone on to Kotagarh. In Delhi they had made plane reservations for their return to England, talked to Edward and Belinda in London, and seen Ramakrishna Rao, who had been most helpful and promised to have a plan ready soon to carry forward Kamala's wishes. On their last evening, they had rung up the incorrigible General Bobby to thank him for the use of his house, dined with him in their hotel suite, and found him considerably subdued by the recent events in Punjab.

As David expected, the leave-taking at Terripur had been painful. On the last day, tension at the house rose to a fever pitch. Servants and delivery boys came round to settle accounts and haggle over baksheesh. Then Kamala, sporting a cane, appeared for a farewell lunch, bringing Sumitra and Sonny. Her usually high spirits restrained, she claimed the trek to Kedarnath had done her in, but Sumitra insisted it was an attack of gout brought on by having eaten and drunk too much on the evening of their return.

All in all, it had been an impossible few hours. There was so much more he'd wanted to say to Kamala. Not only could he not express himself in front of the others, he wasn't sure what he really wanted to tell her. And, of course, it had been impossible to be alone with Sumitra for even a moment. She had, however, cleverly managed to slip him a scrap of paper with her Paris address and telephone number and a scribbled note saying she loved him and would be waiting for his call around the second week of November. With Arjun there glaring at him, Sonny, trying very hard to act the young businessman, had rattled on nervously about the trucking business and bored everyone with innumerable statistics. And then Ravi, obviously unhinged at the prospect of their leaving, had dropped an apple pie in Philippa's lap.

By the time lunch was finally over and Kamala was ready to leave, she didn't look at all well. When he took her in his arms and kissed her, Sumitra and Sonny looked startled and Philippa looked away. Kamala promised to try and come to Kotagarh before they left. Everyone knew she wouldn't, but it made the leave-taking less painful. He found goodbyes terribly depressing and was relieved when they had all gone and he was able to settle down on the veranda, smoke his pipe in peace, and watch the afternoon fade into evening.

After supper, Ravi had come to massage him and begged to be taken along. He prefaced his request with an extremely touching history of his sad life. Confronted by his grave, calm face and pleading eyes, David found it difficult to say no and had agreed to see what could be done; meanwhile, Ravi would come along to Delhi and Kotagarh, and Mrs. Kapoorchand would be notified.

Later, however, he was unable to sleep and lay awake wishing he'd found out just what Ravi told Kamala about Arjun and Philippa. Quietly, he let himself into the bath that separated his room from hers, stood at Philippa's closed door, and listened. Arjun was telling her they probably wouldn't have a chance to be together again, that it would be too difficult in Kotagarh. There were muffled noises, which he supposed meant they were embracing. Then Philippa said something about treasuring the few moments of happiness in one's life, and Arjun said something about once she left he'd never see her again. Feeling like an intruder, David had crept back to bed, watched the old half-eaten moon rise over the mountains, and lain awake having dark thoughts about growing old. He'd been a strong, good-looking fellow and had used his looks to get what he wanted, the way Arjun did now. But he remembered well the time, he must have been in his mid-forties, when he realized people had stopped offering to do things for him. What a shock that had been. It was as though overnight he'd become invisible. Suddenly everything became more difficult. He'd had to work harder to make things happen: in business, with his family, even with women—which made this affair with Sumitra so important he supposed.

The train was in Rajasthan now, and the landscape took on that familiar silvery tone he loved. He went over in his mind how he would approach the subject of Kamala's proposal with Madho Dev. Would their grandchildren really be happier in the West? That was the question Rama Rao had raised, a question neither of them had been able to answer, even though Rao had lived abroad for many years and was most sympathetic. Now they were nearing Kotagarh: he recognized the long stretch of hills to the south that marked the edge of the game preserve and felt a certain excitement, almost like coming home. Philippa put down her book and repaired her makeup. Ravi came in, announced their imminent arrival, and began taking the luggage out.

On the platform waiting for them, Madho Dev was in a sour mood and began haranguing them about the proper attitude of sons toward fathers. When he'd left, Arjun had told them he'd be back in a week. Then he called from Terripur and it was to be one more week, which had turned into two and a half. Such lack of consideration was the reward, he supposed, for all the sacrifices they'd made for him. He was carrying on, thought Philippa, as though Arjun were fourteen.

"We worry about them, we do everything, then they forget we exist. Gayatri too has been most upset. Arjun also neglected his duties in the forest. The moment he got back, he had to rush out there, and will not be home until tomorrow."

"Well, old chap, at least you still have certain traditions about filial responsibility," said David. "We have none. Compared to our Edward, I assure you Arjun is a model of correctness."

Madho Dev melted. "So, you have got to know him, eh? That is good." He smiled at last. "Yes, he is really an excellent son, the light of my life. No doubt I'm jealous of his attentions to others. When he's gone, we seem to wither a bit. That's what comes of this frightful medieval life we live nowadays. When my father was alive, when you and I were young, David, it wasn't like this, was it? We came and went, we were modern; there were so many interesting things to do, so much going on. In our day, the times were hopeful. After the war ended, we felt a wonderful new age was beginning. Now everything is out of joint. We keep to ourselves; we've become introverted, obsessive; we feel the countryside is infested with robbers, dacoits, murderers; we worry that our son won't come back in one piece."

"Anyway," said David, "Arjun did get back, and look at this day:

simply fantastic, what? The best time of year, just after the rains; everything so green, the rain-washed sky. . . . Let's count our blessings."

They passed a pond filled with water hyacinths and crimson lotus. At the edge, water buffaloes were cavorting in the shallows with their young attendants. Philippa asked Madho Dev to stop and snapped a series of pictures with her camera.

Madho Dev laughed. "We're so used to all of this we don't even see it."

"Perhaps you need a holiday, then you'll appreciate it more," said David, thinking it was a good opening for what he wanted to discuss later. "Philippa and I have been talking it over, thought you might enjoy a change of scene, hoped you and Devika might consider visiting us soon. Not that England is so much, but it might be restful to get away from your responsibilities for a while, get a new perspective."

At the house, they found Devika and Gayatri waiting at the front door, with the children—Manoj, Rishi, Sona, Uma and Lakshmi— standing in a row. Seeing them again, seeing Gayatri there smiling at him, her green eyes like two luminous emeralds, David thought he might break down. He glanced quickly at Philippa, who nodded and smiled reassuringly, and while Ravi jumped out of the back of the truck and helped unload the luggage, he hugged each of the children and presented them with gifts. It was a difficult moment, one that took all the courage he could summon.

"You must be tired from your trip," Devika said, with a formality Philippa had not expected from a woman with whom she thought she'd reached a certain level of intimacy and understanding. "Traveling is such a grim affair these days. Come, I have a hot bath ready. You can tell us all about Terripur."

While she bathed behind a screen, attended by a servant girl, Devika and Gayatri questioned her. Nearly thirty-five years had passed since Devika had been to Terripur, and she seemed stunned by the changes, especially at the Ritz, which she remembered as a very grand hotel. There were probing questions about Sumitra and Sonny, neither of whom Devika had ever met, and a full account of the trip to Kedarnath. When Philippa emerged from her bath wrapped in towels, tea was brought in, and the unblinking eyes of the two women bored into her as Devika spoke of Arjun's irresponsibility, how unthinking it was of him to have stayed away so long; a trip to Kedarnath was certainly the chance of a lifetime, but . . . ! Her tone suggested to Philippa that both women thought she and David should have had the sense to send Arjun home and were letting her know in a polite but firm way that they held her responsible. Philippa tried subtly to shift the blame to Kamala: Kedarnath had been her idea; a younger man had really been necessary. She told them about the landslide and how Arjun had probably saved them all by his quick thinking. But nothing she could say seemed to placate them, and though the conversation finally evaporated into pleasantries, their searching eyes told her the whole story. Here were two women who felt trapped, desperate for information from the world outside, yet jealous of anyone who had been there. Certainly it would be good for both of them to get out of Kotagarh for a while.

That evening, after Madho Dev's durbar, especially crowded as people had heard of the return of the English sahib and memsahib and wanted to glimpse them, the entire family dined together. As a special favor to Philippa, who had requested it to please David, all five children had been permitted to eat with them, an unheard-of privilege. With their father gone, however, they proved more difficult than expected and by the time the curry course had arrived, all but Manoj and Uma had been hustled off to the women's quarters with their ayahs and the talk turned to events that had taken place in David and Philippa's absence.

Since June, Madho Dev disclosed, Harbinder Singh and his family had been under constant surveillance. The authorities were certain they must be hiding the three missing Sikh soldiers. And Harbinder Singh had received more news from his relatives in Punjab. As soon as the wheat crop was in, they had written, there would be general disruption. The entire Sikh population, especially the young students, was still furious with Mrs. Gandhi for sending the army into the Golden Temple. In the past, whenever the army had moved through Punjab to protect India's borders with Pakistan, they could always count on the support of the people, particularly the Sikh women, who had always fed and doted on the soldiers. Now there would be no support. In fact, if trouble came with Pakistan, there was no telling whose side they would be on.

David had been trying to watch Gayatri without actually looking at her and was finding it hard to follow Madho Dev too closely. Although he could see now how she resembled Kamala, she also bore a striking resemblance to photographs of his mother, who had died of typhoid in Bengal when he was six. How proud he was of her, sitting there next to Manoj, a handsome lad of fourteen, and Uma, her golden eyes like those of a young female lion.

Devika was reciting the number of senseless killings and murders that had occurred in broad daylight. Using hit-and-run tactics, terrorists on motorcycles had attacked prominent Hindus and even Sikhs who did not agree with them. The police in Punjab had been infiltrated by terrorists. Mrs. Gandhi was surrounded by sycophants like Kamala's friend Ramakrishna Rao, who only told her what she wanted to hear. She had no idea that things weren't improving and that her so-called "healing touch" was no more than a slogan people were already making jokes about. There had been many more threats on her life. Sikh leaders had organized a march on Amritsar that was due to take place any day. Trains had been derailed. Buses had been stopped, their Hindu passengers dragged out and shot. Sikh priests were excommunicating everyone who had had anything to do with Operation Blue Star or helped in the reconstruction afterward.

What a blessing to have been out of touch with these grisly events, thought Philippa. She hoped Madho Dev could be persuaded to take advantage of Kamala's generous offer. On the surface India seemed so peaceful it was difficult to imagine the situation was as serious as he made out. Perhaps the insularity of their lives here made the outside world seem more threatening, or was it television that was making Devika and Gayatri so sensitive and jittery?

Philippa was mistaken about Devika, however. It was not events in Punjab that had set her nerves on edge but the change she'd noticed in her son on his return from Terripur. She couldn't understand it. Like a kite broken loose from its string, he seemed to be flying out of control. Could the altitude at Kedarnath have affected him, or was it Philippa? She'd been watching Philippa carefully, scrutinizing her every move for some clue to Arjun's strange lightness. Philippa was a beautiful woman. It was unthinkable that Arjun could be in love with her, but why else would he have stayed away so long? She would be relieved when the Bruces left; their arrival had been attended by inauspicious omens. And seeing his old friend again, Madho Dev had become dissatisfied and had begun to complain about the most insignificant things.

The dinner ended with Philippa offering to read stories to Manoj and Uma, who were perfecting their command of English. Although she was terribly tired, she sensed Devika's disapproval and wanted to make an effort to win back her confidence.

"One bedtime story"—she smiled—"then I must sleep, for I'm exhausted."

"What is 'exhausted'?" asked Manoj.

They all laughed.

"At your age you wouldn't know," said Philippa. "Come, I'll explain exhaustion when we start reading, but first you must pick out a story."

Madho Dev and David retired to the study. The sound of crickets and night birds drifted in through the window on the cooling breeze, and an old servant prepared a hookah that was placed between them.

"Nothing like the hubble-bubble," said David as he sucked the water-filtered smoke through the long tube. "And a jolly good one too."

"Baghwan Singh's been making hookahs all his life; he's a great artist." Madho Dev glanced at the old man, who squatted in one corner of the room.

"Do I detect a bit of opium?" David asked.

"One doesn't mention it, but yes, I believe there might be some. He must think we need it, just a hint, and probably a dozen other things we're not aware of. I leave it up to him; he seems to know what suits the mood. We grow five different kinds of tobacco for him, and he uses aromatic barks which he collects in the forest and dries; God knows what else. After one of his specials, sometimes you can't get up."

A young boy padded in with a bottle of brandy and glasses on a silver tray.

"I say, old man, what do I see?"

Madho Dev grinned. "From Father's collection, one of the few things the government didn't find when they took over his property. We discovered a whole cache of bottles in a secret cellar a few years ago and brought them here in the middle of the night. It's quite a collection, probably worth a great deal; the old man was a connoisseur."

"If I were to order this in London, if I could even get it, it would cost well over two hundred quid."

Madho Dev poured the brandy, and they puffed on the hookah in silence.

"Haven't had a chance to tell you about Kamala," David said at last. "As you predicted, it was a frightful shock; I barely recognized her."

"Always a jolt to see one's friends after a long absence. She drinks far too much."

"She does? I didn't notice."

"Solitary drinker, worst kind. After she stayed here, we found empty bottles chucked under the bed; perhaps she's better now."

David stared off into space. "Why didn't you tell me I'd got her pregnant? You knew I was looking for her, knew how much I loved her."

"My dear chap, I had no idea."

"You swear it?"

"I swear it. But it wouldn't have worked out; you're much too different. Great romance. Marriage would have been disaster."

"You think so?"

"I know it. Kamala's very spoiled, always was; your life would've been hell." He blew smoke rings across the room. "I suppose if she told you that, she told you everything."

"About Gayatri, you mean."

"Yes."

David stopped smoking and stared at him. "At least you could have written."

"Believe me, I had no idea you were involved. When she brought Gayatri to us, she didn't tell me who the father was, not till after we'd lost touch. Devika still doesn't know."

"If I'd known, I certainly would have returned."

"Are you sure? Philippa's smashingly beautiful."

"I met her well after Gayatri was born. Wouldn't have married her if I'd known. As it is, we've never been that close: Afraid Kamala's specter was always there haunting me."

Madho Dev shook his head. "Too many barriers here between men and women, between foreigners and our own people. You were probably closer to Philippa in the first years of your marriage than you would ever have been with Kamala."

"But you and Devika seem happy."

"We've shared the burdens of a hard life." Madho Dev sighed. "Like Draupadi in the wilderness, she's been a faithful companion through difficult times. Never cut out for this sort of life, you know, but she doesn't complain. Yet there is always a distance between us. Perhaps that's why we've survived."

"You've had mistresses then?"

"I had, until a few years ago, when I decided it wasn't worth all the trouble. The girls were getting younger; I was getting older. Remember what an idiot my father made of himself over young girls? I didn't want Arjun to think the same of me, so I gave it up."

"In your father's time people expected it."

"But times have changed." Madho Dev chuckled. "We can't get away with what we used to. Here in Kotagarh they've become more puritanical than ever. Did you know Father's real reason for setting up the hospital was to have his prospective concubines examined? Terrified of disease, I suppose, and wanted to make sure they were fit to weather his libidinous onslaughts!"

They fell silent. The sound of the bubbling hookah filled the room.

At last David spoke. "Kamala has made a will leaving everything to our grandchildren."

Madho Dev looked surprised. "What about Sumitra and Sonny?"

"They've been taken care of by their fathers. This is her own money."

"That could be true."

"She hopes that Arjun, Gayatri, and the children will want to emigrate. Most of the money is abroad, and someone must be there to look after it; she wants me to help. Seems to think the country is heading toward some form of police state."

"Heading!" Madho Dev chortled. "Doesn't she know it's here already? But of course, she really wouldn't, she has the money to pay off the proper officials, and that Rao fellow looks after her interests."

"At least one can still leave."

"Not that easy. You have to have a passport and find a place to go. Thousands of people are waiting for visas."

"That's where I come in. I'm to grease the hands and smooth the way."

"Has anyone consulted Arjun? Does he know you're his father-in-law?"

"Of course not, she made me promise not to tell him, but I've sounded him out vaguely. He feels he'd like to try it; thinks the situation here is pretty hopeless, not much chance for the children. Hopes you'll leave too."

Madho Dev sighed. "What a mess, eh? You spend your life making a place for your children, and the government is so bad it spoils everything. Governments should not spoil people's dreams. What kind of trouble does she expect?"

"Some sort of controlled uprising from the bottom, Maoist type."

"India's too stratified for that."

"She thinks not, says people are more informed; expectations have been raised which will be impossible to satisfy. She feels there's a distinct possibility of widespread disruption and a subsequent crackdown. At least her money is safe abroad, but to use it freely, our grandchildren would have to live there . . . at least for a while."

"Where?"

"Australia, perhaps, you could have a farm there. But if Australia doesn't appeal to you, there is always America. Almost a million Indians live there now.

"America might be an excellent place. The children would have a better chance than Australia, less discrimination. More opportunities."

"So in principle you agree that it's a good idea?"

"We should consider it seriously, but we're going to have a damned hard time explaining why Kamala would be so magnanimous; the family hardly knows her. However, if they must leave, it would be wise for them to go while the children are still young. Arjun will have a difficult time adjusting, not to mention Gayatri; she's very traditional." He puffed on the hookah. "Clever bugger, eh, that father of Kamala's?"

"How did he manage it?" asked David.

"Flew it out. Expert pilot, had his own plane, saw what was coming in '47, and before the new government gained a foothold, he got it out."

"Got what out?"

"Gold, my dear fellow, hundreds of kilos. Nothing, of course, compared to the gems and jewelry: natural China Sea pearls, big as Ping-Pong balls. Packed 'em up in old trunks and flew 'em out himself. As I recall, some Brits helped him. In those days—before jets, you know—it was quite an adventure. He had to stop in out-of-the-way places to refuel, finally reached Cairo, and from there it wasn't hard to go on to Switzerland. Imagine the guts it took to fly around with all that loot! Over the years, everything's been converted to financial instruments, I've heard. Indeed, our grandchildren may be quite well off."

"Proves how important it is to flow with the times," said David, "have the foresight to change."

Madho Dev sighed. "Much as I would like to keep Arjun here with me, it would be better for him to go. You say he knows nothing about Gayatri?"

David puffed on the hookah. "I haven't told him. I'm not sure what Kamala has said. As you know, she can be rather impulsive."

Madho Dev remembered how he had lost his head and told Philippa everything. "Does Philippa know?"

"Yes, I told her after Kamala told me, and I think ultimately you should tell Arjun."

"He could be quite upset; we never gave him much of a chance to choose anyone but Gayatri, and it wouldn't be wise to tell her now."

"You must talk with Arjun soon, say I've invited you on a holiday and you wish him to accompany you; that would start things off."

"Is there a rush?"

"Kamala seems to think there is. I'm to get the ball rolling in Delhi with Ramakrishna Rao before we leave. I don't much like the idea of leaving, but I have a feeling I'll be back."

"Really?"

"Really, I've seen the world many times round, and in spite of all the horrors, all the stupidity and greed, there's still a sense of humanity here that's rare."

"You call the way people treat each other here human?"

"Indeed I do; with all the human frailties. The rest of the world is becoming standardized. People have become automatons. I wouldn't mind settling down some place here near you."

"You'd have no problem having a full love life. Our girls find old men very attractive." David groaned. "You have to face facts, my friend. Although we're quite well preserved, we're already wandering on the shores of old age."

"Waiting for the ferryman, eh?" said David. "Perhaps after I get Arjun and his family settled somewhere, you'll find me a house where I can spend six months of the year. I really dislike our English winters."

"What about Philippa? Can't see a glamorous woman like her living here."

"Philippa has her own friends in London. We might get along better if I were gone part of the time. Then you and Devika could come back to England with me in the summer, miss the monsoon."

"I wonder if I'd really like that?"

"Probably not. It's not the England your father used to tell you stories about."

"In fact, old chap, it's what I said before. Old age is setting in for both of us."

They smoked in silence.

"But wouldn't you give anything for just one more passionate love affair?" David said at last.

Madho Dev laughed. "Sometimes after one of these hookahs, I fall into a trance and see troupes of narrow-waisted damsels with buttocks like she-elephants cavorting around me."

"Hope you're able to let off steam occasionally. Wouldn't want you to develop prostate problems."

Madho Dev smiled a leonine grin. "I'll let you in on a little secret: there's a place I could take you to right now, a hut near the river, where a woman lives with her five daughters. No one knows where they came from; south India, perhaps Assam; arrived here out of the blue some years ago. They work in the fields and do odd jobs in the neighborhood. People like them because they're reliable. When they first came, the youngest daughter was just ten, the eldest around eighteen. The mother was barely thirty. Would you like to visit them?"

"Now?" David grinned. "What about our desirelessness?"

"That's what made me think of them. Talking with you has aroused old memories of former exploits. Or it could be the hookah. Come, it's only a ten-minute walk."

"But what if they're asleep? It's terribly late."

"It's not late. The hookah slows things down. In any case, for me they would get up in the middle of the night if necessary. I championed them when they first appeared here. People were suspicious of them, but I let it be known they weren't really human beings but heavenly spirits, divine apsaras, nymphs. In fact, I'm not sure I wasn't right." Madho Dev rose and pulled David up. The room whirled before his eyes. "You aren't used to the hookah," he said. "Come."

They shuffled out of the house, past the barn, and down a path between two irrigated fields. A balmy wind blew through the tall grass, crickets sang, and the light from the stars was like moonlight. Madho Dev led the way, flashlight in hand, carrying a long stick for snakes; David staggered on behind. In time they came to a wooded area where the path widened and they strode beneath old mango trees.

Madho Dev stopped and listened. "Hear the drums? We're in luck. The celestials are dancing; their drums are calling us."

David glanced doubtfully at him but realized he was perfectly serious. "Of course, old boy, carry on."

Walking steathily now, they approached a thatched mud hut and, opening a gate in a primitive picket fence, stood in the shadows. In the soft glow of oil lamps, a beautiful large-breasted woman was playing the drum while several young girls danced.

"We're doubly in luck: they're alone. See how important it is to follow one's instincts?"

Taking David by the hand, Madho Dev led him inside. Three girls were dancing while a fourth played a tambourine and a fifth tended a small fire in an open pit. In one corner an altar with a gaily painted statue of the blue-skinned Krishna playing a flute was garlanded with scarlet hibiscus flowers.

When she saw them, the woman stopped playing and the girls giggled.

"I have brought an old friend of mine to see you," said Madho Dev in Hindi. "May we come in?"

The statuesque mother motioned them inside. As she measured out pinches of herbs and powdered barks into a brass pot, the girl tending the fire smiled ingenuously.

"Hope that isn't bhang," said David.

"Do not ask, it's a potion," said Madho Dev. "These women are famous for them."

"Let's hope it's a love potion," muttered David. "Do you think it will mix with the hookah?"

"Leave that up to them. Remember, they're really mythological beings."

The mother started to beat the drum again. A girl of fifteen or sixteen began to dance. She was tall and lithe like her mother, with full breasts, a high narrow waist, ample hips, and jet black hair which hung in a single braid to the calves of her legs. Though not muscular, one could tell she had worked hard. One by one, she extinguished the oil lamps until she was dancing in the firelight.

The brew was served. Two other girls materialized with mattresses and pillows, took off David's sandals, and began to massage his feet. From somewhere came the haunting strains of a bamboo flute. The room whirled about. One of the girls was dancing around the fire, a small tambourine held high over her head so that her freshening breasts quivered to the syncopated beat as her hips swayed and stopped, swayed and stopped. Another girl had removed his clothes and was massaging his legs. Lazily he stared across the fire to where Madho Dev was lying. The youngest sister squatted above him, massaging his stomach with oil like a woman grinding wheat into a mortar. The girls massaging David reached his inner thigh. His blood rose. They smelled like fresh-cut grass in Surrey. From its somber beginnings, the flute had moved into a lilting raga which carried everything with it. Across the room he thought he saw Madho Dev standing on his head in some impossible yogic pose with two girls. No one could get into such a position; it was too ridiculous. He closed his eyes and gave way to the touch of firm breasts, buttocks, probing fingers, lips and mouths. Love is God, he thought.

Deep guttural groans from Madho Dev and delighted cries from the girls brought him back. He opened his eyes to see almond eyes staring quizzically into his. The fire had burned down and he could not make much of the tangle of undulating copper flesh from which Madho Dev's voice came. For his own part, he could not remember whether he had had an orgasm or not. The eyes staring into his were attached to a head and body gyrating on top of him in a most delicious way, causing energy concentrated in his loins to pour out into some warm, pulsating place. He gave way to them, fell into a bottomless sea, every orifice of his body licked by desire as breasts, mons veneris, and clitoris brushed his lips and tongue, showering his cheeks with female nectar.

Then Madho Dev was standing over him, extracting him from a prolonged orgasm, and they strode away naked, their clothes in their arms, to an irrigation ditch and slid into the warm water. Madho Dev washed himself vigorously, taking in water and expelling it through his nose like a hippopotamus.

"You have enjoyed?" he roared.

"Immensely," cried David, splashing himself. "Now I understand why you look so young. You have a fountain of youth right here in your backyard. Not many Englishmen find their way to such a spot."

"Why do you suddenly refer to yourself as an Englishman?"

"Did I?"

"Yes, and it's the first time."

David paused to consider. "Something in that hut: case of confused identity, I suppose."

"You were born here; you will die here too. You are Indian, not English."

"What an odd thing for you to say, old man. We must be smashed."

"Attar of roses and bitter herb tea." Madho Dev grinned.

"What makes you think I'm Indian any more than English?"

"You have no choice. Besides, you should want to be—we are culturally superior."

"Oh, come off it."

"It's true. Didn't the Brits finally have to leave us without firing a shot? Worshiping the past, we have preserved certain attitudes and techniques of social organization that disappeared from Europe centuries ago. Our present predicament is that they are being eroded by so-called modern technology. But is there any proof this technology has made people happier? In fact, it may destroy everything. Meanwhile, we who are often unable to organize our day-to-day lives, and may be living on a mountain of shit owing to lack of sewage systems, are culturally superior and can expel or absorb foreigners at will as we have done over and over in the past."

"I never realized you disliked the British so."

"With a passion. We are sensualists, dreamers, and philosophers, perfectly willing to let the other fellow run things if he does a decent job. The Brits were good organizers, but they flogged us with racism, the white man's burden—all that rot."

"Nonsense." David laughed. "White-skinned supremacy has been promoted here for thousands of years. 'Fair Brahmin boy desires to marry light-skinned girl from good stock.' How many times have I seen that ad in the papers? And what about that great national hero Ram? Fair Rama of great intelligence defeats evil dark-skinned Ravana, king of the south. Wouldn't you say the British just exploited a fatal flaw?"

He helped Madho Dev up the bank, and they stood in the warm wind.

"What we hated was they lumped us in with all the others, with Africans, and called us natives."

"Aha!" exclaimed David. "See what you're saying?"

"You were never expelled from a railway carriage by a group of low-class Brits as I once was."

"It must have been a mistake."

"I don't think so. Of course, my family was never mistreated by the viceroy or his friends, but standing just behind them were these hoodlums from Lancashire and Yorkshire. That's what we resented, the fact that no one at the top objected to the behavior of those mindless fellows and always backed them up."

"My uncle was like that," David said thoughtfully. "I hated him for it."

"That's why you're really one of us," said Madho Dev, hugging him. They dressed and staggered back toward the farm. "That's why I've always loved you." He stopped and took a packet of biscuits from his pocket. "And now I shall demonstrate how to get into a house without rousing barking dogs."

David paused and took his arm. "You still agree it would be a good idea to get Arjun and his family out?"

Madho Dev nodded. "If they want to go, yes. The world is becoming one. The kind of patriotism I just expressed is very out of fashion, but then, so am I."

"Let's tell them tomorrow and get things moving."

"But you won't tell Gayatri you're her father?"

"Of course not. You'll do all the talking."


THE next day after lunch, Madho Dev broached the subject of Princess Kamala's proposal. Arjun, who had returned in high spirits from the forest that morning, filled with plans for the Diwali festival, which would take place in five days, was squelched by a withering glance from his father and fell silent.

"I've never told you much about your parentage"—Madho Dev addressed Gayatri—"but the time has come when you should know what I know."

At the opposite end of the table, Devika stared into space. Why couldn't her husband speak to Gayatri privately about these things?

she wondered. The poor girl was terribly embarrassed. Had he no feelings?

"Perhaps you should have been informed earlier, but it was the wish of your mother that you should not be told until you had a family of your own. I won't draw things out. My child, the fact is you are Princess Kamala's daughter."

Sitting cross-legged on her mat at one end of the table, Gayatri nodded imperceptibly and smiled. Arjun looked down at his plate, and held his breath. "And my father?" she asked. Her question hung in the air.

"Your mother won't reveal that," replied Madho Dev, "except to say that he was of high birth. I'm sure you need not be ashamed of your father's blood." Hoping no one sensed his sudden relief, Arjun breathed out slowly. "There is good reason to tell you this now," Madho Dev went on. "As you know, your mother is a rich woman. The fathers of both Sonny and Sumitra left them well provided for, so your mother wishes to place her own personal fortune at the disposal of you, Arjun, and the children."

Gayatri glanced shyly at Arjun. He had often mentioned to her his feelings about leaving India, and, although it was difficult for her to imagine life anywhere else, she was more devoted to him than he knew and would follow him to the ends of the earth, if necessary. Perhaps now that he would be able to realize his dreams, he would find peace of mind.

"As the bulk of your inheritance is in Switzerland," Madho Dev continued, "your mother feels it would be wise for you to settle outside India and has enlisted Captain Bruce to help her in this matter. That is why I have spoken of these things in front of him. If you agree, Captain Bruce is ready to look around for suitable places, take you to see them, and generally facilitate the whole process. It doesn't mean you'll not return here. Once you establish residence abroad you can come and go as you like. It means our family will have one foot in another land and your children's future will be more secure."

Devika sat stoically, her hands folded in her lap. From the first day she'd suspected the Bruces' visit boded no good for her family. Their coming had been announced by a road accident in which a number of victims had been claimed by Goddess Kali. Foreigners always brought trouble and disruption. Now they were conspiring with Kamala to take away her son, Gayatri, who was even closer to her than her own daughters, and her dear grandchildren. Why was Arjun not satisfied with their peaceful life in Kotagarh? It was Madho Dev with his stories of past glory and his constant criticism of the government who had given the boy wrong ideas. She would have to speak with him. The woman Philippa was involved in it too; she knew because there was something about Arjun's coolness toward her that was unnatural.

"And what is your own view about this, Father?" asked Gayatri.

"I feel it would be a prudent move. You have your whole life before you, your children's lives and educations to think of."

"But we have land here, we have a good life," Gayatri said sadly. The reality of leaving the warm familiarity of hearth and home suddenly overwhelmed her.

Sensing her panic, David thought he might break down, excused himself and fled to the bathroom. How he longed to hold her in his arms, calm her fears, and tell her that everything would be all right. First he had to get them out of the country, away from all these stupid prejudices. Then he could talk to her, tell her what was in his heart.

When he returned, Madho Dev smiled at him. "Well, it's all settled."

David laughed. "In Hindustan is anything ever settled?"

Delighted that he understood the impossibility of making plans in a country where people didn't believe in planning, they all laughed explosively. The tension in the room unwound like an invisible spring.

"Nevertheless, I think we can try," he said. "I've an important business meeting in Paris in mid-November, and after that I could begin making the necessary arrangements."

"Would you be coming too?" asked Gayatri, looking nervously at Devika and Madho Dev.

"No, my child, it's too late in life for us to make a shift like this, but once you are settled outside, of course we will visit back and forth."

"But how will you manage without us?" asked Gayatri. "You need our help; you will be at the mercy of all these servants."

"You can come back for intervals of six months and help us to keep them under control." Madho Dev smiled. "Also, don't forget, we have many good friends in Kotagarh, Arjun's sisters and their families are not far away, and there's always Harbinder Singh, Harpal, and Hardev—they're grateful to us for acceptance in this community and will always support us."

"I'm not certain they're in a position to support anyone," said Devika, breaking her silence.

"Nonsense," barked Madho Dev. "Everyone knows they are hard-working, solid people; that's what counts. These difficulties will soon blow over."

Arjun, who had been maintaining an expression of studied indifference, now spoke. "You've all been so busy talking about the distant future, you've completely forgotten Diwali. It's only five days away. There are many things to decide. We must make a trip to town tomorrow for fireworks or they'll be sold out."

"You act as though David has said nothing!" exclaimed Madho Dev. "Aren't you the least bit interested in what we've been talking about? You've been longing to leave India. What is your opinion of these plans?"

"My opinion," said Arjun, "is that the goddess has truly smiled on us and I am very grateful. Yet I have the same reservations about leaving you and Mother as Gayatri does. And there are so many details to attend to, the arrangements could take years. Let us wait and see what happens." He hoped he was sounding sufficiently indifferent. "Meanwhile, who are we going to invite for the evening of gambling? We have to make up a guest list."

"I doubt David and Philippa would be interested in that," said Madho Dev.

"I say, speak for yourself, old man," said David. "I'm very keen on Diwali. In fact, I think I remember celebrating it once here in Kotagarh; we played cards till dawn."

"You lost a fortune too," said Madho Dev.

"What on earth is this holiday about?" asked Philippa.

"It commemorates the return of Rama to Ayodhya after his defeat of Ravana, the sorcerer king of the south," said Madho Dev. "Victory of light over darkness. That's why we have all the lights, one in each window, and fireworks."

"And Lakshmi, goddess of wealth, is worshiped on Diwali," said Arjun. "Rich people open their safes, display their wealth to an image of the goddess, and do puja to her . . . and their money." He laughed. "That's why there is gambling. Gambling and money go together."

"You mean, you actually spend the day worshiping money?" asked Philippa.

"Not us," replied Devika haughtily. "We are Kshatriyas. Only the shopkeepers and moneylenders do that."

"My dear," said Madho Dev, "you may not remember it, or perhaps you didn't know, but both your father and mine performed Lakshmi puja in front of their treasure vaults on Diwali."

"A lot of good it did them," Devika said crisply. "And we don't."

"We don't because we have no treasure to do it to."

"Ah, but you're wrong, Father," cried Arjun. "We must find a map of Switzerland, put Goddess Lakshmi in front of it, and do a puja. After all, we have treasure there now."

"What a crazy idea!" Madho Dev said. "But you are right. Now we must decide who we are going to invite."

"And we must try to get some really good fireworks," said Gayatri enthusiastically. "Last year we had too many duds; the children were terribly disappointed."

# 18

THE FOLLOWING MORNING David awoke from a startling dream, the first to plague him in some time. In fact, it was so real, so vivid, that when he came to he was looking down at himself, yelling "This is not right, this is not right!" That was the end of it. In the beginning he had been wandering through the streets of old Lahore, city of lights, the Paris of Asia. It was 1945 and he was on leave from the army. Spotting a beautiful young girl sitting in a café, he had followed her down spacious boulevards through the old section of the city to an outlying suburb, where she had suddenly stopped in front of a hut with a thatched roof and beckoned him inside. Excited at the thought of having this sensuous young animal, he followed her into a dark room, only to find when his eyes became adjusted that he was face-to-face with a very fat naked woman, her hair disheveled, smoking a big black cigar. Her complexion was swarthy, her large eyes bloodshot; she was adorned with gold earrings, bracelets, and anklets. Thick black hair grew under her arms, between her thighs, and down her legs. Her ugliness was magnetic. He felt a deep urge to embrace her but turned away in disgust. "See me, come to me, touch me," she whispered, and winking at him, she spread her legs and opened the lips of her vagina. It was huge and unfolded before him like a huge jungle flower, purple, magenta, pink, and pale lavender, whose petals seemed to ooze nectar. Only an elephant could satisfy such a woman, he remembered thinking as she stood up, tore off his clothes, and embraced him. Somewhere a sleazy band was playing. They began to dance and he looked down at his feet, which had sprouted hooves, and saw his penis grown the size of a horse's. Thrusting it brutally inside her, he whirled her around and around. They fell to the floor. He buried his head between her breasts and was just reaching a climax when he realized she was covered with thick hair and looking up, saw her face change into the face of Durga Baba. Overcome with fright and embarrassment, he tried desperately to disentangle himself but too late. As the apparition grinned hilariously and changed back and forth between the face of the Baba and the strange female, he came like a gushing fountain. "Come, come, come to me, I am waiting," a voice cried, and then he was naked in the Baba's cave looking down at his cloven—yes, cloven—feet; and he woke up crying "This is not right, this is not right!"

Filled with shame and loathing, he leapt out of bed and stumbled into the bath. What a hideously disgusting dream, yet so vivid; what could it mean? He felt possessed and scrubbed every inch of his body several times. After that he dressed and went into the dining room, where to his immense relief he found Philippa and Madho Dev sipping coffee. But when he told them he'd been dreaming again, and Madho Dev pressed him for details until he felt himself going crimson, he suddenly fled; an action he immediately regretted.

Back in the room, however, an irrational fear that the phantom might appear again seized him. Imagining he might never sleep again, he lay on his bed and stared into the corners of the room expecting to see her. What shocked him was not so much her appearance, which was certainly awful enough, or her changing into Durga Baba, but a certain familiar quality that permeated every aspect of the dream.

Fortunately Arjun came round and asked if he would help them with the truck—they were taking out the engine and needed an extra hand—so he had gone with him to the yard behind the barn, worked hard all morning, and managed for brief periods to forget himself. As they were cleaning up for lunch, however, he glanced up and saw Durga Baba's face grinning in a small open window. Madho Dev asked him what was wrong, but he was so surprised he could only point. Finally he was able to tell them he had very distinctly seen Durga Baba's face looking out of the barn, and insisted they look for him. Madho Dev glanced at him as though he'd gone mad but accompanied him inside, where, of course, no trace of the Baba was to be found. David was horrified: now he was dreaming in broad daylight.

After lunch he was exhausted and thought perhaps he could nap. Just as he was falling off, however, there in the corner of the room stood the Baba again, his skin powdered white with ash, his eyes outlined in kohl, leering at him. He actually pinched himself hard to make sure he was not asleep. Then he asked the Baba why he had come and what he wanted but the Baba, or apparition created by the Baba, only beckoned.

Hadn't the ugly woman in the dream said "Come to me, come to me"? Was it too farfetched to think the Baba might be sending him a message? Hadn't he promised to visit him before he left? Somehow he must find the time.

That evening he asked Madho Dev if he could borrow the jeep the next day. He would leave first thing in the morning, spend three nights with the Baba, and return the morning of Diwali in time for the celebrations. Arjun insisted on accompanying him but Gayatri and Devika refused to hear of it. There was too much Arjun had to do to prepare for Diwali. Devika suggested Ravi should go. David was glad Arjun wasn't allowed to leave, as he wanted to be alone. And when for form's sake he invited Philippa and she declined as well, he felt relieved.

Before dawn the next day he packed a few things in the jeep and was ready to make his escape when Madho Dev appeared with Ravi. He had hoped to avoid taking Ravi but Madho Dev insisted, fussing about, kicking the tires, and examining the toolbox.

"You're sure you want to do this, old chap? I don't think it's a very wise idea. Seems to me you're going off a bit half-cocked, if I may so. Not like you at all; you look a bit possessed." David laughed. He *was* possessed; it was the reason he was going. "Well, at least you've got this fellow with you if you have any problems." Madho Dev nodded toward Ravi. "And we'll expect you back day after tomorrow at the latest. Take care and remember not to get out of this vehicle in the forest. Have you got your rifle and your .38?"

They hugged each other and David drove off. The sun was just rising through the October haze. Silhouetted against the mist, formations of wild geese coming south from the Russian steppes soared and wheeled in great arcs over the fields and marshland. It was good to be alone at last. On the farm in England he always managed to find time to gather his thoughts. Every Saturday he spent alone on his horse. It cleared his mind to have one day in which to erase the voices and conversations of the previous week. He hadn't lived so closely with Philippa in years, if ever, and the feeling that he must make conversation with everyone they met had become burdensome. Families were wonderful, but they could be frightfully oppressive. Now that he was going to be alone, his spirits lightened and he chatted with Ravi, explaining that he was not going to take him all the way into the forest because it would be too frightening for him. Ravi seemed relieved.

Like many devout Hindus, he was desperately afraid of Babas and would only go to one if confronted with a major crisis.

They came to the crumbling battlements that marked the entrance to the park, and David dropped Ravi off with the guards. Following a map Arjun had made for him, he then set off past lakes now teeming with waterfowl of every description, through herds of sambar and nilgai, up onto the plateau of bush country beyond which lay the valley in which the Baba lived.

Arriving around noon, he got out of the jeep and walked quickly toward Baba's cave. The trill of a flute over the lazy sound of buzzing bees told him the Baba was there, and David found him sitting in the sun at the entrance to his cave, his cow beside him, her chin on his knee, enjoying the music. The Baba's eyes were closed but David knew he was watching him. Hoping there were no tigers about, he put down his rifle, came closer, and stopped. A scarlet bird with long iridescent tailfeathers alighted in the upgathered knot of the Baba's hair and sat in it as in a nest. At last, taking the flute from his mouth, the old man raised both arms.

"I am Lord of the Universe," he declared, winked, shook himself, and suddenly became the monstrous dancing girl of David's dream.

"Why are you doing that?" David asked.

"What are you seeing?" returned the Baba.

"I am seeing ugly woman with chest hair, then I am seeing you. I saw her in a dream night before last, and I since have seen you during daylight hours. That is why I have come."

The Baba chuckled and turned back into himself. "Very good, Vruce, very good! She is one of my assistants; you don't like?" He arched one eyebrow inquisitively.

"What?" said David incredulously.

"Do not try to stand under it, Vruce." The Baba smiled. "These things cannot be known with words; only to show you I can. But fear you should not be having. Later you will know everything." He waved his hands expansively. "Now you take me for jeep ride. We go, I show. That is why fat lady has come for you." He patted his cow, got to his feet, and led her inside. David thought of running away but found he was unable to move, and soon the Baba reappeared, carrying a small cloth bag. With his right hand he made a strangely obscene gesture. "Come," he said. "We take ride, I show you something. You plenty gas got?"

David nodded and followed. The Baba flew ahead from rock to rock, down the slope. "Where are we going?" David asked as they got in the jeep.

The Baba gestured ahead. "Some distance, a secret place. I will show." As they drove past the cottage and out the road on which David and Philippa had become lost, the Baba played melodious passages on his flute. Late in the afternoon, they descended into the bottomland of a river valley luxuriantly forested with ancient trees, where huge vines thick as elephant trunks arched up, birds called, and monkeys chattered. David thought of Winchester Cathedral, with its towering vaults, buttresses, and branchlike windows. Even the echo was the same. Under this canopy of green they drove until the road disappeared into a path and they came face-to-face with three tall young men in tunics. The Baba put up his hand and David stopped. With their coppery skin and mahogany-colored hair cascading in curls to their shoulders, their large eyes and aquiline noses, David thought they looked more Greek than Indian. Most curious of all was the way they were each balancing on one leg, like herons or flamingoes. Gold earrings depended from their enlarged earlobes and they wore gold anklets on their bare feet. He was just wondering whether they hadn't been conjured up, and for what purpose, when the Baba jumped out and carried on a conversation with them. Finally they turned and walked down the path. The Baba motioned David to follow, and soon they came to a clearing under a huge tree where the three young men swept the ground and constructed a fire pit.

"We stay here," said the Baba when they had finished. He spread out several cloths and a deerskin, and sat down.

One of the young men brought wood and lit the fire with a flintstone. Another brought bunches of long grass which grew nearby and spread them on the ground around the fire. David sat down too, and the three young men squatted on their haunches, lit a big oversized country cigar, and passed it around. It looked like the cigar the woman in the dream had been smoking, and David avoided inhaling it.

After some time, they were joined by two older men. They smiled at the Baba, touched his feet, presented offerings of fruit, vegetables, and milk to him, and carried on an animated conversation in a language David could not understand.

"I telling them you very good man, Vruce," said the Baba affably. "These headmans must give permission for you, me, stay here. They think you look good. In their whole life they see only one foreigner like you. They admiring you." He giggled.

The sun set and the jungle grew dark around them. The two older men left and the Baba got up and bathed in a nearby stream while the three young men smiled benignly at David and puffed their cigars.

The Baba returned, dusted his body with powdered wood ash from a small pouch, and began cutting up a pumpkin and some fruit. One of the young men ground roots and spices which the Baba handed him, and soon the whole lot was bubbling in a brass pot.

"Food," said the Baba. "We eat, feel better, then we go with these fellows."

From a distance the sound of drums echoed through the forest. Playing in tandem as if engaged in some cryptic conversation, one maintained a steady cardiac beat in a deep timbre, while others in different locations answered in sharp bursts of staccato counterpoint.

"Where we are going, is there a religious observance?" asked David.

The Baba, who either didn't understand him or preferred to ignore the question, sat stroking his beard and staring into the fire through half-closed eyes.

"Why you come to me when I you called?" he asked at last in a low voice.

"I was frightened. I want to stop having dreams; they drive me crazy," said David. "Also, I wanted to say goodbye. I'm going away for a while."

"You no crazy, you good man, only cracked." He imitated the motion of cutting something in half with a large knife, accompanied by appropriate guttural sounds. The young men laughed. "I put you together, no problem, make you feel young again. You stay with me. You need stop thinking too much, is crazy making you."

"It's the dreams," said David.

"No, no," said the Baba. "Is too much thinking."

Withdrawing a large wooden ladle from his bag, he stirred the contents of the pot and said something to one of the young men, who slipped into the jungle and returned shortly with six big leaves. The Baba ladled the contents of the pot in equal portions onto the leaves and deposited one in the fire as a sacrifice.

"For goddess," he said and repeated the words to the young men in their own tongue.

They sat watching, as the fire devoured the food. Then they ate their own portions. The combination of pumpkin, fruit, and spices was delicious. The young men scraped their leaves delicately with long fingers, smiled at the Baba, and smacked their lips in appreciation. Two of them got up to go, touched the Baba's feet, and disappeared. The Baba put more wood on the fire and began playing his flute in time with the distant drums. The firelight on the trees seemed to animate them.

David glanced at the Baba and was horrified to see the fat woman sitting beside him. She whispered something in the Baba's ear and gestured toward David. He wondered if the young man sitting across the fire from him could see her. The Baba nodded and listened and nodded and listened, as if agreeing with what she said; he treated her with great respect. Then he shook his shaggy mane, was surrounded by an effulgent blue light, and the woman was gone. The young man smiled at the Baba in a peculiar way.

"You saw her?" the Baba asked.

David nodded.

"Very good, Vruce." He picked up his flute and began playing again.

Above the sound of the flute, David thought he could hear a chorus of otherworldly voices. The siren song that lured Ulysses toward the rocks must have sounded like that. The young man across from him swayed from side to side. Moved by the haunting sounds, so familiar yet so utterly strange, David's body began to jerk uncontrollably. The Baba's dark eyes bored into him from across the fire. Still playing his flute, he got up and began to dance. His canescent body undulated back and forth, head and neck moving from side to side. If I could dance like that, I'd be free, thought David as the Baba reached down and pulled him up. He tried to imitate the Baba's movements. The youth seated across from him rose slowly to his feet and danced seductively in front of the Baba. Somewhere inside, David felt his neural synapses fusing. He glanced down at his feet, thought how ridiculous he must look in his sneakers, khaki shorts, and bush jacket, and began throwing off his clothes. The Baba took his hand and danced him round and round the fire. The young tribal whooped approvingly, clapped his hands, and led them off toward the sound of the drums.

Through a curtain of vines, they came to a vast grassy meadow, the size of a soccer field. Squatting and standing around fires at its edge were men of all ages. Their bronzed naked bodies glowed in the firelight as they smoked and laughed and beat on their drums. In the center of the meadow, silhouetted against the starry sky, was an enormous columnar stone around which, in the crepuscular light, David thought he saw hundreds of women dancing in concentric circles, singing a haunting siren song. Was this another of Baba's grand illusions? When he danced up behind the Baba, the men nodded approval, threw garlands of flowers over his shoulders, offered him the pipes they were smoking and a cup of tea. They grinned and patted him on the back, pointed toward the women, and made jokes among themselves.

"Very good, Vruce? Very good?" The Baba chuckled.

From the sidelines, a naked male would now and then dart into the clearing, catch one of the women, and carry her off. Cries and groans of pleasure sounded from the edge of the forest: David looked down and was embarrassed to see his penis erect. The men around him laughed and clapped, nodded approval, and nudged him out toward the stone. Taking up his flute again, the Baba danced away and David reeled up the slope after him, drunk with joy. The black stone, higher than a man, glistened with libations. Frenzied women and girls crowded around it, adorning it with flowers. Some threw milk on it from brass pitchers, some stood worshipfully or lay prostrate before it, while still others fell to the ground in fits, uttering guttural cries and moans. An exceptionally beautiful woman came up and, removing her tunic, began to embrace the smooth stone. Her full breasts pressed against it; her thighs and buttocks twisted and turned ecstatically. The Baba nudged him and David rushed toward her. She laughed at him, dodged away and he ran across the meadow after her. But just as he caught her in his arms, a clutch of old women rushed up and dragged him to the ground. The stars spun round overhead. Suddenly the fat woman of his dreams was straddling him, staring at him implacably and fondling him while another woman waved incense and still others poured milk over him. Then a band of girls came up, pulled the fat woman off, and tried to drag him away. Soon the crowd of women was fighting over him, pulling his arms and legs, even his hair, until he was literally lifted from the ground. He yelled and cursed them. A group of men ran out, pulled the women off, carried him into the jungle, and pushed him through the door of a long bamboo hut.

Inside white teeth flashed in the darkness. Hands stroked him and tongues licked him until he ached with desire. Bright eyes floated in space. Lovely female faces loomed up and became men with beards. Sable arms enfolded him. Swarthy youths grew breasts and kissed him with soft lips. Sighs of satisfaction filled the air. His body began shaking uncontrollably. He closed his eyes and was taken in every conceivable way. His mind merged with a collective soul that floated from body to body.

When he regained consciousness, he saw sunlight slanting through the trees. It was dawn. He was lying on his back by a fire. Two old men were massaging him with warm oil and he became aware that the Baba was seated at his fire chatting with people, lecturing them and dispensing small packets of herbs.

"I see you wake up, Vruce," he said. "Very good. I think you have fine evening, no?"

"I lost you," said David. "What happened? I feel completely empty."

"Very good." The Baba smiled benignly. "You take rest, sleep, I work. These very good people, very old. Worried by outsiders trying to steal land, government mens, cutting-down-tree mens, all bad people encroaching. No doctors. I am helping."

The steady stream of visitors continued all day long as David drifted in and out of consciousness. Sometimes one person would be rubbing him; sometimes he would wake to find five or six people laying hands on him. At one point a young man was brought in panting and frothing at the mouth. The Baba passed a hand over his head, then plunged his fist into the boy's stomach, withdrew a bloody mass, and threw it in the fire. The boy got up and walked away. Unable to believe what he had seen, David groaned and turned over. The Baba giggled. Near sunset, the youth who had been with them the previous evening nudged him awake and handed him a cup of tea.

"Ah, you wake, Vruce, very good." The Baba smiled. "You sleep, now you wake up, I make food. Azur, here, he been looking after you. You feel good?"

"A bit weak," said David. "Like a baby, if that's possible."

"Anything possible," laughed the Baba. "Last night you see that is so. You always chasing women, now woman chasing you, huh? Those ladies plenty tough, eh? Very good."

"Did that really happen last night? I mean, it wasn't one of your creations, was it?" David asked.

"What is really and not really?" The Baba smiled. "Everything real is and everything no real. No separate pieces, just different views, that's all."

"I mean, there was a celebration of some sort," David said. "There was a meadow—Azur here led us out to it—a black stone, all that."

"Ah, yes," said the Baba. "Once each year it happens with these people. Anybody can do anything. Then all are peaceful, no jealousy, no envy. You enjoyed, eh?"

"I wouldn't say I enjoyed, it was more like dying. Something inside me died. I feel new."

"I putting you together again. Not to worry. This only beginning. Tomorrow we go back to cave, I show you more."

That night, David slept soundly, dreamlessly, and the next day, after the Baba had said goodbye to a stream of visitors, patients, and well-wishers, they drove back to his cave. The Baba would not let David drive; said he'd just been born and was too young, so Azur, who knew something about driving (but not much, David decided), drove barefooted. But the Baba was right. As they bumped along the jungle road and Baba played his flute, David realized he was still highly intoxicated. Perhaps exhilarated was a better word: his eyes seemed more sensitive to light, everything around him seemed alive and charged with meaning, the landscape seemed to be smiling and winking at him, and he saw faces between the leaves in the trees, even in the sky!

When they arrived back at the cave, they found the cow, who'd been penned up in an alcove where the tigers couldn't get her, was very hungry. The Baba sent David out with Azur to cut grass. When they returned he had prepared a light meal, which they ate outside in front of the cave. The afternoon was warm and still. Somewhere a tiger was calling. David was overwhelmed by the wild beauty of the landscape and realized he'd never really seen it before. He sighed and said he wished he could stay forever, but as Diwali was the next day and he'd promised Arjun's father he would be back, he'd have to leave in the morning.

The Baba stared at him seriously, one of the first times he hadn't smiled or made faces. "This Diwali is nothing," he muttered. "Shopkeeper's holiday. And this Rama they are worshiping, he is also nothing. You stay here with me, you see real Rama. You very good man, Vruce. I teach you some things." He looked suddenly very old.

"What kind of things?" asked David.

"Everything I know, you can learn. I never found anyone who could, but maybe you can. You very strong, very hard work it is."

"What?" asked David.

"Come," said the Baba. "I show you the beginning." He got up, and David followed him inside. The Baba picked up a lamp and his small pouch, lifted a cloth hanging in the wall behind his fire, and disappeared through a crevice in the rock. "Azur should not know about this," he said after they had squeezed through. "You follow me." They crawled on their hands and knees up a long tunnel that was barely wide enough in places to squeeze through. A number of other tunnels seemed to branch off it. Finally they came to a series of large rooms, so large the lamplight barely reached the ceiling. "This very big place, Vruce," the Baba whispered. "No one knows. My guru, he is bringing me here many years long time back. I was Azur's age then." He led the way out of the room, up and down through a maze of tunnels, and finally squeezed through another small opening into a room not quite high enough to stand in, shaped like an egg and painted pale blue. The floor was white sand. "This my special place," said the Baba, "You stay here till I come for you. Plenty water there"—he pointed to a large pottery vessel in the corner. "You want learn see, you stay here. After some time, I come back. You not go outside door, you get lost. Extra wicks and oil for lamp, here. Now listen." He lowered his voice. "You sit there." He pointed. "You put lamp here." He placed the lamp on a stone protruding from the wall. "You stare at lamp, but you no blink. When feeling desire to blink, shut eyes, rest, but no blink. You get tired, you lie down, sleep. You get hungry, you have water. While watching lamplight, you repeat two things: AUM and MA. You say," he nodded.

David repeated the two syllables.

"You keep repeating AUM and MA over and over. While staring at flame and saying AUM and MA, you think of sex organ of your father in the womb of your mother just when they are making you." He slapped him on the back. "You, whoever you are, soon you will see everything. If light goes out, don't worry. You won't need. I will return after some time, but do not try to get out yourself. Many other animals are living in cave. Roll the stone in front of the opening when I leave."

"Conveniences?" asked David weakly. At first, the Baba did not understand. "Latrine?" David said.

"That you must live with," he said cryptically. "Now give me your clothes; you must not wear clothes."

"Why am I doing this?" David asked.

"Because you have done everything else and found no satisfaction. You have fought, killed, loved, had children and much wealth but not satisfied. You are good man, Vruce, very strong. For this you are now ready."

# 19

AT KOTAGARH, a considerable debate had taken place about whether David should have been allowed to go into the forest alone with Ravi. Philippa had wondered aloud over breakfast what would happen if Durga Baba gave them one of his potions or what Ravi (who couldn't drive) would do if, for some reason, David became disabled. Although Arjun was secretly pleased because he thought he might be able to spend more time alone with Philippa, he gallantly offered to drive in with the Ambassador and get David if everyone was so upset. The plan, however, was vetoed by Madho Dev: after all, David was a grown man, had had a lot of jungle experience in Burma and elsewhere, was in excellent physical condition, had driven in to the Baba's place twice before, and even rescued Arjun when the jeep tipped over. Moreover, he'd taken along Madho Dev's Purdy and a .38, had extra petrol, even an ax, and a machete; what could go wrong?

The truth was Philippa, who'd been trying to put Devika off the track, was really more concerned that she'd been left alone in the guest room. As long as David had been there, no one would have thought much about Arjun's coming to their room. Now, there would be a problem. Devika had been treating her with considerably less warmth than she had on their first visit, and Philippa felt she must have noticed a change in Arjun and become suspicious. Certainly, she or some servant whom she'd delegated would be watching. Then, of course, there was the possibility that Madho Dev, who eyed her when no one was looking, might very well try to visit her . . . and bump into Arjun? It was all too ridiculous, yet as she'd become involved with this family, she was determined to see things through without causing a scene. No wonder Arjun wanted to get out. The sooner it could be arranged, the better!

Before lunch she asked if it would be possible for her, while David was away, to move into the women's quarters (nauseating as the idea was) and gave the silly excuse that she wasn't really used to sleeping in a room without her husband. As she thought, her move caught Devika off guard. She seemed, if not pleased, at least relieved and sent a servant to fix up one of the extra rooms near the children.

"Perfect," Philippa said. "Now I'll be able to help amuse them while you and Gayatri do whatever you have to do for this Diwali celebration."

The glance Devika gave her told Philippa she'd won a round. But when she found herself alone for a few minutes after lunch with Arjun, he was furious. Didn't she realize they hadn't been alone together since Terripur? Had she no heart, no feelings? Was it possible she didn't understand how painful it was for him to be constantly with her yet unable to express himself? In fact, he had intended to come to her that very evening after everyone was asleep. Didn't she realize they might not have another chance to be alone before she left?

She couldn't very well tell him he might have bumped into his father on the same mission. Instead, she reminded him that men can hide things from the world, even from their wives, but never from their mothers; Devika was suspicious, was watching them constantly, and there was simply too much at stake, their whole future together, to make a wrong move. Being patient had worked to their advantage before. Why should they risk everything now?

The morning before Diwali they all crowded into the Ambassador and drove to Kotagarh to shop. The bazaar was jammed with holiday crowds, and Philippa and Gayatri had their hands full managing the five children. Despite his frustration, Arjun was pleased that Philippa was being so helpful.

Madho Dev had gone off to visit the District Superintendent of Police, the Supervisor of Police, the District Magistrate, and lesser citizens, such as judges of the court, Dr. Kapoor, and the manager of the chemical factory. His mission was to invite them and their families to drop by the farm the next evening for food, drink, and gambling. It was a once-a-year sacrifice he and Devika made to maintain what power they still had in the community; in fact, it was expected of them. Doggedly pursuing his rounds, Madho Dev was greeted warmly in each office. The fact was, he was bored to death, but duty was duty. Inviting people of a lower caste into his house because they were now important professionals still seemed strange to him, but it meant the difference between being ignored by the political system or making it work for him. The more his guests won gambling at Diwali, the fewer bribes he'd have to pay to get his work done during the coming year. Nevertheless, it was exhausting, and the tea he had to drink in each office was not very good.

Philippa was enjoying herself tremendously. Compared to drab Terripur, the Kotagarh bazaar was gay and colorful. Gayatri explained that Diwali was the time one bought new pots and pans, especially as the wedding season was coming up, many brides-to-be and their friends would be shopping, and indeed the cookery shops with their brass and stainless steel wares hanging from ropes and artfully displayed in gleaming pyramids were packed with people. There were also special shops selling mass-produced plastic statues of the gods. At this season, statues of the elephant-headed Ganesh, of Rama and Sita, and of Lakshmi were popular items and came in every conceivable color combination: pinks and pale lavenders, oranges and greens, silver and gold.

But for the children the most important shops were those selling fireworks. Already, on this day before Diwali, one had to watch one's step because crackers were exploding everywhere. They stopped at the largest fireworks display, and of course the children wanted everything in sight. Philippa bought five large bags, one for each child, and Arjun stocked up on the more exotic displays like pinwheels, fountains, Roman candles, skyrockets, and wall-size hangings that were supposed to give you sparkling images of the gods but rarely worked. Then they had to purchase small clay lamps, which would be placed in each window the following evening at twilight, together with cotton for the wicks and the sesame oil to fuel them. Last but not least were stops at the liquor store, the meat store, the vegetable wallah, and the grocer, Ramchand, who would deliver everything early the next day.

That evening there was a big gathering in the courtyard. Everyone was in high spirits. On the night before Diwali, it was Madho Dev's custom to distribute gifts of money to all the servants and field workers so they could make purchases for their own celebrations the next day. Along with the regulars who often came to Madho Dev's nightly gatherings, forty men and women and an equal number of children sat in long rows before the fire. The singing and drumming were especially boisterous, and the old bard was in top form. Several young men got up and expertly performed a wild dance with swords. Then, they all lined up and passed in front of Madho Dev, who gave them each some food and a small packet of money according to their seniority, station, and present salary.

After dinner when he went in to say good night to his children, Arjun found Philippa there alone with them, reading dramatically from an English translation of the *Mahabharata*. This sudden vision of familial solicitude upset him even more. Here was the woman he loved surrounded by the children of a woman to whom he felt bound by duty, not love. Moreover, the children themselves had David's blood flowing through their veins. Now that he knew the truth, he could see the resemblance, particularly in the two girls, Uma and Lakshmi. What a pity he and Philippa would never have children. Making love to her, knowing they might be creating life, would have been everything he could have hoped for. When David returned tomorrow, Philippa would move back to the guest room and they must arrange to be alone. If necessary, he would say something. Certainly David must have sensed something was going on between them. He despised the way David kept his feelings to himself. After all, David had been having an affair with Sumitra; he should be willing to cooperate. But could he risk upsetting the man who was going to do so much for him? He slipped out into the courtyard and found his mother alone, sitting in front of the shrine of Mombai Devi, her eyes closed. He knelt down beside her and kissed her forehead. After some time she turned to him, took his hand in hers, patted it, and smiled up at him.

"I'm asking her for special protection," she said. "We are moving through a time of troubles. It is not a good period. The signs and numbers are very bad, but I know she will help us as she has many times in the past. If it weren't for her, none of us would be here now."

Humoring his mother, Arjun touched his forehead to the stones in front of the small altar. Above him, the night wind stirred the leaves of the pipal tree. Then he lit a small lamp, placed it in front of Mombai Devi, and repeated the mantra she had taught him as a child.

"You must pray to her for guidance," said Devika softly. "At the time of need she will come to you and tell you what to do as she has done for me many times, especially now that you are thinking of leaving me."

Arjun wished his mother wouldn't put it that way. Whenever she wanted to influence him, bind him to her with the silver chains of motherly love, she made it sound as if his decisions were aimed personally at her.

"I'm not thinking of leaving you," he said, "I'm thinking of accepting someone else's plan, the plan of one of your best friends. How do we know it is not due to the grace of Mombai Devi that Princess Kamala has left all her money to Gayatri and our children? And it won't be like leaving. As you have heard, as soon as we are established outside, we can spend as much time here as we like and you and Father may come and visit us wherever we are. It's not such a big thing."

"To leave one's hearth and home, one's native land, is a very big thing," said Devika. "You will see. After a few years you won't recognize your own children, they won't respect you. I have seen it happen so many times with friends who have gone abroad."

"Do you want to let all that money slip through our hands?" Arjun said. "I think it's a gift from the Goddess. Both you and Father lost your inheritances, and Mombai Devi gave you money to start over. Now she is giving money for your grandchildren. You should accept it and be grateful."

As she lay in bed, trying to fall asleep, Devika thought of what a fine day it had been, what a good time she'd had with her grandchildren, and how much she would miss them, and prayed to Mombai Devi to keep Arjun and his family in India. "I have done your puja for many years now," she said to the Devi. "Please grant me this small request."

\* \* \*

"How shall we explain David's absence?" Devika asked as she and Madho Dev stood with Philippa in the hall waiting for their guests to arrive.

All through the long October afternoon, as the sun slanted into the courtyard, they had waited for David to return, and several times Madho Dev, thinking he had heard a jeep, had rushed to the front door, only to return cursing. Now Arjun, with Gayatri and the children, were placing the oil lamps in the windows.

"We can't very well let on he's gone to visit a yogi; they'd think it very peculiar," said Madho Dev. "Especially as the yogi in question isn't supposed to be where he is."

"Can't we say David was suddenly called to Delhi on business?" ventured Philippa.

Madho Dev nodded. "I should think that would work. I'll go tell Arjun." Damn David, he thought, as he followed the sound of the children in search of his son. He'd counted on him to help handle some of these boring people; to have a former captain in the British army there would have put them on their best behavior and given them something to talk about for months. Especially Mrs. Sharma, wife of the D.S.P., the Madame Bovary of Kotagarh. He found Arjun and the children placing the last of the lamps in the windows in Devika's wing of the house.

"Doesn't look like David's going to make it back. People are going to wonder where he is. Think we'd better say he's tied up in Delhi on business, eh?"

"Mmm." Arjun nodded.

"Perhaps he'll arrive yet. If he comes in the middle of the party, someone should warn him not to say anything. Wouldn't do to let on he's been in the forest with Durga Baba."

Arjun followed Gayatri and the children down to the courtyard to turn on the twinkling lights they had strung in the pipal tree and around the eaves of the veranda. When the lights went on, everyone clapped.

A wave of sadness stole through Philippa as she thought of Christmas in England. Yes, it was like Christmas Eve. She saw Edward and Belinda as children, like Arjun's children now romping around her; saw the mayor, the sheriff, and Vicar Farmsworth with their wives, dropping by for eggnog; saw David standing in front of the fireplace. David, where was he? It was very naughty of him not to have come back when he said he would. No doubt he'd realized he'd have to make conversation with a lot of dull people and decided to avoid it. And now, of course, she'd have to spend another night under Devika's watchful eye. Poor Arjun. He'd planned to come and get her after David had fallen asleep; now he'd be grumpy, and God only knew when they'd have a chance to be alone.

After performing puja in front of the fire in the courtyard, Madho Dev took a burning twig from it and, followed by the children, Devika, and Gayatri, marched through the house lighting the lamps in all the windows. Would this be the last time they would all be lighting the lamps at Diwali? he wondered. No one would know how much he would miss them, because he would have to keep up a brave front and spend his time consoling Devika. Well, times changed and one had to change with them or go under.

When all the lamps were lit, Arjun placed a series of fountains at the base of each pillar around the veranda and let Manoj and Rishi light them. While the hookah maker, Baghwan Singh, played the drums and the children began to set off their firecrackers, the old bard played the harmonium and sang songs about Rama and Sita, their trip to Sri Lanka, and the defeat of the wicked Ravana.

Soon the guests began to arrive: the men in their polyester safari suits, the ubiquitous social uniform of bureaucratic India, made stilted conversation; the women in heavy silk saris with gold borders, wrists jangling with bracelets, nodded and smiled while their children—young boys in shorts with high socks and polished shoes, little girls in blouses and long skirts—ran into the courtyard shouting and throwing firecrackers. The servants brought drinks and passed hot snacks. Arjun lit the pyrotechnic mural, which materialized not as Ganesh but as a blazing Lakshmi—the first time in years it had really worked.

"No doubt, wealth will be coming into your house this year, Madho Devji," said the factory manager, Mr. Dass.

"Let us hope so." Madho Dev laughed.

Arjun passed out Roman candles and began launching the rockets. The sky was filled with loud explosions and showers of proliferating colored sparks.

Philippa stood talking with Mr. Mishra, the D.M., and his wife, Reka, young provincial copies of the Ramakrishna Raos. How much they were like the socialist mayor and his wife at home in England! Mr. Mishra was explaining to her how often people at his level were moved about to keep them from becoming involved in local politics. Though tall and handsome, he was consumptive looking, wore a perpetually worried expression, and kept asking Philippa what impressions of India she would be carrying back to her friends in England. He seemed concerned about his country's image and obsessed by what he thought was the unfair opinion of India held by the rest of the world. While her husband droned on, his attractive wife shifted from one foot to another, which kept her hips, like those of Sylvia Singh's at Terripur, in constant motion. Philippa wondered where the habit came from. Reka also shouted at her four children, who ran this way and that, throwing crackers under the ladies' saris, but did not discipline them. She told Philippa she was from Poona, had won a beauty contest there and began a career in films, but didn't like the life and went to college instead. She and Mr. Mishra met in college and were married after he had passed his first Indian Administrative Service examination. No doubt she was bored with Kotagarh and hoped to move on soon to a more interesting place.

Mr. Sharma, the D.S.P., and his wife joined them. He was a swarthy young man with a handsome blank face and military bearing that reminded Philippa of a Nazi officer in a 1940s war movie. Like the wives of most men of his type, Mrs. Sharma was very beautiful, pretentious, and quite stupid. She smiled, preened, posed inanely, and pretended to ignore her husband as he stared at Philippa. One could hardly avoid the lubricious stare of those large saturnine eyes. Philippa felt he would like to do something terribly nasty with her if he had the chance and amused herself by staring back at him until he had to look away.

The Kapoors arrived, and their teenage sons immediately took charge of the other children. It was clear from the condescending manner in which he was treated by officials like the D.M. and the D.S.P., however, that Kapoor was considered an eccentric: someone who had to be put up with because he was a doctor and whose opinions were to be patronized and not taken seriously. It was equally plain to see that Kapoor chafed under this slight to his station by people whom he considered his intellectual inferiors. Real feelings of hatred and vengeance seemed to lurk just beneath the bare-toothed smiles and polite remarks that passed back and forth between these people, who were, after all, supposed to be members of some sort of community. No wonder Mrs. Gandhi had to constantly threaten them with the machinations of a "foreign hand," thought Philippa. Yet whenever she tried to analyze her judgments, she felt there was something terribly important she was missing, something really basic about India she would never understand.

In the dining room, a sumptuous buffet of curries, kabobs, various rices, deep-fried delicacies, chutneys, and sweets had been set out.

After the fireworks had subsided and the children were shooed away to be fed in the women's quarters, they all went in, helped themselves, and sat at tables for six set up on the veranda. Philippa found her place at Madho Dev's table between Sharma and the factory manager, Mr. Dass. Dr. Kapoor's wife and Reka Mishra were the other two ladies. Mrs. Kapoor seemed quite ill at ease and could hardly eat, while Reka Mishra gave every appearance of one who, though trying to remember her table manners, was so beautiful she knew if she ate with her feet she would be forgiven. Obviously Madho Dev was having some perverse revenge in making them all use utensils, when he knew perfectly well they would have preferred eating in the traditional way with their hands. Philippa wondered why. Reka Mishra pecked at her food and laughed stridently at Madho Dev's jokes as he exchanged verbal salvos with Sharma, the D.S.P., who regaled them with tales of famous dacoits he had caught, leered at Philippa, and slowly pressed his knee harder and harder against her thigh. No doubt diabolical Madho Dev, aware of his habits, had seated her next to this man just to see what would happen. She let him press and did not press back. He had one of the cruelest mouths she had ever seen. She'd read unbelievable accounts of police brutality in the Indian Press, but as she watched Sharma she could believe them all. Here was a young tough so obviously fascinated with crime and punishment it was really immaterial to him which side he was on, as long as he could act out his sadistic obsessions.

When the meal was over, the women seemed relieved to get away from the men and Philippa couldn't blame them. In fact, some of them remained in the women's quarters for some time, gossiping with Devika, and only emerged much later to gamble at a separate table of their own. Philippa suddenly thought perhaps she'd been seeing this separation of sexes the wrong way. Perhaps it was really a women's idea; perhaps it worked in their favor. After having coffee, however, Gayatri, Philippa, Reka Mishra, and the petulant Mrs. Sharma rejoined the men in the dining room, where tables for gambling had now been set up. Arjun enlisted Gayatri to run the bank. One of Madho Dev's prides was a roulette wheel, made in Paris, that had belonged to his father. Roulette was the first game of the evening, and Philippa was certain Arjun was rigging the odds, for all the guests came out ahead and had plenty of spare cash to play cards and dice. Dr. Kapoor had fantastic luck at dice and won several thousand rupees from the D.M., who did not look pleased. After dice, a tray of pan was passed around and they all settled down to poker and blackjack. Philippa, who declined the betel nut over the protests of the others, was pitted against the baleful Sharma in several hands and won heavily from him. She'd played a lot of poker in boarding school and was an expert. She could tell Madho Dev was furious at her but didn't care; she had awfully good cards and wanted to get even with Sharma for his behavior at dinner. Sharma stared at her malevolently, as though he would like to throw her in jail, but she persisted and had won almost all the money on the table when Madho Dev suggested they play a game called Indian. At first she thought it most unfair but then realized, as Madho Dev's guests would resent a foreigner winning all their money, he had no other choice. Indian turned out to be a ridiculous game in which the players drew cards and, without looking, held them up to their foreheads face out. The idea was, while taking into account the cards on the foreheads of one's opponents, to bet on your own card, which you could not see. High card won. The odds against guessing were enormously high: in fact, as far as Philippa was concerned, there was no skill involved. Everyone looked so silly staring from under their cards, she couldn't concentrate and began to lose.

"Ah, Mrs. Bruce, your lucky streak is running out, I see," croaked Dr. Kapoor gleefully, rolling his eyes. "Now you are seeing a game that is quite different, I think, from your English games." He lowered his voice. "You have to see the card on your forehead with your third eye, that is the trick."

Philippa smiled. "And how do I do that?"

"Oh, that is a great secret, it takes much practice. You come to my office someday and I will show you."

Everyone but Philippa laughed. However, Dr. Kapoor did seem to have an uncanny ability to guess the card on his forehead and began winning again. Then the trend reversed itself, and Mrs. Dass and Sharma were neck and neck. Finally, when Sharma had won back all the money he'd lost that evening and more, he looked at his watch, appeared surprised that it was already two-thirty in the morning, and, raking in the rupee notes with his big hands, announced he would have to be leaving. Philippa thought he was probably anxious to get to the jail and torture someone. She wanted to cry "spoilsport," but to her surprise no one objected. Obviously it was wise to appease this childish young man by letting him win. A final round of drinks was passed, the sleeping children of the guests were rounded up by the ayahs, and everyone stood around making polite remarks.

"Well, Mrs. Bruce, it has been a great pleasure for me to meet you," said Sharma, one corner of his mouth turned up in a cynical fuck-you expression. "Perhaps you will be coming to my bungalow for tea with your husband before you are leaving Kotagarh, eh?"

"I'm sure we'd be delighted, Mr. Sharma. It's been awfully nice to have met you and your wife," murmured Philippa.

Then he kissed her hand and clicked his heels. Perhaps he had seen those Nazi war movies after all.

Finally everyone was out in the front yard getting in their cars. There was the rumble of engines starting up, horn blasts, and final farewell shouts.

"And so ends another Diwali," said Arjun, as the last cars wheeled out of the gate.

"We'd best be getting to bed," said Madho Dev. "It's late, and tomorrow, if David doesn't show up, we'll have to think about finding him." He went inside and began banking the fire in the courtyard. They all stood watching as he covered the glowing logs with ash. Devika, Gayatri, and Philippa went to bed. Arjun squatted down beside his father and stared into the glowing embers.

"I suppose in the end it's this fire that would keep me here." Madho Dev sighed. "Strange, isn't it, being attached to a fire?"

"I'm sure the D.M. thinks you're very extravagant." Arjun smiled. "I saw him out here looking at your woodpile."

"He knows there's something to it, though," said Madho Dev. "He doesn't say anything because he's afraid."

"Is there something to be afraid of in a fire?" asked Arjun.

"Tradition," said Madho Dev. "This fire is very old. The D.M. knows the story of how it was kept going even after your grandfather died; how before that it had been burning for five hundred years. People like the D.M. are scared to death of tradition."

"How will you come visit us if you have to tend this fire, Father?" asked Arjun.

"Let us see," said Madho Dev. "You do what you must do. We live in unsettled times, my son. All I know is that if things happen easily in an auspicious manner, one ought to pursue them, whereas if obstacles present themselves, one ought to think twice." He got up and stretched. "Will you drive in and look for David tomorrow?"

"Let's hope he comes back himself. I'm not keen on taking the Ambassador on those roads."

As he went to sleep that night, Arjun prayed fervently he would never have to endure another Diwali evening. Though he enjoyed lighting the lamps with the children and setting off the fireworks, enjoyed watching their happy faces as the rockets zoomed off into the night sky, the idea of playing the solicitous host to people like the D.M. and the D.S.P. galled him. By this time next year, he hoped, they would be settled outside India. "Outside"—the word had wings.

The next morning he woke up late and sat on the veranda with a hangover having tea. David had still not returned. He supposed there was nothing to do but drive in and look for him. Damn inconsiderate, especially as David was meant to be in Delhi seeing Ramakrishna Rao in four days and on a plane to England after that. But wait! His mind came awake; the clouds parted. Of course, he was seeing it all wrong. Why not take advantage of the situation? Philippa was David's wife; she must be worried about him. Naturally she would insist on driving into the jungle to find him. At last they might have a chance to be alone, really alone.

He finished his tea and began taking down the lights he had strung up around the veranda. Philippa came out and helped and asked what he thought could have happened to David.

"Listen," he said quietly as he worked. "The gods are favoring us. If he doesn't come back tonight, tomorrow we will both go."

"We?" said Philippa.

"Naturally, Mother will insist I take some servant. You're right, I've been watching her. She's suspicious. You, however, must act very concerned, and as David's wife you have every reason to accompany me. You must insist upon it. She might want Father to go along too, but as she doesn't like to be left alone overnight, I doubt she'll push it. Just be firm and you'll see. Everything will work out."

At lunch things went as he expected, and the conversation finally turned to David.

"He may still come today," said Madho Dev, "but if he doesn't, you'll have to drive in and see what's happened. First thing tomorrow."

"If Arjun takes the Ambassador," said Devika, "that will leave us without any transport. The truck is in pieces."

"Perhaps he can borrow Harbinder Singh's jeep," said Madho Dev.

"I would like to go too," said Philippa. "I can't just sit here and do nothing."

"But wouldn't it wise for you to take one of the servants?" said Devika. "Baghwan Singh? In case anything happened?"

"You think he'd be any help? He's awfully old," said Arjun.

"I think I'd be more help than him," said Philippa, "and if anything has happened to David—" She broke off and looked down at her plate as if she were going to cry.

Arjun was delighted by her performance.

"Of course you must go," said Madho Dev, who couldn't stand to see a woman crying, "You must be very worried. Look how upset she is. You can take Baghwan Singh along, but as Ravi is already out there, perhaps it's not necessary."

After lunch, Arjun drove to Harbinder Singh's house and found that Harpal had taken their jeep to Jabalpur, where he had gone on a business matter and would not be back for two days.

"So it's the Ambassador, I guess," Arjun told them at dinner that evening. "I hate to take it on those rutted roads, but what else can we do? Anyhow, when I get to park headquarters, I can borrow one of their jeeps and leave the car there."

"Will you take Baghwan Singh?" asked Devika.

"If you insist, Mother," said Arjun, "but he'll be useless baggage."

"He could dig if you got stuck," Devika persisted.

Arjun laughed. "Baghwan Singh dig? He's done nothing but make hookahs for years; he'd break his back."

"Why not take him?" said Philippa, seeing that Devika would not give up until they were properly chaperoned. "I think your mother is right. I'd feel better if he came along."


THE next day, shortly after lunchtime, they arrived at park headquarters to find a distraught Ravi, who greeted them with the news that he'd been left there by the sahib and told to stay until he returned. Now many frightening nights had passed with tigers roaring all around him, and sahib had not come. He would have gone searching for him but didn't know where to look. Arjun wondered what David could be up to and ordered Ravi to remain there with the car while they took Baghwan Singh in a borrowed jeep. Although Ravi would have been more help in an emergency, Arjun didn't trust him. Baghwan Singh didn't know a word of English.

As soon as they finished lunch, they were on the road again, bouncing along toward Durga Baba's retreat. Arjun was now in high spirits. "We'll find David, spend the night in the cabin, and return tomorrow," he yelled over the engine noise. "Perhaps we'll have to spend two nights?" He grinned. Philippa glanced back quickly at Baghwan Singh. "Don't worry, he can't understand a word," Arjun shouted. "I haven't told you how beautiful you look today; how madly in love with you I am; how I would like to stop right here, tear your clothes off, and chase you through the jungle. It seems like years since we last made love."

Philippa laughed gaily. "I suppose I can't put my hand on your knee," she cried. "That's what I'd like to do."

"He doesn't understand words but he'd understand that." Arjun grinned. "But you can talk about it, tell me how it would feel to put your hand on my knee, how you would move it to my thigh, and what you would do after that. He looked down at himself. "See what you're doing to me?"

They drove on through the autumn haze. Arjun sang and laughed, telling her how he was going to make love to her all night long, David or no David, and by the time they reached the path to the Baba's cave, the excitement he managed to generate between them seemed almost unbearable.

"Shall I drop Baghwan Singh here and tell him to go up while we go to the cabin for a few minutes?" said Arjun, his voice hoarse from yelling.

"I don't think he'd appreciate that," said Philippa. "We'd better not."

"I suppose you're right." He held her eyes fervently. "Come on, then."

They struggled up the rocky path to Durga Baba's cave and found him sitting outside in the sun playing the flute with his cow and a strange-looking young man whom Arjun identified as a tribal. Upon seeing him again sitting there, his skin glowing, his piercing eyes flickering under ropes of matted hair, Philippa was frightened; what an astounding human being—if he was human. As the Baba spoke little English and she understood almost no Hindi, she had to rely on Arjun's brief asides to discover what was going on. After a few pleasantries, Arjun came to the point and asked politely if he had seen David.

The Baba responded by wagging his head and smiling. Yes, of course, he had seen him, he was there.

"Where?" Arjun asked.

"Inside," said the Baba. Arjun started to poke his head through the door. The Baba laughed. "No, no, him not there," he said with a deprecatory gesture, "he deep inside mountain in dhyan."

Arjun asked why David was meditating.

The Baba grinned. "He wanting to see."

"See?" said Arjun. The Baba pointed to his forehead.

Arjun nodded and told Philippa that David was somewhere inside the mountain doing a meditation that was supposed to open his third eye. Philippa looked baffled.

"Didn't he tell you he was to return two days ago?" said Arjun.

Durga Baba nodded again. "He has told, but he is not wanting to go back so stay here. You wait, I will bring."

# 20

DEEP INSIDE THE MOUNTAIN, the magnitude of his experience had left David in a highly charged state, one in which the borderline between the real and the unreal had been so thoroughly destroyed he was not sure he was still alive in the usual sense. To begin with, he'd become terribly upset about having to perform his functions in the same small space in which he was confined and had tried to go out into the passageway to relieve himself. But when he rolled the stone back and held the lamp up to go out, the head of an enormous snake reared up and hissed at him. Frightened out of his wits, he rolled the stone back in place, finally had to defecate in a corner, and, unable to clean himself, had broken down and cried. Only then, out of desperation, had he begun staring at the lamp as the Baba had suggested, repeating AUM and MA out loud and imagining the moment of his own conception. Why had he let himself in for all this? Surely deep inside he was really crazier than he'd ever suspected. The flame slowly gave way to a negative space in which he saw two figures copulating. Although he had never been able to remember his father or mother and, except for a few old photographs, had no idea what they looked like, the reality of the image was of such a high order he was sure it was them. They were there in the room with him, and he was surprised and delighted that they were enjoying themselves, that he had come about as the result of such an act of pleasure. Then his eyes had grown tired, the vision faded, and he was staring at the lamp again. Slowly he became aware that he was not alone and turned to see the fat woman sitting in a corner. He was horrified. Although she was younger than he remembered, she was even uglier. Masses of thick, crisp hair grew between her breasts, on her back and legs. Desperately he chanted AUM and MA as loud as he could, hoping she would dematerialize, but not only did she disappear, she suddenly picked up his feces and began smearing them over his body. He screamed and yelled and grappled with her but she was terribly strong. He became sick, started to throw up, and lost control of his bowels. Overpowering him, she squatted down on top of him and fondled his penis as she had in the meadow. He remembered rolling out from under her, getting to his feet, and dodging away, but he was no match for her and finally found himself lying there, filthy and exhausted, as she ran her hands over his body slippery with sweat and ordure and sang to him sweetly. Slowly, against his will, he realized she was arousing him. He remembered taking her huge breasts in his hands and sucking on them until milk gushed forth in great quantities. Though he knew she was a created being, it made her no less real. Her body was hard and muscular and gave off a ferocious smell. He glanced about him and saw several huge yellow dogs watching them, panting, the scarlet tips of their sexual organs protruding from furry sheaths.

"I am yours and you are mine," she whispered cloyingly. "Have no fear. I am with you always and will protect you, but you must promise to love me or I will destroy you."

Then she had laughed and vanished along with the dogs and he had lain there on the floor, his eyes closed, desperately chanting AUM and MA. The sounds seemed to act as an anchor to keep him from being swept away entirely by mysterious waves that threatened to engulf him. After some time, he realized the awful smell of the hairy woman had been replaced by the scent of lilacs. Yes, it was lilacs. He opened his eyes, half expecting to find himself lying on a bed of blossoms, and propping himself up on one elbow, looked around. The lamp was very low and he was about to get up and search for the box of wicks the Baba had left when he looked down at himself and noticed to his horror that he had grown breasts, his male sex organs had disappeared, and his skin glowed with a strong violet light.

Collapsing back on the floor, he lay staring at the ceiling, fondling his breasts in disbelief, inserting his finger between his legs. How could he still think as David Bruce when his body had been transformed in this manner? He sat up and examined himself again. The smell of lilacs was overpowering. The walls of the cave glowed a phosphorescent green, and his body, the color of amethyst, was definitely female. Definitely female, he remembered thinking, and must have passed out, for the next thing he knew he looked up to see the figure of a smiling youth standing above him. His body was broad-shouldered, narrow-waisted, and bright blue in color. Epiphany. He closed his eyes, hoping the phantom would disappear, and appealed to

Durga Baba to save him. He was still David Bruce but felt he couldn't
hold himself together much longer. Then a cool hand stroked him,
causing a prickling sensation wherever it touched his skin, and he
opened his eyes to see the godlike face bending down to kiss him. His
brow was of a sapphire hue, his eyes were crimson. David turned his
face away, but the creature held his head in a viselike grip and kissed
him passionately.

Like a looking glass hit by a rock, something inside him shattered.
The creature was kissing his breasts now, watching him, smiling. He
remembered wondering whether this was the fat woman in another
form or an altogether new creature. At first he tensed and struggled
and felt sharp pain as the youth's member ravished him. Then waves
of femininity overwhelmed him and against his will he found his new
body responding the way so many women in his life had responded to
him. His arms wrapped themselves around the youth's neck, his legs
locked themselves around his waist. The creature, effulgent with
light, alive and breathing, mounted him, red eyes bored into him, and
suddenly they were no longer in the cave but flying through the air at
great speed. Magenta clouds billowed up beneath them, penetrated
by giant green fronds waving in copper skies.

They sped on through lightning bolts and thunder and broke
through pink clouds, beneath which he now caught glimpses of
golden cities he easily identified. For some time they hovered over
Athens, but not the Athens of today with its rows of ugly apartment
houses, for the Acropolis stood newly built in all its splendor. Speeding along over the wine-red Mediterranean, over Rome and Mar-
seilles, they turned northward and paused over the unfinished
cathedral of Chartres rising above its plain. Next a wartorn London
spread out beneath them, and then New York. But New York was a
ruin. Rusted girders of buildings loomed up out of islands of rubble,
surrounded by water. He remembered asking a question, but the
youth silenced him and pointed ahead as they sped on over the Pacific,
China, and the peaks of Himavat. Locked in the arms of this being
who seemed so impossibly real, he felt tremendously secure, as
though after a long time he'd been reunited with a lost friend, brother,
or perhaps even his own double. A great feeling of happiness surged
through him. Despite his consternation at being in a female body, he
knew he was at one with something he had always been searching for.

Then, as suddenly as it began, he was back in the cave again. The
lamp had gone out, and it was black as pitch. He reached down
cautiously, discovered he had returned to his masculine form, but was
surprised that it didn't seem to matter much anymore what kind of

body he had. The scent of lilac had vanished and although he was again filthy and disheveled, he now felt strangely exalted. He was convinced beyond a doubt that life as he had known it was as illusory as stage scrim, which could be pierced, and that beyond lay other worlds with different laws of time and space in which past, present, and future were one. Elated, he forgot his disreputable condition, found matches and a wick, lit the lamp, and began the procedure again. Once more he met supernatural beings, and now that his fear had fallen away, he became increasingly adept at directing himself wherever he wished to go.

When the Baba rolled away the stone and appeared at the opening, David had just been visiting London and had managed to look in at Belinda's flat, where she was giving a dinner party. At first he was unsure whether it was the Baba who'd interrupted him or another of the supernatural beings with whom he'd been in contact. Taking his hand, the Baba led him back through seemingly endless passages. He had the impression he was traversing the intestines of some colossal monster, and by the time they reached the Baba's room and emerged from the crevice behind the cloth, it seemed years had passed. Following the Baba outside, at first he failed to recognize either Philippa or Arjun. Their flesh had a peculiar dead look, as if made of some fibrous vegetable substance. Their movements seemed spastic and their eyes darted this way and that, like the eyes of large rodents trapped in a cage. Though he felt sorry for them, they were so frightening he felt a strong desire to run back into the cave. But that would never do. If they looked strange to him, what must he look like to them?

Philippa was appalled. Her hand inadvertently flew to her mouth. David's beard had grown out, he was naked, and smeared with something that looked and smelled like excrement. In a voice suffocated by fear, she asked him what he thought he was doing, how he had got so dirty, why he hadn't come back when he said he would. Had he forgotten they were supposed to be in Delhi in four days?

David stared at her in amazement. She sounded completely unreal, like a wound-up talking doll or a nanny who has discovered a child with soiled diapers. Seeing her, it was obvious to him he had stepped into another world from which it would be hard to come back even if he wanted to. And why should he? He'd come so close to solving so many important riddles that had plagued his life.

Arjun started yelling incoherently. "What have you done to the sahib? What drug have you given him? This time you have gone too far!"

David thought he might be going to strike Durga Baba, so he stepped between them and held up his hand. "You don't know what you're doing," he said. "Stop making a fool of yourself, he's a very great man." He told them that although he might look terrible, for the first time in his life he felt whole and didn't wish to be involved with their problems any longer. He told Arjun he thought it was a great mistake for him to think of taking his family out of India and that he, David, was going to stay, stay there with the Baba. He went on to say he knew all about what had been going on between them. Philippa tried to interrupt but he silenced her. "At first I was jealous," he said, "even though I had no right to be, for I was having an affair with Sumitra. Now, standing here with the two of you, I realize I'm not jealous. Along with a lot of other useless emotional baggage, I've lost that too." He raised his hand and blessed them and told them they were free to do what they liked, that men were born free, and all the rules and regulations they saddled themselves with did nothing but stifle their energy: kill them while they were still alive.

Arjun reminded him he'd promised Kamala, who was after all the mother of his child, that he would help get them out of India, and it was his duty to do so.

David replied that he'd gone beyond duty and that Philippa was perfectly capable of doing everything he would have done. "As you may guess by my appearance, I've had a shattering experience; onto something frightfully important, I believe, yet my condition is fragile. I don't feel strong. If I went to London or even Delhi, I might lose everything. I don't want to risk that and I hope you'll understand, as I am understanding your love for each other."

Arjun thought if he could just get David to agree to come back to Kotagarh for a few days he might return to normal. "All right," he said. "I'm enough of a believer to admit you've had an extraordinary experience. I also see your point in not wanting to stop now; in fact, it might be very dangerous for you to do so. But at least come back with us tomorrow and remain in Kotagarh until Philippa leaves. If she's to carry on in your place, she'll have to have some very clear instructions from you, perhaps even letters, powers of attorney, and so on. If you're going to break with the world, it must be a clean break. I'm sure the Baba would be the first to agree." He repeated his suggestion to Durga Baba in Hindi.

The Baba closed his eyes. "If he going, I think he not return, but I not keeping any man against his will. Let him spend night here. By morning he will know."

Philippa realized Arjun thought David had gone mad and was humoring him. She was furious. What he needed was a good thrashing. He was acting like the naughty spoiled child he had always been.

They got up to leave. It was decided Baghwan Singh would stay at the cave, where Azur would see that he had a place to sleep. The Baba asked to ride with them to the pond, where he and David would bathe. "That woman no good for him," he muttered. "Vruce, he very good man." No one translated what he said. They stumbled down the path to the jeep and drove to the cottage.

With only a nod and a smile, David turned and followed the Baba toward the pond. From the deck of the cabin, Philippa watched them bathe and walk back along the road. She was thoroughly shaken; she felt she'd aged ten years in the past two hours. Or was it that David looked so much younger?

Arjun came out and stood beside her. "Well, there he goes," she murmured, "walking out of my life. It's incredible. After all these years." She wondered why he was so dirty, covered with excrement. "He must have been drugged," she said. "How else can you explain it?"

"Tantric practice," said Arjun. "It exists; we all know about these things, but few of us have the guts to do what he's doing. Still, once we get him home he may come out of it."

"If we get him there."

"Mmm," said Arjun. "Just now he is very much under the influence of the Baba. They put people in trances when they teach them; that's the method. In a few months, you might very well find him walking with tigers. But he was much too aware of what was happening to have been drugged. If we can physically separate him from Baba for a while, the trance will fade. He may be on that plane to London with you after all."

"But what can he possibly hope to gain from all this . . . mumbo jumbo?" asked Philippa. She turned away and burst into tears.

Arjun took her hand, kissed it gently, and held it. "Anyway, he knows about us and doesn't care; that's a burden off my mind. I was feeling very bad about it."

"You still haven't answered my question: what would make a perfectly sane Englishman like David, someone with everything in the world to live for, do what he's done? I simply cannot understand it." She wiped her eyes with her handkerchief.

Arjun smiled. "To begin with, who is perfectly sane? No one knows that, and there is no way of finding out. Perhaps it's curiosity. He's been having all these dreams; he felt the Baba was harassing him.

Then again, he might not be as contented as you have imagined. He spoke to me several times about coming to live with the Baba."

He took her in his arms and embraced her, but she felt drained empty, incapable of feeling any emotion at all. How was she to explain it all to Edward and Belinda? She could hear Belinda now: "But, Mummy darling, what did you do to send poor Daddy running off to a cave?" Or her friends, the whole village, gossiping, laughing at her, saying her husband had "gone native."

"I suppose he's known about us for some time." Philippa sighed. "Now he's getting even."

"Give the fellow some credit," said Arjun. "What he's doing is very difficult. I don't think he'd be doing it just to get even. And you heard him; he wants us to be happy together, gave us his blessing."

"Permission," said Philippa. "As if I need permission from him!" She twisted out of Arjun's arms and paced up and down on the deck. "And now while he returns to childhood, I'll have all the responsibilities; it just isn't fair."

It was difficult for Arjun to understand what had come over her. Here they were, alone at last as they had never been before, and she was suddenly acting peculiar. Was it that although she didn't want David for herself, it hurt her pride for him to leave her? He'd heard of that in some women. "At least you can't say he left you for another woman," he ventured.

"I might feel better if he had, instead of for that disreputable old man."

"What you need is a drink," he said. "I'll go and fix one. . . . Anyway, at least he's waited until your children are grown and you're financially secure," he shouted from the kitchen. "Here in India, many men become yogis and leave their wives and children destitute." He handed her a strong Scotch and water. "He hasn't left you, he's just pursuing something that interests him."

"I suppose you think it's interesting to sit in some dark cave and foul yourself like a . . . an idiot." She clutched the railing of the deck and looked out over the darkening jungle. The moment they'd landed in Bombay, she'd known coming to India was a dreadful mistake. But she'd been a good sport about it, hadn't complained when he'd refused to leave, and now thirty years had ended—poof! just like that. Perhaps if she were to go to him now, this evening, before the Baba had a chance to do anything more. . . . "I think I'll go up to the cave and talk with him again," she said. "If he's left with that Baba, no telling what will happen. Would you mind driving me?"

"You'll just make things worse," said Arjun. "Forget him; think of us. Here we are, it's what we've been looking forward to for so long. We're alone, no servants, just the two of us."

"If you won't take me, I guess I'll have to walk," she said, turning to go.

He caught her arm. "You are not going to walk there. How many times do I have to remind you of the dangers?"

"Well?" she said defiantly.

"And I am not going to drive you."

"You aren't?"

"No." He had never encountered such strange behavior in a woman and did not know how to deal with it. He put down his drink and tried to hold her in his arms again.

She struggled to free herself. "Let me go, will you? I don't feel like making love. Can't you see how upset I am?"

"You're just making yourself upset," he said. "Don't you feel anything? Doesn't it mean anything that we have the whole night to ourselves?"

"It is still very early. I want to go back to that cave and see David, talk some sense into him."

"I'm sure he'll be asleep."

"So you won't take me?"

"No, and I won't let you go either."

She slapped him hard on the cheek and struggled to free herself. He held her by her shirt. It ripped and she slipped out of his arms. He caught her on the stairs and picked her up and carried her kicking into the bedroom, where he dropped her on the bed, slammed the door, and began taking off his clothes.

"I told you I don't feel like this!" she cried. "And I'll thank you not to treat me like one of your Indian women."

Arjun was outraged. "You should be so lucky that you are treated like an Indian woman," he said huskily. "And I'll thank you not to treat me like one of your Englishmen. You think you can manage them like trained dogs to do your bidding, and when they don't behave, you say they've gone crazy. Like David. I'm sure this is one of the first times since you've been married he's done what he really wanted to do."

"I think you're dreadful. I'm certainly glad I'm seeing the real you before it's too late."

It was difficult for him to know whether she was really angry or just pretending in order to excite him. If that's what it was, she was certainly succeeding. He looked down at himself, smiled, and started toward the bed.

"Arjun, please, you don't understand. So much has happened; please, you must give me time. I swear, if you come any closer, I'm going to scream."

He jumped up on the bed and threw open one of the small windows near the ceiling. "Go ahead, who will hear you? Scream, it might make you feel good."

She got up and lunged past him for the door. If she could get to the other bedroom, she could lock herself in. He caught the edge of her skirt, grabbed her, and ripped off her remaining clothes.

"If you'd seen Gayatri in David's condition," she panted, "would you feel like making love?"

"With you, yes." He smiled. "My feelings toward you have nothing to do with her."

"You'll never understand anything!" she cried and pounded on his chest with her fists.

"Just a dumb Indian," he shouted, "but pretty sexy to fool around with on holiday, no?"

"That's unfair. You know I don't feel that way."

"You're acting that way."

"And you think all you have to do is take off your clothes, exhibit your beautiful body, stare at me with those big dark eyes of yours, and I'll swoon. Well, I'm not that kind of woman."

"What kind of woman are you then?"

"I don't know, but I'm not so overcome by the physical as you might imagine."

He picked her up again. They fell on the bed and he struggled to find her mouth. Her sharp nails dug into his back. He caught her wrists, pinned them to the pillow with one hand, and held her hair with the other. She turned her head aside. He turned it back, found her mouth, and kissed her. Suddenly her body heaved and she began to cry. He licked her tears away and drank them, kissed her forehead, her neck, and breasts, returned to her mouth, and found her tongue. At last her body went limp. He released her arms, and she ran her hands through his hair.

"That's better," he said quietly. "There is nothing to be frightened about. You have me. You don't need David anymore, forget him." She wrapped her legs around his waist. He flowed into her. She began to moan and thrust herself violently against him. He kissed her gently. "Surprise," he whispered. "It's just the beginning; we've got all night."

She looked up at him. The cloud hanging over her seemed to have passed, and she smiled. "I don't know what got into me."

"You were frightened. Seeing David that way touched something very deep inside you. Fear is a terrible thing."

"Thank you for persisting," she whispered.

"Don't thank me. I would expect the same understanding from you."

"O tiger among men." She smoothed his forehead. "O bull of Bharat."

"I shall have to teach you that in Sanskrit, it sounds better," he said. "I noticed you reading the *Mahabharat* to the children."

"It's very beautiful, so human."

"If you know the *Mahabharat*, then you know us." He stared into her eyes.

"When I look into your eyes," she said, "I fall in."

"And when I look into yours, I see the limitless sky." He nuzzled her breasts. "I feel very comfortable with you; is that the correct word? As though we have known each other forever, or like friends who have met after a long absence."

"Do you think we were lovers in another life?" she asked.

"And now we are joined together, two halves become one. And those whom God has joined together, let no man tear asunder. I think they say something like that at your English marriages." Her teeth began chattering. "You're so funny when you do that," he said. "Your teeth go—" He clicked his teeth together. "It's very amusing to me."

"It started happening when I first met you. It's you that does it to me."

He took her face between his hands. "You are in many ways such a child. Why should your teeth chatter when you are enjoying? Teeth chatter from cold or shock; you aren't cold, are you?"

"I was cold before, thinking of David in that cave, but you're very warming."

"Don't think of him."

"You're right, I'll stop. He must be free to do what he wants, and I shall do everything he would have done. It's more important to me than ever that you should get out as soon as possible. I'm going to miss you terribly."

"You're not going to call me a dumb Indian again tomorrow?"

She giggled. "I did not call you that, and you know it."

"Would you like another drink?" he said.

"Why not?"

He went into the kitchen and poured out two more drinks. "Come," he said at the bedroom door, "see how warm it is outside." They stood on the deck and sipped their drinks.

"Remember the first time we stood here together?" she said.

"Did you know how much I wanted you? How nervous I was?"

"I knew you were nervous, I didn't know why." She glanced around her at the darkness. "I feel quite strange standing here like this, naked in the middle of the jungle."

He put down his drink, went to the bedroom, and returned, dragging a mattress. "Let us stay here for a while, see the stars and watch the new moon."

She sank down on the mattress, pressed herself against his thighs, and looked up to see him smiling down at her. What sort of mystery was hidden behind a mouth that never expressed despair or discouragement?

"What are you smiling at?" she murmured.

"I am enjoying watching you." He reached down and held his stiff penis in his hand. "Do you not think it is admirable? I am very proud of it. Five children have come out of it." He squatted down beside her. "But Gayatri has never seen it, would never look at it." He lay down with a sigh and gazed up at the moon.

She ran her tongue over his body. Never had he felt anything so pleasurable. He turned and let his tongue slide down between her thighs and began to nibble at her like ripe fruit. She became excited. The melonlike muscles of her buttocks divided above him and swayed back and forth. Never had he been able to explore a woman's body like this. Never had a woman used his body so freely, with such honest pleasure.

"Whether we ever marry or not," he whispered, "I tell you this night we are one, and if something should happen and we were never to see each other again, you know you have been properly married to a man who loves you."

Without uncoupling, he sat up, folded his legs beneath him, and lifted her into his lap. She felt his blood throbbing deep inside her. He kissed her breasts and neck and gazed into her sky-blue eyes. "Don't move." He smiled. "Relax completely and look at me. This is the position favored by the rishis of old; have you seen it in the statues?"

She nodded.

He kissed her and sucked her lips and tongue. The whites of his eyes were like mother-of-pearl. When she gazed into their dark pupils, she felt herself diving toward the warm center of creation.

He licked his lips and laughed, felt flames mounting up his spine, shooting out the top of his head, and then a warm flood anointed his lingam.

She kissed his smiling lips and felt him discharge inside her in bursts that shook his whole being. His eyes rolled back in his head, and he began to laugh and yell.

"Stop, stop!" she cried. "It's too much."

His eyes came back into focus; they dropped to the mattress exhausted and lay trembling in each other's arms.

"This is the real marriage ceremony," he whispered. "Wherever we may go, we will never forget this night, and in the next world we will also remember it and find each other."


BACK in Kotagarh the next afternoon, David had gone directly to his room, where he'd slept through the night and most of the following day. Saying goodbye to the Baba had been difficult. After they had bathed and returned to the cave, they sat at the fire. The Baba urged him not to leave, told him part of himself had died in the cave and, like a snake losing its skin, he was now in the process of being reborn: fragile and subject to influences he might not be able to control. Finally he'd persuaded the Baba that no harm would come from leaving for a few days to fulfill his responsibilities; he'd only be gone till Philippa left and would return as soon as possible after that. But the next morning, after picking up Ravi and the car at park headquarters, when he'd been obliged to drive the jeep back to Kotagarh, he realized how right the Baba had been. Not only had his spatial perceptions changed, he was so physically disoriented he could hardly steer. Then the Ambassador had hit a rock and sprung a leak and when he'd tried to help Arjun patch it up, found himself quite incapable of using his hands properly. So by the time they arrived at the farm and he'd apologized to Devika and Madho Dev, who'd stood gaping at him in the front hall, he'd been so exhausted he'd gone straight to bed.

Now light was filtering through the heavy curtains of the guest room, and he was just wondering how long he'd been there when a knock sounded at the door. It was Madho Dev.

"Afraid I'm causing problems," David said. "I'm sorry. Is it time for dinner?"

Madho Dev smiled. "It's time for lunch; you've slept nearly twenty hours. I thought I'd better wake you. Philippa is leaving tomorrow, so there are things you must attend to."

David sighed, fell back on the pillow, and stared up at the ceiling. "I suppose Arjun has filled you in on the dramatic events of the past few days?"

"Vaguely." Madho Dev nodded. "He says you've decided not to

leave, that you're going to live with Durga Baba. We were all quite surprised. Can you tell me what brought on this sudden change of plans? You think he drugged you?"

"No, definitely not. Not any more than you do with that hookah of yours. I don't think he has to use drugs, he does it all with . . ."

"With what?"

"His mind, I suppose; rather a shallow word to describe whatever he has: mind. It's so much more than that."

"What happened?"

David scraped his throat and looked away. "That's just it, I'm not supposed to tell anyone, but I can say it was awful and wonderful at the same time. I have the feeling I learned more about myself in those few hours than I have during the rest of my life put together, but I couldn't possibly put it into words. And I feel younger."

"You look younger."

"I feel quite different, though I'm not certain just how, and the world—people, things—everything looks very different."

"How?"

"Dead."

"Dead?" cried Madho Dev.

David nodded. "This everyday world in which we live is basically dead, but it has these cracks in it. If you know where to look for them you can look through to the real world—at least it seems that way."

"You've got more guts than I have," said Madho Dev.

"You don't think I'm crazy, that I'm having hallucinations?"

"I didn't say that, old man, you may well be. I said it takes guts; it's not something you'd find me doing."

"But you've completely transformed yourself," said David. "It's one of the reasons I wanted to do this."

"It took forty years; naturally I've changed."

"I haven't got forty years. I have to do it all now."

"But why, what's the point? You have a wonderful life."

David sighed. "That's a relative matter. The point is I wanted to stop dreaming. I couldn't get any sleep. I became afraid to fall asleep, exhausted all the time; then one thing led to another. On top of that, I'd decided I really didn't want to go back to Europe. I think it was the night you took me to that hut by the river—we did go there, didn't we? There were girls there?"

"You're not sure?"

"Not really, at this point."

"Yes, we did."

"Ah, well, but it wasn't the girls, girls one can find anywhere, it was the sense of peace I felt standing in that irrigation ditch later on. I told myself it was time to do what I wanted to do, not what other people planned for me. Now this business with the Baba has started, I want to see it through. And beyond that, I want to be near my grand-children and Gayatri. I know they may leave, but this is where they belong and where they will always return."

"Hmm," said Madho Dev. "You think Philippa can manage all this business with Rama Rao and in Switzerland?"

David decided it was better not to tell Madho Dev about Arjun and Philippa. While it might not last, it would certainly motivate her. "Yes, I do. She's an extremely capable woman."

"I'm not keen on having Arjun move away, I can tell you that."

"I think it's nonsense; they should all stay here."

"You think so? That makes me feel better. But having had one fortune slip through my hands, I think it's important, as long as Kamala has offered another, to do the necessary things to secure it—which means their taking up citizenship abroad for some time. You know as well as I that if they aren't there to watch it, the money will vanish. Once they are established outside, it can be used here."

"I quite agree, and Philippa can and will do it. And if there are any real complications, I promise you I'll put on my clothes and go back into the world and deal with them. I might as well tell you another reason I didn't want to go back to Europe. I fell madly in love with Kamala's daughter Sumitra."

"You what?"

David nodded. "Yes. She's very beautiful, more beautiful than Kamala was. I'm supposed to meet her in Paris in about three weeks."

"You must have had a complicated time up in Terripur."

"Quite. Kamala found out about it and was furious. But when she told me about Gayatri and I realized I had grandchildren here, the affair with Sumitra seemed unimportant. Still, I know myself too well. Sumitra is irresistible. If I leave, I'll go to her, and if I do, she'll drive me crazy with jealousy. This came through very clearly at the Baba's after I'd meditated in that cave and been flying around with this blue-skinned young fellow."

"What blue-skinned young fellow? What are you talking about?"

"One of the creatures I met while I was in the cave. But I forgot, I'm not supposed to discuss that. It's one of the reasons I have to go back . . . another mystery to unravel."

Madho Dev slapped his knees and got up. "You'd better be careful you don't unravel yourself, my friend. Will you come to lunch now?"

David yawned. "I think not. I'll rest for a while and then I'll get up this afternoon. Where's Philippa?"

"With your grandchildren. I believe she's become quite attached to them."

"When you see her, will you ask her to wake me at teatime? We can go over the arrangements then."

Madho Dev went out into the bright sunlight of the courtyard, muttering about blue-skinned creatures, and crossed to the dining room, where Devika, Arjun, and Gayatri were already eating.

"Where is Philippa?" he asked.

"Having lunch with the children," said Devika. "It was her idea. She wanted to have a lunch party alone with them before she left. She's become very fond of them."

"You have been with David?" Arjun asked his father.

Madho Dev sat down and sighed. "To see one's old friend in such a state, not realizing he's making a fool of himself, is very sad. I would say he's close to a nervous breakdown. Just described to me how he was flying about over the world with some blue-skinned young fellow."

"Krishna," said Gayatri calmly.

"What?" said Madho Dev.

"Krishna," Gayatri repeated. "He must be flying with the Lord Krishna, who is blue in color."

Devika stopped eating and narrowed her eyes at her husband. "Durga Baba is a sidh, a man of power, and a very accomplished tantric too. One can tell it by looking at him. To become a disciple of such a man is most dangerous but very brave. If that's what David wants, we should support him in every way. He must know that he has us to fall back on if he needs to. He may go quite mad before he attains realization, but he has reached the time in life when a man is permitted to retire to the jungle or an ashram."

"An ashram is one thing; to live in the jungle with a hermit like Durga Baba is quite another," said Madho Dev.

"There is nothing we can do about it," said Arjun. "He seems quite determined. When he came out of that cave, it was very strange. He was naked and filthy. Philippa was most upset."

Devika thought about Philippa and how Baghwan Singh had given her the information that she and Arjun had spent the night alone in the tourist cabin. She was so pleased, however, that Philippa was leaving the next day, and so certain that, once gone, she would not have the energy or drive to accomplish Kamala's plans, that she had decided to put the matter out of her mind.

"I admire David," Arjun was saying. "I wish I had the courage to do it."

"As a householder, your place is with your family," said Madho Dev harshly, "until your daughters are married. Then you may go off to the jungle if you like. Meanwhile, you must promise not to get involved with Durga Baba; it could be very dangerous for you, Gayatri, and your children. David and what he is doing is another matter."

"Perhaps he will become a saint," said Gayatri.

"David Baba." Madho Dev laughed.

"Don't laugh," said Devika. "Many foreigners have become saints here. Think of Mother Teresa. Then there was Aurobindo's wife, the Mother of Pondicherry, and a famous saint from England; his name was Ronald Nixon. My mother's guru, a woman, was his guru; he became a saint near Almora and was called Krishna Prem. Today there is Father Bede Griffith in the south, and who knows how many others?"

Madho Dev changed the subject. "Do you think Philippa will be able to make all the necessary arrangements David would have made? I wonder if I ought to get in touch with Kamala and let her know what's happening."

"She's very competent," said Arjun. "Nothing seems to faze her. You should have seen her digging out the center of the road so the car could get through. Baghwan Singh was useless. But I'm afraid we knocked a hole in the oil pan coming back. We'll have to leave the car with Dr. Kapoor's son when we take Philippa to the train."

"Imagine coming to a country and having your husband refuse to leave," said Gayatri. "It must be very hard on her."

"Let's hope this is just David's way of taking a vacation," said Madho Dev. "He's been leading a busy life, he's been under great pressure. We're the same age, but when he first arrived he looked ten years older. What can one say about something like this? I suppose it's our fault for taking him to meet Durga Baba."

"No, no, no," said Devika. "Thousands of people are taken to babas and don't stay with them. You have to be touched. Many times I have thought that, in times of need, the gods send spirits in the form of ordinary people and work through them to help other people. We don't really know why David is here. We must let things happen and not interfere. Only in that way can we discover the intentions of the gods. It is when we interfere that we cause trouble. Instead of questioning and meddling, we must spend more time in prayer and devotion."

* * *

THAT evening, Madho Dev made a special effort to see everything should go off smoothly. The gathering in the courtyard was an intimate one. Harbinder Singh, Hardev, Harpal, and their mother were the only guests. The fire burned brightly. David had pulled himself together and appeared in fresh white pajamas with Philippa. Arjun sat with Gayatri, surrounded by their children.

Although he felt almost suicidal, Arjun made a valiant effort to look cheerful and unconcerned. By this time tomorrow, Philippa would be gone. Would she vanish forever like some celestial created by the spirit world?

Philippa prayed the next few hours would pass quickly. Not that she wanted to leave Arjun, but as she must, to see him sitting there, knowing what must be going on inside him, was too painful. And there was Devika, an expression of contentment on her face, obviously relieved that the foreign temptress would soon disappear. And sweet Gayatri, oblivious to everything that had gone on; and Madho Dev, deeply disturbed about David. The old bard was singing the last section of the *Mahabharata* in which King Yudhishthira refuses to enter heaven without his faithful dog. Madho Dev translated it for her as they went along.

"It is said that abandonment of one who is devoted is infinitely sinful," sang the bard. "I shall not abandon this dog today from desire of my happiness. And when Sakra, the Lord of Heaven, saw that it was impossible for him to dissuade King Yudhishthira from bringing his dog, that he refused to enter without him, the dog was transformed into Agni, god of fire, and accompanied Yudhishthira on his heaven-bound ascent.

"And the entire welkin blazed with his effulgence," went the chorus. Baghwan Singh beat the drums. "And the entire welkin blazed with his effulgence." The children rang cymbals, and Devika and Mrs. Harbinder Singh shook tambourines. The rousing music, the look of devotion and triumph on all the faces, brought Philippa to the edge of tears. At the end, Madho Dev did puja before the fire and offered food, spices, and ghee, which he spooned into it. The fire blazed up and gave off a scent that she would remember for the rest of her life.

They retired to the dining room, where Devika had arranged to have all the dishes Philippa liked best. The children were allowed to join them and managed to keep the grown-ups from becoming too depressed. Philippa had no appetite but heaped her plate and tried to eat heartily. Looking about her at the family gathered round the table, she realized she would never understand them. They were too intense, their emotions were too powerful for her to cope with. If she stayed much longer, even she might end up in Durga Baba's cave.

After dinner they all wandered back to the courtyard. She couldn't bear looking at Arjun, so beautiful, trying so hard not to show his emotions but only managing to look more distracted than ever. And when they went in with Gayatri to say good night to the children and tuck them in, he seemed to be projecting waves of desire toward her. She felt faint, and her teeth began chattering again. She said good night quickly and fled to her room. David was in bed reading. When she sat down in a chair and stared into space, he put down his book.

"What's the matter?" he asked. "You look worried."

"This leave-taking, it's too depressing, and naturally I'm worried about you. Everyone is acting so cheerful, and I feel awful. Did you have a fight with Madho Dev?"

"Not a fight. He says he can't understand what's got into me, that I'm acting childish and should be careful; that under the guise of teaching, babas often capture people's minds to do their bidding."

"But what could the Baba want from you?" Philippa said.

"Absolutely nothing, that's just the point. If he were in an ashram with a big following, there would be some reason to suspect his motives. But he's out there in the jungle; he wants nothing."

Philippa got up, closed the window, and pulled the curtains. "Why do you think you're staying on? Is it because of Arjun and me?"

"Definitely not. Oh, I was angry at first when Kamala told me— apparently Ravi had seen Arjun go into your room—but when I thought about it, I realized you had as much right to freedom as I did. No, what bothered me most was that I felt Arjun had deceived me, seeming so friendly, all that uncle business. Then Kamala made me realize his wanting you had nothing to do with his liking me." He laughed. "When I saw it that way, I stopped feeling betrayed. No, it's not you and Arjun. I've been thinking of staying on ever since we arrived. I know it's been hard on you. It's not your fault. You didn't really want to come, and you tried to get me to leave, but you have to remember, I spent my youth here, it's part of me and now I'm getting old—"

"You aren't."

"Oh, yes, I am. Time's wingèd chariot is just around the corner. You were only eighteen when we were married; there's years between us. You have the best part of your life ahead of you. Believe me, I'd go now; I'd do all this business even though I really don't think they'll be happy elsewhere. It's just that at this moment I think my future peace of mind depends on carrying this thing through with the Baba. My resolve is not that strong, quite frankly, and if I leave now I'd get so caught up in the world, I'd never get back; and regret it for the rest of my life. But if you have any problems with Ramakrishna Rao or anyone else, postpone them. Give me six months; by that time I ought to know what I'm doing. One reaches a point where one is haunted by all the things one hasn't done in life, or left undone; all the accumulated emotions and feelings that lie buried and unresolved come to the surface and have to be faced down. That's why I say go ahead, don't suppress things. Have your relationship with Arjun. Suppression is death. But I'm afraid, like all such relationships, it may prove more painful than you expect. Perhaps the real reason behind my staying on is that I just want out of the whole business. I really don't know. As you can imagine, many things went on in that cave."

Philippa changed into her nightgown and sat on the edge of the bed. "I suspect it's rather like a speeded-up psychoanalysis you're going through," she said.

David looked away. "I'm afraid you were dealt a rather bad hand when you married me. You never knew how much in love with Kamala I was, and I never told you. I was sure it would fade, and it did. Then recently I began to realize that when she had run away and I came back to England, it was a turning point, a replay of my childhood—only worse. The war with all its romance was over, I was twenty-three, and suddenly there it was again: cold, gray, monolithic Britain. I had to suppress everything."

"Which you did extremely well." Philippa smiled.

"Until recently, when I began feeling useless," he replied. "It was that feeling of uselessness which drove me back here, and though I'm sure I'm just as useless here, I don't feel that way."

She stroked his forehead, got into her bed, and turned out the light. He stared at the ceiling. Why was everyone patronizing him, everyone except Devika?

# Part Four

# 21

A T ONE THE NEXT AFTERNOON, they were at the
station. The children stood in a row with Gayatri and Devika
as the train came down the track. Philippa kissed them all.
When she came to Arjun, he gripped her arms, held her very stiffly,
pecked one cheek, and then the other. "Love is God," he murmured as
he released her. She would have fallen into his arms but for David,
who propelled her up the steps and into her compartment, where he
kissed her goodbye. She had to sit smiling and waving until the train
moved. Arjun saluted, the children waved and blew kisses, and
Kotagarh slipped away. She felt part of her life ending.

The train picked up speed. She sat in a semicomatose state holding
back tears, feeling helpless, overwhelmed by an undefined sense of
loss: her body on the train, her heart with Arjun. After a long time,
she opened her eyes and gazed out at the passing landscape, which
seemed suddenly drab and lifeless. The compartment was stuffy. She
was the only woman. Across from her, two businessmen in safari suits
were drinking tea. Beside her a rather large young man was trying to
engage her in conversation. He was from Mysore and had recently
graduated from medical school; his marks had been very high, and he
was on his way to Delhi to be married to a Kshatriya girl whose father
was in the government. The bride's father was giving him a postgradu-
ate medical education in the United States, an apartment in Bombay,
and a Mercedes car as dowry payment. He had never seen his bride
but didn't care. She looked presentable enough in photographs, and

the family pundit had pronounced the horoscopes to be correct. He was provincial and pushy, but after the strain of leaving Kotagarh, his ridiculous behavior came as a relief. Gorging himself on some snacks he'd purchased, he pulled up his silk kurta and fondly stroked his large young belly, a gesture so outlandish it disarmed her completely and she started to giggle.

He smiled and asked her to call him Nirendra, offered to escort her to her hotel when they reached Delhi, and casually propositioned her. "My wedding party does not arrive for three days and the bride's family does not expect me yet. Let us spend some time together; you will not be disappointed." His thick lips curled under a youthful mustache; his stout legs wobbled back and forth. "I will show you things that may surprise you."

Philippa thought she was surprised enough already. Now he stared at her with dark bovine eyes; she sighed inwardly. It was one of the worst problems of India for her, these dark eyes boring holes into you until you felt your innermost thoughts leaking out all over the place.

"May I ask at what hotel will you be staying?" he said in a commanding voice.

"Majestic," she replied, knowing somehow he would find out.

"I am not knowing the hotels in Delhi. Myself, I am booked into Maurya Sheraton, but I will accompany you to yours. A woman like you should not be going about alone at night."

The air of Delhi was still heavily polluted. In the chilly fall night, people squatted around roadside fires, and the lights of the city seemed to hang like lanterns in a brown haze. She remembered it was the night before All Hallow's Eve, when the world cracked open, you could see into the past or future, and the dead rose up and walked again. And here she was rattling through the streets of New Delhi in a decrepit taxi with an insouciant youngster from south India—an unlikely set of circumstances, to say the least.

The taxi wheeled up Vivekananda Road and into Connaught Circus, once the ornament of British Hindustan, its grand design now obliterated by a forlorn patchwork of billboards, shop signs, and peeling paint. In the center a modernistic fountain played in a forlornly deserted park. Up Janpath Street the taxi lurched, through the gates of the old Hotel Majestic, down the drive lined with royal palms to the entrance. The hotel was surrounded on all sides by encroaching shops, built against an outer wall that separated its compound from the city. She peered doubtfully out the taxi window. She had wanted to stay at the same hotel where they had stayed before, but it was fully booked. A tall Sikh doorman opened the taxi door, smiled at her, and frowned when he saw Nirendra emerge from the other side. Philippa was determined that he should leave then and there.

"Well," she said, brushing off her suit, "thank you very much for seeing me here. Do ring up sometime tomorrow; perhaps we can have lunch." She had no intention of lunching with him but thought it a good ploy to send him on his way.

"But I must be seeing that you have a room. These places are not to be relied upon."

Ordering the taxi to wait, he strode into the hotel lobby, approached the desk, and demanded to know if Mrs. Captain Bruce's reservation was there. The clerk nodded at Philippa and, thumbing through his reservation file, withdrew a card.

"Ah, but you see, they are quite reliable here," said Philippa, taking up a pen and filling in the card. "Now I must thank you again for your courtesy and say good night, Mr. Nirendra. Thanks to you I've had a most delightful journey, but I'm afraid I'm awfully tired."

She tried to make the words sound like an official utterance, something he would obey. The clerk looked on with amused interest. Admitting temporary defeat, Nirendra saluted casually and retreated through the lobby.

An ancient room boy conducted her from the lift down cavernlike corridors to a room on the third floor overlooking the hotel compound. Putting down her bags, the old servant fidgeted about, turning back the bedcovers and switching on the TV. A picture of Mrs. Gandhi addressing a large open-air gathering fluttered on the screen. Philippa was about to turn the set off and paused. It was hard for her to believe this was the woman she'd met barely four months ago. Her skin, drawn tightly over her cheekbones, was deeply lined. Mrs. Gandhi's voice faltered: "I do not care whether I live or die. I have enjoyed a long life and I am proud that I spent the whole of my life in the service of my people. I am only proud of this and nothing else. I shall continue to serve until my last breath and when I die, I can say every drop of my blood will invigorate India and strengthen it."

Why was Mrs. Gandhi talking about death and blood? The brave woman's voice sounded exhausted. A feeling of foreboding crept through Philippa's bones. She switched off the set, tipped the room boy, showered, and got into bed.

Immediately her mind became filled with images of Kotagarh. Now they would all be singing at the fire. What dear people they were, even Devika, and how she missed them! What she would not have given to have had Arjun there beside her. David had been right. It was going to be painful.

\* \* \*

THE following morning dawned sunny and cool. It would be a beautiful day. She walked to the airline office to reconfirm her reservation and cancel David's. After that she would return to the hotel and call Ramakrishna Rao, who should then be in his office. The Swiss Air office was empty. She gave her name to the clerk, who punched it into his computer. Just then the phone rang and she watched curiously as a look of disbelief, then horror, spread over the young man's face. For some moments, mouth agape, he listened. Then he replaced the receiver. The blood had drained from his face. There were tears in his eyes and he looked ill.

"The P.M. has been shot," he said quietly.

Philippa was confused. "You can't mean Mrs. Gandhi?" she said.

He nodded. "The P.M. She has been shot at her house, over an hour ago. By her daughter-in-law, Sonia Gandhi, she has been taken to All-India Medical Center."

"You can't mean her daughter-in-law shot her?"

A small crowd had suddenly gathered around them.

"No, no, of course not. Sonia Gandhi has taken the P.M. to the hospital."

"How did you get this information?" a man asked.

"My brother works at All-India Medical Center, he saw the car come in bringing the P.M. She was covered with blood. He helped carry her into emergency surgery. He is just now having his coffee break and rushed to phone me."

Philippa thought of the weary face of Mrs. Gandhi on television the previous night, the cryptic words about shedding blood.

"You are scheduled to fly out at noon on the third via Indian Airlines to Bombay, from where you will catch our flight to Zurich and London," said the dazed-looking agent. "In view of what has happened, you might want to leave earlier. Shall I see what is available?"

Philippa shook her head, picked up her ticket, and walked out the door. The first thing that impressed her was that nothing had changed. The streets were still filled with the same bustling traffic and gawking tourists, the same men lounging around pan shops, and the same hustling beggars. Outside the gates of the Majestic, Sikh taxi drivers wrapped in blankets blinked up at the sun and drank tea. She walked into the hotel, where she noted a small crowd had gathered around a teleprinter, and took the elevator to the third floor. As she was letting herself in her room, a voice with a French accent called to her from down the hall and a smartly dressed young woman with short blond hair approached.

"Have you heard the news?" she asked.

"You mean about Mrs. Gandhi?" said Philippa.

"But of course," replied the young woman.

Philippa stood in the open door. "Do you suppose there is anything on television?"

"You must be joking." The woman laughed. "It doesn't even come on till six in the evening. Why don't you come with me? I'm going over to the All-India Medical Center. It's only a short distance; we will find out what's happening."

"Why not?" Philippa smiled, then suddenly remembered she'd meant to call Ramakrishna Rao and asked the young woman to wait while she dialed his number. She let the phone ring for some time but there was no answer. If there was going to be some sort of national crisis, it might be wise to know about it first, she thought. "My call doesn't seem to be going through, I'll try it later. Shall we go?"

"My name is Iris," the young woman said as they walked to the lift. "I'm in the rag trade." Philippa looked blank. "Rag trade is American slang for clothes," she explained. "I supervise manufacturing here in India for several American firms. Over the years I've come to know these people well. They're very emotional. If Mrs. Gandhi's been killed, all hell could break loose!"

"You don't think it's really possible?" asked Philippa after they were settled in a taxi.

"Who knows?" replied Iris. "That's why I want to go to the hospital. If something serious has happened, I want to know before people start reacting. In that case, our next stop will be the grocery store."

"Grocery store?"

"To lay in supplies. I can see you haven't been around very long. Whenever something happens here, people go crazy. Food deliveries stop. I'm going to be prepared."

At the All-India Medical Center cars of the police, government officials, and white-clad Congress Party members had already created a mammoth traffic jam. Iris told the driver to wait, pushed through the thick crowd, and began asking questions.

"She was bleeding profusely when she was brought in," said one man.

"My cousin who is an intern here says the Surgeon General is operating this very moment," said another.

"Who shot her?" Iris asked, looking around.

"No one knows," said the first man.

"I heard one of her bodyguards did it," put in another.

A group of politicians in Gandhi hats pushed past them, almost knocking Philippa down.

"*Mon Dieu!*" cried Iris. "Where are your manners? Don't you have any respect for ladies?"

"Is her son here?" Philippa inquired.

"No," said someone else, "he is in Calcutta. The President is in the Middle East. No one is here. Only the daughter-in-law, the secretary, and the cousin were in the house. They will have to wait until her son returns to make any announcement."

"Come, let's find our driver before he goes off," cried Iris over the noise. "This looks serious. I want to get to the market before other people get the same idea."

Regaining their taxi, they drove to a residential shopping center. No one at the store seemed to know anything about the assassination attempt. Iris bought several boxes of canned goods, crates of mineral water, cheese, butter, and bread. When it turned out she didn't have enough cash with her, Philippa paid half the bill. Then they drove off to Iris's bootlegger and stocked up on gin, Scotch, and brandy, returned to the hotel, and distributed the food between their two refrigerators. Before lunch, Philippa tried to call Kotagarh but was told all outgoing lines from Delhi were engaged. Then she tried Ramakrishna Rao again but there was still no answer.

After lunch she and Iris went to the hotel garden, where they warmed themselves in the autumn sun and watched as a few brave souls swam in the pool. After so many months alone, Philippa found it relaxing to be with a European woman again, despite her rather odd manner. Other Europeans were sitting in the garden. Someone had a portable radio. Between long stretches of classical Indian music, All-India Radio broadcast terse bulletins of noninformation: "There has been an assassination attempt on the Prime Minister's life. She is in the All-India Medical Center where doctors are now operating."

"Perhaps it's not too serious," Iris said. "Perhaps she'll recover."

Around three an Englishman came by with a portable shortwave radio and said the BBC had announced Mrs. Gandhi was dead, that she had been shot by two of her Sikh bodyguards, and that she had died on arrival at hospital that morning or shortly thereafter. Everyone gathered around the radio, but the news bulletin had ended.

At the garden entrance, Nirendra, the young man who had introduced himself to Philippa on the train, now appeared and stood watching the sunbathers. Just as Philippa thought he hadn't seen her and was going to go away, he waved and lumbered across the lawn. Iris looked up from her copy of *Paris Match* with amused Gallic disdain.

"Ah, I am finding you at last," he puffed. "You must leave this hotel at once. I am told it is owned by a Sikh family. The BBC says the P.M. has been shot by Sikhs and is dead. Announcement is due at six o'clock. There may be trouble. I thought of you here and came to warn you on the basis of what I have heard to come to the Maurya Sheraton. You can have the suite next to mine, which is reserved for my wedding party. I think they will not be coming just now."

At Nirendra's news, Iris put down her magazine. "He's quite right, you know, this hotel *is* owned by Sikhs. I hadn't thought of that."

"We don't know definitely that Mrs. Gandhi is dead. The radio could be wrong," replied Philippa, not wanting to believe the worst.

"By the time we hear definitely, it will be too late," predicted Iris.

"But we have plenty of food and people are too civilized here in Delhi for any violence," said Philippa. "After all, it's a world capital."

Iris and Nirendra exchanged glances and laughed. "Oh, dear, I see you don't understand," said Iris. "I deal with these people every day in my business. The Hindus and Sikhs hate each other. It sounds to me like the Sikhs are paying the Hindus back for Operation Blue Star. If it's that, the Hindus will now revenge themselves. It could be very bad."

"Perhaps it has all been set up to look like that," observed Nirendra. "It could be something else, something deeper."

Philippa was surprised at this astute observation. He might be worth a Mercedes after all. Thinking it over, however, she decided to stay put. If she moved, no one in Kotagarh would be able to find her, and she didn't relish being in the same hotel with eager young Nirendra.

"It's very kind of you to offer, but it would be better for me to stay here. I'm expecting my husband to call from Rajasthan, and other friends may try and reach me. One can't trust these hotel operators to forward messages." Nirendra looked defeated. She felt sorry for him. "It was very sweet of you to think of me. I'm going up now for a nap, but why don't you come over later on and we'll all have dinner together?"

"The food here is horrible," said Iris, "but we could go to Nirula's for pizza."

Philippa saw Nirendra to his car and returned to her room, where she tried again without success to reach Rama Rao. Setting her alarm, she dozed fitfully and dreamt of her guide at the Red Fort, who kept pointing out places where he claimed various Moghul emperors had assassinated Indira Gandhi.

At six she woke up and turned on the television. A pale-faced announcer was reading the news. Mrs. Gandhi was dead. Her son, Rajiv, had rushed to Delhi from Calcutta, and someone had appointed him to succeed his mother as Prime Minister. The country must now rally around him. That was the message.

There was a knock on the door and Iris, slightly drunk, came in with a French couple, whom she introduced as Marianne and Paul, and sat on the bed, prophesying doom.

"What a tragedy for India, what a tragedy for Indian women," she moaned.

Philippa recalled the vibrant, intelligent woman she'd met just a few short months before and found it impossible to believe anyone would want to shoot her. "What is shocking is that two young Indian men would gun down an unarmed woman."

"*Exactement*," cried Iris. "*C'est horrible. Alors*, we all need a drink. Why don't you get dressed, I'll fix us something."

Marianne and Paul sat on a sofa and stared blankly at the television. A group of musicians were now playing mournful Indian classical music while images of Mrs. Gandhi floated across the screen. Philippa showered and dressed. Iris brought a bottle from her room, and they all sat watching as the President of India swore in Rajiv Gandhi as the new Prime Minister.

"The Queen is dead, long live the King," observed Philippa sadly.

"This is not a real democracy, I think," said Marianne. "What qualifications has he to be a prime minister? He is only an airline pilot."

Her boyfriend Paul withdrew a small box containing white powder, which he sniffed with a straw.

"Whoever said it was a democracy?" scoffed Iris.

"Indians say it," said Paul. "The world's largest democracy. It's really funny, don't you think?"

There was a knock on the door. It was Nirendra. "So you have heard the news," he puffed. "I am afraid there will be trouble."

"Don't you think you might be exaggerating?" said Philippa.

Nirendra shrugged. "Who can tell? But what about dinner, are you not hungry? I have brought a car. Places may be shutting down. I think we had better go to your pizza place soon."

"On second thought," said Iris, "I think we should eat right here, bad as it always is."

"My hotel is very nice and has many restaurants," said Nirendra. Please allow me to take you as my guests."

"What an excellent idea," cried Iris, not one to turn down a free meal. "I believe there's a good tandoori place there." She introduced Paul and Marianne to Nirendra. Paul offered him some cocaine. At first suspicious, Nirendra was pleasantly surprised, soon agreed it was superior to pan, and proceeded to sniff up several lines.

DOWN in the lobby, a number of well-to-do Sikhs were standing in groups, and there was a crowd at the desk checking into the hotel. The men looked grim, the women frightened. As they waited for Nirendra's car, a Mercedes limousine pulled up, two distinguished-looking gentlemen in turbans got out, opened the trunk, withdrew half a dozen rifles, and handed them to a bearer.

"Did you see that?" Iris whispered. "Something funny is going on here."

"It doesn't look very funny to me," said Philippa. "Do you think we should risk going out?"

Just then Nirendra's car drove up and he hustled them inside. Outside the hotel compound the streets were empty. A deathly pall seemed to have descended over the city. Their driver took a peripheral highway, and they arrived at Nirendra's hotel in half the usual time. Here, too, Philippa noticed a large crowd of Sikhs around the reservations counter, and although the restaurant was open, the diners were subdued.

As they waited to order, Iris observed that it was difficult to know just how to take the whole affair. In any other society the shooting of a prime minister would be seen as a heinous act but not really a national tragedy. In India, however, Mrs. Gandhi was not an ordinary prime minister but an icon. People could remember her as an adolescent girl standing by her father's side, as a young mother of two very different sons, as the mother of a dead son: mother and goddess. And, of course, there was her famous dark side: Kali, Chaumundi, Durga, and Kapalani Devi. But everyone in India knew this was only proper; the goddess did have a dark side. Worshiping it in the moment of need brought powerful forces to your aid. And so the masses of religious Indians had worshiped Indira.

"She was more than just a P.M.," concluded Iris. "She was the symbol of womanhood struggling in a man's world."

Nirendra guffawed and ordered enormous plates of tender lamb kabobs, tandoori chicken, and Punjabi bread, which he proceeded to wolf down.

Iris groaned. "How can you eat so much at a time like this?"

Nirendra ignored her. "Have you no feelings, no compassion, no thought for the dead?"

"I am a south Indian," Nirendra replied, his mouth full of food. "We never liked her much, always interfering in our lives. She was a Kashmiri Brahmin; they are all part Muslim and look foreign to us. Just because she has got shot, does that mean I should go without my food? Someday I will be food for the worms too. When that day comes, you please go on eating." He swallowed another kabob and winked at Iris, who lit a cigarette and stared at him. She had been coming to India for fifteen years now: first, overland as a hippie, then as a dope runner from Goa, and for the past five years as an increasingly important person in the world of international fashion. Young men like Nirendra fascinated her. In her business she had to deal with many like him, sons of textile manufacturers, wholesalers and distributors who worked for their fathers. Their grossness appalled her, but she had had several interesting encounters with them and they were usually very generous. She sighed and nibbled at her dinner.

"I suppose you're right. After all, we did dash out and buy food, didn't we, Philippa?"

Philippa smiled at her. She'd been talking with Paul and Marianne, who had just come from a photographic assignment at the ashram of some yogi who lived in the jungles of Madhya Pradesh. She thought of David's plan to live with Durga Baba in the forest. How hard it was to realize that just a short distance from where they were sitting, yogis were walking in jungles with tigers.

After dinner, Nirendra suggested a visit to the hotel discotheque, but Iris, Paul, and Marianne wanted to go back to the Majestic and do more coke. It was not a night for dancing in public, declared Iris; they had tapes at the hotel, and Nirendra could dance in their room. While they stood in the hotel lobby arguing, Philippa heard a familiar voice. It was General Bobby; his face looked drawn.

"What are you doing here?" he asked as she separated from the others.

"I had dinner with those people, I'm flying out in three days. The young Indian chap has a car and driver. But what are you doing here? You look worried."

"We're all in a state of shock," said Bobby.

"It's a great tragedy. You were so close to her, it must be very difficult for you."

"We fought constantly, but I loved her and will miss her terribly. I knew her for thirty years. She was a great woman."

"Are you checking in here?" asked Philippa. Bobby nodded. "Is something going to happen? Will there be trouble?"

"There could be, best not to take chances. Anyway, these telephones work better than mine. I'm setting up shop here for the time being."

"What are you expecting?"

"Riots, perhaps. Members of my community have killed Mrs. Gandhi. There will be reprisals from the other side. Where is David?"

"He's still in Kotagarh with Madho Dev. I had to leave early— things to attend to at home. David will stay on a little longer."

"Kotagarh should be safe," said Bobby. "Where are you staying?"

"The Majestic."

Bobby frowned. "I shouldn't speculate about what is going to happen, but it could be nasty. Delhi is famous for violence. Why don't you shift here? The Majestic is likely to be a target. I can get you in; they know me well."

Philippa smiled at him. If she hadn't met Arjun, she might very well have said yes.

"I haven't had a chance to apologize for scaring you that morning when I called, but I couldn't resist," said Bobby. "Will you forgive me? If you come here now I promise there will be none of that. It's for your protection I'm asking you."

She didn't know whether to believe him or not. "David is going to call me there. I think I'd better stay put." She could imagine what life would be like for three days in the same hotel with Nirendra and General Bobby.

"I'll call tomorrow, but please be careful."

"Until tomorrow then," said Philippa.

"Friend of yours?" asked Iris when she rejoined them.

"An old friend of my husband."

"Handsome, well preserved too. He looks like an army man."

"He's a general, almost retired."

Iris rolled her eyes. *"Très impressive."*

They went to the hotel entrance and waited for their car. The doorman and the driver, both Sikhs, exchanged a few words in Punjabi.

"They're saying gangs of Hindus are gathering, stoning taxis and cars driven by Sikhs. The doorman advised him to speed up and run over any people he sees on the road," reported Iris, who understood Punjabi.

Marianne, Philippa, and Iris sat in back while Nirendra and Paul sat in front with the driver. On one of the new bypasses that ringed the city, they came upon a large crowd in the street, armed with clubs and sticks blocking the way. Their driver, a serene-looking young Sikh, lacked the nerve to hit anyone, and at the last moment, although Nirendra was urging him on, he stepped on the brake by mistake. The car stalled. Philippa saw two youths approaching with clubs and cans of petrol.

"Start the car, hurry, hurry!" screamed Iris as something hit the windshield and a spider web of cracks appeared. The driver cranked the starter.

"Flooded." Paul cursed. "He's flooded the bloody thing."

Then, abruptly as it had stopped, the engine started again and the vehicle lurched forward, knocking several people over. Two more climbed on the hood. The driver threw the gears in reverse and pushed the throttle down. The car screeched backward. A second car approaching from behind narrowly missed them and plowed through the crowd. Nirendra cheered. The driver jammed the gear in second and rammed through the mob in its wake. Philippa winced as she heard the thud of bodies against the bumper and voices screaming.

"Shabash!" cried Iris as they cleared the crowd. "Well done, *très bon*. You must come up and have a drink when we get to the hotel."

Philippa's heart beat wildly and she sat on the edge of her seat, peering ahead down the dark streets. At the Majestic all seemed quiet, but the gate was closed, guarded by Sikhs with drawn swords. The cots for off-duty drivers had been moved inside the hotel compound. The guards looked into the car and opened the gate, waving the driver through. Several Sikhs came up and asked what had happened. They spoke in the quiet, steady voices of fighting men.

"Park your car and come have a drink," commanded Iris. "Room 302."

The driver grinned broadly. They walked through the lobby, which was now mobbed with people gathered around a television set watching the new Prime Minister, Rajiv Gandhi, address the nation.

In the lift, Iris turned to Nirendra. "You must not risk going back to your hotel, it's too dangerous. We have plenty of room."

Nirendra glanced eagerly at Philippa, but when they reached the third floor and arrived at her room, she bade them all good night.

Nirendra looked disappointed and hesitated but Iris took his arm. "Come, you can stay in my room or have Paul and Marianne's if you like. The night is still young; we'll have some drinks and dance. Paul has a portable tape recorder and all the latest music."

Philippa got into bed and tried to phone Kotagarh but was told there would be a six- to ten-hour delay. Then she called Ramakrishna Rao's house and managed to get Mrs. Rao, who was polite but cool.

"My husband is extremely busy, so many things to be done; in fact, he's with the Prime Minister at this very moment. And tomorrow he will be meeting many of the dignitaries coming for the funeral. But I will give him your message. I know he has prepared the papers your husband asked for. It's only a matter of finding the time to explain things to you."

"I understand," said Philippa. "Thank you so much. I'm at the Majestic."

"Oh, I see," said Mrs. Rao.

Philippa could tell by the tone of her voice that Mrs. Rao did not approve. "I'm due to leave on the third."

"Yes, of course," said Mrs. Rao. "I'll see he gets in touch with you."

Philippa turned out the light and burrowed under the blankets, still trembling from the encounter with the mob. No wonder Arjun was so anxious to leave. All his predictions were coming true. How she missed him. Sleeping in his arms was such bliss. She turned the light back on and got the hotel switchboard.

"I know the delay is ten hours, but why don't you tell the long-distance operator we'll give her something extra to get my call through? And there will be something for you in it too." She smiled to herself. Arjun would be proud of her; she was learning to handle herself like a real Indian.


THE next morning around nine the phone rang. At the same time there was a knock on Philippa's door. It was Iris in a long silk wrapper, holding a cup of coffee. Philippa beckoned her in and rushed to the phone. It was General Bobby.

There had been some incidents, he explained; it would probably be wise to stay off the streets until further notice. What a shame they weren't in the same hotel. Philippa told him about the mob they had encountered the previous evening.

"You see," he barked, "I told you to stay here; it's just luck you're still alive. I'll ring back around five to see how things are. You should call David." He rang off.

"That was the general," said Philippa, putting down the receiver. "He says we're lucky to be alive."

"Now he tells you," said Iris. "Why weren't the police out on the streets last night? And what is the general's army doing anyway?"

"You look rather tired," said Philippa. "Didn't you sleep?"

"Oh, *ma chère*, that young man you picked up on the train . . . he's too much."

"Where is he?"

"In my bed, finally asleep."

"I see," said Philippa.

"Yes," said Iris, her eyes bulging, "and after me, he got it on with Paul and Marianne."

"Really?"

"I'm afraid I did too much coke. Would you by chance have any downers?"

"I have a few Valium."

"I need something stronger." Iris groaned. "But I'll take a couple. I don't usually do things like this; you must have a bad impression of me. It's just I was so upset by what happened last night on the road, I needed some human warmth."

"Of course, I understand. I'm sure Nirendra was quite warm."

Iris raised her eyebrows. "These big ones are *très intéressants, plus actifs.*"

The bearer came with tea and toast and Iris departed. Philippa switched on the television and was confronted with a view of Mrs. Gandhi's body laid out on a flag-draped, flower-bedecked bier. In death she resembled one of the garlanded statues of the goddess Philippa had seen in temples and calendars displayed in shops across the country, the stern, grim, old-looking embalmed face of India. At last, something real on television.

The camera pulled back to reveal officials circumambulating the bier. One woman was lighting bunches of incense, another bathed Mrs. Gandhi's face. There were glimpses of the family: of her son, Rajiv Gandhi, the new Prime Minister, standing with dignitaries, his Italian wife, Sonia, and their two children sitting on the floor to one side. She caught a glimpse of Ramakrishna Rao's hawklike face in the background. The unctuous voice of the Indian commentator Melvin de Mellow was describing Teen Murti house, "the home of the Nehru family since 1947." After dwelling on the body of the slain leader in excruciating detail, the camera cut over to a view outside Teen Murti house, where, passing in front of the open front doors, troops of young men shouting "Indira Gandhi forever!" and "Indira Gandhi martyr!" marched past, catching brief glimpses of their fallen leader. Television, the all-seeing eye; television as religious spectacle. But not too well thought out, for, after watching for a few minutes, Philippa realized she had seen the same young men passing in front of Teen Murti house several times.

A few minutes later, Iris was at the door again, trailed by a glassy-eyed Nirendra. She was holding her miniature Sony shortwave radio to her ear.

"BBC is reporting that Hindus are killing Sikhs in Delhi, Rajasthan, Punjab, Jammu, Kashmir, and U.P. They say the Indian army is being called out to deal with the situation."

Philippa reached for the phone and tried to find out why her call to Kotagarh had not come through. What of Harbinder Singh and his family? She could see that dreadful D.S.P., Sharma, leading an attack on them. Could the farm be in danger? The shifts of long-distance operators had changed, and no one knew anything about her call. She rang up General Bobby and asked him what he knew about the reports of violence.

"It is all true," he said, "but the army is not being called out despite the announcement and the police are doing nothing."

"Why?" asked Philippa.

"That's what many of us would like to know, but we can't find out. The lines of authority are very shaky just now. Someone is playing a very dangerous game."

"You mean the politicians?"

"Who knows? Because he's in mourning, everyone is afraid to explain the situation to Rajiv Gandhi. We in the army are trying to get through to him, but he is surrounded by people who refuse to disturb him and insist we are exaggerating. Someone is fixing the police. As usual, BBC is better informed than we are."

"Bobby, I must go to Kotagarh. I can't get through on the phone. I'm so worried; can you get me a car?"

"Are you mad? At a time like this, it would be suicide!"

"I thought you might loan me one of yours. Don't you have some sort of vehicle with an official flag on it?"

"My vehicles are all in use, but I'll try to get through to Madho Dev on a priority line and call you back. You must promise me not to—" The line went dead.

Philippa got the hotel operator, who told her there must be a break in the line. Iris and Nirendra had settled themselves on the sofa and were sniffing cocaine.

"I didn't take the Valium," said Iris. "Thought it was more important to stay awake. Have some coke, *chérie:* very high quality. I have a feeling this is going to be a long day."

"Never touch it," said Philippa and went to the window, drew the curtains back, and looked down on the street. Several fires were burning in the direction of Connaught Circus. The swimming pool looked normal; a number of hotel guests were sunning themselves. She felt jittery and decided, despite the cool weather, that a swim might relax her. She called the operator again and asked him to direct any calls to the pool. After a swim, she would see about hiring a car.

"I'm going down for a swim, care to join me?"

"Fantastic idea," cried Iris, "absolutely *fantastique!*" She tugged at Nirendra's sleeve. "Come, we will all go down for a swim."

"I am not knowing how to swim," said Nirendra, "and it is much too cold."

"Well, I would adore to swim and you must come too. At least the walk will do you good."

The hotel pool was in one corner of the large compound, surrounded by a high wall. At one end was a pool house resembling a ship's forecastle, with changing rooms, an open bar, and stairs that led up to the roof, from which one could see beyond the wall to the street. A color TV had been set up on the bar facing the pool. An incongruous scene: the sad-faced mourners at Teen Murti house, the body of the murdered leader; the swimmers at poolside—mostly Europeans—having drinks, applying suntan lotion, munching on sandwiches. The thundering traffic noise which usually blocked most conversation was absent, but sounds of rioting could be heard in the distance and Philippa noticed there were men with guns on the hotel roof.

"Nero strummed and we shall swim while Delhi burns." Iris giggled, leading a slightly knock-kneed Nirendra in a swimsuit borrowed from Paul to the shallow end of the pool.

Just as Philippa was about to dive in, a crash and the sound of yelling voices in the street beyond sent a number of sunbathers rushing up the pool-house stairway. Philippa turned and followed them. Directly below in the street, a taxi had been turned over and the driver, a Sikh, was struggling to climb out through the window while a group of well-dressed young men were beating him back. Then a man with a large rusty can came up, threw its contents into the car, lit a match, and set the driver and his passengers on fire. Philippa screamed. A German woman began to cry. Another cab drove up. The mob turned on it, stopped it, dragged the driver out, beat him senseless, put him back in the car, and set it on fire. Several policeman stood looking on, calmly guiding pedestrians around the scene as though it were some construction site. A sunbather on the roof had a camera and lifted it to take a picture.

One of the young men leading the mob yelled in English and pointed a pistol at the pool-house roof. "Take any pictures and I will shoot you!"

The sunbather dropped his camera.

"Why don't the police do something?" cried Philippa.

"Obviously been told not to," said a beer-guzzling Australian standing next to her.

Oblivious to everything, Iris and Nirendra stood in the shallow end of the pool splashing each other.

Philippa wrapped a towel around herself and ran back through the grounds. A large group of tense Sikhs with drawn swords stood by the gate. Everywhere she went, there seemed to be television sets broadcasting the scene at Teen Murti House. Dashing to her room, she showered, changed, and called the operator. Her call to Kotagarh could not be completed because no one at the Kotagarh exchange was answering. Filling a flask with bottled water, she went downstairs to the lobby. The atmosphere was tense. She made her way through the crowd, approached the doorman whom she'd been tipping liberally, and offered an exorbitant sum, three times the usual amount, if someone would drive her to Kotagarh.

"No Sikh will drive you, madam, much too dangerous."

"Surely there must be a Hindu driver here?"

The doorman shook his head. Several drivers were listening.

"I will take her," offered a husky young man. "I have just cut my hair and shaved my beard." He grinned. "I went to the hotel barber for the first time. See, if I smoke, they will not believe I am a Sardar." He stuck a cigarette in his mouth and everyone laughed. "I am also having a gun. But the price will be twice what you have offered. Six times the normal fare."

"But that is outrageous!"

"It is outrageous to risk our lives trying to get to Rajasthan," he replied, still grinning.

# 22

I N   T E R R I P U R the day had dawned clear and cold. At Prospect Point the maid drew the heavy damask draperies aside, revealing the icy Himalayan massif in all its splendor. It was Kamala's custom to sit before the open French doors of her boudoir in the morning sun and perform yoga asanas, breathing exercises and certain meditations. This morning, however, the maid pointed to the palace grounds and shrieked. "Look, Your Highness, look! Something terrible has happened."

Throwing on a pashmina wrapper, Kamala rushed out to the balcony and gaped. "What on earth?" she exclaimed.

The sight that met her eyes baffled her powers of imagination. The beautiful grounds and gardens, sloping away in terraces of marigolds, dahlias, asters, and roses of every hue—suddenly her beautiful gardens were filled with trucks and cars. Kamala screamed, a long piercing scream, like the dying cry of one who falls from a high place.

Below in the library, Sonny, who was resting after a hard night's work with Kirpan, jumped up and, half expecting to see his mother come flying out a window, rushed to the front door. Realizing the scream had come from her bedroom, he dashed up the great marble staircase, three steps at a time, to find three or four attendants and Miss Cartwright, her English secretary, trying to calm her.

"I have seen a vision," she cried, "a terrible vision of the future. I looked out the window and the gardens had been turned into a parking lot. Sonny darling, promise me this will never happen."

Sonny quickly turned on the television set and ordered the bearer to bring some brandy. Mrs. Gandhi's dead face materialized on the screen and diminished in size as the camera awkwardly pulled back, showing the inner sanctum. Having heard the news of Mrs. Gandhi's death from Ramakrishna Rao the previous afternoon, Kamala had retired early. She had always disliked Mrs. Gandhi, thought her spoiled, neurotic, and pushy, but for an Indian woman to be gunned down in this manner was simply unbelievable. What had the country come to that this was possible? How could men who but a generation before had been so peaceful, had invented the nonviolent protest that inspired the world, now gun down an unarmed woman in cold blood, never mind who she was? That had been her first thought. She had loathed old Mahatma Gandhi, thought Nehru an obsequious fool, and, yes, admit it, really hated his daughter, but that did not mean you went out and shot her. What sort of person could be persuaded to do such a thing?

Ramakrishna Rao had called after lunch, four hours before the official death announcement was made. When he told her all the details and the first shock had worn off, she asked if he thought it was simple revenge or a palace revolution.

"What difference would it make?" he observed. "We will never know the real truth, but the result will be the same. Rajiv is on his way back from Calcutta, he will be appointed by the party to succeed her, and elections will then be called within a few months." Kamala sighed. The Nehru dynasty was continuing. Rao went on. "Can you imagine? They have had an ambulance standing by her house for weeks in case of an emergency like this but the drivers were off having tea. That's why Sonia had to take her to the hospital. Can you believe that when her secretary called the Commissioner of Police, his servant refused to put through the call, saying his sahib was in his bath and could not be disturbed?" Kamala chuckled. "One of the assassins was killed on the spot, and except for one quick-witted officer, both would have been killed! Well, we must forget about these things, think only of India, and get behind the new leadership."

"Ah, yes," said Kamala, remembering from the tone of his voice that, exalted as he was, Rao's phone was undoubtedly monitored. "Of course, you are right. It's a terrible tragedy, but Rajiv will be able to surmount it. He's a solid young man and we must all stand behind him. Goodbye then. Call me whenever you can."

Even though it had been early afternoon, she had taken a sedative, gone straight to bed, and told her maid not to disturb her for any reason. The strain of the expedition to Kedarnath, seeing David again after so many years, and getting Sumitra off to Europe, not to mention all the Diwali entertaining she'd done, had left her exhausted, and for the first time, talking to Rao, she felt palpitations in her chest. Best to go to bed. At this altitude, palpitations could lead to heart failure.

The television had shifted to Palam airport in New Delhi, where delegations from foreign countries were arriving for the funeral. The Russian delegation was getting out of its plane and walking across the tarmac where reporters waited at the gate. In their fedoras and top-coats the Russians looked to Kamala like thugs from an old American gangster film she'd once seen. As they approached the gate, a young Indian reporter thrust a microphone toward the leader, but one of his burly bodyguards struck the reporter with his arm and sent him reeling into the crowd. Kamala gasped and looked at Sonny. The screen went blank and then suddenly Mrs. Thatcher's face was there, being interviewed in London on her departure for Mrs. Gandhi's funeral. Kamala thought the faces of the world leaders looked criminal and sinister.

"Can you tell me what is happening?" she asked Sonny.

"Sacrificial rites, Mummy," he replied with a grim smile.

Remembering her earlier vision, Kamala got up and went to the balcony again. "Is it real?" she gasped, drawing back in horror.

"Yes, Mummy, it's all my fault. But we were warned in the night. The television is not reporting what's happening; it's only stirring up emotions and making things worse. Sikhs are being killed by the hundreds, perhaps thousands, their properties burned and plundered. It started last night. We moved all our trucks off the plains and I gave the order to bring them here, along with any Terripur Sikh taxis that need shelter. Down below, in Sonagar, it is very bad—riots and mobs; we would have lost everything. Even now there is a mob here in Terripur gathering in the bazaar. Some Sikh is supposed to have passed out sweets to celebrate Mrs. Gandhi's assassination. A lie, of course, but they have burned every Sikh place in town and are heading this way."

"But we are not Sikhs," cried Kamala, looking down at the truck drivers warming their hands around a fire they had made in her rose garden, a fifty-year-old garden of rare hybrid roses now utterly destroyed.

"You haven't brought me up as one, Mummy, but my father was Sikh and I am doing business with them. A Sikh is living here. I am protecting Sikhs. Don't forget, Kirpan is a Sikh and all our drivers too."

Kamala looked down from the balcony and saw Kirpan, in a black turban again, talking with several other black-turbaned young men.

"They are carrying guns," she observed. "Sonny, this cannot be; you'll have the army down on us."

"I wish the army were here. Where are they? BBC is saying the army has been called out but they're nowhere in sight and the Terripur police are standing by, watching and doing nothing, while the Congress goondas incite the rioters."

"No doubt our brave police are scared to death," murmured Kamala. "Where is the mob now?"

"Coming from the lower bazaar. They have almost reached the clock tower."

"Go down immediately and tell Kirpan to do nothing until I appear. I'll dress and be right down." If her son had not taken up with a Sikh, none of this would be happening, thought Kamala. Yet rule by mob must be put down. Dispatching all her attendants except Miss Cartwright, she picked up the telephone and booked an immediate call to Ramakrishna Rao in Delhi. He was more or less responsible for the police in India—what was wrong that this sort of thing was being permitted? It was outrageous!

She dressed quickly in a flowing red sari, the color of a wedding sari—or the sari one is cremated in, she thought morosely. Red, the color of heroism and sacrifice, the color of the gods! Ordinarily, she would have worn a tweed suit at this time of year, but if she had to confront an ignorant mob she had better be wearing a sari. She would appeal to them on an emotional level—Maa-baap: I am your mother and father—the way the rulers had always talked to their people. She paced the floor, waiting for her call to come through. Now she could see smoke rising on the mall near the library. The phone rang. Miss Cartwright answered.

"All the lines to Delhi are broken, madam," she said. "Calls are not going out or coming in."

"So we are in a state of siege," muttered Kamala, adjusting her sari before the mirror. Applying a heavy line of kohl around her eyes, she placed a large red tilak mark on her forehead. The effect was theatrical. She knew the mob would be able to see her eyes. She had seen her father hypnotize angry throngs by twitching his sinister-looking mustache and exaggerating his expressions, and she intended to do the same. Leaving her room, she swept down the marble staircase and out onto the terrace overlooking the drive.

Kirpan greeted her. He was all business. "They are down near the clock tower," he said brusquely. "We estimate there are several hundred of them. Very few caste Hindus—all rabble: sweepers, coolies, young goondas, recruited by local Congress-I people."

"You must be joking. They wouldn't dare!"

"But I am not joking, Your Highness, it is a fact you will soon see for yourself. We may have to fight for our lives."

"Kirpan, I will not have any violence."

"Mummy darling, you don't understand, there has already been violence," said Sonny, joining them. "In the bazaar they have already beaten up people, doused them with kerosene, actually burned people alive. And Sonagar is in flames."

"Unbelievable." Kamala shivered. "And you have moved every Sikh taxi wallah and truck in the district into my garden."

"It was necessary, Mummy," pleaded Sonny. "I must defend my people."

Kamala did not answer. It was plainly too late to be concerned with flowers. Something else, something far more important, was at stake. She gazed down the hill, where she could now hear the distant babble of voices, and watched Kirpan out of the corner of her eye. Her son's lover. The thought pained her, yet he was hardworking and successful, and she had to admire that. As a Rajput princess she would always stand up for the Sikhs, and, of course, Sonny's father had been one. For the first time since he'd died, she wished he were standing beside her now. And David: had he left India safely? The priests in the mountains had been right after all. A time of trouble was beginning.

"All the gates are closed, I hope," she said.

"Of course."

"How many guns do you have?"

"Five," replied Kirpan. "But you have many more in your armory."

"My father's tiger and shikari guns, all very old, I'm afraid. And not much ammunition for them. They haven't been used in years."

"Let them be given out among my men," he urged. "It will make a good show."

Kamala smiled wanly. "Listen to me, Kirpanji, I'll have no violence here today. You have five guns, that is enough. First I will speak to the people at the front gate, from the lion statue. Have three guns there, send the other two guns to cover the other two gates. I don't want the people to see those rifles until I talk with them."

"You should let us handle this," protested Kirpan. "They have no guns. When they see ours, they'll run away. A few shots over their heads will scare them off."

"But you are forgetting we must go on living here. Both Sonny and I must go on living in Terripur. Think of Sonny. If we resort to a show of force, it means our power is diminished. We do not rule by force, we rule through tradition."

Sonny shook his head. "Kirpan is right, Mummy, these younger people do not respect tradition. They have none. Most do not even know the names of their fathers. They respect only force."

The ragged mob, brandishing lighted kerosene torches on bamboo poles and carrying cans of petrol, had reached the gate and were beating on it with sticks.

Kamala strode down the drive between the parked trucks and lorries, followed by Sonny, Kirpan, and his men. When she reached the two colossal pedestals on which lions crouched, forming the two sides of the great wrought-iron gate with the gilded crest, she ordered Sonny and Kirpan to lift her up. When they saw her standing there, the mob fell silent.

Kamala stared angrily down at them. "What have you come here for? Why are you misbehaving in such a manner? Go back to your work, go back to your wives and children."

"Indira Gandhi forever!" someone yelled.

"Indira Gandhi martyr!" another bellowed.

"Have you come to tell me that?" shouted Kamala, her inflection filled with disdain. "Indiraji was my friend. She has stayed in this house many times. Why are you coming here?"

"It is a lie," screamed a shabbily dressed young man. "She never came here. You were her enemy, she arrested you. That is why you are harboring Sikh murderers, it is a big conspiracy. You are all in it together."

"Yes, yes," cried the crowd. "He speaks the truth."

"Ek haath say taali, nahin baitery; you cannot clap with one hand," retorted Kamala.

Impressed by her knowledge of one of their folk sayings, that there are always two sides to a dispute, they quieted again and grinned up at her.

"These men are not murderers," she said, gesturing to the men around Kirpan. "They have murdered no one."

"Celebrating the P.M.'s dastardly assassination, they have distributed sweets," cried one of the leaders.

"Indira Gandhi forever! Indira Gandhi forever!" the mob screamed.

With alarm, Kamala realized she was facing a gang of mindless hominids aping what they had seen on television.

"Revenge for Indira Gandhi's murder," cried a tall man in a frayed Gandhi hat. "We don't want you; we want those men who are hiding in your undergarments, those cowardly Sikh traitors, visegules, cocksuckers."

Kirpan's men fingered their rifles but kept them well hidden.

"Two wrongs do not make a right," shouted Kamala. "It was wrong that Indira Gandhi was murdered, a wicked terrible thing, but killing innocent people, people who loved our P.M. as much as any of you, is not going to bring her back. She wanted us all to love one another, she was always fighting for the country's unity against the foreign hand. It is the foreign hand that is behind this tragedy, not these hard-working young drivers."

"Yes, yes, it is the foreign hand," cried the crowd.

"Don't trust her, she has the teeth of an elephant: one set to show and one to eat you with," screamed an old man.

"Idiot!" Kamala raged back. "Yes, I have teeth and they are getting ready to bite too." She put both hands on her hips and stared down at them. If she could just keep talking, they would soon get bored and go home. It was almost lunchtime; they would be getting hungry and tired. "We must live in peace," she continued in a quiet tone. "If you destroy these truck drivers, who will deliver your food? Some of you are coolies, I see, that is certainly an honest occupation. If these trucks are destroyed, what goods will there be for you to deliver? Return to your work. How else do you expect to eat?"

The crowd mumbled among themselves. Some of those in the rear were beginning to wander away.

"You don't work and you eat," screamed a scruffy-looking young man. "Everyone in this town knows how much food you consume. You spend thousands on food while some of us have to pick up the excrement of cows and wash it with water to find undigested particles of grain with which to feed our children. How can you even talk to us? Get down off your pedestal."

"Khanna, khanna, khanna," wailed the crowd.

"This man is a liar," cried Kamala. "I am an old woman, I eat very little. My son is not often here, my daughter is always away. So I ask you, who am I feeding? I am feeding my servants, their wives, and children. I am feeding politicians, your elected officials, who come here and eat me out of house and home. By living here, I am indirectly feeding all of you and am putting money in your pockets. If I leave Terripur, overnight there will be one hundred unemployed hungry people on the streets."

The mob fell silent. They knew what she said was true. Then the scruffy young man who had spoken before about food picked up a large rock and hurled it. Everyone saw him do it. No one thought much about it and watched diffidently as the stone arched through the air. Kamala saw it too and dodged, but not in time, and was hit squarely on the forehead.

"Beware of stones in the sky," the old priest in the mountains had said. That was her final thought as she fell into Kirpan's arms. Pandemonium broke loose. Kirpan's men jumped up on the pedestal and began firing.

"Now dance, do the bangara, you bhen chots, you sisterfuckers!" they yelled.

Those in front turned and trampled the people behind them. Kirpan's men continued firing until the mob had dispersed. Then they rushed out of the compound and pursued them back down into the bazaar.

"Where is the S.P.?" shouted Sonny hysterically. "Where is the D.M.? How could conditions deteriorate like this? Where are the police? They are nowhere."

Carried to her room, her head bleeding profusely, Kamala had not regained consciousness. Lying on her bed, she was at Firpo's in Calcutta, with Captain David Bruce, the handsome young friend of her cousin Madho Dev. Glasses were tinkling, jewels sparkling, the band was playing the latest Noel Coward hit, and she was in David's arms dancing cheek to cheek. Outside her lovely dream she could feel people crowding around her, felt waves of fear, and wanted to tell them it was all right, she was happy, she was dancing in her lover's arms and nothing else mattered. Her old nurse patted her face lightly with a damp cloth.

"The doctor is coming soon," panted Sonny, running into the room. Kirpan had left to pursue the mob, and he felt totally incapable of handling the situation. If only Sumitra was there, she would know just what to do. But she was gone. He cursed his luck and ordered Miss Cartwright to put through a call to Ramakrishna Rao in Delhi immediately.

"I have," replied the secretary. "The lines are out."

Gazing down at his mother, whom he both feared and loved, Sonny was filled with conflicting emotions. How would he manage without her? Could he live his own life finally without her interference? But what would he do? Could he forget this fiction of hers that there was still a place in India for people like them and live abroad? At least in Europe or America one could be just another rich person lost in the crowd; here it was impossible. He enjoyed the common people yet he was not supposed to. Even ordinary men like Kirpan, who he loved and who he hoped loved him in return, would never completely trust him and, not trusting, would always be playing games with him. What if his mother went into a coma and lived on and on for years like a vegetable? Would he be trapped in this wretched mausoleum for the rest of his life, drinking himself to death?

Either live or die, he repeated inwardly. I love you, Mummy, I truly do, but for God's sake don't leave me in limbo. He stared down at her still beautiful face, her forehead auspiciously unlined, now hideously bashed in, and began to cry. The stone had hit her right at the hairline. Her hair was filled with clotted blood but she was still breathing, even smiling. Suddenly he realized he should be doing something but didn't know what. Racing downstairs to the library he found a large medical encyclopedia and had just located the section on concussions when he heard a commotion at the door and the voice of young Dr. Joshi.

"Ah, Doctor-sahib," he cried, rushing to greet him. "We are all going crazy here, so good of you to come. I was just looking up concussion in the medical dictionary but here you are, thank God, no one has the faintest idea what to do. You must see my mother at once."

Just then Kirpan strode through the door, rifle in hand, and shook hands with the doctor. "We got the sisterfucker," he announced triumphantly, "the one who threw the rock. He was a student at the degree college and a drugrunner for a gang of goondas from Sarangpur."

Sonny kept seeing the rock as it arched across the crowd toward his mother, cursing his own helplessness, and how she had misjudged its direction and ducked the wrong way. It was as if the rock, like some guided missile, had swerved in midair on purpose to strike her down.

"Come," said Kirpan, slapping him on the back, "let us take Doctor-sahib to see your mother."

Outside her suite they found two of her maids wailing and groaning. Sonny dashed into the room and stopped. His mother's face was ashen, her eyes wide open, her mouth agape like the goddess Kali.

"I couldn't do anything, I couldn't do anything," an old nurse screamed in Hindi, cringing and dancing around the bed, certain that Sonny was going to beat her.

The face of death. He had seen it too many times not to recognize it, and went to the bed, closed his mother's eyelids, straightened her mussed hair, closed her mouth, and repeated the mantra given to him on his twelfth birthday. Then he folded her hands across her breasts and kissed her on the forehead. The moment his lips touched her skin, he realized she wasn't there anymore. It was just that simple. All that was left was a mass of insensible matter. Her soul had gone off. He smiled inwardly, thinking she was probably still in the room, watching him, then put his arms around her waist and wept, knowing that his wonderful, beautiful mother, the only woman who would ever really love him, was gone forever.

Kirpan and Dr. Joshi stood silently at the door. All the details that would now have to be attended to rushed through Kirpan's practical mind. They must get in touch with Ramakrishna Rao immediately. Sonny must go down and sit on the old throne in the durbar hall, attended by his friends with their guns. If word got out that Princess Kamala was dead and no authority had replaced her, the servants and workers would at once misbehave. Pilfering and stealing would begin. And what of her jewels and other valuables, the black money and gold? Did Sonny know where the keys to her locked boxes were? It was important they have some time alone away from the eyes of servants. If action was not taken quickly, there was a great deal to lose. Under no circumstances should the Princess's body be left alone in this room, unguarded by some trustworthy person. But who? He trusted no one. Ah, yes, there was Miss Cartwright; she was honest. Moreover, with her employer gone, Miss Cartwright would probably return to England. She'd never think of reporting what had gone on.

When would Sonny be up to it? If he brought these all-important matters up now, Kirpan knew he'd be accused of coldheartedness and gross materialism.

At that moment, Miss Cartwright appeared. After she recovered from the shock of seeing Sonny crying inconsolably over his mother's body, Kirpan advised her to go down to the post and telegraph office with Dr. Joshi and stay there until she got hold of Sri Rao. Then she must summon the Superintendent of Police and the District Magistrate and have them come to the durbar hall at five o'clock to explain themselves. And there was the business of Princess Kamala's cremation; she had always expressed the wish to be cremated at Konkul on the Ganga, just below Hardwar. Her body would have to be transported to Konkul by tomorrow afternoon. Miss Cartwright should make all these arrangements, but most important was to find Ramakrishna Rao.

After the doctor and Miss Cartwright had left, he dismissed the wailing servants, coaxed Sonny to his feet, and held him in his arms. "Your mother's soul has left her body," he said gently. "There is no reason for you to cry. You must gather your strength for the days ahead. You know I will always stand by you."

# 23

THAT MORNING in Kotagarh had dawned a perfect autumn day. The fields were tilled and ready to be planted at the auspicious moment with winter crops. Madho Dev, following his usual custom, arose at five-thirty, built up the fire in the courtyard, and sat meditating before it. About seven Devika came out and sat beside him. It was unusual for her to be up so early, but she had awakened in the middle of the night from a dream and was unable to fall asleep again. In her dream, her feeling had been one of imminent danger, of falling off a cliff or being carried off by something that had swooped down from the sky. She had repeated a mantra that had always calmed her but had been constantly interrupted by the foreboding voice of an old hag telling her not to let Arjun leave India. It was most disturbing. What did it mean? Had her horror of hearing of

Mrs. Gandhi's death carried over into her dreams, or was it something else? She had gone to the kitchen, made tea, and brought it out to Madho Dev.

"What are we coming to that this sort of thing can take place in India?" she asked herself aloud.

"If the cow kicks, kick back," muttered Madho Dev. "That is our philosophy. As long as people believe that way, there will be no peace. The Sikhs have taken revenge for the destruction of their Golden Temple; now the Hindus will take revenge—you'll see."

"Will it never stop?" asked Devika.

"No one has ever taught us to turn the other cheek."

"But we have been warned against taking too much action."

"To take no action when one is angry is very difficult, some say cowardly."

"And for the average person it is impossible." Devika sighed.

"One must take action if one is to live, but one must not become attached to the fruits of that action."

"Now you are sounding like a swami." She smiled.

"No, just reciting scripture."

"Then we should not be attached to our children or grandchildren. Aren't they the fruits of action?"

"One should not be; that is the teaching."

"You know very well," stated Devika, "that you are attached to everything. I've never known a man more attached to things—your land, your family—than you are."

"That doesn't mean I don't know what is correct," he said, "even if I am unable to practice it."

Later Madho Dev brought out the television set and they watched in silence as a news commentator listed all the dignitaries who had arrived, or would be arriving, for Mrs. Gandhi's funeral. Segments were shown in which the various leaders talked to the new Prime Minister, Rajiv Gandhi, in a room with Mrs. Gandhi's garlanded portrait. David came into the courtyard, carrying a small shortwave radio. Arjun joined them, and Gayatri brought straw mats. The five children straggled out and sat silently watching while Darshan, the cook, served breakfast.

"BBC says there's been a lot of trouble in Delhi," reported David. "Rioting, burning of Sikh businesses, widespread killing of Sikhs too. Sounds rather bad; hope Philippa is all right."

Madho Dev glanced at David. "Hadn't we better try and call Delhi? See if Philippa is safe?"

"The Majestic is owned by Sikhs, as I remember," said David. "There could be trouble there."

Madho Dev nodded to Arjun. "Ring up the operator, tell him we want a lightning call."

The picture on the set had shifted to live coverage of the dead body, and the cameras had pulled back to reveal the parade of Congress Party workers passing in front of Teen Murti house yelling patriotic slogans, shaking their fists in anger. The children looked on in wonder.

"How can Mrs. Gandhi live forever when she is dead?" asked Manoj, the oldest boy. "Look, there she is dead."

"Her memory will live on," said Gayatri.

"What is memory?" Manoj asked.

"Be quiet and eat your breakfast."

"But I'm not hungry."

"I think Mrs. Gandhi will be forgotten quickly," said Madho Dev. "People have increasingly bad memories. In a few years she might as well have lived a thousand years ago. No one will ever know the difference."

Arjun returned from the phone, his face pale. "I reached the operator, but the lines to Delhi have been cut. There are disturbances in Kotagarh and he says Jaipur is very bad."

"So BBC is right again," said Madho Dev. "No wonder the government hates them. Can't cover up any secrets when they're around."

"Father, may I speak to you alone for a moment?" Arjun signaled with his eyes that it would be better if they talked inside. David followed them.

"I didn't want to upset the children," said Arjun when they reached the study, "but several Hindu groups are stirring up trouble in town. Some Sikhs have been killed, burned alive, their shops sacked. Some have fled to Harbinder Singh's for protection, and the operator said he has heard the mob could be heading toward us."

"You think they would come all this way?" asked David.

Madho Dev shrugged. "Nothing else to do. Shops and offices are all closed, nice fall day—perfect for burning a few Sikhs. Arjun, you'd best take the jeep, run over to Harbinder Singh's place, and see what is happening. Tell him I have plenty of ammunition and he's welcome to send his women and children over here. He can leave a few men there to watch the farm but his sons' wives, the other women, and all the children would be safer here."

"You're going to help him?" Arjun was incredulous.

"He's our neighbor; we are friends," Madho Dev said. "His brother Paramjit was a classmate of mine in school. Can you think I'm going to let a gang of Congress junglis make trouble for him?"

"You can't mean the Congress is involved?" asked David.

"Must be." Madho Dev sighed. "If it were the R.S.S., the police would be doing something to stop it. I can imagine what's going on in Delhi right now. The Congress has always been good at inciting riots."

"People are being brutally killed," protested David.

"They'll call it 'teaching those bloody Sardars a lesson.' The Congress jackals will show their teeth, unleash the have-nots against the haves. It's easy to recruit as many angry have-nots as you want. Costs almost nothing and frightens a lot of people into obedience." Madho Dev glanced at Arjun. "Go immediately to Harbinder Singh's and report back here to me within an hour." Arjun rose to go. "David and I will break out some guns and ammunition, eh, old friend? Are you still a good shot? Oh, and Arjun," Arjun stood silhouetted in the door. "Please ask your mother to come in here for a moment."

The sense of doom that had beset Devika since she awakened increased as she watched her son coming across the courtyard toward her. At the same time, her Rajput genes rose up and commanded her to behave in a manner befitting the memory of her ancestors, who had fought, died, and immolated themselves on funeral pyres in Chitor and Ranthambor. She followed Arjun to the study.

"There may be trouble today; the children are to stay inside, as well as you and Gayatri," ordered Madho Dev. "Arjun is going to Harbinder Singh's house. His women and children may come over here."

Although she did not much care for Harbinder Singh's wife, daughter-in-laws, and grandchildren, Devika's sense of duty toward her husband was such that she would never have thought of objecting.

"Because of my premonition that something might happen today, I had already planned on keeping Gayatri and the children in the house and intended to conduct school here and read stories. The younger ones can paint and the boys are learning to knit."

"Knit? My grandsons?" Madho Dev laughed.

"Yes," she replied. "It is good for the mind and makes the hands dexterous. If you had learned to knit, perhaps you could pound a nail straight or repair a light fixture."

That Madho Dev was incapable of doing anything with his hands except drive, play polo, and shoot was a well-known fact which they all laughed at. In fact, when they were married Devika discovered on their first morning together that he was almost incapable of dressing himself. As a child he had his personal servant, a little boy a few years older; when he went on to school at Mayo's, a still older servant and his own cook had accompanied him; and in the army there had always been his batman. It was only in combat in Burma that he had finally been forced to dress himself, and he was never very good at it, often getting things wrong side out. Even when they had been down and out in Bombay, Devika had helped him dress every morning. Arjun was embarrassed by this and thought his father extremely old-fashioned.

"Arjun, go now to Harbinder Singh. See what is happening and come back immediately," said Madho Dev, assertively. "We don't want to worry about where you may be."

Arjun disappeared and Devika and Gayatri hustled the children into one of the big rooms off the rear of the courtyard near the kitchen.

Madho Dev and David went back to the courtyard, sat down on the grass mats by the smoldering fire, and watched television. The camera was focusing on the central hall of the Teen Murti house, where ministers and notables in the political world were now paying their respects.

"See how pompous they are, how they are seeking the limelight, even on such an occasion," muttered Madho Dev.

"I say, the lines to Delhi aren't working but do you think there's a chance of reaching Terripur? I have a strong feeling I should call Kamala. I want to speak with her before I go out to the Baba's cave."

Madho Dev shook his head. "You'd best not think of that cave business till this blows over. The car is at Dr. Kapoor's, the truck is in pieces, so we'll need the jeep here. As for calling Terripur, all calls must go through Delhi. When traffic on the lines gets heavy, the operators just give up and take a tea break. But this time I think the wires may have been cut."


HARBINDER SINGH'S house was a copy of Madho Dev's except that while the roofs of the latter were tiled, Harbinder Singh's roofs were thatched. Arjun preferred thatch but it was more expensive to keep than tile and could very easily catch on fire. Glancing back at the smoke rising from Kotagarh, he turned in the drive. It was strangely quiet. Usually at this hour there would be vendors coming and going, workers doing various odd jobs, children playing. Even the great teak doors which usually stood open were closed.

Arjun knocked and waited. After some time an old servant ushered him into the courtyard, where he found Harbinder Singh and his two sons cleaning and oiling their guns. Another servant sat on a mat sharpening kirpans, swords. An old shortwave radio was tuned to the BBC.

"We have heard there's trouble in town," Arjun advised the gray-bearded Harbinder Singh. "My father sent me to offer our help in whatever way you deem necessary."

"As you can see, Arjunji," said the old man, "we are preparing to defend ourselves. Ordinarily I would not be worried, but some of our Hindu workers from Kotagarh town did not show up today. We hear they believe we have gold. Mrs. Gandhi's assassination would give them the perfect excuse to try and find some."

"My father has said that perhaps you would like to send your women and children to our house," said Arjun.

"Achcha." The old man smiled. "That would be a great burden off our heads. We have just been discussing that very problem. There is Harpal's wife and his four children and his widowed mother-in-law. There is Hardev's wife, who is expecting a baby, their five children, and his wife's sister, who is here helping out. Then there is my wife and three old Hindu servants who are faithful to us. So that is nine children, three wives, a mother-in-law, a sister, and three servants, seventeen in all. Can you handle that many?"

"Yes, of course, no problem," answered Arjun.

"Along with the women I will send bags of wheat, rice, dal, sugar, and three cows. The cows I was just sending into the jungle with two boys. I will divert three to your place."

"Father thinks it should be done now. He's rather worried."

Hardev stood up and embraced Arjun. "Hindu-Sikh bhai-bhai," he murmured. "I will tell them to make ready and load our jeep. We will take them in two convoys. Although it is only a short distance, we must take no chances."

Hardev strode off to the back of the courtyard, and Arjun sat down beside Harpal and examined the automatic rifle he was cleaning.

"Russian," explained Harpal. "We bought it from a man who bought it from an Afghani refugee. We have five hundred rounds of ammunition for it."

The old man snorted. "Think of the irony. We who do not trust the Russians, who disapprove of the way Mrs. Gandhi has invited them into our country, now find our best weapon is a Russian one."

"When the women and children are gone, I must fire it to make sure it is working," said Harpal. "Three years have passed since it was last tested. I hope we do not have to use it."

"That is in the hands of God, my son," said the old man.

"How many men do you have here who can be trusted?" asked Arjun.

"About eight," replied the old man, "but two have never fired a gun."

"Is your phone working?"

"That is the other thing that made us suspicious. We tried to call you and discovered the phone is dead. The line must be cut somewhere."

"The trouble could be in Kotagarh," suggested Arjun.

"But then at least we could have called you."

Arjun nodded. Harbinder Singh's success in farming had created considerable jealousy among the Hindus of the area, but then, of course, none of them remembered how hard Harbinder Singh had worked in the days before his sons were old enough to help.

Hardev came back with his mother, three old women servants, and the mother of Harpal's wife, who would ride in Arjun's jeep. The twelve others would ride in two shifts in the other jeep, which was now waiting in front of the house loaded with foodstuffs, ready to go. Harbinder Singh's wife, a distinguished-looking white-haired woman in a white tunic and voluminous Punjabi trousers, had tears in her eyes, and the servants were moaning. Only Harpal's mother-in-law, Usha, seemed to have control of herself, thanked Arjun vociferously, and said she thought it was very wise of them to make the move. She put her arms around Mrs. Harbinder Singh, who protested that she did not want to leave either husband or home, and led her to the front door. Hardev tossed Arjun a pistol and, picking up two rifles, followed the group to Arjun's jeep and helped his mother and the other women into it.

"I'll be right back," he told his father. "Shouldn't take more than half an hour."

Arjun started up his vehicle and the caravan set off. Across the shimmering midday landscape, smoke was still rising in the direction of Kotagarh. Crowded into the rear of the covered jeeps clutching their children, the women were blissfully unaware of the danger the men sensed as they drove down the ominously empty road.

"When an old tree is pulled up by its roots, the earth shakes." It was a proverb that everyone knew. Arjun prayed the earth would not shake too much in Kotagarh that day.

Devika and Gayatri were standing just inside the courtyard, hands pressed worshipfully together, waiting to greet the women and children of Harbinder Singh's family. While they conducted them to the women's quarters, Arjun helped Hardev and the foreman unload the provisions.

"There was no one on the road," said Hardev. "Not a good sign, but then, just as well no one saw us coming."

"If we are attacked, it will come at night," said Arjun.

"In the day we could easily pick them off, but at night it will be more difficult," said Hardev. "We will post our men on the roof of the house and hope for the best."

Arjun stared long and hard at his childhood friend. "You had better go now; your father will be wondering what has happened. I will send one of our men to check the telphone lines. If anything happens, send someone immediately for help."

"There is an old tunnel," said Hardev. "Thinking of the Pandava brothers and their escape from the burning house of lac, my father when he built our house many years ago constructed an escape tunnel from the cellar underneath to a place behind the granary. Do you remember it? We used to play there when we were children. It is well made, of stone, and has for years been used for storage. We have just now cleared it."

Arjun nodded. "I remember it."

They embraced each other. "I must apologize for not believing you about the young Sardars you took into the jungle," Hardev said. "I know you did all you could to help them."

"It's all right. I knew you didn't mean it," said Arjun.

His hands holding Arjun's, Hardev repeated the vow of the Sikh soldier:

"Grant me, O Lord, this boon,
That I may not falter from doing good;
May I entertain no fear of the enemy when confronted by him in
    in battle,
And may I be sure of my victory!
May my mind be so trained
As to dwell upon thy goodness,
And when the last moment of my life should come,
May I die fighting in the thick of battle."

After embracing Arjun again, Hardev got in his jeep and drove off. Arjun stood looking after him, wondering what would happen next. Then he returned to the courtyard, where his father and David were moving the television set into the cool darkness of the study.

"Let us not upset the women and children with this nonsense," said Madho Dev. "It's bad enough that we have to look at it."

To his mind there was something indecent about the grotesque spectacle of Mrs. Gandhi's body decaying before the nation's eyes: the air conditioners and fans aimed at her rotting corpse, the whole shoddy presentation by the government television network. What a price she had paid for her egomania. And now her elder son, standing there so quietly by her bier, who had removed himself from her influence by becoming an airline pilot and marrying a foreign woman, now this inexperienced young man had been thrust into a position of power and was somehow expected to lead a nation of eight hundred million. Madho Dev was sure his elevation was illegal and all this dwelling on a dead body was a smoke screen. If, as Hindus believed, the body was a husk, a shell, what other reason could there be for this impious proceeding?

Suddenly the television switched to the airport. A group of men were exiting from a plane.

"Russians," muttered David. "See how disgruntled they look."

Madho Dev watched intently. "Unattractive-looking bunch." He nodded. "Look at those clothes, they need a good tailor."

"Why do they look so angry?"

"Mrs. Gandhi was very close to Russia," said Arjun gloomily. "They have just lost a good friend."

"It went deeper than friendship," said Madho Dev. "I have heard that when she declared her Emergency a number of KGB officers were brought in to advise her; supposedly they are still here."

"Whose side is the son on?" asked David.

"Who knows?" Madho Dev shrugged. "If he's wise, he'll build a strong fence and sit on it."

"Mind you, last night Radio Moscow accused the CIA of killing her," observed David.

"Denied by the government of India today."

"Do you think the son will turn away from his mother's Russian friends?"

Madho Dev laughed. "Really, you know, we pretend to welcome everyone here. We smile and agree, but we go on clinging to our old customs and never actually accept anyone."

He paused and looked affectionately across the room at Arjun. "So, my boy, are all of Harbinder Singh's women and children here now?"

Arjun nodded. "That was your order, Father, and I have carried it out, but I am not in favor of it. By taking them in, we have made ourselves a target. Why should we defend Sikhs?"

"How can you say that when you have grown up with Harpal and

Hardev? They are your brothers. Sikhs are a sect of Hinduism. Also, they are the defenders of the gurus and they have—"

"But not the defenders of India," interrupted Arjun.

"What do you mean by that?"

"But for them, in 1857 we would have liberated ourselves from British rule."

"Yes"—Madho Dev snorted—"and have been ruled again by Islam. Who teaches you this nonsense?"

"It's in all the textbooks; the Sikhs came in on the side of the British and helped finish us off."

"They finished off the Moghuls," corrected Madho Dev. "Up till then we were ruled by them. From the time of the tenth Sikh guru in the reign of Aurangzeb, the Sikhs fought against the Muslims and kept them from completely destroying Hindu India. When they saw the chance to finish off the Moghuls once and for all, they joined the British; that was all there was to it. Forty-five years later the British turned on the Sikhs and massacred them at Jawallianbagh. From then on the Sikhs were in the forefront of the Independence movement, helped organize the first nonviolent demonstrations with Gandhi. No one can say they aren't patriotic people. In recent times, the best part of the army has been Sikh. Their only problem is they're a bit hotheaded; comes from eating too much meat—we Rajputs eat meat too, but not so much as the Sardars do—and onions. Onions cause quarrelsomeness." The three men laughed.

"Still, we are now a target." Arjun sighed.

"Nonsense," said Madho Dev. "They wouldn't dare attack my house."

"You don't know the people's minds as I do," protested Arjun. "Actually, you have never known them."

"Minds," said Madho Dev. "They have no minds. Even if they are stirred up and cause momentary violence, as happened in '47, these violent fits do not last long because they become distracted and forget. The power of concentration is simply not there. Today we may be the target; tomorrow they'll be touching my feet."

"It only takes a second to shoot someone dead," said Arjun.

"As it is said in our *Mahabharata*," Madho Dev replied, " 'Even like a doll pulled this way and that by threads, man in this world moveth, swayed by a force not his own.' "

# 24

PHILIPPA peered apprehensively out the window of the hired car as it sped through the deserted streets of New Delhi. As they passed through the outlying quarters of the city, she felt overwhelmed by a sense of inevitable doom that seemed to hang like a pall over the dusty streets, where smoke now rose from burning buildings and packs of angry men ran here and there like wild dogs. What on earth was she doing, she kept asking herself, risking her life to return to a husband who'd rejected her, gone mad? Or had he? Perhaps it was she who'd gone mad. Or was it Arjun who had driven them both crazy, Arjun whom she was running back to?

The young Sikh, Harsh, who had volunteered to drive her the hundred and fifty miles to Kotagarh, placed a cigarette at a jaunty angle between his white teeth and glanced nervously from side to side. She tried to imagine what must be going through his mind. Just then they passed several cars burning on the side of the road and saw two lone Sikhs being clubbed to death by a gang of bullies. Harsh glared ferociously but drove doggedly on. At the next intersection a number of taxis, their drivers bound and gagged inside, had been piled in a pyramid and set on fire. Rage welled up within her. Wasn't this the India of the great Mahatma Gandhi, of peace and non-violence? Why was one group of people being singled out for persecution while their fellow countrymen, including the police, stood idly by? She thought of her lifelong friend Irma, who had somehow managed to escape from Vienna with her mother in 1938. Her account of the mobs burning and looting on the night of broken glass when Hitler's men burned the synagogues had left an indelible impression on her. Was this India's *Kristallnacht?* How could the country's leaders, supposedly civilized men educated at Cambridge and Oxford, permit this to happen?

The car suddenly slowed to a halt. On the road ahead, a mob had caught three more Sikhs, tied their hands behind their backs, thrown old tires over their shoulders, doused them with petrol, and set them on fire. Agonized screams rent the air. Philippa buried her face in her hands and broke into tears.

"Why is no one stopping these madmen?" she sobbed. "I can't believe this is happening."

"No one is interfering, madam, because they would be killed," said Harsh, quietly fingering a pistol that lay concealed under a sweater on the seat beside him. "These are my Sikh brothers you see suffering. Can you imagine my anger? And if it is happening right here on the main road, think what is happening on the back streets." He cursed under his breath but when several men with clubs looked at him suspiciously, he lit his cigarette and puffed nonchalantly. The men turned away. Harsh stepped on the accelerator, swerved purposefully, hit them, and sped away down the road. "Two for my side," he barked and threw his cigarette out the window.

Philippa glanced back. Two bodies lay kicking in the dust. The mob shook their sticks and ran down the road. "You took an awful chance there," she said, trying to control her trembling. "What if they'd had a vehicle to chase us in?"

"Those idiots?" snorted Harsh contemptuously. "Brainless fools— lucky to have a cycle. Let us hope their deaths are slow and painful."

Philippa wiped her eyes and wrapped her head in a scarf against the dust. At last they seemed to be out of Delhi, and the highway, except for an occasional oxcart or pedestrian, was empty.

"We will be all right till Madhgarh," said Harsh. "No telling what we will find there."

Even before they reached Madhgarh, however, they could see smoke rising, and as they approached the ugly industrial town, they began to pass clutches of youths and poor people armed with sticks.

"We don't want to get stuck here," Philippa said quietly. "Isn't there a way around?"

"No, madam," replied Harsh steadily. "We will just have to hope our luck holds."

They had slowed down behind a covered jeep filled with grinning policemen.

"Well, at least that's a hopeful sign," said Philippa.

"I wouldn't say so, madam," replied Harsh curtly. "They won't be doing police work today. More likely they're out for gain. First they will let the mobs do the dirty work; then in the night they will come and confiscate the looted goods. That is how it is done. Just because they are in police uniform does not mean they will help anyone, especially of my community."

The streets were jammed. It was impossible to pass the jeep and so they crawled along behind it, the object of countless staring eyes. Each time the driver halted, Philippa thought the windows might be bashed in and they would be dragged out and beaten. Harsh lit another cigarette and grinned bravely. They passed a crowd watching a color television set outside a shop. It was garlanded with marigolds, and incense had been lit in front of it. The reception was bad, but images of Mrs. Gandhi's body lying in state could be seen, flickering in livid polarized colors; green, burning orange, saffron, and purple.

Did they actually think she looked like that? Philippa wondered. Yes, probably.

At the center of town, the police jeep pulled over and they were again able to pick up speed. At the southern end of Madhgarh, the highway was deserted but on both sides they could see the smoke and flames of houses burning and passed the charred remains of two trucks. Harsh told her the next town of any size was thirty-five miles away. Philippa offered him water from her flask and settled back, hoping to get some sleep. Even if they made good time, it would be dark when they reached Kotagarh. No telling what they would find there. Images of the day's madness lingered in her mind's eye. Beneath India's apparent calm lurked something out of control, brutish, remorseless. No wonder Arjun was set on leaving. Arjun—where was he? Until now she hadn't really understood how much she loved him.

The colors flashed by—umber and burnt sienna, white dhotis, dark skin; violet, pink, and red saris—and, over all, the silver dust of Rajasthan. They passed a vast herd of camels guarded by tall, fierce-looking tribesmen. Then herds of sheep and paddy fields. At last they were coming to the small town where Harsh said they might stop for tea. He suggested she could even try calling Kotagarh from there.

But they were never to reach it. At a junction that branched off toward Jaipur, a roadblock had been set up. To her amazement, Philippa found herself suggesting they speed up and run through it. About a hundred yards later, however, Harsh saw no alternative but to stop and turn around. The barricade was too big; there were too many people. They would have to find another way. Just after he had successfully reversed directions, a tire blew and the car stalled. They gazed back down the road toward the mob, which seemed occupied searching a bus. Some of the leaders had seen them turn back, however, and came running toward them. Commanding Philippa to remain in the car, Harsh calmly took the spare tire from the boot and began to jack up the axle.

A group of men soon surrounded him. "You are coming from which place?" one of them asked threateningly. "Your good name?"

Harsh gave a Hindu name.

"I don't believe him," said another, obviously the town bully. "Let us see your license."

Philippa watched in the rearview mirror as Harsh's confident expression crumbled. It was obvious he hadn't planned on showing his papers.

"His hair looks freshly cut and look, he's got a Sardarji bracelet," said the leader.

Three men grabbed him from behind. "Your papers," they barked. "If you are who you say you are, your papers will prove your innocence."

"In the glove compartment," shouted Harsh bravely.

Philippa leaned over and picked up Harsh's gun. When the man reached in for the papers, she sprang out of the back seat and pointed it at him. The sight of a foreign woman holding a .38 pistol caught him off guard. Gesturing obsequiously, he slunk back among his friends.

"See, a foreign spy. Spy, spy, spy!" shouted a younger man, wearing the boy scout uniform of the Hindu brown shirts movement, the R.S.S.

More people came running up but all now stood at bay, gaping at Philippa.

"Release this man!" she shouted, surprised at how steadily she was holding the gun. "There is no reason for you to see his papers. They are quite in order." They let go of Harsh.

"It's an English memsahib," yelled someone.

Harsh shook himself free and returned to his work.

"You help my driver change this tire—now!" she ordered, jerking the gun at them.

Several men squatted down and pretended to help but by now there were other figures running across the fields and down the road.

"Hurry up," Philippa commanded sternly, realizing that if the crowd grew too large there was no way she could control it.

Knowing this too, the men fumbled with the tools. Time seemed to slow down. The ludicrous nature of her situation became obvious. She felt like laughing and crying at the same time—to die here on a country road in Rajasthan at the hands of a people she had hoped to love and thought she understood. It was too much.

Sensing her faltering will, the leader taunted her abusively and harangued the crowd. "No doubt this foreign woman helped killed Indiraji," he screamed, "and is even now trying to escape."

"Yes, yes, escape!" they yelled. "Grab her, kill her!"

The sun was a fiery ball suspended in the western sky, blood red. Philippa felt faint. At any moment the pistol was going to fall from her hand—the hand of an English memsahib, great-granddaughter of a viceroy, on November 1, 1984, holding off an Indian mob; defending a Sikh. If the crowd knew all this they would have seen it as a remarkable omen, that she was atoning for her family's sins. Each turn of the wrench by the men who were unscrewing the bolts of the flat tire, removing it, and putting on the new one, seemed a lifetime, a horror film occurring in diabolic slow motion. On the periphery of her vision she saw more men converging, many with sticks. In a few more minutes it would be too late.

"Jeldi, jeldi; faster, faster," she commanded as the hubcap was replaced and the old tire lifted into the trunk.

Then, without warning, she was grabbed from behind and held aloft like a prize. The pistol went off in the air and was batted out of her hand. She kicked furiously as another group of men overpowered her driver, began tying him up, and doused the car with petrol. Just then, the bus which had been the former object of the mob's attention, came down the road, scattering the throng, and pulled to a screeching halt. Out jumped several well-dressed teenagers who muscled their way to her side, grabbed her driver, formed a cordon, and carried them both into the bus. The doors slammed shut. The bus driver stepped on the accelerator. The mob, furious at having their prey snatched away, threw petrol on the front of the bus and ignited it. With a screeching crunch, the bus leapt forward over the bodies blocking its path. Flames obliterated the driver's view. The occupants of the bus, all teenagers, cheered him on. One of them turned on the windshield wipers, the view cleared, and the bus swerved to miss a bullock cart piled high with fodder.

Philippa collapsed on the stairs. Two boys helped her into a seat and untied her driver's hands.

"These animals are stopping every vehicle looking for Sikhs. Four of our classmates are Sikhs. They are being sat on and hidden in the back seats," the boys explained.

There was another cheer and laughter as the four Sikh students were uncovered and sat up, blinking.

"I think you just saved my life and that of my driver," whispered Philippa. "Are you students?"

"Yes, at the Connaught Public School in Delhi. We've been on a field trip to Jaipur and Amber. We are seniors in the eighth form. From which place are you coming?"

"I was on my way from Delhi to Kotagarh." Philippa sighed. "Now I guess I'm going back to Delhi."

"We are expecting trouble in Madhgarh," said one of the boys.

"We passed through several hours ago. There were crowds but nothing violent at the time."

"Is there no way around Madhgarh?" the student called. The bus driver shook his head.

"Then we had better cut their hair and beards, it is not worth the risk," said a girl sitting behind Philippa.

Suddenly everyone was shouting for a scissors, razors, and combs. Three of the young Sikhs refused, said their fathers would kill them. The fourth boy's hair and youthful beard were clumsily cut with small scissors but it was too bumpy a ride for them to shave him close.

"You are from which place?" asked one of the boys standing near her.

"England," she replied.

"Oh, very nice. I have lived in London. My father was posted there for three years."

"Your father is in the government then?"

"Ministry of External Affairs," he replied. He was a tall, pale youth with a shock of straight black hair hanging over his brow. "My name is Tiwari and these are my friends, Vijay Agarwal and Rajesh Verma. Why were you going to Kotagarh?"

"To join my husband who is visiting an old friend there. I was worried there might be trouble. When I tried to call from Delhi, the operator said the lines had been cut, so I hired a car. It's a wonder my driver agreed to come, but he'd cut his hair and beard. Then they asked for his identity card."

"We'd better tear up the identity cards of our Sikh friends," said the boy called Verma.

"Why are they killing Sikhs?" exclaimed Agarwal. "Just because Mrs. Gandhi's assassins were Sikh fanatics doesn't mean every Sikh is guilty."

"You can bet someone else has given them the idea," said Tiwari. "These fellows never have ideas on their own."

Philippa smiled. "You talk as though you were discussing a foreign race."

The boys looked at each other and laughed. "In some ways, they are," one admitted.

"What is your name?" one boy asked.

"Philippa Bruce. My husband is David Bruce. He was born in India and was a captain in the army here during the war."

"The war with Pakistan?"

"The Second World War."

"He must be very old," said the boy.

They fell silent. The bus rumbled on through the deserted country-side. The autumn sun had set, and by the time they arrived at Madhgarh, it was dark. Mobs roamed the streets, throwing bricks, looting, and burning shops. They passed a tree with two corpses swinging on ropes and came to a roadblock. As the bus came to a halt, the students in the back sat on their Sikh friends again. But the bus driver, furious at being stopped, had other plans. Heaving the vehicle into reverse, he backed up and, shifting gears, lumbered toward the barricade. When the people standing in front of the makeshift road-block saw what was about to happen, they scattered. There was a deafening crash as the big vehicle hit the empty oil drums, and then they were free. Philippa uncovered her face, which she'd hidden in her hands, and tried to control her trembling.

"Now we'll certainly get through," cried Tiwari as they broke into a rousing school song.


ONCE in Delhi, the students insisted the driver take Philippa to the Majestic. Outside the gates an angry mob had gathered. The gates, guarded inside by armed men, swung open, letting the bus pass through, and immediately shut again.

"This hotel is owned by Sikhs," said Tiwari. "Our friends will be safe here too."

"I owe my life to you," said Philippa, still trembling. "I don't know how to thank you."

"No mention," said the students. "Between friends there is no need for thanks."

Philippa got out of the bus with her driver, the four Sikh boys, and three girls who were also Sikhs. Inside the lobby the students were joyfully reunited with relatives and whisked away. Philippa paid her driver, who then demanded ten thousand pounds for his burned car. "Later," she stammered, "I'll see you later," and made her way through the lobby to the crowded bar, where people were watching eulogies of Mrs. Gandhi by prominent persons on television. Ordering a double Scotch and soda, she stared numbly at the screen. She needed to get slightly drunk, stop trembling, and go to bed. Suddenly General Bobby was there beside her.

"I couldn't get you all day," he said. "The desk clerk said you'd gone to Kotagarh. When you returned just now they called me; I came right over. You must be mad, going out like that!"

"I was almost killed. My driver was almost killed too." She explained what had happened. "Where is your army, the police? Why is no one doing anything to stop this madness? We were rescued by a busload of students. My driver is now demanding I give him ten thousand pounds for his lost car."

"He has a right to ask for something, but not that much. I'll deal with him later. You're lucky to be alive. Why did you do it?"

"I was worried sick about everyone in Kotagarh. I saw two Sikhs murdered right outside here this morning." She held her head in her hands. "I'm exhausted. Did you get through to Kotagarh on the phone?"

"No."

"Is there no way we can reach them?"

"I've tried everything. Kotagarh is an out-of-the-way place; even the police communications are not functioning. You'll simply have to be patient. I'm sure everyone is all right. After all, David and Madho Dev are both army men; they won't let anything happen."

"If you could have seen the mobs in those small towns, the road-blocks."

"To you it must seem unbelievable but to us it's no surprise; we lived through the bloodbath of '47. I'd certainly like to know who is responsible for inciting these people, though, and I intend to find out."

"I've seen Congress Party hats and people called R.S.S."

"They say we'll be called out shortly. We're all waiting for our orders, but they're not coming."

"Meanwhile Delhi and other places are burning."

"While Rajiv attends his mother's corpse." Bobby nodded. "Come, let's have some dinner. You probably haven't had a solid meal all day."

"I'm more in need of a bath than food." Philippa sighed. "I must wash off that mob's hands."

"Let us go to your room then, I will arrange a special dinner which you otherwise would not be able to get. How about champagne, some caviar, and chicken?"

"You must be joking."

"Oh, no, we have plenty of caviar from our Russian friends, and I have brought the champagne and chicken in my car. I'll have them sent up."

Philippa retired to her bath. Outside the window she heard gunshots and explosions and could see smoke and flames rising in the distance. How important it was to be in the right place at the right time. This afternoon she had definitely been in the wrong place. What of Arjun, was he in the right place? And what of Ramakrishna Rao? The least he could have done was to have called and left a message. In forty-eight hours she would be leaving, leaving for England and sanity. Or would she?

"Ah!" Bobby beamed when she returned to the sitting room in a silk caftan, her blond hair glowing. "You look yourself again. Come, have some champagne." He uncorked the bottle with a flourish. "What a strange turn of events that on a night like this I should find myself here, alone with you." He grinned and filled two iced glasses. The telephone rang. He answered, grunted at someone on the other end, and spoke gruffly in Hindi. "The orders have finally arrived," he said, hanging up the receiver. "It may take us a week to act on them, but meanwhile, cheers." He saluted her with his glass.

Outside, the explosions and gunshots continued. Philippa rose, went to the window, and parted the heavy draperies. The general got up and stood behind her, his arms around her waist, and nuzzled the back of her neck.

Philippa stepped away. "Please, I've been through too much today."

"Can't we pretend this is the week you said we'd spend alone together?"

She laughed. "I said no such thing and you know it."

His arms fell to his side. "I'm sure you must be very tired. Tomorrow you will see things—"

There was a violent knock on the door and Philippa heard the voice of Iris calling her.

"*Mon Dieu, mon Dieu,*" she shrieked, bursting into the room, the bulky Nirendra lumbering behind her. "Where have you been, I've been so worried! Oh—" she stopped, seeing General Bobby. "I see you have a guest. We won't disturb you."

"Not at all," said Philippa. "Are you all right? You look terrified."

"She thinks the hotel will be attacked at any moment," said Nirendra, "and the women and children raped." He looked questioningly at General Bobby.

"Oh, sorry, you haven't met," said Philippa. "Nirendra, may I present General Singh." General Bobby nodded. The disdain with which the two men confronted each other went unnoticed by Philippa, who was now greeting Marianne and Paul as they trailed through the door carrying an open bottle of brandy.

Angry over the interruption, Bobby sat down and poured himself another glass of champagne. Why didn't she send them away? They weren't her kind of people.

"But, *mon général*," cooed Iris, who was obviously tired of Nirendra, "why is the army not patrolling the streets? There has been such violence. Now they are sending rockets of fire onto the roof of this hotel."

"Impossible," said Bobby. "They don't have rockets."

"But I have seen them out my window; that is what has disturbed me so. Come into my room." She took his hand. "From there you may see them."

"Sorry." Bobby smiled. "I must stay on top of this phone. I'm expecting a call."

Iris paced back and forth and went to the window. "Look, you can see them from here."

Bobby went to the window. Flaming petrol-soaked missiles were being catapulted from beyond the compound wall toward the roof, where they were thrown down by men who were stationed there. The phone rang. Bobby picked it up and listened to an excited voice on the other end. Then he slammed down the receiver and cursed under his breath. Why was life so filled with interruptions? "I must go," he said.

"I hope you'll come back soon and give us some news or call," said Philippa, seeing him to the door. "And please try to reach Kotagarh."

He took her hands and kissed them. "I'll be back soon. As David is absent, I feel responsible for your safety. If this place should catch fire, you must come to the Maurya Sheraton."

"I will. Be careful."

Nirendra sank down in the place vacated by the general and stared absently as Paul shaved cocaine from a white cube with a Swiss Army knife and arranged it in lines on the coffee table. When he was finished, he passed out short straws and turned on his portable tape recorder. "Put on your red shoes and dance," sang David Bowie. Nirendra and Marianne sniffed up five lines. Paul offered Philippa a straw.

"I'm sorry," said Philippa. "I've had a ghastly day."

"Don't be sorry," said Paul. "I have a feeling we will have to stay awake tonight. Come on, it will give you a lift." Against her better judgment, she took a straw and sniffed. Perhaps it would steady her nerves. Paul smiled. "Now the other side."

Just then there was a knock at the door. Paul put away the cocaine.

A frazzled-looking young American bolted into the room, looking for him. "Some people downstairs said you might be interested in what I have," he said. He claimed he'd been on a train from Punjab when it was stopped; Sikhs had been dragged out and killed. He held up a roll of film. "I just happened to have my crummy little Instamatic with me. It's all on this film."

"He wants to sell it," exclaimed Paul, looking at Iris. "Why sell it to me?"

"Only one thousand rupees," said the frightened-looking young man. "I have to get out of this place. I've run out of money. I'm going crazy."

Suddenly Harsh, the driver who had accompanied Philippa on her ill-fated journey, burst in, collapsed in tears at her feet, and began to groan and cry in Punjabi. Overwhelmed, Philippa backed to the sofa and sat down. The driver threw his arms around her knees.

"He is saying," translated Iris, obviously stunned, "that when he left you he went home to where he lives, not far from here. He said a terrible massacre has taken place there, the women raped, all the men and boys killed in the most horrible ways. His three sons are dead, he found their mutilated and partly burned bodies; his wife and daughter have disappeared, nobody knows where." Iris broke into tears. "Oh, why have I stayed here so long? Why can't I leave this horrible country?"

At a loss for words, Philippa sat stroking the head of Harsh, who was sobbing quietly. The demented American with the film was still trying to negotiate a deal with Paul. Paul was shaking his head.

"*Alors*, listen, man, some press photographers have set up a lab on the floor below: room 213, I think. Take your film there, get it developed. If it's what you say, you'll get much more than a thousand rupees." He put his hand in his pocket and withdrew a wad of notes. "Take this money, go on down, and get it developed. Ask for Raoul, he's a friend of mine."

The boy staggered out of the room.

"Look," said Iris, wiping away her tears. "Things are getting pretty bad, no? This place could easily be stormed and taken. If things like this driver says are really happening, we should be prepared."

"For what?" asked Paul.

"For this hotel catching on fire, idiot. It would be easy for them to blow a hole in the wall and storm in here. There are gangs of thugs out there, just ask Philippa."

"Hmm," said Paul dreamily.

Nirendra and Marianne stared at her glassy-eyed.

"Do any of you have weapons?" asked Philippa.

"*Exactement!*" declared Iris. "None of us has anything. But I know where we can get some. After all, we must be prepared for the worst. In the rear of the hotel compound, behind the swimming pool, there is a gardener's shed." Her voice became a whisper. "I have seen old pipes, hoes, rakes, and shovels there."

Paul looked doubtful.

"It's better than nothing," cried Iris impatiently. "I'll show you where the place is. We'll put on shawls and sneak the tools in underneath them."

"What about him?" asked Nirendra, indicating the driver, still sobbing on Philippa's lap. "Shall we take him too?"

"Don't be crazy," scoffed Iris. "He might go insane. Let him stretch out on the sofa. Hey, Sardarji, just put your head on this pillow. We'll be back in ten minutes: das minutes." Philippa got up and they lifted him onto the sofa. "Das minutes, eh?"

The driver groaned.

"Here is the Valium you gave me before," said Iris. "I never took it, give it to him." Philippa poured a glass of water.

"Excellent." Iris smiled and turned to the driver. "You must drink this water—pani pigiay—and take this little pill, ji? You will relax. You have suffered, you are in shock, this pill will help you." Lifting the driver's head, she stuck the pills in his mouth and made him drink the water. He slumped down and began crying into the pillow. Outside, a loud explosion shook the glass in the windows.

Quickly throwing long shawls around themselves, Philippa, Iris, and Marianne, followed by Paul and Nirendra, took the lift to the lobby, slipped out a side door, and crept steathily around the building. Outside on the streets they could hear the yells and cries of the mob, the sound of breaking glass, and occasional shots.

"Stay in the shadows," cautioned Iris. "See the men on the roof with guns? They might shoot us by mistake."

Reaching the shed, Iris produced a small flashlight. "What did I tell you? Pipes!" She brandished one and hit the side of the hut with it. "And look, there are some grass-cutting knives—cutties—and an ax. Take that and the two hoes also."

Concealing their find under shawls and coats, they made their way back through a side door and up the stairs to Philippa's room.

"Hide these things in the closet where we can grab them fast if necessary," ordered Iris, unloading her share of the tools. "I don't trust these room bearers; half of them are Hindus, probably hate the

Sikhs who own this place. You never know what will get into their bird brains."

"Let us order some dinner, some khanna," said Nirendra when they had settled down.

Philippa idly wondered what had happened to the dinner ordered by General Bobby. Did his cook go on duty with him? The television was still on; a group of serious-looking musicians with long hair were accompanying an old man playing the sarangi.

"*Merde.*" Paul groaned. "Must we hear that wailing? Turn it off."

"Put on the Boy George tape, something cheerful," Iris suggested.

Marianne made a face and turned off the set. "Personally, I adore the sarangi, it is my favorite instrument. Don't you feel sad about what is happening? Have you no feelings?"

"Why should I feel sad?" returned Paul. "These are not my countrymen, every day they make it clear to me that I am ferenghi. Well, I *am* foreign. I'm French and glad of it, and I refuse to share their self-created sorrows even if they are genuine. Just a day ago they were all reviling Mrs. Gandhi. Everywhere one went people were putting her down, wishing she would retire, and now they are moaning and carrying on because she is gone. Tomorrow they will be picking her bones, digging up scandals to discredit her, and in a few years they'll be doing the same to her son. Indians have no sense of obligation. What do they say in English? Ingrates. Yes, that is what they all are."

Iris, who had stopped listening to Paul, had gone to the window, opened it, and was gazing out over the hotel compound to the street and the mob, which had grown in size and was batting bricks and flaming missiles over the wall. A large group of Sikhs was at the gate, brandishing swords, preventing anyone from climbing over. At the door, Nirendra was ordering food from a bearer.

Paul laughed. "Even the end of the world would not prevent you from having your dinner on time, would it?"

"Brahman is food and food is Brahman," recited Nirendra. "The violent habits of these north Indians are a well-known fact. As you say, why should it disturb me?"

"There is something important that we have forgotten," cried Iris, turning from the window. "Weapons we now have, but what if this building catches on fire? They are still throwing flaming missiles toward the roof. They could also break through the back wall and start a fire in the central kitchens. It would be so simple; there are dozens of propane tanks there. What would we do?"

"We'd have to jump out the window." Philippa sighed, wishing Iris weren't so paranoid.

"It's too far, much too far," proclaimed Iris. "Come, have a look." She paced up and down, then strode to the door and pressed the button for a bearer.

"We need six bed sheets," she said imperiously when he appeared. "Please bring six bed sheets—jeldi, jeldi!"

The room boy, an old man with a humped back, craned his neck, staring past her at Nirendra and Marianne. No doubt the sheets were wanted for some sexual purpose, he was thinking. Having worked all his life in hotels he had seen many strange sights, but the foreign dancing women were the oddest, always doing queer things.

"For what purpose will madam be wanting the sheets?" he asked.

Iris, an old India hand, had already anticipated this question. Smiling her most beatific smile, her eyes glistened like a cat's with its prey, as she said triumphantly, "For my puja, of course. I am going to perform a puja," and closed the door.

Paul, setting out lines of cocaine on the table, guffawed. "Why are you asking for bed sheets?" he asked sarcastically and passed Philippa a straw.

"We are going to tie them together into a knotted rope in case we have to climb out of here," said Iris, her eyes bulging.

"I think you have been in this country too long and are becoming hysterical." He patted the seat beside him. "Come, sit down here, I have another line for you."

There was a knock on the door and the bed sheets were delivered. "For your puja, madam." The old servant smirked.

Iris tipped him generously, locked the door, and began laying out the sheets.

"Let me help," said Philippa.

"You'll need twelve sheets to reach the ground from here," said Paul.

"We'll rip them in two lengthwise," said Iris. "They'll still be strong enough."

"Why not use the sheets on these beds?" asked Philippa. "There are four in this room and we can use two from your room; that will make six more. They'll be stronger then, and we won't have ruined six sheets."

There was a terrific crash and a flaming brick bounced into the room, narrowly missing Marianne and Nirendra.

"Quick!" shrieked Iris. "Somebody throw it back outside."

Casually picking up the flaming brick with his bare hands, Nirendra tossed it out the window.

"*Mon Dieu!*" cried Iris. "You are a hero after all."

There was a knock at the door. Philippa opened it and a bearer wheeled in a room service table complete with silver ice bucket, candelabra, and a large bouquet of roses. A second table with braziers containing hot dishes followed.

"You ordered all that?" Iris laughed. "At a time like this, with our lives in danger?"

"For the puja," said Nirendra solemnly.

"For the puja," Paul said to the curious bearer, who stood watching Iris and Philippa tying sheets together while Nirendra paid the bill.

No sooner had the bearer left than two young Frenchmen burst through the door with the sick-looking young American.

"Paul!" they shouted.

"Raoul, Jacques," yelled Paul, embracing them. "Where have you been?"

"Outside, we have been out trying to take photographs, almost we are killed," said the one called Jacques.

"Can you imagine," said Raoul, "the barbarity of these people, the cruelty? We come upon a tree, just in the block behind this hotel, the thugs had tied these young Sikhs by the hands, hung them from the low branches, and were slitting their guts open. Meanwhile, other people were passing on the street quite normally and there were police watching."

"I held up my camera to take a picture," said Jacques, "and a young fellow came up to me, very polite and smiling, pointed a pistol at me, and said in perfect English, 'If you take a picture, I'll kill you.'"

"Beasts," cried Iris. "Fucking animals!"

"Come, have a hit," said Paul.

Marianne turned up the ghetto blaster and began to shake wildly.

"Are you weak-minded or something?" cried Iris. "Here we are, trapped in this hellhole, bombs exploding outside, people being disemboweled, and you are dancing like a maniac. Come over here and help us; take the other end of this sheet and pull tight."

"May I ask what you are doing?" said Jacques.

"I am making a rope, monsieur, how do you think we'll get out of here when this place catches fire? Get on the other end now with Marianne and pull. The knots must be tight."

Nirendra sat quietly down at the table and began serving himself dinner.

"Another animal," muttered Iris. "Constantly thinking of his stomach while all around him his countrymen are dying."

"Sit down and eat something; the dal is good, so is the subjee. Nothing is going to happen," said Nirendra.

"Cool it, Iris, you're getting too excited," said Paul.

"Did you send this fellow to us?" asked Jacques, referring to the American boy who was pacing up and down. Paul nodded. "We have developed his film. Sensational! How much does he want?"

"He said he wants a thousand rupees," Paul replied. "Let me see what pictures you have." The boy passed over a proof sheet. Paul whistled. "Excellent, the best yet. *Paris Match* or *Stern* will buy these in a minute. Is the telex working?"

"Broken down," said Jacques.

"How about five thousand rupees?" asked Paul.

"We have offered that but he refuses."

"An hour ago you were giving them away; now five thousand doesn't satisfy you?"

"That was before I saw the film," said the boy in a hoarse voice. "Give me eight thousand; that will get me home to California."

"That's too much," said Paul.

"Then I'll take them to UPI," replied the boy stubbornly. "These are real good pichers."

The three Frenchmen looked at him. "We'll give you seven thousand five hundred," offered Paul, "eight thousand minus the money I loaned you: the price of a ticket to California."

"I dunno, look at this one here, it's real clear. Look, this guy has just sliced the other guy's head off; pretty far out, wouldn't you say?"

Marianne darted to the bed to look at the proof sheet.

"Real gory, wouldn't you say?" The boy grinned.

"Horrible, absolutely horrible." Marianne shivered.

"I can see this on the cover of *Time* or *Newsweek*," persisted the boy. "I met a guy from *Newsweek* a little while ago—"

"This is completely outrageous," said Philippa, "bargaining over the misfortune of others. I will donate the extra five hundred rupees just to get him out of here."

Ever the stubborn Frenchman, Paul took a wad of notes from his pocket and counted out seven thousand five hundred rupees. From her purse, Philippa produced the other five hundred.

"There you are," she said, putting all the money in the boy's hand. "Now go, get out. That poor man over there has lost three sons, his wife, and daughter. Get out of my room immediately."

The boy handed over the film can and proof sheet to Paul and started for the door. "*Un moment,* stop, *s'il vous plaît,*" called Paul, moving toward a lamp. "How do I know these are the right negatives?"

Philippa turned away in disgust. She'd never liked the French much and was now convinced they were the most impossible people on earth. How could she get these people out of her room?

Paul took the roll of film out of its can, held it before the light, and nodded. "*Alors,* it's all right. Sorry, but you could have pulled a fast one on me, couldn't you?"

The boy shrugged and opened the door. Thick smoke poured in from the hall, and he slammed it shut again.

"What was that?" gulped Iris.

"Smoke," said the boy.

Not believing him, Paul strode to the door and opened it. Smoke billowed into the room.

"Just as I predicted," screamed Iris, her hands on her hips. "Stuff pillows against the door so the smoke doesn't come in under it. I was in a fire once in Amsterdam. I know what I'm talking about."

Marianne took the pillows from the beds and stuffed them at the bottom of the door.

"It's time for us to get out of here," commanded Iris. "Everyone get their money and passports. Don't forget that kid's film."

Philippa shook her head. "What are we going to do about my driver? He's asleep, poor thing."

Iris and Marianne were feeding the knotted sheets out the open window.

"Try to wake him up," Iris shouted distractedly.

Nirendra, still at table, had finished his meal and sat staring at the bouquet of roses, patting his mustache with a napkin and sniffing the air. "It doesn't smell right," he said quietly.

"What are you mumbling about?" said Iris crossly. "Get up and get ready to move out."

"I said it doesn't smell right," he drawled. "It is smelling like burning fat, not like a burning building." He got up calmly, went to the door, kicked the pillows aside, and opened it.

Philippa was amazed at the relaxed way in which he seemed to handle any situation, how quickly he could move when he wanted to. Perhaps it was the knowledge that he might never make it down Iris's makeshift ladder. Or was it all the food he had just eaten, which, in certain breeds of dogs she knew, led them to furious action?

"Hoy, bearer," Nirendra shouted into the smoke-filled hall and closed the door behind him.

"He's crazy, going out there," moaned Iris. She ran to the door and opened it. "Nirendra, come back here immediately," she yelled. Then, gasping for air, she stepped quickly back inside and stared angrily at Philippa's driver asleep on the sofa. "We must get out of here now! Can't you wake him up?"

While Paul and his two friends tied the end of the sheets around a pipe leading to the air conditioner and tested it, Philippa prodded the young driver awake.

"We must leave," she said urgently. "The building is on fire. We have made a rope, you must get up and climb down it, out the window," she pointed.

The driver sat up, stared wildly about the room, slumped down, and went to sleep again.

"Wake up, wake up," pleaded Philippa, "You must wake up!"

"Marianne, you go first," ordered Iris. "You are the lightest. The heaviest people come last in case a sheet rips. At least some of us will get out."

Marianne peered out the window. "You don't expect me to go down there?" she shrieked.

"What do you think we've been doing the last hour? Of course you are going to go down. Look, just sit on the ledge, put your feet on the first knot, and climb down."

"Why don't you do it if you're so sure it's going to work? I'm not going to be your guinea pig!"

"*Merde*, if you want to be burned alive," blustered Iris. "I was just trying to save your life." Shoving Marianne aside, she backed out onto the window ledge and started down.

Suddenly there was a pounding at the door.

"Wait," cried Marianne.

"Get the pipes out of the closet," yelled Paul. "It might be some crazy looters."

Marianne opened the door cautiously and Nirendra, coughing heavily, bolted in.

"No problem," he puffed, "there's a kitchen on each floor. Some cook was frying puris, cooking oil has caught fire, he is throwing on water, making it worse. Then someone else is smothering it with flour. No problem; it is out."

"Where is Iris?" said Philippa, looking around.

They all rushed to the window and looked out. Iris was halfway down the building, dangling from the sheets. The mob had seen her and was pelting her with stones. Standing below, several Sikhs waited to catch her.

"Come back," shrieked Marianne. "There is no fire, come back."

# 25

AT THE FARM near Kotagarh it was now evening. The family sat around the fire listening to Madho Dev, who was reading aloud from *The Mahabharata*.

"Therefore ye tigers among men, arise and arm yourselves without delay for rescuing those that have sought our protection. Who is there (amongst these standing around me) that is high-souled enough to assist even his foe, beholding him seeking shelter with joined hands. The bestowal of a boon, sovereignty, and the birth of a son are sources of great joy. But ye, sons of Pandu, the liberation of a foe from distress is equal to these three together."

Madho Dev put down the book and gazed out across the courtyard. Two cuckoos droned monotonously from the old pipal tree. The fire crackled. He took up his harmonium and began to sing. David watched proudly as Manoj, his eldest grandson, just turned fourteen, joined in, Uma, seated beside Arjun, played a drum, and Lakshmi rattled a tambourine. And there was Rishi, a skinny boy of seven nicknamed "The Thinker" hunched over a book, and Sona, the youngest, between Devika and Gayatri. In the west the sun had disappeared into the smoke that was still rising from Kotagarh. The long afternoon had been tranquil. David prayed the worst was over.

Although he had assigned the Nepalese foreman, Norbu, to watch and report anything unusual, Madho Dev's nap that afternoon had been restless. Knowing the foreman might doze off, he had kept one ear cocked for any disturbance. But there had been none and he had awakened feeling that, after all, everything was going to be all right. In India, palace revolutions had come and gone for thousands of years. The earth around Delhi was soaked red, as red as the sandstone of its buildings, with the blood of fallen tyrants and liberators alike, but this house here in Kotagarh was a safe haven.

Waking up in this frame of mind, he hadn't bothered to turn on the

TV but had bathed, changed his clothes, and gone to sit by the fire, where a small heap of coals glowed on top of the mound of powdery gray-white ash. Placing two small logs around the remaining embers, he had coaxed them to life again, thrown a handful of jasmine flowers on the flame, and thanked the god and goddess of the fire for the peace and tranquillity of his hearth and home. He was not a templegoer, a seeker of yogis, nor did he consult pundits; he was not a religious man in the ordinary sense, but he believed as a practical matter in the gods of his ancestors and that they should be propitiated through offerings.

As a youth, these things were as foreign to him as to the British tutors who trained him. It was only after his father died and everything was lost that he began to believe. One day in the depths of depression when he was driving around Bombay in his wreck of a taxi, he happened near the temple of Mombai Devi, the goddess for whom Bombay was named. Hot and tired, he had stopped at a stall selling sugar-cane juice. Not far away, a disreputable-looking dark-skinned figure, his long black hair matted with filth, squatted half naked on a piece of burlap and held out a small plaster statue of Mombai Devi, crudely painted and gilded, juggled it in his hands in a strange way, and tried to catch Madho Dev's attention. Pretending to ignore him, Madho Dev had walked back to his taxi.

"You are having bad luck," the creature yelled after him, attracting several onlookers and embarrassing Madho Dev. "Take this statue of Mombai Devi, and before you touch any food offer it to her on a small silver dish. She will take the essence from it and will be pleased with you. Later, set the plate some distance away and let flying and crawling animals eat the remains. Do this and you will prosper."

To keep the man quiet, Madho Dev had taken the small plaster goddess, given the fellow a few rupees, and forgotten the whole incident until Devika had found the statue among his belongings. Recognizing from her husband's description that a good-luck boon had been bestowed on him by the goddess through the squalid-looking ascetic, Devika immediately followed the directions he had given Madho Dev and set up the plaster statue in a place of honor. The fact that the man had been dark-skinned and thoroughly disgusting looking had struck her, for it was well known that when the gods wished to favor you, they often appeared in the guise of a filthy beggar to test you. And so she began offering food to the statue on a silver plate.

Within weeks their luck changed; Madho Dev was parked near the rubbish heap of a vacant lot where he and other taxi drivers often parked. It was twilight. He had overslept his nap and the other taxis had all driven off. He went to piss and, while he was standing there, his eye was attracted to a shape that looked like the end of a cardboard box. Poking it with a stick, he managed to push the object to one side. Its heaviness intrigued him. It was tied with string and was as filthy as the rubbish heap in which it lay. Suppressing an instinctive revulsion at touching anything so unclean, he picked the box up but, not wanting to open it there where anyone could see him, had thrown it in the trunk of his taxi. That evening when he had arrived home and opened it, he discovered two gold bars weighing at least five kilos each. Ten kilos of gold! Both he and Devika were convinced it was the result of Mombai Devi's boon, and from that moment on, even though they often felt ridiculous in doing so, they had faithfully worshiped and waited upon the little statue.

And now that statue was tucked in a shrine between the roots of the ancient pipal tree, which Devika had picked out as the place where they should build their house when they returned to Kotagarh. The house had been constructed around the tree, which shaded half the courtyard. It had also been Devika who had told him to dig the fire pit in an auspicious place and helped him keep the fire going after it had been brought in by his father's old priest. The goddess in the tree, the daily offerings of food, which had even attracted a family of cobras who lived in the tree, and the fire itself had created a zone of peace that extended for some distance in all directions. They had prospered here, and their lives had been happy and full. Sitting there in the dusk with his son and his old friend, surrounded by his family, it was difficult for Madho Dev to imagine that anything or anyone could penetrate this serene refuge.

As the night grew chilly, they all went inside to the family dining room for a light supper. Sounds of laughter and scolding drifted across the courtyard from where Harbinder Singh's women were cooking their own food separately. Madho Dev saw no reason why everyone should not have eaten together in the manner followed on feast days, but Devika and Arjun wanted to keep Harbinder Singh's people away as much as possible from their own servants. Servants were the source of all gossip and intrigue, and it would be soon enough that the entire neighborhood would know they were sheltering Sikhs. They hoped the servants would not have the opportunity to gossip with their neighbors until after Mrs. Gandhi was cremated. When pictures of her body stopped coming on television and people came to know that her son had broken her skull with a long pole as her corpse burned on the funeral pyre, thus releasing her soul to be reborn, they would forget their anger.

After the children had been taken off to bed, David sat with the family over coffee and wondered whether Philippa, in the midst of the chaos that must have engulfed Delhi, had managed to see Ramakrishna Rao. The fact that Mrs. Gandhi had been gunned down in cold blood by two young soldiers horrified him. Could Arjun's view that the country was being maneuvered into a state of confusion and anarchy to justify the government's imposition of ever more dictatorial powers be correct? If so, it was time for them to act quickly.

Madho Dev ordered the hookah to be prepared and brought in. Gayatri and Devika retired, and the three men sat smoking on the veranda. The night was still. Down by the river a nightingale was singing and they could hear dogs barking in the distance. No matter what happened to him when he retired to Durga Baba's cave, thought David, part of him would always be here in this tranquil spot.

Then Arjun cupped his hand to his ear and listened, stepped into the courtyard and listened again. Working in the jungle, his ears had been fine-tuned to any discordant sound. David and Madho Dev joined him. Madho Dev frowned and shook his head. A sudden gust of wind brought a louder noise, a high-pitched roar that died out at once. David pointed to the sky, where a dull glow lit the mist which often settled along the river near Harbinder Singh's. Arjun climbed the pipal tree to get a better view and quickly climbed down.

"They must be setting fire to his house. What shall we do?"

"Are you certain?" asked Madho Dev.

As he spoke, they heard several sounds, like firecrackers popping at Diwali.

"Hear that?"

Simultaneously, there was a sharp knock at the front door. It was Norbu, the Nepalese foreman. A servant had come to say that a mob surrounded Harbinder Singh's house and was setting fire to it. Although the roof had been saturated with water, one part had caught and the fire was spreading.

"We must help them," said Madho Dev. "Even though they have sometimes been arrogant and unfriendly, it is our duty. We must!"

"We helped them last June and see what a mess it got us in," said Arjun. "Now we are keeping their women and children for them. They have an automatic weapon, rifles, and kirpans; surely that is enough to keep a mob at bay."

"Yes, and send them on here," replied Madho Dev. "Once it gets going, a mob wants to accomplish something. Come, we must get our guns and attack from the rear, station ourselves near the exit to their escape tunnel in case they are trapped. Let us not waste time."

"I will go, Father," said Arjun, swallowing his distaste for the affair. "David and Norbu will come with me, but you must stay. It is your place to be here."

"Of course I am not going to stay," blustered Madho Dev. "Do you think I'm a coward?"

"Who will guard the women and children then?" asked Arjun. "Is there anyone else we can trust?"

Madho Dev looked at his son, a long thoughtful look as if he was wondering whether to call the whole thing off. Then he nodded. "Yes, naturally I must wait here and keep watch. If it comes down to it, your mother is also a first-class shot."

He saw them off at the door, indignant that he was not able to go with them. Waiting was always worse than getting involved, infinitely worse. Women knew how to wait; he had often asked himself how they stood it. Flashlight in hand, he walked back through the house, checked the fire in the courtyard, and found the old hookah maker, Baghwan Singh, asleep on a charpoy under the pipal tree. Baghwan Singh had once been a subedar, in the Kotagarh state militia, and Madho Dev had known him all his life. Waking him gently, he asked the old man to prepare tea and bring it to his study. Then he crossed the courtyard to Devika's room, sat down on the bed, and nudged her awake. When her eyes opened, she stared at him for a long time.

"They have attacked Harbinder Singh's house?"

"Yes." Madho Dev sighed. "One of their servants came running on foot to ask for help. Norbu, Arjun, and David have gone. Come. Baghwan Singh is making tea. We three must keep watch here."

She threw a heavy shawl around her shoulders and followed her husband. In his study they found Baghwan Singh squatting on the floor, pouring out tea.

"I see the sky glowing the color of saffron, sahib. I think there must be trouble at the Sardarji's."

"I have sent Norbu, Arjun, and David-sahib to find out what is happening. We must hold the fort here. Do you think you can still shoot straight?"

Baghwan Singh smiled. "Of course, sahib, one doesn't forget that." As a young man he had often accompanied Madho Dev and his father on the shikar. He had even saved Devika's life once, and she his.

"Like old times, eh?" Madho Dev said as he sipped the strong tea.

A wave of affection for her husband swept through Devika. In thirty-eight years their marriage, though filled with love and devotion, had become a humdrum affair. The days of shikari house parties and elaborate celebrations were dim memories. In the struggle to survive, duty had come first and the magic of their lives had withered, but now she felt the old thrill rising inside her—adventure, companionship—and was grateful that he had come to her in this time of need.

Far off they could hear hoots and cries. "Bloody animals," muttered Madho Dev. "Come, both of you, let us select our weapons. They were cleaned just last month."

Unlocking a large wooden chest, he began examining its contents. "Here is the twelve-bore you used on tigers"—he handed Devika a magnificent Purdy—"and here is yours, Baghwan Singh, as good as when you last used it; and plenty of ammunition."

Outside, the wind had risen and was rattling the leaves of the pipal tree. Devika's face went abruptly pale. "I forgot to give tea to Mombai Devi before I drank," she whispered, gazing out toward the old tree.

"She's well fed," said Madho Dev. "I'm sure she won't mind this once."

"But it's been years since I put anything to my lips without first offering it to her." The vibrations of the night seemed to deteriorate, a shudder passed between her shoulders, and she walked out under the ancient tree where an oil lamp burned and prayed to Mombai Devi for forgiveness.


ARJUN, David, and Norbu had driven off in the jeep and managed to get within a few hundred yards of Harbinder Singh's house when Arjun stopped. Across the intervening fields illuminated by the flames of the burning roof, they could see a group of men preparing to scale the compound walls and another readying a battering ram to force open the front door. Occasional gunshots sounded from inside, but where was the automatic rifle? Had they exhausted their ammunition? One sweep of the deadly Russian gun, and Arjun was certain the crowd would run. They listened intently and soon heard the ominous thud of the huge log as it crashed against the massive teakwood doors protecting Harbinder Singh's compound.

"We'd better get moving," Arjun said. "That door will never hold." Climbing out of the jeep, he dropped to the ground and led the way as they crawled across the open space toward the granary. If only they had worn dhotis or kurta pajamas, he thought, no one would have paid any attention to them and they could have taken the crowd by surprise from the rear. Successfully negotiating the bare fields, they finally reached a thicket of castor bean plants, tall as trees, and the security of the granary wall. Moving slowly around it, they came to the tunnel entrance, cleverly disguised to look like a pit into which trash and sweepings were thrown.

A rather precarious spot, thought David. At any moment the mob that was on the other side could descend on them, or someone might come to piss and find them there. "Where's the entrance?" he whispered.

"Under there." Arjun pointed to the trash pit. As a high-caste Kshatriya, he could not touch it; God knows what had been deposited there. But to his amazement David squatted down and began digging with his hands. Arjun was shocked: an Englishman polluting himself with the gods knew what! Obviously his ordeal in Durga Baba's cave had deranged him.

David had uncovered a large cement slab and was struggling to raise it. Arjun bent over and helped him stand it on end. The entrance to the tunnel, a small square space just large enough for a person to squeeze through, was now open. David's heart was in his throat and he sat down, wiping his hands on the grass.

"The stupid thing about all this is it's so damn senseless," mumbled Arjun. "In my grandfather's time, these lawbreakers were stomped by elephants, had their hands chopped off. That made quite an impression, one they could remember." He cupped his ear and bent forward to the opening of the tunnel. "Someone is coming," he whispered.

A bony hand appeared on the side of the opening, and old Harbinder Singh's turbaned head and gray beard followed.

"Careful, he is wounded," said the voice of Hardev from behind. "Pull him up gently; there is a bullet in his thigh."

Arjun and David lifted the old man to the edge of the rubbish pit, where he lay panting. Hardev pulled himself out.

"Where is Harpal?" asked Arjun.

"Dead," said Hardev flatly. "That bloody Russian machine gun jammed, a piece of junk. We were counting on it. It worked earlier, but when he started firing rapidly, it jammed. What we need is a few grenades. Those bastards."

Tears streamed down Harbinder Singh's cheeks. David could see he was in great pain.

"I say, Arjun, we should take a look at that leg."

Harbinder Singh shook his head. "I have looked at it, no need for you to also look. It is Harpal I am shedding tears for. He was on the wall. They got him in the shoulder, and he fell outside the compound. They butchered him; no telling what indignities his corpse will suffer." He looked about. "We must leave this place quickly."

"We can't go back the way we came. Carrying you, we'll be spotted," said Arjun. "We'll have to detour the length of the orchard to the river, along that to the bridge, and backtrack up the road to my jeep."

"One of us could go for the jeep," suggested David, "and meet the rest at the bridge."

"I will carry my father," said Hardev. There was loud cheering from the other side of the granary. "They've broken into the house," he said. "Come on, let's go."

The conflagration had increased, the light now clearly illuminating the field over which they had crawled earlier.

David shook his head. "No chance now of getting back to the jeep that way. We'd better stick together. If we keep in the shadow of this building, we can escape into the orchard."

Hardev, a strapping elephant of a man, picked up his father, and they crept away from the granary into the thick foliage of a guava orchard. Reaching the river some ten minutes later, they sat down on the bank and rested. Over the tops of the trees, the fire cast a lurid glow.

"We should push on," said David. "If that mob starts looking about, they may discover the jeep."

"I'll go ahead and get it," said Arjun. "I'll be waiting at the bridge when you reach there. Norbu, come with me."

David slapped Arjun on the shoulder and watched as he disappeared down the river with Norbu.

"I fear this is the end for us, Captainji," said Hardev.

"Listen," David said. "Your wife and children, your mother: they are all safe. Believe me, this will pass. You will rebuild your house. I will help you."

David saw that Harbinder Singh's pajamas were soaked with blood, which now covered Hardev's chest and shoulders. He wanted to apply a tourniquet but the old man refused.

"No, no, we must not delay. Let us be on our way. The path is uneven here and we must go slowly. By the time we get to the bridge, Arjun will be waiting."


CROUCHING and running, Arjun and Norbu finally found the overgrown side road where they'd hidden the jeep. Norbu sniffed the air. He was famous for his sense of smell. Often out hunting, he had led them directly to a wild boar, tiger, or leopard. Now he sniffed the air and listened intently. Apparently satisfied that there was no one around, he stood up and they ran for the jeep. Turning on the ignition,

Arjun started up the engine and bumped back onto the road. Then shots rang out.

"Ambush," cried Norbu in Pahari. "Ambush!"

Arjun gunned the motor. Norbu turned and fired in the direction of the shots where numerous white-clad figures had unexpectedly appeared. There was a volley of shots and Arjun felt a searing pain in his back just under his shoulder blade. The jeep sputtered and back-fired as he lost control. He glanced at Norbu. His face lay slumped against his chest, the back of his head blown off. Arjun pressed the accelerator down, but the engine was flooded and the jeep lurched along the road in fits and starts. In the rearview mirror he could now see torches. The gang of men was well out of range but coming up fast. He threw the jeep out of gear, coasted, and revved up the motor to burn up the excess gas. The engine cleared, and he sped down the road to the bridge and stopped. There was no sign of the others. The pain in his chest was white hot. He honked the horn; no point in being quiet when he could plainly hear the whoops and yells of the mob coming down the road. David came out of the underbrush carrying Harbinder Singh, staggered up the embankment, and managed to roll the old man into the back seat.

"Where is Hardev?" Arjun gasped.

"Slipped on a rock," panted David, "fell on his back, twisted or broke his leg, can't tell; he's right behind me. The old man may be dead, hit his head when Hardev fell." He looked at Norbu. "What happened?" Then he noticed blood spreading across Arjun's back. "Oh, my God!"

"Ambushed," said Arjun faintly. "Get in quick, they're right behind us!"

Appearing over a rise in the road, the leader of the mob let out a whoop.

"Can't wait here much longer," choked Arjun.

David grabbed his gun, braced himself on the jeep's roll bar and fired.

The advancing men halted momentarily. Hardev came out of the bushes and struggled up the embankment. Arjun, weak and short of breath, barely able to keep his foot on the accelerator, knew it would take all his remaining strength just to shift gears. David pulled Hardev into the back, shoved Arjun toward Norbu's dead body, jumped in the driver's seat, and started off. From the sides of the road came more shots. The windshield shattered into a cobweb of cracked glass. It was collapsible, and he managed to push it flat against the hood. Heavily scented night air blew in against his face and in one sudden rush of certitude, he realized he would never leave India again. With all its horrors, stupidities, deprivations, its exalted madness, he knew he belonged here and every moment spent elsewhere had been a ghastly mistake.

"Are you all right?" he shouted. "Want me to stop?"

Arjun's face was pale, his voice barely audible above the drone of the motor. "I feel sick."

"Hold on, just hold on, I'll get you home," cried David, slowing down.

"That's better," Arjun muttered. "Sorry to grab you like that, but it helps to hold on to someone." He knew enough about guns and killing to realize he was badly hurt and might actually be going to die. As many times as he had tried to imagine what death would be like, as many times as he had contemplated it with fear and loathing, nothing he had imagined had prepared him for what he now felt, something between relief and abandon, perhaps even joy: relief to be done worrying about life, and joy that death might not be as bad as he had thought. He prayed for Philippa's safety.

"Promise me, promise you'll get Gayatri and my children out of here," he shouted hoarsely, struggling for breath.

"You have my word," said David. "But you will also be going. We'll get you fixed up in no time."

"I think not." Arjun smiled wanly. "Funny, isn't it, I who most wanted to leave? Yes, I'm going to leave, but not how I imagined. As Father says, if you can understand the accidents in your life, you will see the real plan; that is what Durga Baba says too. I want to be reborn in the forest."

"Where?" asked David, not understanding.

"In the forest, with the tigers."

David found his voice catching in his throat. As they drew closer to Madho Dev's and swung into the drive, the enormity of what was about to happen overwhelmed him. At the front door Madho Dev and Devika stood silhouetted in the light from within, holding their weapons. Above them on the roof stood Baghwan Singh and the cook, Darshan. Sensing disaster, Devika dropped her gun and ran screaming toward the jeep. Madho Dev followed.

"See if you can get Norbu out," said David quickly. "He's dead and Arjun is hurt, badly hurt but—"

Devika's wailing stopped and she stood wide-eyed, biting the knuckles of her hand, as David and Madho Dev lifted Norbu's body out of the jeep and carried it inside. Hardev, his face wracked with pain, stood up on one leg next to his father and managed to hand him into the arms of two servants. Devika climbed into the jeep and spoke softly to Arjun, cradling him in her arms.

"Go quickly," Madho Dev commanded her. "Awaken Gayatri, Manoj, and Hardev's wife. Do not waken the others or we'll have a scene on our hands. Have them bring mattresses and clean sheets into the dining room. Where is Harpal?"

"Harpal is dead," said David. "Harbinder Singh was also wounded but made it through the tunnel with Hardev. Hardev was carrying him to the jeep but slipped and hurt his leg. Then we were ambushed."

Devika gently passed Arjun into her husband's arms. It had been years since she had held him like this, her baby boy, her firstborn.

"Be careful, Dev, be very careful. Arjun, can you hear me? Can we move you?"

Arjun's eyes opened wide. "Of course, why not?" He smiled and closed them again.

"He has lost much blood," said Madho Dev. "Quickly, we must get him inside. Go and get the other women, David will help me. And wake Ravi."

Madho Dev and David made a chair of their arms and carried Arjun into the dining room where Hardev, limping around on one leg, was helping out. He stroked his long black beard and gazed at Arjun. His father had been laid out nearby. Hardev didn't know whether he was dead or alive, but he was an old man and to die in battle was glorious. But Arjun! . . . He rolled his eyes, closed them, and opened them again. His thick black lashes were wet with tears, his massive body tense with the desire for revenge, to kill whoever had shot Arjun. Thinking of what would happen if Arjun died, he closed his eyes again. What would he do? How could he bear the guilt he would feel for the rest of his life, the terrible debt he would owe Madho Dev?

"Give me a gun," he said, "your best. You've got a semiautomatic, yes?"

Madho Dev, crouching on the floor beside Arjun, looked up.

"I'll go out along the road somewhere; I'll find cover and hold them off."

"You mean they're coming this way?" said Madho Dev.

"They know your jeep. They may very well come. If they don't, I shall go after them."

"He's right," said David, "and you and I should station ourselves on the roof in case they come across the fields. Whoever they are, they're damned tricky; ambushed us very neatly. Someone intelligent is leading them."

"Congress-I youth," said Hardev, "and R.S.S. They are leading; the others are idiots."

"They wouldn't dare attack this house," said Madho Dev.

"Are you such a friend of the Congress Party then?" said Hardev grimly. "If I can delay them till near dawn, they will run away."

"I am not letting you go out there alone with one leg," declared Madho Dev. "You are as much a son to me as Arjun. Your brother is already dead; we can't lose you both. If they come, they will come to the front door. David and my wife will cover me from the roof, Darshan and Baghwan Singh will protect the back of the house. You will position yourself in the small building in front that houses the generator and pump. Lock yourself in that building; there's a small window facing the house. If they start anything, you'll be behind them. If one shot is fired, kill as many as you can."

Devika returned with Harbinder Singh's wife and the two daughters-in-law. Harpal's wife was moaning and pulling out her hair. Then Gayatri and Manoj came carrying mattresses and sheets, and the other children trailed in, sleepy-eyed. Seeing Arjun, Gayatri burst into tears, ran to him, and helped Manoj and Devika lift him onto a mattress.

"They were awake," said Gayatri, looking helplessly at her other children.

"Can either of you shoot?" Madho Dev asked the wives of Harpal and Hardev. They shook their heads.

"I can shoot," said old Harbinder Singh's wife, leaning over her husband.

Usha, Harpal's mother-in-law, appeared in the doorway. "I cannot shoot but once I was a nurse; let me help."

"You two go back with your children," Madho Dev commanded the wives of Harpal and Hardev, "and take ours with you. Uma," he said to his eldest granddaughter, "you help them. Lock yourselves in and keep quiet."

Usha had been examining Arjun and Harbinder Singh. "I need hot water, Dettol, and cotton cloths. Do you have any antibiotics?"

Devika ran to get the boxful of medicines she kept in her room.

"Manoj"—Madho Dev addressed his eldest grandson—"you stay here with your father and Harbinder Singh." He handed him a pistol. "If any strangers come, shoot them."

Wide-eyed, Manoj looked from his father to Madho Dev and back. His whole world had suddenly fallen apart.

"I think we had better take up our posts," said David. "Give Harbinder Singh's wife a gun. She says she can shoot, let her sit outside the women's quarters and keep watch."

"Let me be with my husband," declared the old woman.

"Yes, of course, you must stay here," said Madho Dev. "You and the boy can help Usha. You should apply a tourniquet immediately above Harbinder Singh's wound. Also look at his head; when Hardev fell down he said his father got a nasty hit."

Madho Dev knelt down with Devika beside Arjun and took his hand. "Can you hear me, son?" he whispered. "If you can hear me, squeeze my hand." Feeling Arjun's grip tighten, he continued. "I must go now and take up my post in case those fellows come here. I am just now sending David's servant to Kotagarh to get the ambulance. You must go to the hospital. Lie perfectly still and you will be all right. We love you and nothing is going to happen. You have Gayatri and Manoj right here beside you." Gayatri stroked her husband's forehead. He opened his eyes and smiled. "Don't talk," said Madho Dev as Arjun's lips parted. "We will all be here if you need us."

Nodding to Usha, he got up and left the room with Devika and David. Hardev hobbled to the pump house and locked himself in. Ravi appeared and Madho Dev scribbled a note for him to deliver to Dr. Kapoor.

"You will find a cycle at the kitchen door. Go quickly, it is a matter of life and death. Here is a map with directions to the doctor's house and the hospital."

Never having seen a map before, Ravi wondered how he would follow it. The idea of traveling alone at night in a strange part of the world frightened him. But after the doctor had been found, perhaps he would visit Baga, a young girl he had met the week before on his day off. At his age, to attract a young maiden was most unusual. Perhaps she was a goddess in disguise and would bring him good luck? He would ask her to pick a lottery number. But first he must find the doctor. Otherwise, if Arjun-sahib died, they would blame him. Why did the sahibs always arrange things so if they did not work out, it was your fault?

Lying on his mattress, Arjun tried to concentrate his will, accept his pain, and relax as much as possible, but the room went in and out of focus and he felt his life force ebbing. Manoj was sitting beside him, and Gayatri was stroking his forehead with a cool damp cloth. Obviously Madho Dev thought he was going to die or Manoj would not be there. According to the Shastras, a proper death could not be had without a son to see you off. The boy's hand was warm and made it easier to bear the pain. How strange existence was! Having done many dangerous things, dealt with tigers in the jungle, climbed mountains, and taken ridiculous chances with his motorcycle, never had he been injured. Now a bullet fired from the barrel of a country-made weapon from a good distance had connected with a moving object, himself. Who were the gods that controlled such things? Had he angered them by being unfaithful to Gayatri? If he had been slightly to the left or right the bullet would have gone past him, but it hadn't. The idea that one's luck was the result of action in past lives was too easy; he could not accept it. As he lay pondering this question, he realized his attempts to accept the pain in his chest were not working. He tried to form the word for opium, ajim, squeezed his son's hand, and managed to whisper in the boy's ear. From a clinical point of view he was certain his lung had been pierced and he was bleeding internally. No tourniquet or antibiotic could heal that. He watched as Manoj understood and spoke to Usha, who produced a small ball of the stuff from the medicine chest. The problem then was to swallow it. Gayatri propped him up. The ball of ajim was in his mouth, a glass of water at his lips. He let his mouth fill with water and swallowed, almost gagging in the process. Gayatri lowered him back onto the pillow and Manoj kissed his cheek. Tears filled his eyes, not of sadness but joy. He had been hard on Manoj as was the custom with eldest sons. The full weight of his fatherly ambitions, his frustrations, even his failures, had always fallen on Manoj. Often he felt the two of them were caught, like two bulls, in a senseless deadlock that would never end. At times he thought Manoj hated him or thought him a fool. He waited for the opium to deaden the pain but nothing happened. In fact, it was getting worse. Usha had finished dressing Harbinder Singh's wounds and wanted to have a look at him. When she saw how the blood had caked and hardened on his shirt, she frowned and asked if the opium was working. He wished he had the strength to grab the pistol from Manoj's hand and shoot himself. But what a terrible memory for his son to carry with him for the rest of his life. No, he would have to be brave, as fathers are supposed to be, and sweat it out.

The room where they had eaten so many happy family dinners was closing in on him; he felt oppressed and longed to be lying in the courtyard as he often did, under the open sky, letting his soul float out to the stars at the edge of space and time. If he died in this room, he might turn into a bhut, a ghost. He squeezed Gayatri's hand and managed to whisper that he wished to be taken near the fire.

"Pull mattress out door," he murmured. "Want to see stars."

Together, Gayatri and Manoj pulled him out into the courtyard. Seeing the fire eased the pain: something stable, something to rely on. The paving stones near the fire pit were warm. Manoj brought blankets and wrapped them around him. The boy's face was pinched and serious. Arjun hated himself for getting shot, for putting them through such a harrowing experience. Why hadn't he been killed instantly?

"That's better," he whispered.

"Better?" said Manoj.

"Yes."


AT THE front of the house, Madho Dev paced back and forth, calling to Devika and David, who were on the roof and could see some distance down the road. His idea was that he would stand at the door and harangue the crowd while Devika and David, hidden behind the crown of the roof, would cover him from above. Hardev was in the pump house, Baghwan Singh and Darshan were on the flanks, so the mob would be trapped in a deadly crossfire. He looked at the sky, then his watch. Three full hours before the first light of dawn. He knew the rioters could not risk the morning light, for if their identities were known, there would be reprisals against them. He hoped the majority of them were looting Harbinder Singh's house, digging under foundations, hoping to find gold. Smiling inwardly, Madho Dev thought that if Harbinder Singh had gold buried anywhere, it was most likely under the new latrine he'd constructed for his workers' use. No one would want to dig under a latrine.

On the roof, Devika, her Purdy beside her, lay flat on the gently sloping tiles listening to the night sounds, waiting for some unusual break in their rhythm that would signal someone's approach. She longed to be down in the courtyard with Arjun, whom she could see lying by the fire with Manoj at his side. Arjun, her crazy boy. Only yesterday it seemed she was holding him in her arms, nursing him. Having only one son was almost worse than none at all. One became protective, indulgent, with the result that the child became oversensitive and hot-tempered. In that way, Arjun was very much like her own father, whose fits of temper had been legendary; almost caused the British to reduce their state's salute. She thought of all the times she'd worried over Arjun and nothing had happened, how she'd fretted about his going abroad. Now this awful, senseless thing and all because her stubborn husband had insisted on helping these Sikhs. Or was it because she had forgotten about Mombai Devi when she had taken tea? Glancing toward the shrine of the goddess, she prayed the Devi would be able to forgive one lapse and save her son. Silently she repeated a mantra to awaken the powers of protection that Mombai Devi could bestow if she desired. "O Devi, I have worshiped and served you all these years," she whispered. "Now in this time of need please see what is happening to my only son, look after him, and protect us from these lunatics who are roaming around the countryside."

At that moment, far down the road, she saw the glow of torches. From the halo of light moving under the huge old trees, she would have thought, if she'd not known better, that a wedding party was approaching. She signaled to David at the other end of the roof, who yelled down to Madho Dev that they were coming.

"Tell Baghwan Singh and Darshan to keep a special watch at the rear of the house," he called back. "They may try to surround us."

Now Devika began to hear sounds of a drum: *rum a tum a tum, rum a tum tum*. It was the rhythm to which the dancing girls of old escorted the gods in the temples while ecstatic devotees rolled in the dust . . . and the rhythm that accompanied the dead to the cremation ground. She flattened herself against the tiles and released the safety catch on her rifle.

Madho Dev went inside. He intended to apply kohl around his eyes, wax his black-dyed mustache, and put on one of his grandfather's turbans, not a state turban with plumes and jewels but one of the everyday turbans printed with the pattern once used by the state guard; that would be quite enough. He would greet them in his beige achkan, holding his gun. He ran to his room, changed, applied makeup, tweaked his mustache, and wound a turban cloth around his head with a carelessness befitting a raja's son. Surveying himself in the mirror, he practiced some haughty, angry looks and hoped David wouldn't laugh when he saw him. He could hear the whoops and slogans of the crowd as it turned in at the drive, the same jargon chanted by the hired mourners parading in front of the television cameras at Teen Murti house in Delhi. All this staginess, he thought, like a Moghul court. How little times had changed, how gullible and weak-minded the masses were. What a grim harvest they were about to reap from this crop of neglected souls!

The mob poured into the yard. The leaders were husky young men who looked to David like off-duty policemen. It was they who were exhorting the rabble with slogans, they who were armed with guns. Behind them were some local thakurs, former noncommissioned officers in the army. Many wore the white hat of the Congress Party. Pouring into the large open area in front of the house, they came to an

abrupt halt some forty paces from the big door. It was obvious some of
them knew exactly who Madho Dev was, and those in front displayed
a certain reticence about going farther. But as the crowd jammed into
the yard, the pressure from behind mounted. David was amazed at
how young most of them looked: only teenagers.

Finally one of the leaders stepped forward. "Madho Dev Singh," he
yelled, "we want to talk to you. We have nothing against you personally, but we know you are hiding that traitor, Harbinder Singh, and
his family. You must give up these people or face the consequences of
our wrath."

It was a very dramatic presentation, and the mob cheered. Just
inside the door, Madho Dev waited, knowing they did not expect him
to respond immediately. Harbinder Singh's wife stood behind in the
hallway, covering him with her gun. Another spokesman now reit-
erated the ultimatum and elaborated on it, asking what Harbinder
Singh and his family had ever done for Kotagarh that they should be
spared the punishment due to all traitorous Sikhs. Stones thrown by
the impatient mob now began to bounce off the front door.

Madho Dev would have liked to prolong the preliminaries, playing
for time and the coming of daybreak, but the crowd, most of them
drunk, might get out of hand. He threw open the front door dramatically and strode onto the raised threshold. Seeing him, some of the
leaders shrank back. Some touched their foreheads, and a few raised
their hands prayerfully.

"Who has ordered you to come here?" Madho Dev thundered. "I
want to know who has given you permission to go about destroying
other people's property, eh? You chootiyas! Don't you know that
tomorrow or the next day you are going to be brought to justice? Half
of you are known to me. I don't want to have to give evidence against
you."

"The police are on our side. Who will put us in jail?" shouted a
young man, waving a torch.

"Where are they? I do not see a single constable here among you,"
retorted Madho Dev.

"Ha, that proves they are with us," said an angry-looking man who
spat into the dust. "Otherwise they would be here."

The insolence of the remark caught Madho Dev off guard. He
wasn't used to being addressed in such a tone. "In India," he shouted,
"every citizen is a policeman and every policeman is a citizen. All
must obey the laws of the land. The policeman may be looking the
other way now, but when the Inspector comes he will swear he saw
you doing these bad things."

A feeling of uncertainty rippled through the crowd.

"Don't listen to him," exhorted one of the leaders. "Indira Gandhi is a martyr."

"Indira Gandhi martyr!" the crowd yelled back. "Indira Gandhi ki jai!"

"What has Indira Gandhi got to do with this?" demanded Madho Dev over the noise.

"They have killed her," shouted the leaders. "The Sikhs have killed her."

"You have killed her," boomed Madho Dev. "She was like your mother. You, with your lazy, disobedient, and jealous ways, have killed her. You and millions of other greedy good-for-nothings, always wanting things from her; like beggars you wore her down. You have seen on the television how old she looked. Yes, from running here and there trying to solve your problems. Now because her assassins happened to be ignorant young Sikhs, you are using that as an excuse to again satisfy your greed. Your jealous and disobedient natures can think only of taking advantage of people's weaknesses: let us burn his shop and carry off his stock of goods; let us burn his house and steal whatever is inside it. That is arson, that is robbery; they are serious crimes punishable with stiff penalties. Now go home. The night is over. See? The dawn is coming. You have done enough. You have already killed one of Harbinder Singh's sons, and my own son is gravely wounded. Go!"

"Give us Harbinder Singh's other son and we'll go," said a tall man, stepping forward with a gun.

Madho Dev released the safety catch of his rifle and raised it slightly. "You bhen chot, you sisterfucker, you dare point a gun at me, I will shoot you."

The man was a troublesome squatter who kept three or four women on land near the edge of the jungle. Men will use any excuse to settle old scores, thought Madho Dev; the man was probably going to shoot him. He lifted his rifle and pulled the trigger. The man fell to the ground.

"Murderer, you have killed him!" cried an old man.

"In self-defense, sir," shouted Madho Dev. "Again I am reminding you of the laws. You yourselves have voted for the people who have made these laws, they are your laws and you must obey them. What kind of monkeys are you that you should behave like this? Let anyone else point a gun at me and the same will happen to him. Now go home to your wives and children."

"Murderer, assassin, just like all murderous princes," the leaders screamed, and soon they were all jumping up and down yelling, "Kill him! Kill him!"

A shot rang out. It was David on the roof. He had picked off a young man who had stealthily climbed an old mango tree and from this concealed vantage point had been about to shoot Madho Dev. People began shaking their fists and raising sticks; their mood was ugly and mindless.

Up until then, Madho Dev had rather enjoyed the whole scene. The people were very dramatic, exaggerating everything like bad Shakespearean actors he had once seen perform in Delhi. Then another shot exploded, and from the corner of his eye he saw David fall backward, heard him slide down the roof toward the courtyard.

He surveyed the crowd grimly and for the first time in his life saw other Indians as the enemy. It had nothing to do with religion or community, for there were representatives of many castes and clans there. No, it was more profound than that: he was fed up with their stubbornness, their greed, their damaged brains; a terrible legacy bequeathed by the policies of his own ancestors, nevertheless a hydra-headed monster that would soon destroy them all. Not enough that they have shot my only son, he muttered to himself, now David. The realization pushed him past reason. He had arranged with everyone that if he threw his turban to the ground, they should start firing into the air to disperse the crowd, but should only shoot at those who had guns. Holding his rifle with one hand, he threw his turban dramatically in the dust and began firing just over the heads of the mob.

In the pump house, it took all the restraint Hardev could muster to keep his gun sighted above the crowd. He strained his vision, searching for someone with a gun. He wanted to shoot at least three of them: one for Harpal, one for his father, and one for Arjun.

From her perch on the roof, Devika had watched helplessly as David slid backward down the tiles and fell onto the paving stones of the courtyard below. When her husband threw his turban in the dust, she started firing over the heads of the people as he had directed. Those at the rear began to break and run but seeing no one fall, they hesitated. Staring through her scope, Devika took careful aim and shot one of them. It was the first time she'd ever raised a gun to a human being, but she was glad she'd done it. Her only son lay dying below. She had always had a horror of outliving him and now it was happening. She was a Rajput princess; these people were the mercenaries of Congress Party politicians who had broken promise after promise and destroyed her family's way of life. Pitting one community against another, the Congress had always used mobs to get its way, expropriating the wealth of others, secreting it in foreign bank accounts. To her this mob, not Pakistan or China, was the real enemy. She stared through the scope of her rifle, squeezed the trigger, reloaded, and fired again and again. The crowd began to disperse. Nothing had happened until a few of them had been hit. She hoped they wouldn't die but didn't really care; why should her beautiful son die and none of these animals? The first pink light of dawn lit up the eastern sky, the dawn before the dawn. She glanced down in the courtyard, where Harpal's mother-in-law had put David on a mattress near Arjun. Then she looked over at Mombai Devi and gave thanks; it could have been much worse. If the mob had stormed the house at the very beginning, they could have killed Madho Dev and broken in. Yes, easily. It had been Madho Dev's bravery in lecturing them like bad children that had thrown them off. Now she must climb down from the roof and go to her son. Where was that idiot Ravi with the doctor?

WHEN David was hit, he laughed, then doubled up and rolled down off the roof. Laughing was the last thing he remembered, and when he regained consciousness and found himself lying next to Arjun, he tried to recall what he'd been laughing about. But a stabbing pain in his stomach as he came to told him, whatever had happened, it was no laughing matter now. He'd been on the roof and shot a man in a tree. Then he thought he'd seen another man raise a gun, but before he could fire—ah, that was it, at that moment he had laughed. Why? Now he was lying out in the courtyard staring up at the sky and Usha was giving him an injection. Then Madho Dev was beside him, looking very worried.

"We're waiting for your Ravi to bring Dr. Kapoor and the ambulance," he said. David's eyebrows furrowed skeptically. "Yes, we have an ambulance in Kotagarh, rather an antique, I'm afraid, but it runs. My father gave it to the town in '38: Rolls-Royce engine." Madho Dev seemed oddly at a loss for words. He squatted on his haunches between Arjun and David and stirred up the fire.

Hardev limped over, supported by a makeshift crutch. "You got that bloody bastard in the tree who would have shot Rajaji, and Devikaji got the one who shot you. I saw her, first-class shot."

They all stared at Devika, who turned away in embarrassment and extended her hand to Gayatri and Hardev's wife, who had just come out of the house. A moaning sound issued from the dining room. It was Harbinder Singh's wife. Hardev hurried to her side.

"He is dying," Usha said quietly. "He says he saw his mother sitting in the corner of the room." It was well known to them all that the goddess often appeared to a person just before the soul got ready to leave the body and usually took the form of one's mother, wife, or daughter.

Devika went into the dining room, knelt down beside Harbinder Singh, took his arm, and searched for the pulse. His jaw was slack, he was breathing heavily, but there was a smile on his lips. Hardev lay down on the floor beside his father, who held his son's hand tightly, whispered in his ear, and then was gone. The women began wailing and praying. Hardev struggled up on his good leg and hobbled back into the courtyard.

"Cuttam—finished," he said, shaking his head. "His injury did not kill him, it was the shock."

"Often the soul is shocked out of the body," said Madho Dev.

"No doubt that is what happened," said Devika, returning to Arjun's side. His breath was coming in fitful, rasping gulps.

Madho Dev paced back and forth across the courtyard, cursing Ravi and the phone, which was still out of order. Unless the ambulance came soon, it would be too late. A mynah bird began singing cheerfully in the pipal tree.

"I'm going to drive the jeep in now!" he announced. "I can't sit around watching them—"

"You'll do no such thing," said Devika. "You'd run into that mob going back to town, then what? Is it not enough that I am losing a son? Do you want to make me a widow?"

"I will go," said Hardev. "Where is my servant?"

"In the kitchen with the cook."

"Buta Singh," roared Hardev. The servant appeared on the run, his mouth full of food.

"Come," said Hardev. "You and I are taking the jeep. We are going to hospital to find doctor and ambulance."

"Your leg," protested Devika. "You're in no condition—"

"It is the very least I can do," said Hardev. "We owe you a great debt. Don't worry, I will find that doctor."

"No, no," said his mother, who had come out into the courtyard. "You are all I have left, the only grown man in the family; you cannot go."

"She is right," said Devika, well imagining the responsibilities that would fall on them if all Harbinder Singh's women and children were left without a man to look after them.

"Of course he cannot go," agreed Madho Dev. "You must stay with your mother, Hardev. Thank you for offering, but it would be best for you to keep out of sight. Darshan can drive. I will send him with Baghwan Singh to see what is happening. I'm afraid Ravi doesn't know the town well." Madho Dev called Darshan and old Baghwan Singh and told them to hurry.

The sun was just rising red over the hills to the east of the river. Before the heat of the day declared itself, they dragged the mattresses on which Arjun and David were lying into Madho Dev's study. Usha, the former nurse, racked her brain trying to think how she could keep the two men alive until the doctor came. She was not a surgeon, had never done any cutting. There were pieces of metal inside them festering, muscle and tissue to be sewn up. She knew both men needed surgery soon.

Madho Dev paced the veranda outside his study. Why had he not finished repairing the truck? The jeep was too small to carry them in. The sun was just rising and, although it was November, it would soon be hot. Why couldn't he hitch the tractor to one of the flatbed carts they used to carry fodder and take them to town on a bed of soft hay? Then he remembered that he had loaned the tractor to Harpal and it had probably been destroyed by the mob. And the Ambassador was at Kapoor's place. Sinister coincidences. But what about hitching two of his bullocks to the same cart? It would be slow going, but at least they would get there. He called to Hardev, who was sitting with his dead father in the dining room, and ran to the farmyard.

ON THEIR way to town, Baghwan Singh and Darshan encountered remnants of the mob walking alongside the road, who shouted but did not try to stop them. Kotagarh itself was strangely quiet after a night of rioting. Paramilitary troops patrolled the streets in front of burned-out shops and godowns. They picked their way between fallen timbers, bricks, and other wreckage. Driving straight to the hospital, they were informed that during the disturbances the ambulance, as it went out to pick up victims, had been set afire and destroyed. Nevertheless, many wounded had been brought in, and Dr. Kapoor had worked through the night saving many lives. He was now asleep. Baghwan Singh explained the situation at the farm and asked that Dr. Kapoor be awakened. Everyone in Kotagarh knew Arjun, and the hospital clerk called the head nurse, a tough corpulent woman not known for her sympathetic nature.

Nurse Jacob, as she was called, informed them the doctor had operated all night, was finally asleep, and she was not going to wake him up. A man called Ravi had come with a note and she had told him the same thing. Yes, the doctor was right there in the hospital but how could he go out to Madho Dev's farm and operate when he had had no sleep? And there were no facilities there. Why didn't they find a truck, load Arjunji and the English sahib in the back, and bring them into town? That would be best. By the time they returned, Doctor-sahib would be rested and able to operate.

The two servants agreed. Who were they to question the pronouncements of the head nurse, an educated woman? Retreating to the jeep, they drove to a tea shop in the center of town, where they discovered Ravi eating a large breakfast of potato curry, chapattis, and fresh curd. Baghwan Singh cursed him. Why had he not returned at once to tell them the ambulance had been burned and Dr. Kapoor could not come? Why, when Arjunji and his own sahib lay dying, was he sitting there filling his stomach?

Shocked to hear about the captain-sahib, Ravi told them he had almost been waylaid by robbers and had to hide in a ditch for some time fearing for his life. The raja-sahib himself should have come. He was a big man; they would have listened to him and awakened the doctor.

"Raja-sahibji had to stay and protect the women and children in case the mob returned," said Baghwan Singh. "Rani-sahibji's orders. We must find a truck quickly to carry the sahibs to the hospital. There is a shopkeeper, Ramchand, raja-sahibji buys his groceries from him. Let us go and borrow his truck."

"First let us put something in our own stomachs," said Darshan. "We were up on that roof all night, no telling when we will get a meal."

Loyal to Madho Dev, Baghwan Singh protested but to no avail. Darshan was already ordering full breakfasts for them both. Over their meal, Ravi boasted about his exploits with the girl, Baga.

"She cannot get enough of me." He grinned. "She is not interested in me, only my prick. I doubt she even knows what I look like, but at my age who can quibble with details?"

"At your age a man begins to have fantasies," scoffed Darshan, a matter-of-fact young man who had come down from the hills only six months before. His goal in life was to get to Delhi, and he had accepted Madho Dev's offer because from Kotagarh he might easily escape to the capital. In the hills he had been earning four hundred rupees a month; at Madho Dev's he was being paid six hundred, but in Delhi a cook who could make Western as well as Hindustani dishes could command as much as fifteen hundred, a vast sum, enough to get married if he could find the right hard-working girl. In Delhi he would be able to live the modern life; no one would care about his caste or that he was an unpolished hill boy, and if he could find a good foreign family to cook for, he would be an eligible bachelor. The worst problem at Kotagarh was the lack of women.

"Well," said Baghwan Singh, noisily sipping the last of his tea, "we must hurry before the bhania goes to his store."

They paid their bill and put Ravi's bicycle in the back of the jeep.

"Tell me, Raviji," said Darshan with a sly doglike look, "where does this wonderful girl you were telling us about live? Will you show me?"

"We must not waste time," said Baghwan Singh sternly. "Raja-sahibji's son is badly hurt, and Ravi's sahib too. They are waiting for us."

"I am driving," growled Darshan. "Just let us drive past the house of this Baga. I am not convinced she truly exists." The fact that Arjun and David could be dying did not concern him in the least. Sahibs were replaceable objects. He had faced death from the mob last night himself and deserved a little relaxation. Ignoring Baghwan Singh, he followed Ravi's directions through the back streets of Kotagarh and came to a colony of tin and straw hovels.

"She lives in there, third on the left," said Ravi grudgingly.

"I'll be right back," said Darshan, jumping out of the jeep.

In tears, Baghwan Singh shouted after him, but Darshan wouldn't listen and neither he nor Ravi could drive. About half an hour later, just as the sun was rising, Darshan returned, zipping up his pants.

"What you have said is true, Raviji." He grinned. "The best cock-sucker I ever met. Thank you for letting me in on your secret. Next time we will go together, eh?"

They drove to Ramchand's house, but he had just left for his shop on the other side of town. Arriving there a short time later, they explained the situation and asked to borrow the truck. Ramchand told them that just then his son was changing the oil, but when he was finished they were welcome to borrow it. But Ramchand's son disliked Arjun, who had always lorded it over him, and took his time. Finally, after a long wait and threats by Baghwan Singh that the raja-sahib might take his business elsewhere, the son handed over the keys, along with an envelope from his father.

"The bill," he said sullenly. "After all, it is the first of the month."

\* \* \*

IN THE cool gloom of Madho Dev's study, his chest packed with the last of the ice, David was certain he was dying. Contemplating what would surely be a strange ending, he began to think about what he would be leaving behind. The fact that he was surrounded by Gayatri and his grandchildren heightened his guilt about Edward and Belinda: the unfinished business of his life. When Edward was a boy, they had been together constantly—riding, hunting, outings in London, summers at Antibes . . . those wonderful summers. Then Philippa had insisted Edward go to Eton, where all the men on the English side of her family had gone. Edward hadn't wanted to go, and David, who had suffered bitterly at public school after being sent "home" from India, hadn't wanted to send him. But Eton it had been, and after his first year there, you couldn't get near him. The boy closed up, refused to communicate his feelings, became a fop and finally an enemy. How had this happened? The mystery haunted him. He longed now to apologize for everything he hadn't done. But what would he say?

And Belinda—he smiled when he thought of her. Philippa had taken her in charge at an early age: the same sort of discipline she used with her Thoroughbreds. He was enchanted with the result, as one is enchanted with a great work of art. Yet like any masterpiece, a hallowed space seemed to surround her, sacrosanct, to which no one was admitted, least of all him. Why? Perhaps these questions would soon be answered in another world.

Views of his grandchildren as they grew up, married, and grew old flickered before him. The years swept by. He saw them on their deathbeds with their children and their children's children standing by. Would any of them remember him, he wondered? What was the point? He began to repeat AUM and MA silently inside his head. Then he was aware of Arjun's gaze resting on him. "Don't think I'm going to make it," David whispered.

"Your body may not, but what about your inner one?"

"You really believe that?"

Arjun nodded. "I think we will soon know all."

David smiled wanly and reached for Arjun's hand. "My dogs," he whispered. He saw them clearly, lying in front of the library fire, their heads between their paws. "What will happen to them?"

"Philippa will take care of them." It was Madho Dev.

Ah, but of course, Philippa. The thought calmed him. How could he have forgotten? She'd escaped just in time, hadn't she? Hadn't expected the real India, a neglected open wound, too much for her. He chuckled. Ah, well, at least she'd had Arjun. He turned and watched Arjun's profile silhouetted against the dazzling light streaming through a window. Gazing at the brightness, the image of the hairy fat woman materialized before him. She was naked, smiling and dancing in the light. Through half-closed eyes he lay watching her as she slowly changed into a voluptuous maiden with multiple arms, legs, and heads all nodding and waving at him. Her lips moved as he tried to form her name. Had she come to save him?

Then Usha was changing his ice pack. The vision dissolved and pain returned. Damn woman was a bungler. He winced. "You are in pain?" she asked. What did the idiot think? "You want morphine?" He didn't want morphine, he wanted opium.

Arjun stirred. Dreams and reality faded into each other. Cuttam, I am finished, he thought to himself, and came back to Gayatri sitting beside him. Gayatri, his child bride whom he had lived with forever and hardly knew; and there was his mother, her cheeks wet with tears. He wanted to tell her not to cry, that he was strong and would come back to her from the spirit world. But when he tried to speak he only heard a cawing, gurgling noise, like a crow. Was he turning into a crow? His mind drifted. In Australia, everything would be green, there would be hundreds of acres of rolling green land, fine horses, plenty of water, few people. In the forest, he had learned that man was the enemy, not nature. In man's world there was no time to think, no space in which to realize one was a separate being with feelings of one's own. That had been Philippa's gift. She had called it "the feeling of being an individual." Thinking of the forest, he saw Durga Baba, remembered something he had to say to his son Manoj, and managed to whisper that he would like to be cremated at the pool near the forest resthouse. The poor boy burst into tears and buried his head in Gayatri's lap.

"What did you say to him?" asked Madho Dev, putting his ear to Arjun's lips.

Arjun repeated what he had said.

Madho Dev stroked his son's forehead. "I've hitched the oxen to the hay cart. In a few minutes we are going to load you both and start for town. Just now we are putting on a tarp for shade."

Beneath his calm exterior, Madho Dev was cursing Baghwan Singh and Darshan. Just then, he heard the sound of a distant motor. They all listened. The sound grew louder. Gun in hand, he went to the front door and opened it cautiously. It was Ramchand's old Tata lorry, the cabin painted bright yellow with scenes from the life of Lord Krishna, and above all the gilded goddess Lakshmi, showers of pink flowers falling from the heavens around her. Inside, behind the tinsel windshield decorations, he recognized the faces of Darshan, Baghwan Singh, and Ravi.

Baghwan Singh explained what had happened: how the doctor-sahib had operated all night and was asleep, how the ambulance had been burned up with several people inside it, how they had gone to Ramchand, who'd loaned them the truck, but only after his son had purposely delayed them a full hour changing oil and adjusting spark plugs. Relating their woes, the old man burst into tears. Ravi, who had rushed into the study to see David, returned crying. What would he do so far from home if anything happened to his sahib? Madho Dev set him to work cleaning the inside of the truck and bedding it down with hay. Then he ordered Baghwan Singh and Darshan to assist in bringing David and Arjun to the front door and asked Manoj to fan them to keep away the flies.

Gayatri and Devika got ready to go to the hospital. In Indian hospitals, especially provincial ones, members of the family were expected to look after the patients. The two women hurried to gather the necessary things. Madho Dev looked down at Arjun and David. A miracle was needed to save them. He believed in miracles—the very stuff of existence, but his faith was running thin.

After a last word with Hardev, who stood at the door with his rifle, they lifted Arjun and David on their mattresses into the truck. Gayatri and the children, Devika, Usha, and Madho Dev climbed in behind them, and with Darshan driving and Baghwan Singh beside him with his gun next to Ravi, they set off for Kotagarh.

The dust kicked up behind them and swirled in around the two injured men. Devika and Gayatri spread their saris over them. Soon they were on the tarred road, which proved worse, however, as it was filled with potholes and the truck seemed to have no springs. Madho Dev shouted at Darshan to slow down, but the obstinate fellow wouldn't listen. Just past the old guesthouse, where he had spent the first nights of his marriage with Devika and where Kamala had conceived Gayatri, there was a jolting bump and the truck shuddered to a stop.

"Fool." Madho Dev cursed under his breath. "Fool!" He jumped out to see what had happened. By the side of the road a pile of bleached bones marked the spot where starving cattle had died in last year's drought.

"Blowout, sahib," Darshan said, assuming a downcast look. "What bad luck."

"We'll have to jack it up and change the tire," said Madho Dev.

Positive now that fate was against them, he went grimly to work assembling various parts of the jack stashed behind the driver's seat. The jack, which was supposed to fit under the axle of the truck, was old and kept slipping. Ravi found an abandoned pile of bricks under an old neem tree, and he and Baghwan Singh ran back and forth between the truck and the tree, stacking them under the axle while Darshan worked the jack. As Madho Dev watched, he remembered the bricks had belonged to a hermit who had built a roadside shrine under the tree. The same hermit had attended the coming-home ceremonies after his wedding to Devika. This neem tree was very old. How many generations of his family had it shaded, he wondered, and noticed that in its roots there was still a small shrine to the goddess Kali. Devika called. He ran to the back of the truck. Arjun was wild-eyed.

"I can't, I can't," he muttered, doubled up, and began vomiting.

Tearless now, Devika looked toward the neem tree and thought of Mombai Devi. Everything became clear; the goddess did not want any of them to leave India and was killing Arjun and David to prevent it.

David had come out of his stupor and held Arjun's hand. The five children looked on terrified. The stalled truck had attracted a ragtag collection of country folk. Crazed with anger and sorrow, shaking his fists at the sky, Madho Dev jumped down and ran to the front of the truck again. His audience watched apathetically as he struggled to wrench loose the tight bolts of the wheel and lift it off. The spare was already in place and he was tightening the bolts when he heard Devika cry out again. Leaving Darshan to finish, he rushed to the back of the truck. The ragged chorus of bystanders followed, gawking, and scratching their bodies. Manoj continued diligently to fan his father. The other children were weeping in Gayatri's arms. Supported by Devika, Arjun was now trying to drink from a flask but blood was trickling from the corners of his mouth and he could not swallow.

"The tire is almost ready," cried Madho Dev. "Hang on, my boy, we'll soon be at the hospital."

"Don't worry, Father." Arjun's voice rattled in his throat. "I'm all right. Yama, the god of death, is standing by me, I can see him." A world-illuminating smile transformed his face. "Love is God," he whispered and slumped into his mother's arms.

Madho Dev buried his face in his hands.

David felt himself beginning to melt into Arjun's mind across the bridge of their clasped hands. Never had he dreamed his life might end in this bizarre way, on a country road in the land of his birth, surrounded by grandchildren. Some unseen hand had bestowed a great gift upon him. Arjun's grip tightened and seemed to lead him on.

Madho Dev kissed his son's forehead, and got up to finish with the tire.

"Don't bother," David whispered. It took all his energy to form the words. "Stay with me. I'm going with Arjun."

He could feel Arjun ahead of him. They were speeding through a long tunnel toward shimmering light, and effulgent gold and silver erupting into ultramarine, rose, and sparkling lavender. His eyes expanded with wonder. Ahead was the dancing goddess. Bells jangled in his ears and grew into a triumphant chorus.

"It's all right." He smiled. "Tell Philippa I'm happy to leave my body here in my homeland. Jai Hind!"

Madho Dev looked around at the impassive faces of the crowd, burdened with loot, straggling home from their night of Sikh killing, to whom death was an everyday occurrence, the turning of the wheel of life. Narrowing his eyes, he stared past them down the road into the bright haze, dismissed Darshan, Baghwan Singh, and Ravi and held out his hand to his grandson Manoj.

"You have to help me now," he said quietly. "Your father's soul has left his body for heaven and you must take his place." They got into the cabin of the truck. Madho Dev turned it around. "Come, take hold of the wheel," he said. "It's time you learned to drive."

# 26

INDIRA GANDHI ki jai. Indira Gandhi amar hey. Jai Hind." As Philippa checked out of her hotel, Delhi echoed with last salutes to the fallen leader. On television sets in the hotel lobby, the funeral cortège with Mrs. Gandhi's body borne on a gun carriage left Teen Murti house for the burning grounds of Raj Ghat, where, near the ancient ruins of Indraprashta, it would be consigned to five thousand years of Indian history. In a car loaned to her by General Bobby who, but for his obligations to attend the cremation, would have accompanied her himself, the now grandiloquent voice of Melvin de Mellow boomed out of a portable radio: Mrs. Gandhi was walking in other worlds; she was leaving her footsteps in the sands of time; she was immortally asleep, the greatest peacemaker who ever lived!

But the streets were empty. All morning long, announcers on radio and television had been exhorting people to go out and see the last journey of their martyred leader—the army had been called out; the streets were safe—but nobody believed them. A state of murder-induced narcosis gripped the city.

Arriving at Palam airport, Philippa stood in line at the Air India check-in counter, watching a portable television set, hoping her flight had not been delayed or canceled. A certain cloying numbness and feeling of defilement dogged her. Inside her head a voice was repeating, "Hang on; hang on, old girl; you'll be out of here soon." It was David's voice. Ah, David, why couldn't you have heard me when I asked you to leave that first evening in Kotagarh?

The gun carriage was just turning into Raj Ghat on the banks of the Jamuna River. She remembered the morning when she'd escaped from Bobby Singh and driven past Raj Ghat in the rain on her way to the Red Fort. She smiled: another life, another me. Though only two days had passed since she'd left the Majestic on her ill-fated attempt to reach Kotagarh, it seemed years.

She remembered being terribly upset with a strange American boy from California hawking pictures of butchered Sikhs. Then there had been Nirendra from Mysore, constantly eating; and her brave Sikh driver, his mind shattered by the discovery of his slaughtered sons; and Iris dangling from her bed sheets and being saved by three young men who brought her up to the room and joined the party.

The evening had degenerated into a morbid farce with half-dressed people wandering in and out of her room and Iris talking to her for what seemed like hours about how dangerous India was becoming. Finally everyone left; her driver had been carried into another room, and she had slept and dreamt of Arjun.

The announcer's voice echoed through the hushed airport waiting rooms. They were unloading Mrs. Gandhi's flower-draped body from the gun carriage and carrying it to the funeral pyre.

Ritual sacrifice.

Arjun.

A call from Ramakrishna Rao had awakened her. She remembered feeling at last something worthwhile, something practical, was going to happen. He would be able to see her at four-thirty that afternoon. She'd gotten up, swept her restive dreams into a remote corner of her mind, and felt happy. It was a beautiful day. Outside, things seemed to have quieted down. Perhaps after all everything was going to work out. Just as she was about to go down for lunch, however, Bobby had called, insisted she lunch with him, and sent a car round to pick her up. The moment she heard his voice she'd been apprehensive, and when she saw him standing at the door of his bungalow, she knew something awful had happened. His suave mask had fallen away, he looked nervous and tired, and finally he blurted out that David and Arjun were dead.

But Arjun and I were . . . she remembered forming the words in her mind, then falling backward as though from a high place into a bottomless pit that seemed to close around her. She was desperately trying to hang on to Arjun, but their hands were slowly being wrenched apart and he was moving away into bright light. But Arjun and I were . . . the numinous vision of their last night together floated in her brain. She felt she was being buried alive. It wasn't possible. How could he be dead? Every cell in her body could still feel him.

Arjun, where are you?

Her luggage had been checked in and a clerk was scolding her about overweight. On television, priests poured clarified butter over the flower-strewn body of Indira Gandhi while her son lit the funeral pyre. The voices of chanting Brahmins echoed through the terminal. Ritual sacrifice.

Deep in the jungle, Arjun's beautiful pure body was burning.

"A husk, a shell," Bobby had said when she regained consciousness and found his sad, expressive face hovering over her. "Don't think of it. David isn't gone, only his body. His inner self can't die. You must think only of returning to your children. Your children are waiting for you in England."

When she came to her senses, she had insisted she be allowed to go to Kotagarh. If Arjun and David were to be cremated the next morning, she could easily make it. But Bobby had refused, and finally she realized he was right. She didn't want to see Arjun's dead body. She wanted to remember him alive. If she went back there, something insane might happen. She might never leave. She had to get out of India; it was not her place. Some people understood it, loved it. For her it had been terribly unlucky.

Bobby had been tender and understanding. He seemed transformed, said he'd gone back to the chaos of 1947 and realized he'd been drawing breath for almost forty years and still thought of himself as the sexy young officer everyone swooned over. And when he'd seen Indira Gandhi lying in state, his life had passed before his mind's eye; the woman he'd fought with and loved dearly for over thirty years was there on the reviewing stand, telling him to shape up, and he knew if he wanted to live with himself and die happy, he'd better change.

At one point she remembered running out the door of his bungalow to catch a cab which she was sure would take her to Kotagarh. Reflex action, no doubt, and he'd run after her and put his arms around her, brought her back and held her until she'd calmed down. Then he told her that Madho Dev had found David's address book and he, Bobby, had phoned Belinda. Belinda would be meeting her flight in London. She had to conserve her energy. Had she forgotten she had a four-thirty meeting with Ramakrishna Rao? Hadn't she told him that on the phone earlier?

What was the point of seeing Rama Rao now? Arjun was gone. Suddenly she saw his rain-soaked, smiling face peering through the car window that day in Terripur. The promise of love returned; his lips, his warm body.

Arjun, amar hey!

Now the flames were rising around Indira Gandhi's body. Philippa stood in the waiting room traumatized by the frightening immediacy of television; the sound of the crackling fire, the wind of north India in the microphone. Who was lighting the fire beneath the bodies of Arjun and David? she wondered. Manoj, of course; son and secret grandson, as he would light fires under Madho Dev and Devika and Gayatri when their times came. And there was Rajiv Gandhi, a good son and father, his wife and children, standing at the pyre. Four more sacrificial victims for Mother India. Once she'd embraced you, you could not leave her. Suddenly Philippa saw herself as an old woman at home in England, sitting in front of the library fire dreaming of Arjun.

What would she do with the rest of her life?

At four-thirty she'd gone to Rama Rao's house. After all, the money was still alive there in Switzerland. Perhaps now Madho Dev and Devika would see it would be wise for them to leave: "make a move," as they said in Kotagarh. Bobby had driven her there and waited outside. Rao was more sympathetic than she'd remembered him at Kamala's party or their last meeting in Delhi. But they'd both had bad news. He had just heard from Sonny that Kamala had been struck down the previous morning. His eyes were glazed. And when she told him David and Arjun were dead, they sat and gazed at each other for some time without speaking, and finally he had wept. How many

times had he warned Kamala to get out of Terripur, that she was
vulnerable there? But she had obstinately refused to listen. What was
the country coming to that these things could go on? Violence everywhere one turned. The new Prime Minister, he assured her, had
known nothing of the horrible crimes committed in his mother's name
over the past few days. He, Rama Rao, and a few others had known
and tried to get the message through to him but were blocked by a
cadre of immediate associates who surrounded him. He described the
scene at Teen Murti house, which he'd found disgusting. How Indira
Gandhi would have loathed it! People were bribing the guards to gain
admittance to the house so they could be seen on television paying
their respects. This was not the India he had devoted his life to
serving. No doubt the television coverage had exacerbated the situation. Unless a strong hand took the helm, the country was going to
disintegrate. He dabbed at his eyes with a scarf and sipped his tea.
He'd made all the arrangements for Madho Dev, Devika, Gayatri, and
the children. He would send the forms to Madho Dev the next day.
Whether they left immediately or not, they should go ahead and get
their passports. Now it would be up to Philippa to go to Switzerland
and obtain visas for them. He gave her Kamala's account numbers and
various letters and documents to show the bankers and said he realized she was in a rather peculiar position. Yes, he knew everything.
Knew that David was Gayatri's father. But did that matter? After all,
children were children.

Then Bobby had joined them for tea and afterward, when she'd
asked to be driven to the Majestic, refused to hear of it: said she could
return there and pack in the morning before going to the airport but
he wouldn't allow her to spend another night in that "nest of the
hippies," as he called it. At his bungalow he'd dismissed his servant,
Anandi, and as the evening sky turned pink outside, they sat in a back
courtyard having a drink and he told her the whole story of the events
at Kotagarh as Madho Dev had related them. Just before he died,
David said, "Tell Philippa I am happy, I am dying in my homeland."
The words had stung her; even in death he was shutting the door on
her. And yet the moment he'd emerged from Durga Baba's cave
covered with filth, looking like a wild man, she'd known. It was an
image she would never forget; his sweat-covered body smelling to
high heaven, his disheveled hair. But if she hadn't insisted he come
back to Kotagarh, if he'd stayed with the Baba?

Ritual sacrifice.

"Did Madho Dev tell you why David stayed behind?" she asked.

Bobby nodded thoughtfully. "When I saw him last June I felt he might be headed for something like that. Perhaps it was the real reason he returned to India, unconscious though it may have been."

"And Arjun?" said Philippa. "Did he say anything?"

" 'Love is God!' Those were his dying words." Bobby sighed. "Strange, no? But he went down swinging, as they say, died like a good Kshatriya should, defending others, nothing to be ashamed of."

"Love is God." She fought back tears, finally broke down, and began sobbing again.

Bobby had been very sweet, picked her up in his arms, carried her inside, sat beside her, held her hand, and stroked her forehead until she stopped. "David wouldn't have wanted you to feel this way," he said. "He was a very understanding fellow. I know, after thirty years of marriage, it's a terrible shock to you, but you must realize he died happy."

"It's not David," she said, barely able to speak. "I might as well tell you, I can't keep it to myself any longer. It's Arjun. We were having— we were in love, madly in love."

His eyes narrowed, a sad, knowing expression hovered around the corners of his mouth. He got up and took off his turban, tied his long hair in a ponytail, went into his bedroom and changed into pajamas, and busied himself in the kitchen.

Finally she got up and joined him. "I suppose I've only confirmed all your worst suspicions about Western women, that we're all whores," she said, drying her eyes. "Well, it wasn't like that at all, it was very deep, very beautiful. If David hadn't been so distracted, perhaps it wouldn't have happened, but there you are."

He took her hands, held her at arm's length, and shook his head thoughtfully. "You've got it wrong. I wasn't thinking that at all. I understand perfectly. As one who has had many affairs of the heart, I understand more than you give me credit for. I was thinking back many years. I too had a tragic love affair. She died just weeks before we were to be married. I was never to fall in love with the same intensity again. I wished fervently for death and have risked my life over and over again, but here I am, alive and still unmarried. Let us not speak of these things. You can help me fix something to eat. The only thing I know how to cook is omelet. Will that be all right? And perhaps you would fix a salad."

They puttered about the kitchen like an old married couple. She burned the toast. He uncorked a bottle of white wine, and finally they sat down at one of the low tables.

"I know it's not much comfort to you for me to say this; our minds forget things but our bodies do not. However, I doubt it would have worked out between you and Arjun. We Indian men are rather unreliable when it comes to fidelity, you know, don't treat our women all that well. In the end, he'd have probably felt so guilty about the whole affair, he'd have left both you and Gayatri for someone else."

She sighed and looked into her wineglass. "You're very perceptive, as I knew you must be when we first met that day in the hotel elevator. You've just said what I've been telling myself for weeks but couldn't bear to face. Still, I had hoped—"

"Ah, yes, hope. It's one of our great human gifts, isn't it? Or shortcomings?"

They gazed at each other. "What I can't understand," she said at last, "is why Madho Dev let David and Arjun go off and help that neighbor of his. You heard what happened in June with those three young soldiers. Wouldn't you have taken that as a warning not to get involved?" She got up and paced back and forth. "As it was, David was in a very shaky state. I think it was monstrous, and all to uphold some antiquated code of honor."

He got up and held her hands firmly. "We are all, each one of us, instruments of a higher force: the gods, fate, call it what you will. I'm sure Madho Dev acted from the highest principles, and I'm sure his grief is much worse than yours because it is compounded with the very guilt you have spoken of."

"Instruments of a higher force," she said, and began to cry again. "That's an awfully convenient way of looking at things. It means no one is responsible for anything."

"Did you ask to be born?" he said gravely.

"I've heard that before too. How do I know? I might have."

"But you really haven't thought about it. If you think about it, you'll see your very existence depends on factors that are completely out of your control. We in the army know this well. Despite our best-laid plans, things go wrong; there is always the unpredictable element we can't account for: human emotions, passion, what have you. That is why military men believe in fate, in the gods. To be sure, one must conduct one's life as though one could exercise control over it; at the same time one should always remember that control is basically an illusion. A paradox perhaps; the foundation of compassion. Do you understand?"

Philippa smiled through her tears. "My mind does. My heart rebels."

They cleared the dishes. His driver appeared at the door with a message. "I must return to my office for a while," he said. "So many details to attend to for tomorrow's funeral. I'll be back later. Will you be all right here alone? You won't do anything rash, I hope?"

She shook her head. He held her and kissed her forehead. "Perhaps you'll allow me to come visit you in England soon. I think I am going to retire early. It's time for me to leave the scene. I know this is hardly the moment for a declaration of love, but I believe you know I'm more than a little fond of you, and under different circumstances perhaps you'll allow me to show you how I feel. I understand you're quite interested in horses. I too am an enthusiast." He smiled. "We could start from there."

Now in the customs line, she watched as one of the priests handed Rajiv Gandhi a long wooden pole. It was his duty, the man next to her explained, to pierce his mother's skull, thus freeing the last part of her soul from the body's prison. He had done the same for his grandfather, Jawaharlal Nehru. The serious face of the young Prime Minister seen through the smoke and flames, the unrelenting realism of the television as it focused on the atavistic rite, had many people in tears.

She went through customs, put her hand luggage in the X-ray machine, and headed for the personal security check booth. That morning when she'd gone to the Majestic to pack, she'd put on the gold chains and bracelets she always wore. Now a truculent woman in the khaki-colored sari of the Delhi police searched her and began examining her jewelry.

"What is this?" asked the woman in a rancorous voice and pointed to a bracelet of dangling gold coins.

"It's a charm bracelet."

"You take it off, please," the woman said.

Philippa undid the clasp. The woman examined it and told her to go ahead. Philippa asked for the bracelet back. The woman said she would have to show it to her superior. Philippa objected.

"It is not permitted for you to be taking so much gold out of India," the woman shouted. "Where are your receipts?"

A male guard came up and led them aside into an alcove so other passengers could pass. "Where did you get the coins on this bracelet?" he asked. "Some of them are Indian gold coins."

"I bought the bracelet in London. I brought it with me when I came in June. Now I'm returning to London and am taking it back with me." She grabbed for her bracelet but the policewoman handed it to the guard.

"You must have a receipt," he bullied her. "You are having too much gold. You may be taking it out of the country for someone."

"I tell you this is my jewelry. I wore it in and I'm wearing it out; can't you understand that?"

"Ah, but when you brought it in, madam, you must have declared it. That is the law. Where is your receipt of declaration?"

"I didn't declare it, I walked right through. Look," she said, "my flight has been called. I'm going to miss my plane."

"You may go if you choose, but you can't take these out of the country." He deftly removed two gold chains from around her neck.

The thought of missing her plane, of being this close to getting out and not making it, brought her to the edge of collapse. "You give me my jewelry," she said shakily. "I'm telling you the truth. Can't you understand that?"

The man pretended not to understand her. "You give me these two chains, I give you your bracelet, eh? It will save a lot of time and trouble for you. Otherwise, I must detain you and take you to my superior."

It was the last straw. She was about to give in when she heard a familiar voice. "I say, Philippa, is that you?"

Akbar!

"I thought I heard your voice," said the poet, lumbering toward her. "What on earth is happening? You look pale as a ghost. Are these people giving you trouble?"

"I think they're getting ready to confiscate my jewelry. They say I need a receipt."

"Bah!" roared Akbar and addressed the two inspectors. "I've been watching you two from around the corner. This woman is a close friend of Rajiv Gandhi's. Give back that jewelry at once and let her go or I shall report you to your superior officer and see that you are canned. Did this man say he would let you pass if you gave him one of your gold chains, Mrs. Bruce?"

Philippa nodded wide-eyed. "Two, it was two he wanted."

"Well," said Akbar impatiently, "are you going to give them back and let her pass or shall I report you?"

The guard asked Akbar in Hindi who the hell he thought he was, interfering like this in a security check.

"I happen to be a very good friend of the P.M., and if you want to find out just who I am, then let us go to your superior. Now! If necessary, we are prepared to miss our flight."

The guard thought for a moment, then with a baleful look returned Philippa's jewelry and quickly disappeared. The policewoman heaved a sigh of defeat and gestured them toward the departure lounge.

"What unbelievable luck," sighed Philippa.

"Fate." Akbar grinned. "I thought I saw your blond head in front of me. Then, after I went through security check and didn't see you, I looked around. Better check your purse; be sure they didn't take your passport while they had you focusing on your jewelry. They know you want to leave, so they've got a certain leverage. Tell me, what would you have done if I hadn't come by?"

"Why I'd have given them the chains, I suppose, considered it an offering. Silly of me to wear them, but many Indian women wear far more."

Akbar laughed. "And once you had given they would only have demanded more. Your proper course of action should have been to have screamed as loudly as possible that they were sexually molesting you." He smiled shyly and took her hands. "It's been an awful three days, hasn't it?"

"I thought you'd gone to Tashkent," she said.

"That's where I'm headed now, via Bombay and Kuwait. You're shaking."

"I'll calm down when I get on the plane. It's all been too much."

"Let's get on the bus, I think they've called our flight."

They hurried through the departure lounge.

"These Delhi police are infamous, a real Mafia," puffed Akbar. "Any weakening of central authority and they turn into dacoits. Just now the power structure is blurred, everyone's wondering how people will be shuffled around, whether their sins will be forgiven or dug up. No doubt you've heard what happened all over the city the past few days." He mopped his brow.

"I was caught in the middle of it," replied Philippa. "Nearly killed trying to get Kotagarh in a hired car with a Sikh driver; saw bodies hanging from trees with their bellies slit open, men being burned alive with crowds looking on."

"Dear lady!" He gazed at her. "You've really had it, haven't you? Nothing like that's happened to me. Some of my Sikh friends moved in with me, lost everything, but we stayed inside and didn't move."

"My driver's whole family was murdered. He found his three young sons butchered."

"You can be sure someone manipulated the police," declared Akbar.

"Who?" asked Philippa.

"It had to be someone in the Congress Party close enough to Rajiv Gandhi to keep him from hearing about it. I'm sure he is an absolutely righteous man. I heard one rumor that when he was finally told what was happening, he immediately ordered the army to be called out, but whoever received the order waited twenty-four hours to execute it. Whoever that man was, he also controlled the police. It's just another manifestation of the greed and hatred that's gripped the country in the past few years."

They boarded the plane and managed to shift seats so they could sit together. Philippa stared out the window, wondering whether she would ever see India again. The plane taxied down the runway.

"As you haven't mentioned it, I suppose you don't know about Princess Kamala," she said.

Akbar sighed. "I do know. I wondered if you knew. I was going to spare you that. After what you've been through—"

"Then you know about David and Arjun too?"

Akbar nodded. "Through Primula; apparently Bobby Singh told her. Don't look surprised, everyone knows Primula; she's a regular one-woman intelligence bureau. I'm terribly sorry. You must feel awful. Saraswati Rao called me about Kamala, really horrible. I just sat and stared into space for hours, I couldn't move. Strange, isn't it, two great Indian women, each so different in her own way, struck down by young men. It's a revolt against something, and it's revolting. It's also the end of an era. I fear things will get worse now. I must tell you the purohit at Kedarnath, Pandu, told me neither David nor Arjun would be alive in six months; he saw it in their hands. And one of the priests at that fire temple told Kamala to beware of stones in the sky—which was how she died; someone threw a stone and it hit her head. I got through to Sonny this morning. They cremated her yesterday near Hardwar. The poor fellow is really shaken up."

The plane was taking off. Out the window, Akbar pointed to the wisps of smoke from Mrs. Gandhi's funeral pyre rising into the limitless blue sky.

"Your attitude toward death here is very odd, almost indifferent," said Philippa. "People grieve, but it doesn't really seem to frighten them. I don't understand."

Akbar turned his eyes from the window. " 'To that which is born, death is indeed certain; and to that which is dead, birth is certain. Wherefore, about the unavoidable thing, thou oughtest not to grieve.' "

The plane soared away from Delhi toward Bombay. At the pond near the cabin in the game preserve, the cremation had ended. The mourners left for Kotagarh, and Durga Baba sat in front of his cave with his cow and watched the plume of a jet plane arch across the afternoon sky. Far off, a tiger roared. Slowly the Baba took up his flute and began to play.

# Glossary

*achkan*  long fitted jacket
*ajim*  opium
*ayah*  maid or nanny
*baksheesh*  tip, bribe
*bhai*  brother
*bhang*  marijuana
*bhangi*  carrier of night soil
*bhania*  shopkeeper caste
*Bharat*  India
*bhut*  ghost
*bidis*  cheap cigarette
*Brahmin*  priestly caste
*budmarsh*  rascal
*chai*  tea
*chamar*  worker in leather
*chapatti*  unleavened bread
*charis*  hashish
*churidars*  tight pants
*dacoit*  bandit
*dahi*  yogurt, curd
*dal*  lentils
*dandi*  sedan chair
*depta*  heavenly being
*dharamsala*  lodgings for pilgrims
*dharma*  law
*dhoti*  long cloth worn by men
*diwan*  prime minister
*Doordarshan*  government television
*durbar*  audience of a ruler
*ferenghi*  foreigner
*ganja*  marijuana
*ghat*  bathing place
*han*  yes
*hejira*  hermaphrodite

*howdah*   sitting platform on top of an elephant
*jawan*   enlisted soldier
*jeldi*   faster
*kirpan*   sword
*kirtan*   singing
*Kshatriya*   warrior caste
*kurta*   high-collared men's shirt
*lingam*   penis, symbol of the god Shiva
*mahant*   religious
*mali*   gardener
*muni*   silent yogi
*mutlub*   intrigue
*nahin*   no
*pandal*   roof
*pan*   betel nut
*pani*   water
*paratha*   fried bread
*Pir*   Muslim wise man
*puja*   service of worship
*punkah*   fan
*roti*   unleavened bread
*sadhu*   wandering holy man
*sadhana*   method of teaching
*salwar*   loose pants
*Sardar*   Sikh
*shaitan*   devil
*shant*   peaceful
*shikar*   hunt, safari
*subedar*   noncommissioned officer in the Indian Army
*subjee*   vegetables
*Sudra*   serving caste
*syce*   groom for horses
*thali*   round metal plate
*thyagi*   renunciate
*tonga*   horse-drawn carriage
*wallah*   seller or dealer
*yatra*   pilgrimage
*yoni*   vagina, symbol of the goddess
*yuveraj*   heir to the throne
*zemindar*   large landowner